Susquehanna

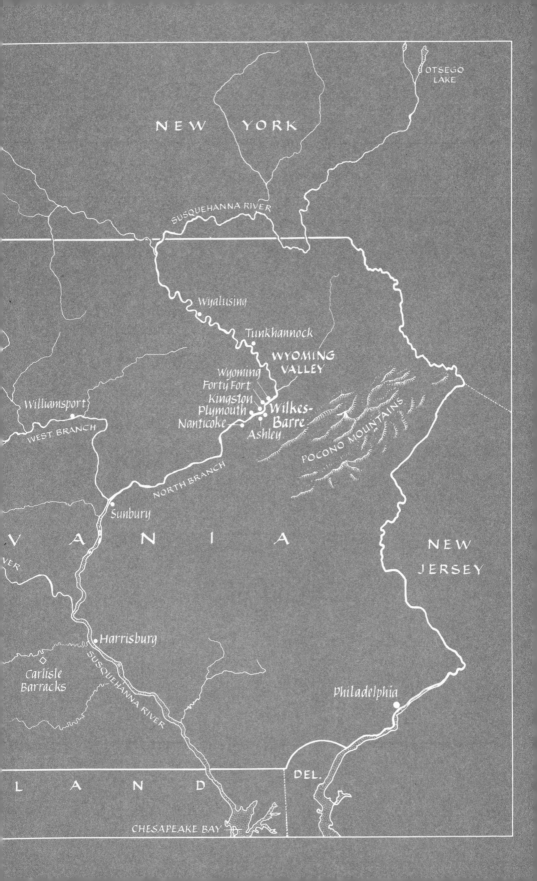

OTSEGO LAKE

NEW YORK

SUSQUEHANNA RIVER

Wyalusing

Tunkhannock

WYOMING VALLEY

Wyoming
Forty Fort
Kingston
Plymouth
Nanticoke

Wilkes-Barre

Ashley

POCONO MOUNTAINS

Williamsport

WEST BRANCH

NORTH BRANCH

Sunbury

VANIA

NEW JERSEY

RIVER

Harrisburg

Carlisle
Barracks

SUSQUEHANNA RIVER

Philadelphia

LAND

DEL.

CHESAPEAKE BAY

Susquehanna

A NOVEL BY

Harriet Segal

DOUBLEDAY & COMPANY, INC.
GARDEN CITY, NEW YORK
1984

"When You Are Old" from *The Poems of William Butler Yeats*, edited by Richard Finneran, Macmillan Publishing Company, New York 1983.

Library of Congress Cataloging in Publication Data
Segal, Harriet.
  Susquehanna.
  I. Title.
PS3569.E42S9 1984   813'.54
ISBN: 0-385-19246-0
Library of Congress Catalog Card Number 83–25320

For Sheldon, who knows all the reasons why . . .
with all my love

and

In memory of my father, Albert R. Feinberg, M.D., who loved and served Wyoming Valley and her people for all the days of his life.

H.S.

ACKNOWLEDGMENTS

This is a novel and all of its characters are imaginary. While it is hoped that they may seem real, any similarity to persons living or dead is unintended.

I must ask the understanding of the citizens of Wyoming Valley, where I was born and grew up, for creating places that do not exist and rearranging some of those that do. I have used the actual names of towns along the Susquehanna because I feel they provide a unique and colorful background for my story. For the same reason I have invented streets and institutions, and taken certain historical events out of context.

I would like to thank the following libraries and reference librarians for their invaluable help: Greenburgh (N.Y.) Public Library; Falmouth (Mass.) Public Library; White Plains (N.Y.) Public Library; Yale University Library, New Haven, Conn.; Grant Anderson, Supervisor of General Reference, Historical Library of the Church of Jesus Christ of Latter-Day Saints, Salt Lake City; and particular thanks to Bernadette McGough and Diane Suffern of the Osterhout Free Library, Wilkes-Barre, Pa., who allowed me to borrow many old and out-of-print volumes on the history of Wyoming Valley for extended periods of time.

I gratefully acknowledge the assistance of the following institutions: Jefferson Medical College of Thomas Jefferson University, Philadelphia; the Pennsylvania Historical and Museum Commission, Harrisburg; the India Government Tourist Office, New York; the Yivo Institute for Jewish Research, New York; the Leo Baeck Institute, New York; the Sisters of Mercy, New York Province; the Church of Jesus Christ of Latter-Day Saints (Mormon), Salt Lake City; the American Museum of Natural History, New York; the Press and Information Service of the French Embassy, New York office.

There are many individuals I must thank for their assistance while doing my research and writing *Susquehanna.* Some of them are old friends. Others I have never met except by letter or telephone. I can only mention a few, but in all cases they have my deep gratitude.

Some of the people who furnished me with valuable information for my work are: Peter Onukiewech, Department of Planning and Development,

City of Wilkes-Barre; Margaret E. Craft, Librarian/Archivist, Wyoming Historical and Geological Society, Wilkes-Barre; Betty Smith, Curator, Susquehanna County Historical Society and Free Library Association, Montrose, Pa.; Leon Stout, Head, Penn State Room, the Pennsylvania State University, University Park; Richard A. Cairo, Secretary, Susquehanna River Basin Commission, Harrisburg; Commissioner Walter J. Vicinelly, Bureau of Deep Mine Safety, Commonwealth of Pennsylvania Department of Environmental Resources, Uniontown; Edward Gardner, collector of railroad memorabilia, Mountain Top; Lloyd Noseworthy, Vice-President for Real Estate, Lehigh Valley Railroad, Bethlehem; Damon Young, Executive Director, Susquehanna River Tri-State Association, Wilkes-Barre; Anicetas Simupis, Consul General of Lithuania, New York; and I wish I could thank an anonymous lieutenant colonel of the United States Army Engineers in Maryland for his eloquent discourse on rivers and their flood plains.

Of the many friends whose interest and aid were important, a few were exceptional: Sumi Mitsudo Koide, M.D., always responded immediately to my frequent requests for medical information, supplying me with dusty tomes from the Albert Einstein Medical College library and injecting her enthusiasm and good humor into our many conversations about things medical. Luigi Mastroianni, Jr., M.D., inspired me with spirited medical narratives and reminiscences from his medical school-internship years. Elaine Pierson Mastroianni, M.D., Ph.D., was constantly available for consultation, not only on medical subjects but on points of Philadelphia and Pennsylvania history, often sending me hard-to-find facts and clippings.

I am very much indebted to Francis C. Wood, M.D., Emeritus Professor of Medicine, University of Pennsylvania, a most remarkable raconteur, who was kind enough to relate in great detail his experiences while serving with the 20th General Hospital in Margherita, Assam (India), during the Burma campaign of World War II. I have drawn on Dr. Wood's account of his assignment in the China-Burma-India theater for background in the section entitled *At War*. Thanks are also due to Daniel R. Mishell, M.D., who was stationed in Assam and answered many of my questions about army life there.

My aunt, Ida Smulyan, shared with me her memories of Wyoming Valley in the early days of the century, taking a lively interest in my project. Cathy Camhy, a fine editor, read and criticized my manuscript, making many valuable suggestions. My friend Rollene Saal became my literary representative and mentor. Her enthusiasm and encouragement were unflagging and I am more than appreciative.

Everyone who has a supportive family thinks there is none quite so wonderful as hers and I am no exception. Except, there really *is* none as extraordinary as mine! From the first glimmer of an idea, my husband, Sheldon, urged me to do a novel. He and our three daughters, Jennifer, Laura, and Amy, not only encouraged me to write this book but enabled me to devote my time to the task by taking over many of my other responsibilities. They cheerfully adapted to a complete change in home life, and not once during those three years did I hear a complaint—at least not about the book! There is no way to adequately thank them.

And to all my friends, who put up with my dropping out . . . thank you for remaining my friends.

Harriet Segal

Woods Hole
August 1983

Contents

Contents

Prologue

There is a place in the northeastern part of Pennsylvania, just to the west of the Poconos, where you can stand on the sunset side of Wyoming Mountain to survey all of the long, narrow valley below . . . much as those who have come before have paused to view it.

Once, there were broad, flat meadowlands of rare fertility in the valley, thick forests abundant with wildlife, glades lush with berries and fruits . . . and always, through the center of the valley like a silver thread, the shining tracery of the Susquehanna, teeming with fish and turtles, its shores edged with wild grains, its shallows gleaming with pearl-white stones.

Far to the north, where the river rises unbidden from subterranean springs, it wanders, a narrow unassuming stream, flowing south. Then, with a change of heart, it doubles back, irresolute to pursue the course. From the towering ramparts, where once ruled the Iroquois nations, the river tumbles down over rocky shoals in earnest haste. On it rushes, increasing in dimension, toward the valley at Wyoming . . . "great grassy meadowland." Here, the river quiets, reflective, as if considering events long past.

When the wind is fresh off the river, it calls to the farthest reaches of the valley, a song of peace. It was not always so. For the Susquehanna's waters have run red with blood . . . red with the blood of conquest, of revolution, and of greed.

And the waters of the Susquehanna have run black—with the dust of coal.

In a time before recorded time, this valley was a place of special sanctity, a place set apart for the repose of the Great Spirit . . . set apart by those into whose keeping the river and the lands were given, the Susquehannocks. The valley was sacred to the river, belonging to no one.

Then came the Yankees from Connecticut, those souls of grit who craved the river lands for their beauty and their promise. They paid dearly for their dream. The Pennsylvanians who challenged them coveted the Susquehanna

Valley, not for love of it, but for the riches it would bring them. These fought to the death. English, Welsh, Scottish, they forgot their brotherhood.

In the end, though, it was none of them who shaped the valley and captured the river. It was those who came after. Those who came because of anthracite coal.

They came, the Irish, to dig the canal . . . and stayed to mine the coal. They came, the others . . . the Germans, Slavs, and Poles . . . the Hungarians, Lithuanians, and Italians. And the Jews.

They came to Wyoming Valley and set their seal on her, made her what she is. They claimed the river and fought its vengeance. They struggled there, sometimes against each other. They all have a story to tell.

This is one of those stories.

BOOK ONE

A Distant River

1877–78

I

Eastern Europe   Summer 1877

"Hold there, *Danika!* Where are you bound?"

The man stood on the dock at Memel, his collar turned up against the gusty Baltic wind, forming a cup with one of his hands, the other holding on to his high gray top hat.

"Kovno bound," shouted Isaac, standing in the bow of the steamer.

"Can you take a passenger to Kovno?"

Isaac signaled for the man to wait. He went aft, looking for his brother. Aaron was in the cabin making notes in the ship's log. He did not look up when Isaac entered.

"Aaron, there's a man asking for passage to Kovno. Shall we take him?"

"Who is he?" Aaron asked, still writing.

Isaac shrugged. "How should I know? Looks to be a gentleman from his dress. He's on the dock."

Aaron put down his pen and looked at his brother. "I don't like taking passengers, Isaac. You can't be too careful these days. You'd better find out who he is. Ask for his papers. Or better still, check with the inspector."

Isaac lowered the gangway and approached the man who was waiting on the dock, the cape of his long traveling coat flapping in the wind.

"Do you have papers, sir? They'll be checking at the Russian border. We're not a passenger vessel."

The man fumbled in his leather pocket case and removed an envelope which bore a large seal. Isaac read the legend on the face of the envelope: "Under the protection of His Majesty, Emperor Wilhelm I." He glanced briefly at the man, whose face looked pale and pinched, although the weather was mild this late summer along the Baltic seacoast. Opening the envelope, Isaac removed a heavy sheet of foolscap embossed with a crest at the top. He quickly read its brief message, in German and in Russian.

Isaac handed the letter back to the man, carefully controlling his words. "You are traveling on official government business?"

"Let's just say that I have the confidence of the Crown."

"It seems odd that you don't have passage. Surely more suitable accommodations could have been arranged for an emissary of Emperor Wilhelm." He indicated his cargo boat with a sweep of his hand.

"I do not require luxury, sir. Only a safe, dry berth, Herr . . ."

Isaac removed his hat and bowed. "Hillman, Isaac Hillman. First officer and part owner of the *Danika.*"

The man returned his bow. "Permit me to introduce myself. I am Leopold Bloch from Vienna. I represent a consortium of banking interests whose mission compels me to take this roundabout sojourn. I should be much obliged if you would grant me passage to Kovno. There seems to be little choice in mode of transportation to that city."

"True enough, Herr Bloch. If you will accompany me to the inspector's shed, we'll have to obtain the required permits. They may refuse you entry at the boundary, even with your impressive document." Isaac smiled to show his goodwill.

They cast off before dawn, using their single square-rigged sail to catch the following wind and conserve fuel. Aaron was always cautious about starting up the boiler too rapidly after they'd been in port. There were frequent explosions on these steamers. Just this week one of the Poliakoff side-wheelers had burst its engine, killing two crew members and scalding several others.

Aaron carefully guided the squat boat through the sheltered harbor, past the moored schooners and merchant vessels which regularly plied back and forth to Sweden, two hundred miles across the Baltic Sea. They were hauling a barge loaded with heavy metal parts for Russian factories, so they'd have to get their steam up soon because the current was against them, although not swift here near the mouth of the Neman River.

This was the return of their long run from Memel, the Prussian city on the Baltic, to their home port, Nemunaitis, 240 miles away. Herring boats were returning with their morning catch, followed by screeching seabirds, when Isaac stoked the furnace with wood. The flat delta swept out on either bank. Soon they were steaming along toward Tilsit, the cylinder pumping smoothly, smoke rising in a trail behind them.

Leopold Bloch sat in the sheltered stern of the steamboat, his myopic eyes shielded from the glare of the bright sun reflected from the rippling surface of the river. He watched the two brothers at work. Although they bore a strong physical resemblance to each other, they were as unlike as any two men could be. The elder brother, Aaron, at the helm, was heavier and not as tall as his more handsome younger brother, Isaac. The brothers had the rugged appearance of men who spent their lives exposed to the elements. Both were fair, with wheat-colored hair and eyes of azure blue. But Aaron maintained an almost sullen silence, while Isaac was friendly and congenial as he tossed fuel into the pit of the boiler, the graceful movements of his long torso rhythmic and practiced, the muscles of his shoulders and upper arms taut beneath his close-fitting shirt. All that energy, strength, and youth, the gray-haired bank secretary envied him.

Bloch walked forward to where Isaac was seated, mending a canvas tarp. Isaac smiled at him, a ready smile, open and inviting, motioning him to sit on a bench along the rail.

"You come from Vienna, Herr Bloch? It must be a grand city."

"Yes, Vienna is a beautiful city. It has a grand cultural tradition. Not so fashionable as Paris, nor as powerful as London, but to a Viennese, the hub of the universe." He laughed at his own chauvinism.

"What brings you to Kovno, if I may inquire?"

"The conditions of life in the so-called Pale of Jewish Settlement is of constant interest to my employers . . ." He hesitated. Discretion was Leopold Bloch's most valued characteristic.

"The Rothschilds have always tried to be of help to the Jews of Russia, I am well aware," Isaac answered.

Now it was the Austrian banker's turn to be surprised. "How do you know that I work for the House of Rothschild?"

"The inspector at Memel is not always as discreet as he might be. In a word, he, like all port inspectors, talks too much."

"Aah, I see. Well, why not? It isn't meant to be a secret. I am employed by the Kreditanstalt Rothschild. What else did he tell you?"

"Nothing much. Only that you had asked for passage previously and he told you to inquire on the *Danika*. We're always a little uncertain about passengers, you see. These are unsettled times along the Neman—indeed, throughout Russia. Especially for the Jews, I think."

"You and your brother . . . you are Jews. Isn't it unusual for Jews to operate a riverboat in Russia?"

"I suppose it is," Isaac said. "But most of the shipping along the Neman and Vistula is owned by Jewish concerns. Much of Russia's transportation system has been developed by Jews, I'm sure you are well aware. What's unusual, I believe, is that we own this boat ourselves and are independent merchant-captains."

"Do you live in Kovno?"

"No. We live in a small town between Kovno and Grodno. But my wife came from Kovno. I went to school there. I know it well."

"Perhaps you can tell me, then, where to find this address." Bloch withdrew a card from an inside pocket and handed it to Isaac.

On the card was the name of Isaac's father-in-law, Michel Belkind, advocate-of-law, and underneath was the address of the house where he had first loved Malka.

The *Danika* docked at Nemunaitis late in the afternoon of a mild summer Friday after unloading her cargo at Kovno, where they had bid good-bye to their passenger, giving him directions to his destination. This was the brothers' home. The main part of the town lay some few versts to the east from the river Neman.

When the decks of the *Danika* had been washed down, the bilges and hold cleaned, the cargo nets set out to dry in the air, Aaron called to one of the hangers-on who loitered around the docks, "You, boy!" The boy scampered on board, holding his hand out for the few kopecks that would ensure his watching over the boat.

The brothers walked through the town, past the busy marketplace with its colonnade of stores around the perimeter and jumble of stalls in the center. The din of vendors hawking their wares, the smoke from the fires of the peasants who sat by the side of the road roasting potatoes for their midday meal, the smell of animals and dung commingled with unwashed bodies rose in their nostrils like a putrid miasma after the clean air of the river.

They headed toward the long, dusty road where the scattered line of carts and foot traffic led to the Jewish settlement, greeting those they passed on the way. In a few hours it would be Sabbath. The brothers always came home in time for the Sabbath meal on Friday evenings.

This was the only time they had for family life, Aaron with his wife and two young daughters, and Isaac with his small son. An old serving woman helped with the cooking and other household chores, and her daughter cared for Isaac's little boy. Their scholarly father, Simon, an invalid, completed the crowded household. Isaac found the press of so many people intolerable after a few days. He was always happy to return to the *Danika* where he could think his thoughts in relative solitude, comforted by the sounds and sights of the river.

They approached the sprawling wooden house with its low, sloping roof and two chimneys. Aaron's daughters saw them when they were far away. "Papa, papa!" they called, running on thin legs with plaits flying. Tanya, the five-year-old, made such strenuous efforts to keep up with eight-year-old Sara that she was red and panting when she reached them.

Aaron caught her up in his arms, kissing the chubby child resoundingly, oblivious of the reproachful gaze of his elder daughter. "How is papa's beauty?" he asked.

Isaac couldn't bear to see a child feel slighted, so he threw down his bundle and lifted Sara in his arms, giving her a hug and kissing her sallow cheek. "Do you have a kiss for your Uncle Isaac, Sara?" He was rewarded with a shy kiss and a smile.

When they entered the house, the smell of freshly baked *challah* and stewed meat greeted them. After their monotonous diet of rye bread, cheese, and porridge on the *Danika,* it was always satisfying to return to food cooked at home by a woman.

Isaac crossed the small front room to his father's sleeping alcove where Simon sat in a chair, propped up with pillows and wrapped in a blanket, despite the warmth of the summer afternoon. He embraced his father, who smiled, happy to see him.

"So, Father, how are you feeling?" he asked.

"A little better today, Isaac," he answered. "I've been reading the entire day. In this weather, my leg doesn't pain so much." He indicated the empty space under the blanket where the leg was missing.

Isaac's face clouded for a brief moment. He forced himself to smile.

"And how is my little Jacob? Has he been behaving himself?"

"He's an angel," Simon answered, a smile lighting his face. Just then, the nursemaid came in carrying Jacob, who struggled to get down when he saw his father.

All the joy in his life centered on this one little son with his light blond hair, round eyes, and slight frame. Never a robust child, he worried Isaac with his susceptibility to frequent colds and fevers. But Jacob's high spirits belied his frail appearance. Still unsteady on his feet, he came running on tiptoe across the room to his father. Isaac hugged the thin body to his large chest, then tossed the youngster high in the air. The child shrieked with glee, throwing his head back, his mouth wide open.

"Ho! Another tooth, I see." Isaac put his finger in the small mouth to feel the bottom gum.

Simon watched his big, handsome son and sighed heavily. He must speak to him again about another marriage. A young, virile man without a wife was not good. The boy needed a mother. There were many young women who would be happy to become the wife of Isaac Hillman, the merchant-captain. A year and more had passed since the lovely Malka had died. It was time. . . .

II

Nemunaitis   1876

It had been a night of revelry, in that March of 1876 . . . the fifteenth anniversary of the edict which freed the serfs, issued by Czar Alexander II in an attempt to bring his vast empire into the modern world. The lot of the peasants had hardly changed. Poverty and ignorance still framed their lives. Nevertheless, celebrations were decreed, and in many taverns throughout the countryside drunken peasants mingled with cossacks, soldiers, and malcontents. In the Jewish towns within the pale it was wise to remain at home, secluded, and away from the attention of the coarse peasantry.

By the next afternoon most of the revelers had returned to their homes, or were sleeping off the effects of the wine and spirits. Malka had ridden to the market in a hired droshky, taking Sorke, the old servant along. It was a lovely day with a hint of spring in the air.

Sorke bundled Isaac's pregnant wife into layers of robes over the hooded cloak she wore. It was against everything the old woman believed for her mistress to go forth in her seventh month. These educated women would come to no good! They should stay at home and sit quietly throughout the months of waiting, eating honey and buttermilk, thinking beautiful thoughts, and guarding themselves against the evil eye. But Malka laughed at Sorke's superstitions, chiding her for believing in such things.

"I'll lose my sanity if I have to stay in the house one more moment, Sorke. You'll just have to come along with me. I need some air to breathe, some sights to stir up my senses."

Stir up her senses, indeed! That's what comes of teaching girls to read Hebrew and Russian. The folly of it all. Imagine, she doesn't even wear a *sheitel.* Her hair was never cut before her marriage. Hah! The old woman threw up her hands, drew her shabby cloak around her, and climbed up into the droshky with her young mistress, whom she adored, as she did each member of the Hillman household.

The bells on the horse's reins gave off a pleasant tinkling sound, the hoofs clapped smartly against the hard surface of the road as they rolled by the houses and fields on their way to the central part of town. Malka had a glow of well-being. Soon, in just two months, she would have a baby, a little one belonging to her and Isaac. And in three more days her husband, her beloved, handsome, wonderful Isaac, would return from his long trip down the Neman River to the Baltic Sea. Malka felt a flush of warmth when she thought of how she would greet him, tenderly kiss him, and how he would hold her close to him. Theirs was a deep love, a passion, their own secret. For it was not considered a womanly virtue to harbor such thoughts, such thrills and delights at the relationship with one's husband.

After stopping at the cloth merchant, they visited the jewelry-maker where Malka had left a small miniature of her grandmother for repair. Its tiny clasp had broken, and Sandor, the artisan, had cleverly fashioned a new one with a small locking device which would ensure against losing the valued ornament. Finally, Malka gave in to Sorke's mutterings and waited in the droshky while the stout woman purchased provisions for the household.

Sorke climbed back into the carriage while the grocer loaded her purchases in front, next to the driver. Then they were homeward bound.

Malka nodded and waved cheerfully to the housewives she knew. "Good afternoon, Malka!" they returned her greeting. She was well received in Nemunaitis, despite her big-city ways and learned pastimes. Isaac had always been a favorite, if maverick, member of the community, and his wife was a pretty, friendly girl whom everyone had grown to like.

On the way down the Long Road, they passed a number of peasants traveling on foot in groups or singly. Dressed in rough garments, many of them knew the young Mistress Hillman and bowed as her carriage passed, removing their caps, if they were wearing them. Isaac was kind and generous to the peasants in the district, as his father and grandfather had been before him. The Hillmans had enjoyed respect from the peasants in the province ever since the days of Isaac's remarkable great-grandfather, Simeon—a large, powerfully built man of action with a thick amber beard and strong white teeth who had become a legend when he organized his fellow Jews to defend themselves against attack.

The droshky arrived at the house. On this day Isaac's father, Simon, had returned home early from the office where he was the local shipping agent for the river trade. Simon was concerned when he discovered that Malka was not at home. Why would she go abroad when she was so far with child? He must speak to her about that. Then he heard the droshky pull up in front of the gate. He hurried out to greet Malka, going to the far side of the conveyance to hand his daughter-in-law down.

"I'm glad you've come home, Malka! I was worried about you. A woman in your condition should not go into the town," Simon chided her, but he did not succeed in making it a reprimand.

Malka laughed down into his face. "I promise this is the last time, Father. Please, don't tell Isaac!"

Sorke and the driver were engaged in carrying the sacks of provisions from the droshky into the house. Simon extended his hands to Malka, who was encumbered by the lap robes tucked around her.

At that instant, from the opposite direction, two horse-drawn carts—the kind peasants use to haul hay and grains—came tearing down the Long Road. Their drivers were stupefied with drink, lashing the poor beasts who pulled them, each trying to crowd the other off the narrow way. So close did the wagons come to each other that their wheels locked together.

"Yo-ho! *Giddap!*" yelled one of the peasants, his face purple.

"Faster, faster!" roared the other, laying on the whip, as he stood in the swaying cart.

The horses were terrified with the wrenching pull of the locked carts, the constant lash of the thonged whips, and the hoarse, drunken shouts of the drivers. When they saw the droshky, with its small, high-stepping mare standing quietly on the side of the road, each tried to go on an opposite side of the two-wheeled vehicle.

The well-behaved little mare reared up, tossing the droshky on an angle just as Malka was standing, ready to step down. She screamed as she was thrown into the road. One of the horses struck her with its hoofs, as it struggled to free itself from its trapped position. Simon, caught between the side of the droshky and the oncoming wagons, tried in vain to subdue the charging animal by dragging on its reins. The droshky disintegrated as it was crushed by the two lumbering wagons. The poor mare went down and was caught in a tangle of reins, horses' hoofs, and wagon wheels.

In a panic, the droshky driver rushed out of the house and cut the reins of the horses, so they ran off from the wagons. Shouting and cursing at the befuddled peasants, he roused them enough so that they realized what havoc they had created. "Dunces! Stupid louts! See what you've done," he thundered at them.

Sorke and Tobe, Aaron's wife, were kneeling over the still form of Malka in the roadway. Sorke was wailing and wringing her hands as a crowd of neighbors began to gather. It had all happened so suddenly, seemingly in an instant.

"Is she alive?" someone asked.

"Get a doctor, quickly," Tobe ordered, and someone else ran off to find the doctor.

They heard a low moan behind them. It was Simon. He was pinned beneath the carts, which were still locked together, his right leg wedged between the wheels, as if in a vise. A neighbor boy came running with an ax. With a few deft blows, the droshky driver split the wheels. They fell away, almost crushing Simon as the weight of the wagons shifted onto his back.

The next hours passed in a haze. . . . Malka and Simon were carried into the old house. The doctor arrived—a worried-looking, gray-haired man with a neatly trimmed beard, dressed in a short city coat.

"Two patients? No one told me there were *two!*" He sent for his apprentice and asked a neighbor woman to stay and help.

Malka regained consciousness. She was in severe pain. The women removed her clothing, cutting away the bodice of the dress. When she'd fallen into the roadway, Malka had instinctively shielded the child in her womb from the flailing feet of the horse, turning her back and side to them. Consequently, her back and ribs had taken the full impact of the draft horse's beating hoofs.

The doctor examined her, told the women to keep a watch over her, and turned his full attention to Simon, the master of the house, whose injuries appeared much more serious.

Simon's right leg had been broken in numerous places, and he was unable to move the other leg. The doctor manipulated the broken leg, only to discover that the limb had been so shattered below the knee that he knew he would be unable to save it.

He shook his head pessimistically. "This is surely a case for the surgeon," he announced.

In Nemunaitis this meant the *feldsher,* the barber-surgeon, an uneducated person with no medical training whose instruments were none too clean. Tobe begged him not to put her father-in-law in the hands of the *feldsher,* whose patients had a high mortality rate.

"But he'll die of poisoning if the leg isn't removed!" the doctor argued.

"Not always. Sometimes they don't die. He will surely die if the *feldsher* saws his leg." The poor woman, little more than twenty-three and unaccustomed to having such heavy responsibilities to bear alone, was distraught. It would be three days until Aaron and Isaac would return from their long boat trip to the Baltic. What should she do? She made a firm decision and no one could dissuade her from it.

"We shall wait until Aaron returns. Meanwhile, please do whatever you can to save his leg," she ordered the dumb-struck doctor. For someone to question his advice, and a woman at that!

He went about bracing the mangled leg, cleaning the gaping wounds and bandaging them. Simon suffered the procedure stoically; however, he was unable to keep from moaning aloud. When the pain became unbearable, he lapsed into merciful unconsciousness.

The doctor had just finished his difficult task when one of the women came in. "Doctor, you'd better come! The waters have broken."

The doctor entered the dim room, surprised to see that the young woman was looking much worse than several hours before when he had first examined her. Her hands were icy, her lips appeared pale and blue and she had a confused look in her eyes. Delayed shock, no doubt, from the fright and injuries. That would account for an early birth.

The long night passed second by second. Dawn was breaking when the tiny little boy was born, more dead than alive. The doctor turned him over to the women, concentrating his attention on the mother.

The women bathed the scrawny creature, hardly more than a hand's length in size, wrapped him in flannel, and placed him in a padded basket with bottles of warm water on each side. He was so small, they didn't expect him to survive. Yet, he seemed to cling to life with a tenacity as large as life itself.

"We must find a wet nurse," said Tobe. Malka was far too weak to nurse her child . . . besides, only the poor and the peasants nursed their own babies.

Simon was gathering strength by the hour. He was in considerable pain, but his delirium had left him. He was asking for tea and porridge, which Sorke gratefully prepared and fed to him, wiping her eyes with the corner of her apron as she did.

"In the name of God, Sorke, stop that sniveling! Everything will turn out. You'll see." Simon, although weak, had little patience.

"Yes, Reb Simon," she would reply and weep twice as hard. Simon was so overjoyed at the news of a grandson that he did not seem to realize the baby or its mother might not survive.

Malka had lost a great deal of blood. Even in her pain and weakness, she asked to see her little son, smiling through tear-misted eyes when they brought the diminutive man-child to her. They laid him in her arms for a few minutes, then removed him and placed him back in his roughly fashioned cradle.

Malka lay there, propped up with feather pillows, her breathing more labored than ever. Each time she tried to move, she was seized with knife-like stabs. She dozed frequently. When she awakened, she would ask for Isaac. Tobe assured her that Isaac would be home the next day.

"Rest, Malka. Tomorrow, the men will be here," she told her sister-in-law. She prayed that there would be a tomorrow.

Too late, Tobe had thought of the telegraph. The shipping office, where Simon had spent his entire working life, had a wireless. From there it was possible to contact all the other shipping offices along the banks of the Neman River. She had sent a message for the *Danika,* telling them that a baby boy had been born and urging them to hurry home as soon as possible. She did not have the heart to tell them that Malka and Simon had been injured, not by telegraph.

When the *Danika* tied up at the wharf at Seredzius, a messenger boy came waving a white paper as he ran from the shipping office on the side of the pier.

"Danika, Danika!" he called. "There is a message!"

Aaron took the paper from the boy who had sprung onto the deck. He read it expressionlessly, then handed it to Isaac, who had been opening the hatch to the cargo hold. Isaac squinted in the bright sun as he read the message. He looked up with a startled glance at the curious boy, then he turned to his brother.

"But, it wasn't supposed to be for many weeks—eight weeks! Aaron, we must leave immediately, something must have gone wrong." Isaac felt a cold dread. All he could think of was Malka, his beautiful Malka. It didn't even occur to him at that moment that he had become a father.

Aaron, for once, had no caustic comments, no arguments. He quickly prepared to get under way. Isaac threw more and more wood into the furnace in an attempt to drive the cylinder faster.

"Careful. We don't want to blow our boiler," Aaron cautioned him. Aaron had taken the boat far out midstream, away from the busy channel where the barges and fishing boats would interfere with their progress.

Isaac stood in the bow looking south, willing his wife to be strong, sending his thoughts of love and support to her. He pictured Malka in his mind's eye as he first had seen her in Sol Lieber's anteroom. She'd come to visit Sol's sister, Lara, and was just leaving after tea. He'd returned home with Sol from the state school in Kovno where he was studying. They often studied together, Isaac always hoping for an invitation to dinner because the food at the house where he boarded was sparse and unpalatable.

Sol had introduced Malka. Isaac was struck with her beauty and self-assurance. She wore her luxuriant auburn hair back in a single braid with full waves in front and on each side of her forehead. Her short, sweetly shaped nose had a sprinkling of freckles on the bridge, and when she smiled there were long creases which formed in her round cheeks. She looked him fully in the eyes, unabashed to be speaking to a man. So unlike the girls in Nemunaitis!

"You have come to Kovno for your education, Mr. Hillman? I hope you are finding our city a hospitable place."

Her speech had been that of a cultivated woman of the city. Later, Sol told him that her father, a lawyer, believed in education for women and had provided his daughter with an excellent tutor when they lived in St. Petersburg. Recently, the family had moved back to Kovno following the death of Malka's older brother.

Their courtship had been a sometime thing. Isaac didn't dare call at her house. For one thing, the family was still in mourning for their older son, who had died of typhus. Isaac spent as much time as he could at Sol Lieber's house, always hoping that he might find Malka there. He was delighted one late afternoon when he walked into a bookshop and saw her.

"Good afternoon, Miss Belkind. Are you browsing?" His heartbeat had quickened at the sight of her.

"How nice to see you, Mr. Hillman. I came for some books my father has ordered." Isaac insisted on carrying the books for her, accompanying her to her parents' house. It was only natural for her to invite him in for tea.

Malka's parents, Michel and Sophie Belkind, and Malka's younger brother, Judah, had been entertaining several guests. They welcomed him into the circle, with scarcely a pause in the lively conversation.

Isaac was catapulted into a different world. Despite his father's interest in worldly subjects and his own secular education, Nemunaitis had been a circumscribed world, truly a backwater. Old customs die hard, and the tenets of Enlightenment, *Haskala,* had not found a nurturing environment in the provincial river town. One must have someone with whom to exchange ideas if a dialogue is to exist, and in Nemunaitis, the exchange of ideas was most frequently limited to traditional scholarly subjects—the Talmud and the Torah.

Michel Belkind was a lawyer who specialized in business law. His clients included Jews and gentiles, and he enjoyed a fine reputation in Kovno, where he'd lived most of his life. Circumstances had taken him to St. Petersburg for several years.

Lawyer Belkind knew many important people. He spoke knowledgeably about international finance, was acquainted with some of the great banking houses of western Europe. He had traveled to Vienna and Berlin, and even to Paris. Isaac listened, spellbound, to the discussions of international affairs.

When the talk turned to the thwarted reforms of a once-liberal Czar, some of Michel Belkind's guests spoke of organizations composed of anarchists like the ones who had twice tried to assassinate Alexander II. The futility of the anarchists' approach was debated back and forth.

"Gradual liberalization, with a constitution and democratic principles such as they have in America, is what the rational man should support," a young man named Reuben Sarnoff argued. And over and over Isaac h

the name pronounced with a regard amounting to reverence . . . America
. . . America.

Those had been heady days. Isaac returned again and again to the Belkind
home, where he was made to feel welcome, like one of the family. He realized
that he was falling in love with Malka and he was reasonably sure that she
looked upon him with favor. But one did not fall in love, marry, and live
happily ever after like the English fairy tales would have you believe. Not in
the time-honored tradition of the Russian Jew.

Isaac pondered his situation. There he was, in his twenty-second year, just
completing his course of study, with the rather unpromising prospect of
spending his life as a shipping agent at a minor port along the Neman River.
And he knew that his father had begun making inquiries about a suitable
marriage for him, discreetly to be sure, but inevitable in its outcome. He
became obsessed with the necessity of having Malka as his wife. But how? He
knew his prospects were not great enough for the only daughter of the Lawyer Belkind.

And then the solution presented itself to him from the least expected
source—the shipping office in Nemunaitis, where his father and brother
worked each day. The "List of Ships for Sale," which he'd seen often enough,
contained several items that caught his eye—all small cargo vessels that had
seen service on the Neman and the Vistula. It didn't take him long to determine that the *Danika* was the sole possibility for him—and then only if his
rother, Aaron, could be convinced to join him in what he realized was a rash
nture. Aaron had reluctantly acquiesced. He'd always been slow to take
nces, but Isaac suspected there was a core of the adventurer in his sober
r brother. He'd seen the look in Aaron's eyes as he sat over the endless
  in the shipping office, envying Isaac his freedom in Kovno.
  ir father, Simon, was stunned at their recklessness. To set out on the
  'eman as merchant-captains? No one they knew in Nemunaitis had
  e such a rash thing! As for the townspeople, the Jews? They'd always
  ere was a wild strain in the Hillman blood. . . . After all, they
  sent their sons to *cheder!*

   left Kovno to begin his new life as a merchant-captain, he had
   d to speak to Malka, to tell her in some way of his love for her
   vait for him. He'd spent many restless hours in the still of the
   hat another suitor had presented himself to Michel Belkind.
   roached the Belkind house he would torture himself with
   ngagement would be announced.
   d walked out along the twisting streets near the bend in
   y talked of inconsequential things. Malka seemed dis-
   ly. He approached his subject warily.

"Miss Belkind, I shall miss your family. I have a . . . great affection . . . for your family. They've been so kind to me."

"Yes, Mr. Hillman," she replied laconically. "They also have an affection for you. I know my family will miss you too."

"I shall miss the hearty discussions. I've enjoyed all of your father's friends . . . and your friends . . ."

She did not answer. It was going badly.

"Do you suppose I may come to call on your family when I stop at Kovno in the future?"

"Will you be stopping at Kovno?" she asked.

"Yes. I should think so. Perhaps once in a week or two weeks."

"Yes, then, by all means do call on my family when you stop at Kovno."

Suddenly he had turned and, all caution thrown to the air, said, "I feel a very deep affection for *you,* Miss Belkind. I feel a deep . . . love for you." There, it had been said, and whatever the result, she would know his feelings. He had looked at her with pleading in his eyes.

And she had smiled, the most wonderful smile. For the first time that day her eyes were alive with their customary brightness.

"Love? Did you say you feel 'love' for me?" In his vulnerable state, he mistook her tone for ridicule.

They were standing still in the street, facing each other. Isaac was tall, youthfully slim and handsome, his blond head bare in the late spring breeze. A look of torment and pride darkened his blue eyes as he said, "Do not mock me, Malka. I had hoped that you might harbor some regard for me. But I see that I am mistaken."

Impulsively, she touched his hand, forgetting where they were. "Oh no, you are not mistaken! Don't you see, Isaac? I, too, feel love for you. From the first day, when you carried my books, I have loved you."

A great burden lifted from his heart when Malka said those words. He was filled with life, purpose, and direction. For many long months their love remained their own secret. But Lawyer Belkind and his wife were not such fools. As time passed, although nothing was said, they saw that their daughter was in a state of perpetual exhilaration, only to change to *intense* exhilaration when Isaac Hillman came to visit on his frequent port calls at Kovno. They admired the young man. Michel Belkind thought he possessed a fine mind and the ability to succeed. And Malka's mother saw the tenderness and devotion in the brawny man's gentle eyes when he looked at her daughter.

In six months on the river, Isaac had grown broad-shouldered and muscular. Unable to hire a hand, the brothers did most of their own hauling and crew work. As a result, not only had they become robust and physically hardened, but their cargoes were among the best on the entire length of the river, always arriving on time and in perfect condition. The services of the *Danika* were much in demand. Many merchants were willing to pay a surcharge for their goods to be shipped on the boat of the Hillman brothers.

Aaron, surprisingly enough, had turned out to be the more natural seaman of the two. He quickly took to piloting the broad-beamed vessel, learning the ebbs and flows of the long river as naturally as if he'd spent his life on the water. It was Isaac, however, who was the planner and visionary.

Isaac realized that the government stores of grains were low when he overheard a conversation between a merchant and a government purchasing agent on the docks one day. He set about buying up all the grain he could from the merchants in Grodno, paying them a fair price and arranging to store it in an empty shed in Nemunaitis. Three months later he sold the entire shipment for five times what he had paid for the grain, again at a fair market price. Similarly, he traded barrel staves for kerosene in the summer, storing the oil until the demand for it grew as the shorter days of winter approached. In this way, always with complete honesty, they were able to pay off the debt on the *Danika* within a year of her purchase, much to everyone's amazement—not the least, their own.

Meanwhile, Isaac and his brother were building a reputation of enviable proportions on the river. Their reliability and character were beyond question. There were occasional incidents of an anti-Jewish nature, but for the most part they enjoyed good relationships with the various factors on the river. They were aware that some shipping agents farther away from Kovno and Grodno took them to be Russians. Be that as it may, it did not worry them.

One day as they steamed along toward Kovno, Aaron said to him, "Where do you go all the time in Kovno, Isaac? You must have many friends there from your student days."

"I have some friends, Aaron. You met Sol Lieber once. You know my friend Reuben Sarnoff . . . Reuben has gone to America. He left a few months ago. There was a party for him at Malka's house." The name had slipped out before he was aware of it.

Aaron smiled to himself. A little while later he asked, "Who is Malka?"

Isaac seldom confided in Aaron. At that moment, though, Isaac had an urge to tell his brother about the young woman who had captured his heart.

Aaron had listened with unconcealed astonishment as Isaac described how he'd met Malka, fallen in love with her, and she with him. He shook his head in mock dismay.

"Isaac, I should've known you wouldn't do *anything*, even get a wife, in the way other people do!"

"Times change, Aaron. Many young people in the cities choose whom they will marry. I haven't yet spoken to her father, but soon I shall do so. Now that we've paid for the boat, I can save enough money to support a wife."

"But, that's not the way it is done," Aaron protested. "Our father must do the speaking, Isaac. And it's the girl's family that gives the money for a marriage. That's the way it was with Tobe and me."

Isaac didn't wish to offend Aaron by pointing out that his brother had scarcely known his quiet, rather plain wife before their marriage. Tobe had come from a good family, one with background and education, although she herself had intellectual limitations. To Isaac's observant eyes his brother's placid marriage seemed nothing short of dull.

Still, he took Aaron's words under consideration, and the next time they docked at Nemunaitis, on the afternoon before the Sabbath, he decided he would speak to his father.

After the Sabbath meal the men went to the synagogue to pray, while Tobe remained at home with her two small daughters. When they returned, Aaron went into his part of the house, presumably to discharge his marital obligations, because, according to custom, every devout Jew must cohabit with his wife on the eve of the Sabbath. Isaac, ashamed of his impious thoughts, envied his brother the opportunity, but not the object, of conjugal bliss. He decided this was the moment, so sought out his father, who was reading in the dim light of an oil lamp.

Simon smiled with pleasure when his tall, manly son drew up a chair. "How is the *Danika,* your soul's delight, Isaac?" his father asked, half in jest.

"Fine, Father. You know, we've not only paid off the debt, but we've put aside some money. I knew that owning a steamboat would be a good thing for Aaron and me, but I didn't expect it to be so profitable at this early stage."

Simon smiled knowingly. "Acting as a grain broker is something in addition to hauling cargo, Isaac. And holding futures in lamp oil goes beyond the scope of a merchant-captain."

"So, you know about those ventures, Father! Well, I wasn't sure it would work out profitably, so I didn't want to worry you with my risks," Isaac answered, surprised that his father had heard about his investments.

"I'm proud of your business ability, Isaac. You certainly didn't inherit that from me." Simon poked fun at himself.

"Father, there's another matter I want to discuss with you."

"Not another steamboat, I hope."

"No, not a steamboat." He hesitated, then went on. "A wife."

"Ah, Isaac! I'm not such an old man that I haven't thought about a wife for my son! Of course, you want a wife. And I shall find her for you. In fact, I've already been making inquiries. I've been told that there are some wonderful families with daughters of marriageable age in Vilna and Kovno." Isaac kept trying to speak, but his father continued. "If your mother, of blessed memory, were still alive, it would have been done long ago. Imagine, my son, that you should have to ask me to get you a wife!" And Simon laughed at his own joke.

"Father," Isaac began, and found much to his distress that he wasn't sure how to go on. "I'm not exactly asking you to 'get' me a wife."

"I know, Isaac, I know. Of course, you'll have the opportunity to become acquainted before the agreement, before your betrothal. These are not the Dark Ages, after all."

"That's just it, Father! These *aren't* the Dark Ages. I knew you would understand that. I meant that it wouldn't be necessary for you to *arrange* a marriage for me . . . because I've already met the woman I want for my wife."

Simon Hillman of Nemunaitis, graduate of the gymnasium at Vilna, a scholar and advocate of Enlightenment, had never conceived of the idea that his son would not depend upon him to arrange a marriage for him. Was it not his duty, his privilege to do so? And yet, here was his son, who knew more about the world beyond Nemunaitis than he himself. Isaac had always been a good boy, although independent, and he loved him dearly. So, he listened while Isaac told him about Malka and her family and how he'd spent many hours around their table, getting to know them and finding them so congenial. And it made sense to him.

"And so, you would like me to talk to Lawyer Belkind, Isaac. To arrange a marriage with his daughter."

"Yes, Father. That's what I'm asking. But, Father, no talk of money, please. I wouldn't have them think that I don't want Malka without a dowry. You *do* understand?"

"Understand? I'm not so sure I have to understand, my son."

Not long after that, Simon Hillman boarded the *Danika* and accompanied his sons to Kovno, where the brothers and their father called on Lawyer Belkind. The two fathers went by themselves to another room, and when they emerged, everyone had some *shnaps* and honey cake and toasted the happiness of the blushing couple, Isaac and Malka.

Isaac had often pondered during his long night hours on the river about the meaning of love. How could it be that one smile, one pair of laughing eyes, one dear face should make the difference between joy and despair for him? Yet it was so.

And now that fragile happiness was threatened. He prayed to God that all was well with Malka. If there was danger, as there certainly must be—for why else had the telegraph message said to come as soon as possible?—please God, let it not be his wife!

The *Danika* steamed her slow way up the Neman, each hour seeming like ten. When finally they caught sight of the ancient castle, a familiar landmark, Isaac's anxiety had become unbearable. The moment they touched the dock, Aaron urged him to go on ahead, knowing his need to reach home.

Isaac entered his house in a state of combined dread and relief to be there at last. Tobe was waiting, dark circles under her eyes, hair unkempt.

"Where is she, Tobe?"

Tobe motioned toward the stairs, unable to speak. Isaac's heart turned over. He took one look at Tobe and raced up the stairs to the room where his wife lay in bed.

Malka's eyes were closed. He could see that she was breathing in shallow gasps. Her face was deathly white, her eyes sunken. Her lovely auburn hair lay in two braids on either side of her shoulders and over the counterpane. Isaac sat down next to the bed and took one of her hands in his. It was so cold, so limp. Malka's eyelids fluttered open.

"Isaac, my dear, you came . . ."

"I am here, my heart. Everything will be all right now. You'll be well now, Malka." He kissed the hand and leaned over to kiss her brow.

"Oh, Isaac, we have a son. Do you like your son?"

He couldn't help the tears that coursed down his cheeks. He shook his head in denial. He knew that she was dying and he didn't want a son. He wanted his wife, only his wife.

Her voice was weaker. "He's such a little baby, so small." Then: "Bring him to me."

Isaac rose and walked over to the basket, which he'd failed to notice before. He looked down at his sleeping son. The baby was smaller than any he'd ever seen. Could he possibly live? He reached in and picked up the tiny bundle. The child stirred but did not waken. He carried him over to the bed and laid him beside Malka, placing her arm around him, for she was too weak to move.

"I want to call him Jacob. After my brother. Will you do that?"

He nodded his agreement, afraid to speak.

"Please love him, Isaac. He needs you." Her eyes pleaded with him.

Isaac sat down and leaned over the two of them. His wife and his son. How wonderful it could have been. If only . . .

"I *do* love him, Malka. He's part of you, part of our love. Our little Jacob."

Malka smiled, contented. She slipped into a state of unconsciousness soon after. Her breathing became quieter and quieter until it simply stopped. Isaac had never left her side, holding her hand and watching her face until the end.

The doctor said that one of her ribs had been broken when she was trampled and while she labored the break must have separated. The jagged end of a bone had pierced her lung, causing a hemorrhage.

Later, Isaac couldn't remember much about that week. He had walked behind his wife's casket to the small Jewish cemetery. He went through the motions of accepting visitors, sitting *shiva,* saying the prayer for the dead, the *Kaddish,* but it was unreal to him. He still imagined Malka alive, speaking to him, waiting for him in their bed.

Simon was making a slow recovery. Isaac would sit with him for hours, staring into space while Simon talked or just watched his grieving son with a heavy heart. He had lost his own wife, but that was after the boys were past childhood, and she had seen them grow tall.

Isaac wasn't aware of when he first noticed the odor. It was a smell of decay, reminding him of the hold when there had been rotten fruit, or they carried a cargo of chickens. Simon had not complained of any new pain in the leg, but Isaac unwrapped the bandages one afternoon and was horrified to see that the toes and part of the foot were dark and festered and there were red streaks running upward to the knee. When the doctor came and Isaac showed him the leg, he reminded Isaac that he'd said it couldn't be saved from the first day.

The brothers carried Simon out of the house to a cart. He was taken aboard the *Danika,* once again to travel to Kovno. But no happy celebration awaited them this time. Weeks later, when they brought Simon home, he had lost most of his leg. He would never walk again because he could not move the other leg.

Simon, the Enlightened, had an explanation for it all. "It is God's will," he said.

III

Summer 1877

Tobe entered the house, her face flushed and shining, with damp ringlets showing beneath her kerchief. Isaac knew she had returned from the ritual bath, the *mikvah,* to which all the devout women went each Friday before the Sabbath, to be purified and made clean. . . . Malka hadn't gone to the *mikvah,* preferring to bathe at home. The memories. Everything reminded him of what it had been like when Malka was there. . . .

They had talked about America often. Reuben Sarnoff was in America. He wrote to Malka's brother, who read the letter to them.

> . . . I'm working on a newspaper—for an Irishman! He's a good
> sort. I engrave plates and set type. It is not exactly art, but it's a
> good living. . . . We are expecting a child in the spring. Our baby
> will be an American citizen! . . .

What would it be like to go to America? she had asked. There, everyone was free to do as he wished. Jews were the same as everyone else . . . no pogroms, no Pale of Settlement.

"Reuben says they are not rich, but it is a land of opportunity!"

Maybe, someday, they had mused. Oh, but it would be so hard to leave Simon and her parents in Kovno . . . they had already lost their older son. It wouldn't be right. But maybe . . . we'll see. . . .

Isaac had written a letter to Reuben Sarnoff, asking about life there, in America.

Sorke lifted Jacob from his father's lap. "We must bathe for the Sabbath, Yaki," she said, as the little boy tried to escape from her grasp.

The girls were dressed in white. Sara stood placidly while the servant plaited her freshly washed hair. Tanya shifted impatiently from foot to foot when her turn came.

Isaac and Aaron had bathed in the large wooden tub which rested over a bed of hot embers in the annex behind the stove. Dressed in fresh clothing, the brothers relaxed in the late afternoon hours before the Sabbath meal.

"Aaron, I'm worried about our father. He's growing weaker. His leg doesn't look right to me," Isaac confided to his brother when he was sure they were alone.

"He's getting older, Isaac. He's weak because he doesn't move about." Aaron tried to reassure his brother. He knew that Simon's disability only served to remind Isaac of the accident that had cost Malka her life.

Isaac shook his head. "No, I'm almost sure it's more than that. When I washed him, I could tell the entire stump was painful and the pain went up into the hip. Father tried not to let me see how great was his pain. He won't return to Kovno to see the surgeon. He says he prefers to die, rather than have him remove more of the leg."

A month later Simon Hillman died—as he had lived—quietly and thoughtfully, at peace with God and himself. Isaac and Aaron stood at his bed, not aware that the end would come so soon. Simon smiled, took Isaac's hand, squeezing it briefly, then turned his face away and breathed his last.

The brothers grieved for their father, for his gentle spirit, and his generous nature. Again, they walked to the old cemetery, returning to the shrouded house to sit *shiva*. Isaac felt weighted down with endless sorrow. Surely life was meant to be joyful, a celebration of work and creativity—not this heaviness, this somber desolation that had etched his heart since that fateful day in March a year and a half before.

"Shall we make a long route to Memel next month, Aaron?" Isaac asked his brother as they were returning from Grodno one evening in October. "We can get a contract from the Poliakoff Line. They have more cargo than their ships can handle. If we had another boat, we could be twice as booked."

"Another boat! That's all we need. But a run to Memel before the winter sets in—yes, we should do that. We'll just have local trade during the coldest months."

"Next time we make port at Kovno, I'd like to spend the night with Malka's family, Aaron. They're getting old. You know, I haven't taken Jacob there for a long time. They look at him with such unhappiness. I'm afraid he'll notice and misunderstand."

"It's natural for them to mourn their daughter when they see her child . . ." Aaron didn't finish.

"The child who caused her death? That's what everyone thinks, you know. I felt that way myself when Jacob was first born. Malka was afraid of that. She asked me to love him. . . . But it wasn't the baby's fault. The birth would have been perfectly normal if those drunken bastards hadn't come along. And what happened to them? A fine! That's all. They were out getting drunk and celebrating afterward. Well, why not? It was, after all, only a *Jewish* woman." Aaron had never heard his brother speak with such bitterness before. Not in all the long, sorrowful months since he had lost his wife.

Michel Belkind had aged. His beard was almost totally gray now and the shiny pate of his bald head was fringed with silver. He smiled widely when he saw Isaac, embracing him heartily. "Come in, come in, my boy! This is indeed a pleasure—an unexpected and welcome pleasure. Sophie, Sophie, come see who is here!"

Malka's mother, so like her dead daughter that it gave Isaac's heart a wrench every time he saw her anew, came into the salon. "Isaac! Oh, my dear, how wonderful to see you!" She embraced him, and when she withdrew, he saw her eyes swimming with tears. He had a difficult time controlling his own.

"We were so sorry about your father, Isaac. It was too late, when we heard, for us to come. So much sorrow . . ."

"Yes, thank you, Mother Sophie. I received your letter. Father had suffered enough, I think. He had a peaceful end and we are grateful for that."

Michel took out the *shnaps* and Sophie brought kuchen and the shining copper samovar. They sat and talked of events of the world. At the same time, Isaac was aware that their own world had shrunk.

"How is Judah?" he asked.

Sophie threw up her hands. "He talks of settling in Palestine now!"

"Palestine?" Isaac laughed. "I thought it was America."

"It was. But his friend Lazar Weinberg came back from America. He said it's not so easy for a Jew there. So now they say they want to go to Palestine together, to join a community of young Jewish Socialists, to build a Jewish homeland there."

"He wants us to go with him," Michel said casually, but something in his tone made Isaac pay close attention.

"And would you do that, Reb Michel?"

The older man sighed. "If I were twenty years younger, I might. But I think I would go to America before Palestine. That's just my feeling, mind you. I don't see a Jewish homeland in Palestine within my lifetime, or yours either. But, in America, for all that Lazar Weinberg says, it's still a free country, a place where even the poor have rights."

Later, when Sophie had retired and the two of them were sitting in front of a fire, sipping the fiery plum brandy that Michel loved, the conversation became more serious.

"This continuing conflict with the Ottoman Turks is draining the treasury, causing economic unrest unparalleled," Michel stated, gesturing with his cigar. "All the big Jewish financiers say they're dealing with a government bankrupt in spirit as well as in gold. Rothschild won't float a loan, even if Poliakoff requests it personally. The Czar doesn't even realize how much he *needs* the wealthy Jews—how much they've *always* needed them. Who would build the railroads? Who would develop the industry?"

As always, Isaac felt stimulated when he talked to Michel Belkind. The broad knowledge of the man still impressed him. From this small provincial city, his connections in the world of international finance and politics were surprising.

"I met a man named Bloch several months ago. He works for the Rothschilds. He took passage on my boat . . ."

"Ah! Leopold Bloch. Yes, he came to see me about some financing." Michel hesitated for a moment. "The French Rothschild—Louis—is interested in supporting a settlement of Russian Jews in Palestine. It's still very confidential," Michel warned.

"I won't mention it to anyone," Isaac assured him.

Now Belkind said something that chilled Isaac:

"To be a Jew in Russia has always been difficult. But never so difficult as it's going to be in the near future. Whenever Russia has seen hard times, it has gone badly for the Jews."

Isaac said to him, "I've been thinking about the future, Reb Michel. I don't like the things I read in the Russian-language newspapers. I don't like the remarks I hear along the docks, either. There's a tide of discontent. And too often I hear sentiments against the Jews. I agree that there will be troubled times, particularly for the Jews."

They were silent, Michel puffing on his cigar and sipping brandy. "You say you've been thinking about the future, Isaac. What are your thoughts, then?"

Isaac stared into the flames for a long moment. Then he raised his head and looked into his father-in-law's eyes.

"America," he said.

Memories assaulted Isaac when he retired to Malka's old bedroom. Here they had spent the first nights of their marriage before he returned to the *Danika*. Was it only four years ago?

He had lingered in the salon that first evening after the wedding celebration, allowing Malka some time and privacy, admittedly a little nervous himself. In the small anteroom with its wardrobe, Isaac had discarded his coat and vest. Then he'd removed his high-collared shirt and tie. Bare to the waist, he had knocked on the door to the sleeping chamber.

Malka was standing in front of the mirror brushing her long, heavy hair. She had laid down the ornate silver brush and, bending her head sideways, was braiding her chestnut hair into a thick coil, holding it in front of one shoulder. She stopped when she saw him, smiling and flushing with pleasure.

Isaac walked across the room toward her, his eyes drinking in her loveliness. She was wearing a loose-fitting white gown which trailed on the floor. Its wide neckline and broad sleeves were trimmed with heavy lace. In the soft glow of the single oil lamp, she looked ethereal.

He took the braid from her hands, bringing it to his lips, breathing in its perfume. Loosening the strands, he gently unraveled her hair, brushing its silkiness back from her smooth, high forehead. She turned her lovely face up to him, placing her palms against his chest, her hands moving up to caress his shoulders and back. He bent his head to kiss her brow. His lips traced the curve of her cheek, her eyelids, her answering mouth. Holding her close against his lean, muscular body, he felt her soft curves. They aroused feelings within him of mingled desire and protectiveness. As his hands stroked the contours of her body, he felt her tremble.

"Isaac. Oh, Isaac," she whispered.

"Don't be afraid, my beloved."

"I'm not afraid," she answered. "I love you so much, Isaac. So very much."

Standing next to the high bed with its draped curtains, Isaac had untied the ribbons on the front opening of her gown, spreading it back from her shoulders and allowing it to fall to the floor.

He thought then he had never seen anything so beautiful as her lush, nubile body. In her, he saw everything that was womanly beauty, all the allure of femininity. Her eyes had not wavered when he stripped off the rest of his clothing. Dreamily, voluptuously, they had loved each other, relishing the sensuality of their young, lithe bodies. When they had finally joined, in the perfect harmony of their desire, she had cried out in love and joy.

Later, held in her arms, his lips against the smoothness of her throat, he listened to the combined measure of their heartbeats.

"Now, you are truly my husband," she had murmured sleepily.

"And you are my wife. . . ."

Lying alone now with his memories, in the cold emptiness of Malka's bed, Isaac spilled his seed and wept dry, bitter tears for his lost love and the bleak void in his life.

IV

On the Danika at Kovno   Summer 1878

"Hah! And what have we here?" Isaac lifted the urchin from his hiding place between two drums of kerosene, holding him high with one hand by the collar of his tattered jacket. The boy was scrawny, but strong; however, his strength was nothing in the grasp of the muscular riverboatman. His fists and feet flailed in the air, his pinched face contorted in fear and anger.

Isaac's keen eyes spotted the newly cut hair where the side curls had been, even in the poor light of the boat's hold. "A *yeshiva bucher,* hmmm?"

"Niet, niet! I don't know what you're talking about," the boy cried, his face blanching even paler.

"Sssh! Don't worry, my young fellow. We are Jews, too. You're safe with us." He put his hand over the boy's mouth to silence him and held him against his broad chest until the youth stopped struggling.

"We'll have to do something about your hair, though. And these clothes! You wouldn't fool a half-blind inspector with that cut-off *kapote* . . . you might as well have left the *peyes* if you wear that hat. Anyone would spot you as a Jew."

Isaac held the youth away from him and gently removed the telltale round black hat of a pious Talmudic student. The boy immediately clapped his hand on top of his head.

"You're going to have to learn to go bareheaded if you want to be taken for a gentile. We'll make you into a river rat and put you to work . . . get you to Tilsit. After that, with God's help, you'll be all right."

The boy's eyes moistened, but he showed no other signs of emotion. Then they heard footsteps on the deck above. Isaac doused the dim lantern, pushed the boy behind some crates, and started up the ladder.

"Hallo! Who's there?" he called in Russian.

"Who else would it be? You were expecting the Czar, maybe?"

"Aaron! Come quickly into the cabin. I must talk with you," Isaac said. "Don't joke. We have a problem." He turned and spoke in a low voice to the boy below. "Stay hidden and don't worry. We'll come right back. It's only my brother."

In the cabin, Isaac told Aaron of his discovery.

"So, you propose we take this unknown foundling from God knows where and smuggle him to Prussia. Then we get caught and hanged, and make a widow of my wife and an orphan of your son."

"But, Aaron, we can't let the soldiers catch him. He's so thin now. One month in the army and he'd be dead."

Aaron sighed. "Well, let's have a look at him," the gruff brother answered.

When Isaac had brought the boy to the cabin, he stood him before Aaron, straightening his dirty shirt and rumpled coat like a father preparing his son for an introduction to a friend. The boy stood squinting in the light of the cabin, bewildered, yet wary.

"Where is your home?" Aaron was the grand inquisitor.

The boy swallowed. "Near Garliava."

"Who are your parents?"

"My father is dead. My mother makes hats and I am all she has."

"What is your name? How old are you?"

"My name is Yekhiel. I'm twelve"—and when Aaron looked doubtful—"almost fourteen."

"You're running from the soldiers? And you're the only son of a widowed mother? You expect us to believe that? Think of a better story!"

"It's true, I tell you! My father was a tailor. He died. I had a brother. He was taken to the army three years ago. He died in the winter from the cold. There is a draft in our district—for the canton there—they are taking second sons. We are poor and can't pay the fee. My mother told me to run away."

Aaron was silent for a few minutes, while Isaac watched him and the boy watched Isaac.

Finally: "All right, we'll let him come with us." He looked the boy in the eye. "But one wrong move and we turn you over, understand?" The boy nodded. "Get him cleaned up, but not too much. Those clothes have to go. And, for God's sake, do something about that hair!"

"Are you hungry?" Isaac asked. But there was no answer. The boy was lying crumpled on the floor of the cabin.

They set out after dark, the hold full of containers of lamp oil, sacks of grain, and wagon-wheel staves. By the time the first rays of dawn were spreading across the sky, they had passed Veliuona. They were preparing to pull into the wharf at Jurbarkas when Isaac awakened Yekhiel, giving him some work clothes he'd found in the rear compartment.

As they pulled alongside the pier, Isaac threw a line to the longshoreman who waited on the dock, and jumped off himself to push the boat away from the pilings in case there should be a sudden wash from a passing boat. He checked the thick braided hemp bumpers, made sure the fore and aft lines were fastened securely, then hurried back on board to help with the manifest, which must be presented to the inspector at each port along the way.

"Go see that the boy stays out of sight," Aaron told him.

Isaac went back to the cabin where the boy was just finishing an entire loaf of bread and some cheese that Isaac had given him.

"I see that you were hungry. How long since you had a meal?"

"I finished the bread and salted fish my mother gave me two days ago. Nothing since." At the mention of his mother, the boy's voice grew unsteady.

"No matter. We'll make you a better meal as soon as we set out again. But for now, you must hide because we're at Jurbarkas and the inspector will come on board. Get in this compartment and don't make a sound." Isaac opened a storage area filled with ropes, blankets, and matting. The boy crept in and settled on a bundle.

"Put that blanket over you and keep very still," said Isaac. He handed the boy the chunk of cheese. "Here, let this keep you company."

Back on deck, Aaron was directing some dockhands with the unloading of drums of lamp oil. An inspector stood on the dock counting the containers as they were put ashore to be weighed by the master of scales. At each station along the length of the winding Neman, a fee was collected according to the weight of the cargo.

The inspector climbed on board, requiring Aaron's signature on his clearance papers. He was friendly enough. The brothers, although Jewish, were known and liked along the river. They were honest. They spoke Russian, Lithuanian, and German. You could actually have a conversation with them without feeling they were afraid of you, or thought they were better than you —ridiculous though that was! Everyone knew the *zhids* were a deceitful bunch, wont to smuggle and cheat. But for Jews, these two, they weren't bad.

The routine questions. "Destination?"

"Memel."

"Cargo?"

"Crude, fifty barrels; wagon staves, thirty-five crates; grain, a hundred and twenty sacks; forty hemp bales; some chickens, some eggs."

"Pigs?"

"On my boat? You must be joking!"

Ha, ha, ha, he laughed. It was a ritual.

"Passengers?"

"Just me and my brother, as usual."

"Taking on anything?"

"Some stores for ourselves."

When they were under way again, Isaac took the wheel while Aaron made tea. "Just one more stop at Neman, and then we make it for Tilsit," said Aaron.

"Maybe we should go direct to Tilsit and hit Neman on the return," suggested Isaac.

"Ah, you're just edgy. Better not deviate from the routine. That would raise some questions."

Yekhiel was allowed out of the stuffy compartment. Isaac gave him *farfel* in a thick broth and some tea. The boy held a chunk of rock sugar between his teeth as he sipped the steaming liquid.

"You'll have to stay hidden below when we reach Neman. It's darker and not so pleasant down there, but better be safe," Isaac told him.

They approached Neman. Here they would have to go through a Russian checkpoint before crossing the Prussian border. Isaac took Yekhiel below, lifting him into a barrel that had holes in its sides. He placed sacks of grain around the boy, leaving some air space for him to breathe.

"Keep this over your mouth in case you sneeze or cough," he said, handing Yekhiel a square of cloth from his pocket. "Don't make a sound, no matter what you hear," he cautioned. Then he hammered a top on the barrel and rolled it into a corner behind some other cargo.

Two soldiers were lounging on the dock when they made fast. Isaac felt the vise of fear at the back of his head. He leaped back on board, seemingly busy with the lines. "Look! Soldiers!" he whispered in Yiddish to Aaron as he bent over.

"I see them. Just stay calm. Bluff is the only way."

There was a grating sound as a wooden plank was set against their side, and an inspector came aboard followed by the two soldiers, their bayoneted rifles held before them.

The inspector addressed Aaron. "You are the captain?"

"Yes, I am the captain."

There was no joviality in this inspector. "Papers."

He inspected the manifest which Aaron handed him. "Identity papers!" he barked.

Aaron and Isaac reached for their documents.

"Jews, I see. Where are the beards?"

"Not all Jews have beards these days, Inspector," Isaac answered, an edge to his voice. Aaron flashed him a warning glance. "We are of the new generation," he added in a less emphatic manner.

"Let's have a look at your quarters." Isaac gave a small prayer for having moved Yekhiel from the cabin. The inspector was thorough, opening all compartments and poking around inside.

"And now, your cargo," he said coolly when they had left the cabin.

Isaac's throat felt dry. He motioned below. One of the soldiers stood aside and with a nod of his head indicated that Isaac should go first. The soldier followed him down the ladder.

"Put on a light, *zhid*," he said, contempt in his voice. Isaac fought hard to control his anger. He lit a lantern, making sure that the wick was low so as not to cast much light. He was sharply aware of the other soldier, poised above him, weapon ready, halfway down the ladder.

The first soldier gazed around the dark hold. They could hear the sound of the bilges swishing, smell the oil mixed with a sour sewage odor, but Isaac could hear only the thudding of his heart and smell his own sweat. The soldier poked a few sacks of grain, thumped on the oil drums methodically. Each one sounded dully with the tone of a filled container. He had turned toward the ladder when he spotted the barrel with some sacks of flour leaning against it. He walked over, examined the top for a moment. Then, with a motion so sudden that Isaac was caught completely off guard, he lunged at the barrel with his bayonet, driving it into the soft wood up to its hilt. Isaac's strangled cry was muffled by the cursing of the soldier as he tried to withdraw the bayonet. It finally came free. He examined the blade in the dim light before replacing it in its scabbard.

"Nothing here," he shouted as he climbed up on the deck.

Isaac felt weak, but doused the lantern and scurried up the ladder. Aaron was talking now with the inspector, who seemed to be a little friendlier. They quickly concluded the formalities.

As soon as they left the pier, Isaac told Aaron what had happened. He hurried below, pried off the top of the barrel, and removed one of the sacks of grain.

Yekhiel was there, his head thrown back, his eyes closed. The other sacks were soaked with red blood.

"If it doesn't become septic, he'll live," said the doctor. "He probably won't have full use of the hand, though. The tendon was almost completely severed. It's amazing that it's such a clean wound for that sort of accident."

"We keep our tools clean and free of rust on our farm," Isaac replied. His blue eyes met the doctor's questioning look directly. "It was an unfortunate accident."

"He is your nephew?"

"Yes, my nephew. An orphan."

The doctor busied himself packing up his bag of instruments. Isaac had insisted on finding a Western-trained doctor and supervised him while he washed his hands before touching Yekhiel. The boy had lost much blood. Now he slept fitfully on the cot in the back room of Rivka's bakery. Isaac had cared for him in the cabin after convincing Aaron that they must cruise back upstream. They had hastily disposed of their cargo at Tilsit, not taking on any return cargo for the intermediate ports along the way. They passed the border without incident. Not until they reached Vilkija did Isaac feel safe. Here, closer to Kovno, he felt comfortable. Every town, every little hamlet had its ties with the network of Jews within the pale, of course, but the closer to home you were, the more you could trust others. No Jew would inform on another unless he was a complete scoundrel, but it was better to be careful. The two brothers were known and respected in Kovno *guberniya* even by the traditional Jews, who disapproved of the secular education their father had provided for them.

"Take care of him, Rivka. I'll check back in a week when we come this way. Say nothing. If anyone asks, he's a relative. One thing now, he won't have to worry about the army. He can go to his mother and learn to make hats with one hand." His tone was bitter.

"You're a good man, Isaac. God bless you," the stout woman said as Isaac placed some kopecks in the ceramic jar on the table.

He walked along the muddy streets, passing the central market area, and hailed a farmer with a cart.

V

On the Neman River   August 1878

"*America!*" It was not often that Aaron's gloom lifted. "What kind of *mishegoss* are you talking, Isaac?"

"It's not craziness, Aaron. I've given it months of deep thought, and . . ."

"I *don't* want to hear anymore, Isaac. Just as things are settling down you always come up with some nonsense, some scheme that disrupts everything. You can forget about America as far as *I'm* concerned!" He stalked into the cabin, leaving Isaac alone on the deck of the *Danika*.

They were at anchor in a small lagoon in the heart of the fertile Lithuanian plain. It was a rare moment of repose for the two brothers. Sitting out on the deck, under a moonlit sky, Isaac could hear the distant music of the Lithuanian harvest celebration in one of the farmhouses in the broad river valley. The rich tone of male voices raised in minor harmony floated across the fields and over the still water of the cove. The silvery moonlight bathed the fields of grain with an unearthly beauty, touching a place within Isaac's spirit, creating a mood of nostalgia. He and Aaron had been drinking tea, talking quietly, and he had chosen that moment to approach Aaron with the idea that had grown to a determination. Aaron's reaction didn't surprise him—he knew how to handle his irascible brother. After a few minutes, he followed him into the cabin.

"Aaron. I've made up my mind. Listen to me. . . . What kind of a country is it where soldiers will hunt down a boy and run him through with a sword? Where a public servant, an inspector at a river port, will stand by while ignorant peasants spit '*zhid*' at a merchant-captain?"

Aaron sat stolidly, his eyes on the deck.

Isaac continued. "Our father was an educated man. He shaved off his beard, wore the clothes of a Russian businessman, and gave his children a secular education. Even his employers, the Jewish owners of ships and railroads—wealthy and respected beyond imagination—are *suffered* to live in Moscow! Do you realize that? They couldn't live in Moscow until a few years ago! Do you understand what that means? . . . We speak Russian, Polish,

Lithuanian, German. We are the owners of our own steamer. Yet we are treated with contempt—by this . . . *scum!*" He spat the word.

Aaron looked up. "Do you think I enjoy making the same old jokes about pigs with the inspector? Giving him a bribe so they won't tear the hold apart?" Aaron's eyes were dark with the remembered indignities. "But, we are making a living, Isaac. What will we find in America?"

"Whatever we find, it will be better than our future here. I don't want my son to grow up in a land where there is hopelessness for him. I tell you, Aaron, a very bad time is coming for us, the Jews of Russia. I read it. I see it. I *feel* it in everything around me. I want to *go*—away from here—to America."

Now Aaron's voice softened, as he said with resignation, "You always had ideas, Isaac. And I always followed you. As a little boy, you wanted to peep at the *mikvah,* and who was punished for it? You wanted a boat, so here I am, on the river . . ."

"That's not true, Aaron! Are you not the chief, the captain? Do I not honor you as the older brother?"

"As it amuses you, you allow me that honor." He spoke without rancor, in a sad, kind tone of voice. "You think I don't know how you control things?" He held up his hand. "It's all right. Without you, I'd still be a junior clerk in the marine freight office of Nemunaitis—barely able to feed Tobe and the children. . . . But, Isaac! We *have* our boat, we have regular cargo, we're trusted and respected the whole length of the river Neman. Is that not *enough* for you?"

"*No! Not* enough." He slammed his hand down on the table. "Because it will last just until the next disturbance. The next pogrom, and your fine friend, the inspector, will be the first to slit your throat and rape your daughters."

Aaron sighed. This brother of his, he always had been one for visions. He couldn't stay here without him if Isaac was determined to go, but he didn't want to think about selling everything and going so far, to the unknown.

"How will you know where to go there . . . in America?" he asked.

He was immediately sorry, for Isaac pulled a crumpled letter out of his pocket. He unfolded it, smoothing out the paper, and said, with unconcealed excitement, "Listen, Aaron. Just listen to this! I had this letter from Reuben Sarnoff—you know, my friend Reuben Sarnoff from Kovno—just a month ago he wrote. He writes from America, from a place called Nanticoke in Pennsylvania *guberniya.* Listen to what he says." He scanned the letter until he found the passages he was looking for.

> . . . so, Isaac, I think this place is a good one for you and your brother. It is not so crowded as a city. The people are friendly and honest . . . there are enough Jews nearby to make a *minyan,* and there's a *shul* in Wilkes-Barre, the big town right up the river. . . .

There are many small settlements along the river and here you
could earn a living in one village or another. . . .

Again Aaron sighed. "How would we go? I don't think we can afford it,
Isaac."

"Yes, we can, Aaron. We can sell the boat. We'll get a good price from
Pilsky in Grodno. We'll also sell the house—that shouldn't be too difficult, it's
a sound house, well-kept. We take the family on the *Danika* as far as Grodno,
then by train to Warsaw. From there to Hamburg, where we'll take a small
freighter—that way we can have a cabin—and sail to Philadelphia. That's the
port in Pennsylvania *guberniya.*" Isaac shook his head emphatically.

"Well . . ." Aaron said dryly, "I see you have it all planned out."

"I've been thinking about this for a very long time, brother. Malka and I
wanted to go together since before we were married." He took a deep breath.
"Malka isn't here. Our father isn't here. There's nothing to hold *me* here
now, Aaron. Only you. And I want you to come with me."

And so it was that the brothers sailed away from Nemunaitis for the last
time. They bade farewell to the friends and neighbors they had known all
their lives. They visited the graves of their parents and of Isaac's young wife,
Malka, dead for over two years now.

Aaron's wife, Tobe, wept and his young daughters wailed, clinging to their
mother, as the ancient, ramshackle river port grew smaller, and finally disappeared from their sight.

Isaac stood at the rail of the *Danika* holding Jacob in his arms. The excited
boy kept waving long after they were under way. He had taken the child to
say good-bye to Sophie and Michel Belkind in Kovno. Michel had been
happy that they were going.

"I wish you would come, too," Isaac had told his father-in-law.

"We're too old to start again, Isaac," he had answered with his customary
dignity. "Here I'm someone, for whatever that may count. But in America I
hear they would call me a 'greenhorn.' I'm not prepared to face that at my
age. For you, it's different. You're young, strong, and energetic. You can show
them a thing or two about making a success! Good luck, my boy. God be with
you." Michel's eyes had been moist when he embraced Isaac and his daughter's son.

Sophie had clipped a lock of hair from Jacob's head and placed it in a
locket which she wore around her neck. She kissed his cheek tenderly and
whispered a blessing in his ear. Isaac thought she had aged ten years since he
had last seen her a few months before.

"Write to us, Isaac," she said. "You'll be in my prayers."

"And you'll be in mine, Mother Sophie. You are as dear to me as my own
parents. I don't want to believe that we'll never see each other again."

"So, you're not ill," he said, raising his voice above the wind.

"No, not ill. I feel better out here in the air. It's so close in the cabin. And the woman who shares my cabin *is* ill." She grimaced. Then she looked at Jacob and smiled. "Is this your little boy?"

"Yes. This is Jacob. And this is Miss . . . ."

"Solweiss," she said. "Rachel Solweiss."

"I am Isaac Hillman." For a long moment their eyes met. Then, flushing, she looked away. She turned back and took Jacob's hand, making little sounds that women make to small children. Jacob, for his part, reached out and pulled at the veiling on her hat.

"Niet!" Isaac scolded, slapping his hand away. The child looked crestfallen.

"Oh, please don't scold him," Rachel pleaded. "He just wanted to see what it felt like. Didn't you, *Liebchen?*" And she put out her arms to him. Isaac was amazed when the child went into her embrace.

"He never goes to strangers," he told her.

She answered with a bright smile. "That must mean he likes me!" Who wouldn't like you? Isaac said to himself.

They found a narrow, sheltered space on the port side, away from the wind, where they could sit on a bench. The ship rolled constantly, occasionally pitching sharply, so that Isaac held on to Rachel while bracing himself against the bulkhead opposite. This was not unpleasant. Not at all.

The next several days were calmer and many passengers went out on deck. Isaac managed to spend hours each day with Rachel, taking Jacob along. Aaron and Tobe kept to the cabin. Aaron would leave his wife and daughters only when Isaac stayed with them. So none of them saw him with Rachel.

Two weeks sped by. They would be landing in Philadelphia in three days more. Isaac had much on his mind. He could see a future in which Rachel was by his side, but how would he dare to speak to her? He was wise enough to know that he must seem like a coarse, uneducated rustic to this city-bred German girl. And yet, he knew that she liked him. And she and Jacob had become such good friends. He would like to ask someone what to do, but the only person to ask was Aaron. . . . Isaac knew what that dour man would have to say about such matters.

They were standing at the rail, side by side. They talked of inconsequential things . . . the terrible food on the ship, the strange-looking couple who marched up and down religiously every day at precisely the same time. And then they were silent.

"How long will you stay with your cousins in Philadelphia?"

She shrugged. "I don't know. A few months. They say they want me to stay for a long time, perhaps permanently."

"And would you do that?" His heart was beating faster.

"I don't think so," she answered. "I am German, after all. I don't think I want to stay in America." His spirits fell.

"But, if you were to marry there? You would stay then." He couldn't believe his courage.

"That's all everyone talks about. Marrying! As if that's all there is for a woman to do with her life." She said this with such vehemence, it was like a splash of cold water in his face.

"I . . . I didn't mean . . . forgive me, Miss Solweiss . . . Rachel. It is only my high regard for you that prompted me to ask . . ."

He could see that she was crying as she looked out to sea. She fumbled for a handkerchief and took it out, turning away from him. "Oh, please!" he said. "Please don't cry. What have I said? What have I done?"

She just shook her head. "Nothing. Nothing. . . . It's not your fault," she said finally, recovering her composure. "That was very foolish of me."

Isaac took the handkerchief from her hand and gently wiped her cheek where the trail of a tear remained. "Tears we must not have on so beautiful a face," he said in a soft voice.

She gave him a small smile.

"Will you stay in America awhile, then?" he asked.

"I might stay . . . for a while." He put his large hand over her small one where it rested on the railing. He felt such happiness. If only it can be, he prayed.

The Port of Philadelphia was teeming with passengers, cargo, stevedores, and anxious relatives scanning the crowd of arrivals for a familiar face.

A kinder port of entry than New York, it nevertheless had stringent health regulations. Isaac worried that Jacob or perhaps Aaron's wife, Tobe, or one of the young girls would be refused entry. One never knew if the chest was becoming consumptive.

He'd bid good-bye to Rachel, who was only visiting, not immigrating. His longing was tinged with envy as he watched her go through the magical doors where she would be greeted by her waiting cousins. He had made hasty introductions to his brother and family as they grouped together on the deck while docking. Aaron had looked at him suspiciously, but he'd turned his back and stood with Rachel, holding Jacob in his arms, speaking quietly of his plans for establishing himself in the Pennsylvania river valley, which was his ultimate destination.

BOOK TWO

Wyoming Valley
1878-1914

I

Wilkes-Barre, Pennsylvania   November 1878

Reuben Sarnoff met their train. Isaac hadn't seen Reuben for six years, since
the gathering at the Belkind house before Reuben left for America.

What a shock! Look at him! A real American. Can a few years make that
much difference? The hat, the suit, the haircut . . . and he speaks English,
just like he'd spoken it all his life!

But how *wonderful* to see him! A warm embrace, a grin, a jumble of breathless words rushing out. . . . What of Reb Michel and Sophie? . . . And
what about Judah? Your father . . . a shame. Sol Lieber . . . did you see
him? The voyage, was it terrible? So, this is little Jacob . . . just like Malka.
. . . Poor Malka. Aaron . . . a pleasure! Come, come little girls. . . .
Dear Tobe . . . you don't mind if I call you Tobe? In America, we use the
familiar . . . you'll soon get used to everything. . . . Come, Miriam is
waiting. . . .

Reuben had taken a bride before he left—an arranged marriage to a distant
cousin. Miriam Sarnoff was a warm, energetic woman who gathered people to
her bosom as naturally as she breathed. Before they knew what they would do
or where they would go, their bags and bundles were piled on a wagon and
they all climbed into a carriage to be driven off to the Sarnoff apartment on
Vine Street in Plymouth—a new apartment, above the printing press.

Reuben had recently joined in a newspaper venture. The Wyoming Valley
Sentinel was a penny daily whose liberal young editor championed the rights
of coal miners to form a union. Garrick Flannery, the courageous Irish journalist, was the publisher and editor of the *Sentinel*, but he needed Reuben
Sarnoff's skills. An expert engraver and typesetter, Reuben also had a good
understanding of business details. Together, they had become a team . . .
partners! That was the way Garrick Flannery wanted it. Share the risks, share
the profits . . . the American way!

For six weeks Isaac and his family lived there over the newspaper office
with Reuben, Miriam, and their two small children. Isaac found this acutely
uncomfortable. Never, never in his life had he been in such a position. . . .
To have to depend on the friendship and hospitality—no, the *charity*—of
others. He, Isaac Hillman—the merchant-captain. Proud, independent, re-
sourceful, Isaac found this a humiliation.

But Reuben insisted that until they found work, a regular income, they could not rent their own place to live. He knew. He'd been through it all, and Isaac could believe him and trust his advice.

"Save your money, Isaac. You'll need it," he cautioned. Besides, Miriam was lonely. It was a joy for her to have her *landsmen* there with them, eating, talking, laughing, and reminiscing together. A pleasure for both of them!

Soon, he told them, it would be easier . . . everything became easier, once you could bring yourself to do it . . . going about bareheaded, without a *yarmulke,* eating *treyf,* forgetting to *leg tefillen* . . . too easy. In America, too easy to become like all the others, because you were treated like everyone else . . . almost.

The beginning in Wyoming Valley was difficult. Isaac had to remind himself that he had expected no more. In Russia, despite his worries, Isaac had been one of the fortunate Jews—a man of property. They'd had enough money to share with the poor. The Neman River had been his security, his livelihood. As a merchant-captain, he had known respect and good friendship in Kovno *guberniya* and beyond.

And what of the Susquehanna, the river that had brought him to this community?

"Truthfully, Reuben, it's an unimpressive body of water," Isaac told his friend.

Shallow at this time of year, it depended on spring rains and freshets to provide enough depth for commercial transportation. The North Branch Canal, running partway along the river, then cutting inland behind the town's central part, permitted shipping and passengers to travel as far as Philadelphia by canal boat, if they so desired. Most people preferred to take the train.

Isaac and Aaron found work on the canal, but it was low-paying, backbreaking work as a poleman or stevedore. The captain of a canal boat was generally a man unaccustomed to gentle ways. Those who worked under him were even less so. In Europe, to own a boat meant something in the community. Here, as Isaac discovered, it was not necessarily so.

"What happened to you, Isaac?" Tobe cried in alarm when she saw his torn shirt and blackened eye.

"Those thieves! Thought they could get away with stealing from me," he told her, wincing as she bathed his eye with witch hazel. Half the polemen were drifters, who worked just long enough to finance a drinking spree. When their money ran out, they looked for work on the canal again.

"That's not for me, the canal," he declared to Aaron.

Aaron was eager for them to buy a barge and go into business for themselves. "If we own our own barge, we won't have to bother with such trash, Isaac. It will be the same as it was on the Neman," his brother urged.

Isaac convinced him to wait. "We must learn more about the Susquehanna, Aaron, before we buy any kind of boat. We don't know enough of how business is conducted here in America. Wait. There's time." He paid heed to Reuben Sarnoff's advice, certain that it would end in disaster if they used their limited funds to buy a barge without knowing whether they would have regular customers.

Isaac looked around for other work, and soon he was doing whatever came his way—driving a dray, loading cargo, signing on as an extra hand on a construction team. Reuben's partner, Garrick Flannery, was a help to him.

"The company that supplies us with newsprint and engraving materials needs a drayman, Isaac. I told the owner that I had a friend who wants work," Flannery told him.

Within a week, Isaac had a regular job driving a dray for Star Printing Company. The pay was good, and the owner a fair-minded man.

Isaac stopped at the *Sentinel* plant to thank the journalist. He liked Garrick Flannery, a forthright man with smiling green eyes, who always treated him courteously. Flannery was in his shirt sleeves, getting ink on his trousers, as he struggled to repair the roller on the press.

"Here . . . I help you," said Isaac, in his halting English. He was frustrated not to be able to express himself in English. Isaac knew five languages, but here in America, he could see that people thought of him as an ignorant, uneducated man because he could not speak their language.

He turned to Reuben Sarnoff. "Reuben, ask Mr. Flannery, does he know a teacher of English?"

So, on Wednesdays, as soon as he delivered his last order of newsprint, Isaac would go to the home of a young English teacher named Ethan Carpenter to study the language of his new country. Carpenter was an earnest young man about the same age as Isaac. He was impressed with Isaac's knowledge and experience.

"You mean you speak *five* languages, Mr. Hillman!" he exclaimed in German, their only language of communication during the first few lessons. He asked Isaac many questions about life in Russia and about the Jews. Ethan Carpenter had never known a Jew before, and those he had seen were dark, bearded men with an air of mystery about them. This blond, handsome, clean-shaven Russian Jew intrigued him. And Carpenter interested Isaac.

"Where did your people come from, Mr. Carpenter?" Isaac asked.

"My ancestors were among the first English settlers in Wyoming Valley," Carpenter told him with pride. "There were no white men living here then, a hundred and seventeen years ago. My great-great-grandfather fought in the Battle of Wyoming during the American Revolution." That was about as American as you could get!

Isaac learned rapidly. Within six months he was reading books on American history and literature which Mr. Carpenter lent him from his own collection. When he had finished reading a chapter, he and Ethan Carpenter would have a discussion about it. Thus, the lessons became an enjoyment for Isaac. He looked forward to his weekly visits to Carpenter's house.

"You don't need to come here any longer, you know," the teacher told him one day. "You're learning as much by reading as I can teach you."

But Isaac was reluctant to give up the English lessons. He realized that they were one of the few pleasant diversions in his life. "My pronunciation improves when we have our conversations, Mr. Carpenter. Do you mind if I come and we just talk together?"

"I'd like that, Mr. Hillman. But, we must consider that you are visiting me. I can no longer take a fee for lessons." And for a few months Isaac did visit Ethan Carpenter more or less regularly. But as time passed, Isaac became so busy that the visits to his English teacher occurred less and less frequently . . . and then, not at all.

One of Isaac's first temporary jobs after arriving in Wyoming Valley had been as a drayman for Wilkes-Barre Dry Goods Company. One afternoon Solomon Lang, the owner, saw Isaac driving a team from Star Printing, his new employer, and hailed him.

"Hillman! I've been looking for you!" he called in German. "Where have you been for all these months?"

"I've found a permanent job, Mr. Lang, making deliveries for Star Printing Company," he told the merchant, a Jew who had come to the valley from Germany some twenty years before.

"I must talk to you, Mr. Hillman. Please come to see me when you're finished with your work."

Isaac went to the dry-goods store to see what Lang had in mind. It was an offer of another job, making deliveries.

"I don't know, Mr. Lang. I have this good job. It pays well. What I really have in mind is to buy my own delivery wagon and horses—to go into business for myself. I'm not a man to work for someone else for long," Isaac answered.

Lang thought about that for a few minutes. "Maybe we can work something out. If you will agree to work for me, I'll give you a part interest—a commission on whatever goods you transport for me, and the right to use the dray for any independent business you may be able to transact. We can make an arrangement that will guarantee you will own a dray as soon as you can pay for it. I'll top whatever you're earning now by ten percent."

Isaac was cautious. "Why do you do this now, Mr. Lang? You didn't have a permanent job for me before."

"You're an honest, hardworking man, Hillman. I'm getting too old to worry about people cheating me, ruining my merchandise with careless handling. I'm doing it because it's good for my business. Trade is picking up, I have more customers than I can handle—yet I don't have a reliable man to transport my goods."

Solomon Lang presented Isaac with figures. Isaac could see that it would take many months, even years, for him to own a dray and team outright.

"Ummm . . . I don't know, Mr. Lang. Let me think about it."

"What is there to think about? Would it be any worse working for me with this arrangement than, for Star Printing, earning less?" said Lang, a humorous look in his eyes.

"I suppose not," admitted Isaac.

"So, you work for me . . . I pay you more than Star, you get a commission, and you do your own business on the side. As for the dray—that will be something you can decide in the future. Agreed?"

"Agreed," said Isaac.

Aaron chafed under the routine of going home to Tobe and his daughters every evening. He missed the freedom of the river life, the feel of a steamboat's wheel under his hands. Riverboating, it seemed, had become an integral part of him. He was fortunate enough to find steady work in one of the several boatyards that lined the banks of the river. Aaron became fascinated with boatbuilding. At the same time, he was curious about the rest of this picturesque river, below Wyoming Valley, where the channel was deep and broad.

"Someday, Isaac, I will own a boat again—with or without you! I am a boatman . . . because of you. You have only yourself to blame!" he said with a grin. Aaron was determined. If Isaac would not be a partner in this, well, he would see what the result would be. . . .

They lived in a few rooms on a little lane off Main Street in Plymouth, not too far from the Sarnoff's place. On the Sabbath he and his brother prayed with the other Jews from Plymouth and West Nanticoke. Sometimes he went to the *shul* on South Welles Street in Wilkes-Barre, B'nai Jacob, but it was far to walk in the winter, and he felt reluctant to ride on the Sabbath. The other synagogue in Wilkes-Barre, B'nai B'rith, was attended by the German Jews, some of whom had lived in the valley since 1839. The ritual there was different and Isaac did not feel comfortable in that congregation. . . .

The seasons changed, the children blossomed like the spring flowers, chattering away in English with neighborhood children from varied backgrounds. Sara and Tanya, Aaron's daughters, attended class in the small, wooden schoolhouse. Jacob missed them when they were away from home, but he spent as much time with the Sarnoff boys as he did at home—in fact, he considered them his cousins, too. Isaac did not have to worry about Jacob's welfare as he worked each day from before sunup until after dark. But that was not to say that he didn't have much on his mind.

Living together as they did, with so little privacy, Isaac longed for a place of his own. He was accustomed to having his separate apartment in the house in Nemunaitis. It hadn't been a luxurious house, heaven knew, but it was commodious, with each brother having his own wing, so that he had not always been aware of the intimacies of Aaron's family life. It depressed him to see the relationship between Aaron and Tobe, so unaffectionate, so reticent.

At night Isaac would often hear the sounds of Aaron's and Tobe's lovemaking, if that's what it could be called. No gentle laughter, no soft murmured endearments, no cries of joy sounded through the thin walls of the apartment. But the creak of the bedsprings, followed by his brother's growl of satisfaction, was enough to stimulate his own yearnings, so long unmet.

Often during those early months as he drove along in the dray, his thoughts would return to Rachel Solweiss. He saw her lovely face. . . . He remembered her kindness, her affection for Jacob, her concern for him and his family when they had landed at the Front Street pier in Philadelphia. . . . He wondered how Rachel fared. . . . Should he write to her? Would she answer him if he did? Then he had traveled to Philadelphia with a shipment of goods, and visited her briefly. . . .

Malka was a sweet, dim, remote dream of a memory to him here—as if he had left the reality of his young, first love back in the stark graveyard on the banks of the Neman River. Three years now since her death. It could have been another lifetime.

As their second winter in America drew to a close, Isaac realized that he must make some changes in his life. His mind began to mull over an idea that had been slowly growing for the past several months. . . . It had started one day when he noticed an old empty building up on the hill in Wilkes-Barre. Of solid construction, it was clean and dry, with a second floor that could easily be made into a large, airy apartment. . . .

Isaac sat down with pencil and paper to figure out his financial condition. . . . Next, he visited the supply company on Canal Street . . . he had heard they needed a drayman. Then he spoke to several farmers about the goods they required. . . . Jackson, from the livery stable, had a horse for sale. . . .

Satisfied with the plans that were formulating in his mind, Isaac was engaged in furious activity for the next six weeks. He barely had time to come home for his meals, and then, he would eat hurriedly and fall into exhausted slumber, to be up before anyone else in the house was stirring, on his way to Wilkes-Barre by the time the first rays of light appeared in the eastern sky.

When he told Aaron the result of these weeks of planning, dreading his brother's disapproval, he was surprised at Aaron's mild acceptance of his actions—indeed, if appearances could be an indication of feelings, it looked like Aaron heartily approved.

"*Mazel tov,* Isaac!" his brother congratulated him heartily. "You always did have a good head on your shoulders."

Relieved, Isaac now turned his attention to his other problem . . . his loneliness. This was a matter not so easily solved.

Philadelphia Spring 1880

Isaac pulled the door chime of the house on Spruce Street a second time. He didn't want to seem impatient. He shifted uncomfortably from foot to foot. What if no one was at home? What if Rachel had left—maybe gone back to Germany? But surely she had received his letter. She would have written—someone would have informed him. Perhaps she would refuse to see him. What a fool he was to think that such a refined and beautiful German lady would be interested in having him call on her—him, a Russian immigrant, no longer a merchant-captain of his own steamer on the great river Neman, but a doer of odd jobs, a drayman, from Plymouth.

He must have been crazy to buy this new suit from Simon Long's store in Wilkes-Barre—at a cost of an entire month's earnings, too. The tall hat, the white shirt and cravat! If Aaron had seen him, he'd have some explaining to do.

The door was opened by a plump maid dressed in gray with a white ruffled cap and apron. "May I help you, sir?" she asked in English.

"Is Fräulein Solweiss at home?" His English was halting.

"Who is calling?"

"Isaac Hillman."

"She's not at home now," the maid answered, and his spirits fell. She opened the door wider. "But you're to come in and wait. She'll return by four o'clock."

That was in only a quarter of an hour. She would return, and he was to wait! Isaac stepped into the narrow hallway and handed the servant his new gray hat. She led the way into a tiny parlor, all crammed with heavy mahogany furniture and dark red hangings. Isaac sat down on a settee. The maid disappeared.

He looked around the overfurnished room. Had it really been more than a year since he had first entered this house? How fortuitous it had been that he had met Rachel on the ship. When he and Aaron had come through the immigration shed with their family and their baggage, there she had been with her cousins, Anna and Mordecai Franke, waiting for them, waiting to help them in this new America. So tenderhearted, so concerned about the children and Tobe. She had prevailed upon Mordecai to seek out the Hebrew Immigrant Aid representative who found them a lodging and helped them to arrange their travel to Wilkes-Barre, even sending a telegram to Reuben Sarnoff, announcing when they would arrive.

The night before they left Philadelphia, all of them had gone to the Franke house for dinner. They had bathed and were dressed in their finest, of course, looking far more presentable than they had after the difficult sea voyage.

Mordecai had been gratified that these Russian immigrants could at least speak a civilized tongue, German. He had softened somewhat when Isaac proved to be more than an uneducated laborer from the waterfronts of the pale.

Aaron hadn't liked Mordecai at all; it was a mutual disaffection. Mordecai was a stiff, overbearing sort of man, but he had offered his hospitality and some good advice about enrolling immediately in an English class, how to establish credit, what to do with the bank notes they carried—their entire fortune. Isaac knew that the fact that they were not penniless was another attribute that made them acceptable in Mordecai's narrow view.

Once, not long after their arrival, Isaac had come to Philadelphia with a drayload of goods. On that occasion he had sent a letter to Rachel asking whether he might call on her the next afternoon. She had answered, telling him that she could see him for only a short time because the family had an engagement.

He had presented himself, feeling awkward in his clean but old and mended clothing from Nemunaitis. By then his eye had grown accustomed to the variations in fashion and he was aware that he looked like an immigrant —a not very prosperous immigrant. They had sat in this parlor, the four of them—Mordecai, Anna, Rachel, and Isaac—making stilted conversation in German. He had left after half an hour, dejected, losing hope of ever winning her affections. But at the door, when they were alone for the briefest time, she had squeezed his hand and whispered, "I'm very glad you came, Isaac."

"If I write to you, will you answer me?" he had asked.

She had smiled eagerly in response. "Yes! I should like to hear from you. I will answer."

They had corresponded several times. Her letters had been an inspiration to him. He kept them together in a small carved box from his father's house, one of the few things he had brought along from Europe. When he decided to come to Philadelphia, he had sent a letter saying that he would call on her this afternoon, but there had been no time for her to reply. He had come to court Rachel, or at least to make a beginning to that process.

How difficult it seemed. He did not know the rules here. He had to laugh at himself. . . . When had he ever obeyed the rules? Not with Malka, certainly. For a moment he even thought it would be nice if someone were here to perform the task in the traditional way. How should he begin? *Rachel, I want you to be my wife.* No, too cold, too direct. *Rachel, I would like to have permission to call upon you as a suitor.* Ridiculous! *Miss Solweiss, do you think you might consider . . .*

"Isaac! I'm sorry to have been delayed. Have you been waiting long?" Rachel appeared in the doorway, pretty and flushed, wearing a simple gray striped silk dress with a high collar and tiny little pearl buttons going down the front. She wore her curly light brown hair piled on top of her head with soft wings on either side. She looked younger and lovelier than he had remembered.

Isaac rose, a gentle smile lighting his face as Rachel came forward. He took her extended hands in his own. How small they seemed, but firm and capable.

"You are beautiful," was all he managed. He gazed tenderly down at her upturned face.

"How is little Jacob? Does he like his new home?" She withdrew her hands and seated herself on a small oval-back chair with ornate carvings of flowers on its curving splats. Isaac settled himself again on the velvet-covered settee with its high upholstered back and lacy, carved mahogany frame.

"Jacob is wonderful. He is blooming. His health has improved so much." Isaac relaxed in the warmth of her presence. "Why wouldn't he be happy? All day he plays with his cousins, no one to tell him 'no'—he needs some discipline, a mother."

Rachel looked down at her folded hands in her lap.

"And how is your work? Have you found a boat to travel the river?"

"The river is not so wide or navigable as our Neman River. This river—the Susquehanna—is very beautiful, but has many shallow, rocky sections. I'm told it is a broad, deep stream with much navigation near its mouth, around Harrisburg. There is a canal in Wilkes-Barre, for barge traffic and flat-bottomed boats, but I think it is not wise for me to invest in a boat. Dray and railroad are the preferred means of shipment there."

"I'm sorry. I know you wanted a boat," she answered in a sympathetic tone.

"No, no. I don't mind. My brother, though! Aaron cannot get a boat out of his brain. He is going to buy a barge and transport coal and wood downriver. I think I won't join him. It is only a one-man enterprise."

"And your house? Have you found a comfortable place to live?"

"I have just moved to Wilkes-Barre. I was living in Plymouth with Aaron and Tobe, but it was too crowded. Now I have my own apartment with room downstairs for a business."

"Oh, you are going into business?" Rachel sounded genuinely interested.

"Yes. I have bought a dray for transporting goods. Soon I shall have another. If I can't take cargoes by steamer on the river, well then, I will take them overland. And, as on my boat, I can invest in goods and sell them at a profit."

"That is very clever of you, Isaac. You sound happy. I am glad for you." Her smile was enchanting.

"I would indeed be happy if only . . . ." he began. The little, corpulent maid came bustling into the room with a tea tray.

"Where shall I put it, Fräulein?" she said in German. It angered him to think she had let him struggle with English.

"Here on the table, Hella." Rachel leaned forward and placed a small ornate silver box out of the way on the tripod tea table with its claw and ball feet.

After setting out the teapot, cups, and a plate of small cakes, the maid left them.

Rachel poured tea and handed him the delicate gilded china cup and saucer. Isaac wasn't sure what to do with it so he sat holding it suspended halfway between his lap and his chest. He sipped the hot tea, trying not to make noises—the way they did in Russia. So many things here were different. Would he ever learn them all?

"I have been helping the Female Hebrew Benevolent Society, teaching sewing, cooking, and home sanitation classes to immigrant girls. They know *nothing*, Isaac. How could they have lived?"

"Where do they come from?" he asked.

"Mostly from Romania or Turkey. A few come from Russia. They are victims of war, of riots."

"Usually the people who can afford to come here are not ignorant, Rachel. Perhaps they are confused. What language do you speak to them?"

"Why, German, of course."

"But, they aren't German! They probably speak Yiddish, but certainly not German. Can't you speak Yiddish?"

She shifted uncomfortably. "No, not really. It isn't a real language, you know."

"Not a real language? Millions of people speak it as their only language. It's as good a language as any other. In fact, a good deal more precise than some. You know, it is supposed to be close to Old German. Languages change —like people." His voice sounded sharp, but he didn't care.

In a conciliatory tone, she said, "Perhaps I'll try to work with someone who can speak Yiddish to them."

She picked up the plate of cakes and offered it to Isaac. He took one in his left hand, still holding the teacup in his right. Balancing the cup and saucer on his knee, he reached for one of the small linen napkins on the tea table. The cup of tea turned over, fell to the floor, spilling its contents over the carpet.

Isaac went down on his knees to pick up the china, cursing himself for his awkwardness. He noticed that the hem of Rachel's gown had been splattered by the tea. He patted it with the napkin.

"Ach, what a clumsy fool am I! An ignorant peasant. Like an ox. You shouldn't invite me to tea in your parlor."

How could Isaac have known his words echoed those of Mordecai Franke to Rachel the day before, when she had told him the Russian riverboat captain was coming to call on her?

Rachel leaned forward and clasped his hands, crying, "No, no! Don't say that! You are kind and wise and strong. Life is, after all, not a tea party!" Her eyes were brimming with tears.

Isaac raised his head and looked into Rachel's eyes. "My life would be beautiful indeed, if you were to share it with me."

She smiled down at him. "Are you asking me to marry you, Isaac?"

"I think I must first speak with your Cousin Mordecai. That would be the proper way. But, only if you agree."

She leaned forward and kissed him tenderly on the lips. "I agree."

They were married by Rabbi Marcus Jastrow at the Rodef Shalom Synagogue one week later . . . a year and a half since they had arrived at the Port of Philadelphia. Mordecai Franke had been a gentleman through it all. Magnanimously, he offered to host a reception at his home after the ceremony for the small group of friends who had known Rachel.

Everyone agreed that the groom was an unusually fine-looking man, tall and distinguished in his vested suit and high hat. His English was poor, of course, but he spoke German well enough. Mordecai would have felt happier if Rachel had married one of the men from Philadelphia's German Jewish community, several of whom had been interested in his wife's cousin. But, all in all, she was off his hands now, and since they would be living in Wilkes-Barre, would present no problem for him.

Isaac sent his dray with its cargo of merchandise for Wilkes-Barre Dry Goods Company back with his driver who had accompanied him to Philadelphia. He would not take his bride on such a conveyance over the poorly maintained roads to her new home. They traveled by train, on the Philadelphia & Reading Railroad to Bethlehem, where they changed to the Lehigh Valley coach for Wilkes-Barre.

Anna and Mordecai bade them farewell at the railroad station. Anna wept, but Rachel was radiant. "Anna, don't cry. I am very happy. We'll visit each other often. You'll see."

The ride was long and dusty. As the train snaked over the mountains between Lehighton and Mauch Chunk, Rachel looked out of the window exclaiming, "Such beautiful country, Isaac! Even more beautiful than Germany."

Isaac had sent a telegraph message to Aaron several days before, telling him he was marrying Rachel and would return with her on the Sunday evening train. When the train chugged into the Lehigh Valley station at Wilkes-Barre, there on the platform were Aaron, Tobe, Sara, Tanya, and four-year-old Jacob, who jumped up and down with excitement.

Isaac helped Rachel down from the railroad car. Tobe embraced her, smiling and happy to see Isaac with his new wife.

Aaron said, "Welcome to the family. I wish you happiness." But Isaac could tell that his enigmatic brother had some reservations about the unexpected turn of events. He hoped it was only temporary. Maybe Aaron was feeling slighted because they had married without his presence.

The two girls stared at Rachel in fascination, noting her fashionable traveling outfit. Rachel stooped to take Jacob in her embrace. "Hello, Jacob, little darling. I've come to be your new mama." Jacob regarded her gravely for a long moment, then threw his arms around her and gave her a kiss.

With Rachel, Isaac never found the same kind of exultant sexual satisfaction that he had enjoyed with Malka. Malka and he had been innocents. Their love was simple, direct, and unexpected—therefore wondrous.

Rachel was more complicated. She was the product of a self-conscious minority group within a society so steeped in decorum that it stultified all normal reactions. She loved Isaac. She was prepared to be an obedient, supportive wife in all areas of marriage, including the baser aspects. Unfortunately, her cousin, Anna Rosenmaier Franke, was the only woman to whom she might turn for guidance in these matters. The sole purposes of sex in the marriage of Anna and Mordecai were the quick satisfaction of Mordecai's carnal needs and the carrying on of the Franke family name. Both of these objectives had been met with decreasing frequency. Thank God.

Isaac, though not a subtle man, was by nature patient and loving. He instinctively understood that all women were not as Malka had been. Therefore, when Rachel awaited him in their marriage bed wearing her voluminous high-necked, long-sleeved nightdress, lying rigid and silent in the darkness, he sat on the edge of the bed quietly talking, waiting for her tension to ease.

"Jacob is happy, Rachel. See how he smiled when you kissed him good night?"

"He is a sweet child," she replied in a small, tight voice.

"You will like the apartment better when we buy more furniture."

"The apartment is fine, Isaac."

"It needs nicer curtains for the windows. Don't you think so?"

"Yes."

"Do you know how to sew, Rachel?"

"Yes, Isaac. I like to sew."

"That's *good*, Rachel! That's a *wonderful* talent for a woman," he said, with more enthusiasm than this deserved.

Eventually, chilled to the bone by the cold night air, he slid beneath the comforter. Drawing her to him, he gently caressed her face and hair, kissing her soft lips.

"You are so lovely, Rachel . . . a beautiful woman." He stroked her back until he felt her relax and soften.

She never said a word. . . . Her dutiful submission to his advances left him only partly satisfied, with a vague feeling of unrest.

Had he not experienced the beauty of a woman enjoying love as much as he? Surely this silent endurance was not going to be Rachel's lot throughout their marriage.

Each night, Isaac tried to stir Rachel's senses, loosen her inhibitions. And after several patient weeks, he began to imagine some results from his efforts. She seemed to await his caresses at night, and on the few occasions when he fell directly asleep, he sensed her disappointment.

Then, one night, her responses became warm, sensual, and Rachel was carried beyond herself on the tide of her emotions. Triumphant, Isaac held her naked body against his own, whispering words of endearment.

"My sweet! My dove!" he murmured against her trembling lips, covering them with impassioned kisses. "Oh, Rachel, my beloved wife!"

But his happiness, like a fragile crystal, was shattered by her fierce reaction. So appalled was Rachel by her own wantonness, her depravity, that she wept in angry humiliation, convinced that she was unfit to be his wife.

"What must you think of me?" she sobbed, choking on the words. "What kind of woman am I?"

Bewildered, Isaac tried to reassure her that she was a normal, loving woman. "This is the way it *should* be, my dear one! Between a husband and wife, this is right. A husband is also a lover."

But Rachel had found it so painful to lose control of herself to such an extent that she made supreme efforts to resist the rush of feelings which threatened to overcome her each time Isaac made love to her.

As for Isaac, hadn't he the proof that Rachel could feel that special joy the same as he? He took it as a challenge to bring her to an acceptance of her own sensuality. To his credit, he never entirely relaxed his efforts.

As time passed, the babies arrived, and family life, as well as business demands, became the matrix of their existence together. Rachel yielded gradually to the natural, affectionate warmth of Isaac's exuberant personality. And Isaac's ardor became more subdued. Their happiness was nearly complete.

> Paris
> 1 August 1880

My Dear Isaac,

We rejoiced to receive your letter telling us that you have taken a new wife. Rejoiced with tears in our eyes, I must admit, for, you understand, as you made clear in your letter, that it is with mingled sorrow and happiness that we receive this news. What's done cannot be undone, Isaac, and it was a burden on our hearts to think of you so alone without a wife, your little son Jacob without a mother. We pray that you will find happiness with Rachel, that you will be a happy family together, the three of you, and that you will be blessed with more children.

We received your letter just two days before we left Kovno for Paris to join Judah. That is why we have not replied before this. We plan to stay here for an indefinite period, as long as Judah is here.

He is studying law now. You will forgive a fond father for saying that he is more than pleased that his son has decided to follow in his path. Judah is getting married to a lovely girl, Renée Blum. She is very dear to us. To be near them means so much to Sophie.

Sophie's health is not good, Isaac. She looks quite frail. The medical care in France is another reason why we have come. . . .

. . . and so, my son—for I still think of you as my son, and always will—we wish you and Rachel mazel tov, good health, and a long and happy life together. Please write to us now and then. Tell us about our grandson, how he grows, what mischief he performs! Well I know that boys cause more trouble than girls. But we love them just the same.

Sophie and Judah send you their love and good wishes for your marriage.

I am, as always, your devoted father-in-law,

Michel

Isaac took Jacob and Rachel to a photographer to have a family photograph made so that he could send it to the Belkinds in Paris. At least, from time to time, they could see a picture of their daughter's child. . . .

When the year 1881 brought the terrible pogroms in Russia, followed by the May laws of 1882, forcing many Jews in the Pale of Settlement to relocate, Isaac was thankful that the Belkinds had remained in Paris. Sophie was too sickly to travel, Michel wrote, although she was able to enjoy short walks in the park and visits from Judah with his wife and infant son.

So, it looked like Reb Michel and his wife would become permanent residents in France. Michel reported that the French had a tolerant and civilized attitude toward Jews. . . . There were a number of Jewish officers in the French Army, he understood. How different from Russia!

Wilkes-Barre
10 October 1881

My Dearest Anna,

It was wonderful to receive your letter with such diverting passages about the dear children. I long to see all of you, although I am so happy here—happier than I ever dreamed I would be. I have joyful tidings! We are going to have a child, Anna. The birth will be in four months' time. If you should be able to come to help me, I would be forever grateful. But, if that is too much of a burden to place on you, I will understand. Miriam Sarnoff, the wife of Isaac's friend from Russia, will come to me. Also, my sister-in-law, Tobe. So, I will not be alone. At a time like this, however, it would be comforting to have one's own dear family, instead of even the kindest people with foreign ways.

Little Jacob is an adorable child. So sweet and solemn a boy. But

I know how to make him laugh. I bake the jelly kuchen and he places a walnut in the center of each cake. How he claps his hands when I bring them from the oven, all fragrant and brown! I now supply several fine ladies with tea cakes each Thursday afternoon. It is a pleasure for me. You know how I enjoy to bake, and we cannot possibly eat all the cakes and confections I make each week. It started with the wife of one of Isaac's customers. . . . She told her friends . . . and now, I have too many clients!

I am glad you like the tea towels I embroidered. It is a design I composed myself.

I must fly now, Anna. With love to all of our dear, dear Franke cousins—handsome Herman, sweet Celia, and a kiss for my darling little cherub, Rose. Please deliver my most respectful wishes to Cousin Mordecai. And for you, dear Anna, who are like a sister to me, my most loving embraces.

Rachel

II

Wilkes-Barre   Spring 1884

"Come in, Mrs. Crittendon. How nice to see you!" Rachel ushered the wife of the city's leading banker into her sitting room, where she had been stitching a ruching on a new lavender gown she had copied for herself from an illustration in *Godey's Lady's Book.* "Sit right down. I have your *Linzer Torten* and the *Apfel Strudel* all ready. I'll just go wrap them."

Ordinarily Mrs. Crittendon sent her driver for her weekly pastry order, but it was a brisk spring day, and she was a hearty woman who enjoyed driving out in her sulky with her new trotting pony.

While Rachel put together the pastries, she served the woman some tea and a chocolate cream-filled puff pastry. Mrs. Crittendon promptly ordered a dozen of those for the following week—which had been Rachel's intention, of course.

Mrs. Crittendon's attention was on the almost finished dress, which was laid over the back of Rachel's chair.

"Mrs. Hillman, are you making that gown yourself?"

"Yes, Mrs. Crittendon. I make all of my own gowns," she answered, as if it were the most ordinary thing in the world.

There were a number of dressmakers in Wilkes-Barre. None of them, however, had a sense of high fashion or a flair for stylish fit. When Mrs. Crittendon or her friends—the wives of the mine owners and professional men of the valley, who were among its wealthiest citizens—wanted an outfit for a special occasion, they traveled, at considerable expense and inconvenience, to Philadelphia or even to New York to a fine dressmaker. Then, without a final fitting, the garment would be sent to them by train and a local seamstress would handle any necessary adjustments. It was a tedious and frustrating business at best.

Mrs. Crittendon had an inspired thought. "Mrs. Hillman! *Would* you be willing to make some gowns for me? I would pay you whatever you consider a fair price."

And so, Rachel was not only in the pastry business. She became a custom designer.

Meanwhile, Isaac's transport business was growing. He now owned a dozen large wagons for hauling heavy merchandise, and several closed vans, which were protected from the elements. He had given up any attempt at long-distance hauling. The roads were impassable in certain areas, long neglected since the rise of the railroads. Warehousing and transporting within the valley were sufficient to keep him and his hired men fully booked.

As his business prospered, Isaac purchased two adjacent buildings, which shared a common wall. Rachel's bakery business soon took up the entire first floor of one of the buildings, where she supervised her small staff of bakers. Eventually the dressmaking business occupied the second floor, spreading out as the need for space grew. Rachel employed four seamstresses full time, and she had a waiting list of clients.

One morning Isaac came in to their apartment full of excitement. "Come, my dear, come see what I've done!" He ushered her out to the front sidewalk and together they walked one block farther up the hill on Prospect Avenue.

"This," he said, "is our new home!" He stopped in front of a large white house with a wrought-iron fence and a brick stoop with a balcony above. It was an imposing house, Rachel thought, and it commanded a splendid view of the valley.

Isaac preferred to live on the hill rather than down in the flat areas of the city. He knew that the flats were the flood plain of the Susquehanna River, and although there hadn't been a flood since 1875—before he had come to America—there *had* been severe floods in the past, and he had no doubts that there would be in the future. The Susquehanna had low-lying natural banks in Wyoming Valley. This was a wily river, one you couldn't trust.

They moved into the big white house on March 15, 1885—Jacob's ninth birthday. Now they had two daughters, Simone and Sonya, and soon Rachel was pregnant again. The following winter, another son, Jonas, was born.

Isaac looked at his beautiful growing family and his loving wife. . . . He could have taken pride in his modest success, had he been that sort of a man. Instead, he was merely grateful . . . to God, and to America.

Wilkes-Barre   1886

On Saturday nights Rachel supervised the ritual of the bath. The housemaid, a German girl from a large family in Hanover, whose father had been killed in the mines and all of whose brothers were miners, would drag out the big tin tub, fill it with steaming water from kettles on the stove, and one by one the children would be wet down, lathered with the big bars of white soap, then dunked in the hot bath. Jacob loved to watch the soap melt down until the blue Hebrew letters became blurred and its sharp edges had rounded. Gerda would allow him to play in the water longer than his sisters because he was a "little man" and would not catch cold as easily. As he grew older, he realized that she enjoyed looking at his little man's body, and this made him self-conscious, so he told Rachel he wanted a screen around the tub when he bathed. Gerda was replaced with another German woman, this time a widow whose husband had been killed in a mining accident, and who had sons of her own, so was not interested in little men or their bodies.

Rachel usually came to the kitchen to be certain that Jacob's hair and ears were completely clean before he finished his bath. She was preparing to pour clear warm rinsing water over his head when she noticed the long red welts on his back. She almost dropped the kettle in shock.

"In the name of heaven, what has happened to your back?" she cried. Then she ran to fetch Isaac.

Isaac found Miss Althea Schmidt sitting in her classroom correcting spelling papers. She wore a high-necked light blue cambric dress, which had rings from perspiration under the arms, and she had an unclean body odor about her, redolent of a fish market.

Isaac introduced himself. Miss Schmidt looked at him over her spectacles and asked in a cold voice, "Well, Mr. Hillman, what is it you wish to talk to me about? As you can see, I am rather occupied at the moment."

Isaac told her why he had come.

"America is a Christian nation. It was founded on Christian principles. If your son is in my classroom, he will learn to respect the name of Christ."

"My son respects everyone's religion, which is more than I can say for you, madam. But no one—do you hear me?—*no one* will force him to sing Christian hymns, nor strike him for refusing to do so. I did not come to America for my son to be beaten because he is a Jew!"

"In my classroom, Mr. Hillman, every child is required to recite Morning Prayer and sing a hymn in praise of the Lord. I consider it a sign of disrespect when Jacob clamps his lips shut over the name of Jesus. And now, if you will excuse me . . ."

Isaac went to see the new principal of the public schools. A secretary sat in the outer office at a big table, stacking composition books. Without looking up, she said, "Do you have an appointment?"

"No, I do not. I need only five minutes for what I have to say. Tell him it is Isaac Hillman—his English pupil."

The young woman disappeared into the inner room. A moment later Ethan Carpenter came through the door, smiling. "Mr. Hillman! What a pleasure! Please come in." Isaac felt the hard, bitter lump in his chest begin to ease.

"Sit down, Mr. Hillman," the new principal said in a gracious tone. Isaac congratulated Carpenter on his appointment. Isaac could see a remarkable change in the man in six years' time. From a raw-boned, shy young English teacher, who had retreated behind his thick-lensed eyeglasses, nervously attempting to hide his frayed cuffs, he had become a relaxed, genial, confident man. Well-dressed, self-assured, he smiled at Isaac, rejoicing in his professional success.

"And my wife has just presented me with a new son!" he announced. "We've named him Wallace Hobson, after my father," he added.

"Ah. Too bad your father couldn't have lived to see his grandson," lamented Isaac.

"Oh, he's still alive, Mr. Hillman! And very proud, as you can imagine."

"Wonderful," Isaac answered, realizing this was another American custom, naming babies for the living. Rachel often said he had to stop thinking like he was still in Russia. . . .

That made him remember why he had come. He told Ethan Carpenter about the beating—about his ten-year-old son's back covered with swollen, raised lash marks from a cane.

"In our religion, Mr. Carpenter, a righteous man does not mention the name of his own God, much less that of another's. Jacob is a more observant Jew than I am. It would be against his principles for him to sing a hymn of praise to Jesus. He did not mean any disrespect."

The principal was troubled, Isaac could see. His receding forehead furrowed in concentration and distress. Two dark red spots formed on the curve above his cheekbones.

"Just leave this matter in my hands, Mr. Hillman. You need not concern yourself again about this affair."

After a few more minutes of conversation, Isaac rose to leave, thanking Ethan Carpenter for receiving him, and wishing him well. He hoped that Miss Schmidt would not hold it against Jacob after she was reprimanded by the principal.

Two weeks later Isaac learned that Jacob had a new teacher, a round, cheerful person named Miss May Simpson.

"What happened to Miss Schmidt?" he asked Rachel.

"I don't know. She left the school, I was told. They've had a substitute teacher until this week."

Again, Isaac presented himself at Mr. Carpenter's office. This time the secretary ushered him in immediately.

Isaac was dismayed to hear that Althea Schmidt had been summarily dismissed and had left town.

"But . . . but, I didn't mean . . . I would not want her dismissed because of Jacob . . ." he stammered.

"Mr. Hillman. My philosophy is that if you have a rotten apple in the barrel, you cast it out before it spoils some of the other fruit!" He told Isaac not to worry. Althea Schmidt had taken a job as a teacher in a private academy in Altoona, and no doubt she had learned a valuable lesson.

West Nanticoke 1887

Monday, June 9, dawned clear and mild. Isaac reached Heatherdale, the Matlin Coal Company colliery, hours after the men on the early morning shift had settled into the newly opened single shaft of the furnace-ventilated mine.

Heatherdale. A name to conjure up pleasant images of pastures green and fragrant . . . neat white houses surrounded by quince and rambling roses . . . a clear bubbling millstream, with perhaps a shepherd and a flock of snow-white sheep in the distance.

Was it a poor joke? A fanciful invention of mine owner Abner Matlin's, this poetic title for the blighted mining patch on the west side of the Susquehanna?

The mountainside, crowned by the high, skeletal breaker, was black with culm banks. A crooked line of grayed wooden company houses jumbled lower on the hill along the unpaved way. No park, no flower bed, no bright spot of color relieved the drab, smudged sameness of the hamlet. Matlin was fond of describing "his" miners as "strolling" to work from their "cottages." Fine stroll, up a blackened hillside while others slept! Fine cottage, two rooms, no window glass, a cooking stove for a hearth!

This, then, was Isaac's destination. He reached the company store at eight o'clock, seeking the purchasing agent, who would settle the monthly account and give him an order for the following month. While his man unloaded the cartons of provisions from the dray, Isaac went over the inventory with the mine's agent, trying to quell his own indignation at the outrageous prices the company charged the miners for the goods it ordered from him. The miners had no choice but to pay whatever was asked. There was no other store nearby where they could buy food or working clothes, and even if there were, what good would it do them? They were paid in scrip, redeemable only at the Matlin Company Store! Even here in America, Isaac saw how the poor were exploited, powerless as the miners were to do anything against the wealthy mine owners.

Just as Isaac was making out a receipt for the delivery, there was a piercing whistle that sounded in a repetition of sharp releases . . . once, twice, and again. The signal for disaster!

Isaac and the purchasing agent stared at each other for what seemed an eternity. Isaac felt a prickly bitterness at the back of his throat, spreading through his neck and over his scalp . . . a remembered dread from the past which he had hoped never to again experience. It meant danger.

"Is it . . . ?" he began, but couldn't finish. The alarm shrieked again, repeatedly.

"The colliery!" shouted the agent, finding his voice. Isaac rushed out of the shop, the purchasing agent close behind. From every one of the company houses along the steep incline emerged women, children, and a few old men. In a steady line they converged toward the mouth of the coal mine.

Isaac raced up to a point where he could see the top of the breaker. His heart stopped. Bright red-orange flames shot a hundred feet in the air, billows of thick oily black smoke swirling in plumes behind them. The air roared with the sound of the flames. As he neared the summit he caught the stench of the enormous conflagration, felt the intense heat radiating from the colliery. There was a series of short, muffled reports as he rounded the bend just below the breaker. And suddenly the fire was shooting out of the headhouse, the entire structure a pillar of flames. Below him on the mountain there was a swelling moan from the crowd of women and children.

Later, trying to reconstruct the scene, Isaac decided it was indescribable. He would never forget a single detail of what his eyes beheld that day. Each image was etched in his memory forever. The anguish of the women who stood, some weeping and wringing their hands, others praying or standing vacant-eyed, knowing they were widowed many hours before the shaft would yield the terrible truth . . . that husband, brothers, and sons were all entombed there.

An hour before Isaac Hillman had awakened that morning, Jamie Morris had walked up the steep path to the Heatherdale colliery. A month ago Jamie had come home from Pennsylvania State College, armed with his ideals and a brand-new degree in mining engineering. He had studied hard and he had learned everything there was to know about anthracite coal mining. His major interest was mine safety and he knew about safety equipment that had been invented and was being used elsewhere. But he also knew that thousands of miners would suffer and die before the anthracite mine owners of Pennsylvania would deem it more profitable to use modern ventilating and safety measures in mines such as Heatherdale, with its single shaft.

Jamie's first job after graduation was a good one—inside boss at the Matlin Coal Company's Heatherdale mine. This meant he was the first man into the tunnel each day. He tested the air for blackdamp or methane gas, using a lighted candle, since Heatherdale was not equipped with the safety lamp developed in Wales. The air quality was fair—as good as could be expected without a second shaft and a ventilating fan. Satisfied, Jamie rode up on the hoist to the surface and checked in his crew in the predawn chill that Monday morning.

It was almost nine o'clock when Jamie told the chief engineer that he didn't like the way the furnace flue was acting. "I'll be with you in a few minutes," said the engineer, who was busy talking to some men from the railroad company. Half an hour later, he gave his attention to Jamie, who was examining the top of the brattice at the headhouse.

"There must be some obstruction in the flue, Mr. White. It just isn't drawing right . . . I think I'll go down there."

White shrugged. "Go ahead, then, Jamie. I doubt you'll find anything." These young fellows, he thought. Always have to show off their college learning. He had learned on the job.

Jamie descended the shaft slowly, peering out where the flue ran along the side. He put his hand on the surface, exclaiming aloud as he pulled it quickly away. It was searingly hot! Then he looked more closely. There were strips of sheet metal . . . some brick . . . but he was interested in the other component. He took out a pocket knife and scraped at the joint. His breath caught in his throat. The wood was dry as a bone, and dangerously hot! Quickly he went to the bottom of the shaft. Thin trails of black smoke were threading from the firebox and the opening of the flue, which was cut through solid coal. It *wasn't* drawing well. He had been right. Either there was an obstruction partway up the flue or the fire was too hot for the capacity of the furnace. In either case, it meant trouble. He grabbed a bucket of sand to dampen the fire. There wasn't even a man in attendance, for God's sake!

"Furnaceman!" he shouted, running toward the tunnel. The entire brattice, partitioning the shaft and tunnels, was constructed of pine. My God! There are 180 miners down here, he thought. I've got to get them out right now! How would he ever manage it without causing a stampede?

Jamie moved into the first tunnel, calling for the crew. Two helpers, young boys, were guiding a mule cart loaded with raw coal. "We're going out," he said to the first boy. "The furnace is acting up. Get the mules out of the way so they won't block the exit."

But the two bolted, leaving the mules and cart on the tracks, blocking the exit. Jamie slapped the mules so they moved forward, clear of the tunnel, then went in looking for the work crews scattered in chambers throughout the maze of tunnels. I'll probably get fired for this, he thought, but I don't care. These were all his friends, the boys he had grown up with, them and their fathers and uncles. . . . He started to run, bent over, because even here, where the coal had long been mined out, the tunnel was low.

The mule boys who had run out of the tunnel had reached the bottom of the shaft. But the cage wasn't there! They yanked the signal rope frantically, to have it let back down. Men began to come out of the tunnel. Black smoke was pouring from the flue now, choking them and causing them to back off. They retreated toward the tunnel—the only direction in which they could move.

Suddenly there was an explosion of flame and smoke from the furnace. The flames shot out and around the bottom of the pit and leaped up the shaft in a tower of fire. The retreating miners pulled the heavy wooden door at the mouth of the tunnel closed behind them. How long they could survive in the tunnel without fresh air, they didn't know, but they'd all be dead in minutes if the tunnels filled with smoke.

As they closed the gate they heard the distant shriek of the colliery whistle, high above them, three hundred feet up that single shaft. Over the roaring of the flames, the high, keening siren sent out its repeated signal of disaster. It was the last message they heard from the world. It was their death knell.

Isaac had busied himself from the start in joining whatever effort—sand and bucket brigades, removal of explosives, carrying away of fainting women —seemed needing of his help. Toward the end of the afternoon, the fire was under control. An enormous amount of water had poured down the shaft, but it would be hours before any attempt could be made to learn the fate of the men within the mine.

Exhausted and covered with soot, Isaac stumbled down through the press of people to find a place to sit. At that moment he saw Reuben's partner, Garrick Flannery, the newspaper editor, standing on the wooden planking in front of the company store. He, too, was in disarray, smudged with coal dust, wide-eyed with distress at the terrible scene.

"Isaac Hillman! I thought I recognized you there, working." He rubbed his face with a blackened handkerchief, shaking his head in disbelief. "Horrible! Horrible! These poor people . . . what will they do?"

Isaac didn't reply. The two men stood there silently, gazing up at the smoldering ruins of the breaker, keeping the vigil with the bereaved families of the trapped miners.

Garrick Flannery's eyewitness account of the Heatherdale mine disaster and its aftermath dominated the pages of that week's Wyoming Valley *Sentinel*. In an impassioned editorial, Garrick placed the blame for the tragedy on Abner Matlin, the mine's owner. When Isaac read the Irish journalist's fiery call for greater safety measures in anthracite mines and recognition of the miners' organization—the Workingmen's Benevolent Association—by the coal companies, Flannery became for him a hero, a standard-bearer for compassionate, crusading American journalism.

Tunkhannock Autumn 1889

Joseph Sanduski was one of Isaac's early customers. A farmer, he lived up on the West Side near Harding, with his wife and five sons—enormous men, whose working overalls had to be specially ordered for them. Isaac supplied them with these oversize garments, as well as with farming tools, burlap, seed, harness, and all manner of sundries he happened to pick up on his travels. Joseph owed him a large amount of money, but Isaac hated to press him for payment. He knew Joseph would pay him when he had the money.

Isaac would take the long trip up to Joseph's farm himself instead of sending his hired boys. He loved to ride along the old river road. It was a relaxation for him and he looked forward to the once every few months that he sat with Joseph over a glass of mulberry wine or home-brewed brandy, speaking in Polish about the old country, comparing experiences.

"Yah, Isaac, first I worked the mines. . . . A mule boy, I was. Dirty, smelly work! In no time, I had lung fever. Can't take the coal dust, the doctor told me. So, I had to quit the mines." He poured Isaac another glass of wine. "Yah! Best thing that ever happened to me. . . ."

Joseph had found work as a hired boy at a stable over near Forty Fort. One day this farmer, a German, from up near Bowman's Creek, comes along, takes a liking to young Joe, who was a fine-looking fellow, he thought, with a strapping body and a good honest face on him—even if he was a Pollack. . . .

"To make a long story short, Isaac, I married the farmer's daughter!" The only one of the German farmer's children to live—imagine! And he'd married her! When the old man passed on, all of his property went to Irene . . . and Joe and their five sons. A lotta property, too! "No money, Isaac, but lotta land, lotta corn, lotta wheat . . . cows, horses. . . ."

Big problems, though. So far from the river, the railroad. Costs a fortune to get the crops to market. "Now, listen . . . I've got a proposition for you. There's this piece of land I own near the river . . . it's just a couple miles from here. If you'll take a piece of land to settle our bill, and in return for carting my harvest down to Wilkes-Barre . . ."

And that is how Isaac came into possession of five acres of wooded land on the west bank of the Susquehanna, in the countryside a few miles south of the Tunkhannock Bridge.

There was an old stone foundation there with a massive chimney from a long-vanished homestead. It stood on a bluff above the river in a grove of tall

Scotch pines. What a location! How wonderful to rebuild a house over the solid chimney base—a summer house for his growing family. Land! That was something of value, something worthwhile you could always count on. For Jews, owning land hadn't been easy . . . had never been too successful either . . . always on the move, as they were in Europe, forced out, fleeing this edict and that pogrom. But, here in America, Isaac would own land.

Joe's immense sons went to work on the old place. The following summer the Hillmans spent two weeks in August in the rustic wooden lodge overlooking the sweeping curve of the Susquehanna.

How delightful to breathe the fresh country air! To walk through the pine-scented forest, to wander down along the shore of the tranquil river. Here the Susquehanna was clean and clear. Not like the dirty water downstream in Wyoming Valley, where the coal companies had killed the river.

Isaac bought a rowboat and built a small wooden dock. They cleared away a spot on the bank for picnics. Rachel enjoyed it, too, although she could never bring herself to bathe in the stream.

Of all his accomplishments in America, Isaac was most satisfied with this wooded glen on the river bank. He named their summer retreat Hillside.

                                                          Wilkes-Barre
                                                          23 March 1891

Dearest Anna,

It is too long since I have written. So much to do, with four children and the house, in addition to my businesses. Only you can understand this—you, who are so good to come for my confinements. Whatever would I do without your kindness?

Now that Tobe is gone—and, I really cannot say that I am sorry they moved away to Williamsport, for you know that I always considered Aaron a stubborn and disagreeable man. Still, there is something between kinswomen, even if they are not related by blood. Tobe is a nice woman, a trifle dull perhaps, but kindhearted and loyal. I would miss her if I weren't so busy. What a comfort it is, though, to know that you and I will always be close! No matter that we don't see each other as often as I would wish.

Simone, Sonya, and Jonas are thriving. They are sweet children, but Jonas is so full of mischief! Jacob has grown up. Such a nice, handsome boy. I can hardly believe it has been two years since you were here for his Bar Mitzvah. Jacob talks all the time about his "little Rose," and asks when we shall see her again. Do not forget that we are expecting Rose to stay with us at Hillside this summer.

Until next time, Anna dear, I send warm regards to Cousin Mordecai and many kisses to you and the children.

                                                          Your loving,
                                                          Rachel

Wilkes-Barre Spring 1892

Rachel was putting the final touches on a gray bombazine dress for Mrs. Matlin, wife of the president of Wyoming and Susquehanna Coal & Navigation Company, who insisted on having the overexaggerated bustle she had seen in the *Ladies' Illustrated Monthly Book,* despite the fact that it added unnecessarily to her already ample proportions.

"Perhaps a modified version, Mrs. Matlin," she had suggested tactfully. "This would be awkward, getting in and out of carriages and seated in church or at dinner—don't you think?" Rachel had continued, trying to gently dissuade her from the style.

Mrs. Matlin would be coming for a final fitting within the hour. She was an important customer, so it was wise to humor her wishes. But to have her going about in a ridiculous outfit would do Rachel's business no credit!

Isaac came in for the midday meal. She had prepared the usual thick soup that he liked—today a pea porridge with potato dumplings. Isaac loved her soups, even though he said they were "German" soups. He said the same thing about her sauerbraten, her potato kugel, her gefilte fish, and her sweet and sour tongue—but he ate everything with gusto. It was a wonder he didn't grow fat like Mordecai, with the amount of food he consumed! But Isaac worked hard and walked a great deal, remaining firm and lean, still as handsome a man as he was the day she married him fifteen years ago.

Isaac had gone to Williamsport recently to visit Aaron and Tobe, taking Jacob with him on the train. Rachel was glad not to join them, even though she was curious about the city on the West Branch of the Susquehanna. Somehow, she could never bring herself to feel warmth toward Aaron. He had not been pleased when Isaac married her, she knew, anticipating that she would be a patronizing presence in the family. She had been nothing of the kind! Even if she *had* influenced Isaac to act in more American ways. After all, they *were* Americans now. They had become citizens of their new country, and it was only sensible to adapt themselves to new ways.

She herself had made adjustments. In Germany she certainly wouldn't have baked and sewed for a living! She would have been married to some stolid banker or businessman and living in a dark apartment with a servant to bring the tea tray, and she would have been . . . so bored, so completely, utterly bored. How much better to be here in Wilkes-Barre, busy and creative, helping her husband to build a comfortable estate. And what a husband! Rachel shook her head in wonder to think that she and Isaac had found each other on that ship, the *Vrieland.* How good life was!

"And how do Aaron and Tobe live in Williamsport?" she had asked Isaac when he returned.

"They have a nice house, a large white wooden house, with big columns in front. It has many rooms—I don't know exactly how many, but more than they need for the four of them."

Rachel had sniffed and said nothing. Isaac reported that Aaron was prospering. He owned a successful factory in which he made wooden parts for small boats—everything from masts to hatch covers. He then shipped them down to the shipbuilding centers—Philadelphia, Baltimore, Wilmington, even to Pittsburgh. He would like Isaac to join him in business.

"Isaac, it's a big business, more than I can handle. I have no sons. I can use you here with me. Believe me, it wouldn't be a mistake for you to come here."

But Isaac was happy in Wyoming Valley, building his own transport service. When he was with Aaron, as pleased as he was to see him, he realized that he had always had to accommodate himself to his brother's sour personality.

Aaron had come to visit several times since he had left Plymouth. On his way to Philadelphia he had stayed with them about a year ago. After he left, Rachel had said, "Your brother's success hasn't done a thing to improve his disposition, Isaac."

"Now, now, Rachel. Aaron means well. He's just a little . . . serious."

She had patted his cheek and kissed him, slowly, and fully on the lips—right there in the kitchen, in broad daylight! He had been startled, flushing, and awkwardly putting his arms around her.

"Thank God, you don't take after your brother, Isaac. I don't like 'serious' men."

III

Philadelphia   Summer 1896

Isaac never had cared much for Mordecai Franke. Mordecai was such an austere man, completely humorless. To Isaac, this was a character defect without equal. The man who couldn't enjoy life, laugh a little, was not as God intended him to be.

Mordecai had treated Isaac fairly—he had to admit that. But he knew, without anything being said, that Mordecai had always felt that Rachel married beneath her when she became Isaac's wife, and Isaac resented it.

Now, Jacob and Rose, the youngest child of Anna and Mordecai, wanted to be married, and it was up to Isaac to speak to Mordecai about it, because Jacob didn't have the courage to do it himself. They were young—too young to be married, in Isaac's opinion. Rose had told Jacob that her father had mentioned the son of a certain rich Philadelphia banker—a German Jew—

several times, and her instincts told her his casual references to the young man were purposeful. If Jacob didn't request her hand soon, it might be too late! The two young people were so unhappy, it both saddened and amused Isaac. He remembered his own love-smitten youth in Kovno, when he approached Malka's house each day with the certain knowledge that Reb Michel would tell him she was betrothed to another. God willing, these two children would have a happier fate than he and Malka.

"Isaac! Come in. How was your trip?" Mordecai had put on many pounds since the day eighteen years before when Isaac had first met him. He was a portly, bald man who looked all of his fifty-four years. His elegantly tailored black bengaline frock coat barely met across the expanse of his abdomen. The vest beneath had been let out from behind several times to accommodate his added inches. Isaac, scarcely changed in physique from the day he had landed at the Front Street pier, was still a strong, hardy man who enjoyed physical labor and kept in good health by walking long distances in winter and chopping wood at Hillside in the summer.

Isaac declined the cigar Mordecai offered him, but took a glass of brandy. They sat in the little dark red parlor, unchanged all these years, save for new drapings at the windows and an even greater accumulation of bric-a-brac.

"How is business, Isaac?" Mordecai inquired.

"Business is going well, Mordecai. I have recently signed a contract with the railroad to handle their transfers from the canal." Isaac sipped his brandy. "The day of the canal is almost over. I give it another five, perhaps ten, years. Before long you'll see automotive shipping used in place of inland waterways, even taking business away from the railroads."

"Nonsense! Those ridiculous machines? They're nothing but a fad. Be finished in a decade." Mordecai relit his cigar, puffing nasty-smelling fumes in Isaac's direction.

"I don't think so, Mordecai. I'm intrigued with these machines—in fact, I've made a small investment in a company manufacturing them, up in Old Forge. It's an invention that will be improved and will catch on. You mark my words. In twenty years, we'll all be riding around in our own horseless carriages."

"Prepost'rous!" And that was Mordecai's final word on the subject.

Mordecai now turned his attention to the political scene. He instructed Isaac on the fine points of the presidential campaign, which was gaining momentum. William Jennings Bryan had just made his "Cross of Gold" speech at the Democratic National Convention in Chicago, and Mordecai had contributed to a fund started by eastern businessmen in support of the Republican William McKinley, who favored protective tariffs.

American politics were an endless fascination to Isaac. The idea that the people could participate in this wonderful democratic process was by far the overriding issue for him. . . . William Jennings Bryan, William McKinley, what did it matter? It wasn't the Czar!

"Mordecai," he said finally, "I have come to discuss our children with you. My son Jacob is very fond of your Rose. And, I believe, she has similar feelings for him. They have known each other all their lives. I would like to propose that they should marry."

Mordecai did not react one way or another, but was paying inordinate attention to his cigar. Isaac regarded him for a while from under his brows. "Well, what would you think if they were to become engaged now, and then marry after a period of time?"

Mordecai cleared his throat several times. He gazed at the ceiling, the floor, across the room, and at the tip of his cigar—anywhere but directly at Isaac. Isaac continued to look steadily at the pompous banker, not the least intimidated by him. He had taken Mordecai's measure long ago and knew what to say, and when to say it.

"It is not usual for cousins to marry each other, Isaac," Mordecai finally managed.

"Come, now, Mordecai, they're not even related. Jacob is not Rachel's own son."

"They're very young to be married . . . Rose is not yet eighteen, and . . . and . . . how old is Jacob?"

"Jacob was twenty in March. He's a serious young man, not given to youthful misbehaviors—never has been. Jacob has been helping me in the business for over four years. He will have the clothing business as his own, once he is married. Rose will never lack for security if she marries Jacob. As for their youth, most young people marry early these days."

Mordecai sucked in his jowly cheeks and adjusted the pince-nez that was clamped on the bridge of his short broad nose under his dome-like forehead. "Rose is a cultivated girl, Isaac. She is accustomed to a certain scale of living and entertainment in Philadelphia. I'm not so sure she would find Wilkes-Barre . . . shall we say, agreeable?"

"Rose would not have much of an adjustment to make. She feels at home with us," Isaac answered. "Rachel will be a second mother to Rose. I have seen a nice house not too far from us which is for sale. They would start out in their own home, with a maid, so Rose would not be in reduced circumstances." Isaac could not resist this last comment, enunciating it with a certain relish.

Mordecai did not reply immediately. Isaac was wondering how the man would manage to raise the point which was closest to his heart . . . or whether he would have the courage to do so. Isaac knew that Mordecai was a little afraid of him. The Philadelphian had never been able to dominate the Russian immigrant, and he didn't understand why he couldn't.

"To tell you the truth, Isaac—and I say this in the strictest confidence— one of our leading Jewish citizens in Philadelphia, a colleague of mine whose family ties go back to the same part of Germany as ours, has mentioned Rose to me in regard to his own son, a fine young man of twenty-four, well-established, an educated person. . . ." So, Rose had been correct! It was time to play his card.

"Yes, I can imagine that a lovely young woman like Rose would have many suitors. Of course, Mordecai, you would want to be certain that she is valued for herself, and not for her family's wealth. You love your daughter, I'm sure, and would want to ensure her happiness. For Jacob, all he wants is Rose's hand in marriage. Because he loves her and wants her for his wife, he would not require any financial settlement. In fact, in our family, we do not like the custom of asking for a dowry." He sat back now to let his cousin-in-law digest this information, while he sipped his brandy and toyed with a little Dresden figurine of a shepherdess on the overladen table.

Mordecai's pasty, flaccid face had unusually high color today, Isaac noted. The man could scarcely control the glint in his eyes, behind the thick lenses.

"You make a very good point about Rose's happiness, Isaac. You are correct that I have a deep affection for my daughter. It is important to me that she be married to someone she cares for." Mordecai was calculating how many thousands of shares this arrangement would save him.

"Well, then, Mordecai . . . am I to understand that you would give your consent to an engagement now, and to a wedding in the autumn, shall we say, if Rose is in agreement?"

Mordecai's sigh indicated that he was still weighing the considerations—he had, no doubt, counted on the advantages of the connection to the banker's family. But he extended his hand with a shake of his head, and he actually smiled.

"Yes, Isaac. I give my consent." He poured another glass of brandy for both of them. Isaac drew a breath of profound relief before downing his brandy.

Wilkes-Barre

In the early dawn of a March morning in 1902 nothing marred the clear, blue innocence of the sky. The river was still frozen in its northernmost reaches, where blocks of ice six feet deep could be cut to put in the storage cellars for preserving foodstuffs. But spring was on the wind and the fishermen were preparing their boats for the coming season. Furrows of freshly turned earth traced their patchwork design over the contours of the softly rolling farmlands of New York and Pennsylvania.

That afternoon the temperature suddenly dropped ten degrees, then twenty. By midnight it was below freezing and a strong gusty wind came roaring down from the Canadian plains, bringing with it heavy, dark clouds laden with moisture. A slow, steady snowfall began, the flakes large and thick. By morning the accumulation had reached eight inches. It continued to fall throughout that day, and the following night, until it had blanketed the entire region of the upper Susquehanna under many feet of silent whiteness.

For several days the hardworking people of the northern Susquehanna Valley luxuriated in the unaccustomed respite from labor. Doors and windows were drifted shut and the howling wind never ceased. Fires were stoked, needlework taken out, the stores delved into for feeding, and families drew closer together, reminiscing about times past and enjoying the sharing of one another.

And then, as suddenly as it had arrived, the wind and the cold departed. The sun returned, melting the huge snowfall and loosening the great mounds of ice that had jammed together, sending them downriver like fairy ships of crystal. Farmers standing along the riverbank at Towanda looked down at the dark waters, remarking at the great amount of ice navigating the stream. Downriver, near Tunkhannock, people stood on a flimsy wooden bridge and watched apprehensively as the water level rose to within a foot of the boardwalk. At Kingston the sheriff assigned deputies to measure the river level every four hours, reasoning that although there wasn't likely to be rain after three days of snow, it never hurt to be extra careful.

That night it began to rain. A leaden sky dropped four inches of rain on the New York–Pennsylvania border near Binghamton and Owego within forty-eight hours. At Tioga Point a sudden thaw released a huge ice mass which lazily began its way downstream. Mountain brooks came cascading down rocky precipices to spill over the already saturated earth.

And at 2:00 A.M. a wall of water rushed over the banks of the Susquehanna in Wyoming Valley, drowning the countryside and all of downtown Wilkes-Barre.

The Hillman family, from their safe bastion on Prospect Avenue, offered their help and their homes to less fortunate friends, as did many of their neighbors. A dormitory was set up in the parlors, while Rachel and her daughters cooked constantly for the growing number of people whose homes had been inundated.

When Isaac had chosen to remain in this part of town although it was not as fashionable as the lower areas near the river, his reasoning had been that a river is entitled to its flood plain, and periodically will lay claim to it, as a sort of rite of eminent domain. The foolish people who originally built their forts and houses along the riverbanks and, later, those who followed had acted out of ignorance or obstinacy. That didn't mean that he would go along with their short-sightedness, even if most of the prosperous people in the valley did.

The result of this foresight was that Isaac repeatedly witnessed over the years the distress of those who lived in the flat areas of the valley, while his home and businesses remained safe from flooding.

Rachel's dressmaking enterprise had changed drastically. With the advent of ready-to-wear clothing and less complicated design, few women required custom-made clothes. Isaac had bought a building in Hanover Township where the factory produced housedresses, work shirts, and overalls made of a heavy twilled cotton fabric, firm and durable, which was popular with farmers and laborers. Jacob had taken over this business when he married Rose. Isaac thought that his son was not innovative enough, but he was careful not to offer unasked-for advice. Jacob was a young man who needed to gain in self-reliance and self-confidence. Marriage to Rose had done wonders for him, Isaac had to admit. Jacob was happier than Isaac had ever seen him. Quiet, simple, kindhearted, but reticent to the point of painful shyness, there must be something magical in their relationship with each other, Isaac mused. Rose gazed at her husband adoringly whenever he was in sight. They preferred to be alone together to almost any other activity. Love! A wonderful thing. Only God could have invented love!

Jacob was about to sign a contract to supply work uniforms for the Wyoming and Susquehanna Coal & Navigation Company when a young man named John Mitchell, head of the American Federation of Labor and the United Mine Workers of America, succeeded in convincing the 150,000 men who worked the anthracite mines of northeastern Pennsylvania to go on strike for higher wages and fairer treatment. It was May of 1902, and everyone thought it would be only a matter of weeks until the miners were forced to go back to work. How long could they live without an income? But no one reckoned with the charisma of Mitchell or the determination and stamina of the miners. Somehow, this small, unassuming man was able to bring together Irish and Welsh, German and Pole, Italian and Slav. Traditional enemies became brethren in their single cause.

Months passed, the mine owners refused to bargain, men left the valleys of the Pennsylvania coal regions to look for work elsewhere, and the public began to panic with the coming of cold weather and the promise of unheated homes. To say nothing of the railroads, without fuel. President Theodore Roosevelt threatened to send in troops to run the mines if the coal operators refused to negotiate a settlement. On October 13, 1902, the mine owners gave in and agreed to submit to arbitration. The men of the hard-coal towns went back to work, there was coal for the furnaces of America, and in March of 1903 a commission awarded the miners a 10 percent wage increase, union recognition, and the expectation that their future might bring further gains. It was a time of quiet hope in Wyoming Valley.

The Wyoming Valley *Sentinel*'s young editor, Matthew Flannery, wrote an inspiring editorial about the great victory for everyone in this triumph of recognition of the rights of the workingman. It was, he said, a portent for the future of American labor relations. His father, Garrick, was proud of his son's full-blown style. It looked like the *Sentinel* would continue in good, crusading journalistic tradition, once Garrick decided to hand over the reins to the next generation of Flannerys.

Jacob Hillman had been planning to discontinue the dress component of his factory, to concentrate on work uniforms and overalls. He had even considered opening a plant to produce the durable cotton material called jean fustian, or *denim*, by those who preferred the French name. The long strike had frightened him, however. Mining was the chief industry of the area, and one crippling strike like that could put him out of business! So Jacob kept on manufacturing cotton dresses, produced work uniforms for a single, independent coal company, and put aside his plans to produce jean fustian. Isaac thought his son had made the wrong decision, but when Jacob did not immediately follow his suggestion, he refrained from offering more advice.

Simone, Isaac's and Rachel's older daughter, was married to a hardworking, pleasant young man who helped Isaac at the transportation company, Hillman Express. He was respectful of his father-in-law, and the association was proving to be a satisfactory one. Sonya, their younger daughter, whose wedding had been celebrated recently, lived in Scranton, where her husband was a partner in his father's law firm.

That left Jonas, their youngest child. Isaac sometimes worried about Jonas . . . his head always in the clouds. Jonas had attended the Wilkes-Barre Academy, a private institution. Not like the others, who had graduated from the public high school. Jonas had gone off to Lafayette College—the first of his family to go to college—where he was in his third year. He didn't appear to have any interest in working in a family business—or working anywhere else, for that matter. Children! A joy and a responsibility.

The grandchildren, though! That was a different matter altogether. That was pure joy. To hold the small babies in his arms as he had once held his own children. To feel the pulse of life in the chubby, warm little bodies. To fondle and kiss the rosy cheeks, gaze into the big wondering eyes for signs of his own image . . . what a pleasure, a *mechaieh!*

First had come Nathan, Rose's and Jacob's oldest. A long, sturdy boy with a strong disposition, bright beyond his years, a born leader. A year later, Frieda had arrived. A sweet, pretty little girl. Both of the children had Rose's dark hair and brown eyes.

And then, on a sultry Wednesday, the second day of July in 1901, Rose had given birth to a second son. They named him Arthur Franke Hillman.

This child was fair and beautiful from the moment of his first breath. He had inherited all of the good looks of the Hillman-Belkind line, the robust strength of his paternal grandfather's forebears, the sunny disposition and grace which were Isaac's, and the kindhearted, strong character of his mother, Rose. Blond, blue-eyed, tawny-skinned from the sun at Hillside, he was the most beautiful boy anyone ever knew. And he had a manner to match.

As the years passed and Isaac watched this child grow into a winsome, smiling boyhood, such a love for him formed in his heart that it sometimes frightened him. To love anyone that much, it was dangerous! He had never been one of those superstitious Jews, the kind who spit or tossed salt, but he silently asked God's protection on this favored grandchild whenever someone admired him.

Who wouldn't admire such a boy! Handsome, spirited, bright, he lit up a room when he walked in. The older children doted on him—never jealous of the attention he received. People would stop to look at him when he was a baby in his carriage. . . . When he entered school, he became the favorite of the teachers, and his classmates, too.

Arthur excelled at sports from the time he was a small boy. Fleet-footed, agile, coordinated, he swam, fished, rode bareback, skated over the frozen pond sooner and better than his older brother, Nathan, who was too impatient and rash to master the technique of a sport. Nathan slammed into an activity, managing to conquer it by sheer willpower and devil-may-care derring-do. Arthur approached it slowly, with quiet contemplation, then, after studying the matter, performed it effortlessly, with finesse. Most people were a little in awe of him, except that he was so modest and unaware of his talents and charm that they soon forgot their wonder.

Isaac loved all of his eleven grandchildren dearly, but for Arthur he felt a special bond. He saw something of himself in the boy . . . as if, through this grandchild, he would live on into the next generation.

June 1914

Sitting in the sanctuary of Congregation B'nai Israel on the day of Arthur's Bar Mitzvah, Isaac was lost in a haze of haunting memories. Shadowy impressions of timeless sacraments administered by generations of high priests flashed across his mind. . . .

He was back in the small wooden *shul* in Nemunaitis at his own Bar Mitzvah. . . . Walking through the fields of barley with an ever-young Malka, auburn tendrils blowing across her face in a warm summer breeze. . . . Her grandson . . . her legacy . . . taking his place among Jews today. . . .

He watched as this beloved grandchild read the portion of the Torah in a clear, resonant voice. Tall for his age, not yet a man, but showing promise of a handsome maturity, Arthur had none of the gawkiness of adolescence. His brilliantly blue eyes shone, the firm, determined mouth threatened to break into his radiant smile as he exchanged a glance with his grandfather. To Isaac, who knew Arthur in a way he was certain no one else did, the boy's most appealing characteristic was his fineness—a quality of forthright honesty, of inner reserves, of dreams to be dreamed and challenges to be met.

Isaac watched as Jacob laid the *talis,* the prayer shawl, over Arthur's shoulders, an uncommon display of emotion playing across his restrained features as Jacob reenacted a ritual performed by countless fathers for untold generations. Arthur bent his blond head over the scroll, slowing a moment over a difficult word, the rabbi nodding approvingly as he continued the passage.

Isaac had a sudden memory of another thirteen-year-old boy . . . the stowaway child, Yekhiel, fleeing the Czar's soldiers on the Neman River . . . just Arthur's age . . . thirty-six years ago. What had become of him? What had become of all the thousands and thousands of Yekhiels in Europe . . . those Jewish boys whose futures contained hopeless misery?

The goodness of their lives in this land of freedom was enough reason to thank God at every turn. How fortunate he was! How blessed were they all—the Hillman family—to be here in America, celebrating the coming of age of his grandson, the Bar Mitzvah, Arthur Franke Hillman.

BOOK THREE

A Native Son

1914–28

I

Tunkhannock   Summer 1914

They always spent their summers at Hillside.

Near the end of June they packed a big carriage full of baskets and boxes of household necessities, tied valises on the top and back luggage racks, crammed children and cats into the seats, and traveled out the old road toward Dallas, through Kunkle and Beaumont to Eatonville. There they went off the main road onto a narrow country track that wound down toward the Susquehanna, past cornfields and rolling acres of wheat, past cow pastures with lowing brown and white milk cows from which Rose obtained their milk and butter all summer, past Joe Sanduski's farm where the boys got jobs when they were old enough.

Two years before, Jacob had purchased a Model-T Ford. Rachel refused to make the trip to Hillside in that contraption, so she and Rose took the train with the girls, while Jacob, Isaac, and the boys drove the automobile. They had two pierced tires along the way, arriving at Hillside after sundown, dusty but triumphant. What an adventure! The age of motor travel had arrived in the Hillman family.

The old stone and wood house with its great veranda stood in a grove of hemlocks and Scotch pines high on a promontory overlooking the broad deep channel of the Susquehanna. On the opposite shore, the steep, forbidding palisade rose to the level of the narrow roadbed along Sullivan's Trail. Behind it, the rounded hump of Sunrise Mountain climbed gently to the winter world beyond.

One of the nicest things about his family was that all the members were allowed their own private moments, in a place of their choosing. Arthur liked to lie in a hammock strung between two white-barked birches whose leafy branches filtered the sun so that its rays speckled the pages of his book in curious patterns. That was his special retreat, away from view of the house, set down the broad bank a little to the north, in a boulder-protected crescent overlooking a dense glade of feathery ferns. From there, he was able to see the sweeping bend in the river before it curved eastward out of sight toward Osterhout.

In that summer of 1914—after mornings filled with ceaseless activities . . . fishing, chopping wood, working on Joe's farm—he would come back to the cool, sprawling house, make himself a picnic lunch of egg-salad sandwiches, Damson plums, and raisin cookies. He would take the latest book borrowed from Tunkhannock's small public library down to his glen, there to spend an hour or two wallowing in a newly discovered eroticism. He had stumbled upon a wealth of little-noticed literature on a neglected, dusty shelf in the library—a collection of books from the estate of Phineas Hobson Gentry, Esquire, according to a bookplate in each of them. Arcane tales of ancient Mogul India and China's imperial court, of eunuchs and concubines and thwarted loves, described in flowery, romantic language, so specific in its biological detail that he spent a good number of that summer's afternoon hours in a state of tumescence.

At regular intervals he would run down through the fern fronds to the sandy beach made by his grandfather, dive into the sparkling river, swim out to the raft against the strong current, returning to shore presently to read another passage until compelled to splash into the cold water again.

His room looked across the river to the forested mountain. The long, lonely wail of the Lehigh Valley night freight as it followed the winding course of the Susquehanna sounded across to him each moonrise, beckoning him, reminding that there were other places, other worlds—disturbing his complacence.

His favorite mornings were those when he arose before the sun was up. Sometimes his Grandfather Isaac joined him on the river. At other times, Nate or one of their cousins. They rowed the skiff upstream, then dropped a drag anchor which had been filed down so that they moved slowly with the current. Isaac had shown them when they were very young how to set out trawling lines in the squared-off stern to catch the bottom feeders, usually drumfish. Arthur liked to sit and watch the dome of Sunrise Mountain form a fuzzy pink line, etched with charcoal, turning orange along its edge, and finally the orb of molten yellow gold would lift over the brooding mountain, causing him to squint against its blinding brilliance.

But the very best was to cast his line far out in a soaring loop, let it fall and sink in the deeper channel near the eastern bank, then the reeling in a little, waiting, his eye on the tip of his light, slim rod, his hand lightly fingering the line. Then the excitement when he felt a nibble, mounting as it grew to a tug, and at just the right moment to snap it upward and wind in, in a smooth, coordinated rocking motion, keeping just the right tension on the line so that the fish couldn't twist itself loose. It hurt him to see the fish struggling, truthfully, although he would never admit it, but the thrill of the catch was overriding. How often they had taken buckets full of catfish, carp, drumfish— and in the earlier days even river trout—home to Hillside, where they sat on the back porch cleaning, scaling, and boning the fish for their mother, who would fry it for breakfast, stuff and bake it for dinner, or prepare it in a sweet and sour raisin sauce to be eaten cold as an appetizer. . . .

Sometimes they would tramp through the woods to Indian Rocks, where they would play for hours in the caves. Once they took candles and matches with them to see what was inside. It had been a revelation. People had lived in there! They found the blackened ring of a long-extinguished campfire, some broken pottery shards . . . and, in an inner chamber, the skeletal remains of three unfortunates . . . two adults and a child. Arthur told Miss Hester Jones, the librarian at Tunkhannock, who was secretary of the Wyoming County Historical Society, about their discovery. They led her there with some men from Eatonville who took photographs. The caves were sealed as a permanent tomb for the victims, who they said had been captives, left to die there by Indians, over a hundred years ago. The Methodist minister said a blessing. Arthur wondered how they knew the dead had been Methodists, but perhaps that didn't matter.

They didn't go to the caves to play after that. But on their walks they often found arrowheads imbedded in the mossy floor of the birch and pine forest.

So many things to know, to experience! Sometimes he felt he couldn't wait to get on with it. With life. That here, in the Susquehanna Valley, he was marking time. Waiting for the day when he would leave. Out to the world beyond. To college, to the unknown, the challenges that awaited him. To dance another rhythm in another place where the beat would quicken.

At other times he welcomed the protective surroundings of his birthplace. Secure in the warmth of his loving family, the friendships, the comfort of the familiar.

From his older brother, Nathan, and from the boys on the Sanduski farm, he expanded his knowledge of sex. Heaven knows, his father wouldn't talk about it, and he didn't want to ask his mother. . . . But it was from his grandfather Isaac that he learned about love. Isaac spoke of love naturally, simply, but with feeling. He made it sound like it was an integral part of life, important and beautiful. Something wonderful that would happen to him someday.

"A man is nothing without the love of a woman, Arthur. Remember that. To find the right woman for your wife, one who loves you and whom you love in return—that is happiness—that is success. Marriage, children—those are the most important things in life. Without those, all else is empty."

"Did you love my grandmother very much?" he'd asked. They were skipping stones into the river, upstream from Hillside.

"I still do," Isaac answered, amused.

"I meant my real grandmother—the one in Russia."

Silence. A long sigh. "Yes. Very much." Then he smiled and said, "When I met Rachel, she drove away my sadness. That's another thing to remember, Arthur. The human spirit cannot be crushed. We always come back from defeat or sorrow. No matter what bad things may happen to you in life—and, my boy, no one goes through life without some disappointments—there is always a measure of joy to balance our setbacks. I always like to count the happy things and not dwell on sadness." He skipped a flat stone expertly, skimming the surface. "Let's see you match that!" he shouted.

Arthur liked it when Isaac rambled on about life. He enjoyed the times they walked through the woods together or went out on the river in a boat, just the two of them. Somehow he could never feel as close to his father as he did to his grandfather. Jacob was such a quiet man, so reticent. Isaac smiled a lot. He was fun to be around.

"When I was your age, Arthur, I had no idea I'd be living in America one day. You have to remember that life is full of surprises, unexpected turns of fate. That's what makes it exciting."

One day Arthur asked, "How did my father's being born kill his mother, Grandfather?"

"*What?*" Isaac's voice was like a whip cracking. "What did you say?"

He was scared. "I . . . I . . . well, that's what Cousin Tanya said once when she was visiting from Williamsport. That giving birth to Jacob killed his mother . . . I heard her say it to Aunt Simone."

Isaac looked so stricken that Arthur wished he hadn't mentioned it. "Listen, my boy. Your grandmother—your real grandmother, whose name was Malka—died from injuries. Two drunken peasants came along and hit her carriage with theirs, knocked her into the road, and the horses trampled her. Her baby—your father—was born two months early because of the accident. He almost didn't live himself. Malka's death was not because of the baby. It's evil of Tanya to say that."

"My father thinks it was because of him, Grandfather," Arthur said quietly, but with firm conviction.

"How do you know that? Are you sure?"

"I know it. I'm sure."

Arthur didn't know exactly what happened after that. He knew that Isaac and Jacob had a talk, and he thought Jacob seemed happier afterward.

By late summer of 1914, Europe was at war. The Hillman family left Hillside early that year because Nathan was going to college at Pennsylvania State University. Arthur had a letdown feeling as the end of August approached, thinking about Nate leaving home. He and Nate—well, they were really close. More like pals than just brothers. Most brothers he knew argued a lot, but Nate never had picked on him or teased him, even when they were young. He'd never resented Nate, either. They'd always loved each other, enjoyed spending time together. Arthur didn't want to think about the lonely days ahead for him, with Nate away. His sisters were fine, but they weren't especially fun to be with—Frieda was quiet and dull, and Dorothy, three years younger than Arthur, was sort of silly, in addition to being self-centered.

After Nate left for State College, Arthur began a feverish round of activities which lasted throughout his high school years. He filled his afternoons and weekends with club work and friendships. Occasionally he helped his father in the factory during the busy seasons. Jacob was not, however, anxious to have his sons work in his business. He had always disliked the business world; had wished—too late—to have been in a more intellectual profession. Nathan wanted to be a lawyer, an idea he favored. And Arthur was good in chemistry and zoology—wouldn't it be a good thing for him to study medicine? A doctor in the family. Jacob liked that thought. He must mention it to Arthur. Or maybe ask his father, who seemed to have a way with the boys. Jacob had a difficult time talking to them, getting his ideas across to them.

When Nathan came home on vacations the house rang with happy laughter, the boys' deepened voices sending a thrill through Rose as she watched her sons mature into handsome, vigorous young manhood. Nathan's dark, dashing good looks—such a contrast to Arthur's golden, blue-eyed brilliance —made him extremely popular with girls. There was always a bevy of young women in middies and serge skirts, or soft white dresses with pastel sashes, smiling and laughing at Nathan's antics, harmonizing in a circle around him at the piano while he played and sang lustily in his strong baritone.

Life in the house on Prospect Avenue was warm and full. The war in Europe was remote. Thank heaven, it was not *their* war! Not *their* sons who would have to fight! As each year passed . . . 1915 . . . 1916 . . . and war clouds loomed on the horizon, Rose comforted herself with the thought that Nathan was only seventeen . . . then, only eighteen. Even if the United States entered the war, he would not be old enough to fight.

She looked to Jacob for reassurance. "If we enter the war, Jacob, they won't enroll boys under twenty, will they?"

"We won't get into the war, my dear," her sage husband assured her. Jacob, in his wisdom, had sold the uniform plant at the end of 1915. It was the least successful part of his business and he'd had a good offer from a New Yorker who had recently moved to town. Isaac had been dismayed when he learned of it, but it was too late for recriminations.

On April 2, 1917, President Wilson told a stunned America that they were going to "make the world safe for Democracy." How had they lulled themselves into thinking they could keep out of it?

Men aged twenty-one to thirty were subject to the draft. Rose prayed the war would end before Nathan's twenty-first birthday, in January of 1919.

A frenzy of patriotism seized the nation, and nowhere so keenly as on the university campuses. At Penn State, military training was increased, austerity programs put in force, and all student capers canceled. When Nathan came home from State College in May, the end of his junior year, it was Corporal Nathan J. Hillman of the United States Infantry reporting.

Nathan had become part of the war.

Wilkes-Barre   September 1917

A bell clanged. The stationmaster's voice blared from a megaphone: "This is the Pennsylvania Railroad Coach to Nanticoke, Retreat, Shickshinny, Wapwallopen, Berwick, East Bloomsburg, South Danville, and SUNBURY . . . with connections to Lewisburg, Glen Iron, and BELLEFONTE-STA-A-ATE COLLEGE . . ."

A sudden weakness gripped Arthur. His heart tripped a beat as he thought, *This is IT!* The moment of departure had actually arrived. After all the months of anticipation. He picked up his coat, the box of food his mother had prepared, the book bag his "Uncle" George Sarnoff, Reuben's son, had given him as a graduation present containing his dictionary, Latin grammar, and slide rule. One of his cousins took his suitcase, and the entire family moved out onto the railroad platform.

Arthur noticed Harry Steiger, who'd been a year ahead of him at high school, standing with a group of several boys, talking to two girls who were dressed in navy-blue suits, wearing straw boaters.

As the engine quieted to an impatient puffing, waiting for the passengers to board, he turned to embrace his mother, then his sisters, Frieda and Dorothy, his Aunt Simone, Aunt Sonya, and his cousins.

"Good-bye, Arty!"

"Don't forget to write us!"

"God bless you, son. Good luck to you." At the last moment, his father hugged him in a rare display of affection. One last embrace for his mother. . . .

"Abooooaaard . . ." called the conductor.

Arthur swung up the steps, the conductor helping him with his heavy valise, which he stowed in a space behind the last seat in the car. Arthur looked at it dubiously.

"Don't worry, it will be all right," the man said kindly. "No, no . . . don't bother," he put up his hand to stop Arthur's motion toward his pocket. Arthur wasn't sure about tips. His experience at traveling alone was limited to the Laurel Line from Wilkes-Barre to Scranton.

Moving up the aisle, he bent to look out the grimy window at his family, grouped together on the platform in little islands, the girls talking, the boys standing with their feet apart trying to look grown up. Dorothy, his kid sister, always the clown, was making faces at him. Rose waved a lacy handkerchief. His father, standing apart from the others, was lost in thought. *He looks worried,* Arthur thought with a pang. The aunts and uncles were clearly impatient for the train to leave now, so they could get back to their own affairs.

The whistle sounded a short blast. There was a last cry from the conductor, a ring of metal on metal as the doors slammed, and the train moved slowly forward, jerked, catching him off balance, then settled into a smooth motion. At the first hiss of the locomotive, his family moved along the platform with the car, waving, his mother in tears by now. Arthur felt a great lump in his throat as he returned their waves. He sat down, pressing his face against the glass to catch a last glimpse of them as the train gathered momentum. It moved out of the station, past the freight yards with an accelerated chug-chug-chugging of its engine. Through the industrial area the train rolled, near his father's dress factory with the large painted white legend, *Hillman Mills.*

Weathered board houses lined the track on the outskirts of the town. As the train started its climb, the culm banks and breakers in the distance—idle on this Sunday afternoon in September 1917—spoke a mute farewell to him, a native son gone out from his home.

Arthur walked forward to the lavatory, locked himself in, and gave in to the tears that overwhelmed him. After a few minutes, his breath came evenly. He looked into the murk of the mirror above the washbasin and spoke aloud to his reflection. "Grown men don't cry, Arthur. Remember that."

He splashed cold water on his face, using his handkerchief to dry himself. He felt much better. Opening the door, he stepped out into the corridor and faced Harry Steiger, who came swaying toward him.

"Hey, Art, I've been looking for you. Come join us in the next car. I met some friends from State."

Once inside the other car, Harry led him to a group of three boys and the two young women he'd noticed on the platform. They were sitting facing each other, one fellow balancing on the arm of the girls' seat, an easy confidence in the way they carelessly talked, spontaneous and sure. There were other groups of students in the car, all relaxed and in high spirits. At ease, they represented an unknown world to Arthur. For a brief moment he wished he hadn't boarded the train, but had remained safe in the haven of his family, in the familiarity of old friends.

"This is Arthur Hillman," Harry was saying. Harry pointed to each as he named them . . . there was Jean Matlin, Shirley Davis, Tom Crittendon, Bill Johnson. The girls were typical of what his Aunt Simone would call *shiksas*—his mother did not use such Yiddish expressions.

Tom and Bill nodded, then went on with their conversation. "And that big lummox sitting next to Shirley is James Aloysius Flannery, Esquire," said Harry.

A large, sandy-haired boy stood up, extending his hand, and greeted him with considerable friendliness. "I know your brother, Nate," he said to Arthur, motioning him to a seat behind the two girls. "Real nice guy." He had an appealing face, light brown eyes that seemed to know a delightful secret, and a peculiar grace of manner for someone who looked like a halfback.

Harry leaned over. "Where're you going to stay, Art?"

Stay? He hadn't thought about it. He just assumed that when he reached State College he would register at the university and be assigned a room. That's what Nate had done. Harry explained that it was much better to board in a rooming house or, after freshman year, in a fraternity house with a group of friends.

"We don't know what's going to happen this year with the wartime campus. I heard the Army might take over. If so, we'll all be in the Reserve and subject to military discipline . . . drilling, curfew, and all that. . . . Half the junior and senior classes enlisted last year."

A shadow passed over Arthur's face. "I know. My brother was one of them. He's in France now."

"That's right . . . I forgot about that. How is Nate?"

"All right, as far as I know. We haven't heard from him for a long time. My folks weren't so happy when he enlisted, but they're used to it now. My father's really proud of him." Arthur spoke with a measure of pride himself.

"Say, meanwhile, Art, why don't you come stay with us, and we'll see if we can get you set up with a room? Is that O.K. with you, Jim?"

"Sure thing, Steeg," said Jim Flannery.

Jim and Steeg instructed Arthur in the mysteries of freshman behavior at Penn State . . . the wearing of the green dink . . . not walking on the grass . . . and no smoking, for starters. But the worst deprivation of all, they informed him, was that the lowly freshman was not permitted to call on or converse with a female person until House Parties Weekend on Pennsylvania Day! Since Arthur did not know any "female persons" at State, he did not expect this to be much of a deprivation. In general, though, it appeared that the role of a sophomore was to see how miserable he could make the life of a freshman.

"Are you a frosh?" asked a silky voice. Jean Matlin was kneeling on her seat, looking back at him with a teasing expression.

"Yes," Arthur answered, at a loss for what to say to this hazel-eyed, smooth-skinned girl with the pert mouth. "Are you?"

"Yes, I am!" she said. "Jimbo, trade seats with me for a minute, will you?" The large youth moved over next to Harry, saying, "Might as well take advantage of it, Art. This is your last chance!"

Jean slid by Shirley and seated herself next to Arthur. He was unused to girls acting in such a bold manner. In fact, he realized, he was unused to girls . . . period. Except for his sisters and cousins, but that didn't count.

"Do you come from Wilkes-Barre?" Jean asked.

"Yes. What about you?" Sparkling conversation, he thought, feeling ridiculous.

"I'm from Mountain Springs. I went to the Wilkes-Barre Institute." This was a little more interesting. He knew about Mountain Springs—a wealthy residential area around a small lake—restricted, so he had heard.

Jean was sizing him up with a frank, appraising look. "How old are you, Arthur?"

"Seventeen," he lied. He wouldn't be seventeen until next July, but if he said he was sixteen, he was sure she'd get up and move away.

"What courses are you planning to take?"

"Chemistry, biology, trig . . . and German, I guess. I'm not sure what else. Maybe Latin or English."

She looked at him quizzically. "Are you going to medical school, or something?"

He nodded. "Yes. I'm going to be a doctor."

"My father's a doctor." She smiled in approval.

At every station stop, more and more students boarded, until the car was full. The train wound its way along the Susquehanna Basin, each mile carrying Arthur farther away from Wyoming Valley.

II

State College   Autumn 1918

A tremendous red-orange moon hung low in the night sky like a giant balloon, seeming close enough to touch. The hay wagon swayed slightly as it rolled along the winding country lane in the strung-out caravan. Someone in one of the other wagons had a ukelele and a medley of male and female voices floated back over the rolling farmland, sweet and mellow . . . ". . . shine on, harvest moon . . . da-da-dee-dah . . . up in the sky . . ."

Arthur burrowed deeper into the prickly hay, forming a cradle for himself and Thelma in the fragrant hay mound.

"Comfortable?"

"Ummm . . . very comfortable."

He smiled down at her. "What do you think of your first hayride?"

"It's like being in a nest."

He blew on her bangs, which fluffed up. Then he bent his head closer. He could smell her sachet, sweet and floral. His lips touched the silky bangs, the smooth forehead. Her eyes closed. She stirred slightly and seemed to move closer—or was it his imagination?

With his finger Arthur traced the contour of her ridiculously small nose, the outline of her curving mouth. Her eyes flew open for a moment as he pressed his lips tentatively to hers. He was afraid she would pull away, but her arms encircled his neck and she kissed him in return, a full, warm, slow kiss to match the full, lazy, harvest moon.

Arthur felt the sharp jab of broken straws boring into his left elbow. His arm was beginning to go numb, but he was afraid to break the mood by shifting to a more comfortable position. This was, in fact, the most romantic situation he'd encountered in the year since he'd been at Penn State, and he wanted to make the most of it. However, it was becoming difficult to hold his breath for such long intervals.

It was Pennsylvania Day. This was the first big college weekend they had been permitted since America had entered the war. Although the dance wasn't being held, SATC rules had been relaxed, for there was the expectation of victory in the air, and everyone was in high spirits. Arthur had become eligible for the Student Army Training Corps at age seventeen. He rather enjoyed the marching and drilling . . . the patriotism.

On Friday afternoon the busloads of young ladies began to arrive from points near and far. Tonight's hayride was sponsored by the Interfraternity Council. A regimental review was planned for Saturday, to be followed by the football game against Rutgers, and a jazz concert in the evening. Thelma Hoyt was his date . . . a friend of Steeg's girl, from Lancaster.

There was silence now all around, broken by an occasional giggle from one of the other couples in the wagon. The moon had risen high in the night sky, painting the fields whitely lustrous. Arthur sat up. Thelma patted her hair, smoothing the long strands with both hands. She had glistening, light brown hair, which shone in the silvering moonlight.

"Hey, you two, coming up for air?" It was Jim Flannery, with his crooked grin and smiling Irish eyes.

Thelma threw a handful of hay at Jim. "Look who's talking," she retorted. Jim laughed and threw hay back. Suddenly everyone was throwing clumps of hay at one another. In this mood of hilarity they reached the end of the field between Fraternity Row and the college barns where an enormous bonfire had been lit. There were large vats of cider, an unaccustomed treat during wartime.

Milling around in the crowd surrounding the bonfire, Arthur saw Professor Chase, whose classics course he'd taken the previous term. Chase walked over. "Hello there, Arthur. How was the hayride?"

"Lots of fun, Professor Chase. It's a beautiful night."

"Yes . . . lovely. Arthur, didn't you tell me you have a brother who's serving with the Forty-second Infantry in France?"

"That's right . . . my brother, Nate. He's been promoted to First Lieutenant. Why do you ask, sir?"

"Um . . . no special reason. I heard some news about the Forty-second on the radio earlier this week. There's been some action, but everyone seems to agree that the war is drawing to a close."

"That's good news for me, sir. My brother was supposed to go to law school at Penn, and I know my parents will be relieved when he comes home."

They said good-bye and the professor moved away. Arthur took Thelma's hand. "Come on, let's go find Jimbo and Steeg . . ." They circled the crowd until they found the others. Arms around their girls' waists, they all headed for the fraternity house.

When they reached the front hall, Arthur noticed a slip of white paper in his box. "Call your family" was its terse message. He excused himself and went into the closet under the stairs where he cranked the telephone until he heard the operator's voice.

"Get me Wilkes-Barre 3-7543, please . . ."

His father answered, sounding old and tired. When he heard Arthur's voice, he made an attempt to speak more cheerfully. But the news was bad, as Arthur knew it would be.

"It's Nate, Arthur. He's in a hospital in France."

What does it take to make a boy grow up? In Arthur's case, it took a telephone call. At one moment he was a carefree college boy, spooning in a hay-filled wagon under a harvest moon, not a thought in his mind beyond the night's adventure. With his father's words he had the most certain feeling that his youth had come to an end.

Other families had suffered, had even lost sons. They mourned, recovered, and continued with their lives as before. Arthur knew that would not be so with his.

He packed his bags, bid his friends farewell, and boarded the train for Wilkes-Barre. His house was not hung with crepe, nor were the women dressed in black, but the prevailing mood was one of bereavement. Isaac had already cabled Malka's brother, Judah Belkind, who lived in Paris. Judah's son, Rafael, was a doctor, and he was able to arrange for Nathan to be moved to a private hospital in Reims where he would be well looked after. The cablegram said that Nathan had been gassed.

Rachel was practically hysterical. The Germans, her former countrymen, had done this to Nathan! Frieda sobbed when she saw Arthur, and Dorothy, effervescent Dot, was disconsolate. Rose was the pillar of strength for them all, especially for Jacob. His father grieved as Arthur had never seen a man grieve.

"Come on, everyone, he's not dead!" Arthur tried to cajole them. "Let's cheer up, for Nate's sake." He felt he succeeded in raising their spirits after a few days, but they lived in continuing anxiety, awaiting word from France, wondering when their son would be sent home to them and what his condition would be when he arrived.

November 11, 1918, was a bittersweet occasion in the Hillman family. Nathan would be sent home as soon as the French doctors said he could travel. They were cautious. Influenza stalked the world, snuffing lives. In Europe and America hundreds of thousands were dying. One of every four

American soldiers lost in the war was felled not by bullets but by influenza and its spectral accomplice, pneumonia.

Arthur, who had been studying at home, went back to State College for his examinations. The Penn State campus was in disarray following a disastrous fire which had destroyed the engineering building, its chief pride. Arthur had been so preoccupied with his personal tragedy that he had paid little attention to news of the fire. Seeing the ruins of the building reminded him that he had lost touch. Arranging with his professors to complete the year's work over an extended period of time, he returned to Wilkes-Barre so that he could spend these days of waiting with his parents.

He found out, in this trying time, what friendships meant. Jim Flannery and Harry Steiger, particularly, were his mainstays. Through them, he maintained a link with the college, with his other friends, who might well have forgotten him in his absence. Jim and Steeg came to Wilkes-Barre often, bringing assignments and lecture notes for him, offering to help him with missing material.

Jim, whose family were the wealthy and powerful owners of the Wyoming Valley *Sentinel,* one of the state's most important newspapers, had decided to forsake journalism for the study of medicine. His friendship with Arthur, who was a premed, had influenced his decision. Jim was able to give Arthur considerable help with the mathematics and science classes he missed. Steeg, who planned to go to law school, with an eye on a political future, was good for moral support. Arthur wondered how he would've made it through those months without the two of them.

New York City   January 1919

Arthur and Isaac went to New York to meet Nathan's ship. They convinced Rose that it would be better for her to remain at home with Jacob, who was recovering from one of his frequent attacks of pleurisy. Arthur was sure the illness was brought on by his father's anxiety about Nathan, if it was possible for disease to be a product of emotional stress.

The big steamship with the Red Cross painted on its side looked fit and nautical as it was eased into its berth. A band was playing, streamers were flying out of nearby windows, and there was a holiday atmosphere as expectant relatives strained to catch the first glimpse of a loved one.

First came the ambulatory cases—the convalescents and the walking wounded. Cheers rent the air, shouts of recognition and glad cries of greeting as a mother clasped her son, a wife her husband, a sweetheart her soldier boy. Next, an honor guard formed, and several dozen sealed coffins were carried down a second gangway, from the ship's hold. A murmur of sympathy rolled through the crowd. Men removed their hats, women wiped their eyes a little. It was a reminder that things could have been worse, much worse.

And then the file of stretchers began. There were sharp intakes of breath, an exclamation, a stifled cry. . . . A hush fell over the throng assembled there as these remnants of America's sons were carried back on their native soil. Armless . . . legless . . . armless and legless . . . without sight . . . without hope . . . they were borne down by men and women who had spent these most private, intimate days with them, knowing them in a way their families never would . . . the Red Cross nurses, doctors, and workers who had become skilled at crying without tears while they provided solace for the inconsolable, balm for the wounds of the spiritless.

Arthur heard a sound behind him. He turned to see his strong grandfather, Isaac, still tall, upright, indestructible, standing there unashamedly with tears rolling down his cheeks. "God in heaven!" Isaac addressed his Maker. "Why? For what?"

Somehow they found Nathan. Or, Nathan found them. Because they would never have recognized him. In the frantic milling about of those seeking their wounded kin, Arthur held high the placard with the number he'd received from the Red Cross coordinator.

An orderly touched his sleeve and indicated the wheelchair with its sunken-cheeked, cadaverous occupant. Arthur thought, as he hugged Nate, that if he didn't pass out from shock, he must be a lot stronger than he'd given himself credit for.

Isaac embraced Nathan, smiling and in complete control of himself. Amazing! The man was indomitable. Arthur would've bet anything that he would break down, after seeing him cry earlier, but he maintained a calm cheer, bringing a wan smile to Nathan's face and infecting Arthur with his happy mood.

"It's . . . good . . . to . . . be . . . home . . ." Nathan gasped. That effort seemed to cost him his entire reserve of energy.

Was this the reward one got for high ideals? Was this what happened to heroes? Nathan had turned twenty-one a week ago. He was finally eligible for the draft.

Wilkes-Barre 1919

Rose practiced her own brand of medicine . . . nutritional medicine. The pot of chicken soup was simmering constantly. Fragrant roasts, potato puddings, mouth-watering apple dumplings and cherry cobblers emerged daily from the big iron range to appear in tempting array. The aromas from Rose's kitchen could awaken pangs of hunger in the body of the most abstemious monk. Unfortunately, they did little to combat the effects of chlorine gas.

Nathan's condition remained shockingly poor throughout the winter. He spent more time in the hospital than at home, for he was subject to wracking attacks of bronchitis that left him blue-faced, gasping for air, and caused such severe chest pain that Rose feared he was dying of a heart attack. At those times he needed oxygen and a carefully controlled temperature and humidity. The hospital was the best place for him.

Dr. Davis had been the family doctor ever since Rose and Jacob were married. He was a good, solid physician with much experience; however, Nathan's case frightened him. The doctor seemed at a loss when it came to alleviating Nathan's pain. To look at Davis's somber face was enough to prepare everyone for the end.

"I think Nate needs a doctor with more experience in handling lung problems," Arthur told his grandfather. He didn't like to worry his parents with his concern.

Isaac called Reuben Sarnoff, and Reuben asked his former partner, Garrick Flannery, who knew everyone in town, for the name of a physician who might be able to help Nathan.

Dr. Wallace Hobson Carpenter was a general practitioner who had practiced in the valley long enough to have seen many miners with chronic lung ailments. Isaac was certain Dr. Carpenter was the right man as soon as he discovered that this was the son of his old English tutor, the retired superintendent of Wilkes-Barre City Schools, Ethan Carpenter. "How is your father, Dr. Carpenter?" Isaac asked upon meeting the doctor, an attractive man in his early thirties.

"Father is doing well, Mr. Hillman. He's getting on in years, of course. Not as active as he was." Ethan Carpenter was Isaac's age.

Dr. Carpenter referred Nathan to a pulmonary specialist in Philadelphia for a consultation. The specialist thought that Hobson Carpenter could manage Nathan's case well enough, but other than that, he was not very encouraging. Carpenter was a confident physician, and while Nathan's wheezing and attacks of bronchitis concerned him, they were not beyond his abilities.

"Dr. Carpenter, may I have a few words with you in private?" Arthur asked one day when the doctor came to pay a house call.

"Of course, Arthur. What's on your mind?"

"I'm very worried about my brother," Arthur said.

Carpenter nodded. "Yes, I'm worried about him, too. I can't tell you much at this time, Arthur. It's going to take a long period of recuperation until Nathan is able to resume a normal life."

"Will he? Resume a normal life, I mean?"

The doctor looked sorrowful. "There's just no way of predicting what will happen, Arthur . . . but I do have hope for him."

With the milder spring weather, the attacks tapered off. Nathan was sleeping well, and he developed an appetite for all the tempting trays his mother served him. Arthur, who had been dividing his time between State College and Wilkes-Barre, returned home after his exams in late May to see a noticeable improvement in Nathan's appearance.

"You're looking good, Nate! Have you been getting out of bed at all?"

Nathan gave him a withering look. "Yeah. I walk to the bathroom. Now I can pee standing up."

Nate's bitterness was impossible to get through. Arthur knew it was because he hated their pity, and he interpreted every word of concern or kindness as pity.

"What about Barbara?" Arthur asked him. Nate's girl friend from college had called to inquire about him a number of times.

"What about her?"

"Aren't you going to call her?"

"What for?" he asked angrily. "So she can come hold a wake over the body?"

"Nate, Nate . . . c'mon, buddy . . ."

"Well, what else would it be, Art?" He was wheezing. "Even if she were inclined to stick by me out of loyalty, her family would object. Hell—I wouldn't let her do it." His eyes had a haunted look.

"You're not being fair, Nate. At least let her know you think about her. She'll think you don't care."

"It's better that way." He had a spasm of coughing. When he was able to speak, he said, "See what I mean?"

"That's no way to talk, Nate. You're getting better. It'll just take time." But he didn't sound convinced.

"Art, I know and you know that I'm never going to be better. I may improve for a while, but one of these days an attack will get me . . . one of them will be the one to finish me off."

His heart sank. "Did Dr. Carpenter tell you that?"

"He doesn't have to. I can tell by looking at him . . . and I can tell by the way it feels when I'm running out of air."

By the end of July, Nathan felt strong enough to go to Hillside. Arthur was certain that just being up there in the fresh country air would be good for him. It improved his spirits. He sat out in the sun, gaining some color in his face, and he was more talkative, more like the old Nate.

Arthur spent all the time he could spare with Nate. He hesitated to ask him about the war, sensing his reluctance to relive those terrible days. "What was it like being out there . . . in the trenches . . . I mean, did you ever actually *see* the enemy?"

Nate nodded. "They were just people, like us, Art. Young. Scared. Lonely . . ."

One day a letter arrived from the Department of the Army. Since Nathan had never spoken about his battle experiences, its contents came as a surprise to the entire family.

ORDRE de l'ÉTOILE NOIRE du BÉNIN

Know all whom it may concern that Nathan Julius Hillman, First Lieutenant, 42nd Infantry, having distinguished himself in the service of the United States Forces in France, is awarded this citation for bravery by the Government of France, for gallantry in action on the twenty-sixth day of September, 1918, during the offensive at Meuse-Argonne.

In the face of heavy artillery, machine-gun fire, and gas attack, Lieutenant Hillman led his men, taking over when his superior officer was killed, in the attack on an enemy stronghold at Sedan, France. When directing his men, he removed his gas mask at his own peril, to urge them forward until the position was secured.

That was the only time Arthur ever saw his mother cry during all the months of Nathan's convalescence.

In later years Arthur would look back on this period of his life as a time of forging and tempering. It was a time when he was tested, subjected to stresses, molded and formed in character and temperament . . . a time of strengthening.

The abruptness of Nathan's invalidism drastically altered his plans, plunging him into the role of part-time student, requiring that he divide his attention between his studies at college and his family's needs at home.

The continuing reality of his brother's ill health had an even greater influence on the shape of his future. Onto Arthur shifted the obligations of the elder son. He felt the intentness of his parents' expectations of him—as a future medical student, as the one they would come to lean on in the ensuing years. Gradually he moved from being the younger, quieter, more introspective brother who sought counsel from Nathan. The role reversal was an ongoing process—Nathan retreating within himself, while Arthur emerged.

III

Wilkes-Barre 1920

"Your brother tells me you want to study medicine, Arthur," Dr. Carpenter said to him one day when he had accompanied Nate to the doctor's office. Nate was getting around pretty well now, although he became short of breath with the slightest exertion.

"Yes, Dr. Carpenter. I'm not sure where I can go to medical school. At this point, I'll be glad to get through college. I've lost a lot of time since Nate's illness."

Carpenter wrote something on one of his prescription blanks, handing it to Arthur. "Why don't you drop a letter to Dean Christian Rutledge at my school, Jefferson Medical College, in Philadelphia. It's a fine place. Dean Rutledge was my professor of medicine when I was at Jeff. You tell him I suggested you contact him." Dr. Carpenter gave him a friendly smile before going into his examining room to look at Nate.

Arthur graduated from Penn State in June of 1921. The following fall he entered the Jefferson Medical College. By the time he left for Philadelphia, Nathan had made remarkable progress—far more than Dr. Carpenter had expected.

"You can work a few hours a day, Nathan," Carpenter told him. "See how it goes. Don't overdo things. Take it slow, until you learn how much strength you have." Nate was able to spend a few hours a day helping his father in business. His plans to attend law school were something he never mentioned. It took a certain amount of stamina to study law, and stamina was something in short supply for Nathan.

The days of a first-year medical student are bewildering. *Gray's Anatomy* became Arthur's bible . . . memorizing the names and classifications of the thousands of individual parts of the human body, a seemingly impossible task. Histology, bacteriology, embryology, physiological chemistry. Night and day he studied, attended lectures, worked in the laboratory—sleeping no more than five or six hours a night.

For the first time in his life, money had become something of a problem for Arthur. Nate's medical care had drained the family coffers. The army pension did not cover the cost of expensive specialists or extended private hospitalization. Jacob's penchant for doing poorly in business had not changed. Isaac had stood by helplessly as he watched his oldest son let a hugely successful business run down. Isaac was paying for Arthur's medical education—the only way that Jacob would accept his help.

Jim Flannery, in his second year at Jefferson, proved once again what a loyal friend he was. He swept Arthur under his protective aegis, convincing him to join his fraternity, which was supposed to have the best food and the most comfortable rooms at bargain prices.

It was through Flannery that Arthur had his first, and only, encounter with the nurses. The student nurses at Jefferson were closely guarded by Clara, the ever-watchful directress. The rules were simple and unbreakable—no student nurse was permitted to go out alone in the company of a medical student or doctor. Like all such rules, there were ways of getting around this one. The risk was entirely on the nurse's part, since she could find herself out of nurse's training the very day she was discovered in a breach of the edict. As for the med students, "boys will be boys" was the prevailing attitude.

Jim had found himself a pretty probationer named Louise Macy, an Allentown girl. Louise and another "probie," Nancy Dillard, agreed to meet the two of them at their friend's, Mark Holden's, apartment on Pine Street after the Friday night lecture. Jim and Louise disappeared for hours, leaving Arthur in the living room with an extremely nervous Nancy.

The girls had to sneak back into the nurses' residence at midnight. Arthur kept waiting for a summons, but several days went by with no word. Finally, he met Nancy on the street one afternoon.

"What happened, Nancy? Did you get caught?"

"No, Arthur, we were lucky that time. But I'll *never* do that again!" So much for the nurses!

Arthur's would be the one hundredth class to graduate from Old Jeff, as it was lovingly referred to by her loyal sons. As each year passed, Arthur was known increasingly as a popular, much-admired man by faculty and students alike. Unaware of his personal magnetism, he still retained that small-town, unassuming air, which only seemed to add to his charm.

From time to time his uncle, Herman Franke, Rose's older brother—a Philadelphian to his core—would pay attention to Arthur, as it suited his whim. These were usually painfully dull occasions, and Arthur tried to avoid them as much as possible.

Philadelphia   Fall 1924

"Hey, Hillman, phone call for you," a fraternity brother yelled from below.

"Who is it, d'you know?" Arthur was trying in vain to read a chapter in Da Costa's *Manual of Modern Surgery* before attending "Dr. Jack's" surgery that afternoon. The great John Da Costa was one of his idols. He wished he'd gone to the library instead of attempting to study in his room at the Nu Sigma Nu house.

"I dunno—some old guy. Sounds important. Ya better take it."

Arthur grimaced, but clattered down the three flights to the lower hall where the phone was located, its receiver dangling.

It was Uncle Herman. "Arthur, my boy, how goes it?"

"Fine, Uncle Herman, just fine. How are you?" This meant he was going to be asked to do something, Arthur knew. Something he wouldn't want to do.

"Arthur, I want you to join me for dinner on Sunday evening at my club. Come by the house at six o'clock promptly." Wrong. It was not a request. It was a command.

"Uh . . . that's very kind of you, Uncle Herman." For a moment, he thought of saying he had a class, a meeting, anything. "I'd like that very much," he finished lamely.

"Of course, you have a lounge suit."

"A what?"

"A dinner jacket. You know, we dress for dinner at the club." Faint irritation, overt patronization.

"Oh . . . of course. Yes, Uncle Herman, don't worry. I'll be dressed."

Ralph Soames, the house dandy, was in the second-floor hall when Arthur walked back upstairs. "Ah, just the man I wanted to see!" Arthur greeted him with a winning smile. "We're about the same size, aren't we, Soames? Have you got a dinner jacket I can borrow?"

"Well . . ." the young man hesitated. Arthur was an upperclassman and a house officer. "Yeah, sure. I'm not as broad-shouldered as you are, Art . . ." By this time they were in Soames' room, with the closet door open. Ralph's many suits hung neatly on a row of hangers.

"This'll do just fine," Arthur said with enthusiasm. "Now, the tie . . . the shirt . . . the waistcoat—great! The trousers may be a trifle short . . . but that won't matter. Too bad my feet are too big for your slippers. I'll have to wear my own black shoes." He whistled as he returned to Da Costa's study of surgical technique.

"Evening, Mr. Arthur," Thomas, Uncle Herman's houseman and general factotum, greeted him when he arrived at the narrow, four-story town house on a little cul-de-sac off Walnut Street. Thomas led the way into the small drawing room to the right of the entrance foyer. "Mr. Franke will be with you in a few minutes." As Arthur waited—he had arrived promptly at six o'clock, as he had been instructed—he wondered whether Uncle Herman did these things purposely to manipulate people or whether he was just offhandedly careless of other people's time.

"There you are, my boy! How grand to see you." The old codger wasn't so bad, after all. He did have a nice smile, an expansive manner, and seemed to be genuinely fond of him. Arthur rose to greet his uncle, who appeared in the doorway with a cape over his exquisitely tailored dinner suit, his ever-present walking stick in hand. Suddenly Ralph Soames' tuxedo seemed practically like civilian wear.

"Let us be on our way. Thomas will be waiting with the car." The genial Negro had indeed driven the Packard limousine to the front of the house and was waiting in his chauffeur's uniform at the door.

They arrived at the Nightingale Club, a scant four blocks away on Locust Street, in less than five minutes. The homely building housed the eating and social club most favored by well-to-do German Jewish Philadelphia families, in this clubbiest of all cities. In a zeal of patriotism, its name had been changed from the German Club at the outbreak of the Great War. With the alighting of the Nightingale had come the membership of a select number of Russian Jews. The unpretentious lobby and lounge were carpeted in dull brown velour. Worn leather sofas were placed around the lounge, with ashtrays on stands at every hand. Drab wallpaper and unremarkable draperies in an ocher and beige print did their best to add to the impression of stodgy, unrelieved, old-money boredom. Uncle Herman made a little ceremony of handing his cape, gloves, and ivory-headed walking stick to the liveried footman who greeted them.

"Hello, Herman, I haven't seen you in weeks," said a deep, familiar voice. Arthur turned to see Dr. Roland Silverberg, associate professor of surgery at Jeff and lecturer in his section on thoracic surgery.

Uncle Herman shook hands with the surgeon and presented Arthur. "Roland, perhaps you know my nephew, Arthur Hillman? He's studying at your place."

"Ah, Hillman . . . Yes, I believe you're in my section? Good to see you out of the amphitheater, so to speak."

Arthur shook hands. "Good evening, sir. It's nice to see you, Professor Silverberg." He felt a little ill at ease. Silverberg was a much-admired teacher, but he lacked the warmth of Da Costa, Gibbon, and some of the others. He was pleasant enough on this occasion, however.

"I didn't realize that you were Herman's nephew, Mr. Hillman. Arthur, isn't it? Yes. Well, have you brought him around for dinner, Herman?"

"Yes, Roland. I like to come for Ladies' Night, but I dislike dining alone. Thought it would be good for Arthur to get away from the books for a change. He's my youngest sister, Rose's boy. From Wilkes-Barré, you know." Arthur smiled to himself at Uncle Herman's affected pronunciation—Wilkes-Bah-*ray*.

"Ah, yes, that explains it," said Silverberg.

Explains *what?* Arthur wondered.

They rose slowly in the ancient brass lift to the third floor, where the hum of male voices mingled with the counterpoint of feminine laughter.

"Shall we have a sherry, Arthur?" Uncle Herman led the way into a round parlor. Arthur was taller than anyone in the room, so that he felt conspicuous standing there. A trim, distinguished man with dark hair graying at the temples came over to Uncle Herman. They exchanged a few words and Uncle Herman turned.

"May I present my nephew, Arthur Hillman, Fred. This is Frederick Grant, Arthur, an old friend of mine."

They shook hands. "Now, whose son is this?" he asked Herman Franke.

"My sister Rose's. She married Jack Hillman from Wilkes-Barré. I don't know whether you've ever met Rose."

"Oh, yes, years ago," Grant replied, his eyes scanning the room. "There are my ladies. Come say hello to Claudia and Emily, Herman. I know they'll be happy to see you." He led the way across the crowded room toward the small portable bar where a waiter was pouring sherry into thimble-sized stemware, in genteel defiance of Prohibition. Grant approached his wife and daughter, Arthur watching as if he were a camera, the lens capturing each movement in a separate frame.

Her eyes were friendly. They looked at him with level, clear appraisal, and responded with warmth. Light gray translucent irises with dark pupils were outlined by hazel rings. She had clear, smooth, vibrant skin, with a tawny blush where the high cheekbones molded her face. Above her well-shaped forehead, her hair was a shiny, silvery blond, worn straight back and falling to her shoulders. She was tall, holding herself with a willowy grace in the simply draped blue crepe dinner gown. Frederick Grant's voice intruded.

"And this is Herman's nephew, Arthur Hillman. Mrs. Grant, and my daughter, Emily."

I like his face, she thought. Not just good-looking, more than that. There's something in his eyes, a depth, warmth. They go on and on, drawing you inward. And his smile. There could be a path of broken hearts somewhere from that smile. He must know it. No one could be that attractive and not know it.

"Herman tells me you're a medical student, Mr. Hillman." Claudia Grant spoke easily, sipping her sherry, and giving him her full attention.

"Yes, Mrs. Grant. I'm in my last year at Jefferson." He realized that he had missed a part of the conversation in his preoccupation with Emily Grant, the visual Emily.

"Do you live in Philadelphia?"

"No. I'm from Wilkes-Barre. Although by now I feel like Philadelphia is home."

"Claudia . . . Arthur, let's go to the buffet. . . . We're going to share a table." It was Herman Franke. "Emily, my dear, everyone must tell you what a stunner you've become." He beamed at the young woman, who smiled back at him.

"Thank you, Mr. Franke. Your telling me makes it special," she answered in a confiding manner. She took the arm he offered and moved smoothly into the dining room.

Arthur was alert through the meal to any morsel of information about Emily Grant. Uncle Herman presided at the head of the table, flanked by the two ladies, engaging first one, then the other in conversation, so that Arthur found himself speaking mostly to Frederick Grant and his wife, with barely a word between himself and Emily. The bits of information he gleaned from the conversation told him that the Grants lived in Haverford and that Emily was in her junior year at Bryn Mawr College, where she majored in fine arts. Emily was the younger of the Grants' two children—the older, a son, was at Harvard Law School after graduating from Yale, like his father.

After dinner the ladies withdrew to the library for coffee, while the men went into the lounge for brandy and cigars. There were a few young men present, but for the most part the gentlemen were middle-aged and beyond. The conversation was of financial and international affairs. Arthur, accustomed to the high jinks of student life overlaid with clinical talk, found this an alien but fascinating environment. He kept hoping, though, that they would rejoin the women so he could see Emily again.

Half an hour later, as the talk switched to the Teapot Dome Scandal, his eyes glazed. He had been up late the night before, studying; now, under the influence of the brandy and cigar smoke, he felt drowsy.

Uncle Herman interrupted. "I think we should be going, Arthur. It's late for me at my age. I have to be at the society bright and early tomorrow morning." Uncle Herman spent his retirement years as secretary of the American Philosophical Society, founded by Benjamin Franklin, an honorary society whose members were an elite group of humanists, scholarly and erudite.

Frederick Grant rose, saying, "I must go reclaim my ladies."

In the lobby, waiting for Uncle Herman's cape and cane, they once again met the Grants, who were also preparing to leave. Emily turned to Arthur, putting out her hand, which he took, holding longer than necessary.

"We haven't had a chance to talk. I hope I'll see you again," he told her.

Her face lit up, beginning with her eyes and ending with her smile. She was an extraordinarily beautiful young woman. "From what I've heard, medical students seldom have time for fun."

He returned the smile. "We manage now and then." Intriguing, that's what she was. He wondered whether he would have the courage to call her.

Uncle Herman asked Thomas to drop Arthur at his fraternity house. He bid them good night, thanking Uncle Herman for the evening.

"That's a lovely young woman, Emily Grant, Arthur. You ought to ask her out. Fine family."

That did it! He'd be damned if he would.

Mr. and Mrs. Frederick Norman Grant
request the pleasure of your company
at a supper dance on Saturday, the
twenty-fifth of October, nineteen
hundred twenty four, at seven o'clock
in the evening.

Briar Hill
Winding Brook Lane
Haverford
The favor of a reply is requested.

Arthur turned the invitation over. It was engraved on heavy ivory stock with the monogram embossed at the top. October 25, that was in two weeks.

He spent a busy weekend helping Professor Schaeffer unpack books and records for the Anatomy Department office in the newly constructed Jefferson Hospital. Arthur's was the first graduating class to receive instruction in the tallest hospital building in the world. The dean had asked Arthur to stop by to see him the following Tuesday to discuss his plans for next year. Arthur hoped that meant he had a good chance at one of the Jefferson Hospital internships. They had all been dismayed when it was announced that the Philadelphia hospitals would not make internship appointments until the first of February—too late for the deadlines at other first-rate hospitals around the country.

Preoccupied with these considerations, Arthur forgot about the invitation from the Grants. When he returned to his room on Sunday evening, he saw it lying on his desk. He thought about it. Why not? It would mean he'd see Emily again. He wrote an acceptance to the Grants and put it in the mail on his way to his obstetrics clinic on Monday morning.

Arthur took a taxi from Bryn Mawr station. The driver knew Briar Hill. They drove along a winding wooded residential road with large mansions on either side. At the big stone gateposts to Briar Hill, they were stopped by a guard. Arthur gave his name, and after consulting a list, the guard waved them on. Lights shone from every window of the huge Georgian mansion at the end of the long, tree-lined sloping driveway. The cab circled around in front of a tall, pillared portico. Arthur paid the driver and mounted the steps with some feeling of trepidation. He had never been in a home as grand as this.

The door was opened by a butler. Arthur entered a large circular entrance hall with a curving staircase. String music was coming from a parlor to the rear. He gave his coat to a maid and followed the butler, who ushered him to a reception room on the right where Claudia Grant was receiving her guests along with her son, Freddy.

Mrs. Grant greeted him warmly. "How nice to see you again, Mr. Hillman." She introduced him to her son. "This is Arthur Hillman, dear. He's a medical student at Jefferson."

They shook hands. "Good of you to come all the way out here." Freddy had already acquired the urbane diffidence of the elegant men Arthur had seen entering the Chestnut Street buildings where the best law firms had offices. As tall as Arthur, he was more angular, with thin, sensitive features, brown hair, and timid gray-blue eyes. He was tailored to perfection from custom-made tail coat to patent-leather dancing pumps.

Claudia smiled at Arthur approvingly. "Mr. Grant is circulating, and I believe Emily's dancing at the moment. Do go in. Have some refreshments and enjoy the dancing. We'll be having supper at eleven. . . . There are some very special young ladies here tonight!"

He walked into the ballroom where a small group of musicians was playing a medley of fox trots. Looking over the crowd, he spotted Emily dancing with a dark-haired young man, laughing and talking.

"Hello. You're Herman Franke's nephew, aren't you?" It was Frederick Grant, Sr.

"Hello, Mr. Grant. Yes, it's Arthur Hillman," he said, shaking hands.

"Right. Arthur Hillman—from Scranton, or was it Wilkes-Barre?"

"Wilkes-Barre, sir."

"Nice to see you, Arthur. Won't you have something to drink? There's a good punch over here." He led the way to a table where a smiling black woman was serving punch and small finger sandwiches. "Nellie, Mr. Hillman would like some of your excellent punch. It really has a 'punch,' too, Arthur, so beware!" Arthur smiled at the unimaginative joke.

"Yessir. Here you are, Mr. Hillman. I hope you're enjoyin' yourself this evenin'." Nellie's voice was rich, with southern warmth.

"Thank you." Arthur took the cup. "I certainly expect to. I just arrived." Nellie beamed at him. She surveyed the room with satisfaction, as if it were her own party. Arthur suspected that it was—at least in the execution.

Several couples danced over to the punch table. A pretty brunette wearing a peach dress sipped her drink and spoke to him, but Arthur didn't hear . . . Emily was approaching. Their eyes met and she smiled in recognition. He moved toward Emily as the band began to play another set.

That's how it began. A dance. Her tall, willowy body turning in his arms as they moved across the floor. They didn't say much. Emily didn't attempt to make bright conversation for the sake of filling silence. She looked into his eyes directly, a faint smile lighting her lovely face. They danced until there were no more dances—moving gradually closer and closer. Her forehead pressed against his cheek and his lips brushed her fine, silky hair. No one cut in on them. Arthur wasn't certain what he was feeling, but he did know something important was happening.

The Grants felt more comfortable as Jews in the Quaker community of Haverford than the more Episcopalian suburban towns on the Main Line. One branch of the Grant family had actually become Quakers in the early part of the nineteenth century. The Meeting was an easy transition to the Christian world. A shoot from that Quaker twig was said to have later adopted the Episcopal faith, thus making the connection to Judaism even more remote. Like laundered money, it was sometimes impossible to retrace the origins of some of Philadelphia's best families.

For old German Jewish families like the Grants, Philadelphia had always been an easy city. In the eighteenth and early nineteenth centuries, there were a number of wealthy Jews among Philadelphia's elite. Secure in their position, the descendants of these families had enjoyed an enviable place in the City of Brotherly Love.

With the wave of eastern European immigrants who flooded American cities after 1880, that had changed. By the time Claudia and Fred were married, one was conscious of which community would provide the most hospitable environment. It was an uncomfortable feeling which infuriated Claudia and made Fred nervous.

The Grant household was constantly in preparation for one event or another. Claudia, with her endless social and organizational activities, held dinner parties, afternoon teas, morning coffees, committee meetings, and readings in the large Georgian mansion. That the Grants were Jewish was overlooked by most of Main Line society who attended these functions. Claudia's family, the Allenbergs, predated the American Revolution, and Fred's great-grandfather had been one of the financers of the Pennsylvania Regiment during the War of 1812. The Grants were cultured, attractive people, a lively couple, and above all . . . very wealthy.

Arthur took Emily out every weekend. Sometimes they had dinner with Mark Holden or Roy McLean, who had become Arthur's closest friends since Jim Flannery had graduated the previous June.

Flannery was interning at St. Anne's Hospital in Wilkes-Barre. He had married Louise Macy, the nursing student, over Thanksgiving weekend of his senior year. Arthur had gone to the wedding in Allentown.

"I'd like you to be an usher, Arthur, but the priest says you have to be a

Christian to participate, even if it isn't a high mass. Can you beat that? I
swear, if I could resign from the Church, I'd do it!" Arthur had been touched
that Jim asked him, and disappointed that he couldn't. "You're an honorary
usher, Art. I expect you to give a toast at the reception," Flannery had told
him.

Now Louise and Jim had a baby boy, born at the end of August, "nine
months and ten minutes after the wedding," according to Jim.

Louise and Jim came down to Philadelphia for the Penn-Cornell game—
their first break since the baby had been born. They went out to all the old
spots—Gonnam's, Ziess's, and the Studio.

"That's some classy female you've got there, Hillman," Jim had said to
him later. "I wouldn't blame you if you fell for her in a big way. She's a
knockout!"

After football games they often went over to fraternity parties at Penn,
where some of his old friends from home or Penn State were in graduate
school. One of them, David Benjamin, was at the Law School. They double-
dated with David and his girl, Ruth Sandover, a couple of times. There was
always some kind of party to go to.

Emily invited him to have Thanksgiving dinner with her family. Her
Grandmother Allenberg was there, as well as a number of aunts, uncles, and
cousins. Although there were over twenty people seated around the large
dining-room table, the room was not crowded. No one made much of his
presence, welcoming him as a friend of Emily's just as they welcomed Freddy's old roommate from Yale. Arthur reflected that if *he'd* brought a girl
home for a holiday there'd be plenty of notice taken by his various relatives.

The last weekend before Christmas, Emily invited him to a formal dance at
the Bellevue. She stayed at her grandmother's house on Rittenhouse Square.
He called for her there, taking a corsage of camelias. She was wearing a deep
wine-colored velvet gown, square-necked and low-waisted, its new, slim silhouette becoming to her tall figure. She'd caught her pale hair in a roll at the
back of her neck.

Arthur had been browsing at Sessler's, a shop specializing in old and rare
books, when he'd come upon a pair of volumes. They were English romantic
poetry, bound in soft blue leather, and boxed in a blue velvet case with a
carved ivory border and a small brass clasp. He had bought them for Emily.
When they were alone in her grandmother's library, he presented them to
her.

Emily was enchanted with the books, as he had been. "Thank you, Arthur!
I've never seen anything like this before."

"They made me think of you when I saw them," he said. "I guess it's a sort
of Chanukah . . . or Christmas . . . present. Which do you celebrate?"

She smiled brightly. "Both!" She ran her fingers over the carved ivory. "It's
a very special gift."

"For a very special girl, Emily. I'm glad you like it."

"Here's something for you." He opened the box from Strawbridge and Clothier. It was a white silk evening muffler with a diamond-shaped monogram at one end, fashionable and tasteful. He leaned over and kissed her smooth cool cheek. She smelled faintly of lily of the valley. The lamplight enhanced her classic blond beauty.

Before leaving for Wilkes-Barre, he went out to Briar Hill for the Grant's annual Christmas party. Every window of the big house was lighted with candles. On the front door was an enormous Christmas wreath with a large red bow and pine cones.

There was not one, but two Christmas trees. As if the Grants were determined to usurp the gaiety of the Christian holiday denied them by birth, and thus make it by adoption even more their own. "Merry Christmas," one said, in place of hello and good-bye, Arthur soon learned.

He couldn't very well monopolize Emily at her own party. He wandered around, observing the mannered behavior of the Grant's large circle of elegant friends. There were many young people, all of whom seemed to know one another well. There was much talk about clubs, parties, and Christmas dances . . . the sort of conversation that excludes outsiders.

He drifted from group to group, recognizing a few people from the dance he'd attended in October. One was the dark-haired young man who had been dancing with Emily when Arthur had first seen her on that occasion. The fellow walked over to him, his hand extended.

"I don't believe we've met. I'm Bill Beckinger," he said in an accent Arthur had learned to recognize as Good Eastern Boarding School.

"Arthur Hillman," he replied, smiling and making an effort to be friendly.

"Where'd you prep?" asked young Beckinger in a clipped voice, his lips barely moving.

"Wilkes-Barre High School," Arthur answered blandly. That effectively brought their conversation to a halt.

Arthur left the party early, explaining to Emily that he had to pack for the morning train to Wilkes-Barre.

Emily took him aside into her father's study after he put his coat on. "Have a nice vacation, Arthur. I'll see you in 1925!" She was going to spend part of the vacation in Palm Beach with her grandmother.

He put his arms around her. "I'll miss you, Emily. Happy New Year." He kissed her, a real kiss, for the first time. She sighed and moved into the kiss, her hand softly caressing the back of his neck.

How long they stood there embracing, he didn't know. It was a rich feeling. A mood of glittery, expensive, high-placed sophistication wafted through the rooms of the Grant mansion . . . in the strains of the string instruments playing light popular ballads, the hum of gay, holiday conversation, the trills of feminine laughter. Emily was scented and silken in the curve of his arms.

She stood framed in the doorway, the light from the foyer behind her, until his taxi had disappeared from view.

Emily Alicia Grant was an April baby. Exquisite, with silvery blond hair, she resembled her mother, Claudia, long and narrow in structure. From her earliest years, Emily lived a secret life in a place of fantasies so vivid that sometimes she was unable to separate the dream from reality. Her nanny, Irene McCord, would hear her speaking to someone who wasn't there.

"Don't sit in that chair! You'll hurt Skipper," she would cry in alarm when her grandmother entered the sitting room.

Nurse McCord, plain, sensible, with a reassuring calm in her Scots-accented voice, would take a reasonable view of these flights of imagination. "All children have imaginary playmates," she told Grandmother Allenberg when that woman expressed concern at the little girl's odd behavior. "It helps to conquer the loneliness within."

"Cordie" knew a good deal about loneliness. She had left her native land at nineteen, orphaned and unmarriageable, without dowry or beauty to smooth the way. At Briar Hill she cared for the two Grant children from their birth, until Freddy was sent to Phillips Academy at Exeter and Emily entered the Finchley School.

At Finchley, Emily was an innovator, popular and outgoing. She grew tall and slim, her good looks becoming even more striking as time passed. An athlete, despite her light bone structure, she played center forward on the field hockey team. She excelled at golf, tennis, and horseback riding.

The Grants summered at their family "camp" on Sunrise Lake in Maine, where the children were encouraged to compete with their cousins and the progeny of the other well-to-do families on nearby estates.

Scholarship was important in the Allenberg-Grant clan. Emily graduated with honors from Finchley, then entered Bryn Mawr, living in the dormitory to partake fully of the college experience. It was convenient to be near home, to invite friends for dinner or the weekend. Freddy was in demand to squire Emily's classmates to tea dances or the theater.

Claudia Grant often reflected that Philadelphia was the ideal town in which to live and rear one's children. So gracious, so unhurried, and yet stimulating. The near perfection of her life pleased her enormously.

The Faculty and Senior Class
of
Jefferson Medical College
announce their

One Hundredth Commencement Exercises
Friday, June the fifth
nineteen hundred twenty-five
twelve o'clock
Academy of Music
Philadelphia

Arthur ran his fingers over the soft embossed leather of the commencement program, examining again the pages listing the faculty and members of his class.

The Class of 1925, the Centennial Class! Four years, passed so quickly . . . a strange feeling, realizing they were behind him. What lay ahead, according to all reports, was work, work, and more work. The student life was over, his friends leaving, scattering to various hospitals around the country for their internships.

He was one of the lucky ones. He and Roy McLean were among those few who would be interning at Jefferson Hospital. In three weeks, he would begin the practice of medicine. . . .

". . . Arthur Franke Hillman, Doctor of Medicine . . ." He started as Dean Christian Rutledge announced his name. Moving quickly down the aisle, he went up to the podium to receive his diploma. Dean Rutledge shook hands, giving him an extra squeeze of friendship.

"Congratulations, Dr. Hillman! It'll be nice having you at Jeff next year." Arthur wondered whether it was the same thrill for the others to be addressed by that title.

Emily was in the audience, next to Mac's current girl, Priscilla Curtis—she had felt shy about sitting with Arthur's family. In the melee after the ceremonies, he introduced Emily to his parents and Nate, praying that Uncle Herman would be discreet. He need not have worried. Herman Franke was on his best behavior today, preoccupied with greeting the various trustees and professors he knew. Isaac remained seated with Rachel, whose health was frail, so he missed meeting Emily altogether. Nate guessed immediately that this was the girl—but nothing ever escaped Nate. His mother hardly paid attention, she was so proud of her son becoming a doctor.

Uncle Herman took the family to lunch at the Nightingale. In the afternoon there was a reception for the members of the class and their guests. Arthur had considered inviting Emily along, but she had to leave for Cambridge, where her brother was graduating from Harvard Law School. Privately, he was glad to escape the necessity of having Emily with him on this family occasion. He wondered why he felt that way—after all, he'd spent plenty of time with her at her family's homes. But there was no denying that he was avoiding the encounter.

Jacob presented Arthur with a gold pocket watch, monogrammed with his initials. Arthur was touched. Rarely had his father given him a personal gift, something he could keep always as a memento of a special event. Maybe now that his father viewed him as an adult, they could have the sort of closeness that had always eluded them.

From Isaac and Rachel, Arthur received a new black leather doctor's bag, outfitted with a stethoscope, blood-pressure apparatus, and a set of instruments—everything he would need to make house calls.

"It's perfect! The best thing you could've given me," he told them.

Isaac looked as if all of his hopes had been realized that day, his fond gaze returning again and again to rest on Arthur. For Isaac Hillman, each milestone in the lives of his children and grandchildren was a *mitzvah*—a blessing—an occasion to thank God for granting them the privilege to live their lives in an America where a Jew could conduct his affairs in the same manner as other citizens . . . where his grandson could graduate from one of the foremost colleges of medicine that this bountiful nation had to offer.

So ran the thoughts of Isaac Hillman on a day in June 1925, when an Austrian ne'er-do-well, a rather comic figure, who had been prematurely released from a Bavarian jail the previous year, was putting the finishing touches to a manuscript he had composed while in prison. It was entitled *My Struggle . . . Mein Kampf.* To Adolf Hitler, an achievement such as Arthur's—for a Jew—would have been a cause for lament. . . . But who could have foreseen that this rabble-rouser across an ocean could take any action that would affect the lives of Americans?

IV

Philadelphia   Spring 1926

It was after five o'clock on a Friday afternoon in mid-April when Arthur finished with the last ward patient's chart. An hour past the time when he was supposed to go off duty. He'd been up all night on an emergency the night before.

"Boy, am I tired," he said to his roommate, Roy McLean, who had just come on duty.

"Why don't you go home to bed?" suggested Roy.

"I've got a date with Emily at six—at this rate, I'll just make it. So long, Mac. See you Sunday." He and Mac were seldom at home together because of their differing schedules.

Arthur hurried along Sansom Street to his apartment building, sprinting up the two flights to the third-floor railroad flat.

Arthur had showered and finished shaving when the doorbell rang. He put on a robe and went to open the door for Emily, who carried a bag of groceries.

"I brought dinner, Arthur. I thought I'd cook for us tonight."

"I think you must be a witch!" he said, taking the bag of groceries. "How did you know I was so tired that I don't feel like going out tonight?" He set the bag down and kissed her warmly. For a moment, she relaxed against him, returning his kiss fully. He felt a rising excitement, enhanced by the knowledge that they were alone in his apartment, on his turf.

She broke away from him, a little breathless, and laughed regretfully. "I'll go start dinner while you get dressed," she said, taking the groceries to the small kitchen.

Arthur rummaged in his laundry case for clean underwear and socks. His thoughts were on his relationship with Emily as he dressed.

For over a year, they'd been dating regularly. Arthur cared deeply for Emily. He supposed he was in love with her. It would be easy to just drift along, become engaged, and then marry when she graduated in June. He knew this was what everyone in her family expected, including Emily.

Then, why didn't he just go ahead and do it? He reflected on all the reasons as he pulled on gray slacks, a white shirt, and dark blue sweater.

All the reasons? It could be summed up in one word—money. He had none of his own, and she had a great deal. Or, rather, her family did, and that amounted to the same thing. The Grants had the kind of wealth that dictated a whole different way of life than the one he envisioned for himself. His own family, even before Jacob had business reverses, had never known the equal of the Grant fortune. Emily was accustomed to a life-style that could come only from great inherited wealth.

During all the time they'd dated, Arthur had been a frequent guest at Briar Hill, or at Camp Repose, the Grant's summer lodge in Maine. There were the restaurant dinners, the formal dances, the plays, ballets, and concerts, and the dozens of charity affairs a girl like Emily was expected to attend in Philadelphia. At first, Arthur had been embarrassed, not knowing how to tell Emily that he couldn't afford all of this. She seemed to sense it without his saying anything, often inviting him to events casually: "Oh, Arthur, Daddy has tickets to the opening of *Pygmalion* next Saturday. Will you join us for dinner first?" or "Mother is on the committee for the Lighthouse dance. Will you go with me?"

They were always so gracious to him, the Grants. He wondered what they thought. Did they believe that he was interested in Emily because of their money? If so, they never, by even a flicker of an eyelid, betrayed this. Claudia Grant was warm, welcoming, and approving of him. Frederick acted as if Arthur had come to visit *him* rather than Emily, taking him for long walks and tennis games in Haverford, on canoe rides and fishing expeditions at their lodge on Sunrise Lake in Maine.

Herman Franke was hoping against hope that Arthur would marry Emily.

When Arthur had graduated from Jefferson, Uncle Herman had given him a sizable check as a graduation gift.

"That's far too generous, Uncle Herman," he had protested. It made him uncomfortable to accept money from his mother's brother.

"Don't be silly, my boy," the staid gentlemen had answered. Then, he had added, "You can't squire young ladies around without sufficient funds, Arthur." Arthur's annoyance must have shown in his face, because Herman Franke continued in a placating tone, "I don't have any children, Arthur. Your dear mother is my baby sister. Poor Jack can't help it if he . . . is in poor health."

Arthur would dearly love to have told him to keep his money, but he knew he would never have been forgiven.

Money. It was a problem when you didn't have any, and when you did.

After dinner, they listened to records on the phonograph in the cramped, sloped-ceilinged living room. Arthur put his arm around Emily. They sat on the scratchy horsehair sofa, lumpy from broken springs. He bent his head to kiss her. Emily was marvelous at kissing, despite her cool, ladylike exterior. Long, soulful, romantic kisses, tender-lipped and tantalizing, building up to peaks of excitement that often left him aroused beyond the point of endurance.

In all the months of their romance, there had been heated petting sessions . . . in parked cars, in the boathouse of the Grant's Maine house, Camp Repose, in the various secluded sun parlors and sitting rooms at Briar Hill. With a girl like Emily, one could kiss endlessly, advancing to the use of the tongue, fondle her breasts through her clothing, and, in time, she might wear soft sweaters which enabled you to slip your hand underneath, eventually making your way through the layers to the silky flesh within.

But, never, absolutely never, below the waist. As far as the Emily Grants of the world were concerned, there *was* nothing below the waist until you were married. If, in a frenzy of excitation, Arthur should press himself against her so that she became aware of an unmannerly swollen male presence, she would immediately withdraw, and that would be the end of that particular romantic interlude.

Arthur knew those were the limits with college girls from nice families—especially one who was Jewish. A gentleman did not take unfair advantage of the girl who seemed in danger of forgetting them—not if he cared for her.

Emily, for her part, had no problem with these restraints. It was utterly delightful to spend hour upon hour kissing and petting with Arthur. Seeing his handsome features become hazed over with passion, his firm mouth grow tender with arousal from their deep, languorous kisses gave her a sense of power over him. The long sessions of kissing and touching were an end in themselves, purely gratifying.

There was no question of Emily Grant "going all the way" with Arthur. The girls who did that were known to be "fast." The word got around that they were "damaged goods." Everyone at college knew about poor Betsy Holcomb. She had committed suicide after finding out she was pregnant and that her lover was engaged to someone else.

But, tonight, as Arthur kissed her, Emily found herself losing her sense of detachment. She felt warm and floaty, as if she could drift in his arms forever. She loved him so much, if only she could tell him . . . if only he would say he loved her. He had to love her, he just *had* to. . . .

Emily sat up and straightened her sweater. "It's getting late, Arthur. I think you'd better take me home. I'm staying at my grandmother's tonight." Her grandmother was very strict about hours.

When he kissed her good night at the door of her grandmother's Rittenhouse Square residence, Emily said, "Next Saturday evening there's a benefit for the museum, Arthur. Mother would like us to come. She's on the board."

"I'm 'on' next weekend, Emily. You know that."

"Can't you switch with someone?"

He sighed. He had explained to her often enough that he couldn't switch his duty unless there were overriding reasons. A fund-raising dinner dance did not strike him as a compelling reason for an intern to get out of his hospital assignment. It was just such priorities that worried him about Emily. Away from her family, she was down-to-earth, understanding, and real. But in that rarefied world in which the Grants existed, as pleasant as Arthur sometimes found it, Emily became too caught up in the cult of benefit committees and charity dances. Arthur wondered whether Claudia Grant would be nearly so interested in milk for orphaned babies if it didn't ensure her photograph on the society page of the *Bulletin* several times a year.

Emily was hurt. There may have been some maternal pressure brought to bear. In fact, Arthur would have bet on it, since the following Sunday the Philadelphia papers reporting the affair mentioned that the lovely Emily Grant, daughter of Mr. and Mrs. Frederick Norman Grant, was escorted by William Beckinger II, the department-store heir. The *Bulletin* featured a picture of Emily and Bill dancing, a striking pair, both of them smiling broadly, looking like they were having a wonderful time. Arthur would never have seen it, not being a regular reader of social news, if Roy McLean hadn't brought it to his attention.

After that, Arthur found that Emily was often busy on a weekend unless he called her well in advance. This put them back on the footing of their early dates, when he was overawed—knocked flat on his face, in the words of Jim Flannery. He knew Emily was seeing Bill Beckinger. He was jealous, but he didn't know what to do about it.

As summer approached, he was winding up his internship. The dean had informed him that he had been selected for a residency at Jefferson Hospital for the next year. His brother, Nathan, was going to enter the University of

Pennsylvania Law School in September—nine years later than he had originally intended. Their parents were afraid that Nathan's health wasn't up to the challenge of law school, so Arthur had promised Nate he would spend as much time as possible at home to bolster him against the concern of Rose and Jacob.

"Would you like to come up to Maine for two weeks during your vacation, Arthur?" Emily asked him, unexpectedly. He would love to have accepted. The Grant's rustically sumptuous summer estate was the perfect vacation spot. But he had only a month off, and he had planned to spend it at home.

It was probably just as well, he reasoned. His relationship with Emily was becoming too complicated.

Haverford   Summer 1926

Emily graduated from Bryn Mawr at the end of the first week in June. She called Arthur to remind him that he was invited to attend the exercises with her parents.

The Grants gave a luncheon reception at their home for Emily's friends and their families. Emily's brother, Freddy, who had finished at Harvard Law School the previous year, would be joining his father's firm shortly, after clerking with a distinguished judge. He was following in his father's footsteps, Arthur was told by a gushing matron. Yes, observed Arthur, he was indeed: Freddy gazed adoringly at Martha Von Pforzen, a painfully thin brunette with a flapper hairstyle whose family was reputed to have vast holdings stashed away in numbered Swiss accounts.

For Freddy, there would be no quandry should he fall in love with the wealthy Miss Von Pforzen. Rich German Jews loved it when their offspring united. The tidiness of the Grants' existence fascinated Arthur . . . the apparent freedom from crises of conscience, the neatly tied parcels of their various destinies.

There was Emily across the room, smiling serenely, so poised and contained as she spoke to one, then another, of her friends' parents. Some of these people, Arthur could tell, were out of their element in the impressive Grant mansion; he noticed several of the women look around surreptitiously at the paintings, the sculptures, and the displays of rare porcelain from Claudia Grant's collection.

Arthur sensed a milestone had been reached. Emily's graduation. Although she was dating other men, he thought she was in love with him. He did care for her, deeply . . . but was it *love?* He had trouble deciding what to do. He couldn't make up his mind to marry her . . . yet he didn't want to give her up. Soon he must decide.

Philadelphia   Autumn 1926

Emily had registered for studio art courses at the Philadelphia College of Fine Arts. She lived at home in Haverford with her parents and her brother, Freddy, who was engaged to Martha Von Pforzen. Each day Emily drove to the city in the sea-green Dusenberg coupé given to her by her parents when she graduated from Bryn Mawr. She often went out with Arthur, but she was gradually seeing more of Billy Beckinger, regarded as the best catch among the moneyed Philadelphians of their set.

Emily's parents had never put any pressures on her about men or marriage. She was beautiful, popular, and talented. It would be her prerogative to choose from the ranks of suitors who flocked at her door. Many of them were drawn by the Allenberg-Grant name and fortune, no doubt, but with a daughter like Emily, the Grants had always been more than confident she would marry well and happily.

Frederick Grant, a sweet, mild sort of man, was still relaxed about the matter. But his wife, Claudia, was becoming uneasy. What was going on between Emily and Arthur Hillman? She had been certain that Arthur would come to them after Emily's graduation, asking for her hand in marriage. She was prepared to give them her blessings. Arthur did not have a fortune, but with his looks, charm, and medical education he was bound to be a success in Philadelphia, particularly with the Grants as in-laws and his relationship to the Franke family. And Emily would have enough money—more than enough—to support them well until he became firmly established.

Perhaps Arthur was naïve—after all, he came from Wilkes-Barre. Claudia had never been there, but she had heard it was little more than a coal town, no sophistication, no elegance. Maybe Fred ought to have a gentle talk with him, let him know that although he might not think he could marry Emily now because he was unable to support her on a resident's paltry salary, that need not prevent him from pressing his suit. Otherwise, he might lose her. You couldn't expect a girl like Emily to sit around waiting for years.

Claudia broached the subject with Emily. She had to be careful. Emily was sensitive and rather strong-minded. "Are you and Arthur discussing marriage at all, Emily?"

"I don't think he can afford to get married yet, Mother."

"Well, surely, dear, that's a temporary state of affairs. Many young doctors marry when they're still in medical school. The families usually help out for a while."

Emily hadn't replied, so Claudia didn't press it, although, as the weeks passed, from time to time she would try to speak of it again. She began to get the impression that Emily thought Arthur might not *want* to marry her. In that case, she offered, why waste your time? If he doesn't intend to marry you, it should be broken off now.

"He's a nice enough young man, dear, but you must have more pride than that. If he doesn't love you enough to become engaged now, how do you know he'll change? Either he loves you or he doesn't."

Emily tried not to listen to her mother. She loved Arthur so much that she had to believe he loved her. She knew she was the right person for him, was positive they were meant for each other. He was the only man she had ever loved, ever wanted. She walked around on the verge of tears all the time, with a filled-up feeling. If only her mother would just let it go for a while, she was positive it would work out.

But Claudia persisted. "Emily, dear, you have everything to offer, everything any man could want in a wife. Don't belittle yourself by letting Arthur treat you this way. Billy Beckinger would walk hot coals for you. Isn't that better than a luke-warm husband? . . . And the Beckingers come from our set, even if they *are* in trade."

They own four department stores, and she calls that being "in trade," thought Emily, not responding.

"Look at Freddy and Martha, how well-suited they are," her mother continued. "You know, dear, there's more to marriage than a love affair. Everything has to fit . . . family background, social position . . ."

And as Emily protested, "Oh, Mother! . . ." Claudia softened her tone, "Those aren't the only things that count, dear—I'm not saying that. But they are important. They smooth the way. Daddy and I . . . well, we had an easy adjustment to married life because we agreed on the important matters. We came from the same sort of families."

"What's *wrong* with Arthur's family? I thought you said you liked his uncle, and you used to know his mother." Emily was annoyed and unhappy.

Claudia attempted to be gentle. "The Frankes are lovely people. . . . His father's family are Russian Jews, I'm told. They're . . . *different,* Emily. They don't have the same way of life. . . . Their entire background is unlike our family's. Arthur grew up in Wilkes-Barre. It has no symphony, no theater, or ballet. Whatever would you do there, dear? I suppose he'll stay in Philadelphia, so you would live here. But these are all things to be considered before a marriage, not after, when it's too late."

"Well, you don't have to worry about it, Mother. Because he doesn't want me! You're so busy trying to decide why *you* don't want me to marry *him*. Save yourself the trouble!" She burst into tears and ran out of Claudia's room.

Wilkes-Barre   Autumn 1926

Arthur and Nathan went home to Wilkes-Barre for the Thanksgiving week-end. Their parents were lonely and Jacob's health worried Arthur. His father had had minor seizures on two occasions, losing consciousness each time, yet he refused to pay much attention to it, brushing off everyone's concern with stubborn irritability.

The entire family assembled in the house on Prospect Avenue. The table was extended with all its leaves and extra boards, so that it reached through the arched dining-room doorway into the adjacent sitting room. There were twenty-two chairs and a high chair for Frieda's two-year-old son.

The turkey was a monster, golden brown, with a crispy crust, the way their mother always made it. When they were children, they used to string cranberries to make a necklace for the turkey. No one had made a necklace this year . . . sad.

Everyone seemed to talk at once at the table. Rose sat at the head, while Eva Schleicher, who had done their housework ever since Arthur could remember, helped serve. The amount of food! They all ate too much, but wasn't that what Thanksgiving was all about?

No wine was served with dinner. Some of the men had a shot of whiskey before dinner in the living room, almost surreptitiously, as if they were going to be raided. Arthur thought about all the parties in Philadelphia where the alcohol flowed freely, the women wore paint and smoked, and the conversation was cleverly brittle. He realized, with a sudden recognition, that his family was provincial. They would be considered dull by people like the Grants and their friends. Well, that was all right with him. He loved them the way they were.

Arthur felt sorry for his grandfather, who looked lost and distracted. Isaac sighed often, not saying much. At seventy-nine, he was still a vigorous-looking, handsome man. His hair had turned snow white, his complexion was florid, but his eyes had not lost their sparkle until the previous year, on the day Rachel had passed away. Rose asked him to move in with them, but Isaac remained in the house he had bought for Rachel, two blocks away.

Before he and Nate left for Philadelphia, Arthur went for a long walk along the river with Isaac. "The Susquehanna has a wonderful history, Arthur. Many important events occurred on the river. Did you know that the founder of the Mormon religion was first baptized in this river? Joseph Smith was his name . . . it was upriver, near the town of Susquehanna. The Mormons were greatly persecuted in this country, you know. Like the Jews in Europe."

Isaac spoke with an intonation characteristic of the valley. He had lost all but a trace of his foreign accent, had worked hard to do so, pronouncing each word with care in his deep, resonant voice. "It is such a beautiful river. They should have passed laws to prevent the coal companies from dumping in the stream. It should have been dredged, the channel made deeper and developed for pleasure boating. My brother Aaron, may he rest in peace, recognized that."

"You have to have boating in your blood, Grandfather. It *is* a beautiful river. I remember when I was a little boy, I used to get such a thrill out of the idea that the river at Hillside was the same river as it is here in Wilkes-Barre. Kids are funny."

Isaac smiled and patted him on the back. "You were always such a nice boy, Arthur. The best." Then he asked, "Have you got a girl, Arthur?" There was a twinkle in his eyes.

Arthur knew he was blushing, but he couldn't help it.

"Sooo . . . you have a girl!"

"Well, Grandfather, yes and no. I mean, there is a girl I've been going out with, but I'm not sure about it. I just don't know. She's beautiful and very nice. But I'm not sure I want to marry her."

"What's her name?"

"Her name? It's Emily . . . Emily Grant. Why?"

"Emily Grant. Is that a Jewish name?"

"Yes. She's Jewish. Her family lives in Philadelphia. They're friends of Uncle Herman's. That's how I met Emily. I went to the Nightingale Club with Uncle Herman once, and she was there with her parents."

Isaac was looking at Arthur from under his brows, a curious expression on his face.

"What's the matter?" Arthur asked.

"I suppose they're *Deitchen* if they're friends of your Uncle Herman's."

"*Grandfather!* Seems to me the Jews ought to stick together instead of worrying about who's German and who's Russian."

"*They* started it, Arthur. The German Jews always think they're better than anyone else. Mordecai Franke thought Rachel was marrying beneath herself when she became my wife. Cold-blooded fish, he was. Never cared for the man. Well, I suppose we shouldn't carry our prejudices over into the next generation. Still, if you're going to marry into a German Jewish family, I would be very sure you're in love with the girl."

Arthur didn't say anything immediately. He drew a deep breath. "Grandfather, my mother is a German Jew, too," he said quietly.

"Yes. She is. And her father tried to prevent that marriage. Your mother and father were in love for years, from the time they were children. That story almost didn't have a happy ending."

Arthur was startled. He had no idea that his parents had encountered opposition to their marriage. Rose and Jacob deeply in love, a romance? Why did it surprise him? He couldn't imagine his subdued, reserved father in the throes of passion—nor his mother, either, for that matter. He dismissed the thought. It made him feel uneasy.

Back in Philadelphia, Arthur was working so hard that he saw his brother only once before the Christmas holiday, when he and Emily met Nate for dinner. Nate was with a girl from Penn, Susan Landau. It was a pleasant enough evening. This was the second time Nate had met Emily. Arthur couldn't tell what he thought of her.

Nate and Susan seemed unhappy. They held hands, and Susan watched his face with such a serious expression when he talked. She was in love with him, Arthur could tell, but he couldn't figure out his brother's feelings. Nate was always nice to people, gallantly courteous, displaying a warm sense of humor. His years of ill health had made him an inward person, though.

It troubled Arthur that he and his brother had distanced from each other.

Sunrise Lake, Maine   Winter 1926

Emily invited Arthur up to Maine for the week after Christmas through the New Year holiday. The Grants had decided to have a house party up there, since their lodge had been winterized the previous spring. They left before Christmas for Camp Repose, so Arthur spent a few days at home and then took the long train ride up to Skowhegan, the nearest stop to Sunrise Lake. Emily met him at the station in a horse-drawn sleigh driven by their caretaker, a taciturn Downeaster whose total vocabulary consisted of "Ehyup" and "Noap" and "Geeyup." Arthur, for the life of him, couldn't tell which was the affirmative, which negative, and which intended to spur the pair of shaggy white horses to action.

A huge Christmas tree dominated the main sitting area of the house with its great stone fireplace. Claudia Grant loved to decorate for holidays and parties. She had wound garlands of evergreens gaily tied with red velvet ribbons around bannisters and newel posts, across doorways and over windows. Bunches of holly with shiny green leaves and small scarlet berries nested in unexpected corners. Groupings of thick, tapered hand-dipped candles studded mantels and windowsills, surrounded by graceful arrangements of pine cones and branches. The piny aroma was everywhere, almost overpowering.

It was a week of sledding, skating, and sleigh rides. Great, fragrant roaring fires burned all day and into the night in the game room, and the big living room. Someone was forever popping corn, pulling taffy, baking cookies, or mulling wine. Huge wheels of Vermont cheese and tubs of rosy apples were placed every afternoon on thick wooden planks in the game room. Couples constantly engaged in serious contests at the billiard table or the chess board. Ice hockey was played in earnest. The Grants were fond of games, frequently organizing ingenious treasure hunts or charades. Claudia and Fred, Sr., and the Von Pforzens, Martha's parents, as well as Emily's aunts and uncles, joined in with the wittiest, most worldly verses of all.

Arthur tried to imagine Rose and Jacob in this setting. He almost laughed aloud as the incongruous picture formed in his mind. His mother, whose Rosenmaier-Franke relatives had much in common with the Grants, had been an unformed, sheltered girl of seventeen when she married Jacob and moved to Wilkes-Barre. Her horizons had been limited to Wyoming Valley for the past thirty years. Still, he thought, his loyalty asserting itself, I'd take one of her in place of a dozen Claudia Grants.

On New Year's Eve everyone decided not to dress for dinner—a major decision. Arthur was gratified, since it had not occurred to him that he would need a dinner jacket in the Maine woods.

During the earlier part of the evening, great mounds of caviar appeared in silver bowls, accompanied by champagne. At midnight, after everyone had toasted in the New Year, there was a magnificent buffet of roast pheasant, smoked Canadian ham, cold poached salmon *glacé,* and Maine lobsters that had been cut up and put back in their shells with a tangy sauce. Dessert was meringue with ice cream and a flaming brandied plum sauce which the servants carried in while Freddy dimmed the lights for a theatrical effect.

If ever a year had been ushered in with proper spirit and elegance, it was 1927.

After dinner all the young people—mostly friends of Freddy's and Martha's—donned warm, hooded mackinaws or furs and heavy boots to go tramping through the knee-high snow. A light, new snow was falling. The air was so still and icy, Arthur could imagine it crackling into a million reflective prisms. Someone threw a snowball and then another, and the battle was on. Even in the still of night, this group of overachievers had to compete!

He and Emily were down on their knees behind a tall, spreading Norway spruce, pushing snow into a wall for a fortification. They made a supply of snowballs, Emily continuing to replenish their ammunition while Arthur let fly with the arsenal, making contact every time with deadly accuracy. At least this was one game where he had the upper hand.

The others soon tired of this sport and continued on their way toward the lake. Emily had snow under her hood from the last direct hit. He removed his glove, which was soaking wet anyway, and fished out some icy chunks, brushing her hair back from her forehead and adjusting the hood. Her eyes were shining, her face rosy, and she was still a little high from champagne and laughter.

He tilted her chin upward and kissed her. It had been a long time since they had kissed, really kissed, like this. They sank back into the deep snow, their lips barely losing contact. The snow formed a cocoon around them.

Emily tightened her arms around his neck, kissing him wildly, wildly. She broke away and held his head against hers. "Oh, I love you! I love you so much," she cried. "Why can't you love me the way I love you?" And she began to weep.

Arthur was overcome with a mixture of conflicting emotions. He didn't know if one of them was love.

"Honey!" he said, kissing the tears from her eyes and cheeks. He had never seen Emily cry, lose her self-contained serenity. "Emily, darling, please don't cry!" He continued to kiss and soothe her, sitting up now and holding her against his chest.

She presently regained her composure, looking at him ruefully. "I should know better than to drink more than two glasses of champagne," she said, attempting to lighten the mood. "I'm sorry."

He shook his head. "Don't be sorry, Emily. I'm the one who should be sorry." He felt awful. Why couldn't he love her? Maybe he did. He really didn't know. There were too many attachments to loving Emily Grant. . . .

New Year's Day was sunny and clear. They slept late, then went snowshoeing and sledding. He and Emily were never alone, never had a chance to talk in private. The following morning he left early for the train.

In January and February the weather was especially severe. Philadelphia was practically closed down with three successive snowfalls. Emily didn't come into town on the weekend and Arthur had night duty almost every week night.

He was doing a lot of chest surgery these days. Professor Silverberg was urging him to consider an additional three years of surgical training.

"I am hoping, Arthur, that you'll decide to stay on at Jefferson . . . we get on well together. There would be a place in my practice for a young man like you."

"That's . . . very flattering, Dr. Silverberg. I'd certainly find it a wonderful opportunity, sir." He was overwhelmed. Silverberg rarely complimented anyone.

Dean Christian Rutledge called him in to his office for a conference. Arthur was especially fond of Rutledge, a handsome, distinguished physician who had always gone out of his way to be friendly to Arthur.

"You've done a splendid job this year, Arthur. We're renewing your residency for next year. You've got a good shot at being chief resident," the dean told him.

"That's wonderful news, Dean Rutledge! I can't tell you how pleased I am to hear it. I've had a great year here at the hospital."

"I hope maybe you'll continue at Jefferson when you're finished with your training, Arthur. If I'm still around, I can promise to recommend you for an instructorship. I think you would like academic medicine, and Philadelphia is a good place in which to practice."

Arthur felt great about that part of his life. Maybe now, with spring approaching, he could sort out his feelings about Emily. He missed her when they didn't see each other. They had a date for Friday night. He enjoyed a sense of anticipation at the prospect of being with her.

Emily was withdrawn, preoccupied. "What did you say, Arthur? I'm sorry . . . I wasn't paying attention."

"I said, I won't be on service next weekend, so we can go out Friday and Saturday," he replied.

"I'm sorry, Arthur. I can't. I'm going to Palm Beach to visit my grandmother."

"How long will you be gone, Emily?" He was disappointed.

"I'm not sure. A few weeks."

"Let me hear from you," he said when he kissed her good night.

A month later, Emily announced her engagement to Bill Beckinger.

Philadelphia   Autumn 1927

By the end of November, Arthur was doing some of the complex procedures with Professor Silverberg looking on. The battery of students in the amphitheater, and the fourth-year men who had scrubbed, no longer bothered him. In fact, he was completely unaware of them, absorbed as he was in tissue, fascia, blood vessels, and organs. The hush of the operating room, the muffled voices behind surgical masks, the emphatic thump of an instrument slapped into his outstretched hand by the precise surgical nurses were all part of a background for his focus of concentration, the surgery itself.

"Hold that retractor up, *Doctor!*" he would snap to the intern, remembering somewhere in the recesses of his mind his own terror when he had first begun assisting at surgery.

Dr. Silverberg had developed a smaller, more refined instrument for use in rib resection. He was often called upon to demonstrate his technique to visiting groups of students and other physicians, always selecting Arthur as his assistant in the surgery.

When the prestigious *Archives of Surgery* invited Roland Silverberg to submit a paper, he asked Arthur to draft the text and check all references for him. He submitted the paper without changing a word, giving Arthur a coauthorship. That was enough to put Arthur on the invitation list to many symposia.

In December, Silverberg told him that he had been asked to present his work at the thoracic section of the International Congress of Physicians and Surgeons to be held in Vienna in early April. He invited Arthur to attend the congress with him, indicating that the department would pay his steamship fare.

"You would probably like to take some time to see a little of Europe while you're there, Arthur. You can have a few weeks vacation at the time—before beginning your new residency." In this way it was announced to Arthur that he had been awarded the coveted surgical residency at Jefferson Hospital for the next three years.

As the end of 1927 rolled around, Arthur was enjoying a new sense of freedom. He had saved enough money from his earnings of the previous summer so he had some spare cash for concerts and plays. He and Roy had moved to a better apartment where the rent was lower, surprisingly enough, than the railroad flat they had lived in for the past two years.

At first he had felt some sadness that Emily had gone out of his life. He missed her. But he soon acknowledged a sense of relief that the decision had been taken away from him. He recognized his weak attitude and regarded it as a character defect.

He spent more and more of his free time with Roy McLean, who favored the smart social set in Philadelphia and the Main Line—a small, wealthy group of high livers who were bored with stodgy Philadelphia and tried hard to emulate New York café society. Arthur knew they were a shallow bunch, but they were fun and lighthearted. The girls were beautiful, flirtatious, and somewhat daring. They smoked, wore rouge, made a big show of drinking too much, and were sexy as hell, as Roy was fond of saying. Arthur could only agree with him.

Then Chessy came into his life.

They met at a tea reception in honor of Dean Christian Rutledge's fiftieth birthday. The tea was held in the library at Jeff, and as was true of all such gatherings, inclined toward the stuffy side.

She came up to him and asked him to hold her cup of tea for a moment. Taking out a miniature silver flask from her purse, she divided its contents between her own cup and his, retrieved her cup, raising it in salute, and moved away without saying another word—leaving him to look in astonishment after her.

It had taken him only a minute to collect his wits and follow her across the room.

New Year's Eve, 1927

"New Year's Eve is always such a bore," she drawled. "Everyone out to prove he can have a mad time." Chessy leaned back against the plush upholstery of her Pierce Arrow coupé and took a long drag on the Turkish cigarette in its silver and onyx holder.

Arthur, at the wheel of the car, double-clutched as he shifted into low gear. He had to go slowly. It was a snowy night with a thin ice layer under the newly falling blanket of white. He was having trouble seeing the road. The clink of the tire chains was annoying, and he hated the odor of the sweet-smelling tobacco. He opened the window, waving the smoky air toward it.

"You really shouldn't smoke those things, Chessy. They're bad for your lungs," he said irritably.

"Oh, Arthur, what do I care about my lungs," she laughed, a rich, throaty, sexy sound.

"You wouldn't say that if you saw the lungs of a cadaver who smoked!"

She roared. "That's what I'll be when I grow up. A cadaver who smoked!"

"Christ, Chessy, what a thing to say." He shook his head in exasperation. "If you don't care about your own lungs, you might consider mine."

"Oh, all right," she said, stubbing out the cigarette and putting the holder into her beaded bag. She drew her fox cape closer around her shoulders, shivering a little. "What a rotten night! It's just down the road, on the right, darling. That big gate."

They rolled up the curving drive of the Main Line Cricket Club to the large white clubhouse. An attendant took the auto from Arthur while a doorman helped Chessy out, deferentially tipping his hat and saying, "Good evening, Mrs. Baird."

"Hullo, Reilly. How are you?"

"Fine, thank you, ma'am. And yourself?" He looked at Arthur appraisingly.

"Do I have to submit to a blood test at the door?" Arthur asked in a stage whisper.

The throaty laugh again. "That's what you've got in your veins? I thought it was ice water."

"Now what's that supposed to mean?" he asked.

"Nothing, darling. Nothing." She patted his cheek as she sailed through the door, making her entrance.

Chessy always made an entrance. She was effective now in her silver lamé gown, trailing her fox cape on one shoulder, the shining cap of her brilliant blond hair catching the light from crystal chandeliers overhead.

Each time Arthur was with Chessy he considered why he kept going out with her. It was true she was marvelous company—when she didn't smoke those awful Turkish weeds. She was almost his age, exciting, moody, attractive. Her tastes were expensive—far more so than Arthur's limited funds could provide. Most evenings when he was with Chessy they went either to private parties or had dinner at his apartment or her house. But New Year's Eve was a special occasion, and he had consented to attend the annual dinner dance at her country club, the exclusive restricted bastion of Main Line society.

Chessy's lighthearted manner and acid sense of humor covered a certain vulnerability which he detected underneath. There was a mystery about her, but at the same time she was as direct as an arrow, never playing games, saying exactly what was on her mind. Arthur decided it was the uncomplicated relationship that he liked. That, plus the fact that Francesca Worthington Baird was a very alluring woman.

She had been married when she was seventeen, eloping from boarding school with a spoiled, rich, good-looking Yalie whose family had despaired of his ever settling down. Chessy was the daughter of what Arthur thought of as impoverished plenty—all that money just there for the asking, but all it seemed to do was to increase her misery.

She had eloped to punish the father who lavished neglect on her in the form of nannies, summer camps, lonely trips to exotic places, and boarding schools—many of them, since she was forever getting herself expelled. Shortly after her father's fifth marriage, Chessy had run away to Maryland, conveniently close to the latest select school, where she and Reginald Baird had been married by a sleepy justice of the peace. Chessy had done her best to settle into the role of Main Line wife to the now reconciled scion of one of Philadelphia's wealthiest and most establishment families. The marriage had lasted four years.

Arthur followed Chessy into the large dining room, which had been cleared for dancing in the center. Several people looked at them and looked away. One or two waved, but kept on dancing or drinking. "Let's dance," said Chessy. Arthur moved out on the dance floor with Chessy, holding her close, enjoying the fragrance, the feel of her slithery gown against his fingers, and the way she had of making him seem to be a good dancer.

The crowd looked expensive. Soignée women wore rich-looking gowns, simple but elegant jewels, and brightly rouged mouths. Somehow that spoiled the effect, Arthur thought. Chessy didn't redden her lips with pomade, but she did wear a lot of dark stuff on her eyelashes. And she had powdered her face with something that sparkled. Her shoulders and back, too. Intriguing.

The men all had that tall, athletic, easy look. Like life was a round of golf.

The band was playing a medley of Cole Porter tunes. Arthur loved the syncopated tempo. As a slim young man at the piano sang the sophisticated lyrics, Arthur swung Chessy around and caught her to him in a grandstand motion. She smiled up at him adoringly, also playing a part. I know why I'm doing it, he thought—I don't belong here, so I'm out to prove I do. But what's Chessy trying to prove?

They went over to the bar, where champagne was being served. Chessy introduced him to a number of Bobbys and Billys, a couple of Scotts, a Tiger, and one quite plastered Lonnie. No one bothered with last names. They were friendly enough. One or two women drifted over to speak to their husbands or escorts, but Chessy was the only woman drinking at the bar. Arthur was going to suggest that they sit at a table when one of the Bobbys asked her to dance. Arthur stood, one elbow on the bar, sipping his champagne, observing the couples on the dance floor.

"You here with Chessy?" It was Lonnie.

Arthur gave him a sideways glance. "Yes."

"Anything you wanna know 'bout Chessy, jus' ask me."

Arthur shook his head and turned his back on Lonnie. One of his friends—was it Tiger or Scotty?—said, "Come on, Lon, let it go. Let's go find Tish."

"Lemme alone. I d'wanna find Tish. I wanna talk to this chap 'bout Chessy. I gotta tell'm 'bout Chessy." He pulled away from his friend and walked around to Arthur's other side.

"Look, Lonnie," Arthur said, "let's not talk about Chessy now. You've had a lot to drink. Why don't you go with Scott and have some coffee or something?"

"Hey, listen you . . . what's your name, anyway?"

"Arthur. Arthur Hillman," he said, trying to keep his temper. Reasoning with a drunk was a matter of not letting him get to you.

"Ooooh! So, *you're* the doctor?" Suddenly Lonnie didn't seem nearly so inebriated. He looked at Arthur with narrowed eyes.

Just then Chessy and Bobby returned. Lonnie said, "Well, here she comes, the hottest little number on the Main Line."

There was a brief silence in which his voice seemed to echo with sharp clarity. The startled few who were nearby began speaking in loud, hearty voices. Arthur grabbed Lonnie's shirtfront, not giving a damn where he was.

"You watch your words, buster, or I'll teach you a lesson in good manners. You understand?" He had all he could do to keep from slapping the weak, pretty face with its marcelled hair and slack jaw.

"Why . . . why . . . take your hands off me! How dare you!" All the Bobbys and Billys and Tigers gathered around, soothing Lonnie, separating the two of them. Chessy had been watching the scenario with detachment, a wary look in her eyes.

Lonnie raised his voice. "Never should've let your kind in here. Go back where you belong, you . . . ." Someone clapped a hand over his mouth.

Now Chessy said, "Come *on,* Arthur. Let's get out of this stuffy place. What a bunch of pretentious drunks!"

They found their coats and had to walk around to the side lobby nearest the parking area. Lonnie was there with three of his friends, who were arguing with him. When he saw them, he pulled away and staggered over to Arthur. He fingered Arthur's white silk muffler with its open-work monogram—a gift from Emily. "Well, look at the silk scarf. The Jew boy's wearing a silk muffler!" And he yanked at it with sudden force, tearing the fabric at the edge of the diamond-shaped monogram.

Arthur later admitted he'd lost control, but not all that much. He drew his hand back in a fist and punched the foolish, weak-looking face right in its straight, short, Anglo-Saxon nose. Just enough to draw blood, but not do serious damage. It was a cool, contained loss of control.

The Billys and Bobbys were dragging on Lonnie's arms—holding the two men apart. Blood spouted from the assaulted proboscus, dripped down on Lonnie's starched white shirtfront.

"Blood! I'm bleeding! Look at that."

"Yeah," said Arthur. "What do y'know. It's red."

Chessy drove home. They barely spoke on the way to her house. Arthur felt a strange elation. Maybe I ought to hit people more often, he thought to himself.

Chessy spoke. "Arthur, I am really sorry. I had no idea he would be there. I thought he was in Palm Beach."

"Who? I'm afraid you've lost me, Chessy."

"Lonnie." She paused. "I guess you didn't know. Lonnie is my former husband—Reginald Lon Baird . . . the Third."

"Uh-oh." Arthur threw his head back. "I can see the headlines now. 'Doctor Assaults Ex-Husband of Beautiful Socialite in Love Triangle.' "

"I don't think there'll be anything like that, Arthur. The club is very private, very discreet."

"So I was informed," he answered dryly.

"That was inexcusable. Please accept my apologies. Lon was drunk and he tends to take this class thing too seriously even when he's sober."

"How could you have married a cad like that, Chessy? Even at seventeen, you should've known better."

"Arthur, I've spent the last seven years asking myself the same question." They had reached her house. "Come in for a nightcap?"

"I don't think so, Chessy. It's late. I think I'll just call a cab."

"It's New Year's Eve, Arthur. We haven't even welcomed in the New Year."

"Golly. I'd forgotten. What time is it?" He took out his pocket watch. "Ten to twelve. We're just in time."

Chessy brought out a bottle of champagne, nicely chilled. Prohibition certainly doesn't seem to affect anyone around here, he thought. Arthur pulled out the cork with a pop and the wine bubbled over nicely.

"Perfect!" she exclaimed.

"Happy 1928," he toasted, touching glasses with her. They drank.

Arthur put down his glass and took Chessy's, setting it down on the table. "Happy New Year, Chessy," he said, kissing her.

They sat on the couch, listening to phonograph records. Chessy had changed into a dark green velvet hostess gown, becoming with her platinum blond hair.

Arthur kissed her again. She was exciting. A lot softer and more feminine than he had thought.

"So, it isn't ice water after all," she said. In answer to his questioning look, she said, "In your veins."

"No. It's the same stuff as Lonnie's. Red Blood."

"Lonnie again. I was hoping we could forget about him."

Arthur smiled. "We can. I'm sorry if I spoiled your New Year's Eve. I mean, I don't usually go around punching guys in the nose."

"You know, Arthur, you're really very attractive when you're mad." She stretched languorously. Then she said, in her unusual, throaty voice, "Do you suppose I can seduce you?"

Arthur reached back and turned out the lamp on the table behind the couch. "Why don't we try and see," he said.

V

Vienna, Austria   Spring 1928

Vienna sparkled in the spring sunshine, a froth of a Hapsburg city, self-consciously aware of her legendary romance. Arthur stopped for a newspaper at the stand in front of the Hotel Sächer. He was on his way to its restaurant for coffee and the rich pastries, which were a Viennese treat. A printed announcement caught his eye. *My German's not as good as I thought. That poster can't say what I think it says! KOLLOSEUM Nuremberg. RASSE und ZUKUNFT! Hitler. Juden haben keinen Zutritt!* appeared in bold black letters. *Race and Future? Jews are not admitted? He must remember to ask someone about it. . . .*

Arthur had grown up in the protective cloak of American Judaism, seldom encountering prejudice, comfortably secure in his equal status. There had been occasional incidents from time to time—a chance acquaintance who let slip a bigoted remark, even a teacher, or the parents of a friend. But nothing that seriously affected *him*. Childhood taunts were like being teased for having red hair, buck teeth, or wearing glasses. Unimportant, soon forgotten. The encounter at Chessy's club had been a singular experience, and he had gained his satisfaction in resorting to unaccustomed violence.

His name, his face, his total appearance were American. They eased him into non-Jewish circles, and made him positively desirable among Jews. He didn't think about it much, but if he had, he would have regarded this as an asset.

Something had happened to alter that feeling as soon as he had reached the Austrian border. He'd had to fill in forms, endless forms, each one asking his race, his religious affiliation, and the national origin of his parents. Suddenly he was Arthur Franke Hillman, male Jew, with Russian and German lineage, who carried an American passport. He was mighty grateful for that passport. He took it everywhere with him, slept with it under his pillow. Without it, he would have felt naked.

Once in Vienna, however, the heady environment of the International Congress combined with the *Gemütlichkeit* of the "Queen of the Danube" to lift his mood. There he was treated as a younger colleague by men whose names had been bywords since he first began at Jefferson seven years before.

Professor Silverberg included him in the luncheons and dinners which made up the social part of the program, introducing him to the mighty names of medicine and surgery . . . Cushing, Graham, Albee. After a few days of this, Arthur wryly admitted to himself that he might have been suffering from the paranoia of the unseasoned traveler, unaccustomed to passport and customs controls. After all, the Austrians were a Germanic nation, and the Germans were known for their meticulous keeping of records.

Arthur boarded the train for Salzburg at the end of the congress. He planned a day in that quaint city, and another in Innsbruck, before stopping in Munich, where he was to meet his mother's cousin, Professor Gunther Rosenmaier. The professor was a physician whose private clinic was supposed to be the best in the Bavarian capital . . . so Uncle Herman, who had made the arrangements for his visit, had informed him.

Traveling by train in Europe was a civilized experience. The trip had been noteworthy as much for its superior service, the delicious meals, and the general holiday conviviality of his fellow passengers as it was for the breathtaking Tyrolean scenery. As the train left Innsbruck, Arthur seated himself in the dining car. A waiter served him from a large soup tureen. First came a hearty vegetable bisque with tiny dumplings, followed by thin pancakes rolled with spicy Austrian ham, topped with a creamy white sauce. Accompanying this was a carafe of chilled Traminer. Arthur startled the waiter by refusing the next course, schnitzel and fried potatoes. How everyone in Europe managed to eat such hearty midday meals and stay awake during the afternoon was a mystery to Arthur. The closer he came to Germany, the more ample were the proportions of the citizens.

As Arthur helped himself to the bowl of green salad, a couple seated themselves at a table across the aisle at an angle from him. The woman was tall, with dark blond hair worn in a braid at the nape of her neck. Her clothes were man-tailored and she carried expensive accessories. Her companion, not as tall as she, was a fleshy man whose head was shaven. He wore a monocle on a thin silver chain and was dressed in a dark loden suit which was tailored like a uniform, although it bore no insignia or military emblems. When they crossed into Germany, the German passport officer showed these two considerable respect. Arthur thought they must be in the government.

He was looking out at the charming Bavarian Alpine towns, his interest in the neighboring diners forgotten, when he heard a disturbance behind him. Arthur turned in time to see his waiter thrust the tureen of soup into the hands of an astonished captain and hurry from the dining car.

The captain approached the table of the Prussian-looking couple, greeting them respectfully. Arthur's curiosity was roused, and because few other diners were in the car, he was able to overhear the words that they exchanged. Elementary though his German was, he had no difficulty understanding this conversation, which was loud enough, and clearly stated.

"I merely informed him that I did not wish to be served by a filthy Jew! That is my privilege, is it not?"

Arthur's sense of well-being vanished. He felt that he might vomit the lunch and the wine. The captain spoke to them in soothing tones, seeking to mollify them, glancing nervously over his shoulder at Arthur, who was glaring at them from his seat. Deferentially, the captain served their soup, poured their wine.

Arthur left the dining car abruptly, returning to his compartment, several cars to the rear. In the vestibule between the last two cars stood the waiter, smoking a cigarette, looking out at the passing landscape. He turned when Arthur opened the door, eying him hostilely.

Arthur hesitated. "I'm sorry about what happened in there . . ." The man gave him a disparaging look. Arthur took out some coins. "Here . . . I didn't have a chance to leave something for you . . ." He held the money out to the man, who didn't make a move to take it. "Please, it's for the service . . ." Arthur wanted to beg the man to take it. He pressed the money into the waiter's flaccid palm. The man would not look at him; the muscles of his jaw were rigid.

"Who was that man?" Arthur asked.

There was no answer.

"It's important to me to know . . . I'm a Jew." He realized as he said it that he expected the thin, sallow, dark-eyed man to show some fraternal recognition. Instead, he was regarded with a long, discerning scrutiny.

"An American."

"Yes. I'm an American Jew."

"Consider yourself fortunate," said the waiter. "That man is a Nazi. You probably never heard of the Nazis."

Arthur had heard of the Nazis. Weren't they a bunch of hoodlums, though, not to be taken seriously? That's what he had been told in Vienna, when he'd asked about the poster he had seen. Yet the man in the dining car had been treated with respect, almost servilely, by both the customs official and the dining-car captain.

It was a perplexed and unsettled Arthur who arrived in Munich on a sunny April afternoon in 1928.

The stone building bore the carved date "1730" on its venerable doorpost. He climbed the ancient staircase, whose stone treads were worn into a concave, almost satiny smoothness by generations of feet. He was in the Old City of Munich, where it was fashionable for well-to-do academic families to live in the refurbished apartments of these antique buildings.

At the second level he pulled a bell handle. Almost immediately the door was opened by a slim, severely attractive young woman with an alabaster complexion. Her oval face was framed by copper-colored hair, gathered into what seemed to be the German national hairstyle—that braid and tight cluster at the back of the neck.

"I am Arthur Hillman," he said.

She smiled and her face took on an aristocratic beauty. "Cousin Arthur! I am Leisl. Please come in." Her British English was perfect, the soft accent lending charm to her low voice.

They were genuinely happy to see him, the family Rosenmaier. Despite Gunther Rosenmaier's cool, correct demeanor, he was interested in everything Arthur had to tell him about his American relatives. He had met Herman Franke years before when the Philadelphian had visited in Munich. Herman kept up a regular correspondence with them, repeatedly inviting them to come to America for a visit. Gunther, however, had never been inclined to travel to that distant land. This young man, his second cousin's son, from America—a doctor, training to be a surgeon—was a welcome guest in his home. There weren't too many relatives these days—an unmarried Solweiss cousin was the last of her line.

Arthur spent an interesting day with Gunther at his clinic, a small private hospital with a well-equipped surgery and an impressive staff of doctors and nurses. Here many of Munich's elite came for their medical and hospital care. Gunther's son, Kurt, was a medical student at the university and would soon be joining his father at the Rosenmaier Clinic. Uncle Herman had not been exaggerating when he spoke about the prestigious nature of Gunther's position. In addition to his private medical practice, Gunther held a professorship in medicine at the University Medical College, where he lectured.

At dinner the first night in Munich, Arthur met Kurt and his good friend and fellow medical student Armand Brandt. Kurt, a likable fellow, outgoing and hospitable, had an engaging smile. He was good-looking, with dark hair and long, dark eyelashes, which framed his blue eyes. Armand, by contrast, was a remote personality, blond and pale-eyed, who had little to say. When he did speak, it was in a stolid, Germanic, almost toneless voice.

"And how did you find the sessions at the congress in Vienna, Herr Doctor?" he asked Arthur. Arthur did not appreciate being addressed as "Herr

Doctor," but after several attempts to get the man to use his first name, he gave up.

"They were instructive, Armand. I must admit, though, I was more interested in the conversation *between* sessions—in the corridors and the coffee houses. That's where I heard about the newest techniques. You can read these papers in the journals, the proceedings of the meetings. . . ."

Armand seemed to disapprove of his irreverence.

"I'm taking Arthur on a tour tomorrow," Leisl announced. "We're going all over Munich and into the countryside. He must see something besides hospitals while he's here, or else he'll leave with the impression that everyone in Germany is sick!"

Armand looked at Leisl with surprise and said something to her in a low voice, in German. She shrugged, then looked at Arthur and nodded her head affirmatively.

"You will be alone with Leisl, Dr. Hillman," Armand said. "You will be on your honor, as a gentleman."

Arthur was startled. What a curious statement! Then he smiled and nodded. "Of course." Privately, he decided it must be the language barrier. . . . Armand didn't speak English as well as the others.

They spent the morning visiting museums, then Leisl took him to a beer hall for lunch—wurst and dark bread and the famous Bavarian lager. It was a noisy restaurant filled with students and young businessmen, a jostling, good-natured crowd. Arthur enjoyed it, and Leisl smiled and relaxed, her face taking on a warmer color after drinking her second beer.

Later they strolled through a park full of spring flowers, colorful and groomed to perfection.

"Although I am alone with you, Fräulein Rosenmaier, I am on my honor, as a gentleman!" Arthur mimicked Armand, his words comically stiff and sober.

Leisl giggled, then laughed outright. She seemed to find it enormously funny, peals of laughter welling up again and again.

"Is he always that pompous—Armand?" he asked her.

Leisl nodded. "Yes, always!" And she began to laugh once again. She stopped, taking pity on him. "I must share my joke with you, Arthur. You see, Armand and I are engaged . . . to be married."

Arthur was speechless. He felt the color rush into his face. "Leisl! I'm . . . I apologize . . . I had no idea . . ." And as the full realization of it hit him, he said, "I really am sorry, Leisl. I should never have said that, I hope you can forgive me."

"Forgive you? But it's true, Arthur! He *is* pompous. 'You vill be on your honor as a chentleman,'" she repeated his mimicry. "Poor Armand, he really doesn't have much sense of humor."

"Are you . . . in love with him, Leisl?" They were sitting on a bench near the shore of a small lake, where swans glided gracefully over the surface.

"In love?" She seemed to be considering it. "Probably not in the sense that Americans mean it when they say 'in love.' "

"Then why are you going to marry him?"

"It's more or less expected. You see, our families have known each other forever . . . at least, it seems like forever. Our mothers were like sisters, before my mother died. Our fathers have been friends for most of their lives . . . the families are from a high station . . . it's hard to explain. It just seems right. I've known for a long time that we would marry, even before he asked. . . ." She smiled sweetly, then looked down at her hands.

Arthur said nothing. But he could not imagine Leisl, revealed as this fun-loving, vibrant woman, married to that prig!

Was this how most people married, he wondered—because it seemed right, because it was expected? Had he been foolish to let Emily go when he wasn't sure that he loved her enough? How do you measure love? By degrees, with a thermometer—wouldn't it be nice if you could? . . . To what degree had Emily been in love with him? Had he been in love with her at all? Was there such a thing as a "great love" for him? Perhaps he expected too much . . . he was still that little boy listening to his grandfather tell him that love for a woman was the most beautiful thing in life. In a way, he envied Leisl and Armand the rightness of their marriage, the fulfilling of everyone's expectations.

Companionably, they walked back toward the Old City along a cobbled way in the university district. At the end of the street a small platoon of uniformed men, wearing red armbands with a strange Greek-cross figure in black printed on them, marched across the *platz* and into a building, bearing aloft a banner with the same symbol. Arthur felt an icy trail of chill run down his spine.

"What are those men?" Leisl didn't seem to have heard him. She had stopped walking and was looking at the building at the far end of the block where the marchers had entered. Her face was contorted with disgust—and, yes, with fear. The same fear he had seen in the eyes of the Jewish waiter on the train. A wary, animal look.

"Are those Nazis, Leisl?" he asked, his voice sharp, cutting into her abstraction.

"Uh . . ." She let out a shaky breath. "Yes. Yes, Arthur. They're . . . they're *crazy.* They're bullies—lazy, won't work. Terrible people! They're a blight on our city—on Munich!"

"It's not just Munich, Leisl. There was one on the train, coming from Innsbruck—I saw a notice in Vienna, about a lecture in Nuremberg. It was a talk against the Jews. I couldn't believe that such a thing could appear in the streets of a civilized city." They were approaching the building where the Nazis had entered. On its facade were placards.

OHNE LÖSUNG DER JUDENFRAGE—
KEINE ERLÖSUNG DES DEUTSCHEN VOLKES!

(Without solution of the Jewish problem—
there can be no salvation for the German people!)

Leisl wanted to turn the other way, but Arthur was curious. A boy was handing out handbills, and Arthur took one, although Leisl recoiled from the boy's extended hand. With horrified fascination, he read:

Judentum ist Verbrechertum . . .

(Judaism is Criminalism . . .)

"Leisl! How long has this sort of thing been going on here in Germany?"

"Oh"—she waved it away with her hand—"for years and years, Arthur. It doesn't mean anything. There are always political agitators—crackpots. They have no following."

"I hope not! Because, if they did, you and your family and all of the Jews would be in jeopardy." He continued reading the most appalling anti-Semitic cartoons. "If I lived here, I would leave! I couldn't live in a place where such a thing went on as an everyday occurrence."

"You just don't understand Germany, Arthur!" Her tone was angry. "We are Germans! We have been one of Munich's first Jewish families for generations." She stood tall and slim, her elegant head tilted up, the patronizing smile on her beautiful German face almost a smirk of self-satisfaction.

Gone was the sweet-smiling, gaily laughing girl of the afternoon. In her place stood Fräulein Leisl Rosenmaier, daughter of *der Geheimrat Professor Gunther Otto Rosenmaier von München.*

That evening they were invited to the home of Baron Franz von Würtemberg. Gunther had saved the life of the baron's only son fifteen years before, and in gratitude he had helped Gunther to finance an expanded clinic, making Rosenmaier's hospital the foremost of its kind in Bavaria. Of course it had proved to be a lucrative investment for the baron, but Gunther was nevertheless grateful for his patronage.

The baron was a genial host, clearly paternalistic toward the Rosenmaiers, and they were ingratiating to him. The son whose life had been saved because of Gunther's skill as a physician made a brief appearance to prove that he was a fine physical specimen, and then excused himself to attend to more pressing matters.

Arthur barely spoke during dinner. Once the baron addressed him, "You have come to study medicine in Vienna?"

"Not exactly, sir," he replied. "I've completed my studies in Philadelphia. I attended a medical meeting in Vienna."

He continued, as if Arthur had not spoken, "Vienna's medicine is the best in the world . . . the best place to study."

Arthur had the feeling that he almost didn't exist for the baron. But when they were leaving, the baron said, with a twinkle in his eye, "Philadelphia has good medicine, too." When Arthur smiled and extended his hand, he shook it warmly, thanking him effusively for coming to dinner.

Arthur had one more day in Munich before leaving in the evening for Paris, then almost two weeks to spend as he wished until he sailed home from Southampton.

In the morning, Leisl drove him out to see one of the picturesque castles above the Isar River from the early days of the Wittelsbach rulers. There was a strain between them now—the easy camaraderie of the previous afternoon had vanished.

If she mentions the baron in that smug way once more, I'll explode, he said to himself, as Leisl went on about the important families in the Munich area.

"You're so quiet, Arthur. Is there something bothering you?" Leisl finally asked.

"Yes, Leisl, something is bothering me. I don't see how you people can be so blind to how you are treated. Even your precious baron . . . why, your father's his pet Jew! He uses him like a toy. Professor Rosenmaier dances on a string at his whim."

"How do you *dare* to speak like that!" She was furious, and slammed the car into gear, driving at high speed until they reached the outskirts of the city.

Arthur spoke first. "I'm sorry, Leisl. I seem to keep saying inexcusable things that offend you. It's just that I'm troubled about this thing of the Jews here. We're not accustomed to anything like this in the United States."

"Is there no anti-Semitism in your country?"

"Yes. I guess there's no place in the world where there isn't anti-Semitism —unless it's a place where there are no Jews. However, it's nothing like this. I've never seen anything like this. We have the Ku Klux Klan, in the South— they do terrible things to Negroes . . . burn crosses in front of their homes, beat them, sometimes even kill them. But it's not something I've *seen*."

"So, Arthur, is that so different from this?" she asked, in a reasonable tone of voice.

"In the States, everyone speaks out against the Ku Klux Klan. People *hate* them. Here, I get the idea that the Nazis are admired." He tried for a change of mood. "Look, this is my last day. Let's you and I be friends. I'm sorry if I've offended you. I hope you're right and I'm wrong. I really do hope so."

When they reached the Rosenmaier's home, a cablegram was waiting for Arthur.

FATHER HAS SERIOUS STROKE. SUGGEST
YOU RETURN SOONEST POSSIBLE. NATE.

BOOK FOUR

Returning

1928-30

I

Buck Run
Mountain Springs, Pennsylvania
May 15, 1928

Dear Dr. Hillman:

Your letter was directed to me as President of the Luzerne County Medical Society. It appears that you would be a welcome addition to our local medical community.

I need not point out to you, a native son, the many fine attributes of this area. Suffice it to say that I am the fifth generation of my family to live here, and I wouldn't think of living anywhere else.

There are a number of well-established surgeons in the Valley. I doubt that you would find enough work in a surgical specialty to keep you busy, despite your surgical training. My advice is to begin by opening a General Practice.

Wilkes-Barré has several hospitals. My own is County Hospital, an excellent place, and the largest. Another possibility is St. Anne's, run by the nuns. You would have a little trouble getting on staff there, I imagine.

As soon as you are settled in town, please come to see me.

Very truly yours,
William J. Matlin, M.D.

One Grandview Terrace
Wilkes-Barre, Pa.
May 30, 1928

Dear Arthur,

What a pleasure it was to hear that you are returning to Wilkes-Barre to practice medicine. I hope that being among old friends will compensate for leaving Philadelphia.

You will have many opportunities to use your excellent surgical skills within the scope of a general practice. While it is true that there are several men here specializing in surgery, most of us refer our more complicated cases to one of the large medical centers where the support staff and facilities attract the best surgeons.

I am now chief of staff at St. Anne's Hospital, and I would be pleased to nominate you for admission to our staff. Despite its Catholic affiliation, St. Anne's welcomes patients and physicians of all faiths. I myself am not a Catholic.

I will be happy to offer whatever assistance I can to help you get settled. Good luck to you.

Cordially,
W. Hobson Carpenter II, M.D.

Wilkes-Barre 1928

Since Arthur had returned to Wyoming Valley, he'd had to come to terms with living again in a small town.

As Dr. Matlin had reminded him, he was a native son. What that meant, in practical terms, was that everyone in his family claimed ownership on a segment of his time and attention.

"Arthur, the baby threw up last night and has a little fever," his sister, Frieda, called to tell him the day after his arrival. He was about to leave his parents' house on Prospect Avenue to keep an appointment with Dr. Matlin at County Hospital.

"Well . . . Frieda . . . I was just on my way out. Don't you have a pediatrician? I haven't been taking care of babies much lately." Frieda was easily offended.

He couldn't as readily put off his aunts and uncles, all of whom seemed to have saved their chronic medical problems, just waiting for him to hang up a shingle in Wilkes-Barre.

The people who needed him most were least demanding of his time. His parents. Arthur had come home from Europe to find his father partially paralyzed, with his speech impaired. Rose devoted her days to caring for Jacob, who couldn't do anything for himself. Arthur knew they felt guilty about his having to give up the remaining years of his surgical residency at Jefferson. They hadn't asked him to do it, but he thought he had no choice. Nate couldn't leave law school, and they'd agreed that one of them should be here.

Jacob finally understood that old Dr. Davis might not be the best physician for him. Arthur spoke to Dr. Hobson Carpenter.

"I'll be happy to take care of your father, Arthur. Dr. Davis will understand, I'm sure. He's getting on in years," Carpenter told him. Arthur was reassured to have his father looked after by someone in whom he had confidence.

Accustomed to the independence he had enjoyed in Philadelphia, he was determined that he was not going to permit his moving back to Wilkes-Barre to stifle him. It might not be easy, but if he was anything, he was an optimist!

Having grown up in the valley, he knew and was known by "the whole town," or at least the part that "counted"—meaning the Jewish community and most of the affluent gentiles, with the exception of those few who considered themselves so patrician that they disdained to associate with ordinary folk. This last group included some of the principal mine owners, several bankers, an occasional lawyer, and not a few clergy. They were, almost to a man, members of the self-consciously selective Northampton Club.

Much to the displeasure of the Medical Society president, William Matlin, Arthur had elected to join the staff at St. Anne's. When he'd called to thank Dr. Matlin for his interview, and to tell him of his decision, the chief at County Hospital had been astonished.

"That's very surprising news, Dr. Hillman," he had said coldly. "Very surprising, indeed."

Arthur had consulted Jim Flannery, Tom Sloat, and several other friends from Jeff who were on the St. Anne's staff. Jim had spoken to him confidentially. "They have a lot of post-op complications at County, Art. I think they have some problems with sanitation, nursing care, things like that. Hob Carpenter runs a tight ship at St. Anne's . . . and Sister Francis, on surgery, is a terror."

It was nice to have friends on the St. Anne's staff, but his decision was made because he felt it was the better hospital—efficient, well-equipped, and humanely run by the nursing Sisters of Mercy.

The distinctly Catholic appearance of St. Anne's, unfamiliar yet vaguely attractive to him, lent an air of peaceful calm and reassuring comfort to patients of all creeds. As the seasons passed, Arthur felt increasingly that he belonged at St. Anne's. He looked forward to entering her imposing double doors each day. The large oil paintings of the Crucifixion and the Madonna which adorned the entry lobby, the stained-glass windows of the small chapel with its font of holy water at one end of the corridor, the dark paneling and well-used leather sofas of the physicians' library had an appealing dignity for him. In their flowing black or white habits, the nuns glided along the polished floors of the hallways, smiling and devoted in their ministrations to the sick. Their standards were exacting, the nursing staff better than any he had known. By comparison, County Hospital seemed a cold, commercial institution.

Dr. Carpenter, whom he hadn't seen in years—not since Nate had been a convalescent—couldn't have been nicer or more helpful. Through him, Arthur had found his rented offices and apartment, both in the same building on Northampton Street.

"Living above the shop, Arthur! That's the way I started out. I still have my offices at home. It simplifies life. Not so much tearing around."

Dr. Carpenter conducted staff meetings at St. Anne's with democratic regard for his colleagues. An aristocratic-looking man, now past forty, he was friendly and outgoing.

By contrast, Arthur's impression of William Matlin had been that of a pompous, self-important windbag. He was confirmed in this opinion after attending several of the monthly meetings of the Medical Society.

Those meetings were fun, typically small-town. Many of the issues were piddling, seeming of little consequence to Arthur. Inordinate concern for appearances pervaded the discussions. Some of the older doctors were overly preoccupied with the image of the physician in the community, Arthur thought. Accustomed to the stimulating scientific discussions of the Jefferson colloquia, he was sometimes amused, but often impatient with the lack of attention to medical affairs and issues of social consequence. No one had to tell him that his role was one of observer in these first months. A young doctor, like a novice in any calling, must defer to the sager heads around him.

Not all of his associations were in medical circles. He'd met a whole new crowd through the Flannerys and his old college friend Harry Steiger, who was practicing law in Wilkes-Barre. Steeg was active in Pennsylvania politics, spending so much time campaigning around the state for various Republican candidates that they didn't see much of him.

Then, in July, Arthur's phone rang late one night. "Hello, Art. I've got some good news for you!" Steeg's hearty voice—a great voice for ringing rhetoric—came over the wire.

"You're running for Congress!" responded Arthur.

Steeg laughed. "No-o-o. Guess again."

"You're in jail," joked Arthur.

"You're getting warmer . . . I'm engaged!"

"No kidding! What poor unfortunate woman would have the bad judgment to marry you?"

"Good thing I didn't have her meet you first, Hillman. Her name's Marilyn Sneed. My folks are having a party for us Saturday after next. Will you come?"

Steeg's fiancée was the daughter of the commonwealth's lieutenant governor. Standing next to Harry, Marilyn looked like the wife of a future congressman—svelte, well-groomed, self-assured. Harry Steiger would be running for office one of these days, Arthur had no doubt. Everyone predicted a brilliant political career for him. He was what the state needed—a creative, energetic, honest politician. A breath of fresh air.

At the engagement party, Arthur met the Wintermuths, a couple who were also good friends with Louise and Jim Flannery. Lowell Wintermuth was a brash, attractive man, dark-haired, with a moustache. A little rough around the edges, but smart, genial, and charismatic.

Arthur was told that Lowell came from a poor family in Exeter, over on the west side of the Susquehanna. Thanks to a scholarship, he had graduated from Lehigh with a degree in mine engineering and gone to work for Wyoming and Susquehanna Coal & Navigation. Lowell had proved to be such a fine engineer and brilliant administrator that he rose steadily until the company appointed him its superintendent of mines. It was in this capacity that he had met Phoebe, the only child of Cyril Hess Buckland, president of Wyoming and Susquehanna.

Buckland ran his empire in much the same way a feudal lord oversaw his vast domains. It could be said that Cyril Buckland viewed the men who worked his mines as his serfs—so, when his willful daughter eloped with her father's superintendent of mines, only his wife's intervention prevented Cyril from firing Lowell and cutting Phoebe off. It was also at Martha Matlin Buckland's insistence that Lowell was made a vice president of the Wyoming and Susquehanna. Cyril Buckland was said to be the only chief executive of a major corporation who communicated with one of his officers, who happened to be his son-in-law, by written memorandum.

Lowell had always been a popular superintendent with the miners. Up from the ranks, they knew him, and felt he understood them.

"There are those who say Lowell's forgotten where he came from since he married the boss's daughter . . . but you know how some people are. I think it's sour grapes," Louise Flannery once said to Arthur.

Arthur liked Lowell Wintermuth. "Lowell, I've never been down in a coal mine. I'd really like to do that sometime."

"Sure, Arthur. I'd be happy to take you down a shaft." Lowell set it up for the following week.

It was a singular experience, one that Arthur did not care to repeat. The wind was the most surprising feature. The damp chill and the sensation of always having to clear his throat the most uncomfortable aspects. He didn't much care for the feeling of sinking hundreds of feet beneath the ground, either. Lowell took him to one of their most modern collieries, of course. If that had been a model mine, Arthur was glad that he didn't have to spend his life underground, digging coal for a living.

Perhaps his closest friends in the valley, in the sense of solid, old, comfortable ties, were the Benjamins, Ruth and David. Arthur had known David most of his life. They'd gone to Hebrew School together and played on the same basketball team at the "Y." They'd become even closer friends in the months since Arthur's return to the valley. Arthur was particularly fond of David's wife, Ruth. They were a deeply devoted couple. There was one disappointment in their life together. In five years of marriage, they had not had a child.

These were the people who made up the inner circle of his friendships in town. They were wonderful friends, warm and caring. They, like his sisters, however, were always trying to bring him together with one or another of the valley's unmarried women.

One Friday evening when he had dinner with his parents and his grandfather, his sister Dorothy was there with her young family. As usual, Dorothy wanted him to take one of her single friends to a temple dance. . . .

"Why not, Arthur? She's a lovely girl. You'll have lots of fun, and we'll all be together," she urged.

Arthur had met some of Dorothy's friends. "I'm busy that night," he answered, as he kissed his mother good-bye.

"How can you be busy? I haven't even told you which night it is!"

"I know, Dot, but I'm busy, whenever it is . . . good night."

"*Honestly,* Mother! What's the matter with him? He's the best-looking man in town, and what good does it do him?"

The trouble with taking someone out in Wilkes-Barre was that the moment he did so, everyone knew about it. If he should ask her out a second time, he was almost under an obligation to continue the relationship, with the expectation of its becoming a serious romance.

There were, it seemed, no such women as Chessy Baird in Wyoming Valley.

Ashley   Fall 1928

The priest opened the door wide for Arthur. Our Lady of the Mountain rectory in Ashley, Pennsylvania, was a pretty seedy-looking residence, even for a priest with his vow of poverty, Arthur thought.

"Right on time, Dr. Hillman. Come in."

He entered the dreary hallway. Drab, drab institutional was the refrain from the parlor to the left. An odor of cooked fish lingered in the air. He followed the cleric into a bookshelf-lined study, more welcoming than the outer rooms.

The priest had an engaging smile. He was young. Arthur judged him to be in his early thirties. They had met in August, three months after Arthur had joined the staff of St. Anne's Hospital. Arthur had passed Jim Flannery standing in conversation with the priest in the front entry.

"Father John, this is the man I was telling you about who's interested in lung diseases in the coal industry," Jim had introduced him. Father John Riordan had an eager enthusiasm. He had seemed a pleasant, genial man with a natural manner. Arthur didn't know many priests, and in general did not care for the "clerical" personality, be it priest or rabbi.

"May I give you a call, Dr. Hillman? There's something I have in mind that I'd like to talk to you about. Jim, here, says you'd be the right fellow." He clapped Flannery on the back.

Arthur had agreed without hesitation, and a few days later the priest had called, inviting Arthur to visit him at the rectory.

Arthur had never been in a priest's house before. For that matter, he reminded himself, he didn't remember ever having visited a rabbi's home. When he was young, his parents had occasionally invited the rabbi of their Conservative synagogue to dinner. It had always been a special effort for his mother, he remembered. She had to borrow dishes and silver from his Aunt Simone because his family did not keep a kosher house. His mother would carefully supervise everything in the kitchen, putting white butcher's paper down on the counters and buying new dishcloths so that the dishes would remain kosher. He had always wondered why they bothered to invite Rabbi Berkowitz to dinner. The rabbi had been a nice enough man, but he spoke in a manner that Arthur could only describe as rabbinical—heavy, deliberate, with sorrowful overtones. Arthur had always been relieved when it was over, and he knew his mother felt the same way.

He looked around the rectory study with curiosity. He was surprised to see such titles as *The Complete Works of William Shakespeare* and Plato's *Republic* on a shelf opposite his armchair. An immense mahogany desk was piled with papers and file folders. The carpet, an old dark red faded Persian design, did nothing to add distinction to the room.

"I don't take credit for the decor," Father Riordan said with a chuckle. At thirty-two he still had trouble getting people to relax in his presence, even non-Catholics. It added to the loneliness of his life.

"I can't help being curious about a priest's house," Arthur said with candor.

"Yes. I understand that. Right now, this desk and the books are the only things that belong to me. The rest, sad to say, comes with the job. I'm convinced that whoever selected it secretly hates priests."

He had genuine Irish good looks. Dark brown, almost black, hair capped his head, sweeping back from a widow's peak. Deep-set hazel eyes peered from under shaggy brows. His smile was open, the even, gleaming teeth especially attractive. The clerical collar and seminary cassock which he wore today served to enhance his appearance in an ascetic way.

"Would you care for a drink? Scotch, Irish whiskey, gin, bourbon." He stooped a little to look into a cabinet. "That's the whole of it."

"Bourbon," said Arthur.

Father Riordan broke the seal on the bottle and poured an Irish whiskey for himself. He laughed. "My relatives seem to think I need a well-stocked bar for my lively social calendar. Actually, you're the first visitor I've had in months," he said as he sat opposite Arthur, throwing one arm over the back of his chair in a casual, youthful way that made him seem less remote. "Would you mind if I called you Arthur?"

"I'd be delighted."

"And I'd like you to call me John. Would you do that?"

"All right . . . John."

He smiled. "Why do people have so much trouble with that?"

"It must be difficult being a priest at your age, having people treat you so respectfully."

Arthur liked this man. In other circumstances, they might become friends. Why other circumstances? Why not a friendship between two men—a priest and a non-Catholic doctor? He had a feeling it wasn't done, but he would like to be proved wrong.

Father Riordan got to the point. "Arthur, I have many mining families in my parish. Poor mining families. Some are Irish, but most are not. They're Polish, Hungarian, German. I'd like to ask you to care for some of them. I must be frank . . . there's nothing in it for you. They're a pitiful group. So poor, you wouldn't believe it. They live in company houses, with no indoor plumbing, no furnace, none of the conveniences. There are five, seven, nine children in a family—I do not consider that to be a blessing, unlike many of my colleagues! The mothers are sick, the children malnourished, the fathers coughing their lungs out. They need help. They need good medical care. And they can't afford their next meal, much less a doctor bill."

"I'll be glad to take care of them, John. I set aside a certain amount of my practice for patients whom I don't charge. That's an obligation I feel. A decision I made when I first opened my practice," Arthur told him.

John Riordan knew a lot about men. You get to know all sorts of things about people when you're a priest. Good things and bad things. This man struck him as a strong character, a good person.

"I won't saddle you with too many, Arthur. Jim Flannery has been handling a lot of the cases, but I don't think he can take on any more now. . . . Here are the names of the five families I am most concerned about. If you can manage to see them over the next five or six weeks, that would be wonderful."

John Riordan told Arthur he had grown up in Hazleton, studied at a seminary near Easton, and then served in the bishoprics of Harrisburg and Scranton.

"They sent me here to Our Lady four years ago as an assistant to Father Vincent, who was getting on in years. Unfortunately, he died a few months after I arrived, and I've been here alone ever since. Sometimes I think they've forgotten about me!"

"Isn't it a mark of success for a priest to have his own parish so early in his . . . uh . . . career? I guess you call it a career," Arthur asked him.

"Career, or ministry, is fine. . . . I don't think they meant it to be a reward for excellence in my case," John said, with a humorous grin. "I would much prefer to have served in foreign missions, or at a university. The active life, the intellectual environment . . . I suppose it's a selfish wish, but it has more appeal for me." He sighed. "Well, it looks like it'll be many years before either of those wishes is granted . . . if ever."

Arthur wanted to ask him why, but the priest rose then, closing himself off. Arthur knew it was time for him to leave. They agreed to speak to each other after Arthur had seen some of the families.

"I'll call you to let you know how it's going," Arthur said. "Good-bye, John."

Father John stood at the door, his hand raised in farewell, watching Arthur drive down the hill.

Over the following three weeks, Arthur managed to see all five families on Father John's list. This meant more than forty people, because each family had so many children . . . none less than five. The children had rickets, head lice, worms, scalp fungus, conjunctivitis, anemia, ringworm, impetigo, and ulcerative colitis. They were all malnourished. Most of them were filthy, with no sense of sanitation.

The mothers were either pregnant or nursing an infant, old beyond their years, dull-eyed and slack-jawed, ground down with work and worries. The fathers were somber, desperate men, painfully thin, red-eyed, coughing constantly until they were in danger of tearing the linings of their lungs or separating a rib. They wheezed when they weren't coughing. Unable to work because of miner's asthma, they were sick, anxiety-ridden people who had lost all hope.

Arthur had never, even in his clinical training days in south Philadelphia, seen anything like this. He was appalled. Someone had to *do* something—the companies, the union, the city, the Church! How could he have grown up here, unaware that this sort of poverty and deprivation existed in Wyoming Valley?

At least he was able to help a little. He diagnosed two cases of tuberculosis and arranged for them to be sent to the state sanitarium at White Haven. He called Tom Mooney at the Public Health Department and set up a schedule for a visiting nurse to go to the houses twice a week to examine the children and to teach the mothers how to better care for their broods. She would get rid of the lice, the scabies, and impetigo. But who would heal the diseases of the spirit from which these people suffered?

Arthur spoke often to John Riordan, sometimes visiting him after his house calls to the miners' families. He stayed for dinner now and then. John's housekeeper was a motherly woman who was happy when the priest had company.

Over the winter, the miners' plight was so pathetic that Arthur would be depressed for days after visiting any of them. He collected clothes, blankets, and medicines from his family and friends and gave them to Father John for the parishioners.

He got hold of a bottle of Irish whiskey from a patient who was a bootlegger and took it to John Riordan a week before Christmas. The residence didn't look any the cheerier for the season, but there was a fire going in the study.

Arthur had an idea of organizing a group of volunteer doctors to hold a clinic once a month, to identify the real problem cases in the community. He knew there were TB and cardiac cases. There must be cancer. And he would really like to know what percentage of the miners was suffering from severe lung disorders.

"I'd like to get the mine owners to finance a health project, John, but I doubt I'd get anywhere with that . . ."

Father John was listening with growing excitement. This was just the sort of thing he would love to do, had dreamed of doing. But he needed the cooperation of someone like Arthur Hillman to bring it to reality.

"Maybe we can use the parish house for the clinic, Arthur. I think I can do it without permission from my superiors. I don't know. . . . Let me think it through for a while."

The two friends were happy as they parted, their heads full of plans for starting a clinic in the beginning of 1929.

But it wasn't going to be all that easy.

Wilkes-Barre December 1928

"We're all going to the Wolf's Head dinner dance on New Year's Eve, Arthur. Get yourself a girl, because you're going, too!" Flannery directed him one afternoon in the St. Anne's staff room. Wolf's Head was the golf club they all belonged to.

"There's no one I want to take to that thing," he grumbled.

"If you don't come up with someone, *we* will, so better get out the old address book," Jim teased as he waved good-bye.

A few nights later, Arthur was reading in bed when the phone rang. "Did I wake you?" said a familiar, throaty, female voice. Chessy. He hadn't seen Chessy for months—not since his last trip to Philadelphia.

"No, you didn't wake me, Chessy. Matter of fact, I was just thinking about you!"

"I received the message." Her low laugh was full of innuendo.

Chessy's arrival in Wilkes-Barre did not go unnoted. For one thing, her hair was now a flaming red. Her chauffeur deposited Chessy and a vast assortment of luggage on Arthur's doorstep right in the middle of Monday afternoon office hours.

"Good Lord, Chessy, you're not staying *here!*" Arthur felt the heat rise in his cheeks as two stern-faced middle-aged women sitting in his waiting room craned their necks to see what was taking place in the outer vestibule. "I've put you up with friends . . . Phoebe and Lowell Wintermuth . . . here, let me give your chauffeur the directions to their house. I'll call Phoebe and warn . . . uh . . . tell . . . her you're on the way. I'll see you over there just as soon as I finish up here."

Chessy arched an eyebrow and planted a kiss on his lips before taking her leave. She had started to rouge her lips, he noticed, as he used his handkerchief to wipe the rosy smudge away.

"Arthur! She's a vision!"

Arthur looked around, startled. It was Joan Lang, one of his sister Dorothy's best friends. He groaned inwardly. They were standing side by side on the edge of the ballroom floor at Wolf's Head, watching the dancing couples. Chessy was doing a subdued (for Chessy) rhumba with Jim Flannery, the best dancer in town. Her hips swayed subtly under her clinging chiffon gown, a restrained sexiness at which Chessy excelled. Every male eye in the room was on her, the women casting sidelong glances, making elaborate attempts not to appear to be staring.

She was a vision, all right. The simplicity of the rich green bare-shouldered sheath was adorned by a single piece of jewelry—a magnificent emerald and diamond necklace whose fob rested in the soft cleft between her breasts. She and Jim danced well together. Chessy's long, slim arms, encased in elbow-length white kid, swept in an arc of extravagant gestures whenever Jim went into one of his complicated breaks.

That hair! Only Chessy could've come up with a color so obviously *faux*, so superbly right with her costume. Well, if the town liked to talk, she was certainly giving them something to talk about!

Like a brush fire, word of Chessy swept through the valley. Arthur's telephone rang at 9:00 A.M. on New Year's Day. It was Dorothy.

"Good morning, Arthur," she trilled. "Happy New Year."

Too groggy to think straight, he said, "What time is it?"

"I thought you might come for lunch, and bring your girl friend," she answered in an accusing tone. "Did I wake you?" she added as an afterthought.

"Damn right!" He yawned and squinted at the clock. "*Dot* . . . do you know how few mornings I can sleep past six o'clock? I didn't get in until four!"

"Sorry," she answered breezily. "Go back to sleep now. See you at noon." She hung up.

It had to be the first time Turkish pajamas were seen in Wilkes-Barre. Worn with a carnelian-red Chinese silk brocaded jacket, the wide-legged black velvet pants brought polite gasps from some of Dorothy's and Oscar's conservative guests.

Arthur had gasped, himself, when Chessy appeared unexpectedly at his apartment that morning.

"The door was unlocked," she offered as she entered his bedroom swathed in black monkey fur, a cloche of raven feathers all but covering the bright bob.

Ignoring his discomfiture, she appraised the sparse furnishings with a discerning eye and sniffed. "I hadn't imagined you in these surroundings, Arthur. You need Persian colors—reds . . . and dark blues—*definitely* blues."

He let out his breath. "Chessy, would you be good enough to sit in the living room?"

"Why, *ever,* darling? This room is fine!"

Arthur shifted uncomfortably under the covers. "Chessy . . . I have nothing on."

"*Good!* That's the way I like you *best!*"

"Now . . . be a good girl, Francesca . . . *Chessy!*"

Sometime later, she sighed . . . a soft, most un-Chessy sound. "You're really *quite* wonderful, you know. Somewhere, there is a nice, sweet, *horribly* dull woman who is going to be lucky enough to marry you. . . . The pity of it is, she probably won't know what to *do* with you once she has you!"

Arthur expected a phone call from his mother. He had no doubt that both Frieda and Dorothy had described Chessy in elaborate detail—the eye paint, the rouged lips, the extravagant costumes, the lavender cigarettes in the long silver holder—but Rose said nothing when they spoke by telephone, nor at dinner when he went there on Friday evening the following week.

Only after Arthur had walked Isaac back to his house and Jacob had retired for the night did Rose broach the subject. They sat in the sitting room, just the two of them.

"You know, dear," she said in a mild voice, "a young bachelor doctor is at a disadvantage in a community like this. You are expected to be above reproach in your behavior. I personally think it's unfair, but appearances are important to other people. Some of them might be your patients."

Arthur laughed. "I figured you'd get word of it! Chessy is a *nice* person, Mother—a little dramatic for Wilkes-Barre, maybe. She's a good friend of mine . . . divorced. . . . Somehow, even in Philadelphia, which is a conservative city, she doesn't create as much of a fuss as she seems to have done here." He chuckled, then added confidingly, "To tell you the truth, I think she went out of her way to do it."

"Arthur, you're a grown man, and you're entitled to a private life. But when you're just starting out, you have to consider the conventions . . . and the opinions of others."

Arthur rose to leave. "Don't worry, Mother. It won't happen again. That was sort of a 'last act' for Chessy, anyway. She's going abroad for an extended stay." He kissed Rose's cheek. "I can't seem to find anyone in town to take out—at least, no one I enjoy being with."

At the door, Rose said, "Arthur, I am aware of what you've done for us . . . what you've given up to come back here. Not only professionally—I'm afraid it's a most unexciting life for you. I wish it could've been any other way but this. . . ."

"Nonsense! I'm happy to be here, Mother. I have plenty of good times. There's always Scranton . . . and Hazleton!" Rose watched with troubled eyes through the curtained window as he drove away.

During the thirty-two years of her married life, Rose had lived in the house on Prospect Avenue with Jacob. Except for his hospitalization, they had been apart on only two occasions in all that time.

Rose could not awaken Jacob that winter morning when, after waiting for him to ring the bell that was his signal, she entered his room at ten o'clock. He was breathing quietly.

"Jacob. Jacob, dear?" She shook him gently. "Oh . . . please . . . Jacob, wake up!" She held him to her, kissed his face, on which her tears fell. Then she picked up the telephone and dialed Arthur's number.

An ambulance took Jacob to St. Anne's Hospital, where he remained in a coma for three days. And then it was over. His life finished, a month before his fifty-third birthday.

Such a short time to live. Yet, they had had a full, happy life together. Who was to say what was a better measure of life, length or quality? Her parents had been married for forty-five long years when her father died. An eternity, and none of it particularly happy.

Now, she must go on alone, without Jacob, when for all her life he had been her reason for wanting each day to begin anew. Rose did not weep easily. She dreaded a display of emotion before others. Stoic and dignified in public, she mourned in the privacy of her room.

She felt closer to her memories of Jacob when she was alone in the house she had shared with him.

II

Mountain Springs 1929

Cyril Buckland called his wife's cousin, William Matlin, M.D., just before dinner on a Thursday evening in February. The two were neighbors at Mountain Springs, that leafy enclave on Wyoming Mountain where a privileged few could abide in the bracken, secure in the knowledge that they wouldn't be disturbed by undesirable elements.

A guard at the gate ensured that only the expected and welcome could enter . . . and the prying eyes of those who may have wondered at the occasional small airplane that landed on the private airstrip in the gray hours before dawn were effectively prevented from satisfying their curiosity. Some of the eminent citizens of Mountain Springs would not have cared for the knowledge to get around that bootlegging traffic had an overground conduit of which Mountain Springs was a way station.

"Bill, why don't you stroll over here after dinner? Let's you and me have a drink together."

This wasn't an invitation, of course. It was a summons. William Matlin may have imagined himself to be a power in the medical community of Luzerne County, but here he was simply a poor relation to the wealthy Matlin-Buckland clan. He and Lydia lived there in Mountain Springs at the grace of Cyril and his wife, Martha—the only kindhearted Matlin of recent memory. Dr. Matlin lived in a house on the grounds of Buck Run, the Buckland estate, which overlooked a crystal lake fed by the pure potable water of Mountain Springs.

When William was shown into Cyril's study, he wondered what favor his benefactor was going to request of him—for he had no doubt that this sudden nighttime meeting had an intent and purpose. Cyril poured brandy into two large snifters, then settled himself in a comfortable chair.

"There's a young doctor in town by the name of Hillman," Cyril said. "Do you know him?"

Matlin, who never committed himself to anything without first getting the direction of the wind, answered cautiously. "Yes, I know him . . . he's a member of the Medical Society, of course. On staff at St. Anne's . . . I think he's a friend of Hobson Carpenter's."

"He's also a friend of my son-in-law, it seems. Don't know how *that* happened. A Jew, isn't he?"

"Yes, I believe he is. He's a nice enough young man, Cyril . . . well-liked. . . . Of course, as I say, I don't know him well. Why do you ask?"

"Do you know about the clinics he and some of his young doctor friends have been running?"

"Clinics?" Dr. Matlin looked worried. "No . . . can't say that I do. What kind of clinics?"

"For miners and their families. They spend a Saturday afternoon doing examinations, getting the people all upset about their health. Some of the men are complaining . . . saying that their lungs are diseased from working in the mines!" Cyril gestured with his glass of brandy, becoming agitated. "Now, isn't that prepost'rous? *Did* you ever hear anything so foolish? Next thing you know, they'll be suing the company for their medical bills. . . . Why, I bet that's what this is all about . . . those men are trying to drum up some business for themselves!"

William looked doubtful. "Oh, I don't know about that, Cyril. Where is the clinic held? In whose office?"

"I'll tell you where, and you can be sure Bishop Callahan is going to hear about this. In the parish house of Our Lady of the Mountain Roman Catholic Church in Ashley . . . and another one at Holy Rosary in Hanover. Since when does a parish priest have the right to use church property for that sort of thing?"

Dr. Matlin felt it unnecessary to answer Cyril's question. He waited.

"Bill, I want those clinics *stopped*. I'm having enough problems with the union's demands, without adding health care to the list."

"How . . . er . . . how do you suppose they can be stopped? The bishop . . . ?"

"No, not the bishop. . . . *You*, Bill." Cyril flashed a smile at him which glimmered briefly, like a flame, then went out.

Matlin rubbed his hands together nervously. "What can I do about them, Cyril? They're not breaking any laws, are they?"

"You're president of the Medical Society, Bill—I'll remind you that you have *me* to thank for that." Dr. Matlin looked extremely uncomfortable. "There must be some set of rules or regulations that are being broken . . . medical ethics . . . something like that. Create a stink. Drag them before your Ethics Committee . . . Hillman, Matt Flannery's boy, Jim—I'd really like to get that S.O.B. rabble-rousing Communist publisher—and Thomas Sloat, Henry's son. All young, wet behind the ears. Now, nothing harmful— after all, we don't want to make enemies with the Flannerys or the Sloats. They've got too many friends. Just a warning. Maybe they don't even realize what they're doing . . . ye-es, that's the tack to take. Young, naïve, inexperienced . . . now that they've been advised, they'll put an end to the clinics. You'll think of something."

"And if they don't stop?" Dr. Matlin asked.

"Then we'll just have to find a way to stop them, won't we?"

St. Anne's Hospital, Wilkes-Barre   Spring 1929

"Good morning, Dr. Hillman. Lovely day, isn't it?"

"Good morning to you, Sister Francis. Wonderful day. I feel like playing truant."

The nun returned his smile. She had an ageless face, devoid of wrinkles or lines of expression. Her eyes were pale behind steel-rimmed spectacles that grasped her sharp nose firmly at the bridge, leaving red indentations on either side. The spotless white habit flowed in graceful folds, unadorned, save for the rosary with an ornately carved crucifix which hung at the waist from her cincture. Her quiet hands, smooth and immaculate, were the only vanity she permitted herself. On the fourth finger of her left hand she wore the wedding band which symbolized her bond with the Savior. Her mild manner belied the fact that she ran the surgical floor like a martinet. The nurses were all in awe and fear of her.

Arthur consulted the patient charts she had ready for him. "How did Mrs. O'Malley do last night?"

"She had another restless night, Doctor. I gave her a quarter grain of morphine at midnight and again at four A.M. She seems more comfortable this morning." Arthur followed her to his patient's room.

Gently, Arthur removed the dressing from the incision on the young woman's abdomen. He had performed emergency surgery for a ruptured ectopic pregnancy almost a week ago. The patient, in her early thirties, with five young children, had been on the critical list for the first forty-eight hours after surgery. She had stabilized, and was now listed in guarded condition. Arthur knew that one of the main reasons for her survival was the devoted care of the sisters, who had remained with her around the clock ever since the surgery.

His chief problem now was to prevent serious postoperative infection. He was concerned because his patient had been running a fever since the operation. They had given her transfusions of whole blood, but she had lost so much blood from hemorrhage that she was still in an extremely weakened condition.

Arthur probed the site of the incision, regretting that he must cause her discomfort, but needing to determine whether there was tenderness that would indicate infection. "I'm sorry if I'm hurting you, Mrs. O'Malley," he said.

She bit her lip, but looked up at him with trusting eyes. "Am I going to be all right, Doctor?"

"You're going to be fine. . . . In a few days you'll feel much better. Now, does that hurt when I press? . . . No? What about this? . . . Mmm." He smiled and talked softly to her, trying to assuage her fears, as he fashioned a new dressing for the wound. He made a few notations on her chart, conferring with Sister Francis and the special nurse who was attending the woman —a nurse he knew her husband couldn't afford. He had arranged with the sisters to have the nurse's fee paid for by the hospital's Needy Patients Fund.

"How long do you think I'll be in the hospital, Dr. Hillman?" Mrs. O'Malley asked.

"We'll try to get you home to your family as soon as possible. I can't say exactly when, but it shouldn't be too long. I don't want you to worry about anything except getting well. Is that a promise?" He smiled at her as she nodded.

When they were out in the hall, he spoke to the private nurse. "Keep an eye on that drainage fluid and her vital signs, Miss Gage. Report any change immediately."

"Yes, Doctor. Anything by mouth?"

"Only spoonfuls of liquid today. We'll see how she tolerates those. I'd like to get that IV out as soon as possible."

Back at the desk, Arthur saw the black-habited figure of Sister Emmaline, the general supervisor of the hospital and his favorite of the St. Anne's nuns. Her eyes lit up when she saw him coming toward her.

"Ahh, Dr. Hillman! And how are you today?" The tight white coif and wimple pinched in the plump cheeks. She had merry, round features and a deep dimple in her chin. Everything about Sister Emmaline was hustle-bustle. She seemed to be in constant movement and constant good humor.

"I'm fine, thank you, Sister Emmaline. How's yourself?" Sister Emmaline always made him feel like smiling. He noticed there was a new nurse behind the nurse's station, speaking on the telephone, sitting half-turned with her back to them. She wore the double-banded pleated cap on top of her dark hair, which meant that she had graduated from one of the elite nursing colleges run by the Sisters of Mercy. Trim in her starched white uniform, Arthur couldn't help but notice her slender, well-formed legs. He glanced away and met the alert eyes of the cherubic nun.

At that moment the nurse hung up and turned in the swivel chair. She rose respectfully when she saw them.

"I don't believe you've met the new nurse for this service, Dr. Hillman. This is Miss Shea."

"How do you do, Miss Shea."

"How do you do, Dr. Hillman."

She was easily the most beautiful woman he had ever seen. She wore her shining black hair softly waved in a fashionable bob. The natural high coloring in her molded cheeks gave her flawless complexion the appearance of one who has just come from a brisk walk in the autumn wind. Exquisitely shaped, her mouth had lips too generous and resolute to be called delicate. The short nose was slightly tilted at its tip, with small indentations above each nostril creating a sculptured effect. Straight dark brows framed her most outstanding feature—eyes so vividly blue they looked violet under the thick, curling lashes.

Arthur realized he was staring. Sheepishly, he smiled, groping for words. "Where have you been nursing before coming to St. Anne's, Miss Shea?"

"I've been at St. Patrick's in Dublin for the past year. Before that, I was at Mount Mercy." Her tone was correct, neither containing nor lacking warmth.

"A fine background!" He nodded. "Good luck to you here." He turned and walked down the hall with Sister Emmaline.

Miss Shea watched until they had turned the corner to the elevator. With an impatient shake of her head, she returned to her work.

A few days later, Jim Flannery and Tom Sloat were sitting in the doctors' lounge at the hospital having coffee. "Hey, Jim, d'you see the new nurse on surgical? She's a knockout!"

"So's your wife, Sloat," Jim reminded him cheerfully.

"Killjoy."

Arthur walked in and joined them at the table. He pulled out his memo pad to make a few notes to himself about the patients he had seen on his rounds.

"Here's our eligible bachelor." Tom clapped Arthur on the shoulder. "Go to it, Hillman!"

"Go to what, Tom?" Arthur asked pleasantly.

"We were just talking about the new RN on surgical. Have you met her?"

"Miss Shea? Yes, I've met her. Why?"

"Gorgeous, isn't she?"

Arthur shrugged noncommittally. He thought Tom Sloat was far too enthusiastic about nurses for a married man. Arthur had never liked sitting around talking about nurses the way some of his young colleagues did. It made him feel uncomfortable. He was aware that some of the men thought he was a prude.

"Yes, she is, but you know the rules, fellas. 'No doctor-nurse fraternization.'" His tone mocked Clara, the nurse directress at Jeff, whom they all knew from their student days, an easy prey for mimicry because of her distinctive nasal voice. They all laughed appreciatively.

"C'mon, Art, we're not med students now . . . they aren't really *rules* anymore. I wouldn't let a little thing like that stand in my way if I were in your shoes," said Dr. Sloat.

Jim Flannery rose to leave. "Lucky thing for Molly Shea you're not in his shoes, then."

"Molly? Do you know her?" asked Tom, interested.

"Yeah. Our families are old friends. Well, so long. I've got to make some calls before office hours. See you tonight at the Medical Society meeting?"

"You bet, Jim. I'm counting on you guys for moral support. The clinic proposal comes up tonight," said Arthur.

"It'll sail through, Art," Jim assured him as he left them.

Tom had a patient he wanted Arthur to see, a man with chronic bronchial spasms. Arthur already had a reputation for being the person in the valley to call when you had a question about pulmonary problems.

"Is he a miner, Tom?"

"No, he's a factory worker. He makes insulation materials."

Arthur suspected that with lack of air purity in industry, if a worker didn't wear a mask, fibers such as those used in insulating material could cause chronic irritation of the lungs. "I'll be happy to see him, Tom. Have him give me a call."

"You really worried about the clinic endorsement tonight, Arthur?" Tom asked.

"A little. You see, I hope this clinic is just the beginning, Tom. I'd like to develop diagnostic clinics for routine health care on an industry-wide basis," Arthur told him.

Tom snorted. "You won't get far on *that* one, Art. The AMA is against anything that smacks of social medicine. They'll say you're a Bolshevik!"

"They're nuts! And shortsighted, to boot. Trouble is that anyone who gets involved in policy-making in the AMA is usually more politician than physician," Arthur said heatedly.

Tom squinted at him. "You turning into a crusader, Art?"

"Could be," he answered, standing up and stretching. "I better get going. See you tonight, Tom."

Arthur checked at the switchboard for messages, then headed for the side door to the parking lot. Miss Shea was coming down the stairway, so he held the door for her.

"Thank you, Dr. Hillman."

What a smile! Tom was right. She's gorgeous! "How are things going on surgical, Miss Shea?"

"Just fine. Sister Francis smiled at me this morning," was the pert reply.

He laughed. "That's some kind of a record, I'd say." He looked up at the sky. "Nice day."

"Yes. I'm going to have a quick lunch and then take a walk if there's time."

She had the most incredible eyes. . . . Should he? No, better not. You know the "rules" . . . and there's more than one game to play in this town, he reminded himself.

"Have a nice walk. I'll see you around." He got into his car and waved as he drove away.

Driving uptown, Arthur couldn't get her beautiful face out of his mind. Why shouldn't he ask her out? If it were Philadelphia, he would. It wasn't the doctor-nurse thing. That was nonsense. It was his family and the town—Wilkes-Barre. The gossip mill, the prying eyes. It would be next to impossible for him to take Miss Shea out, even for dinner and a movie, without half a dozen people he knew seeing them. That would mean each one of those would tell half a dozen more and . . . the mathematical projections were infinite! Mostly, it would get back to his family. After the Chessy business, better leave it alone.

He sighed as he pulled up to his office. Lot of people coming this afternoon . . . Medical Society meeting tonight . . . *I wonder if Miss Shea has a boy friend . . . beautiful girl like that must have a dozen men falling in love with her. Molly . . . was that what Jim said her name was?*

He ran up the steps to his office, his mind now on the patients who were waiting for him.

William Matlin, M.D., handed the gavel to Charles Means, the first vice-president of the Luzerne County Medical Society.

"Gentlemen. I wish to take this unusual step to comment on the agenda item now before us . . ."

Arthur's heart sank as the pompous physician began to speak. This was the end of their clinic, he could see. They couldn't possibly continue to run it without the endorsement, or at least the tacit approval, of the Medical Society. And William Matlin, its president, was a formidable opponent.

". . . and so, gentlemen, in 1925—before your time here, Dr. Hillman, and therefore I can understand your not being aware of this—the society condemned the practice of 'contract medicine,' that is, the care of an entire family for a fixed fee over a period of time. It was to hold the physician above the station of a common service person—a plumber, if you will—that the society took this action. And now, your proposal undermines that carefully constructed arrangement by servicing the miners and their families, not for a fixed fee, but"—he paused dramatically, and chuckled—"*for no fee at all!*"

There was a buzz of conversation in the rear of the meeting room. Dr. Means rapped for order.

"You are establishing yourselves as something akin to a garage mechanic by doing this, and, at the same time, bringing down the esteem in which the medical doctor is held in this community. Let us, I pray, leave social medicine to the masses in Bolshevik countries!"

Several other members were waving their hands for recognition. Hobson Carpenter rose. As a former president of the society, Dr. Carpenter commanded respect.

"Dr. Hillman, I wonder if we may ask you to fill us in on the background for this proposal. How did you come to make it, and what do you hope to accomplish if the plan is approved?"

Bless Hob Carpenter! Arthur went to the front of the room.

"Thank you, Dr. Carpenter." He flashed a grateful smile. "As a new physician opening my practice, I, more than occasionally, have patients from the poorest of the mining communities. I reserve a certain part of my practice for indigent people who cannot afford to pay for my services." He turned to Matlin. "If that goes against the guidelines of medical practice set up by this society, I sincerely regret it, Dr. Matlin. That is, I regret the *guidelines*. Because it is my belief that every physician owes it to his community to serve without compensation where the need is greatest. We are all charitable men, I'm sure. Using the skills I have learned in medicine and not charging those who can't afford to pay is an act of charity and in no way demeans either *my* station nor the station of my colleagues."

William Matlin was looking down, shuffling papers. Arthur continued speaking.

"One miner would tell another, and before I knew it, I was besieged with miners who needed medical care. Most of them suffer from diseases of the lung. My special interest, as some of you know, is chest medicine. There is no thoracic medicine practiced in Wyoming Valley, so I believe I have not been depriving anyone but myself of income if I don't charge these poor men. In any case, it would be pointless to send a bill. They don't have the funds to buy milk for their children, food for their families, or a winter coat for a wife.

"Gentlemen . . . I have recently completed three years of internship and residency in Philadelphia, where I served on ambulance duty in the poorest sections of that city. I have delivered babies in filthy kitchens, sewed up wounds by candlelight, brought people out of seizures and suicidal comas in the meanest tenements imaginable. And yet, I have seen the worst poverty and the most deplorable health conditions, not in a Philadelphia slum, but *right here in Wyoming Valley,* in a miner's shack up on the mountain, where the dishwater is frozen in the sink on a winter's morning and the windows are covered with nothing but cardboard to keep out the icy wind." Arthur paused. The room was completely still, every man's attention focused on him.

He went on quietly. "In our first two clinics, we diagnosed fifteen cases of miner's asthma, five stenotic hearts, seven tubercular patients who were sent to state sanitaria, a breast cancer, two streptococcal infections of the throat with rheumatic complications in the same family. Those are just the cases that come to mind. There were any number of children with head lice . . . they all suffer from malnutrition.

"Each of these was a patient who would otherwise not have been seen by a doctor. Many of them represent threats to the health of the community, as in the case of schoolchildren with TB . . ." He went on to describe the clinic procedure, outlining their plans for rotating the clinics in different mining areas. He emphasized the medical participation, trying not to call attention to Father John's role.

"The only doctors who gave their time to these patients were those who volunteered their services. They take nothing away from other physicians by doing so, and I believe they have performed a valuable service for this community."

Arthur sat down. The room was so quiet that he was sure he had not won their support.

Hobson Carpenter asked, "Does anyone have anything to add to what Dr. Hillman has told us?"

Both Jim Flannery and Tom Sloat spoke briefly in support of Arthur's proposal.

"Thank you, gentlemen," said Dr. Carpenter. The tall, distinguished physician's gaze moved across the room as he spoke, engaging the eyes of his colleagues. "That was as fine an example of the best that the medical profession has to offer as I have ever heard! You are to be commended, in my opinion, on your high ideals and fine service to these patients. I would like now to move that this society give its enthusiastic and unanimous endorsement to the project set before it in Item Three."

There was a clamor of "Seconds . . ." and the resolution passed unanimously, with William Matlin, as president, abstaining.

Flushed with victory, Arthur, Jim, and Tom accepted congratulations at the smoker after the meeting. Arthur went over to Hobson Carpenter.

"Dr. Carpenter, I owe you a debt of gratitude for what you did tonight. Thank you. I'll never forget your support."

"Arthur, I wish there were more like you around. It was a glad day when you decided to come back to the valley. I want you to keep me abreast of those clinics . . . let me know if I can help in any way."

What a guy, Arthur thought, as he shook hands with Carpenter. It was people like him who made it a joy to be in medicine.

It was unfortunate that he seemed to have further alienated himself from the influential Dr. Matlin.

William Matlin's private telephone rang at half-past midnight. "Well?" said a familiar voice.

"It passed . . . unanimously."

Cyril Buckland uttered an oath. "I can see that we're going to have to teach your young Dr. Hillman a lesson, Bill."

"Now, Cyril," said Matlin, nervously. "Don't you want to think about this for a while? And he's not 'my' Dr. Hillman . . . I hardly know the man."

"Then you shouldn't be too concerned about him," replied Buckland.

"What are you going to do, Cyril?"

"Never you mind, Bill. Just leave it to me. Good night, Bill. Sleep well," said the president of Wyoming and Susquehanna Coal & Navigation in a soft voice.

During Lent the sisters were on retreat. For the week before Easter many of them retired to the mother house, except for a few who remained at the hospital to perform essential duties.

Arthur was still doing some surgery, but he was gradually growing away from it. He was finding that interaction with his patients was becoming more and more important to him. He enjoyed the human contact of his necessarily general practice. The surgical techniques which had fully absorbed him in Philadelphia were useful in his practice, but not enough to sustain his interest here. Too cold, too impersonal.

The chest. That was his abiding interest. Internal medicine, with heavy emphasis on cardiopulmonary disease. That's what he would specialize in, if he could afford not to have a general practice, he would tell himself in moments of self-appraisal.

Fat chance, with all the bills I owe, he chided himself on Friday night as he prepared to go to bed early. It had been a rough week and he was hoping to get a good solid night's sleep.

An hour later, the telephone rang, startling him awake. He groped for the receiver in the dark, pulling himself up to a half-sitting position.

"Dr. Hillman speaking." His voice sounded gravelly.

It was a woman, a nice voice, efficient and apologetic. "I'm sorry to disturb you, Dr. Hillman. This is Miss Shea at St. Anne's. Your patient, Mrs. O'Malley. I'm afraid she's taken a bad turn. I think she's going into shock."

He was instantly alert, as if someone had thrown cold water in his face. "Who's on service, Miss Shea?"

"Wagner. But he's in surgery. Sister Francis is on retreat this week. The 'special' just left and her replacement hasn't shown up. I'm off duty now, so I can stay with the patient."

"Thank you, Miss Shea. I'll be there in a few minutes."

He pulled on a pair of slacks and a sweater, and was in his car within five minutes, racing along the empty, quiet streets.

His mind went back to the frantic late-night telephone summons from Mrs. O'Malley's distraught husband two weeks ago . . . the shabby house . . . the scattered toys . . . the odor of soiled diapers . . . the pain and panic on the young mother's pale face.

He had almost given up hope in the operating room when he saw the abdomen, filled with blood and the products of conception. He'd suctioned out the cavity, removed the ruptured fallopian tube, and in examining the remaining tube noticed signs of inflammation. . . . She was thirty-three, had five living children, and there'd been two miscarriages. . . . Looking at those tubes, he'd wondered about back-room abortions. If he left it in, she could develop infection there . . . or another tubal pregnancy. . . . His eyes had met those of Sister Francis over their surgical masks. . . . *Well?* his had asked. Slowly, she had nodded, and Arthur had removed the second fallopian tube. . . .

Mrs. O'Malley had been doing so well, better than he'd expected . . . she couldn't die now!

When he reached the silent hospital, he ran up the stairs to the surgical floor instead of waiting for the elevator.

Miss Shea was with Mrs. O'Malley. She had raised the foot of the bed on shock blocks and added several blankets to those already covering the patient, who looked faint and damp with perspiration. Arthur noticed that the nurse had brought an oxygen tank in and had it standing by. She was taking the woman's temperature and blood pressure when he entered the room. As a nurse, she could do nothing else without a doctor's orders. She was obviously relieved to see him.

"Pressure?" he asked.

"Seventy over forty-eight." Her voice was firm and in control. He was glad of that. Many nurses would panic in a situation like this. He inserted his stethoscope in his ears, then took the bulb from her and pumped it up.

"Get an intravenous with plasma," he instructed as he placed an oxygen mask over Mrs. O'Malley's pale face. "See if we can set up a donor for whole blood, Miss Shea. Find out if Wagner is free yet. If not, see whether any of the other house staff are available, even if they're off duty. I'm going to have to go in . . . she may have developed an abscess or internal bleeding."

"Yes, Doctor." Miss Shea hurried from the room.

Damn, damn, damn! I was afraid of this. If only the O'Malleys had called him a few hours sooner, before that tube had ruptured and spilled everything into the abdomen. He took his patient's wrist in his fingers for a brief few seconds, looking at his watch. Bad. He raised her eyelids, shining a small light into her eyes.

Miss Shea came back in, bringing the intravenous apparatus. They would have to get her out of shock before he could open the incision and see what had happened. Maybe the drain had kinked. . . .

The next hour was a nightmare. No time to wait for another surgeon to assist. He had only minutes to spare before he lost her.

"Will you scrub, Miss Shea?"

"Yes, Dr. Hillman. I can assist. I called Sister Theresa. She'll do anesthesia." Sister Theresa had recently come to St. Anne's. Arthur hadn't known she was a nurse-anesthetist. It was a good thing that Nurse Shea had still been on the floor when this happened. She had prepared the OR, aroused the sleeping Sister who administered inhalation anesthesia, and alerted Dr. Wagner to come up as soon as he could leave his present emergency.

In the end, it was the three of them . . . Sister Theresa, with Arthur operating and Miss Shea acting as both instrument nurse and surgical assistant—holding retractors, clamping hemostats, handling sponges, cutting sutures as expertly as any good resident might have done. He was grateful for her quiet, supportive presence. She sensed what he would need before he could ask for it. She was quick and efficient. For a slender woman, she was amazingly strong, helping him to move the patient with ease, carefully gentle.

It was just their luck to have this happen in the dead of night on the weekend before Easter, when the hospital was short-staffed. There was an unusual combination of events—Miss Shea told him that one of the interns had a family emergency, while several had taken vacation. He'd have to see how that had been allowed to happen. . . .

It was an abscess, on the posterior wall of the uterus. Arthur drained it carefully, examining the cavity to be certain there was no other site of infection or sign of bleeding. He closed up, hopeful that the septicemia which had thrown her into shock would now abate. . . . At best, it would be a long convalescence.

Jerry Wagner, the resident, a recent graduate from Temple, came in as they were wheeling Mrs. O'Malley back to her room. The floor nurse said, "Dr. Hillman, Mrs. O'Malley's 'special' just called. She said she's ill. I've called for another nurse."

"See that the 'special,' whoever she is, is dropped from our registry," he snapped. "She should have called hours ago."

In Mrs. O'Malley's room, he eased himself into a chair, laying his head back. The patient was out of anesthesia. He'd done all he could for the moment. Now it was a matter of waiting. He glanced at his watch—three o'clock. He closed his eyes.

Miss Shea was at his side, touching his shoulder. "Would you like some tea, Dr. Hillman?" She handed him a cup. He sipped the hot liquid. It felt good, strengthening. He smiled up at her gratefully.

"Thanks. That's good."

"Why don't you go into the residents' room and lie down? I'll stay here with the patient. If there's any change, I'll call you."

"Oh, I don't know . . ." he began.

"Really, Doctor. I don't mind. I'm off for the weekend, so I can sleep late."

It sure was tempting. He was exhausted. Miss Shea and the resident would keep an eye on her. "All right. Thank you, Miss Shea. I really appreciate your help."

Mrs. O'Malley stirred, opening her eyes. "How are you feeling, Mrs. O'Malley?" Molly asked.

She was weak. "So tired . . . my side hurts . . . is the doctor here?"

"Yes. He'll be in shortly." Molly checked her pulse and pressure. "You're doing very well, Mrs. O'Malley. Your pressure is good," she said reassuringly. The woman drifted off again.

Molly went to the small room where there were two cots for residents who were on night duty. Dr. Hillman was asleep, his head turned toward the door. In the dim light from the hall, she thought he looked much younger. He was such a handsome man, so strong and masculine-looking. Yet, there was a sensitivity about him. She had the craziest desire to reach out and touch his face. He was a magnificent doctor. Wonderful to work with. They had been a good team.

"Dr. Hillman," she said in a clear, low voice. He didn't move. "Dr. Hillman," she repeated, now moving to his side and touching his arm. He opened his eyes. Realizing where he was, he sat up.

"How is Mrs. O'Malley?"

"She's improving, Doctor. She woke up and was asking for you."

He went to his patient's room. She was sound asleep, breathing evenly. Her color and vital signs were good. It looked like she was going to make it.

He glanced up to meet the dark blue eyes of Nurse Shea. They smiled at each other in relief.

"I think I can leave now. What about you, Miss Shea? You should really get some sleep. I can't tell you how grateful I am to you. If you hadn't been here and acted so quickly, we would have lost her."

Miss Shea shook her head. "You saved her life, Dr. Hillman."

"I couldn't have done it without your help, Miss Shea. You are one helluva good nurse!"

It may have been unprofessional, but he thought Miss Shea looked especially beautiful when she blushed.

Arthur caught up with Miss Shea, who was walking down the hall to the elevator, carrying an overnight case.

"Let me carry that for you."

"It's not heavy," she replied, but he took it from her anyway.

"Not going back to the Nurses' Residence?" The elevator arrived and he stood aside for her to enter first.

"No. I was on my way home to Forty Fort for the weekend when all this happened."

"I'm sorry. I've ruined your weekend. You'll be exhausted tomorrow."

She brushed aside his apology. "I'm not even tired, Doctor."

He noticed again how lovely she was. She'd been up half the night after working an eight-hour shift, yet she looked luminous.

"I'll drive you home, Miss Shea. That's the least I can do."

When they crossed over the Susquehanna to Kingston, he said, "I don't know about you, but I'm hungry. Shall we have some breakfast?" Without waiting for her answer, he stopped at an all-night diner.

They ordered bacon and eggs, homemade corn muffins, and the coffee that always seems to be better in diners than anywhere else. And then, another cup of coffee.

She had a quick mind, as her handling of the emergency had indicated. She seemed interested in everything he talked about—medicine, Jefferson, Philadelphia, baseball, politics. . . . Arthur found himself leaning forward, smiling into her face, laughing at her small, subtle jokes. He watched her expressive features as she talked. She had the most unearthly skin, velvety and translucent. Totally devoid of makeup, it was flawless, wanting to be touched. Her dark, thick lashes shadowed her cheeks when she looked down. Those fabulous eyes! They had a gamine quality, slightly tip-tilted at the corners.

She became aware of his scrutiny and flushed a little, then stopped talking and looked down at her coffee cup.

"I must compliment you again on the way you handled things tonight. I intend to tell the sisters about it."

"Thank you, Dr. Hillman."

"Do you think you could call me Arthur?" he asked.

"Not at the hospital, I couldn't," she laughed.

"We're not at the hospital now . . . Molly."

Dawn was spreading over the horizon when they drove up to her mother's house on Sunset Lane in Forty Fort. Molly quickly got out of the car before he came around to open the door.

"Thank you." She smiled up at him. "I'll see you on Monday. Good night . . ." They both laughed. "Good *morning!*"

And she was gone. He drove back to his apartment, wishing the last hour was just beginning.

He would like to call her, ask her out. But he knew he wouldn't. There was something about living in the same town with his mother that inhibited him, he decided. . . .

He called the hospital before going to bed, just to be sure that Mrs. O'Malley remained stable. The last thing he thought of before falling asleep was the way Molly Shea had looked when they knew their patient would live.

This had been a good day, Arthur thought, as he left St. Anne's after his afternoon rounds. Mrs. O'Malley had been discharged. What a glow he had, seeing her leave in the wheelchair with her husband, all smiles, a really nice-looking young woman, now that this ordeal was over.

"Dr. Hillman," O'Malley had said, tears springing to his eyes. "We owe you everything! You saved her life. And now we don't have to worry about this happening again."

"That other tube was infected, Mr. O'Malley. I couldn't be certain when I removed it that it would cause problems, but the site of the abscess leaves no doubt. Your wife is lucky to be alive . . . and I couldn't be happier about it."

Sister Emmaline had told him that she'd arranged for a visiting nurse to put Mrs. O'Malley on her schedule for the next few weeks. And their local priest had recommended a high school girl who would help with the children and housework for a while until she was back on her feet.

Arthur drove up to Ashley to make a house call. John Riordan was expecting him to drop by to discuss the health clinics after that. They were getting calls from all the parishes in mining communities requesting them to hold clinics. Father John had received some modest contributions to pay for medical supplies. Isaac Hillman had donated money, as had the Flannerys and Sloats, and Tom Mooney at the Health Department had assigned a public health nurse to assist them, as well as sending them vaccines and culture material.

He pulled up in front of Our Lady of the Mountain as a splendid red sun was setting. A woman came down the steps of the rectory, walking toward him. It was Molly Shea.

"Hello, Molly! What are you doing way out here?"

"I came to see Father Riordan. . . . I might ask you the same question." She still avoided the use of his first name.

"And I'd have to give you the same answer. I came to talk about a clinic we're running in the parish for the miners."

Her eyes lit up. "He told me about that. I think it's wonderful, what you're doing." She opened the door to a black Chevrolet.

"Red-letter day today," he said, wanting to prolong the encounter. "Mrs. O'Malley went home."

"Yes! Isn't that the best news? I saw her to say good-bye before I went off duty. You're her hero, you know." Did every nurse look like that when she talked about a case with a happy ending? "I must be getting home. I borrowed my brother's car and I promised I'd bring it back soon. 'Bye."

He was sorry to see her go. He wondered again why she'd come all the way to Ashley to see a priest.

The dark, cheerless interior of the rectory always struck him as unnecessarily grim. Couldn't the poor fellow do his job just as well if he had a pleasant place to live, a few basic comforts? It might even improve his performance.

"I met one of our nurses outside," he mentioned.

"Oh, yeah. Molly. She's my sister Katherine's daughter."

"Molly Shea is your *niece?* No kidding! That's a surprise."

"Why such a surprise?"

He was embarrassed, but had to say something. "Jim Flannery told me her family is influential in Church circles."

Father John nodded. "And, you're wondering, if that's so, what am I doing here in Ashley?" He laughed.

"Yeah," Arthur admitted. "I guess that's what I meant."

"In a word, pride. I am too proud, too self-indulgent, too ambitious, and I question doctrine. I need discipline. I had the temerity to ask whether I could go for a doctorate with the Jesuits. My bishop did not like that."

"Why not? I would think that would be a commendable quality in a priest, scholarship. Parish priest material must be the easiest thing to come by."

"The bishop is from the school of hard knocks. He thinks the Church has to guard against elitism. My family isn't poor enough for his taste. We have too many monsignors scattered around in our midst. I think he doesn't want to risk having me aspire to such lofty goals. . . . If he only knew, I haven't the slightest desire to be a bishop. My only real ambition was to do something active, something more challenging. Like education or foreign missions." John let out a sigh. "The one thing I was not eager to do was to become a parish priest. . . .

"But, you know something? I'm finding it more and more to my liking these days, Arthur. These clinics—for the first time, I get the feeling that I'm able to do something concrete for my people here. For the first time, I can offer them something more than words and platitudes. I guess you could say this is missionary work. God knows, they couldn't be more miserable, more in need of help!"

"I've got to agree with you there, John," Arthur replied. "Little by little, though, I think we're making a difference in their lives. It's just a beginning."

When they had finished planning the next clinic, Father John asked Arthur to stay for dinner, but he had to get back for evening office hours. For the same reason, he declined a cocktail.

He felt sorry for the priest as he left. It seemed such a lonely life.

Arthur slowed his steps as he walked up the incline of Prospect Avenue with Isaac. They had joined Rose for dinner, as they usually did on Friday evenings.

Isaac had taken Jacob's death courageously, but it had aged him. Breathing heavily from the effort of walking up the hilly sidewalk, he asked, "You came home of your own free will, my boy?"

"Yes, Grandfather. No one asked me to come back. I came because it was the only thing to do."

"I regret that you couldn't stay in Philadelphia. . . ."

"I don't. I did at first, but I'm having a wonderful time with my practice here. There's something very nice about walking down a street and knowing most everyone you meet."

"You haven't married yet. . . ." Isaac left it dangling.

"No . . . there really isn't anyone I want to marry," he answered.

"The young woman in Philadelphia?"

"She married someone else. I couldn't seem to decide to marry her." He gave his grandfather a half-regretful smile in the darkness.

"Then maybe it wasn't meant to be, Arthur. You should go into a marriage as if it's forever . . . with no doubts."

They had reached Isaac's doorstep. He turned and put his hand on Arthur's shoulder. "Arthur, I want you to know that your mother will be well provided for. Although I've turned over the business to Jonas, I have left most of my estate to Rose." His voice had roughened.

Arthur was moved. "Thank you, Grandfather. . . . I have so much to thank you for."

Wilkes-Barre

It was one of those wonderful sunny Sunday afternoons in May. An ideal time to go riding or play golf, but Arthur decided to stay around his apartment in case he had a call. His practice wasn't so well established that he could afford to miss a patient. He thought of changing out of his new three-piece gray suit.

The telephone rang. One of John Riordan's parishioners was calling from a neighborhood store in Ashley on behalf of a family whose small child was sick. Could he come? They had no car to bring her down to see him.

He sighed. No money there, he knew. He never had the heart to charge any of those poor people. The nation might be enjoying a boom, but it hadn't touched the lives of the miners in Wyoming Valley, except to make them appear bleaker by contrast. And as for his own circumstances, they were none too good either. He owed money on everything—his car, which as a doctor, he couldn't do without; his office equipment; his instruments. The list was endless. His family had been some help when he had first returned to the valley, but after his father's death, he refused to borrow any money from his mother, or his grandfather. He had taken out a bank loan instead.

When he reached the weathered, neglected wood house which clung precariously to the steep, unpaved street, he took his black bag and entered the front door. A smell of greasy cooked cabbage and unwashed diapers greeted him. A child of three was screaming, another infant crying, while several older children stood around with scared, pinched faces, curious and apprehensive at his arrival. The father was in his undershirt, unshaven, reeking of alcohol. A wraith of a woman with pale skin and hair, unrelieved beige except for the faded blue of her eyes, wrung her hands together and spoke pleadingly in a mixture of Polish and barely comprehensible English. The neighbor who had called him was on hand to interpret.

He examined the little girl, who stopped crying and whimpered instead when he drew near, then froze in terror when he took out his stethoscope.

The child's abdomen was distended and hard as a rock. She was unable to eliminate, he was told, and he could see that she was suffering from excruciating gas pains. What had they fed her?

It was Sunday, so they had eaten meat for the first time all week. Pork sausage and potatoes. She had been a little glutton and eaten three helpings.

Her temperature was normal, no sign of infection or disease. He ruled out appendicitis or an intestinal blockage, deciding it was a simple matter of constipation and indigestion from overeating.

They did not own an enema bag. He drove down to the drugstore—the owner lived upstairs—and bought one for two dollars.

Back in the rundown house, he had them spread newspaper on the kitchen table. The mother was horrified at the thought of inserting the syringe into the child's rectum, so Arthur had to administer the enema himself. He asked the neighbor to hold the child still. There was no place to hang the enema bag, so he held it above his head with one hand. The child screamed in pain and fright. The other children peaked, round-eyed, through the doorway.

Just then the child vomited with projectile force all over the trousers of his new gray suit. Stepping back too late to avoid the rush of vomitus, he tipped the bag of soapy water over himself, and as if that weren't enough, the final indignity—the child's anal sphincter let go, her bowel emptying itself explosively all over the kitchen table, the floor . . . and the nice doctor.

The little girl was a pretty thing, with a charming smile when she wasn't crying or doubled up in pain. She had remarkable recuperative powers, he observed, as he did his best to sponge himself off with a soggy, sour-smelling dishrag. She was sitting up and smiling through her tears, sucking on a cherry-flavored lollipop he had fished out of his damp pocket. The mother was washing up the floor with a dirty rag mop, while the father had pulled himself together sufficiently to apologize to Dr. Hillman for the ruined suit.

Through the neighbor, Arthur explained to them patiently that a three-year-old child's system could not properly digest great quantities of greasy sausage, that pork did not keep well and harbored disease organisms if left unrefrigerated or served undercooked. It would be better nourishment to serve children chicken, eggs, or even cheese in place of the sausage links, which were at least 50 percent fat, he added. They nodded seriously, but he knew it was a wasted effort.

"Don't let her eat that much again," he warned them before leaving. At least that was something they might remember.

One suit and two dollars shot—and he hadn't even been paid $3.00 for a house call!

When he drove past Our Lady he saw John Riordan walking toward the rectory. The priest hailed him, so he stopped. Father John came over to the car, looked at Arthur's suit, and said, "Holy Mother! What happened to you?"

Arthur told him, laughing now, since the incident seemed hilarious with the retelling.

"Ah, Arthur, what a shame! I feel responsible. You'd never have gotten mixed up with those people if I hadn't asked you to help out here. Come on in. Let me give you something to put on and we'll see what we can do about that suit."

There didn't seem to be much point in going back to his apartment, so Arthur decided he might just as well stay here. Mrs. Farrell, John's grandmotherly housekeeper, took the suit away after giving Arthur a pair of dark gray trousers to wear. They were a little short, but a good fit otherwise.

"When do you ever wear civilian clothes?" he asked the priest.

"Whenever I can get away from here. Not nearly often enough. Hey, listen, please stay for dinner, will you? My niece, Molly Shea, is coming. It'll be nice to have you."

Arthur let himself be persuaded. He enjoyed a sense of anticipation just at the mention of Molly's name.

They were on their second drink by the time Molly arrived an hour later. Arthur felt a surge of pleasure when he saw her. She found them in animated conversation, laughing and telling stories like two undergraduates. Father John's normally quiet, reflective countenance was suffused with mirth. She had never seen him look so relaxed. She carefully controlled her surprised delight when she saw Arthur Hillman.

They had to tell the story of the house call and Arthur's new suit to Molly, who wrinkled her adorable nose in distaste, but saw the humor of it nonetheless. Her smile was elfin. "You see, if you'd stayed in Philadelphia, Arthur, this never would have happened."

She had used his first name! "No, it wouldn't," he answered, looking directly at her, meaning something quite different. Her cheeks showed a touch more than her natural high color.

Mrs. Farrell produced his suit just before dinner, cleaned and pressed. "How did you manage that, Mrs. Farrell?" he asked.

Her eyes sparkled. "Now, that would be telling, Dr. Hillman. It's my secret."

All through dinner he felt happy. Mrs. Farrell had outdone herself today, serving a roasted leg of lamb with browned potatoes and fresh asparagus. She could have saved herself the trouble so far as Molly and Arthur were concerned. They scarcely noticed the food.

Whenever their eyes met, they held a fraction of time longer than necessary, then reluctantly would draw away, seeking the first opportunity to come together again. Instinctively, she addressed her words toward him, and he would turn in her direction whenever he spoke. Father John sensed that whatever was happening excluded him. But then, didn't it always?

When it was time to leave, Arthur said he would drive Molly home. John said that he'd been planning to take her, but his voice died halfway through the sentence. Molly forgot to ask for the customary blessing when she left.

He prayed for them anyway. Something had begun this day. He prayed it was nothing that would cause them unhappiness.

Molly was going back to the Nurses' Residence, since she went on duty first thing in the morning. They sat in the car talking for a long time. Arthur asked her out for the following Saturday evening. She said yes. They both knew they were breaking the "rules."

"Those people are trying to attract your attention, Arthur." Molly indicated a booth on the opposite side of the dimly lit restaurant.

The Levinsons and the Gellers were sharing a table, looking their way with interest. Arthur smiled, waved, and turned back to Molly. He didn't like table-hopping, and he was afraid they'd suggest he and Molly join them. He wondered how long it would take for news of his date to reach his sisters.

"Did you always want to be a nurse?" he asked Molly.

"No. I never wanted to be a nurse at all! I wanted to be a lawyer, like my father." Her face broke into that amazing smile. "It was an impulsive decision to go into nursing, but the right one. I don't regret it."

That was surprising. She was the consummate professional nurse, skilled, sure, and devoted to duty. She inspired trust and reassurance in her patients. Her friendly presence enlivened the entire floor at the hospital, warming patients and staff alike.

Their pasta arrived, served by Tony Perugi, the affable owner of the restaurant, one of the valley's most popular spots for dining out. Tony brought them some red wine in coffee mugs, setting it down before them with a wink.

"You *do* like coffee with your linguine, don't you, Doctor?"

They both laughed. It wasn't so funny, really . . . but it was an outlet for this feeling of exhilaration.

The time passed too quickly. Others came, had dinner, and left, nodding hello. They smiled in return, oblivious, murmuring a courtesy, their attention riveted on each other.

Molly told him about her family . . . amusing tales of a house crammed full of rambunctious children, with a pretty, loving mother, adoring of her husband and adored by him . . . of a father, a successful lawyer whose good looks were matched by his magnetic personality, something of a dreamer, he was . . . a lover of poetry and nature . . . cut off by death in the prime of life. And of a little girl with unruly bangs and pigtails, dressed in a blue cotton parochial school uniform with stiff white collar and cuffs, and black lisle stockings that scratched. Arthur could picture her with her violet-blue eyes, sometimes solemn, often mischievous.

He, in turn, described the summers at Hillside, the early mornings on the river, fishing with his grandfather. He spoke about his father's death the previous year, and his regrets that he had not spent more time with him . . . about his brother, Nate, whom he'd idolized when they were children, and pitied now for the wasted years of his life, admiring his determination to graduate from law school. He told her of his dreams of becoming a chest surgeon in Philadelphia and how he had decided to return to Wyoming Valley. He even mentioned his trip to Germany and how awful it had felt to be a Jew there . . . things he hadn't talked about with anyone.

When he stopped talking, she said, "Why are you looking at me like that?"

"I was wondering . . . how come some fellow hasn't swept you off your feet and married you?"

She laughed enchantingly and leaned back against the booth. "Oh, there was a man in Ireland . . ." she answered. Then, theatrically, "Sean Tower . . . he was full of zeal for Irish union. I was impressed with the fire in his eyes! But that's long over."

"Why did you go to Ireland?" he asked, trying to ignore the prick of jealousy.

"In *my* family, you ask that question?" she laughed. "My Uncle Thomas—actually, he's my father's uncle, my great-uncle—he's a bishop. He gave me a graduation gift, a trip to Ireland. We still have some relatives there. My mother's cousin who's a monsignor, two nuns . . ."

"With all those nuns and priests, how is it you have so many relatives?" Arthur couldn't prevent himself from saying.

"Think how many more we'd have if it weren't for the nuns and priests!" was her saucy retort. "I loved it there. It's so . . . alive! I decided to stay for a while and nurse at St. Patrick's Hospital. But, finally, like you, I thought I should come back here. Mother's all alone. My sister Maureen is in a cloistered convent, my oldest brother, Danny, is with the Marryknoll Missions in Africa . . . Jim's an engineer in California, Tom's in Washington with the government, and Kevin practices law in Harrisburg. That leaves me."

They lingered over dessert and coffee until the restaurant was closing. Then Arthur drove to the Plantation, a roadhouse-speakeasy on the Harvey's Lake road, one of the few late-night places that went on into the wee hours unmolested by the police. If money changed hands, it wouldn't be the first time.

There was a three-piece combo that played slow, romantic music. Couples were holding each other close on the small, darkened dance floor. A few of them were openly amorous, causing Arthur to wonder whether he'd made a mistake in bringing her here. Molly didn't seem to notice. After a while, he asked her to dance.

As she moved into his arms, an indescribably lovely feeling came over him. He was aware of her scent, an elusive, light fragrance reminiscent of heather and meadowlands. He tightened the circle of his arm around her, drawing her close. He brought the slim hand resting on his palm against his chest, clasping it possessively. She relaxed against him, the curves of her young body chastely exciting. Once he drew back and looked into her upturned face. Eyes dreamy, lips parted, she smiled. With a happy sigh, he brought her close to him again. All too soon, the music ended and it was time to go.

It was late when they drove up to the Shea house. At the door, Arthur cupped her face in his hands. "I don't know when I've had a better time."

Her eyes were shining. "It was a wonderful evening, Arthur. Thank you."

"Next week?" She nodded happily. "Maybe we can start earlier. Go riding in the afternoon?" And, when she agreed, "I'll call you."

He kissed her lightly on the forehead, then left, driving home across the river in a state of euphoria.

Molly turned out the single lamp still burning in the living room. In the darkness, she hugged herself, trying to recapture the delicious feeling. Closing her eyes, she whispered his name.

After that first Saturday night, when they had gone to dinner at the Villa Perugi and seen so many people he knew, they chose other places for their dates. Saturday afternoon horseback riding or canoeing on Lake Nuangola . . . dinner at out-of-the-way family restaurants in Pittston, Hazleton, or Scranton—places where they could be together without feeling they were under scrutiny. Occasionally they made plans with the Flannerys, the Wintermuths, or the Benjamins—the only friends who knew they were seeing each other and would ask no questions.

"Arthur, she is *so* beautiful," said Ruth Benjamin, after meeting Molly for the first time. "I really like her. Will you bring her over for dinner one night?" David was more reserved in his reaction, looking thoughtful, wondering.

Phoebe was her usual, slightly scatterbrained, effervescent self, impressed with Molly, who had done so many independent things with her life. "Imagine, going off to Ireland, Molly, and getting a job nursing, all by yourself! Wasn't that a *kick?*"

Lowell treated Molly with gallant courtesy. "I understand your brother Kevin is a friend of the governor's, Molly." Lowell was great, but being a vice-president of Wyoming and Susquehanna did begin to weigh on one's shoulders.

The Flannerys . . . well, they were old friends of the Sheas, and Jim teased her constantly. "I remember when you were nothing but a little pest with no front teeth, Shea!" Did any other woman laugh like that, have such a captivating smile?

Sometimes Katherine Shea invited Arthur to stay for supper with her and Molly on a Sunday night. Arthur liked Molly's mother. She was an older version of her beautiful daughter, with prematurely white hair and deep dimples.

Arthur wondered what Katherine Shea thought about her daughter dating him. He had been ill at ease with her at first, but she was such a friendly, charming woman. . . . What had Molly told her mother about them? For that matter, what *was* there to tell? That they were good friends, they worked together at St. Anne's, they enjoyed each other's company, laughed together, felt warm and close and happy in each other's presence. . . . And then at night, when he had left Molly and was alone in his apartment, he would say to himself, *Who are you kidding, Hillman? You know what's happening* . . . and still, they continued to see each other.

In that other world they inhabited, they kept carefully apart. Each day when Arthur went to the hospital, Molly was on duty at the nurses' desk. She was coolly efficient, always pleasant, with a briskness that would have satisfied any critical observer about the correctness of their relationship.

The nuns would not have taken kindly to one of their nurses going out with a doctor on the staff. The fact that the doctor was Jewish and the nurse a Catholic would only serve to heighten their disapproval. Certainly, there was no enforceable rule they were defying. But surely one of the sisters would have spoken to Molly or to a person of higher authority. Arthur, as a physician, was free from either rebuke or criticism. Unfair, it might be, but that was the way it was. So, they said nothing.

The summer passed. Each week was punctuated by the Saturday evenings and Sunday afternoons they spent together. They guarded themselves and their feelings carefully. A firm friendship was growing. It was no more than that, they reassured themselves—a solid friendship between two idealistic young people who cared about helping those who suffered, two young people who took pleasure from a shared moment of silence in the crimson of a sunset, or the splendor of a star-filled summer night sky.

And yet, he knew—they both knew—it was more than that. . . . Could simply holding hands in a movie be so satisfying? Was riding along a bridle path together, or drifting over the still surface of a hidden lake, with Molly trailing her hand in the water, the only place he wanted to be, the only way he wanted to pass the time? What was it about her? Her beauty? He wasn't such a pushover for a pretty face, was he? Emily had been beautiful. Different, but just as beautiful in her own way. No . . . it was something more, something that came from within Molly.

When she was with him, he felt more alive, more purposeful, his horizons unlimited. She fit his every mood. There was the playful, tomboyish Molly with a quick grin and sharp-tongued, clever humor. There was the Molly of sweet compassion for the sufferings of others . . . of righteous indignation at unfairness and injustice. Sparks flew in kinetic currents when she was seized with enthusiasm for an idea . . . but no one was a more soothing presence when he was worn out from overwork, or discouraged about a patient who wasn't doing well.

There were times when he felt he had never had such a close friend. She almost knew what he would say before he knew himself. And, yes, her beauty was a source of constant fascination to him. He could have studied her face in its various modalities forever, and never have grown tired of it.

She was in his thoughts even when they weren't together. When he paused in the frantic pace of his work, when he drifted off to sleep at night, and when he awakened early each dawn. At times, a sense of desolation overcame him. . . . For what possible future could there be for them if they should fall in love? A Jewish doctor in love with the grandniece of a bishop of the Roman Catholic Church? From all viewpoints, unthinkable.

Better to cut it off now, before they became too involved with each other, he told himself in rare moments of honest appraisal. Yet, as the summer drew to a close, their meetings became more frequent—and more important.

III

Forty Fort   September 1929

Molly was waiting for him on the front porch that Saturday morning in late September. Her hand-knit suit in a heathery shade of lavender matched her incredible eyes.

His throat ached with the loveliness of her. "You look wonderful," he told her.

Molly smiled up at him, her eyes happy. "This is one of the few things I bought in Ireland, made by an old woman who lives in the most awful, drafty cottage, with nothing of beauty to brighten her life."

"You must tell me more about Ireland," he said, as Molly picked up a large picnic hamper and handed it to him. "Shouldn't I go say hello to your mother?"

"Mother's gone to visit her sister in Sunbury. I'm going to the Nurses' Residence tonight, unless we get back after hours. Imagine! I'm almost twenty-three years old and I still have to sign in before midnight."

"We like to keep our nurses in hand." He sometimes liked to tease her.

"You do, do you? I suppose you think it's just dandy that we have to stand whenever a doctor walks into a room," she retorted, rising to the bait.

They'd had this discussion before. "Surely. Helps you know your place!"

He looked at her sideways, as he drove east toward the Poconos, his eyes crinkling in amusement. The absurd customs observed between nurses and doctors irritated Molly even more than they did Arthur. Why anyone should think keeping nurses firmly subordinate to physicians improved medical care was a mystery to both of them.

The Sisters of Mercy trained the best nurses in the profession, but they were a conservative group who rigidly enforced the show of respect a nurse must give a doctor. No matter that the nurse might be a forty-year-old veteran of years on the wards, and the doctor a green intern just out of medical school.

"All that'll change one day, Molly," Arthur told her. "But it's the nurses who are going to have to change it. Leave it to the doctors, and things will stay just as they are."

It was a glorious Indian summer day, crisp and clear, with tinges of fall in the air. The leaves were beginning to change color. Splashes of red and gold brightened the forested hills on either side of the road. They turned off the highway just beyond Bear Creek. Soon they were far out in the country on a winding road. Near Thornhurst, Molly directed him onto an unpaved mountain lane, little more than a bridle path.

"Are you sure I can drive all the way up there?" he asked doubtfully.

"Yes, don't worry. Dad even came up here in the winter. The only time it's really impassable is in the spring when there are heavy rains."

They were driving to a cabin in the Poconos that had belonged to her father. It had been left to Molly, but she hadn't had the courage to go up there since his death. "I have to see it before another winter goes by. Would you like to come with me?" she had asked.

The road was rocky and narrow, with no shoulder. "What happens if I meet another car coming down?"

"That's not likely. This is our own road. My father bought all the private land on top of the mountain. The rest is state-owned and has an access road on the other side."

The road climbed steeply, twisting around, crossing over a stream twice. Molly was silent, looking out of her side of the car. He knew she was thinking about her father. They had been close, father and daughter.

They came to a level clearing. "Here we are!" She jumped out of the car and breathed in the autumn air, flinging her arms wide. "Oh, Arthur, I'm glad to be here. I thought it would be sad, but I feel fine." She looked at him, laying her hand on his arm. "I'm glad that you're here with me."

"So am I." Arthur smiled down at her and gave her a hug. Arms around each other, they walked across the clearing to a grove of pine trees. A small cabin stood on a rise. Slabs of stone formed steps up to it on the side of the hill. Molly took the key out of her pocketbook and unlocked the door. Arthur followed her inside.

It was dark and smelled musty. They drew up the shades and opened the windows, letting in the fresh mountain air. Arthur pushed the button of the light switch, but nothing happened.

"The electricity's turned off," Molly explained.

"Of course. It would be."

Arthur looked around the cabin. One large room served as living room and dining room, with a partition at the end separating the kitchen. The chimney wall was all stone above the large fireplace. A door led to the only bedroom.

In the corner, a staircase went up to a loft where there were camp beds. The main room had a high ceiling with exposed beams. It was rustic, but comfortable and cheery, with a deep, loungy sofa, colorful cushions and afghans, and a large bearskin rug.

Snapshots of happy family outings were tacked here and there on the rough pine walls. Arthur peered at one of a young Molly, around fourteen, holding a puppy and grinning into the camera. At her side, an arm around her shoulders, was a tall, sensitive-looking man who watched her fondly, an uncertain smile turning up the corners of his mouth. There was a poignancy about the picture, as if the man knew he wouldn't live to see his adored daughter in the fullness of womanhood.

Molly was poking around in drawers in the other room. "Looks like we've had some visitors here," she called.

Arthur went into the small bedroom. A double bed was made up with a patchwork quilt. There was little furniture in the room, other than a chest of drawers. Molly was looking inside an open drawer with a moue of distaste. There were some broken acorn shells in the drawer. Arthur recognized mouse droppings.

"You can't expect the animals to stay out if no one's living here," he said. "Open up all the drawers. I'll get rid of these." He removed the drawers and carried them outside one by one, where he dumped the fragments in the woods. Back in the cabin, Molly was examining the main room.

"It's not really dusty. Isn't that strange?"

"It's been closed up and protected from the elements. The air up here is clean. No coal dust," Arthur answered.

"Let's go outside for our picnic. There's a meadow with a heavenly view not far away." Molly took a woolen blanket from a shelf. They went to the car, where Arthur had stowed the hamper of food.

Molly led the way up the mountain through the pine forest. They reached a low stone wall. "What's this?" asked Arthur.

"That's the property line. The man who sold this to my father owned the entire mountain. He gave the rest of it to the State Forestry Service so it would be protected land."

"How did your father find this isolated spot, Molly?"

"The owner needed a lawyer in Luzerne County and he was referred to my father. I think he took a liking to Dad." Then she added, "My father made friends easily."

"I wish I had known him, Molly."

She turned and looked at him. "So do I. He would have liked you, Arthur . . ." Her voice trailed off.

"But he wouldn't have approved of your going out with a Jew. I think that's what you didn't finish saying." He smiled to soften his words. Molly didn't reply.

They came out onto a rolling grassy plain where clumps of wild flowers,

Queen Anne's lace, goldenrod, thistle and black-eyed Susans, proliferated. The view was as breathtaking as Molly had promised. Below them lay the entire mountainside, and beyond, a spreading valley. To the east in the distance, a sparkling lake nestled between two smaller mountains, the landscape undisturbed by any signs of habitation.

Arthur spread the blanket on the grass in front of a large boulder, while Molly opened the hamper and set out sandwiches, cold chicken, cheese, fruit, and a bottle of wine.

"Where did you manage to get wine?" he asked.

"From Uncle John."

"Why, that old renegade. And him a priest, too," Arthur joked.

"Where did you learn to talk Irish?" she asked in surprise.

"Ah, me girl, there's many a talent I have ye're not aware of," he answered, the brogue as thick as he could make it. He leaned over to give her a playful kiss, his lips lingering. Reluctantly, he drew away, feeling a sweet languor seep through his veins.

Molly paused briefly, drawing in her breath, then looked down, continuing to arrange the food. Arthur opened the wine and poured some in the mugs she had brought along.

They ate some of the lunch and sipped the wine and looked at the view, while they reclined on the blanket, not speaking but terribly aware of each other. The wind skipped over Molly's hair, rippling its dark glossiness in the sunlight. Her eyes were bluer than the sky in her ethereal face, still tanned from the summer sun. He smiled lazily at her, drinking in her loveliness.

"I remember the first time I saw you, with Sister Emmaline," she said, leaning back against the boulder.

He replied, "Yes, I remember," recalling how mesmerized he had been by her beauty that day. That hadn't changed.

"Sister says you're everyone's favorite at the hospital. She told me all the nurses are in love with you."

"*All* the nurses?"

Molly blushed. "Well, you know what I mean," she answered. "I think Sister Emmaline is a little in love with you herself."

"I've got kind of a yen for her, too," Arthur said, grinning. He poured a little more wine in their cups. He was feeling heady, and he was sure it wasn't the wine.

She picked a wild daisy, then pulled the petals off one by one, chanting, "For love, for naught, for love . . ." It ended up "for naught" and she frowned. "Your turn," she said, handing him a flower.

He shook his head. "I'm superstitious. I'd rather not know!"

"It's silly, anyway," she said. Then, "Love!" He'd noticed she acted flippantly when she was embarrassed.

He felt a quickening in his chest. "Is that what you thought when you had your romance in Ireland with . . . what was his name?"

"Sean Tower?" She looked uncomfortable.

"That's the one. Sean Tower. How did you meet him?" he asked, curious, but afraid as he said it that he'd touched on forbidden ground.

"He was a friend of my cousin Patrick—Monsignor Riordan—and we just sort of got to know each other. Sean's somewhat older than I am. Actually, he's twelve years older."

"And he's never been married?"

"No. Lots of men in Ireland don't marry—or marry late. It's got something to do with their land inheritance. Sean is committed to his work. He's in politics, working for a united Ireland. He's brilliant, and a persuasive speaker . . . holds an audience spellbound."

"And you, Molly, did he hold you spellbound, too?"

She gave a small, self-conscious laugh and shrugged. "Well, I suppose he did, a little. I . . . uh . . . didn't know so much about men, after all. Going to school with the nuns doesn't exactly give you a wealth of experience with men!" She laughed, then turned serious. "But I think what it was . . . well, he valued my mind. He was interested in my thoughts. He didn't expect me to just blindly believe, accept . . . everything I'd been taught. He had left the Church at one time, but he returned . . ." She gazed into space. "Well, really, that's all there was to it," she said crisply. "Let's talk about something else."

Arthur was relieved when she paused. He had been so afraid. He realized he was jealous, really jealous. Of this unknown, faraway Irish zealot. Sean Tower.

So, the afternoon hours sped away. Nothing intruded on their idyll, high in the Pocono meadow, as Molly and Arthur smiled into each other's eyes, happy together. Suddenly, there was a rumble in the mountains and a strong gust of wind swept over the meadow, scattering the waxed paper in which Molly had wrapped the sandwiches. Arthur glanced up at the sky, surprised to see black clouds moving from the east. A rain squall loomed over the pristine lake in their panorama, a dark shaft in the silvering daylight.

"We're in for a rainstorm. We'd better pack up and head back to the cabin," Arthur said.

They gathered up the picnic, putting the ample leftovers back in the hamper. Molly rolled the blanket up in a ball. They ran across the meadow just as large raindrops began to fall. Going through the pine forest, they scarcely felt the rain, although the lightning and thunder were violent at times. Arthur held on to Molly's hand, helping her over the stone wall. In her haste, she scratched her leg, tearing her stocking. They came to the cabin from the rear this time, by way of another path. Just as they dashed across the last few feet of ground, they were pelted by a drenching rain. They rushed into the cabin, slamming the door. Molly hugged herself and rubbed her hands together.

Arthur closed the windows. He looked at the cold hearth. "Is there any wood? I could light a fire to warm us up."

"Yes, that door near the ice box goes to the woodshed," Molly replied, shaking her wet handknit jacket.

Arthur returned with an armload of split logs.

"I'll start the stove so we can have tea," Molly said. Soon she had a kettle of water on the old wood stove. She lit several candles. The cold cabin had taken on a warm coziness.

Arthur looked around at the wood planked walls. The rough-hewn pine reflected the light from the fire. "This place looks like it was built to withstand just about anything," he said to Molly, who was pouring boiling water into a teakettle.

"It's not really winterized—there's no insulation. But with the fireplace and the iron stove, it's almost like having a furnace."

She put the tea tray on a low table in front of the couch and sliced chocolate cake from the picnic hamper. Arthur was surprised that he was hungry. The hot tea warmed him. He removed the damp Shetland sweater he'd worn over his shirt.

"I'll have to get the car started as soon as this rain lets up," he said. "I hope the wires aren't wet. I should've parked under the trees."

"It certainly didn't look like rain when we arrived," Molly said. "What time is it now?"

Arthur took his watch out of his pocket, the watch his father had given him when he graduated from Jeff. "It's after five. I didn't realize it was that late. The time passed so quickly."

"It'll be dark early. I think we'd better not wait too long," Molly answered. She seemed worried.

"Is something the matter?" Arthur asked.

"Nooo . . . it's just that the road sometimes gets bad when there's a heavy rain."

"It hasn't been raining that long. I'll go out now. I can bring the car closer to the cabin so you can make a dash for it after I get it started."

Molly found an old tarpaulin in the woodshed. Arthur threw it over his head and ran down the hill, across the clearing to his roadster. He pulled out the choke, pushed the starter button. The motor turned over, coughed, but did not catch. He tried a second time. Again, after a feeble attempt, it died. He tried to crank the motor, but that, too, failed. Putting up the sides of the hood, he could see that the entire wiring system had been soaked. He'd never get the car started—not until the wires were dry. The rain was so heavy and the wind so strong that he was soaked to the skin, his shoes full of water. He didn't know how long he had been out there, but it was getting dark now. Soon he'd be unable to see.

He heard Molly shouting above the sound of the wind. "Arthur, Arthur!" She was running across the clearing in the driving rain, a blanket over her head. "You'll catch pneumonia out here in this rain," she called as she approached. "Can't you get the car started?"

"No," he answered ruefully. "It's what I was afraid of—the wires are soaked and no hope of their drying out as long as this rain continues. Here, get in the car, you're as wet as I am." The blanket was already sodden. "This is the worst rain I can remember ever being in."

"Even if you were able to start the car, the road would be very dangerous," she said. "Especially at night without good lights."

He sat down on the seat beside her. "Molly, I'm afraid we have to stay up here until this stops. I'm sorry. It's my fault. We should've started back immediately." He thought for a minute. "Is there anyone around we can call?"

"Arthur, there's no telephone. There isn't anyone around, anyway. Sometimes there's a ranger, but that's on the other side of the mountain. Well, there's nothing to be done. I guess we ought to go back in and dry off. That's better than sitting out here." They ran across the open ground together. By now they were both so wet and muddy that their clothes dripped in puddles on the cabin floor.

Molly took one of the candles up the stairway to the left. She found some large towels, more blankets, an assortment of men's clothing, and two kerosene lamps.

"Here, Arthur, I think you can probably find something to fit you. These belonged to Dad and the boys." She handed him some denim pants and plaid woolen shirts.

"Why don't you change first, Molly. . . . I'd better not let this fire die down. We need all the heat we can get." Arthur went into the woodshed to bring back more wood. He threw several large logs on the fire. It blazed up, radiating warmth.

Molly emerged from the bedroom wearing a red plaid shirt, several sizes too large for her and a pair of work pants which she had rolled up. With her color higher than usual from the wind and rain, her damp hair forming a cap of curls all over her head, she looked ravishing. Arthur stared at her, longing to reach out and take her in his arms, startled by the rush of warm sensations he felt.

"Arthur, you'd better go change before you catch cold," Molly said. "I'll see what we've got to eat. There must be some canned food here, if it's still good. Otherwise, we just have what's left from the picnic."

Arthur took a deep breath. "That's all right with me. There's more than enough," he answered as he went into the bedroom, where Molly had left a hurricane lamp burning. He toweled himself briskly before donning the dry clothes.

They started with soup. They feasted on cold chicken, cheese, and fruit. And each other.

Outside the cabin the storm raged. Safe and warm in their own private world, they looked into the leaping fire, finished the bottle of wine from their lunch, and smiled when their eyes met, touching hands.

The rain poured on and on. Great crashes of thunder followed bright jagged bolts of lightning. Molly pulled the curtains over the small windows of the cabin.

"I've never liked lightning up here," she shuddered. "I'm always sure one of those huge trees will be struck."

"Has one ever been struck by lightning when you were here?"

"Not that I can remember."

"Well, then, I wouldn't worry about it happening tonight," Arthur reassured her, putting his arm around her and drawing her head onto his shoulder. He rubbed his cheek against her soft hair, inhaling her fragrance. His heartbeat quickened as he felt a helpless desire for her.

Rising, he went to place another big log on the fire. The wood was so dry the flames leaped up immediately, crackling and emitting a piney aroma.

Molly sat watching him from the couch as he threw the log on the fire, then stooped to stir the embers with the poker. She enjoyed looking at him, his tall rangy body, his shoulders and back, broad and strong. His blond hair glinting in the light of the flames . . . the shape of his head, the planes of his face were so appealing to her.

She still felt the warmth of his head and shoulder against her, the comfort of his arm around her. He had never held her that way before—so affectionately; only when they danced. She wished he hadn't left her side abruptly, as if he disliked being close to her. She had wanted him to kiss her tonight, to go on holding her. . . . Tears of disappointment stung her eyes. She busied herself clearing the plates away from the coffee table, annoyed at the foolishness of her romantic fantasies.

Molly sat on the bearskin rug facing the fire, leaning back against a table. Her eyes, so dark blue, looked black in the flickering light. The blush on her cheeks was even more intense in the fire glow, in contrast to the whiteness of her throat. With her smoky dark hair, tousled and curling now, she had a wild, untamed look.

Arthur moved to the floor beside her, leaning on one elbow. As she smiled down at him, he felt his heart turn over. . . . He sat up, facing her. She met his gaze directly, the smile fading from her face. He was so near now . . . a wave of longing for him passed through her, leaving her weak.

Arthur reached out to caress her cheek, his fingers moving softly down to fondle her neck. She closed her eyes momentarily, giving herself over to the sensuous delight of his touch.

He cupped her chin in his hand, brushing his thumb across her lips. "You know, we've never really kissed," he said softly.

"Yes, I know," she whispered, her lips giving his hand the smallest suggestion of a kiss.

For an instant, the world stood still while they looked into each other's eyes, pausing to question what was there, sensing that they had reached a fork in life's road and must choose which way to travel.

And then she was in his arms and he was kissing her hungrily, again and again, uttering words which he had never spoken before, to anyone. "I love you . . . I can't help it . . . I love you, I love you! I've tried *so hard* not to love you."

Molly clung to him, returning his kisses deeply, urgently, unable and unwilling to stem the torrent of love and desire which swept over her. His words, his lips, the touch of his strong hands told her what she had wanted to know since the day she had first seen him.

"Arthur! Arthur," she cried, free at last to say what was in her heart, "I've longed for you so. I've loved you from the very beginning."

She grasped his hands, leading them, helping him to remove her clothes, and then his own. Fire-dancing shadows spread their surrealistic images across the ceiling. The firelight played its golden glow over her young, supple body. He held his breath, rapt at the sight of her exquisite beauty.

"Oh, my love," he breathed, as he bent his head to kiss the soft swell of her breast. "My darling . . . my sweet, wonderful darling." Tenderly, he gathered her into his arms. . . .

And this was love . . . the love of poetry and fables and dreams . . . a force so relentless, so powerful it swept over them, catching them up in its wake, and carrying them along with the frenzy of the storm that assaulted their mountain hideaway.

He paid one last heed to conscience. "Molly, I don't want to hurt you.
. . ."

But she was beyond caution. "I don't care, I don't care!"

Wind-whipped howls buffeted the sides of the small cabin, bending the tall lashes of the aged pines which beat upon the roof in fury. . . . Thunderstruck, amazed, they lay spent in each other's arms, overwhelmed with what had happened to them, wordlessly holding on to the precious feeling of newly discovered love.

Arthur listened to Molly's quiet, measured breathing as he stared into the semidarkness. It was cold in the bedroom of the cabin where the fire's warmth hadn't penetrated. He pulled the quilt up around Molly's shoulders, feeling an immeasurable tenderness and protectiveness. He raised himself on one elbow, looking down at her as she slept, her head cradled on her arm, the lovely face so young and innocent in slumber.

How long had he loved her? How many months had these tumultuous feelings been lying dormant within his consciousness, awaiting recognition? Forever, it seemed. Something so profound, so cataclysmic had been unleashed between them that Arthur knew, no matter what happened in their future, nothing would ever be the same for either of them. The stars in their celestial journeys, the order of life on earth, seemed altered forever.

He left the bed quietly, unable to sleep, his mind in turmoil. Out in the living room he found the picnic blanket and wrapped it around himself. The fire had died to a glowing bed of coals. Arthur put some short logs on the grate and stirred the embers. Soon a small fire was burning, warming him.

He sat on the couch, staring into the flames. It wasn't going to be easy for them, he knew. But wasn't this where they had been heading since the first evening they'd spent together, indeed, almost from the first moment they had seen each other? In the sure clarity of his thoughts, he recognized that they had been trying to deny this love all through the sultry summer days together, the soft starlit nights. There would be difficult times ahead, people would try to interfere, but Arthur could not think of giving up this rare and beautiful love. He appreciated how special it was, for he had never experienced such depths of feeling before. Despite his grandfather's long-ago words, he had begun to doubt that it was realistic to expect a love of grand dimensions.

For perhaps an hour he sat there looking into the flames, thinking. Outside, the howling wind died and the rain fell with a steady, quiet rhythm. Arthur acknowledged that what made their love a problem had little to do with the two of them. The religious difference would be a concern for their families, he realized, but for himself and Molly, he was certain they could surmount any difficulties. After all, they were a man and a woman in love. No one could *prevent* them from choosing each other.

Their love had the secure footing of close friendship, of warm companionship. It was not merely a physical attraction, as overpowering as that was. He and Molly had the same values . . . shared the same convictions about basic questions. Hadn't they, time and again, looked at each other in surprise, struck by their identical responses? Their tastes were similiar—the music they both loved, the poetry, the books. . . . Didn't they think alike about their work, about the poverty of so many of their patients? Molly understood him as no one else did, agreed with the things he wanted to do in the community. . . . Weren't their dreams compatible . . . their hopes and life goals? And weren't those things more important than whether they were brought up to worship God in the same way? He was the same God, after all. And Arthur believed their love for each other was a gift from that God.

Making sure that the screen was in place in front of the fire, Arthur went back to the bedroom. He tried to get into bed without waking Molly, but she stirred and opened her eyes.

"Where were you?" she asked sleepily.

He put his arms around her and drew her sleep-warmed body close to him. "I couldn't sleep, darling. I was just sitting by the fire, thinking about us."

She touched his face, her voice full of awe. "I can't believe it Arthur. . . . I never knew there could be anything like this, that I could ever feel like this. Whatever are we going to do?"

"We're going to get married, my love. I don't quite know how this happened, Molly. All I know is that I love you so much, I don't think I could ever stop loving you, even if I wanted to."

He began to caress her again. His hands wandered over her body, lingering, becoming familiar with this new, wondrous being. Slowly, unhurriedly this time, they made love, rejoicing in their rapture. For Arthur, there had never been one person who reached into his soul this way, leaving him enthralled, overcome with feeling. And, for Molly, it was the affirmation of all she had felt for him during these long months, the dreams she had not dared to hope would come true.

The rain beat gently on the roof, soothing them, closing them in from the world outside. As the first light of dawn appeared over the mountains, the rain stopped altogether, and then there was just the soft sound of drops as they fell from the heavy branches of the tall pines.

Forty Fort   1911

"Molly! . . . Moll-leee . . ."

Up in the Fogarty's orchard, Molly sat on a low-hanging branch of an apple tree, munching on her third hard green apple. She heard her brother calling, but kept on eating. When Mommy started calling her name, she knew she'd better get back there pretty fast. Turning over on her tummy, she slid down, stretching one foot in its white button shoe toward the broken-off branch she'd used as a ladder to climb up. The bib of her pinafore caught on the higher branch, and as she missed her footing and fell, she heard the rending tear of the fabric. Oh, oh—she'd be in for it now!

"Mary Katherine Shea! Look at you! Whatever am I going to do with you?" Kitty Shea was standing over her five-year-old daughter, hands on hips in exasperation. "I declare, you are worse than all the boys put together. You've ruined your new pinafore. Come into the house at once." Her mother took her by the hand, walking briskly, Molly running on her short, chubby legs, trying to keep up. She wasn't feeling very well, suddenly. Her tummy had the worst pain, and she'd skinned her elbow and knee when she'd fallen out of the tree.

Kevin was there, gloating. "Boy! Look at you. You're a mess!"

Molly stuck her tongue out at him and threw up on the kitchen floor. Kitty raised her eyes heavenward, but washed off Molly's sad little face and cleaned the scrapes. Her eyes softened and her motherly heart melted when she saw tears welling in the great blue eyes. She tenderly smoothed back dark, glossy curls from the enchanting face.

"I think you'd better take off your dress and lie down for a while, pumpkin. We'll talk about this when you're feeling better. Green apples are not good for little girls."

Molly held back her tears and slowly climbed the stairs. The day had started out so nice . . . now, look at it.

. . . She must've drifted off to sleep because suddenly she could hear Mommy and Aunt Sally.

"That's perfect, Sally. I can shorten it for Molly. Bethy was taller at that age. It's in very good condition."

"Well, she only wore it for First Communion and Easter that one year. It seems a shame not to get more use out of it. It's a little fancy for Molly's type, but I think it'll do."

Molly got off the bed and walked into her parents' room. Her dark violet-blue eyes widened when she saw the white dress with tier after tier of ruffles going down the skirt.

"Here she is! Hello, darling, come give Aunt Sally a kiss."

"Feeling better, Molly?" her mother asked.

"Yes, Mommy." She eyed the dress. "What's that dress for?"

"Aunt Sally brought it for your First Holy Communion, dear. Isn't it beautiful?"

"C'n I try it on?"

They slipped it over her head and buttoned up the back. "Just remove one ruffle and the length will be perfect . . . now, the veil . . ." Aunt Sally lifted the small white veil with bows on each side of the headpiece out of the tissue-filled box. She fitted it on Molly's head, pinning it in place with two hairpins.

"God love her! Isn't she a picture," Aunt Sally cried. "She is going to be a rare beauty, Kit."

Molly's mother frowned in disapproval. "You'll turn her head, Sally. She's defiant enough, without becoming vain on top of it."

"Danny is going to help prepare you for your first Confession, Molly."

Molly followed her big brother out to the summer house under the grape vine. "O.K., Moll. Now, you remember your lesson on Confession?"

Molly looked up at Danny, her favorite of her four older brothers. "Uh-huh."

"Good. Now, what do you say when you get in the confessional?"

Molly just kept looking at him.

"I'll help you get started. . . . 'Bless me, Father, for I have sinned . . .'"

Molly didn't say anything.

"C'mon, Molly, say it—say it with me . . . 'Bless me, Father, for . . .' well, say it, Molly—O.K., O.K., you don't have to say it now. We'll do that later." Danny gave a deep sigh. "Now, Molly, what sins have you committed this week?"

This was better. She felt on firmer ground. "None," she said brightly.

Danny was beginning to wonder about this. "Molly. Everyone commits sins all the time."

"I don't."

"Oh, boy! They'll never believe this . . ." He tried again. "Moll, listen. I'm

talking about lying, disobeying, thinking bad thoughts about people, vanity, envy—things like that. Do you understand?"

"Uh-huh."

"Good. Now, tell me some sins you've committed."

"I committed no sins."

"Molly, for crying out loud, everyone, even Father McCarthy, commits sins. Now, c'mon, tell me some sins you committed."

Molly started to cry. "I didn't! I didn't commit sins!"

"Holy Christmas! Now you've got me committing one—losing patience and swearing!" Hold on, Dan, he told himself. In a patient tone of voice, he continued. "Molly, honey, I'm not talking about mortal sins. You'll be forgiven for your sins. We all commit sins all the time, every day of our lives. That's how people are. But we go to confession, we confess our sins, and we're forgiven. . . . If you don't confess your sins, you can't take Holy Communion."

So. That was it. They wouldn't let her wear the white ruffled dress and the flowing veil unless she said she'd sinned. She might have known there'd be a catch to it.

Wilkes-Barre   Autumn 1929

More than a month had passed since the night Arthur and Molly had recognized their love for each other. Four breathless weeks, during which Arthur's emotions had risen to dizzying heights of happiness, only to plummet to the depths of misery, as he agonized over his feeling for the beautiful young woman and what the future would hold for them.

It seemed to Arthur that nothing had changed. They still sought secluded restaurants for their dinners out together. "I don't know why we can't go to a restaurant in town, like anyone else, Molly," he said one night when they were dining in a steak house halfway to Hazleton.

She looked around the dark tavern with its mahogany booths. "I like this place. It has atmosphere," she said cheerfully.

"It's all right. That's not the point. I only wish we came here because we liked it, not because it's out of the way."

"You know if we walked into the Wyoming or Shettle's, your mother and sisters would receive a dozen phone calls!"

"So what if they do!" His voice rose. He looked around, lowering it. "Molly, I *want* to tell them about us. I *want* you to meet my mother . . . I've wanted it for a long time. I've met most of your family."

"I don't know about that Arthur . . ." She answered in a worried voice. "Let's wait a little while longer."

He hadn't gone to her mother or one of her brothers to formally request her hand in marriage—the way he had always imagined he would in these circumstances. Again, Molly thought it was premature. She had to prepare the way for them, she said, to circumvent the religious opposition they would encounter.

Oh, yes, there *was* one difference in their relationship. And Arthur wasn't entirely comfortable with it. The cabin on the mountain had become their trysting place—a secret hideaway where they could go to be alone, to talk without interruption for endless hours, to walk through the surrounding woods, arms around each other, to laugh together, to dream. . . . And to make love . . . such beautiful, exciting, romantic love. . . .

It was just this that presented another problem for them. Arthur disliked subterfuge, had a distaste for the secrecy of their romance. He thought the necessity of hiding it from people was cheapening—and for anything connected to Molly to be less than honorable was unthinkable to him. As if that weren't enough to consider, he dreaded the possibility that Molly might become pregnant. It surprised him that she didn't fear that possibility as much as he did. She wouldn't use any device to prevent pregnancy—not that there was much available to her. Even if she decided to use a pessary, wherever would she go to obtain it without damaging her reputation?

So they tried to pay attention to the time of month, and Arthur used withdrawal or condoms, trusting neither. And he worried.

Molly didn't like the condoms. "It's a sin, Arthur."

"It'd be more of a sin if you became pregnant, my love," he'd answered. "Besides, it's not a sin for me, so try to forget about it."

Oddly enough, Arthur could understand the seeming inconsistency—Molly would risk eternal damnation by making love with him *because* of her love for him; but she would hazard the disgrace of a pregnancy rather than commit the mortal sin of using a contraceptive device. Mrs. Sanger's message had not been warmly received in Church circles. Even if it had been, the risks were still grave. No wonder birth control was such a problem for his married patients! He knew he'd show more compassion on that subject in the future.

Molly, after considering the sober facts of marriage to a non-Catholic, was not ready to rush headlong into plans for a wedding. He had tried to understand her point of view. Certainly, her family would raise objections. So would his. Hadn't they discussed that on that first Sunday morning in the cabin? They knew the Church would place obstacles in the way. Arthur was a Jew—not even a Christian. Molly was hopeful that she could receive a dispensation to marry him.

"I've heard conversations all my life about priests marrying Catholics to non-Catholics without insisting on conversion," she told him. "I never had any reason to pay much attention to it before this."

They both agreed that conversion, for either of them, was not a solution.

"Your religion is too important to you, Molly—too much a part of your life," Arthur said. "And although I'm not an observant Jew, I *am* Jewish to the core. . . . Being Jewish is more than religious observance. It's a combination of allegiances . . . like being Catholic *and* Irish. Judaism embraces heritage, customs, and obligations as well as religion—all interdependent parts, like the links of a chain. I wouldn't want to be the one to break that chain in my family."

Arthur's religious faith had always sat easily on him. He believed in God— or a concept of God. Whether that meant man was created by God, or the other way around, seemed irrelevant to him. He didn't care which church someone prayed in or whether they prayed at all. In theory, he thought, religion was a force for good. All of the basic precepts of the world's religions were uplifting. Laws for living as set forth in the name of religion made much good sense, in his opinion.

Being Jewish was a way of life for Arthur, unalterable, important, and a source of pride. He explained that to Molly, wanting her to know this part of him, while he endeavored to understand her beliefs.

"I guess I'm basically a man of science and logic. I can accept that there are things we don't know or can't explain. But I'm unable to believe that the explanations are supernatural," he said one evening when they were discussing religion.

"It all comes down to faith, Arthur. If you can accept some basic truths on faith alone, then everything else becomes logical." She looked so earnest, as if puzzling it out in her own mind.

He didn't answer immediately. "That's a contradiction, Molly. Logic doesn't follow the illogical."

They would never agree, but they could live with their disagreement. He took her in his arms. "The only illogical thing I can believe is that I love you beyond all understanding. I'm willing to accept that on faith alone!"

Molly sometimes talked about her father. "I miss him, Arthur. He was so much fun to be with. Just as I grew old enough for him to think of me as an adult, I left home. He was sick one day, then dead three months later." She breathed deeply. "I wish I could believe what I'm supposed to believe . . . that he's with God in heaven, forever. It worries me that I have such doubts." They were sitting on some rocks near a brook. "Where do you think your father is, Arthur?" Molly asked.

Arthur drew in his lips, considering her question. "I think he's dead, Molly." He ran his hand over her hair. "If you mean, do I believe in heaven or hell . . . I don't. But if there were such a place as heaven, I'm sure that's where he'd be. I doubt if he ever did a sinful thing in his life. Poor man, he never could relax enough to have any fun."

"Were you close to him?"

"Not really. Not in the way you were to your father. I regret that . . . very much. He was too held in, too reserved for us kids to unbend with him. I was—and still am—a lot closer to *his* father, my grandfather. You'll have to meet him soon. He's a marvelous man. He was always so full of life and spirit.

Grandfather was the one I went to when I wanted to ask about almost anything . . . religion, career, sex . . ."

"*Sex?* You talked about sex with your *grandfather?*"

"That's right! He was fantastic. He told me sex—well, he didn't call it sex, he called it love, and for him that always meant marriage—he told me that with the woman you love, it is the purest, most beautiful thing there can be between two people. And he also told me not to believe anyone who says it isn't the same for a woman as it is for a man."

"How beautiful!" She leaned over to kiss him. "You mean, that's who I have to thank?"

It was a glorious autumn, emblazoned by their love. Molly seemed determined to ignore their dilemma, delighting in the present, making each time together a thing of magical beauty, trusting that a future of happiness lay ahead of them . . . an ephemeral future in which all of their problems would be resolved.

But, for Arthur, there was only one solution. He wanted to be married as soon as possible. If they had a civil ceremony, at least they would be married while they waited for the Church's decision. For him every day until they were man and wife was an agony of anticipation. Once they were married, everyone would *have* to accept it. A *fait accompli.*

Wednesday evening, the sixth of November; it was one week since Jonas Hillman had lost a family fortune in the collapse of the stock market. Arthur thought sadly about how stricken his grandfather had been at the news that his youngest son had squandered everything he had struggled to build. Inherited wealth caused more problems than it solved, he was convinced. If Jonas hadn't had a successful business handed to him, he might have been more careful with his investments. Jacob, although he hadn't been particularly successful, had not speculated with his money. In the end, he had been the wise one.

It was after six when Arthur drove up to the Nurses' Residence to call for Molly. Today was her birthday and they were going to her mother's house for a celebration.

"Sorry I'm late, sweetheart. I was held up in the office. Have you been waiting long?" he said as she slid into his roadster. He looked around to be sure they weren't observed, then leaned over to kiss her. "Happy Birthday!"

"Thank you, darling. I don't feel twenty-three. Do you realize that my mother was married and already had two children by the time she was my age? I'll never be able to match that."

"If you'd just me a chance, I'd like to try," was his rakish reply.

"Oh, you!" She moved closer and hugged his arm. She noticed he had turned east and was heading up Franklin Street instead of crossing over the river. "Where are we going?"

"I have to pick something up at my office. It'll just take a minute. We still have plenty of time."

"All right. But I know your 'minute' and I don't want to be late."

"We won't. I promise."

When they reached the office, Arthur unlocked a file cabinet and took out a small velvet box. Molly was looking at his framed diplomas on the wall. He walked over to her, opened the box, and held it out for her to see. Inside was a ring—a round sapphire encircled by smaller diamonds.

"Arthur! What a beautiful ring . . ." She raised her eyes to his uncertainly. "It looks . . . old . . ."

"It *is* old. It belonged to my grandmother, my mother's mother. The next person to wear it will be my wife. Molly, will you . . . please, say you'll marry me!" He took the ring out of the box. "May I put it on?"

She held her breath as she allowed him to slip the ring on her finger. She looked at it wonderingly, closed her eyes briefly, then shook her head.

"Arthur . . . darling, it's too soon. Please try to understand me. I'm not saying we can't marry, but we have to give it time."

"Molly, I don't *need* time. I could spend the rest of my life trying to find someone, and it would still be you."

"I know. I feel the same. It's just that I need more time to . . . to convince my family. Believe me, I know them and I know it will be all right, if you'll just be patient. . . ."

His face showed his disappointment. "Will you keep the ring and wear it when we're together?"

"I'll wear it when we're together, but you'd better keep it, darling. How would I explain it if someone else found it in a drawer?" She couldn't bear the hurt look in his eyes. She loved him so much. Her heart ached with love for him. All she wanted in this world was to be his wife . . . to become Mrs. Arthur Hillman, safe, happy, and loved by him for the rest of her life.

She was tempted to tell him she would elope—run away with him and be married by a justice of the peace in someplace like Maryland. Once it was accomplished, what could anyone do? Her mother loved her enough to stand by her. It would be so easy!

But the teachings and habits of a lifetime are strong. For all of her life, even in her rebellious years, she had adhered to Church and duty. How could she not give the Church, which loved her, the chance to bless their marriage? Marriage was a lifelong union. Wasn't it better to wait for a few months than to have the stain of a hasty, ill-considered act to mar their future? She had to make him understand. . . .

"Arthur . . . darling . . . there's nothing I want more than to wear your ring, to let everyone know how much I love you." She reached up and took his face in her hands, wanting to stroke away the dejection she read there.

"It's because I love you so much, because I'll be so proud to be your wife, that I want to do it the right way. I know if we aren't hasty, in the end we'll be much happier. Isn't that worth waiting for?"

He sighed, trying to smile. He had so hoped she would wear his grandmother's ring tonight, thus announcing their engagement. It wasn't going at all the way he had thought it would. In the first flush of new love, all things had seemed possible. Who was it who said "Love conquers all"? That person must have been living on another planet.

They drove in silence over the bridge. It was a clear evening. The lights from the city were reflected in the lazy current below.

Molly attempted to raise his spirits, understanding his disappointment. "I'm really sorry, Arthur. Please don't be angry."

He smiled down at her. "I'm not angry, honey. I just wish it didn't have to be so difficult for us. I still think that two adults ought to be able to decide whether they are meant to be married to each other, and everyone else should accept their decision."

"You make it sound so logical." She brooded for a few minutes. "Let's just believe that it will all work out. Meanwhile, I want you to smile on my birthday."

"Oh, m'gosh! Birthday! I completely forgot." They had pulled up in front of the old frame house on Sunset Lane in Forty Fort. Arthur reached around behind the seat and brought out a festively wrapped package. "This is for you. Happy Birthday, darling."

She carefully removed the silk ribbons and heavy paper with the Saks Fifth Avenue imprint. He had been in New York two weeks before and had taken the opportunity to shop for a gift. "Ohhh . . ." she breathed, as she removed a heathery blue cashmere sweater from the tinted tissue in the box. "The color! My favorite!"

"I hoped it might make up for the sweater that got ruined in the rain." His eyes crinkled as he grinned. He kissed the tip of her nose.

"You've already made up for that." She laid her head on his shoulder. "I do love you so."

From the front bedroom, Katherine Shea peered out. What a handsome couple they make, she thought, as she watched Arthur help Molly out of the car. He was looking down at Molly, and Katherine saw the radiant happiness on her daughter's upturned face in the early evening dusk. She knew what it meant, for had she not had her own true love?

God love them and help them, she prayed, as she let the white curtain fall back in place, and hurried down the stairs to greet them.

Arthur spoke to Katherine Shea. He had pressed Molly into letting him discuss their engagement with her mother. He knew that Molly had told Katherine about their love—as if she had to articulate what was plain enough for the charming woman to see for herself. It went so smoothly that he honestly wondered why Molly had been apprehensive.

He arrived at the Shea house early on a Saturday evening, well before Molly was expecting him. He thought it would be easier for him to speak to Molly's mother alone.

"Arthur! Come in." Katherine opened the door wide, welcoming him. "I was just finishing up in the kitchen. May I give you something to drink?"

That might help, he thought, but he declined. "Mrs. Shea, I . . . I . . . uh . . . purposely came over a little early tonight because I want to talk to you."

Her eyes looked knowing under the silvery hair. "Why don't we go into the study, where we can relax." She led the way into the room where she spent much of her time alone. It had been Dan's place, and it brought her comfort to be there.

"I imagine you've guessed what I want to say." He smiled as he seated himself on the sofa.

He looks so young and touching, she thought. Her heart went out to him—to both of them. She understood how much they loved each other and she wanted him for her daughter, even if he wasn't a Catholic.

"Yes." Her laugh was gentle. "But that's not any cleverness on my part!"

Arthur's face felt warm and flushed as he continued. "You may have known we were in love before we realized it ourselves." He searched for the right words. "I'm well aware that you may not have chosen me for Molly, Mrs. Shea. It would be better if we had the same religion . . . but the pieces of life don't always fall neatly into place. If love and devotion count for anything, I can promise you that no one could feel more for Molly than I do." He paused awkwardly, swallowing. Why was it so hard to express himself?

Katherine was deeply affected by the young doctor's sincere manner. What a fine man he was. It was a perplexing problem. If only Dan were alive! What would *he* have said?

"Arthur, I'll tell you the same thing I told Molly when she came to me about marrying you." Katherine toyed with an inkstand on the desk next to her chair. "As far as I'm concerned, I would welcome you as Molly's husband. You represent so many of the finest qualities I would like to see in the man my daughter marries. But, as you know, in the Catholic Church, it isn't the parents whose opinion is primary. We are all children of the Church, and are guided by her priests and bishops."

"Yes, I know that. Molly said you advised her to write to her uncle . . ."

"Her *father's* uncle," Katherine corrected him. "He has always taken a special interest in Dan's . . . in our children . . . there would be no way to avoid involving him."

Arthur nodded. "I wanted to consult your brother, John Riordan. We're close friends, as you know . . . but Molly didn't think I should do that."

"A priest can do nothing without the approval of a bishop, even if he is a relative," she explained. "And I'm afraid that my brother and Thomas Shea don't always see eye to eye." She sighed. "We'll just have to give Bishop Shea some time . . . to see what he says." Although her voice remained neutral, Arthur had the distinct impression that she disliked Bishop Shea.

"But your feelings are . . . ?"

"As far as I'm concerned, Arthur, I'm praying the answer will be yes."

He heaved a deep breath. "You can't imagine how much that means to me, Mrs. Shea. I was truthfully afraid you might send me away!"

"Oh!" She leaned forward impulsively, patting his hand. "I'd be a fool to do something like that." Arthur basked in the warmth of her approval.

"I think maybe I'll take that drink now," he said.

Winter 1929–30

The old family house on Prospect Avenue always gave Arthur a feeling of his roots. He thought it was foolish for his mother to live there alone. It was much too large, drafty in winter, difficult for her to keep clean. However, she wanted to stay there. It was the only home she and Jacob had ever lived in . . . one of those Victorian monstrosities that is so ugly, it takes on a certain beauty. Its high, narrow windows marched at regular intervals around its perimeter. A covered porch surrounded it on all sides. At the two front corners were rounded bays with little peaked roofs. Arthur used to like to sit in those bays when he was a boy, covering the entrances with a blanket, pretending he was on the prow of a ship at sea like his Grandfather Isaac, who had been a ship's captain.

He drove up there on Sunday morning after making his early morning calls at the hospital. Noticing that the front was looking shabby, he wished that he could afford to have it painted for his mother, but half of his patients couldn't pay their bills these days. It was fortunate that the mortgage had been paid off long ago. His father had never trusted the stock market and had left his estate in gold certificates, so his widow was relatively well off compared to those who had lost most of their holdings.

"Mother," he called as he opened the front door, which was unlocked, as usual. Arthur frowned. She really shouldn't live here all alone without locking the door, he thought. There were so many unemployed desperate men wandering around these days. . . .

"Is that you, Arthur?" Rose Hillman came into the front hall, removing her apron. She was dressed in a long-sleeved dark dress with immaculate white collar and cuffs. Her hair was neatly combed in a bun. No matter what time of day it was, his mother always looked as if she were expecting company.

She smiled as she gave him a kiss and patted his cheek. "I was hoping you would drop by today. Have you had breakfast?"

"Maybe later," Arthur answered. He was feeling nervous. "I have to talk to you, Mother."

She walked into the front parlor and sat down on the Duncan Phyfe sofa, motioning him to a chair. "Well, Arthur, what do you have to talk about?"

"There's a girl . . . a young woman . . . I'd like you to meet." He just blurted it out.

"Arthur! A girl? Who is she?" There was genuine delight on her face.

"Well, she's . . . she's . . . her name is Molly Shea." There was no reaction from his mother. "She's not Jewish," he finished lamely.

"Her name is Molly Shea," she repeated. And then she spoke to the air. "With a name like Molly Shea, he tells me she isn't Jewish."

"Mother, *listen* to me. Please. You'll like her, I *know* you'll like her. She's wonderful. A lovely person. From a fine family." Why was he saying all these things! He began again, in a quiet, firm voice. "I'm in love with her, very much in love. And I want to marry her. I've never wanted anything so much in my entire life."

Rose looked at her favorite child, for she admitted in her heart that he was her favorite. He was so handsome, so sunny in temperament. As a child and as a man he had always been one of the blessed. Blessed with good looks, charm, intelligence, and a personal magnetism that had seen him through every stage of life with success. To her way of thinking, there was not a girl— a *Jewish* girl—in the entire state of Pennsylvania who would not be fortunate to have him for a husband. What was there for her to say?

"Arthur, my dear, have you really thought about what this will mean? For both of you?"

"I've thought of nothing else for months."

"*Months?* And this is the first that you've spoken of it to me?"

"I haven't wanted to keep it from you, Mother. It was Molly who was afraid to have me tell you. She thought that you wouldn't accept it. I told her you would."

"Accept? It is not for me to accept or not to accept, Arthur. I will accept, and try to love, any woman you marry. I have seen too much unhappiness from mothers who will not accept such things. But before you decide to marry Molly, you must consider so many other things. What about children? What about her family? Surely they must feel some objection. I would imagine they are Roman Catholics?"

He gave a small laugh and shook his head. "Oh, yes, they're Roman Catholics all right! I think they must have more priests and nuns in the family than all the rabbis in Jerusalem. Her father's uncle was head of the diocese in Harrisburg."

"Oh, Arthur, my dear! They will never condone this marriage, then."

"They may not condone it, but they can't prevent us from marrying. We're two adults and we have a right to do as we please." There was defiance in his voice.

"There are many ways to prevent something like that. I hope you know what you're getting involved in."

"How do you know, Mother? What do you know about a Catholic family?"

"I've lived a long time, Arthur. And I know many things about different kinds of people. I will be very surprised if her family doesn't object to this—vehemently."

"But, Mother, you will let me bring her here? Friday night, for dinner?"

She leaned forward then and smoothed his hair back with her hand, a fond, motherly gesture. "Yes, dear, bring your Molly Shea for dinner on Friday. And now, it's Sunday morning, so let's have some bagels."

He smiled gratefully. "Thanks, Mother. . . . Have you got any raisin cookies?"

"Arthur, Arthur . . . still the same Arthur," she laughed.

Rose Hillman met them at the door. She kissed Arthur and looked into Molly's blue eyes. "Come in, my dear." She took Molly's hand. "My son has good taste," she said in her direct way.

Molly, obviously nervous, smiled at Arthur's mother. "Thank you for inviting me, Mrs. Hillman."

They went into the parlor, a room seldom used now that Jacob had died. They sat down and made stilted attempts at polite conversation. Arthur felt a little uneasy himself. It had all the indications of being a stiff evening. He heard footsteps in the upper hall.

"Who's upstairs, Mother?" he asked.

"Nathan came home this afternoon. He has an interview on Monday with a local law firm, so he's spending the weekend."

His brother came down the stairs at a fast trot. "Art!" The two brothers embraced.

"Nate, I'd like you to meet Molly Shea."

Nate took her hand and smiled down into her radiance. His warm brown eyes twinkled. "Molly Shea," he said slowly. "Leave it to that brother of mine to find someone like you in Wilkes-Barre!"

They relaxed then, all of them. Nate had that capacity, to warm people. At first disconcerted to hear that someone else was joining them, Arthur was finally grateful for his brother's presence. He sat back and watched while Molly and Nate settled into easy friendliness. Rose served sherry and little cheese turnovers, then excused herself to see to things in the kitchen. Arthur followed his mother into the pantry.

"Well, Mother, what do you think?" His eyes had such an anxious look in them.

Rose was troubled, but she answered, "I think she's a very beautiful young woman, Arthur. I can see why you're attracted to her."

"Mother, come on. What kind of an answer is that? I wasn't talking about her appearance."

"She seems like a lovely person," Rose answered truthfully. "I can hardly make a judgment in such a few minutes, Arthur. If you like her, she must be nice."

"*Love*, Mother . . . I *love* her!" She nodded and patted his cheek before going into the kitchen. Arthur sighed and returned to the parlor, where Molly and Nate were still talking.

"So your father was Daniel Shea! Imagine that! He was helpful to me when I was trying to get into law school. He talked to me about Dickinson, but I decided to go to Penn after all. He was an awfully nice man, Molly. I was sorry to hear he died."

Rose came to tell them that dinner was ready. They went into the dining room, where she had lit the Sabbath candles on the sideboard. There was a fruit centerpiece on the table, which was set with a white damask cloth, and the second-best china. Arthur knew that his mother was treading a fine line between making an effort to please, but not to impress.

Suddenly he had a terrible thought. It was Friday night and he was sure his mother had prepared meat of some sort. He had forgotten to ask her to serve fish for Molly.

He needn't have been concerned. Rose carried a tureen in from the kitchen. It was mushroom and barley soup, which she served with fresh *challah*. After that came baked stuffed sea bass with parslied carrots and buttered green beans. Rose was a fine cook of substantial American-Jewish fare. She had learned from the best—talented Rachel—when she had come to Wilkes-Barre as a bride.

For dessert there was a chocolate roll. It was iced with fudge topping which had a bittersweet flavor resulting from strong coffee added to the icing. The filling was chocolate mousse. The two brothers each had second helpings. It was obligatory to have seconds when Rose served one of her specialties. Molly took a second cup of tea, unable to eat more food.

"Mrs. Hillman, that was a delicious meal. Thank you for having fish. I appreciate that," Molly said with sincerity. She felt much more at ease now with Arthur's mother, who wasn't at all what Molly had expected. She had had a mental image of Rose, thinking of her as a female counterpart of Arthur, she supposed. Instead, she found a tall, strong-looking brunette with brown eyes, more handsome than pretty, more dignified than charming. She did possess warmth, though, and Molly felt instinctively that Rose Hillman did not have a single falseness in her character. On second thought, Arthur *was* like his mother in some important ways. They just didn't resemble each other physically.

Molly helped Rose clear the table while Arthur and Nate went into the comfortable sitting room, less formal than the parlor, where the family had always relaxed when they were together.

Nate cocked a quizzical eyebrow in Arthur's direction. "When's the wedding?" he joked.

Arthur answered with a rueful smile, "If it were up to me, it'd be tomorrow." He shoved his hands deep in his pockets and paced back and forth on the geometrically patterned carpet. He remembered when he was a boy, he had a habit of counting each grouping of octagons on the Afghan design, constantly rearranging them in his mind in groups of threes or fours.

Nate tapped on his coffee cup with his finger. "Who is it up to, then? I assume that Molly's in love with you. That's quite apparent."

"I'm not really sure, but I think it's more or less a decision her uncle has to make—he's a bishop."

"Why her uncle—even if he is a bishop? Molly's of age, isn't she? I would think it's a decision the two of you should make and then ask for her family's approval."

Arthur shook his head in discouragement. "Well, that's essentially what we've done. But Molly doesn't want me to tackle them head on. She thinks if we don't force the issue, she will be given permission to marry me."

Nate frowned. "You mean marry you in the Church?"

Arthur shrugged. "I'm not sure, Nate. She says sometimes priests will marry Catholics to non-Catholics under special circumstances. Her family has influence in the Church. . . . I wish I knew more about it."

"Art, you have to be realistic. She's one fabulous woman, and I don't blame you for wanting to marry her. But I think either you're going to have to convert, or agree that your children will be Catholic, or Molly will have to convert to Judaism . . . unless you agree to have a civil ceremony. Those are your only options—none of them entirely easy."

Arthur stared into space, nodding slowly. "I know," he whispered.

Nate saw them to the car, standing at the end of the walk, despite the cold night air, until they drove down the hill and out of sight. Rose watched him through the front window as he stood with one hand in his pocket, his head bent forward a little in a characteristic stance. Her two sons were so different. Arthur, fair, strikingly handsome, strong and athletic, had developed from a thoughtful, inward child into an outgoing personality. His cares had been thrust upon him at too early an age. Without a complaint he had laid aside his opportunity in Philadelphia to pursue his career with an outstanding surgeon. He had assumed the role of family leader, the strong shoulder on which they could all lean. And now he was asking only one small favor. That she bless his desire to marry Molly Shea.

Nathan came in, closing the door almost reluctantly. Nathan, whom she must learn not to protect and coddle. That wasn't going to prolong his life. Once so fun-loving and boisterous, he had been the dominant one of the two when the boys were growing up. Now his gentleness was almost frightening.

He hadn't been this soft, this sweet before he went to Philadelphia. There had been a restlessness, almost an anger in him during the years after he was gassed in France, when he lived at home helping his father in the business. But since he had left for the University of Pennsylvania Law School three years ago, the bitterness had evaporated. He seemed reconciled now to coming back to Wilkes-Barre to practice law. She thought his resignation had to do with his disappointment over the Landau girl, who had married a doctor last year and was living in St. Louis.

To look at him, six feet tall—almost as tall as Arthur—clean-cut features, not classically handsome, but strong and appealing, with dark brown, friendly eyes and wavy brown hair, no one would ever think that he wasn't in sound health. She sighed, vowing to treat him as if he were.

"What do you think about Arthur's girl, Mother?"

"I couldn't help but like her, Nathan. She's sweet and lovely, and adores your brother. I can see that in her eyes. But I'm very worried about them. I don't think they're going to find happiness."

"You're not going to stand in their way, are you, Mother?" he asked quickly.

"Nathan, I will never stand in my children's way when it comes to marriage. I know how that can ruin lives. Look at poor Joseph Lasker. He would have married the Stolfo girl long ago if it weren't for his mother. I think it's a disgrace!"

"Mother, you're *so* naïve! They *are* married—I thought everyone in town knew that except Mrs. Lasker!"

Rose was astonished. "Well then, for heaven's sake, why not say so? Is it better to pretend they're living in sin than to admit that they're married?" She shook her head. "I will *never* understand some people! What about that little boy, the one they say is her dead brother's child?"

Nate laughed gently and hugged his mother. "Ah, Mother! You know, I don't think she *ever* had a brother—dead *or* alive."

"Do you think she liked me, Arthur?" Molly was seldom timid.

"Are you kidding? How could she help but like you, sweetheart? I know she did—I could tell. And Nate, too. He told me so."

"Nate is wonderful. He really made me feel comfortable. I was so nervous when we first arrived."

They were sitting in the little study which used to be her father's. Now Kitty used it to do her needlework or to read on lonely winter evenings. They had added a log and stirred the embers of the fire, which had burned low when Molly's mother retired. The flames cast a cheery light on the paneled walls. Daniel Shea's lawbooks filled one wall from ceiling to floor. A desk stood, clear and unused, in a corner of the room, nothing but a clean blotter and an ashtray beside the bronze lamp. A pipe rack with six pipes rested on a little table next to a leather easy chair. The chair was well-worn, with indentations where a man would sit or lean his head against the back as he smoked one of those pipes and looked into the leaping fire.

Arthur felt the presence of Dan Shea in that room. What would he think of them? Would he have helped them in their love? Would he have seen that Arthur honored his daughter, would protect her and cherish her all his life? The fragility of life, the elusiveness of love, bore in on him. Two women, his mother and Molly's, alone in the houses which they had shared for all too brief a time with the men they had loved. And now they were left with memories and empty rooms.

These melancholy thoughts suited his mood.

It had taken Nate to articulate what Arthur had really known all along. Their choices were few and simple. If they were to be married by a priest, he would either have to convert to Catholicism or agree that their children be raised as Catholics. He couldn't imagine converting to Catholicism, even if his religious convictions *were* relaxed. As for their children—could he do that? Have his sons and daughters taught that their father and his family were, by virtue of their Jewish faith, denied salvation? With time, wouldn't that cause dissension between them if they took the Church's teachings seriously?

And to be married by a rabbi? It was unthinkable that Molly would convert to Judaism. . . . With her strong religious training, despite her love for him, she would always suffer from anxiety and feelings of guilt.

They could, of course, have a civil wedding and hope for the blessing of a priest and a rabbi later on. They had discussed this, and Arthur believed this would be the best solution. He knew his family would support him in this. But Molly's family, with their strong Church connections, would resist it, certainly.

There was another choice. One which Nathan hadn't mentioned and Arthur refused to consider. Not to marry at all. That was what everyone except the two of them was hoping for, he suspected. It made him feel both enraged and desolate to think of how little encouragement they had.

He sighed deeply, a troubled sound, unaware that she had heard. They turned to face each other at the same moment. Molly's eyes were liquid with unshed tears. "I'm so discouraged," she whispered.

He held her close, covering her face with kisses, wanting to take her into the very soul of him, loving her more than he ever dreamed it possible for man to love woman. He told her that their love was strong enough to protect them against anyone or anything. When she was with him, when he held her in his strong arms and she felt the terrible sweetness of his kisses, she could look into his eyes and believe it was so.

She had made her petition to her great-uncle, Bishop Shea. The reply had not been encouraging. The bishop did not think it would be productive for him to meet with Dr. Hillman at this time. He would, however, be happy to see Molly and try to help her examine her conscience and her frailties and to instruct her in the methods she might use to improve herself. In a separate letter to Katherine, he had encouraged her to remember how important the Church was to her dead husband's family and asked her to support Molly in the perseverance and self-discipline of that faith which was so important to all of them.

Poor Katherine Shea had been the one to advise Molly to write directly to her great-uncle rather than seek counsel from their parish priest or Father John Riordan, whom Molly felt would be sympathetic to their cause. Katherine knew that in the end Bishop Shea would regard this as a family matter, reflecting on his own position in the Church, and he would have the final say. To put her brother in opposition to him would be unwise.

"Darling, please let me talk to your mother again about us. I think it's time."

Molly told him about the letter from Thomas Shea. "Arthur, I know that with time it will be easier. I truly believe that it would be better if we waited for a while. Just a few months. When they see that I'm determined, they'll give in, make a compromise."

"Would you object if I talked to Father John? He's my friend as well as your uncle. And I need some answers. I'm not even sure I know what questions to ask."

Ashley *February 1930*

"You're a sight for sore eyes! Come in, Arthur. . . . Now that the clinics are spread out all over the place, I don't get to see you as much as I used to." John led the way through the drafty front hall into his study, where a fire was burning.

"I see you've made a few changes, John." Arthur looked approvingly at the attractive framed prints on the wall which had replaced the institutional religious pictures. There was an assortment of crewel and needlepoint pillows bunched in the corners of the brown sofa. Two colorful afghans were draped over the arm of the couch and the back of an easy chair.

"My sister Katherine went overboard at Christmas! I don't think there's much danger of the bishop or the vicar paying an unannounced visit," John jested. "I've actually grown fond of this room."

They chatted on about trivial things for some time. Arthur was leading up to something, but John decided to let him find his own way.

"John," Arthur finally began, "if someone who wasn't a Catholic wanted to know more about the religion, how would he go about it? I mean, are there some books . . . something succinct and informative?"

So that was it? He had suspected all along. *Heavenly Father, please help me,* he prayed.

John's face was expressionless. "I have a number of books that would give facts and perspectives, starting with the simple catechism and the missal," he said easily. He walked over to the bookshelf and removed two slim volumes, and then another. "There's this, written by a non-Catholic in a question and answer format. It comes down rather hard on the faith, but I can't argue with the facts. He handed the three books to Arthur. Arthur read the title of the third. *The True Faith? A Protestant Questions the Roman Catholic Church.*

Father John waited for an interval. "Then, there's this one," he said casually. "It's written for someone who may be contemplating marriage with a Catholic, and is considering whether or not to convert . . . or whether to marry at all." He looked steadily at Arthur. For some seconds, Arthur did not meet his eyes, then he stared back at the priest unflinchingly. It was Father John who finally looked away.

"How long have you known?" Arthur asked.

"I've only wondered about it, Arthur. For quite a few months. No one's mentioned it to me."

"John, I wanted to tell you about it immediately. Ever since we discovered it ourselves—since September. Molly was fearful. She told her mother, who suggested she write to Bishop Shea. She tells me he has been . . . difficult. I think it was a mistake to ask him. We should've made our decision and informed him."

"You can't be married by a priest without a dispensation, Arthur. And the Church wouldn't recognize any other marriage. I don't think Molly could face up to a denial of the Sacraments. She may be a bit of a rebel, like me, but she is a true believer. If she went against her faith, I believe it would eventually harm your marriage."

"I'm not asking her to go against her faith, John. I'm perfectly willing to make a compromise, and so is Molly. It's her family—or some of them—who're standing in the way."

John busied himself filling his pipe. "Your family has no objections, Arthur?"

"Objections? Yes, certainly. They don't want me to marry a Catholic. But they like Molly and my mother has told me she would accept my decision, whatever it is. There are some Jewish mothers in this town who wouldn't—in fact, don't. My mother thinks they just cause unhappiness for their children. It doesn't prevent their sons from falling in love. Somehow, it's usually a son . . . mothers and sons. You don't know Jewish mothers, John."

"Ah, mothers . . . mothers. . . . No, I don't know much about Jewish mothers. . . . Let me tell you a story. It's about a family. . . .

"It was a large family, nine children, the last child of three. . . ."

As he spoke, Father John's voice took on the singsong brogue of the born storyteller.

"The father was a good-looking, merry fellow, much given to having fun, despite the admonitions of his pious wife. He was killed one day by a train when he crossed the tracks on his way home from work. He was only forty-nine . . . a foreman at a factory which manufactured mining equipment. He took a shortcut through the freight yards that day because he wanted to hurry home and hide the birthday present he'd bought for his eleven-year-old son. It was an accordian. The boy wanted to learn music. . . .

"One train had just passed out of the freight yards, so he didn't hear a second fast freight approaching from the opposite direction where a switch had been thrown, sending it onto the track he was crossing. There were so many pieces to pick up, he was buried in a child's coffin. . . ."

John swallowed and sucked in his cheeks, struggling for composure, then continued.

"They were an Irish family, and the Irish have a certain way with death. Everyone gathers to console the widow, and so seriously do they take the responsibility that many of them drink themselves into a fine state of consolation, while the poor widow sits grieving.

"It was during this period of mourning that the youngest child, the little three-year-old boy, took ill with a strange malady which no one much noticed, because they were all so preoccupied with the wake. By the time the child's mother tended to her youngest, he was in a coma, his brain and spinal column affected by the disease. Nowadays, I suppose it might be recognized as meningitis.

"They told her he wouldn't live. So she made a novena to the Blessed Virgin that if her baby survived, she would dedicate a son to serve the Lord in His Church. The son she chose—indeed, the only one of her other five sons young enough to influence—was the would-be musician, the eleven-year-old.

"Now this lad was a bit of a high-spirited fellow. And he liked the girls, too, you can believe it. As he approached his thirteenth birthday, he became aware that the girls thought fairly well of him. He kissed a pretty wench or two in the playground, he pulled some pigtails, he played truant, and he got himself in trouble with the nuns often enough, but he could usually charm his way out of it. In other words, a regular sort of a fellow, but with a head on his shoulders and an ability to succeed at his studies when he had a mind to.

"Well, when this lad was thirteen—the age when you had your Bar Mitzvah, if you can recall that time—he was sent away to the seminary, where he spent the next five years completing his schooling with none but the good fathers and his fellow students—a somber, quiet bunch, each in possession of a vocation.

"He was told *he* had a vocation, and when you're told something often enough beginning at a tender age, you don't think of questioning it, or you haven't got the gumption to. So, he went from that seminary to a higher one, and seven years after that, he was ordained a priest.

"His little brother, by the way, did survive. Only, he had severe brain damage and he, too, had to spend his life in an institution of another sort. But, a bargain is a bargain . . ."

John sat looking away from him.

Arthur broke the silence. "I have a feeling I know the priest."

John looked at him and smiled his sweet, slightly sad smile. "None other."

They spoke then about the Church's views on mixed marriages. There were elaborations and special circumstances such as a pregnancy in which the rules were sometimes relaxed, John told him. Quite often, it depended on the local diocese.

"Our local bishop—Callahan—is a strict and conservative man. . . . I wouldn't advise that route," said John. "And even if I were willing to act independently and take whatever the consequences might be, I find the idea of having a confrontation with Bishop Shea a most unhappy prospect!"

"John, that's not why I came to see you," Arthur said. "I wouldn't want to put you in such a position. I'd really like to learn more about the Church, about Catholicism. I think I should try to understand this from Molly's point of view. I had hoped that my impression of our choices might be inaccurate. Unfortunately, it's just about what I expected."

"I wish I could be more encouraging, Arthur. Someday, I believe, the Church will relax its rules on intermarriage. That doesn't help you and Molly much, does it?"

Arthur regarded his friend. "John, would I greatly offend you if I told you that it is incomprehensible to me as a thinking man and as a scientifically trained doctor that a person can be expected to so unquestioningly accept dogma? If I were born to it, I don't believe I could not question it."

John nodded. "You are not the first to say that, Arthur."

"No, of course not," he acknowledged. "That is not to say that what Christianity or any other religion stands for is not my creed. But why not state it that way? Ethics, morality, concern for one's fellow man, everything the Ten Commandments say?"

"Because man is weak and needs supernatural reasons for behaving in the ways of righteousness and justice," answered Father John.

Arthur looked at him quizzically. "Do you honestly believe that?"

John nodded emphatically. "I honestly do. You'll notice, wherever there is a breakdown of law and individual rights, you'll find religion under attack."

"Then how do you explain the Inquisition?"

"I don't," he said. "There are always aberrations we can't explain."

"I just have to believe in man's intrinsic goodness, or else life wouldn't be worth living," said Arthur. "I guess if religion helps him to be good, whether or not I believe in it, I should be grateful for its existence!"

"You know, Arthur, sometimes so much is asked of the priest. To be virtuous, to be all-wise and knowing. He's set above other men, to lead, to counsel. It's a weight to bear. Sometimes, Arthur, I am so unbearably lonely. . . . Why do we think the *priest* has no need of compassion and understanding?"

He sighed. "It's good to have a friend like you. You don't judge me. I don't feel constrained when I talk to you."

Arthur smiled. "Maybe I would've made a good priest!" He rose to leave.

John put his hand on Arthur's shoulder. "If there's anything I think of to help you, Arthur, you can be sure I will."

"Thanks, John." At the door, he shook hands with the priest. "We're very much in love, you know," he said, the emotion there in his eyes.

"My two favorite people, in love," John said, his voice hollow. "That should make me very happy."

He looked lonelier than usual as he closed his door on the world.

"You're a *Republican?* Arthur . . . there hasn't been a Republican in my family . . . *ever!*"

"Gee, Molly . . . I'm sorry," he said lamely. "Is that worse than being Jewish?" he added in a stage whisper.

"I don't know," she retorted, "but I think so."

Winter. The winter of 1930. The nation was in shock. The vital signs depressed. Wyoming Valley had never enjoyed the euphoria of the twenties in the same style as other parts of America, but it keenly felt the steady grinding down of the economy. Unlike the British, America's unemployed had no government programs to turn to. They had to depend on state and local relief organizations—whose funds were rapidly depleted—and private charity. All too often, those in a position to be charitable were the opposite. . . . Andrew Mellon, the Secretary of the Treasury in President Hoover's cabinet, thought it would be good for the workingman if the economy hit the skids. Americans would learn to work harder, he said. They would live a more moral life, have better values. And if they should not survive . . . ? Well then, better men *would* survive, and *they* would pick up the pieces. . . . Tell *that* to those miners up on the mountain.

During those winter months, Arthur and Molly didn't go up to the cabin. It was too cold there, even with a fire and the wood stove, and the road became impassable. Arthur thought that was just as well. Now that their marriage was just a matter of time, waiting for word from Molly's great-uncle, they were obliged to use restraint. In his Wilkes-Barre apartment, as if Katherine Shea and Rose Hillman might march in on them armed with moral indignation, they did not make love. They explored each other, got to know the person each loved.

Molly cooked dinner. They listened to music, read. This wasn't the most appealing living arrangement Arthur had ever had. Three small, odd-shaped rooms with high ceilings and narrow windows. Other than filling the bookcases and putting up some curtains, he'd done a minimum of furnishing after signing the lease. He'd had more interest in outfitting his offices on the floor below. His only reason for taking this apartment had been for its convenience, its low rent, and to prevent a noisy tenant from moving in above his consultation room. When Molly was there with him, however, it was surprisingly warm and inviting—their place to hibernate while the severe winter blustered outside.

Arthur loved poetry; Molly had given him a book of Yeats for his birthday in July, before they had become lovers. Sometimes they read the love lyrics to each other; Molly had a way of reading the Irish poet's works that touched a place deep within Arthur's soul.

There was one short poem which she read mellifluously, in her sweet, rich voice, slowing down at the end, until it was low . . . almost a whisper. A woeful little piece which, when he read it once alone, saddened him with its prophetic melancholy.

> When you are old and gray and full of sleep,
> And nodding by the fire, take down this book,
> And slowly read, and dream of the soft look
> Your eyes had once, and of their shadows deep;
>
> How many loved your moments of glad grace,
> And loved your beauty with love false or true,
> But one man loved the pilgrim soul in you,
> And loved the sorrows of your changing face;
>
> And bending down beside the glowing bars,
> Murmur, a little sadly, how Love fled
> And paced upon the mountains overhead
> And hid his face amid a crowd of stars.

Molly had twice journeyed to Harrisburg to implore her great-uncle to intercede for them. Arthur had driven her there both times, waiting in his car, hoping to be summoned by the bishop.

On the first visit, Molly had come back to the car somewhat encouraged, reporting that her uncle was making inquiries. "He said he'll speak to me again in a month or two, darling. He did ask me to reflect on my decision . . . to realize what a serious step I'm taking." She looked at him. "That's only reasonable, don't you agree?"

"Yes, Molly, I realize the bishop's concern. It is a major step for you to marry me . . . but did he say anything encouraging? Didn't he want to talk to me? I really would like to see him, to try to reason with him, Molly."

"I don't think that would help right now, Arthur. Maybe the next time, we can see him together."

After the next audience, Molly was subdued. The bishop had been unwilling to meet Arthur. She had reacted with anger, telling him she thought he was being unreasonable.

"We are not dealing with Dr. Hillman's personality, my child," Thomas Shea had told her. "I am sure that any man you would consider marrying is an exemplary individual. If I met with Dr. Hillman and then your petition is rejected, it would be interpreted as a personal slight, when, in fact, the person has no bearing on the outcome."

Arthur was terribly upset. "Well, Molly, that doesn't sound very encouraging to me."

"He did say he was working on an idea of how to resolve this 'dilemma'—that was his word," she replied.

It was that flimsy statement on which she was pinning her hopes. But March came, and still there was no word from Harrisburg.

Arthur heard the telephone ringing in his apartment as he stamped the snow off his boots in the lower hall. He had just returned from the hospital after his evening rounds. The roads were slippery. As he ran up the stairs, he hoped this wouldn't mean a house call.

"Doc?" a hoarse voice came over the wire. It was Eddy Valentine, the United Mine Workers Union organizer from Scranton.

"Hello, Eddy. What's on your mind this stormy winter night?" he said pleasantly. He had spoken to Eddy several times over the months since the union man had become interested in the clinics they were holding for the miners. It seemed strange that he was calling at this late hour.

"Listen, Doc, I gotta talk to ya. There's someone somewhere's got it in for ya *bad*. I got wind of a pretty nasty piece that's s'posed to be in the Scranton *Daily Dispatch* next Sunday. It's all about *you*, says some ugly things. The thing is . . . it doesn't say what they really mean to say . . ."

Arthur felt a sense of dread. "What does it *mean* to say, Eddy?" he asked, his tone worried.

"It's on account of the clinics, Doc . . . no doubt about it. My source says that's what's behind it. But y'know how these guys operate . . . they say lots of other things, things to . . . uh . . . discredit you . . ."

"No, Eddy, I'm afraid I *don't* know how 'these guys' operate. People I know don't happen to do things that way. Just what does this article actually say, and tell me how you found out about it." He was angry now. He listened with disbelief and growing rage as Valentine read him the draft from a popular column in the Scranton paper.

"Whew! Eddy . . . what can I do about it? It's all a bunch of *lies!* Can't it be stopped? What if I talk to this guy, Preston Black?" He was scared. Nothing like this had ever happened to him! Had it ever happened to *anyone?*

"Listen, Doc, it ain't gonna do ya any good to talk to Black. In fact, he'd love nothin' better than to have somethin' real on ya—tryin' to kill a piece. I got some friends who I went to school with when I was a kid. We went diff'rent ways . . . y'know . . . I mean, some of them are . . . uh . . . with the mob. For you, I don't mind askin' a favor."

"Absolutely not, Eddy! I appreciate your offer. I know you're only trying to help, but I don't want to have anything to do with organized crime . . . that's all I'd need, for them to think I had connections *there!"* He laughed, despite his alarm.

"O.K., Doc," Eddy soothed him. "Just a suggestion. If ya know anyone in the newspaper business, I think ya better get to them. I'll scout around—see if I can find out anything else."

Arthur thanked Valentine for alerting him. He sat there after the union man had hung up, trying to clear his mind, to digest what he had learned.

Was this where being a crusader led? What had he done that was so infuriating to the mine owners . . . to solid citizens like Cyril Buckland, or conservative doctors like William Matlin? Were his simple efforts to see that a few mining families received medical care so threatening to these men of the establishment that they would try to ruin his reputation and career with this vile, this vicious slander?

Arthur suspected that it would be next to impossible to trace the source of the article. No doubt, if either Buckland or Matlin were confronted, he would claim outraged innocence. Arthur could think of only one thing to do.

He picked up the telephone and dialed Jim Flannery's number. "Jim, I know this is a helluva time to call you, so late at night . . . but I've got a real problem, and you're the only one I can think of who may be able to help."

Jim didn't hesitate. "Come on over, Art. Don't worry about the time. I didn't want to sleep tonight anyway!"

Fifteen minutes later he was at the Flannery home on South River Street, sitting in the kitchen with Jim. He sipped a bourbon and soda, surrounded by high chairs, discarded toy trucks, dolls, and all the paraphernalia of Louise Flannery's big, messy, homey center of operations.

Arthur told Jim what he had learned from Eddy Valentine. Jim was aghast. "Those sons-of-bitches! Who the hell do they think they are, trying to smear you like that? Does he know who's behind it, Art?"

"He's not certain, but it looks like someone like Matlin or Cyril Buckland got to Preston Black, their columnist—he covers coal, railroads, and politics. . . . Maybe through some of the mine owners up around Clarks Summit. But, dammit, if they want to write about my clinic activities, why don't they write about *that?* Why do a personal hatchet job?"

"Coward's way," answered Jim. But Arthur could tell he was worried. He scratched his head and furrowed his brow as he tried to figure something out.

Finally he nodded. "I guess my brother, Don, is the best person to talk to . . . or maybe my Dad. . . . There must be some way to keep that article from appearing. The *Dispatch* is a real conservative newspaper—in the vest pockets of the mine owners. They've never had good relations with our family, unfortunately. But maybe Dad or Don knows someone who can get to them." He shook his head. "That's a filthy, low-down article, Art . . . no one would believe it for a moment"—he grinned—"I don't think! If I didn't know it would harm you, I'd tell you to let them print it, because it's so ridiculous."

"Jim, if Molly or her family ever get hold of that article . . ."

"Don't be crazy! Molly's too sensible," said Jim, pouring Arthur another bourbon. "You two are really serious, Arthur . . . aren't you?"

"Ah, Jim . . ." Arthur sighed. "I'm so much in love with her, you can't imagine."

Jim's face broke into his infectious Irish smile. "I've got a pretty good imagination, Arthur!"

"We want to get married . . . but there are all sorts of problems . . . or one big problem—religion."

"I told you her family was crazy religious. They really take their Catholicism seriously. . . . Not like us."

"Oh yeah, 'not like you' . . . you've only got four kids in six years!"

"I *like* kids. So does Louise. Believe me, I don't think we'll have any more. . . . *Look* at this place!" Jim's arm swept out, indicating the cluttered kitchen. "But, seriously, Molly's family is strong for the Church. Her father's uncle is a bishop."

"Don't I know that! That's our main problem. Her mother is in favor of our getting married, but her great-uncle has to give his consent . . . and so far, he hasn't."

"I don't want to discourage you, Art, but you should ask my grandfather about Bishop Shea sometime. He married my grandparents when he was just a young priest starting out here in Wilkes-Barre. Gramps doesn't mince words, as you know! He says Bishop Shea is a fanatic. Evidently everyone in the Harrisburg diocese breathed a sigh of relief when he retired a couple of years ago. He hung on until he was past seventy-five."

"Thanks a lot! That's just what I needed tonight—some more good news." Arthur gave a short laugh. "How *is* your grandfather, Jim?"

"Still going strong! He'll be eighty-four soon. They don't make 'em like that anymore."

"I know! When I met him at your wedding, he told me he knows my grandfather. They met when Grandfather first came to this country. Mr. Flannery's partner, Reuben Sarnoff, was a friend of my grandfather's from Russia."

Arthur had mentioned to Isaac about meeting Garrick Flannery. "Fine gentleman," Isaac had said. "He helped me get my first job in Wyoming Valley . . . for Star Printing Supplies . . ." Isaac had rambled on, reminiscing, the way he sometimes did as he grew older.

"I can tell you, Art, in Gramps' day, no one would've gotten away with something like this Scranton *Dispatch* job, not if *he* knew anything about it.

He would've blasted them right to kingdom come on his editorial page!" Jim laughed as Arthur rose to leave. "Course, he might've ended up in an alley over it! He was a fighter, that man. I used to *love* to listen to the stories about him when I was a kid!"

Jim walked him to the door. "I'll do whatever I can to stop this thing, Art. And if we can't stop it—we'll fight back."

"Thanks, Jim. It's good to know I'm not alone in this." It had stopped snowing. Arthur enjoyed walking the few blocks to his apartment in the hush of the winter night.

The article had been scurrilous. Phrases from what Eddy had read to him over the phone kept running through his mind: ". . . not content with thwarting the established code of medical ethics, Dr. Hillman is trying to drag some of his fellow physicians in Wyoming Valley down with him . . . a bachelor whose morals can be called to question . . . like many of his race, he has chosen the underhanded way . . . has been seen escorting women from some of the outlying coal patches to roadhouses . . . nefarious purposes . . . his companions of a lower sort . . ."

Surely the laws of libel wouldn't allow a newspaper to print such trash. The trouble was, by the time he claimed libel, the article would have appeared and done its damage. Arthur wasn't kidding himself. A young doctor would not be able to continue practicing in a community if such a notorious column appeared in a newspaper with him as its subject.

He tossed and turned all night, sleeping only in small snatches, until the dawn-streaked sky lightened through his window.

Arthur was never sure precisely which combination of friends, or relatives of friends, killed Preston Black's column.

The Flannerys, father and son, called a few people they knew in Lackawanna County. Phoebe Wintermuth had a temper tantrum in her father's executive office—Cyril Buckland never had been able to control his only child. And when W. Hobson Carpenter, M.D. heard from Tom Sloat what was going on, he picked up his telephone, dialed William Matlin's private line in Mountain Springs at seven o'clock in the morning as Dr. Matlin sat over his breakfast coffee. Dr. Carpenter spoke to Matlin in an uncustomarily harsh manner, causing the corpulent physician to alternately turn florid and pale as he visualized what would happen if "good old Hob" should carry out some of his threats.

Arthur was reasonably certain that he was not beholden to any of Eddy Valentine's former classmates.

There was still one person in the family whom Arthur felt would have to pass judgment on his plans to marry Molly. His grandfather.

Isaac, the patriarch, had been steadily declining ever since Jacob's death. To see that strong tower of a man growing old before his eyes was almost sadder for Arthur than his own father's illness had been. Isaac, who had never let adversity or sorrow conquer him in all his long life, saw his firstborn son, the child of his youthful love, laid into the ground with a resignation that disturbed Arthur. It was as if he accepted, at the end of his life, all the bitter blows it had to inflict, knowing it would soon be over.

Where was the buoyant spirit of his pioneering grandfather? What had happened to the resilience, the determination of bygone years? Were they all, then, destined to a defeated old age?

Arthur visited Isaac often, encouraging him to get out of the house, join the family for dinner, and to continue his daily walks to keep up his vigor. With time, Isaac did seem to have conquered his depression. He had relinquished his role in business to his children, finally, so there was nothing to occupy his days. Isaac turned his attention to God. He spent more time in the synagogue each week than he had ever before in his eighty years, deriving comfort and courage from the ancient ritual, the familiar passages committed to memory in his long-ago childhood.

Reluctant to upset Isaac, fearful of his disapproval, Arthur kept postponing the announcement of his marriage plans. One day, though, he and Molly were together when his mother called, asking him to stop to see Isaac, who had been running a fever and had a deep bronchial cough.

Isaac's housekeeper, Marie, greeted them at the door. "Thank heaven, you've come, Dr. Hillman! Maybe he'll listen to you. I can't do a thing with him!"

Isaac was in the sitting room, the place he and Rachel had always liked best. He was sitting on the floor, stacks of books and papers surrounding him. He had emptied out all the cupboards and drawers and was sorting photographs, letters, and family records.

He coughed heavily before he realized Arthur was there, but rose when he saw him, saying heartily, "Arthur! Ah, how nice you came to see me. Come in, my boy, come have a brandy with me. . . . No? Well, some tea and cake, maybe? Marie! Bring something for the boy."

Isaac was dressed, wearing a cardigan and a heavy woolen scarf around his neck. His eyes were bright and his cheeks had high spots of color. Arthur felt his forehead. Fever.

"Grandfather? You know you should be in bed. What are you doing here on the floor? It's cold in this room." Arthur took out his stethoscope. When Isaac protested, he said, "Uh-uh, the time has come for me to give *you* orders! Sit down and let me take a look at you."

After he had finished examining Isaac, Arthur said, "Hmmm! You don't have pneumonia, but you do have a bad chest cold, and you *will* have bronchitis if you don't take care of yourself. I'm going to send over some medicine, and I want you to promise you'll take it. Get into bed, drink hot liquids, and don't get up until I say so." He shook his head in pretended exasperation. Isaac merely smiled.

Marie had set out a tray of tea and cake on the dining-room table. Molly was standing there when Arthur followed his grandfather into the room. Isaac looked from her to Arthur. Then he smiled broadly. "You're a friend of Arthur's?" He took her hand, looked searchingly into her face.

"This is Molly Shea, Grandfather." He was pleased that his voice didn't quaver. "Molly's a nurse at St. Anne's . . . *and* a friend of mine!"

They had tea and cake, then Arthur escorted Isaac up to his bedroom and saw him settled in bed. He called the pharmacy, asking them to send over a prescription. Then he instructed Marie to keep serving warm liquids and showed her how to set up a croup tent.

"Fifteen minutes of steaming every two hours," he ordered. Isaac made a face. "Don't you give Marie any trouble, Grandfather! I'll come to see you tomorrow."

When Arthur paid a call the next morning, he found Isaac looking much better. He nodded with satisfaction as he removed the thermometer from Isaac's mouth.

Isaac reached over to the bed table and picked up a carved wooden box. His smile was gentle as he absently ran his fingers over its surface.

"I haven't seen this for years. It belonged to my father," he said, opening it. He lifted an oval pin set in gold with tiny seed pearls surrounding a hand-painted miniature of a young woman. "This was your grandmother's, my boy . . . your Grandmother Malka. I believe it is a picture of *her* grandmother. They said Malka was wearing it the day . . . the day she had her accident." He held it out to Arthur. "I'd like you to keep these, Arthur. We don't have too many family heirlooms on my side—not like the Frankes, with their jewels and silver."

Arthur was moved and saddened. This was the kind of thing people did at the end of their lives. "Thank you, Grandfather. I'll treasure it. I hope I have a daughter someday, so she can wear it."

Isaac patted the bed. "Come sit down for a minute, Arthur." When Arthur had seated himself on the edge of the bed, Isaac said, "Now, you're such a big man, a doctor, I suppose you're too old to have a talk with your grandfather."

"No, Grandfather. I'll never be too old for that."

Isaac looked at him with love. "That was a beautiful young woman, your friend," he said suddenly, catching Arthur off guard.

Arthur did not meet his gaze. "Yes, she is," he agreed, toying with his blood-pressure apparatus.

"You're in love with her?"

Arthur nodded, an uncertain smile playing across his lips. "Yes." It was barely audible.

"And she's in love with you." It wasn't a question. Again, Arthur nodded. Isaac laid a reassuring hand on his shoulder. "Love, it's a good thing. Love is important." But his smile was sad.

Less than two weeks later, on a Saturday, Isaac spent the morning at prayer in the synagogue. He returned home, where Marie served him his usual light lunch. Afterward, he went for a walk, enjoying the early spring weather. Then he went to his room for a rest.

Molly and Arthur were in Arthur's apartment that Saturday evening, just before meeting the Flannerys and Wintermuths for dinner, when the telephone rang. Arthur went into the bedroom to answer it. Molly heard him say, "Hello, Mother . . ." Then his voice quieted, finally dropping to a murmur. There was a long silence. Then he hung up.

After several minutes, Molly entered the room. He was sitting there, his back to her, his head inclined, and his shoulders bent. She walked over to him and touched his head lightly. "What . . . ?"

He looked up at her and she saw tears in his eyes. His lower lip quivered, "My grandfather . . . he's gone." He brought her against him, burying his face. She felt his shoulders shaking.

"Darling! I'm so sorry." She held him. He felt her hands, firmly rubbing his back, comforting and soothing. "My love, what can I do to help you?" she asked.

He heaved a long breath and drew away from her. "I'm sorry," he apologized, using his handkerchief to wipe his eyes.

She laid her hand against his cheek. "Why are men afraid to cry? Women know that tears help you bear sorrow."

At Isaac's funeral, Arthur found himself remembering shared moments of his boyhood when his grandfather had introduced him to the beauties of nature. Their walks in the woods near Hillside, the dawn boat rides on the Susquehanna, the moonrise campfires on its banks. He could almost hear the sound of Isaac's deep voice. . . . *Remember, Arthur, without love . . . the love of a wife and children . . . nothing else in life is worthwhile. . . .*

How like his grandfather not to have admonished him about falling in love with someone of another faith. To think that he had been afraid to tell Isaac about her. . . .

Next to the open grave, they recited the *Kaddish.* They ended with the Sh'ma. . . . *"Sh'ma Yisroel, Adonoi Elohenu, Adonoi echod . . .* Hear, O Israel, the Lord our God, the Lord is One." The casket was slowly lowered.

Arthur turned from the place where his grandfather, Isaac Hillman, would lie in the soil of his adopted land, next to Rachel Solweiss Hillman, his helpmate in life and, now, his companion in eternity.

Good-bye, Grandfather, said his heart . . . *rest well.*

His eyes scanned the large crowd standing respectfully in the cemetery. To one side, slightly apart from the rest, stood Molly, looking lonely and frightened among strangers.

Spring came early that year. The earth was soft and spongy underfoot at the beginning of April. Molly and Arthur, arms entwined, walked along a trail through the forest preserve near the cabin. They had aired and cleaned it two weeks before, after it had been closed up for the winter. Today, they wore riding breeches and boots, for they had spent two hours on horseback at the stables near Thornhurst.

Molly's cheeks were full of color and her tilted violet eyes sparkled when she smiled at him. Arthur stopped, looking down at her, taking her hands in his.

"Darling, I'm tired of waiting. I want us to be married right away."

"We *will* be married soon. I promise, darling. Just give it a little more time."

"We've given it more than enough time, Molly. Seven months is a very long time, when all I want is to have you for my wife. Will you give me one good reason why we can't just go get married?" He had patiently refrained from urging this until now.

"Arthur, these things take time. We could just 'go get married,' it's true . . . but it would be ever so much better if we have everyone's blessing."

"By 'everyone' I suppose you mean your Uncle Thomas—God's co-captain!"

She was defensive in the face of his sarcasm. "Bishop Shea has been very kind to my family, Arthur. It would seem most ungrateful if I went off without getting his . . . well, not permission, exactly . . . his agreement."

"Well, what's taking him so long? And why so much secrecy about this? I thought the couple did these things together. I should speak to him . . . or someone. I feel like the man who isn't there!"

"Arthur, please don't be angry," she implored him. "Just one more month, and then I promise that if nothing is settled, we'll go ahead and announce our engagement."

"*Engagement!* We're already engaged, Molly. What I want is marriage— you do know the difference?"

She flushed. "In our case, there isn't all that much difference," she said uncomfortably.

He was exasperated. "You see! That's *just* the problem. I never wanted to carry on an affair with you, Molly. I love you and respect you. I knew you wouldn't feel right about this, and for me, it makes no sense at all. The sooner we're married, the better it will be for all concerned. They'll just have to accept it. It's no one else's business, anyway."

"Don't be difficult, dear. It'll all be over soon." She pulled on his hands. "Let's not quarrel on such a lovely day. I want to go back to the cabin now."

She was so dear to him that Arthur quickly forgot his irritation. She had raised a thorny matter, however, one that had troubled him from the beginning of their affair—troubled them both.

That was the question of sin. Mortal sin.

"Molly, Molly," he shook his head in denial. "How can anything so . . . so beautiful be a sin? I can't even think the word 'sin' in connection with our love."

"That's the problem, Arthur. I don't either. Not when we're together. It's only later, when I reflect on it, and realize I have sinned." She looked down at her hands. "I haven't been to confession for months, because I can't honestly promise not to make love with you again."

His failure to understand this concept of sin was a wedge between them. How could such an act of sincerity, such depth of caring, be sinful?

"When we make love, Molly, I'm filled with feelings of purity, with love for life, for God, for all of humanity. To call that a sin is . . . is immoral!" But he knew he would have to be the one to use forbearance.

"Look, sweetheart. We should have been married by now. That's what we both want. I can't let this become a problem for us, on top of all the other problems. I think we shouldn't make love again. Not until we're married."

Her head lifted abruptly. There was a look of surprise . . . and dismay . . . on her face. He realized she was hurt, disappointed.

He stroked her cheek. "Darling, that's not easy for me to say. It's because I love you so much that I say it. I think it's become too much of a burden on your conscience." He put his arms around her. "We can still love each other . . . that's not all there is to making love." He kissed the tip of her nose. She smiled. "That's better."

He bent his head down to hers. "Kissing you is really a soul-satisfying experience," he said huskily.

Arthur was going on maneuvers with his National Guard unit, the 109th Field Artillery, at Tobyhanna for the last two weeks in May. He wanted to be married soon after he returned. He was confident that as soon as they were man and wife, all the problems would become a thing of the past.

His family liked Molly and would grow to love her. Molly's mother was fond of him. She had made that evident. And as for Father John . . . they were close friends. What did a great-uncle have to do with their happiness? Even if he was a bishop.

Molly had an inquiring mind and a stubborn vein in her character, both of which had been a problem to her during her Catholic education. The nuns did not enjoy dealing with questions on faith or doctrine. Now, in her greatest battle, she was in a struggle with conflicting forces. The force of her love for Arthur, and her loyalty to the Church.

When she was with Arthur, his strength and his logical reasoning reassured her. He made her feel that their love was invincible against anything—family, Church, the world. Away from him, confronted with the staunchness of her family's religion, she was pulled in different directions. Arthur, so self-reliant and secure in their love, did not care about family displeasure or public opinion. Molly, almost obsessed with her love for him, was nevertheless too deeply imbedded in Catholicism to defy the Church easily. As the April sun warmed the earth, the renewal of spring held promise. Arthur's entreaties began to make sense to Molly, despite her misgivings. For them to go on like this, unable to fully share life together, was demeaning to their love. She, too, was impatient to get on with the business of living—marriage, home, family. Molly had always had her wishful dreams of the man she would one day marry. And now she had found him. Arthur, who far surpassed her dreams in all respects, save one. He was not a Catholic.

As much as she loved the Church and had always tried to be a dutiful daughter to it, she had to make a choice. She couldn't give up marriage to Arthur . . . simply *wouldn't.* Life without him would have no meaning for her.

"Arthur, you're right, darling. This has gone on too long. I'll marry you in June, even in front of a judge if we have to—when you come home from Tobyhanna," she told him.

He was overjoyed. "Let's have a party and announce our engagement, Molly! It doesn't have to be large, just the immediate families and a few close friends."

Molly was fearful that her family would try to dissuade her from her course. "I'd rather wait to tell them at the last minute, Arthur. That way, they won't have time to work on me when you're away." She saw that he thought this foolish. "Let's tell the Flannerys and the Benjamins," she suggested. "They'll keep our secret."

Ruth and David Benjamin had a dinner for the six of them to celebrate Arthur's and Molly's engagement. Jim and Louise brought champagne and Molly wore Arthur's grandmother's ring for the first time in front of others. Each of them made a toast to Molly's and Arthur's happiness. Arthur rose, when they had finished, and raised his glass to Molly.

"To the only woman I've ever loved, or ever want to love," he said, smiling down at her beautiful face.

That night they were both ecstatic, full of expectation. The nation might be downcast with the greatest depression in its history, but their world stretched before them, a long road of happiness, as far as they could envision.

"Oh, darling, just having made the decision and told our friends makes it so real!" Molly told him happily. "I've never been so happy."

It was one of life's bright, shining moments. That was why what happened later was all the more difficult to understand.

Arms full of wild flowers, Molly appeared at the cabin door. The May countryside had burst forth in bloom and foliage. Forsythia, mountain laurel, violets, and snow flowers in soft hues grew in wild abundance around the meadow.

Arthur was unpacking the groceries they'd bought in the country store in Thornhurst. "I'm going to cook dinner," he announced, as he scrubbed and pricked the potatoes. One of his patients had given him a luscious-looking apple pie with rivulets of caramelized syrup on its flaky crust; he planned to serve it warm for dessert.

"I didn't know you could cook," Molly said, surprised.

"There're lots of things you don't know about me," he answered, arching one eyebrow.

She stared at him gravely, not moving. "I want to know *everything* . . . absolutely everything." As if it would be her last opportunity.

Arthur smiled. "You will, darling. You're about to begin a lifelong course . . . 'everything about Arthur Hillman'—it's called marriage."

Molly put her arms around him, laying her head against his chest. "Hold me close, Arthur."

He embraced her, wondering at this uncharacteristic melancholy. Pre-wedding jitters? Over the past week she had become distracted, nervous, easily moved to tears. He knew the strain of waiting so long to learn whether the Church would grant her a dispensation had been a trial for her. He was the one who had been willing all along to be married by a judge. Now that the wedding would take place in June, with or without the Church's blessing, it was understandable that she would have some disquieting moments. He hoped that Father John would bless their union, at the very least. That would make them both happy.

He gently disengaged her arms, kissing the top of her head.

"I'll light the fire, then make us a drink," he said. The cabin was chilly in the late afternoon. "Why don't you arrange a centerpiece out of those beautiful flowers?"

Molly did her best to join in his good humor. When she thought his attention was elsewhere, he noticed she was unhappily preoccupied, staring into space.

The chops were delicious and the apple pie of the melt-in-your-mouth variety. Molly barely touched her dinner.

"I'll go home to mother, if you don't like my cooking," Arthur joked.

Molly laughed, reaching out to touch his hand. "Darling! Everything's delicious. I'm just not hungry tonight. Forgive me." She smiled to dispel her gloom. It was bad enough that she had this sense of foreboding, without spoiling their last evening before his departure.

They sat in front of the fire, holding hands and looking into the flames. "I wish you weren't going away tomorrow," she said in a low voice. "I'm going to miss you so."

He fondled her cheek. "It's only for two weeks. And then we'll be together forever. You'll have lots of things to keep you busy, getting ready for our wedding."

An expression of sadness cast its shadow on her face. She looked exquisitely beautiful, her lips trembling, as she whispered, "I love you so much, Arthur. I want you . . . *now."*

They had not made love since the afternoon weeks before when he had made that decision for both of them. Once Molly had agreed to a June wedding, he hadn't even minded. He was willing to wait.

But his resolve retreated to some forgotten corner of his mind as Molly began to make love to him . . . tentatively at first, growing in assurance as he responded to her loving caresses. Until now, in their love, Molly had followed his lead, slowly awakening to the depths of passion within her. She displayed a rare promise of sensuality now. The impact of her vivid beauty, enhanced by the golden fire glow, the delicious sensations he felt at the touch of her hands and lips, was almost too much for Arthur to bear.

"God, Molly," he groaned. "Ohh . . . my wonderful darling . . . my dearest love!"

"I love you, Arthur . . . I'll always love you . . . only you . . . always you."

"How wonderful you are. . . . Oh yes! yes . . . do that . . ."

"I'll never stop loving you. You are my life . . . forever. . . ."

Afterward, she clung to him and cried, as if her heart would break. Arthur rocked her in his arms, kissing her and stroking her back. What was it that had the power to do this to the woman he adored above all others?

Tobyhanna   May 1930

There was a part of him that enjoyed the good fellowship of military life. He had been disappointed when, in his freshman year at Penn State, he was too young for the reserve corps that most of his fellow students joined. Then, in his second year, he was inducted into the SATC, only to be discharged two and a half months later when the Armistice was declared. Perhaps it was a desire to be more like his brother . . . who knew? He had joined the Reserve Medical Corps of the Pennsylvania National Guard in his third year at Jeff and had been assigned as a medical officer, a captain, in the 109th Field Artillery when he returned to Wilkes-Barre.

Each Tuesday night he went to the armory for drill, and once a year they held divisional maneuvers with the 28th Pennsylvania Division at Camp Tobyhanna.

Reveille at 5:30, roll call, mess, sick call, marching, and war games occupied him for those two weeks. Maybe he was an overgrown boy playing soldier, but he enjoyed the complete change from the daily demands of medical practice—physical, invigorating, and uncomplicated.

In a reverie, he would sit on his camp chair in front of the tent talking to his fellow officers as the sun set over the Poconos and the stars blinked on one by one in the dark heavens. Someone played a scratchy record of "Ramona" over and over again on a wind-up phonograph, and the sickly sweet monotony of the song seemed nostalgically romantic to Arthur as he contentedly looked forward to the last few days of maneuvers before returning home to marry Molly.

Arthur took the stairs two at a time as he came back to his apartment on Northampton Street on the night before Decoration Day. It was late, past 10 P.M., and he hadn't had a real shower or shave for the past several days while his unit was on bivouac. He intended to soak in a hot bath, shave, and await the telephone call Molly had promised to make at 11:00 when she was off duty. He wouldn't call the hospital—it was late to make a social call. Besides, they had managed so far to keep knowledge of their romance from the nuns and nursing staff. Well, they'd know about it soon enough!

He opened the apartment door and switched on a light. A pile of mail was on the floor where it had fallen from the mail slot. He threw down his duffel bag and picked up the envelopes, mostly bills. There was a pale blue envelope with no return address. It was addressed to him in a prim, well-formed script. He put it aside while he looked around the apartment and turned on some lamps. He was hungry but the refrigerator was empty, except for some old apples, a few eggs, and a dried-out loaf of bread. He grimaced, then decided to fry some eggs and make toast.

He looked over the bills while he finished his impromptu supper, then opened the blue envelope and withdrew a single sheet of matching stationery. As he read its brief message, he had a sinking sensation within, and his heart began to hammer. . . .

My Dearest, my Only Love—

By the time you read this I will be far away. As I write these words, darling, I weep for the unhappiness in store for us.

In all the world there is no one who means more to me than you do. You must believe that. But I know, as surely as I know I love you, that we are not meant to be married, to have children, to live in harmony together.

If there were just the two of us, Arthur, what bliss we could share. But we are not just two people alone. We have families— yours and mine. We are part of a community where who you are and what you do matter. And I am part of a Church which holds me in a stronger bond than I realized.

In the end, we would be destroyed. I could not bear to see our love turn to something else—resentment, dislike, intolerance.

And so I have done the only thing I can do. We will not see each other again. I believe it will be better that way. I am so weak. If I had to look into your eyes, I think I could not bear it.

Don't try to find me. Please. I ask you that as one last favor. I hope you won't hate me. I'll always love you,

                                                          Molly

Where her tears had blurred the ink, his now fell. A great, strangled animal wail came from deep in his throat. *Molly, Molly! Oh, my God, please let it not be so.*

His grief was so profound that he had no idea how long he sat there, staring into space, then again reading her letter and feeling the sharp sense of loss once more as if it were the first time. He heard the bells of St. Stephen's Church toll the hour twelve times, and then again, once. And still he sat there.

Finally, with a weariness beyond his years, he threw himself down, fully clothed, on the daybed in his sitting room and fell into a fitful sleep. He awakened once, feeling feverish, and pulled a lap robe over himself, dully aware that something terrible had happened, but mercifully sinking back into a dreamless unconsciousness.

The next week passed in a haze. Arthur went through the motions of seeing patients, going on house calls, and making rounds at the hospital. Just to enter St. Anne's was almost unbearable for him. At the nurses' desk on the surgical floor a strange nurse presided, cool, brisk, antiseptic. Arthur barely acknowledged Sister Francis's introduction to her.

"My, he's an unfriendly person," Miss Johnson remarked to one of the other nurses.

"Dr. Hillman? Why, he's one of the nicest people around here. He must not be feeling well," she replied.

Once he called Molly's house. Her mother answered the telephone. He was about to hang up, but then spoke to her. "Mrs. Shea, this is Arthur Hillman. I was hoping that Molly might be there."

Her voice was sad. "No, Arthur, Molly's gone away."

"Won't you tell me where she is?"

"I can't do that, Arthur. I'm really sorry. You must try to understand."

"All I can understand is that I love her and want to marry her. And she loves me. Is that so unspeakable a sin?"

"No, of course not," she replied, kindly. "But, Arthur, Molly decided it was better this way. I know you're disappointed now, but you'll get over it. Believe me, it's for the best."

"I wish I could agree with you," he said. And hung up.

Ashley   June 1930

Father John was working late in his study, preparing his sermons for the next few Sundays. It was always difficult to provide a message with meaning and hope in simple enough language for his multi-ethnic parishioners with their sparse knowledge of English. He was weary, but found it difficult to sleep on these warm June evenings.

The front bell rang. Before he could answer it, someone pounded on the door.

It was Arthur Hillman. Father John was not surprised. "Come in, Arthur. I've been hoping you would drop by," he said, as if it were the most natural thing for someone to come to the rectory unannounced at eleven o'clock at night. Arthur looked awful. Hollow-eyed, pale, distraught, like a man bereaved.

Arthur followed the priest into his study and sat down in one of the leather chairs. John went to the liquor cabinet. "Brandy?"

Arthur shook his head.

"Well, then. Something else? Irish whiskey, scotch . . . let me see, yes, I even have some twelve-year-old bourbon here."

"All right, bourbon." He took the glass and threw the liquor into the back of his throat, grimacing as the alcohol seared the membranes. Without a word, Father John poured him another, and sat down opposite him with a glass of Irish whiskey in hand.

"Do you know where Molly is, John?"

"Precisely where she is . . . no."

"But you *do* know what happened. You must tell me how to find her. I *will* find her, you know. And I'll marry her, despite all of you. You and that bastard uncle of hers."

John did not react. "It's too late, Arthur. I'm sorry," he said in a quiet tone.

"What do you mean, it's too late? What's happened to her?" he asked in alarm.

John sighed. "Molly is married."

He understood what the priest had said, but the words were meaningless.

He sat there in a stupor, staring at John through bloodshot eyes. He shook his head from side to side. "That's not possible. You must be mistaken."

"I'm not mistaken. She was married almost a week ago."

"How can she be married? What are you saying? She loved *me!* I *know* she loved me. How can she have married?" He had risen from his chair and was gripping the priest by his arms, his voice rising in agitation.

Gently, Father John removed his hands and rose to face him. "Sit down, Arthur. I'll try to explain. You deserve an explanation." He paced back and forth, searching for the right words.

"Molly decided of her own free will to leave here. I do believe it was free will. There was a certain amount of pressure brought upon her by her . . . great-uncle, the—uh—gentleman you referred to . . . but basically it was Molly's decision. Once that decision was made, I believe she felt that she had to take an irrevocable step, something that would prevent you from following her and prevent her from changing her mind. There was a man in Ireland, someone she had known. They had cared for each other once . . ."

"*Sean Tower!*" Arthur's hoarse whisper pierced the air.

"You know about him?" John was surprised.

"I should have known. The first time I heard that name, I should have realized . . ." He buried his face in his hands. "My God. How could she have done it?" His anguished voice was muffled.

Father John placed his hand on Arthur's shoulder to comfort him.

"Arthur, you mustn't blame Molly. This is just as difficult for her. She's not in love with Sean Tower. I think you may consider this a marriage of . . . convenience. Time will heal your grief and you'll understand that she acted to shield you."

His rage was uncontrollable. He threw off the priest's hand, and rising up shouted at him, "What the hell do you know about it? Have you ever loved a woman? Have you ever held a woman in your arms? You, and your whole pack of celibate old eunuchs sitting there with your prayers and platitudes, playing God with people's lives. Who are all of *you* to tell *us* that we can't marry, that we can't live our lives together? Do you honestly believe that your God or anyone's God demands such senseless sacrifices? There's more good and truth and beauty in one sincere act of love between a man and a woman than all the masses you'll ever celebrate, if you live to be a hundred." He could have struck the priest in his anger and sorrow.

John just stood there looking at him with compassion and understanding, accepting the harsh words, welcoming them. Arthur's breath came in uneven gasps as he strode across the room, striking the mantel with his hand, then leaning his head against it.

Hot tears burned his eyes. "I love her so, John. You can't imagine how much it is possible to love someone like that. With her beside me, I could have done beautiful things with my life. Now, I feel empty, used up." All anger had gone from his voice. It was replaced with hopelessness. . . .

"I do understand your pain. Do you as a doctor have to have suffered from cancer in order to treat a patient, to know how much he is suffering? I'd like to try to help you, Arthur. I believe I can help you, if you'll let me."

Arthur sat down and held his glass out for the priest to pour more bourbon. He sipped the liquor, welcoming the dulling effect. "How can you help me, John? How can anyone help? The only person who could help is Molly and she's gone from me." He realized as he said it that he accepted it for the first time.

"Talking helps. Time heals. Work is the best medicine I know. I'm here to talk with you. The rest will take care of itself. You'll soon find that life has much meaning."

Arthur closed his eyes and leaned back against the soft leather chair, feeling the spreading warmth of the alcohol. He knew he shouldn't drink more, but he felt detached, uncaring. The priest continued talking.

"You're wrong about me, you know. I don't think I have the right to plot destinies. That was part of why I'm here in Ashley. I wasn't obedient enough, too proud, too questioning."

"I said some pretty rough things, John. I apologize. I shouldn't have attacked you personally. I know you have no responsibility in this."

"I have a *great* responsibility, Arthur. I feel as if I brought you and Molly together. I knew the night you had dinner here with me that there was something of meaning forming between you. I have been greatly troubled."

"It would have happened anyway. We knew each other. It might have taken a little longer, but it was inevitable from the moment we first saw each other at the hospital." Arthur gazed into space, remembering.

"The Church is a hard mistress," Father John mused. "I've known no other life, but I recognize that I am deprived of that special closeness between man and woman—I don't mean sex—the warmth and comfort of a home, children, someone who cares . . . someone to forgive my weaknesses and accept my frailties. So, although I haven't had to give up a particular person, I do understand what you are going through."

"Have you ever thought of leaving the priesthood?"

"Yes, I've thought about it. I think many priests have doubts. I may have more than most. But, on the whole, I'm happy, at peace with myself, deriving satisfaction in the small circle of lives I touch. There's so much need in this community. The poverty, frustration, and constant danger of the miners touches my heart. I want to do so much for them. But I have to move carefully."

"Why so?" He had a sudden feeling of unease.

"There are powerful people out there, my friend. People who have the ear of His Excellency. They don't want their docile miners stirred up, demanding unreasonable things like good health care or adequate food and housing . . ."

Arthur interrupted. "By His Excellency, you mean . . . ?"

His voice, when he spoke, was heavy with sarcasm. "I mean our esteemed Bishop Callahan, in Scranton." John played with his pipe.

"So, they tried to get you, too! I was afraid of that, John. I've tried to keep your name out of this whole clinic debate." Arthur was boiling mad.

John shrugged. "Doesn't bother me, Arthur. What could they do . . . take Our Lady of the Mountain away from me?" He smiled in irony. "I heard about the newspaper column . . . Jim told me."

"I wish he hadn't done that. There was no need for you to know. That was all taken care of, but I'm sorry to hear your bishop is displeased with you."

John dismissed it. "I've crossed wills with him before, Arthur, when I tried to crack the guarded walls of St. Ignatius University. That was when I wanted to take a degree with the Jesuits—I think I told you about that. I had been in a seminary belonging to the Order of St. Mary. I thought I had it all arranged, but at the last minute Bishop Callahan intervened, and that was that."

"I don't understand, John. I thought the Catholic Church was one big brotherhood. What difference would it have made if you went to a Jesuit university?"

"It's political, mostly. Not all that complicated. Just different clubs jealously guarding their turf. When a man becomes a priest, he doesn't change if he's prone to pettiness and envy. There's a lot of backbiting among the clergy. The Jesuits, as you know, are renowned for their intellectualism, which is what appealed to me. I've always felt I was meant for a life of teaching and writing. Hearing confessions and 'playing God,' as you described it, has never been my strong suit. But I'm reconciled to it now. I've grown quite attached to my parishioners." He puffed on his pipe, then went on in a musing tone. "I always wondered whether Bishop Shea had played a role in my destiny . . . he's a member of the Order of St. Mary. . . . One never knows. You see, the hierarchy operates in special ways, in rarefied channels. That's what happened with Molly. She thought her Uncle Thomas was trying to get a special dispensation for her to marry you and not be excommunicated. But she was finally told that unless you became a Catholic, it was out of the question. Meanwhile, Bishop Shea was communicating with Monsignor Riordan in Ireland, and so this alternative presented itself. A family so entrenched in the Church is formidable, let me tell you."

"All families are formidable. But if a person is strong-willed and believes in himself—or herself—that shouldn't interfere with happiness."

"In families, yes. In the Church, no. You don't have anything quite like this in Judaism, I imagine."

"Oh, yes we do! You don't have a monopoly on bigotry. There are plenty of Jews who would sit *shiva* if a son married a gentile girl. There are plenty of rabbis who preach from the pulpit against fraternizing with non-Jews and intermarriage. But in Judaism, as in Catholicism or any other religion, I have disdain for them."

"The motive is a protective one, and I daresay, for the Jews, a necessary one." Father John poured another drink for both of them. "You weren't willing to accept Catholicism, were you?"

"We agreed long ago, at the beginning, that neither of us wished the other to convert, so it never was a point of discussion. Molly never asked me. I'm not very religious, as you know, John. But, no, I wouldn't have wanted to become a Catholic—even for Molly."

"So, you have your answer. And Molly knew that."

They were silent for some moments, each lost in his own thoughts. It was Arthur who finally spoke, changing the subject.

"Tell me about this new project of yours, John—the students. They're all miners' sons?"

"Yes. And daughters. There are two girls in a group of nine. Each one is uniquely gifted and, given the opportunity to go to college or study at an institute of art or music, as the case may be, they will have the chance to do something with their lives other than repeat this pattern of poverty and hopelessness. . . . Why, there are families there with a father who has barely seen daylight for the past fifteen years! The women are old before they're forty from having too many children too fast, and watching some of them die. They drudge from before dawn until after dark. They have no education and they measure their joy in life by the number of days they can provide a full meal for their brood. And we expect them to get by on the Word of God alone? Well, I don't believe that's good enough. I believe we have to offer them more than that! And I say to *hell* with those who stand in the way!" He banged his fist down on the arm of his chair. There was a fire in his eyes and a determination to the square-jawed face under its dark, wavy widow's peak.

"What are you proposing to do?"

"I'm trying to get some wealthy people in the community to fund scholarships for them. If they can get an education, develop their talents, learn a trade other than mining, they can break out of this hopeless poverty and the prison of their lives. I haven't been able to do much for their parents, but maybe I can help them. They've too much promise to spend their lives digging coal."

"That's wonderful, John," Arthur said, wondering how he could help. "There's a union organizer named Eddy Valentine whom I know. He's up in Scranton. Good fellow. Maybe he can get some money for you. That way, your mine owners might be shamed into contributing. I've been discussing my clinic idea with him in a preliminary way. I'd like to enlist the union and the owners in a cooperative effort, to underwrite a diagnostic clinic for the miners and their families."

It was very late. The glow of the liquor had worn off and now Arthur had a headache and knew he'd have an even worse one in the morning. The dull ache in his chest had eased somewhat. There was truth, after all, to the saying that it helped to talk it out, to "get it off your chest." The priest had helped him just by listening sympathetically, by understanding his unhappiness. He had come in anger, but he was leaving with some degree of consolation. Life still would go on. Without Molly it wouldn't be easy, but he had no choice.

"Work, Arthur. Remember, that's the best cure for all manner of troubles. I've seen it help people over and over," said Father John when he bid a weary, chastened Arthur good night.

May 1930

With a despair borne of hopelessness, Molly had traveled one last time to Harrisburg.

Her father's uncle, a remote gray visage beyond eighty, to whom she had curtsied before kissing his ring when he honored her graduation at Sacred Heart Academy seven years before, had received her with comparative warmth. Dressed severely in the informal black clerical attire suitable for nonofficial occasions, he had lunched with her in his residence speaking of inconsequential matters having to do with the Church, the family in the Church, and, finally, Ireland. Her held-in emotions were screaming to burst forth with an impassioned plea to him . . . for her love, for her life. Instead, she had kept herself tightly in rein, suffering through the tedium of his droning conversation.

At last, in his study, she spoke to him in a trembling voice which she tried desperately to control. "Your Excellency. . . . Have you . . . has there been any word from Rome on the matter of . . . of my marriage?"

"Have you done as I suggested, child? And please do call me Uncle Thomas. . . . 'Excellency' is so formal. We are talking about a family matter."

"I have prayed, Uncle Thomas, and I have reflected, as you suggested. I have considered your spiritual advice."

"And you are still determined to marry Dr. Hillman?"

She nodded wordlessly.

"I wonder whether you truly know what that will mean, Molly . . . for yourself, for your dear mother, for your unborn children . . . and for your immortal soul."

He began to speak, and with his words she knew there was no hope for her. Her choices were clear. Her Church, her family, and her immortal soul . . . or her love for Arthur. To dwell in a state of sin, damned forever, if she married him—for the Church would not bless the marriage unless he became a Catholic. Indeed, she had already sinned grievously, but various penances could atone for those sins. There was no room for error, for lack of faith, for doubt. . . .

He spoke in mystical terms, in riddles, using an ecclesiastical jargon which she had heard all of her life, but which now had no clear meaning for her. She could forsake everything, turning her back on her family and the Church or . . .

"Molly, I have a plan I would like to suggest to you," he said in a mild, dispassionate manner.

There were two alternative avenues open to her—the choice was hers to make. She could retire to an order for a period of reflection and service before deciding whether to take vows . . . or she could begin a new life in Ireland as the wife of Sean Tower, who had spoken to her cousin Monsignor Patrick Riordan of his affection and respect for her.

"I do not personally think you have the temperament for the religious life, Molly," the bishop had said. An understatement, if there ever was one, was her wry thought, even in her misery.

Under the aegis of Father Patrick she would find succor and satisfaction in a truly Catholic life. She remembered his precise words, because later they were to prove so important.

"There is more to Christian marriage than physical love, Molly. The loftiest ideals of love are spiritual. You must not let the temptations of the flesh dominate your life. Discipline and prayer, chastity and obedience are godly virtues. Those are the tenets by which we consecrate our love for God and His Church." Oddly enough, she heard him say, "And it is not altogether certain that God in His mercy will not grant you happiness and children, if you are firm in your faith and dutiful in prayer."

He had ended the audience by offering to hear her confession, a singular act of humility from a bishop. She had stumbled through the form, her eyes dull, too distraught for tears, receiving not the slightest comfort from his blessing.

Two days later, she had sailed for Ireland.

BOOK FIVE

***

Moments of Glad Grace

1930–42

I

Wilkes-Barre   Autumn 1930

"Gin!"

"Sonnuva gun! I can't believe it!" Arthur threw down the cards in disgust.

David Benjamin reared his head back and laughed heartily. "Let me see—that puts me three hundred dollars, U.S., ahead of you, Hillman. Why don't you just give up?"

"Never! Not even under torture!" Arthur joined in his friend's laughter. Ruth Benjamin entered from the kitchen with a tray of coffee and chocolate cake.

The phone rang. David excused himself.

"How's your mother, Arthur?" Ruth asked.

"Mother's doing fine. Nate's been living with her since he came back from Philadelphia, so that's good for both of them."

"Is it?" Ruth asked, a bluntness in her voice.

"Well . . . yes! Why wouldn't it be?"

"A good-looking, thirty-two-year-old bachelor lawyer living with his widowed mother is good? Since when?"

"Ruthie, you know Nate's a special case. His health isn't all that good. Mother can look after him and he doesn't have to worry about setting up his own apartment until he's well established in his law practice."

"In my observation, that could lead to a permanent arrangement called 'confirmed bachelor.' "

Arthur hesitated, then said, "I think it's realistic, Ruth. I doubt very much that Nate will marry. I'm not even sure that it would be wise for him to marry."

"I saw him at the YMHA dance last Saturday night, Arthur. It certainly didn't look to me like anything was wrong with him." She gave Arthur a sly glance.

"Oh?" Arthur couldn't disguise the surprise in his voice. "Well, I'm glad Nate's getting out and enjoying himself."

"Which is more than you can say for his brother, hmmm?"

"Ah, Ruthie." Arthur sighed. "You know how it is."

"Yes, Arthur, I *do* know." She smiled at him as she poured another cup of coffee. She was so fond of him, loved him as if he were her own brother. If only he and Molly . . . if only.

David came hurrying in. "Sorry, Art. I couldn't get off the phone. That was Jason Green calling from Philly. I'm doing some work for him in the county." David sat down at the table and took a piece of cake. He spoke in a casual tone. "He's sending his car for us on Saturday morning. We're going down to the Penn-Lehigh game and to a party he's giving afterward. He has rooms for us at the Barclay." He stirred sugar in his coffee, not looking at Arthur.

"Who do you mean by 'us'?" Arthur asked.

"You, me, and Ruthie—that's who." He winked at his pretty wife. "Not necessarily in that order of importance."

"Hey. Wait a minute, Dave. I'm not going. He's your client. I don't even know the guy. Besides, I have patients to take care of, and that's my day for the miners' clinic."

"Arthur, I won't take no for an answer. You need to get away from this burg. You can get one of the other men to take the clinic . . . and you can turn your patients over to Jack Lerner. He's a better doctor, anyway!"

"Why, you so-and-so!" Arthur and David had this habitual banter between them, as playful as their on-going gin game, which had started almost two years before. "Jack Lerner! That's all I'd have to do. I'd have no patients left after that. Those he didn't kill, he'd steal!"

Ruth giggled. "Arthur, please come with us," she pleaded. "You know we'd love to have you. And Jason's parties are always fun. Really, Wilkes-Barre's so dreary these days, we all need to get away. We could never afford to go down to Philadelphia on our own, so why not accept Jason's invitation?"

"Well, maybe. I'll have to look over my schedule and see. I want to be sure no babies are due on Saturday."

"How would you know whether one's due on *Saturday?*" asked David.

Arthur stood and stretched his lanky body. "I think you better have a little talk with Dave, Ruthie. Tell him about the birds and the bees." He kissed her good-bye and walked out the kitchen door to his car.

When they heard him drive away, Ruth asked her husband, "Do you think he'll come?"

"I don't know," he replied. "I hope so. He's been in mourning long enough." David shook his head. "God! A sensational guy like that, mooning after a little snip of a nurse."

"David Benjamin!" She was genuinely shocked. "Molly was exquisitely beautiful and they were deeply in love. That was no frivolous romance. She was a person of real substance and it'll take him a long time to get over it."

"Well, it's *been* a long time," he grumbled. "I still don't understand it."

"Hmph," she said, "maybe you *do* need a talk about the birds and the bees."

Jason Green's Cadillac sedan pulled up in front of Arthur's office on Northampton Street at 7:30 on Saturday morning. The driver rang the bell just as Arthur, in his upstairs apartment, was throwing his pajamas and a change of clothes into his old leather traveling bag.

Why had he agreed to go with them, anyway? He was tired, irritable, wanted to just hole up in the apartment over the weekend, reading, or maybe go for a long horseback ride along the wooded trails in Dallas. Anything but force himself to be sociable, to make idle chitchat at a post-game party in Philadelphia.

He had called Jim Flannery, half heartedly asking him to take charge of his patients and the clinic for the weekend. He was mildly disappointed when Jim immediately agreed, enthusiastically suggesting that Arthur stay over until Monday. "Louise and I have no plans at all this weekend, Art. Go right ahead and have a good time. Do you good to get away." Everyone was so damned concerned with his "getting away."

Waiting in the limousine, David took one look at Arthur and said, "My, you look cheerful today! Really makes me wish I had chosen medicine instead of law. All that contagious joy!"

"Be quiet, Dave," said Ruth. "It's too early for that. How are you, Arthur? Have some coffee and a roll." She handed him a thermos of hot coffee.

Arthur settled himself in the back seat next to Ruth. David was sitting facing them on a deep, comfortable custom-made swivel chair—an arrangement Arthur had never seen in an automobile before. There was a small bar outfitted with heavy monogrammed glasses and lead-glass decanters of scotch, bourbon, and gin. Mohair lap robes hung on ropes in front of their seats.

"All the comforts of home," Arthur remarked. He felt a little better after sipping the coffee.

The chauffeur had secured his bag in the trunk and was seated behind the wheel. He moved the dividing glass to the side. "Are we all set, Mr. Benjamin?"

"Yes, Warren. All set. Next stop, Franklin Field."

"Begging your pardon, sir. Mr. Green expects you for lunch at the Pennsylvania Club before the game. If you want me, just push that white button." He slid the glass back in place ensuring their privacy.

"Such luxury in the middle of a depression doesn't seem right," grouched Arthur. Ruth nodded in agreement.

"Look, we're here. Why don't you just relax and enjoy it," Dave suggested.

"O.K., I'll do that. Sorry to be such a wet blanket. I had an emergency call in the middle of the night and I'm bushed."

Ruth clucked sympathetically.

"That must be hell, being roused out of a sound sleep," said Dave.

"You'd think I'd be used to it by now, but I never fall back asleep easily after being awakened."

"How often does that happen?" Ruth asked.

"Sometimes not for weeks. But lately, half my patients seem to become ill at midnight," Arthur answered. "What really gets me are the people who call to tell you they've had this pain since morning, but they've waited all day and half the night to call the doctor." He leaned his head back against the seat and closed his eyes.

Ruth looked at him admiringly. His handsome face in repose looked younger. The square jaw, with its slightly cleft chin and his straight, definite nose, gave character to his looks, while his firm mouth had a tenderness at the corners. She noticed he had long eyelashes, darker than his brows and blond hair. His lanky, broad-shouldered body was trim and athletic. At his sides, his long-fingered hands, well-kept and capable-looking, lay quietly. He certainly was an attractive man, she mused. Any woman would think so. Surely there was someone right for him—someone other than Molly.

As she turned away from her scrutiny of Arthur, an amused David caught her eye with a knowing look. She smiled in answer to his cocked eyebrow.

"Penny?" he said.

"I'll never tell," she whispered.

The Pennsylvania Club was crammed with old grads in raccoon coats and club ties. Arthur and David pushed a path through the crush to the crowded bar, where they managed to get three cups of Penn Punch, a lethal concoction which Arthur decided must be 90 percent wood alcohol. "We'll all go blind by sundown," he said, wincing as he tasted the stuff.

"I guess we should find our host," said Dave. "Let's try the second floor."

Jason Green, born Jake Greenberg in a tenement in Camden, was a bachelor who had made piles of money in real estate during the twenties. He had managed to hold on to his wealth when the market collapsed, having sold all his stock holdings before the top had been reached. In those crazy days of wild speculation, he sensed that it would all fall apart. Quietly, in small lots, he had unloaded his U.S. Steel and Telephone, his American Can and General Motors, his oil and utilities shares, putting his money into gold certificates, Treasury notes, and business properties. He knew that he had survived because he wasn't too greedy. Having been content with part of the pie, he ended up one of the few to keep what he had.

A self-made multimillionaire civic leader and patron of the arts, Green had never attended college himself, but he had embraced the University of Pennsylvania as his alma mater, contributing large sums for its building funds, cultivating friendships among its faculty and trustees, and attending every football game at Franklin Field, cheering lustily for the red and blue with all the fervor of a true son of Old Penn.

Jason was standing at the door of a small reception room on the second floor, waiting for them. "Ruthie! Dave! You're here. Wonderful! How was the drive? Have everything you need?" He never paused long enough to let them answer his questions. He kissed Ruth, clapped Dave on the back, shook hands with Arthur.

"Hello, Doctor. Glad you could join us. Everyone, go over to the bar, get yourselves a drink. There are sandwiches and hot dishes at the buffet. We have an hour and a half till kickoff."

There was so much energy in Jason Green it made Arthur feel edgy. He was sandy-haired, with a roundish, smooth face and receding hairline. His alert, prominent eyes moved constantly, but had a flat appearance, lacking warmth. He was attractive in a sterile fashion. Of medium stature, he looked fit under his expensive tweed hacking jacket.

Ruth and Dave were stopped by some acquaintances, and Arthur moved away from them, heading toward the bar, where he rid himself of the awful purple gin drink and ordered a bourbon and soda. He turned, sipping his drink, and looked across the room . . . directly into the clear, gray eyes of Emily Grant.

She was more beautiful than ever. Her shining blond hair, still shoulder length, was arranged in a casual wave around her classic face. Wearing a becoming brown Harris tweed outfit, with a silk blouse and matching scarf, she looked not older, but more finished, more defined. He worked his way across the crowded room, moving around the conversation groups. Emily started forward, then held herself in check, poised, waiting for him to come to her.

"Hello, Emily." He let out a long breath. "You look great."

"Arthur. How nice to see you."

"How are you? It's Emily Beckinger now, if I remember correctly."

"No. It's still Emily Grant," she said with a smile.

"But, I thought you were married. What happened?"

"We called it off. I went to Europe to study art. I think we had a narrow escape."

"Now, why should that make me so happy?" he wondered aloud.

She laughed appreciatively, her lovely eyes crinkling, smile lines forming at the corners of her mouth.

"How are you, Arthur? What has happened to you in these two years?"

"*Three* years, Emily. Three long years. And many things have happened. It will take dinner and the evening to tell you about it," he added impulsively.

"You're not married?" she asked, as though she already knew.

"Not married. But I own a car now!" She laughed again. "Ah, Em, it's good to see you." He really meant it. "I'm serious about dinner."

"I wish I could, Arthur . . ."

"Well, Dr. Hillman, I see you've discovered the prettiest girl at the party," Jason Green interrupted them. His voice sounded hearty, but contained no amity. He put an arm possessively around Emily's shoulder. Arthur noticed that she imperceptibly moved from his embrace.

So, that's how it is, he thought. He's got to be fifteen years older than she is, he estimated.

"Arthur and I have known each other for years," said Emily.

Arthur sensed that Jason didn't like that at all.

"I was going to suggest you have some lunch. We'll be leaving for the game in about twenty minutes."

Great, thought Arthur, we're all going to be together at the game, and probably at the party afterward. Excusing himself, he went to the buffet and filled his plate, then looked for Ruth and David. He found them having lunch with some old friends from law school. There was shop talk—Arthur found legal shop talk deadly. He noticed Emily in conversation a few feet away, Jason Green hovering at her side. Once or twice their eyes met and she smiled at him.

Jason had taken a block of seats on the fifty-yard line for his twenty guests, most of whom knew each other. Arthur found himself sitting between a professor of economics from Wharton and an attractive woman who said she worked for Green Enterprises. Emily and Jason sat in the row behind at the other end of the group. Once, when he glanced back, she was looking at him with a grave expression. She slid her eyes away when he turned.

Arthur concentrated his attention on the game. The Pennsylvania team clearly outmatched the brown and white of Lehigh, who made only one first down to Penn's twenty-three. Lud Wray sent in his second and third teams, playing almost every man on the squad. Long passes and runs were the order of the day. The high point came in the final minutes of the first half when Ford, the Penn quarterback, threw a fifty-four-yard pass to Riblett, who scored for a third touchdown. Both men were substitutes. The crowd went wild, and the band struck up with Penn's traditional fight song as the teams cleared the field at half time.

Arthur did his best to get into the spirit of the occasion, rising each time Penn scored, applauding and cheering with the rest. The game was a runaway, with Penn scoring six touchdowns for a final score of 40–0.

Jason had invited throngs of people to a postgame party and there were the usual number of crashers who tagged along. It was, by all standards, a lively, successful party. Jason was a confident, affable host, seeing to the needs of his guests. Two bars kept the company well lubricated with drink, while waiters circulated with trays of hot and cold canapés.

Arthur was feeling more relaxed than he had in months. If he was attempting to avoid Emily, he didn't have to try too hard. Each time he caught a glimpse of her, she was across the room, seemingly unaware of him.

There was a piano and bass combo in the solarium, which ran the length of Jason's apartment off the living room. A group was gathered around the piano singing. Many of the guests drifted toward the music. Arthur walked into a dimly lit library to the right, seeking a moment of solitude. He looked over the leather-bound volumes on the shelves, noting that the collection seemed to have been acquired more for appearance than reading pleasure. Hearing a rustling behind him, Arthur glanced over his shoulder. Emily had been standing in a darkened alcove at a window, staring out at the dusky skyline. She turned, startled, when she realized he was there. They stood silently looking at each other across the room.

What the hell, he thought, and walked over to her side.

"Are you and Jason Green an 'item'?" he said, keeping his tone light.

"Arthur, that doesn't sound like something I'd expect you to say."

"He's too old for you, Emily."

She gave a short laugh. "You sound like my father."

"He's not good enough for you."

"Now you sound like my brother."

"There is nothing either fatherly or brotherly in my interest. Aren't you going to answer my question?"

"What gives you the right to ask?" she said, with a lift of her chin.

"Because if the answer is yes, I'll go away."

"And if the answer is no?" She was defensive, he knew, a wary, vulnerable look in her eyes which he remembered from the past.

"Look, isn't there somewhere we can go? I want to talk to you."

She looked out the window for a long moment, then said in a low voice, "I'll get my coat. Meet me downstairs in the lobby." She walked out of the room without looking at him.

Arthur waited a few minutes, then sought Ruth and told her he was tired and going to turn in early. He felt dishonest, but pushed the feeling aside. "I'll see you tomorrow," he said. "What time are we leaving?"

"Around noon, after a late breakfast," she replied. "Get a good night's sleep."

He rang for the elevator, which came immediately, opening directly into the foyer of the penthouse. As he walked out into the lobby, Emily nodded and went through the front doors of the building. He put on his overcoat and followed her, falling in step beside her as she walked up the square.

"Where do you want to go?" she asked.

"Shall we have dinner?"

"I really don't want anything more to eat."

"Neither do I," he replied. "Is there someplace quiet, where there won't be a lot of people? Where we can just talk?"

She hesitated. "I suppose we can go to my apartment. It's just a short walk from here."

The apartment was, she explained, really her family's apartment, their place in town, scarcely used by either of her parents, who still preferred the Main Line suburbs. It was on the ninth floor of one of the older buildings facing Rittenhouse Square. For Emily it was a convenient place to live while she worked at the Museum of Fine Arts, where she assisted the curator of paintings.

"Did you tell anyone you were leaving?" Arthur asked.

"I left a message with Jason's houseman. I said I had a headache and was going home."

"He'll be furious, of course. He'll know you're with me."

"Yes, I daresay he will." She absentmindedly shuffled through some mail on a lacquer table in the hall, then turned on several lamps. The living room was spacious and inviting, with deep upholstered couches and chairs, warm lighting, and some excellent paintings hanging on the pale buff-colored walls.

"Ummm . . . this is lovely, Emily. You must enjoy living here."

"I'm glad you like it. Mother told me I could redecorate. I didn't do much —mostly changed wall color and added the pictures," she said. "Will you have something to drink, Arthur? Some sherry or brandy?"

"No, nothing, thanks." Arthur sat down on the couch, drawing her beside him. "How long were you in Europe, Emily?"

"A year and a half. I spent most of the time in Paris, with Aunt Lily, my mother's friend . . . the one who finds poor artists and supports them."

"When did you come home?"

"In June. I just started to work at the museum in August." She looked at him with that direct, honest serenity which he'd always admired. "And you, Arthur? Tell me about yourself."

In many ways it was as if no time had lapsed since they had last seen each other. But Arthur knew that he was not the same person, nor was Emily. On the surface, their conversation was easy and familiar, but there was an electric undercurrent, a restlessness beneath. . . .

"Emily, I want to see you again. All this time, I thought you were married."

She regarded him pensively, not answering. The phone rang in the hallway, breaking the silence. Emily hesitated, then excused herself to answer it. Arthur could hear her words without meaning to.

"Yes, Jason, I'm home. . . . No, I'm really fine, just tired . . . headache. . . . I'm sorry, it was a pleasant day. . . . I'm going to see my parents tomorrow. . . . I'm afraid not . . . I'm busy then. . . . Good-bye, Jason."

She returned and stood in front of him, a smile on her face. "Now, where were we?"

Philadelphia   Winter 1930–31

Arthur went to Philadelphia every weekend. On Friday evenings they would have dinner at Bookbinders or one of the hotels. Sometimes Emily cooked dinner at her apartment, gourmet French or Italian dishes that she had learned to make in Europe. Afterward, they sat in front of the fire drinking coffee, holding hands, talking.

Arthur was afraid to rush things. Emily's defenses were up. She had been hurt once. She didn't want it to happen again, and he didn't blame her.

He stayed with Roy McLean, who still hadn't married. Roy was at Jeff doing surgery, following a plan more or less like the one Arthur had expected to pursue. It hurt a little to hear Roy talk about the surgical clinics, Silverberg, Gibbon, and the other eminent men who were now his colleagues. You can't go back, he realized. . . .

"Did you hear about Chessy Baird, Arthur?" Roy asked one Saturday morning.

"I haven't seen or heard from Chessy in over two years, Mac. What about her?"

"She's a countess now! She married a French count . . . Philippe de something-or-other."

Arthur hooted. "Perfect! Can't you just see Chessy playing the part to the hilt. I *love* it!" Roy told him they were living in Paris and, according to the item he had read on the society page of the *Bulletin,* Chessy's husband owned a château in the French countryside.

"You always did read those dumb columns, Roy."

"Yeah, well, a fellow has to keep up with the important news, Art. How else would you have known about Chessy?"

That was true. He hoped Chessy had found the right man for her this time.

On Saturday afternoons he and Emily sometimes visited museums or went to a matinee, if there was one. Then they walked back to her apartment, where they had cocktails before dinner. They had a tacit agreement those first weeks not to mingle with other people, especially her family. It seemed important to get their relationship properly established before becoming involved again with Claudia and Fred Grant.

Arthur felt happier than he had since Molly had left. He could think about it now without the knife-like pain in his heart. He would always regret that she had left him. He couldn't help it. It was a hurt that would never completely go away. But it was a wound that was healing, and since he had found Emily again, the pain had grown duller, the scar tissue forming.

He asked Emily to come to Wilkes-Barre for New Year's Eve. Phoebe and Lowell Wintermuth were having a formal dinner dance. He supposed it was as good a time as any to let Emily see what she'd be getting into if she married him. There was an early reception planned at the Medical Society and a New Year's Day party at Ruth and David Benjamin's house in Kingston. She'd have a chance to meet a broad cross section of the Wilkes-Barre people in his life. And, of course, his family.

"What would you think of coming to my parents' house for Christmas, Arthur?" Emily asked him in the most hesitant way.

"What would *you* think, Emily?"

"I think it would be all right. They're pretty much accustomed to me pulling surprises by now. I don't believe I can shock them anymore. Poor Mother and Daddy! I haven't turned out at all the way they expected."

He laughed, then said softly, "I can't imagine anyone turning out better, Emily."

She looked at him with the most hopeful expression of heartbreaking gratitude. Why should this beautiful, absolutely wonderful woman look that way at him? He took her in his arms and kissed her, not with passion this time, but with great tenderness. For only a moment did she hesitate, then gave herself to him completely—her last defenses gone.

"Darling Emily . . . I love you . . . I love you, Emily," he murmured.

"Oh! I never thought I'd hear you say that. My darling, do you really mean it?" The joy on her face made him want to weep.

"Yes, love, I really mean it. I mean it with all my heart." And he was sure he did.

Philadelphia   Spring 1931

Frederick Grant had a nervous "little talk" with Arthur the morning after the party he and Claudia gave to announce Emily's engagement to Arthur.

"You know"—he groped for the words at the breakfast table, where the two of them were alone—"father-of-the-bride sort of thing."

Poor Fred, Arthur thought, amused. Claudia's put him up to this, and he hates it!

In his private study, Fred said, "I'll be honest with you, Arthur . . . I'm not so good at this, so you'll help me along if you don't display outrage at what I'm going to say. Emily assures me you have some strong views on money matters."

Arthur smiled. "Knowing Emily, she probably said 'stubborn pride.'"

Fred laughed, relaxing visibly. "I can understand your feelings, Arthur, and I admire you for them. We've never questioned the sincerity of your affections toward Emily. Claudia and I used to worry about Emily—that she might marry someone who . . . cared . . . more for her inheritance than for Emily herself. Even with young Beckinger, if you'll forgive my mentioning it, I was concerned that it played a role. Just because someone has wealth doesn't mean he's not interested in acquiring more! I was relieved when Emily broke it off." His eyes met Arthur's. "I'm so pleased you and Emily have found each other again. I feel I can entrust her to your care."

Arthur was surprised to see Frederick's eyes moisten.

"Emily's wealth, or rather her family's wealth, has been a deterrent in our relationship, Mr. Grant. While I've never been poor, my family hasn't had tremendous amounts of money, and what they did have has unfortunately dwindled. My father . . . well, he wasn't very lucky in business, or in health." Ask Uncle Herman, he thought, wickedly. "We're a close family, and I've had a good life. I've never wanted for anything . . . and Emily won't, either, I assure you." He looked around the sumptuous room. "We won't be able to live like this, of course, but I think I can make Emily happy."

"I wonder, Arthur, whether you fully understand Emily. She's been accustomed to having everything she wants. We haven't done the right thing, perhaps, in indulging her. But it's a way of life. She's never known anything else."

How well Arthur knew that. And now here was Emily's father, raising all the grave doubts he'd tried so hard to repress.

"There will be a comfortable . . . ah . . . cushion . . . shall we say, for the time being. Emily's allowance continues, in fact increases at the time of her marriage." Frederick mentioned an amount Arthur found staggering, more than his own annual income, explaining that this would be paid out of a family trust at regular intervals. In addition, he continued, Emily and Fred, Jr., each had trust funds established by their deceased grandparents.

"Emily's properties are administered by the trust officers, with Emily participating as a cotrustee now that she has reached twenty-five. Although you and I are not direct beneficiaries of the Allenberg trusts, because they were set up to . . . ah . . . protect the women—I think Claudia's father was wise in that, by the way—you *will* become a beneficiary of the Grant family trust after one year of marriage, and as long as you and Emily remain married."

Arthur began to look worried. Fred rushed on.

"If Emily predeceases you, and there are no children, you are entitled to twenty-five percent of her share of the trust, so long as you remain unmarried, the rest reverting to the trust. If you have children and Emily predeceases you . . ." Arthur knew that each one of those "predeceases" would have been followed by a "God forbid" if it had been *his* father speaking. What was it that made Frederick Grant different in this way—Philadelphia? Wealth? Or the self-assurance of his position as a fourth-generation American?

". . . the children would be entitled to the seventy-five percent share. If you remarry, your twenty-five percent reverts to them." Fred pretended not to notice Arthur's restiveness. "It's not as complicated as it sounds . . ."

Arthur cut him off. "Mr. Grant!" His voice was too loud. He lowered it. "Mr. Grant, I don't want to sound ungrateful, but I cannot accept any of this. I meant it when I told Emily that I want to support her myself. I truly don't want *any* of her money—won't take any of it. I appreciate it, more than I can say, but I just can't accept your offer."

"I don't think you understand, Arthur. This isn't something I'm offering you. That's the way the trusts are set up. I have nothing to do with it. No one does."

Arthur was silent, thinking what this meant. "You mean, there's nothing I can do? What happens if I don't take the money?"

"It would just sit there in the account and collect interest. I imagine you'll change your thinking after a year of marriage. It takes that long to settle in, get used to things," Grant said cheerfully. "That's why the trust was set up that way."

Arthur shook his head. "Mr. Grant, please try to understand my point of view. I feel strongly about this matter. When we're married, I'm determined to support Emily without her money. It's hers, and she may use it as she chooses, I suppose. But I rather hope she'll let it alone."

Bewilderment on his face, Frederick said, "I admire your principles, Arthur. Can't help but admire them . . ." He seemed at a loss. "I think it will work out. No reason why money should be a problem for you and Emily. It's *lack* of money that causes problems!"

They were both relieved when the talk came to an end. Arthur pushed the disquieting thoughts it raised somewhere into the recesses of his mind. Frederick was right. It was lack of money that was a source of conflict. Once he and Emily were married, living in Wilkes-Barre, away from her family with their opulent life-style, everything would settle into its proper order.

Philadelphia   June 1931

Emily and Arthur were married at Briar Hall on a blooming Sunday afternoon in early June. The ceremony was held under an arbor of rambling roses in the beautiful setting of Claudia Grant's garden, which had taken prize after prize in the Main Line Garden Club's annual competitions.

All of Philadelphia and Main Line Jewish society was there, along with many of the old guard gentiles who knew Claudia and Fred from their numerous civic and charitable activities. Emily's friends from Finchley and Bryn Mawr turned out in throngs, happy to have a festive occasion to celebrate after the grim Depression winter everyone had just gone through.

Uncle Herman was in apparent ecstasy over this marriage. Arthur thought his mother looked regal as she walked down the aisle on Herman's arm. She wore a long gown of mauve chiffon and ropes of the Franke family pearls, which she seldom used. Rose was pleased. Emily was perfect for Arthur. She had looked for signs of regret in Arthur, but if he had any qualms, he hid them well. Thank heaven he had gotten over the disappointment of his love for Molly Shea. It had broken her heart to see him looking so dejected, so joyless for all those months—her sweet, sunny boy weighted down with sorrow.

Shortly before the wedding, after the excitement of the engagement announcement, his mother and sisters had given a reception in Wilkes-Barre in honor of Emily and Arthur. All of his family and friends had been dazzled by Emily's charm and beauty. Arthur had been congratulated over and over by everyone. Everyone except Nathan . . .

"You look like the golden couple, you and Emily," Nate had said, his tone even and neutral. "I hope appearances aren't deceiving, Art."

Arthur had been surprised and slightly annoyed. "Hell, Nate. What do I have to do to convince you?"

Nate had held up his hand in protest. "Whoa! Forget I said anything. You don't have to convince me, Art. I just want you to be happy."

Arthur had been sorry he'd lost his temper. Nate's concern was perfectly reasonable, he knew.

Emily was a splendid bride. Arthur's heart quickened and he felt a thrill of pride and love as he stood watching her glide down the garden path on her father's arm, her slim figure a picture of grace in the simple lines of the silk organza gown. She wore her great-grandmother's lace veil, her pale blond hair parted in the center and pulled back in a loose arrangement at the nape of her neck. Her only jewels were a strand of pearls Arthur had given her as a wedding gift and the emerald-cut diamond engagement ring set with two baguettes.

The antique sapphire and diamond ring which had belonged to his own grandmother still lay in its velvet box in a safe in his office. Molly had worn it whenever they had been together during the year of their love, and he knew he would never give it to anyone else.

Nate was his best man, standing tall and steady at his side, smiling reassuringly when Arthur met his eyes during a moment of hesitation in the ceremony. It was all right between them, he seemed to be saying, and Arthur was warmed and strengthened by his brother's presence.

After a sumptuous reception and dinner, the newlyweds took a train to Canada to the Château Royale in Quebec. The trip was a wedding gift from Emily's parents.

Quebec

Emily emerged from the dressing room of their suite wearing a gown and peignoir of rich ivory silk appliquéd with intricate satin roses and ecru lace. Her blond hair fell to her shoulders, brushed loose and smooth. Nate's words rang in Arthur's mind when he saw her: "You look like the golden couple, you and Emily . . ." He drove them away.

He took her in his arms. "Darling . . . you're the most beautiful woman, Emily. How did I get so lucky?" She was fragrant and warm in his embrace.

"Seems a shame," Arthur said in mock reluctance, as he tossed aside the expensive handmade peignoir, and then the gown. Emily smiled, running her hands over his chest and shoulders and back, drawing him to her.

She offered her body to him as a gift, arching herself against him, presenting her small, beautifully formed breasts for him to kiss and fondle, returning his kisses with ardor.

But it was only when he had turned out the lamp that Emily gave herself over completely to the expression of her love for Arthur. For she did love him, totally. Longing to be possessed by him, she took pleasure from each separate contact of his lean, hard body against hers.

At twenty-five, Emily was still a virgin. In all the years of dating Arthur when he was a medical student, during her engagement to Bill Beckinger, again in the four months since she and Arthur had become engaged, she had limited her sexual activities to everything up to actual intercourse.

She had still retained that old taboo against losing her virginity before marriage.

She lost it now, in rapt abandon, breathing in the special smell of him, the clean, strong, masculine odor of her husband. She rubbed herself against his long, muscular torso, kissing him, touching him, giving herself over finally to those emotions so long kept carefully under control. Arthur was amazed and much delighted. He could not imagine how these unrestrained passions had lain dormant for all the years he had known her.

Emily's trousseau was vast. By day she was a focus of attention in the formal dining rooms of the château, on the golf course, or riding along the trails. Each outfit was a picture of understated elegance, perfectly coordinated, flattering her classic looks and delicate coloring. And each night she appeared in a new confection, night gowns of rose or blue or sea green or apricot in chiffon, silk, and fine handkerchief linen.

"I feel like every night's my birthday and I get to open a new package," Arthur joked after the third night of their honeymoon. "The wrappings are pretty, but I like what's inside best," he said, looking down into her luminous gray eyes. She had a way of staring at him, as she did now, almost as if she were looking inside of him, searching for something, something that wasn't there.

It was an idyllic two weeks. They swam, golfed, rode horseback, and danced each night after dinner, then returned to their suite and made richly satisfying love.

Only one thing happened to disturb Arthur's tranquility. One night during the second week at Château Royale, he had a dream in which Molly was standing with her arms full of wilted meadow flowers, crying, and telling him she would love him forever. He awakened with a start, covered in sweat, his heart palpitating. A pall of sweet sorrow settled on him. He got out of the bed and went to a window. A warm summer breeze was blowing the sheer curtains and a bright moon was shining on the manicured lawns and golf course of the château.

There's no going back, he thought. Life is like a series of rooms. You close a door and you can never look back, never open that door again. But for just those few moments he gazed out at the moon and thought about Molly, wondering where she was, how she was, hoping she was safe and happy, knowing that all his life he would have to guard against the memory of her.

At the end of the week they returned to Wyoming Valley, where Arthur settled back into his busy practice, while Emily took up the happy task of decorating their rented house and becoming a part of Wilkes-Barre life.

Dublin

Her mother's cousin, Monsignor Patrick Riordan, had come himself to meet her with his young curate, Father Brian. She had accompanied them to the cold, drafty residence where they lived. Tired beyond imagination, in a daze, she had sat listening to his gentle brogue, her ear unattuned to the pronunciation, so that she had difficulty concentrating on his words.

Later, when she had time to reflect, she remembered his saying, "I assume that Bishop Shea discussed the special circumstances of this marriage with you, my dear."

"You mean about Mr. Tower . . . Sean . . . that he understood that I have loved another man. And that he would not require more than mutual respect and affection," she had answered, not really caring, her voice toneless.

Patrick Riordan had discussed the weakness of flesh in more humane terms than Thomas Shea, expressing his sympathy for youth, which must contend with it. He assured her that with time and prayer it would pass. And still, she did not fully comprehend what it meant.

Sean was . . . *Sean!* She had never known anyone quite like him. There was a largeness about him that simply filled a room, spilling forth, beyond its confines, catching you up with it until you felt a part of his verve and vitality. You couldn't be somewhere where Sean Tower was without being aware of him. Tall, broad, with a thick mane of crisp dark hair beginning to go gray at the temples, he had hazel eyes that pierced through you, and his resonant voice carried to the rafters, sweeping others in its wake.

He had more or less swept her along that way when she had first met him almost three years before. He had come to have dinner with Patrick Riordan

shortly after her arrival in Dublin. Appointing himself her unofficial guide to
Ireland, he had taken her through the streets of the ancient Viking town at
the mouth of the river Liffey, visiting Dublin Castle and Leinster House, the
Dáil Éireann, St. Patrick's, O'Connell Street, and other historic spots heralded in Irish verse and song. They had driven far and wide in the Leinster
countryside while he delivered lecture-type soliloquies on Irish history and
times. He spiced their conversations with ribald tales of fanciful heroes and
heroines. She had whirled in a centrifuge of cultural impressions, scarcely
realizing she was falling under his spell, captivated by the misty green of Erin.

At twenty-one Molly had never had a serious beau. She had been educated
from nursery school through high school at Sacred Heart Academy, a girls'
convent school. After one term at Misericordia, the new Catholic college in
Dallas, Pennsylvania, she had fled its stifling environment for Washington,
where she entered nurses training with the nursing sisters at Mount Mercy.
Her experience with men was almost entirely limited to her older brothers,
her doting, charming father, and a vast collection of cousins and uncles, all of
them extremely protective of her.

The flashing, dark good looks and brash personality of Sean Tower had
been enough to excite her interest in all things Irish. She had stayed in Dublin
for eight months, nursing at St. Patrick's Hospital, receiving her education in
Irish politics from Sean. Twelve years older than Molly, still single, he had
lived with his mother until her death several years before. The house was now
his. He lived there alone with a creaky housekeeper who cooked for him. A
united Ireland was the central focus of his life. It was this that had finally
driven Molly home, for she had come to the realization that whatever role she
might play in Sean Tower's life would be peripheral.

They were married in the chapel of the chancery by Patrick Riordan.
Molly thought the loneliness of her wedding ceremony was symbolic. She
knew only three people who were present—her cousin, the monsignor; the
young curate, Father Brian; and the groom.

Sean had been more than considerate during the first weeks of their marriage. She was his lawful wife, wedded to him in the Church, and he had the
right to ask her to share his bed. She was ready for that—hoping it might
create a buffer between her and her memories of Arthur. If she conceived, she
would be pleased, for she adored children and wanted to have many. With
time, with a family, and with the energizing force of Sean in her life, she was
sure she would find the strength to continue. She and Sean had never spoken
of her unhappy love affair. But neither did they speak of any love of their
own.

When Molly had moved to Sean's house she was given her own room. It
had a large double bed, a fireplace, and a cheerful, sunny sitting area. She had
been full of gratitude for his sensitivity. But the weeks stretched into a month,

two months, then three. And still he did not come to her room. She tried to indicate in many ways that his presence would be welcome. One night she knocked on his door after he had retired. He was sitting at his desk in his robe, writing. He smiled and put away the papers.

"Sean, would you like to come stay with me tonight?"

"Would you like me to, my dear?" He seemed pleased.

"Yes, I would."

He stayed with her often after that, affectionately holding her in his arms while he talked to her about his work, wanting to hear about her childhood, always amusing and clever. They kissed, sometimes passionately. But nothing more.

"Sean, I am your wife—yours, and no one else's," she finally said to him.

"Of course, Molly. Do you think I don't know that?"

"Well . . . have you no desire for me?" It was almost humiliating, but she persisted. "I intended when I agreed to marry you that I would be your wife in every way. I appreciate your being so considerate, but it isn't necessary . . . not any longer."

He sat up in the bed, looking at her with a frown of concern. "Molly, surely you . . ." He seemed at a loss for words. "They must have made clear . . ." He stopped, searching her face for a sign of comprehension. Finding none, he said, thickly, as if fighting tears, "I have a feeling that . . . that there has been a . . . a *terrible* misunderstanding."

"What's the matter, Sean? What misunderstanding?"

"Didn't they explain to you . . . about me?" He looked ill, drained of color.

She shook her head. "I don't know what you mean. Explain what?"

"Did no one tell you . . . that I cannot be a husband to you . . . in the physical sense? That . . . that I am . . . impotent?" he finally said, his voice heavy with anguish. He knew from the look on her face that she'd had no idea. He closed his eyes, hating them, the churchmen, with their attitudes about sex and sin. Had they condemned this flower, this exquisitely feminine woman in the freshness of her youth, to a life of celibacy with him without her knowledge and consent?

"I wasn't always like this Molly. . . . The doctors don't know, can't tell me why. They say there is still a chance that I can become a . . . a normal man again."

Molly had not spoken.

Sean touched her hair, gentling her. "They told me you understood. . . . Father Patrick said that your great-uncle, Bishop Shea, had spoken to you . . . that you had agreed that there was enough between us . . . that it would be sufficient for us to live together with mutual respect and affection. . . ." Sean's robust voice sounded weak, defeated.

Molly was too stunned to react well. Numb, she saw that her Uncle Thomas hadn't really given her a choice after all. Either way, she was deprived of love, of children, of the warmth of family associations. Molly Shea Tower found that she was capable of hatred.

Molly began nursing for relief organizations. Sean was deeply involved in Eamon de Valera's Fianna Fáil.

He no longer came to her room at night. He avoided physical contact or intimacy of any kind. He was bitter that she had been deceived and offered her the possibility of annulment.

She felt powerless, unable to take the initiative. Nine months passed this way, and she began to think she might return home.

Then her mother sent her a clipping from the Wyoming Valley *Sentinel*. A beautiful portrait of Miss Emily Alicia Grant of Haverford, Pennsylvania, whose parents took great pleasure in announcing her engagement to Dr. Arthur Franke Hillman.

II

Wilkes-Barre   December 1932

Snow fell in great fluffs of whiteness, spinning and swirling in the currents of sharp air. Emily felt encapsulated in one of those liquid-filled glass balls, like her grandfather used to bring; one turned them over to agitate particles of glitter, creating a scenic Swiss mountainside or confetti-strewn Eiffel Tower. She leaned against the wind, ducking her head into her fur collar.

The gaily wrapped packages from Isaac Long's and the Boston Store protruded from the shopping bag. They were getting wet—she should have had them delivered. Eager to have her purchases home, hidden in the hall closet behind the storage rack, she had never been able to wait patiently for things to happen. Now that she had bought Arthur's Christmas gifts, she wanted it to be Christmas Eve, for him to open the large boxes with the velveteen smoking jacket, the Scottish wool plaid robe, and the wristwatch—a new design, simple and fine-looking with its alligator strap and Swiss movement—to replace his old-fashioned pocket watch. She'd been terribly extravagant, but it was the one occasion when she felt no guilt about being a spendthrift. How she wished Arthur would let her spend her money to her heart's content, indulging him and herself in the luxuries they couldn't afford on his income. He was so foolishly *stubborn* about that. Pride, plain and simple. Sooner or later, she'd bring him around, she knew. Meanwhile, it was worth living like a pauper in order to be his wife. His wife! Even after eighteen months, it thrilled her to realize he belonged to her.

Lumbering, she walked on through the snow, the wind at her back now. Emily thought pregnancy was not the most graceful state. She felt fine, never better, and Arthur became more loving, more elated, with each passing week, as he watched her grow larger and larger. It irritated her to think that he loved this—this *thing* that grew inside her—that he loved her more because "it" was in her. That he loved her more because of it than he had loved her for herself.

She didn't consider it their child—not yet. She felt little excitement at the thought that she would give birth in less than four months. A baby. Their baby. She would love it because one loved one's children, so of course she would. But not now, not yet. It wasn't a person, wouldn't be, until it was living and breathing apart from her—an infant in a cradle in the nursery she had furnished—with a starched nurse hovering over it. The obstetrician thought there might be a second heartbeat, but Emily doubted it . . . there hadn't ever been twins in her family.

Emily let herself in the side door, stamping off the snow, laying her packages down on the telephone bench in the small hallway.

"Hannah!" she called. The maid didn't answer. Emily could hear her humming in the kitchen while she rattled pots and platters, preparing dinner. If I can hear her, why can't she hear me? she thought irritably. Heavens, why couldn't her household run with the same efficiency as her mother's? Claudia had always managed the servants so well! Life at Briar Hill and at Camp Repose went along without a ripple in its smoothness. "Hannah, I'm home! . . . Can you come help me, please?" Imagine, if Claudia should walk into her house and no one were there to greet her, to help with her coat, carry her bundles! But then the whole comparison was silly—Claudia would have a car and chauffeur waiting at the curb in front of each shop. Her own life was nothing like her mother's.

"Yes, Mrs. Hillman? Did you want something?" The maid appeared in the pantry doorway which led into the side hall. Emily noted with distaste that Hannah's faded blond hair was unkempt and she was not wearing a fresh uniform—no doubt she hadn't ironed one in time to change before cooking and serving dinner. Emily wasn't prepared for a discussion with Hannah now; she had to quickly bathe and change for dinner before Arthur reached home.

"Hannah, please put these packages with the others in the closet under the stairs—I must have my bath. It's so late. Any calls?"

"Yes, Dr. Hillman phoned. He has to make a house call on the way home, so he'll be late. I'll serve dinner at seven. He said to tell you that he's not having office hours tonight because of the bad weather."

Emily's initial annoyance upon hearing that Arthur would be late vanished when she heard he would spend the evening at home with her. One thing she had not become accustomed to—*one* thing? . . . one of the *many* things— was that her husband worked at night, had office hours every evening except

Saturday and Sunday. She loathed the fact that he must leave the table after dinner and go back to see patients instead of passing a leisurely evening with her.

Emily hurried up the carpeted stairway to their bedroom. She turned on a lamp, taking pleasure in the soft French blue of the carpeting, the paler blue of the patterned cretonne draperies. Bedrooms were important, she had told Arthur when he objected to the lavish use of the expensive material.

She ran a tub, pouring salts into the water. The fragrance, her favorite Lily of the Valley, wafted up with the steam from the hot water. It had a salubrious effect on her. Pulling open the double doors to the closet she had designed, she pushed aside several full-length robes until she found one she thought most becoming—a mauve challis hostess gown, full enough to drape gracefully over the bulge of her abdomen.

Emily sank into the deep foamy water, allowing herself to stretch out, feeling the tautness ease in her long legs and slim shoulders. She closed her eyes and rested her head against the back of the tub.

There was a matter she must take up with Arthur, a subject she had been reluctant to raise before this. Tonight might be the right moment. In her pregnant state, he would be persuadable. He treated her so gently these days. One would hardly believe he was a doctor, accustomed to women and pregnancy. . . . Emily toweled herself dry, patted herself with Lily of the Valley dusting powder, then replaced the mauve robe with an empire style that emphasized her pregnancy.

"But I've *always* had a Christmas tree, darling. All my life. I wouldn't know what to *do* without one!" They were sitting in the library after dinner, a small fire crackling in the hearth. The room was done in provincial style, with natural woods, print wallpaper, and country colors. The gleam of copper and brass pots filled with greens reflected the firelight.

"Emily, my love, I am a Jew. *We* are a Jewish couple. Jewish people do not celebrate Christmas—at least not in a religious way. I'd feel terribly uncomfortable having a tree in our house. . . . I've *never* had one."

"There are plenty of Jewish people who have trees, Arthur. In fact, until now, I've never known anyone who didn't!" she quickly answered. "It's not a religious symbol. It's just a beautiful decoration—a sign of the holiday season."

"I don't agree with you. It's a symbol, religious or not, and I would feel like a hypocrite having one. Look, darling, if you want to decorate with greens, go ahead. But, please, no tree. It would offend a lot of people unnecessarily."

They had spent the previous Christmas—their first as a married couple—in Haverford with the Grants. Fred hadn't been feeling well, so they'd held a simple open house on Christmas night instead of one of their usual lavish supper dances. Emily, thrilled to see all of her old friends, the people she'd grown up with, had looked stunning that night in black velvet, with a thin choker of diamonds and pearls, a family piece from Claudia's safe, around her slender neck. Everyone thought they were a handsome couple, Claudia had told Arthur approvingly.

"Handsome is as handsome does," he'd quipped, his voice light and non-committal. Claudia always required some particular behavior from those whose lives she directed. For that holiday Arthur had willingly played his role.

This year he had been pleased that Emily preferred to remain at home in Wilkes-Barre for the holidays instead of joining her family. But now here they were in disagreement about a tree. He thought when he'd married a Jewish woman that religion was one area where there would be no controversy!

"Oh, Arthur! What harm is there in it? Just a small tree—here in this room over in the corner near the fireplace. Who would ever notice it besides us? It would give me such pleasure, darling!"

Of course, they had a Christmas tree, and a garland of greenery and red ribbons on the bannister, with a sprig of mistletoe in the hallway. Well, if it made Emily happy, Arthur supposed there was no harm in it. He absolutely refused to allow a wreath on the door—but even Emily hadn't expected to have one.

Arthur was properly grateful for the presents she gave him. A velvet smoking jacket was something he would never have thought of wearing, but he put it on and let her admire him in it. The wristwatch was handsome. He felt a twinge, though, at the thought of relegating his father's pocket watch to a bureau drawer; that watch had meant so much to him when Jacob had given it to him.

Emily was delighted with the carved jade necklace and bracelet, a matched set with old gold clasps and filigree ornamentation. He'd seen it in the shop of a patient who dealt in antiques. It had been expensive but the owner had given him a good price. He would have loved to be able to lavish Emily with beautiful things. If ever there were someone who should have elegant clothes and jewels, it was Emily. Someday, perhaps, he'd be able to afford them. But for now he had all he could do to pay his bills . . . and, with a baby coming, they would have more expenses.

Twin boys! Arthur was giddy with happiness as he watched the two infants, asleep in their bassinets in the St. Anne's nursery.

"The Lord has blessed you, Doctor," Sister Emmaline congratulated him as the babies were wheeled away from the delivery room.

How perfect they were! How strong the small grips on his finger . . . how lusty the cries. The firstborn was longer, dark-haired, fists tightly clenched, mouth screwed up in a grimace, while the other was fairer, looking peaceful and relaxed in the second crib. Jeffrey Grant and Robert Lawrence were the names Emily had chosen, named for Jacob and for Emily's maternal grandfather.

Emily was still sedated from the anesthesia. Arthur hadn't been pleased about that, but it had been necessary; her strength had been fading. She'd been in labor for hours and seemed to be getting nowhere. It had been a forceps delivery—the first child coming easily enough, but the second needing resuscitation. Arthur had been present throughout the delivery—he'd promised Emily he would stay with her.

He sat next to her bed, watching her. Poor darling, she'd had a rough time. He felt a tender remorse, looking at her still, pale face. She was so beautiful! He stroked her cheek, leaned over to kiss her lips.

Emily's eyes opened. When she saw him there, hovering over her, his hands touching her, she smiled groggily.

"Is it true, Arthur?" she asked, the words slurred. "We have twin sons . . . ?"

"Yes, my love, it's true." He smoothed the hair back from her damp forehead. "Emily, darling, I love you . . . I love you *so* . . ."

A tear appeared in the corner of each eye and rolled down her cheeks. "Thank you, darling," she whispered. She put out her hand to him. He took it, bringing it to his lips.

It was the happiest moment of her life.

Their differences had really begun over the furnishing of the nursery. From the moment she knew she was pregnant, Emily became involved in the selection of paint, carpeting, fabric for curtains, expensive chests of drawers, a small sofa, an antique rocker and crib. The bill came to an astronomical figure. When Arthur spoke about it, Emily brushed it off lightly.

"Mother and Daddy said it was their gift, darling. Part of the house."

The Grants had been generous when they were married, giving them not only their honeymoon trip, but furnishing their rented house as a wedding gift. Arthur had thought at the time that Emily was being far too extravagant.

"It's a rented house, darling," he'd told her. "Wouldn't it be more practical to buy rugs and use plain wallpaper? Those panels must cost a fortune." He had viewed the swatches for hand-screened fabric walls in the dining room with concern.

"But they're so lovely, Arthur. I'm *mad* about them! We'll be here for years."

After the twins arrived, Emily engaged a baby nurse for the first month. The maid couldn't be expected to take care of two babies and do all the housework, after all.

"Yes, I suppose twins will be difficult to manage at first," Arthur agreed.

"You'll soon get the hang of it, honey," he added, with more hope than conviction.

Mrs. Kelly, the nurse, stayed beyond the first month. Emily's parents were coming to visit, then Emily and Arthur were going to Philadelphia for Roy McLean's wedding. Old Roy had finally been snagged! Predictably, his fiancée was from Main Line society—a member of the Radnor Hunt and all that. After they returned home, Emily caught cold, with swollen glands . . . Six months passed and Mrs. Kelly was still with them.

Arthur admired how Emily managed the household so well. She wrote the checks, paid the bills, and handled their personal affairs, while Arthur took care of his office books, sharing a secretary-receptionist with the eye, ear, nose, and throat man who had taken the adjoining suite of offices.

One afternoon when Emily was out, Arthur needed to cash a check. He went to Emily's desk for the checkbook to their joint account. There were a number of stubs from certified checks spread over the desk. "What on earth?" he muttered. The First Philadelphia Bank and Trust Company . . . Emily Grant Hillman . . . $2,000; Emily Grant Hillman . . . $2,500; Emily Grant Hillman . . . $1,500. . . .

What was going on? But, of course, he knew.

When Emily came in, he was sitting in the small library. "Em, may I see you a minute, please?"

"Hello, darling! My, you look so serious. What weighty matter do you want to see me about?"

"These." He gestured toward the desk.

Emily glanced at the strewn papers and check stubs. "You've been going through my things," she said icily.

"Going through *your* things! Emily, I thought a joint checking account was as much my business as it is yours. You know I wouldn't 'go through' your things. These were out there, just as you see them. I needed a check. Emily, why didn't you tell me about these?"

"Because I knew you'd be angry."

"Then why did you use that money if you knew I'd be angry?"

She looked away from him. "There wouldn't *be* enough money if I didn't use it." Then she turned to him. "It's *my* money, Arthur. Why *shouldn't* I use it?"

"You *may* use it, Emily. But not to support me, not to pay my bills—our bills—buy our food, pay our rent."

"That's not what I've used it for. I've used it for . . . for . . . things . . . things that I like, things I want that we can't afford." She sounded petulant, but that hardness was there.

"Such as?" Now his voice was cold and still.

"Such as *clothes!* Such as a *nurse* to help me with two babies who are a handful! Such as *hairdressers* and *manicures!* Such as *tickets* to the concert series and Little Theater! Such as Christmas gifts for my family, which they *expect,* and *we can't afford otherwise . . . !"* Her voice had risen to a level of hysteria.

Arthur had never seen Emily like this. Even in labor, she had been quiet, in control. He watched in amazement as she shrieked at him, her mouth contorted, her cheeks darkening, her eyes nervously darting.

Arthur stood up and walked over to her, taking her by the shoulders. There was a ring of whiteness around his mouth. "Now, get hold of yourself, Emily." When she continued her tirade, wrenching away from him, he said, "Emily! There are a nurse and a maid in this house, I will remind you, and they needn't be witness to this. You're acting like a spoiled child. This won't help matters at all. You will give Mrs. Kelly two weeks' notice, and you will not deposit any more of those checks in our joint account. Open your own account, if you wish, and buy things for your own use. But don't pay another household bill of ours with your inheritance. Is that clear?" He walked out, left the house, and drove to his office.

Emily was sitting up in bed, wearing a bed jacket over her nightgown when he came in at 10:30 that night. She had been crying, her eyes and nose inflamed. Arthur felt guilty, that sinking in his chest.

"I don't want to fight with you, Emily," he said, putting his arms around her. She dissolved in tears, holding him tightly, her arms around his neck.

"Why? *Why* won't you let me keep Kelly? What's the difference whether I pay for something frivolous for myself or for a nurse to help me?" She drew back from him, an expression of panic on her face. "I can't take care of two babies alone, Arthur. I *can't!* I know I'll be miserable. Please, please let me. I never thought I wouldn't be able to have a nurse for my children . . . it's just something that never *occurred* to me."

"Emily . . . Emily . . ." He shook his head sadly. "You should have married a rich man. You weren't meant to be a doctor's wife, living on an ordinary income, during the Depression. I thought it would work . . . I thought you understood. . . . People here don't live this way, Em. You know that, darling. Who else in town has a full-time maid, a nurse for their children, extra help for dinners, for window washing, yard work?"

"The Wintermuths do."

"Honey, Lowell is vice-president of the largest independent coal company in the anthracite region! I, may I remind you, am a small-town doctor with a general practice—and half my patients can't afford to pay my bills."

"Lowell is vice-president of the W & S *only* because he's Cyril Buckland's son-in-law, as you well know! How is that any different than your wife paying some of the bills with her money? I thought marriage was a partnership. My money is your money, Arthur."

"No, it is not." His mouth had a stubborn set.

"Is your money mine?" she asked.

"That's different, Emily. A man is supposed to support his wife."

"So, if you don't make enough money for me to have things I want, like a nurse for the children, I'm supposed to just accept that, even though I have money of my own? Does that make sense? You know how much I dislike doing things like changing diapers and preparing baby bottles. . . ."

He threw up his hands in exasperation. "Oh, Emily, it's hopeless! I'm ready to drop. I have to operate first thing tomorrow morning. . . . I've got to get some sleep. Do what you want about Kelly . . . you will, anyway."

There were other matters that lay there between them. Large or small, most of them, he discovered, were not worth the torture of arguing with Emily.

Each time he tried to discuss her extravagance, a steel edge would creep into Emily's voice, then high spots of color form in her cheeks, while her eyes flashed in defiance. He learned that this was the prelude to fits of uncontrolled, sometimes violent, temper.

Her rages were not shrewish. Arthur doubted that Emily willed them. There seemed to be an ill-defined boundary between the rational Emily and the woman of these scenes. Arthur, who had never been at ease with controversy—particularly with women—would back off. Delightful as she was most of the time, Emily, if crossed, could make his life hell.

How had he not seen this side of her before their marriage? How could he have not been aware of her tantrums, her unstable nature in all the years he had known her? It was extraordinary!

It did not occur to him to examine his own attitude.

III

Wilkes-Barre   Winter 1935

"Father John Riordan would like you to call him, Dr. Hillman. He says it's important," Arthur's secretary told him when he arrived for office hours.

Arthur hadn't spoken to the priest for many weeks. The health clinics at the parish had been discontinued the previous year after he'd been successful in getting the union to let their volunteer corps of a dozen young doctors hold them on Saturday mornings at their headquarters. It was a small beginning . . . very small. Arthur had not given up his idea of developing a network of diagnostic clinics throughout the coal industry with the joint cooperation of union and management. He really should have kept Father John informed of the latest developments. . . .

But John wasn't calling about his miners this time.

"Arthur, I'd like you to see my sister, Katherine Shea. She's had pneumonia this winter and a nasty cough hangs on. She's still using old Doc Hanran, who's a good enough fellow, but I don't have much confidence in him. I think she needs a consultation."

Arthur was vaguely disquieted at the thought of seeing Molly's mother. He hadn't met or spoken to her since that last unhappy telephone call five years before. . . . Well, he had to forget all about that and assume a professional attitude. He was a happily married man now, with two-year-old twin sons and another child on the way.

When Katherine Shea was ushered into his office, Arthur was shocked at her appearance. Terribly thin, with dark circles under her eyes, she had a pallor which doctors learn to recognize as a sign of morbid illness.

His examination did nothing to contradict his first impression. He was alarmed. When she dressed and was seated in his consultation room, he said, "Mrs. Shea, I'd like to take you into St. Anne's for a couple of days to do some tests. You'll be comfortable there with the sisters. I think we ought to do a bronchoscopy, to be thorough."

She was frightened, he knew, yet she was her daughter's mother, stoic. He patted her hand and smiled encouragingly. "I don't want to worry you. I'm being extra-cautious. We'll get you fixed up. I'll give Dr. Hanran a call and let him know what we're doing."

She asked him about his family and seemed genuinely delighted to hear about his children. It was only courteous to inquire about Molly. He did so in an offhand manner. Katherine said she'd been to Ireland to visit Molly and Sean. They were fine.

"And how many children do they have?" he asked, preparing himself to hear some amazing statistic.

Her eyes dropped. "So far, they don't have any," was her reply.

On her way out, Katherine stopped at the receptionist's desk to pay the bill. She was told there would be no charge. Katherine protested, but the young woman insisted that Dr. Hillman never charged clergymen's families.

Arthur called his old mentor, Roland Silverberg, at Jefferson. "How are you, Arthur, and how is that lovely wife of yours?" Roland had a chilly exterior, but he liked Arthur. He'd been at first angry, then disappointed, and finally grudgingly admiring of Arthur's decision to resign his residency and return to the coal regions, as he called this part of Pennsylvania.

Arthur told Silverberg about Katherine Shea. "As far as I can tell, the other lung is clear. There's a fair-sized tumor in the upper lobe of the left lung, about two and a half centimeters across, I judge. Unfortunately, she came to see me only two days ago. She's had symptoms for over a year."

"Why'd she wait so long to get medical attention?"

"She's *had* medical attention, Dr. Silverberg . . . their old family doctor, who delivered all of her six children and attended her three miscarriages and her final extrauterine pregnancy, which resulted in a hysterectomy."

"R.C., I guess," said the surgeon.

"Yes," answered Arthur, his voice tight. "Mrs. Shea is a fine woman, the . . . sister . . . of a dear friend of mine. Her brother, my friend, is a priest. I would appreciate it if you'd see her. I don't think she can wait too long." Professor Silverberg agreed to examine Katherine Shea. "Oh, Dr. Silverberg, her circumstances are modest. She's a widow, and there's not much money there . . ."

"Don't worry, Arthur. There will be no charge for my services," the starchy professor assured him. I wonder what he'll do with the afghan Kitty will crochet for him, Arthur mused.

Arthur had felt heartsick when he saw the X-rays. He didn't even bother to put Katherine through the discomfort of a bronchoscopy, since he knew Silverberg would want to repeat it. No need to add to the nightmare that lay ahead of her. She would need all of her faith and fortitude in the months to come. He doubted she would live out the year, from the appearance of the film.

He called John Riordon. John agreed to accompany Katherine to Philadelphia. He told Arthur that Kitty's sons were scattered around the country, so they couldn't be counted on for much help.

"You'd better begin to think about who *can* be counted on for help, John. She's going to need care and a place to stay, or someone to stay in her house with her."

John was grave. "For how long, Arthur?"

"There's only one place you'll get the answer to that, my friend . . . and you're in closer touch there than I am."

"Oh, God!"

Precisely.

Roland Silverberg removed Katherine Shea's left lung on a blustery March day in 1935. Arthur drove down to Philadelphia to observe the surgery, as he often did when he referred his patients to a specialist at one of the teaching hospitals. John was grateful that he was there, and Katherine went peacefully under the anesthesia, knowing Arthur would be in the operating room. Arthur was puzzled at his emotional involvement in this case. He kept telling himself that it was just his fondness for Katherine and his friendship with Father John that accounted for the heaviness of heart he had felt ever since he'd made the diagnosis of lung cancer. In the depths of his soul, though, was something he refused to acknowledge.

After all the years he had been associated with Roland Silverberg, he was still impressed with the surgeon's skill. Arthur watched while his professor made a long, curving incision through the skin and underlying layer of fat, delicately pulling back muscle tissue to expose the ribs, placing retractors in position to maintain the field of surgery. This new technique, the pneumonectomy, had been developed recently by one of the great thoracic surgeons, Evarts Graham, out at Barnes Hospital in St. Louis. Few surgeons had performed the operation. . . . Dr. Silverberg worked quickly, but unhurriedly, clamping blood vessels with hemostats, removing a portion of the ribs, invading the pleura slowly and carefully, so as not to shock his patient. He exposed the diseased organ. There was amazingly little bleeding for such a major procedure. The lung was removed and placed in a basin, to be sent to pathology.

The process of closing up was just as painstaking. Each blood vessel tied off, the pedicle carefully sutured, the layers of tissue brought together with meticulous care. Finally, a puncture wound was made in the chest wall and a drain inserted. Professor Silverberg, from long habit, commented as he worked, speaking in a quiet, precise manner, with an economy of words—like his surgery, nothing wasted. After the dressings were applied, the surgeon removed his surgical mask from his glistening face, moist with perspiration. Arthur felt himself relax. He found that his neck and shoulder muscles were aching from tension.

"That was beautiful, Dr. Silverberg. I feel privileged to have watched it," he said to the older man as they followed the patient out of the operating room.

Waiting in the lounge with Father John were Tom and Kevin Shea, two of Katherine's sons, who had come from Washington and Harrisburg to be at their mother's bedside. John walked outside with Arthur. "I can't tell you how much this means to me, Arthur—your being here. I'll never forget it." The priest looked at a loss. Katherine was one of the few people in the world John was close to. And now he must begin the process of saying good-bye to her, because Professor Silverberg had agreed with Arthur that it was a long shot.

John told Arthur that Katherine would go home with Kevin to Harrisburg for the period of her recuperation. After that, they would decide whether she could return to her house in Forty Fort or stay with her sister in Sunbury. John thought Sunbury was a better idea. "It's closer to Kevin and his family, and it's near the convent where her daughter is in orders," he said. ". . . her daughter Maureen," he hastily added. Neither of them spoke of Kitty's other daughter, who was far away, across the sea in Ireland.

Arthur walked slowly to his car. He was always depressed when he knew he would lose a patient. This was worse than usual. It had opened too many old wounds. He drove home to Wilkes-Barre along the newly paved highway, making the trip in record time . . . five hours. He was weary as he drove the final few miles down the long decline of Wyoming Mountain. The valley lay below under a dark, leaden sky, looking bleak and foreboding.

"She looks exactly like you, Emily!" Arthur said, his arm around his wife, as they stood over the bassinet in the newly decorated nursery.

"She has your eyes, darling," Emily insisted. "And your smile . . . that determined mouth, too."

"Whatever or whoever, she's absolutely gorgeous!" he said with paternal pride, squeezing Emily and kissing the top of her head.

Their daughter was two months old, and had succeeded in dominating the household ever since her arrival in April. Her birthday was three days before Emily's. She had been named Ellen Grace, in memory of Emily's two grandmothers.

This birth had been much easier, and Emily had regained her strength and her figure immediately. Mrs. Kelly had taken on the care of another baby with ease, moving the twins into the upstairs sitting room to make room for the baby in the nursery. They were a little crowded, but none of them seemed to mind.

Emily said Arthur was a sentimentalist about his children. He adored them. Each day when he came home after office hours or hospital rounds, he would bound up the steps, calling for the boys, his whistle a signal for them to drop whatever they were doing and rush headlong into his arms. He would scoop them up, both at the same time, hugging and kissing them, beaming at them, loving them beyond imagination. And how they loved *him!* His great, big, tall, strong body . . . his deep, hearty laugh . . . the way he threw them up in the air and caught them, or let them ride hobbyhorse on his crossed leg, bouncing them up and down. He never tired of them, his patience infinite in teaching them to spell their names when they were only two, to say the alphabet, to recite a poem.

"Arthur! It's crazy to try to teach little children things like that at their age," Emily would protest. But he did it anyway. He tossed balls with them, played hide and seek, and acted, in the words of Jim Flannery, "like a total damn fool."

"Who would have believed there is nothing but a doting father under that sophisticated man-of-the-world exterior, Hillman!" Flannery teased him when he came to see Arthur one Saturday afternoon in June.

Arthur remembered that his own father had seldom done anything with any of them. It had always been his Grandfather Isaac who had played the games and taught him things.

"Golly, would my grandfather have loved to see these kids," he said to Flannery.

"Yeah. Mine sure did enjoy ours." Garrick Flannery had passed away at the grand old age of eighty-nine a few months ago. "Well, it's a lucky thing you married that beautiful woman," Jim teased when he saw Ellen. "Otherwise, she might've been ugly, like her old man!"

Arthur and Jim sat down to go over the clinic records. Arthur was preparing some statistics on lung disease for a paper he planned to submit to the *Pennsylvania Medical Journal.* There was increasing interest in the effects of various occupations on health. You couldn't let up, Arthur thought. If you have an idea you believe in, keep at it, and eventually people will take notice.

They had finished dinner when Father John Riordan called.

"How is your sister, John?" Arthur asked.

"She's doing very well, Arthur. Seems to be getting around. She even talks about coming home, although we're coaxing her to stay in Sunbury."

"I'm delighted to hear that, John. Remember me to her when you speak to her."

"I've got some news for you, Arthur. I'm going to Washington! I'll be studying for my doctorate at Georgetown."

"That's wonderful, John! Congratulations." At the same time, he felt a letdown. He would miss John Riordan. They hadn't seen so much of each other since he and Emily were married. Now, Arthur regretted that he hadn't continued their visits. You always think you have lots of time for things like that. "John, you must come for dinner. We have to celebrate. When do you leave?"

"In a month. There'll be lots of things to do before then. I'd like to have dinner with you, Arthur. We better do it soon, before the Rosary Circle lunch and the Communion breakfasts start!" John chuckled, knowing the fuss the ladies in his parish would make when they heard the news.

Emily agreed to have a dinner for John Riordan. They invited the Flannerys, the Sloats, the Carpenters, Dr. and Mrs. Charles Means, and the Harry Steigers—all of whom knew Father John well. They'd wanted to have a larger group, but John said, "Just a few old friends, Arthur. I'll enjoy that more."

After the molded ice-cream bombe with hot-fudge sauce had been served, Arthur toasted Father John, wishing him happiness and success in Washington.

"If we hear rumors about some renegade priest who's down there trying to get the government to spend money on giving scholarships to poor but worthy students, we'll know they're true!" he concluded. They all laughed. John looked touched and amused. Arthur hadn't ever seen Father John so happy, basking in the glow of friendship and affection around the table.

John rose to answer their toasts. He stood, his sleek, dark head bent forward in characteristic modesty, one hand in his pocket, holding his wine glass. He cleared his throat.

"What you learn when you think you've finally been granted one of your fondest wishes is that everything has a price. When I was sent to Our Lady of the Mountain in Ashley, I really thought I must have done something terrible to deserve such a fate." Everyone chuckled. "Well, I'm not saying that it was the bishop, or whoever makes these decisions from on high, who had the foresight to know that these would end up being the happiest years of my life, but, the fact is, that's how it turned out. And much of that is due to the friendships and working relationships I've had with the people here in this room. Arthur . . . Jim . . . Tom . . . those clinics did more for me than they did for the miners, I can tell you. Hob . . . Charles . . . I've enjoyed our association down at St. Anne's so much. Both of you, as physicians and as men, have shown me what men of healing and compassion can be. And Harry . . . I look forward to being your neighbor in Washington when Congressman Steiger is elected next fall."

"Hear! Hear!" everyone called.

"So, you can believe me when I say that I leave with mixed feelings. I'm excited at the prospect of this new challenge and the opportunity to spend the next period of my life in academia. . . . But my heart is heavy when I think of leaving these dear friends behind." He coughed to cover his emotion. "I haven't meant to neglect you ladies." He smiled at them. "I do love beautiful women . . . and you're all so lovely." Everyone laughed appreciatively. "You're the important ones in your husbands' lives, the force that makes them able to be the fine men, the able community leaders they are." He raised his glass. "I'm off to Washington, but I'm paying a price for it. God bless all of you."

When their guests had left, Arthur helped Emily clear away the last of the brandy glasses and ashtrays from the living room before going upstairs.

"That was a lovely dinner, dear," he said to Emily. "Thanks for doing it."

"I enjoyed it, darling. They're nice, all of them. I like Father John. . . . I'm not sure I appreciate his views on women, though!"

Arthur laughed. "I caught that look in your eye! You don't like being the force behind your husband, do you?"

She shrugged. "I don't mind, but I *do* exist in my own right. Women don't always have to be the afterthought, the pat-on-the-head, you're-important-too part of the after-dinner speech."

He pulled her against himself. "You're the *most* important. . . . Without you, I'm nothing." He began to caress her. Emily returned his kiss ardently. "Darling, let's go to bed," he whispered.

They fell asleep in each other's arms that night, wonderfully happy, sharing a rare sense of joy and harmony.

Winter 1936

In the seventh winter of the Great Depression, people were looking for heroes. In January, England's King George V died and the playboy Prince of Wales became King Edward VIII. Less than six weeks later, Hitler sent his troops into the Rhineland. In America, the unemployed rode the rails, lined up in queues at soup kitchens, and begged door to door for a job in return for a sandwich.

The entire northeastern United States was caught in the grip of the worst series of blizzards and rainstorms in history, followed by sudden early spring thaws. The peculiar circumstances of freezing, precipitation, and warming temperatures caused flooding from Maine to West Virginia, from the East Coast to the Mississippi.

The Susquehanna River poured over its banks as far down as Harrisburg. Wyoming Valley was the hardest hit of the Pennsylvania communities.

Arthur convinced Emily to go to her parents' home in Haverford with the children and Mrs. Kelly. Briar Hill was a lonely, empty house with half its rooms unused. Claudia and Fred were thrilled to have company, since they lived there alone with Nellie and the other servants.

Emily had not wanted to leave. "The flood waters have begun to recede," she protested. "We're in no danger."

But Arthur was afraid of disease. One case of diphtheria had already been seen and several of scarlet fever. He was certain that many of the reported sick children who hadn't yet been checked would prove to have contagious diseases, brought by sewer rats and debris in the wake of the flood.

Their house on Franklin Street was on high ground, so Arthur was able to drive them to the improvised stop for the Pennsylvania Railroad above North Street. The low-lying areas of the city were still under water.

Emily kissed him good-bye cheerfully, urging him to take care of himself. "Darling, be sure you dress warmly when you're out in the boats and at the aid station. It's cold and damp. You know, doctors aren't immune to disease, either."

He reassured her as he hugged and kissed them good-bye. "Be good, boys. Help your mother so she doesn't have too many problems without Daddy there."

"We will," they chorused. They might not look alike, but they did everything alike, with Bobby echoing Jeff's every word.

One-year-old Ellen didn't understand what was happening until she realized that Arthur wasn't staying on the train with them. Then she began to cry. Her chubby little face was pressed against the window, watching him tearfully while he waved good-bye to the slowly moving train as it pulled away.

Without his family to worry about, Arthur was able to devote his complete attention to the flood relief work. The main effort was concentrated on the prevention of epidemic.

"The Red Cross estimates that over a thousand houses have been evacuated, but many people have stuck it out and are living up in attics with whatever blankets and supplies they have on hand," the Public Health officer told them when he and his fellow doctors assembled at the Medical Society.

The Coast Guard had sent men in with small powerboats to conduct rescue work in the still-flooded areas. They were conducting house-to-house searches to see who needed aid. The swift eddies and currents in the flooded streets were difficult to negotiate, causing a few of the boats to capsize, throwing their two-man crews into the icy waters. Thus far, there had been no deaths due to the flood, although one family had been asphyxiated from a ruptured gas line. As a result of that accident, the gas had been turned off throughout the valley. Without heat, the medical teams feared that elderly people would die from pneumonia and exposure. The bridges had reopened, the waters were receding, and everyone felt the emergency was over.

And then, heavy rains upstream sent the water level of the Susquehanna up to eleven feet above flood stage, creating havoc in Wilkes-Barre. The community reeled under the immense onslaught of the flood waters; an estimated eight thousand were evacuated by Thursday, the nineteenth of March. Another five thousand were considered in danger.

The 109th Field Artillery was aided by hundreds of volunteer miners and other National Guard units from the state. They worked feverishly to take people from their homes. Power was out in Wilkes-Barre's downtown area. Dormitories for the thousands of homeless had been set up in the courthouse, the armory, in large school buildings, and churches—wherever there was a large, dry, unoccupied space unendangered by the raging waters.

On the Kingston side of the Market Street Bridge, a temporary emergency hospital was set up in two trolley cars. There Arthur and Jim Flannery, as part of the 109th's Medical Unit under Al Feinberg's command, spent their days taking care of the large number of sick and injured persons rescued from the flooded flats of Kingston. Another case of diphtheria, more scarlet fever, measles, and influenza. Two more deaths were reported. The governor declared martial law, ordering more National Guard troops into the valley to bolster the exhausted Field Artillery men. Finally, the flood crested and the river water slowly began to recede. The aftermath belonged to the Public Health authorities and the medical community, whose job was just beginning.

Upriver at Towanda, the checkpoint for flood levels in Wyoming Valley, it was reported that the river was dropping at the rate of an inch per hour. Gradually, the yellow waters of the Susquehanna returned to their natural channel, moving swiftly, continuing the cycle of carving out the silted riverbed.

How long would it be before she lashed out again, taking claim to her flood plain?

Emily returned from Philadelphia alone, leaving the children and Kelly to stay with her parents until she had put their household in order in the wake of the flood. City steam and gas had been turned on, but the water was not yet purified, so it was necessary to boil all drinking and cooking water, and

Arthur insisted she use disinfectant in bath and laundry water. The sewers had overflowed with the flooding, mixing with the waters of the river and the fresh water supply. Everything that had been in the garage or basement had to be either burned or thoroughly scrubbed and aired in the sun. Emily couldn't bear the damp flood odor in the basement. Sensitive to mold, her eyes were often swollen and her throat irritated for weeks after she began working on the house.

April 10 was Emily's thirty-first birthday. They were planning on going to Wolf's Head Country Club for dinner; most of the restaurants were not yet open because of the health hazard. Wolf's Head was halfway to Scranton, on higher ground, and used the Beaver Lake Reservoir, so it was safe.

"I have a surprise for you," Emily said to Arthur just as they were leaving the house. Her eyes shone with suppressed excitement. "I'll drive, darling. But you have to close your eyes!"

Amused, Arthur cooperated with Emily's game. He couldn't tell where they were going. She drove south, turned west toward the river, then north again, slowing down as they drove up a steep incline before coming to a halt.

"Don't peek until I tell you to," she cautioned, jumping out of the car and coming around to open his door. She led him by the hand over grassy lawn. Arthur could smell a fresh springtime odor of budding trees and bushes—something that had been largely missing from the flooded areas where many flowering bushes had been ruined this year. They stopped. "All right. Open your eyes!"

Arthur found himself standing in front of a large house in the English Tudor style. Imposing and graceful, its front entrance was a thick hob-nailed oak door recessed under an overhang, set on the left end of a long, broad flagstone terrace. On either side of the central structure were smaller wings, creating a pleasing balance to the whole. An expanse of leaded-glass windows spanned the front of the first and second floors, reflecting the pink light of the setting sun. Arthur turned toward the sunset and realized that they were standing at the highest point of Grandview Terrace, a rocky promontory set above the tree-lined esplanade of Grandview Boulevard with a commanding view of the Susquehanna just above the elbow, locally called the Great Bend. This was the Hollander mansion, once the property of one of Wilkes-Barre's oldest, most prominent families. He had never been in the house at the top of Grandview Terrace, although he had visited the other two houses that shared the terraced hillock, belonging to Mason Forrest and Hobson Carpenter.

"The Hollander house," Arthur said, giving Emily a puzzled glance. "It's beautiful up here, isn't it? You can't really see the house from below, the way it's set back." He didn't understand what Emily was so excited about, unless she was rediscovering Wilkes-Barre's charms after the ordeal of the flood.

"You can see the back of it from the Westmoreland campus, Arthur. I've always wondered whose house it was and what it was like inside." Emily looked like the proverbial cat who had swallowed a canary.

"Well, I don't know who owns it now. I suppose a family trust or the bank . . . if you really want to see what it looks like." This was pretty silly, he began to think.

With a triumphant smile, Emily held up a key. "*I* know who owns it," she announced. "And I have the key!"

He allowed himself to be led to the entrance and then inside after Emily had unlocked the massive door. He had an uneasy feeling that events were beginning to unfold in a manner out of his control. He suspected he knew what was in Emily's mind, recognized the signs of her determined planning, and he didn't like his suspicions.

From the slate-floored foyer, they walked into a broad entrance hall from which solid-paneled double doors led to large, well-proportioned rooms with beamed ceilings and dark oak woodwork. The sunken living room was a long room with an immense fireplace at one end and a wide window seat at the front, along the leaded casement windows, framed by handsome built-in cabinets and bookshelves on either side. It had considerable light for a Tudor, the warm rays of the setting sun streaming in. Standing in the middle of the room, Arthur could look up and down the river, as far north as the Market Street Bridge and south because of the elevation of the Terrace—as far as Larksville and Plymouth. It was a beautiful sight. Arthur was intrigued, despite his misgivings.

"Emily . . ." he began, hesitantly, "I think I know what you have in mind and it . . ."

She cut him off, taking his arm imploringly and hugging it to her. "Please, Arthur, don't say anything yet! Just come look through it and then listen to what I have to say. . . . Just let me say it all, and then I'll hear you out. I promise!" As she saw a faint smile begin at the corners of his mouth, she said, "Oh, please, darling," in a low, intense voice.

He let out a long breath and nodded. "All right. That's fair enough."

It was an elegant house with a wonderful flow to the arrangement of rooms. Carpeted throughout with old, somewhat threadbare red broadloom, part of the hall carpeting had been taken up so that they could see the lovely parquet floors, well-preserved, needing little more than refinishing. Because of its elevation, there had been no water in the basement, even though the house was so close to the river.

All the Hollander furniture stood in place, dark and substantial. The dining room was large enough to seat eighteen or more at the heavy refectory table. Arthur didn't care for the massive furniture, but the room itself had pleasing proportions. There was another smaller dining room, more like a sun room, which could be used for family dining; then a butler's pantry and a roomy kitchen lined with glass-fronted cabinets. On the north side of the house, with its own side entrance, were four medium-sized rooms and a bathroom, evidently designed to be a separate apartment. Emily had a wise little smile when she showed him this wing.

"Don't say it," he jested. "I know you think it would be perfect for a doctor's offices."

"Well, *wouldn't* it?" She was so excited, like a child. He had to admit, it was about as perfect as anything could be.

There was more: a bookshelf-lined paneled library with fireplace, a tile-floored, solarium-music room, a screened eating porch adjacent to a rear patio overlooking a small garden. From the back of the slope, all wooded with rhododendrons and azaleas under mature trees, there was a view of the spires of the Westmoreland College campus.

Arthur didn't say much—what was there to say? It was one of the most beautiful houses he had ever seen. Just right for a doctor with a growing family . . . *if* the doctor could afford it, which he couldn't.

Emily led the way up the staircase to the upper hall. Directly ahead, at the top of the stairs, double folding doors opened to a broad, fairly shallow room which might have been two smaller rooms that had been joined at one time. At one end was a fireplace flanked by bookshelves. Facing them as they entered were twin window seats with more shelves and cabinets between.

Emily couldn't contain herself. "Wouldn't this be perfect for a sitting room, where all the family could gather on a winter evening . . . the fire going, the children playing on the floor! Arthur, I have *never,* ever loved a house so much in all my life—not Briar Hill, not Camp Repose . . ." She had tears of emotion in her eyes. This was going to be tough! He merely nodded.

The master bedroom was a suite—a large front bedroom, taking up about two thirds of the space of the living room, with the rest used for closets and dressing rooms. It had the same view as the living room, with a fireplace at the end. The best feature, though, was that it had two bathrooms, one a large, roomy traditional bathroom with a tub and stall shower with numerous shower heads coming out of the walls and ceiling, all done in mellow old Spanish tiles in gold and blue. The other was smaller, with just a shower, but equally commodious.

Something in Arthur responded to all this. He could understand why Emily wanted this house. It was obvious that she wanted them to buy it. After the emotional drain of the past month—the flood, the anxiety, the hard work —he did not feel up to a battle with Emily over anything, much less an expensive house. Quickly, they went through the remaining rooms. The house had everything anyone could possibly wish for: a separate bedroom and bath for each of the children, a guest room, a sun parlor, and a maid's wing to the rear, with a back staircase leading to it. On the third floor was a big attic with excellent storage facilities and a wide-open space for a children's playroom.

"And besides that, darling, there's an entertainment room in the basement, a big laundry, and a *wine cellar*—it's carved right out of rock. Wait till you see it!"

Arthur put his arm around Emily. "Emily, my darling . . . I know how much you want this house. I understand that. I love it too. But there's just no possibility that we can afford this on my income. And you know my feelings about living within my income. I don't know how much they're asking for the house. Who's handling it, anyway?"

It was getting dark. Emily turned on a lamp in the sitting room and motioned him to join her on one of the window seats. "Arthur, listen to me. First of all, they're asking a fraction of what a house like this would ordinarily sell for, even in the Depression. The bank has it . . . they're settling the estate and they want to sell. There are no heirs. It's all in a trust and going to the County Home. . . . I have all that money, darling, just sitting there in a trust—*two* trusts—losing value every day. All I can do is collect dividends until I'm thirty-five, *unless* I buy residential property for us to live in. What could be better? This house is a wonderful investment. It would go up in value, especially after I've done things to it. I could have some of Mother's and Daddy's extra furniture that's just gathering dust at Briar Hill—and there are the paintings and prints I bought in Paris when I was with Aunt Lily. It makes such good sense. Don't you see?"

Arthur did see. It did make sense. But his stubborn pride kept getting in the way. "Emily, you don't know what it means to a man to want to support his own wife. Every man wants that. I know it's foolish pride—maybe insecurity. But I don't want my wife to have to buy our house—*I* want to buy a house for *you*, and I can't afford this, even if it *is* a bargain."

She was sick with disappointment. She looked defeated as she said in a sad, low voice, "What's the point of having any money if I can't use it to buy a home like this, which I love? I might just as well give it all away if you'll never let me use it."

Then she looked at him steadily. "Arthur, *I love you so much.* I couldn't possibly ever tell you how much I love you. I would do *anything* in the world to please you. But I am what I always have been. You knew when you married me that I liked living in beautiful surroundings, liked expensive things, was accustomed to being indulged. I know I promised I would live on our income. I've tried so hard to change—and I think I *have* changed in many ways. I've grown to like it here, I like many of the people, even though they may not like me. I know if this were our house, if I could just put the things that are already mine in it, I would grow to love Wilkes-Barre. I think if I lived in this house, I'd never want to leave it . . . as long as you were here with me." Her eyes were swimming with tears now. "Please, Arthur . . . *please*, darling. Let me buy it for us."

Something about the way she looked at him, the way she said it, reached into his heart. He thought at that moment that Emily had been cheated of so much. He knew she loved him more than he loved her—and the worst of it was that she probably knew it too. There was a part of him that would never belong to Emily—would never belong to any other woman, save one—and he had to, in some way, make that up to her. Would this be the way? It seemed foolish . . . a distortion of values. But if it meant that much to Emily. . . .

"All right, Emily. If you want this house that much, go ahead and buy it. I'll love living in it . . . really, I will." He smiled down at her ecstatic face. "But you must buy it in your own name. It has to be your house, not jointly owned."

She was so triumphant that she laughed it away. "Oh, we'll not worry about silly details like that now." She threw her arms around him and kissed him soulfully. "This is the happiest birthday, Arthur," she murmured.

They never did get to Wolf's Head for dinner. Even before it was theirs, they made love in the Wyoming Bank's house.

Emily bought the Hollander house. According to the terms of the trust set up by Grandfather Allenberg, who had died long before Emily had even known Arthur, any residential property which she purchased with those funds *must* be in her own name, so Arthur had his wish, despite Emily's desire to buy the house jointly.

Emily was annoyed. "There's something antimatrimonial about a clause like that," she said. "Grandpa was an old skinflint, if you must know. He was always afraid someone was trying to get their hands on his money!"

The second trust, from the Grant side of the family, couldn't be invaded at all until Emily reached thirty-five. Amazing, Arthur mused, to what lengths people with serious money will go to keep a hold on it—even from the grave.

The house was hers by the twelfth of May, barely a month after she'd taken Arthur to see it. Emily's delight was so infectious that Arthur took pleasure just from observing her happiness. He wondered now why he had hesitated to agree to the purchase of the house. If it made Emily this happy, and it was her money, why should he oppose it? He began to share in her excitement and enthusiasm.

In a characteristic burst of generosity, the first thing Emily did was to have Arthur's offices furnished. At the same time, she arranged to complete all the noisy carpentry in the main house so the remodeling wouldn't disturb his patients. Arthur liked the suite of offices. The waiting room was tasteful and subdued, with the old dark blue leather chairs from his former office resting on the wine red and navy Heriz carpet.

Emily used all the furniture from their old house in the bedrooms and second-floor sitting room. "The children are so young, they should be able to romp on things without my having to worry about fingermarks."

They moved in by mid-June. "We've saved two and a half months' rent!" she proudly informed Arthur. Her husband relaxed, reassured that she was using good sense. Emily occasionally showed him bills, but usually she initialed and forwarded them to the trustees for payment. He sometimes wasn't aware of what she'd spent, or even that a new piece had arrived.

Emily had a sense of what was right for the house, an assurance about her taste. Her eye for detail and color always achieved the right note. She chose sunny hues—golds, soft apricots, and earth tones—accenting them with splashes of vivid blues, greens, and turquoises. She borrowed the custom of the French *atelier,* allowing as much light as possible to enter, using only woven handloomed fabrics to fashion full translucent draperies. Caught back with cords by day, they could be released for cozy intimacy at night.

"Slipcovers? Are you certain about that, Mrs. Hillman?" asked a reluctant upholsterer when she showed him the natural linen painter's canvas, simple and sturdy, she wished to use to cover the deep, comfortable sofas that had been delivered by truck from Briar Hill. Somehow, Emily had convinced him that a well-made slipcover could look like a well-tailored suit, practical as well as correct.

When the parquet floors had been refinished, they glowed softly, providing a rich background in the living room for the twin Portuguese needlepoint carpets in lustrous pastel shades, which Emily had inherited from her Grandmother Allenberg's estate. Silk brocade pillows from China picked up the colors of the carpets and relieved the plain off-white of the heavy, square sofas.

Little by little, some expensive antique pieces began to arrive. A small candle table, a prayer rug, a pair of credenzas for the dining room. The awkward Grand Rapids furniture which had been in the room disappeared, given to the County Home, and in its place, set off by a glowing Kermanshah rug, appeared an antique Sheraton table and an Adam sideboard whose classical lines blended happily with the other pieces. Some of these had belonged to the Grant family, but others were new acquisitions from a Pine Street dealer in Philadelphia.

Most of all, Emily enjoyed designing Arthur's study, just as she imagined he would want it, comfortable and masculine. That first winter they spent almost every evening in there, a fire going, Emily joining him after putting the children to bed. In October, Arthur said to her, "Darling, I've decided to have evening office hours only twice a week from now on—on Mondays and Wednesdays." He'd had no idea that this simple decision could make such a difference in her contentment.

She was happiest when she was surrounded by beautiful objects: paintings, sculptures, exquisite shapes in silver or crystal or wood. She loved the sensation of touching a fine tapestry, a soft leather binding. Nothing delighted her senses more than the first moment of entering a gallery, the length of white wall, with framed pictures hanging in a line. That sense of anticipation she had each time she went to an exhibit never left her.

When the canvases were delivered to Grandview Terrace, a remarkable change came over the understated rooms. For all along Emily had intended the house to be the setting for her real jewels . . . the collection of paintings, prints, and other objects of art she had begun to acquire during the years she had lived in Europe.

She stacked some of the paintings, hanging them two and three deep on the stark, high wall of the entrance hall, transforming the space. With courageous nonchalance, she hung works recognized as worthy alongside those of unknown painters whose work appealed to her.

At first skeptical, Arthur observed and listened when Emily explained a new work to him, and gradually he began to appreciate what had become her passion.

"I still prefer Utrillo and Monet to Picasso," he told her. "But I'm learning."

He had to be honest . . . he took great pride in her exquisite taste, her style. He enjoyed living in the comfortable elegance she had crafted. He even derived a certain wry amusement from the astonishment of certain people when they first viewed the Hillman residence.

At their housewarming, during the Christmas season, Lydia Matlin, wife of Arthur's old adversary, had wandered around inspecting each room with ill-concealed curiosity. Entering the library in search of some brandy, Arthur had surprised the snobbish matron as she examined the hallmark on a silver inkstand.

"Lovely collection of *objets* you have, Arthur," Lydia gushed, to cover her embarrassment. "Your little wife *does* have a way with things."

Little wife, indeed!

"Yes. Emily has always been interested in art and design, Lydia. What do you think of this oil she found in New York?"

He took the unframed nude out of a corner where it rested against the bookshelf. Its frank posture and lush flesh tones so unsettled the portly Mrs. Matlin that she was able to mutter only a few meaningless phrases. Her eyes averted, she made her escape to the buffet, where she heaped her plate full of food and retired to a quiet corner, whispering to her husband.

Alone, in their bedroom, Arthur repeated the incident to Emily when they were discussing the party. Emily was thoughtful. "You see, Arthur, I really have to be careful here. Sometimes I think everyone's waiting for me to fall flat on my face."

Was *that* the problem with Emily? How strange, he thought. How sad.

Nate often dropped by in the evening or on weekends.

"Hi, gorgeous," he would greet Emily, hugging her and ruffling her hair. He was one of the few people who were that informal with Emily, and she seemed to really like his rough affection. Arthur was pleased that they had developed a close friendship. It was surprising, considering that Nate hadn't seemed to warm up to Emily at the time of the engagement.

Emily sometimes thought about Arthur's family and her relationship to them. She liked Rose. A sensible, plain-spoken woman, sincere and unjudging, Emily was comfortable with her. Now and then she dropped by to have a cup of coffee with Rose, relishing the tempting pastries in her mother-in-law's kitchen.

"I can't stand going to those luncheons week after week, with the same dull women, Mother," Emily said one day.

Rose smiled understandingly. "That's why I became so involved with the Women's Club and the Shut-Ins, dear. I perfectly understand why you feel the way you do. As soon as you're settled in the house, Emily, I know you'll find an interest that will be satisfying for you."

Emily could be herself with Rose, more than with almost anyone else in Wilkes-Barre . . . perhaps even more so than with Arthur.

With Nathan, it was a curious thing. She had been so sure that he hadn't wanted Arthur to marry her when they'd first met. And yet, she had been drawn to him. . . .

He was charming, Nathan. He had that slow, warming smile and easy manner which made you relax, made you want to be with him. She knew that Arthur felt sorry for Nate, pitied him because his years of ill health had prevented him from marrying. But Emily didn't feel sorry for him. She suspected that there were plenty of women in Nathan's life. She'd been told that he had a reputation as a heartbreaker far beyond Wyoming Valley. Emily could well understand that. She thought that Nathan was one of the most physically appealing men she'd ever known. She imagined he was a wonderful lover, thinking that he seemed more tender and sensual than Arthur.

The children adored Uncle Nate. "Lollipop, lollipop!" even little Ellen would cry when she saw him. He tossed each one of them in the air, played endless games with them, and never failed to have some forbidden delight in his pockets.

Emily was not especially fond of Arthur's sisters. Frieda was dull, a bore. Dorothy, although she had a sharp, inquisitive mind and was a provocative conversationalist, grated on Emily. Emily thought she was possessive of Arthur, intruding on their privacy. Dorothy always managed to call Arthur early on a Sunday morning or late on Friday evening, when the two of them were relaxing together in the library, or in bed. Emily was certain that Dorothy was jealous of her. They saw Frieda and Dorothy as seldom as possible, on family occasions with their husbands and children, for whom Emily felt a complete indifference. She had some guilt about this and tried to remember birthdays and anniversaries.

Arthur didn't seem to care that she wasn't close to his sisters. His own relationship with them was more dutiful than devoted. "When Dot gets an idea in her head, she seizes on you until you just go along to get her to stop badgering you," he had said more than once when Dorothy had called at an especially inopportune moment.

Emily believed that for all the years the various family members had brought their worries to Arthur, he found it necessary to build up a wall of reserve in order not to be paralyzed by other people's problems. She sympathized with that. All her life she had retreated behind her exterior self, maintaining a calm facade to mask the inner turmoil. *Emily Grant, a cool number,* said the Yalies. . . . *The lovely Emily Grant, daughter of Mr. and Mrs. Frederick N. Grant, looked gracious and poised as she stood in the receiving line with her parents,* reported the Philadelphia *Bulletin.* . . . *One of the things I love best about you is your serene nature,* Arthur had once told her long, long ago.

When she had married Arthur, Emily thought that at last she would know the peace of total commitment. That here would be the one person who would ever completely know and understand her, and who would reveal himself to her in all ways, as she would reveal herself to him. Never to be lonely again . . . never to be afraid.

But it hadn't worked out that way.

IV

Wilkes-Barre   Winter 1938

"Darling, Phoebe suggested that we join the Northampton Club when we were having lunch today. She said Lowell would nominate you, and you can designate two other members to second the nomination. Hob Carpenter and Mason Forrest would be happy to do it, I'm certain." They were having a cocktail in the study before dinner, since Arthur didn't have office hours.

Arthur knew that Emily had been an essentially lonely person since she had come to Wyoming Valley as his wife. In Philadelphia she had an acknowledged position in the community and in the circle of well-to-do families with whom she had associated all her life. Here, in the small-town atmosphere of Wilkes-Barre, Emily felt that many people were not at ease in her presence. Her reserve, her natural grace and elegance, could appear aloof to those who didn't know her well. She couldn't help the way she spoke; her upper-class accent was as natural a part of her as the singsong twang of northeastern Pennsylvania was to his sister Frieda. For some reason that Arthur couldn't explain, he and Dorothy had grown up with a different intonation, lacking a regional accent, while Frieda, and to a lesser extent Nathan, spoke in that pleasant, homespun monotone.

Emily's best friend in town was Phoebe Wintermuth. They spoke almost daily on the phone, lunched together, and did volunteer work at the hospital. When Phoebe had asked Emily to join the Junior League, Arthur had not been in favor of it, because the league did not ordinarily accept Jewish members. Emily had become a provisional member, declaring, "Someone has to break the ice, Arthur. How else will these barriers be removed?" It hadn't seemed important enough to argue about.

But the Northampton Club? "Emily, I've never had the slightest ambition to be accepted in groups that exclude Jews, Negroes, Catholics, or what-have-you. And I'm not at all flattered when they choose to make an exception of me."

"Arthur, most of the members are good friends of yours, or at least people you know. I don't understand why you feel that way. Why, I feel more at home at the parties we've gone to there than I do at some of the Jewish affairs."

"There's a story connected with the Northampton Club that might be funny, if it weren't so pathetic. I was a member of a Medical Affairs Committee shortly after I moved back here. We used to have a dinner meeting at the Northampton once a month, because the chairman liked to meet at his club." Arthur allowed a touch of acidity to shade his words. "You know how they have portraits of all the founders and eminent old codgers up there on those venerable walls? Well, I pointed out that someone named Israel Cohen had been a founder, according to the brass plate on one of the portraits. You may not believe it, but the next time we met there . . . Izzy had disappeared!"

Emily sat very still. "You're teasing me."

Arthur put up his right hand solemnly. "Swear to God. That's the absolute truth. As I said, it would be funny if it weren't so awful."

Emily did not mention joining the Northampton Club again.

On the second Saturday of March 1938, the Hillman twins had their fifth birthday party. Twenty noisy children in gay paper hats blew whistles, popped balloons, made puddles of melted ice cream on their plates, and allowed Emily to blindfold them for a game of pin-the-tail-on-the-donkey while Arthur took snapshots with his Kodak Brownie camera.

As the sleepy-eyed little party guests departed from the Hillman residence in the arms of their mothers, the mothers of Vienna were putting their little ones to bed beneath quilts of eiderdown after the first day of Nazi rule. The Jewish quarter rang with the shouts of marching Nazi toughs, while Jewish mothers cradled their children in their arms to comfort them. . . .

After Phoebe Wintermuth had left with her son, Todd, Emily heaved a sigh and sank onto the sofa in the upstairs sitting room, which was strewn with gift wrapping and discarded favors. "That was fun, dear, but I'm glad it's over. All those shouting children have given me a headache. . . . Oh, Kelly," Emily said with relief as the children's nurse came to take them for their baths, "*do* give them an early supper and let them go to sleep. Too much excitement in one day, wasn't it, my little birthday boys?" She hugged them and kissed their cheeks. Jeff looked grumpy, but Bobby was all smiles.

"I like the party, Mommy," he said.

"Did you, darling? I'm *so* glad you did . . . and what about you, Jeff?" But Jeffrey wasn't in a mood to talk, so Kelly took them away.

Arthur was reading the headlines in the *Evening Sentinel*. He frowned. "The news in Europe looks grim. The Germans have really seized Austria . . . there's going to be a war, for sure. I'm worried about my cousins in Munich, the Rosenmaiers. Uncle Herman says Professor Rosenmaier has been expelled from the Faculty of Medicine at the university, and that he may not be able to keep practicing in his private clinic. If *they're* in danger, no German Jews are safe."

"It's so depressing, Arthur," she shook her head. "I don't even want to *think* about it." She rose. "We're due at the Lang's for dinner at seven. I think I'll take a nap before my bath." With a thoughtful expression on his face, Arthur watched her leave the room.

Everyone present at the Lang home was Jewish. It was a large group, twenty-four, and the conversation focused on Hitler, Nazi Germany, and the growing fear of what its policies—particularly anti-Semitism—would mean for the rest of Europe.

"My relatives left Germany three years ago," said Milton Lang, the host. "They're in Oneonta, spread around with various aunts and uncles. Had to leave *everything!* They owned a big clothing store in Frankfurt . . . my mother's family. They were pretty well off. Now, they have nothing. But they feel lucky to have escaped with their lives. They say Jews are being rounded up and put in concentration camps by the thousands." Everyone looked upset.

"It's getting worse," said Arthur's brother-in-law, Ralph Kahn. "I hear that Henry Goldberg . . . you know, from the restaurant . . . smuggled some of his relatives right out of a concentration camp."

"How'd he do that?" someone asked.

Ralph shrugged. "I don't know. Probably bribed a guard or something like that. . . ."

Arthur noticed that Emily was unusually quiet throughout the evening. They left early because they were both tired. On the ride home from Kingston, Emily still acted subdued.

"What's the matter tonight, dear? You seem a little down."

"Well, who wouldn't be down with that conversation, Arthur? Honestly, is that *all* that crowd can ever talk about . . . the Jews, the Nazis, the Nazis and the Jews!"

"Emily, when people like us are being dragged out of their beds in the middle of the night and thrown into prison just because they happen to be Jewish, it *concerns* me. . . . It should concern *you*. All of those people realize that it's a problem that isn't going to go away. It'll get bigger and bigger until we are forced to deal with it. . . . Listen, I was in Munich ten years ago, in 1928, and the Nazis were marching around with flags then, handing out anti-Semitic pamphlets, painting hate-mongering slogans on walls. Everyone laughed at them, said they were ridiculous, wouldn't ever gain any power. Now, look at them. Hitler is preparing for war, and sooner or later the United States will have to take a stand. It's not just the Jewish question . . . it's much more than that. But, since I'm a Jew and he's singling out the Jews as his scapegoats, it's something *I* can't forget about . . . something that preys on my mind."

When they were in bed, Arthur could tell Emily wanted him to make love to her, but he wasn't in the mood. His agitation from the dinner conversation and its aftermath on the way home was palpable. Whenever Emily displayed this side of her character, her ostrich mentality, it disturbed him. To ignore something unpleasant was to deny its existence.

But there was something more here. The attitude of the assimilated American Jew who wants to deny any commonality with ghetto Jews, with refugees. The Grants and the Allenbergs had been Americans for many generations, yet the great-great-great-grandaughter of the first pre-Revolutionary Allenberg still feared being identified with Jews fleeing foreign tyrants, still felt threatened.

Emily moved against his back, putting her arms around him, slipping a hand inside of his pajamas, stroking his chest, up and down, in ever-widening circles . . . slowly, insinuatingly. She kissed the back of his neck, ran her tongue along the edge of his ear, as her hand moved softly downward. Arthur felt the tingles of excitement begin, despite himself, against his will. She was so tantalizing in bed, he never was able to resist her when she was like this. . . . Why *should* he resist her? He rolled onto his back, giving in to her, letting the waves of desire roll over him.

"Mmmm . . . I love it when it's like this," she murmured in a thrilling voice, as she bent her head down to him.

Arthur sat in his study, staring out across the bend in the Susquehanna. This was his favorite view—the river and the west bank, where he could see the new spring growth of Kirby Park.

Spring was a happy season . . . a season of promise. In all the great religions, there were spring festivals attesting to that. Renewal, uplifting, hopefulness . . . those were springtime words, springtime sentiments.

Then what was troubling him this fair spring day? His life was in order, he loved his family, his practice was successful, his health excellent. Minor frustrations, of course, but that was usual. The health clinic plan for the miners had gone as far as getting the union's official backing, but there it lodged, unacceptable to the mine owners of Pennsylvania's anthracite regions. All it would take was one courageous owner to endorse it, he thought, and the others would follow. He was confident it would come. It was a matter of time.

No, that wasn't responsible for this melancholy mood.

What then? Emily? More likely, Emily and Arthur. How many marriages are like this? he wondered. Did most married couples live together like this . . . pretending, tolerating each other, disengaging so they won't have a confrontation?

He was a lucky man. Everyone thought so. Emily was a gorgeous woman —there was no other way to describe her. At almost thirty-three, she was slender, vibrant, glowing. Heads turned when they walked into a room, whether it was among strangers or old friends. He remembered Nathan's words . . . "the golden couple" . . . an accurate assessment. He knew, the way you know those things, without anyone having to say it, that as a pair they were admired and envied. People thought of them as the perfect match. The beautiful, artistic, aristocratic woman married to the community's popular, outstanding physician.

There were moments when he could agree with that . . . moments when Emily was soft and loving, seeming to care that he was worried about a dying patient, or sharing his discouragement about the health clinic project.

They were rare, those moments. Too often, Emily exhibited a self-absorption, a lack of compassion for those less fortunate, that deeply troubled him. To those she cared about—family and close friends—she was warm, generous, and spontaneous. But Emily could insulate herself from the problems of others with almost complete detachment.

Maybe he expected too much. Perhaps it was unrealistic to hope that he and Emily could have that kind of marital contentment that he had always associated with a good marriage, once the fires of early passion were banked. Not that the passion wasn't still there. Exciting, sensual, innovative, Emily was wonderful at lovemaking. You couldn't spend all your days in bed, however. You couldn't even count on that to keep a marriage alive if other important elements were missing.

What was it he wanted, exactly? Not the dull, old-fashioned humdrumness of a stale marriage, certainly. Just the loyal devotion, the steadfastness of two who know they will grow old together, enjoying it.

"Say good night to Daddy, Ellen." Emily brought the curly-headed, blue-eyed little girl into the library, where Arthur was working on the plan for the clinic.

"Night, Daddy." She ran over to him and put her chubby arms around his neck, kissing his cheek.

"Ummmm. Good night, sugar. You sure do smell nice and look pretty." Children freshly scrubbed and dressed for bed always were at their most appealing. She giggled.

"Bobby blew bubbles and they got in my eyes," she said, speaking much more clearly than either of the boys had at her age.

"Was he being naughty or was it an accident?"

"He was naughty! Nanny 'panked him!" This was a highly satisfactory state of affairs, it seemed, and she happily went off to bed holding onto Emily's hand. Emily gave him a "we're going to have our hands full" look over her shoulder as they left the room.

The phone rang. It was Eddy Valentine, the UMWA organizer, calling from Scranton. "Bad news, Art. Buckland won't buy the clinic proposal. Without him, we haven't got a chance."

Arthur's spirits fell. "Damn, Eddy. Who told you? Did you speak to him?"

"No. Frank Norcross, their lawyer, told me, strictly off the record. He thought we might bide our time and approach it at a better moment, when the economy improves."

"Aw, for Christ's sake, Eddy, they know as well as we do that the main reason they need a health service is *because* the economy's in bad shape. If the miners could afford good medical care, we wouldn't be thinking about a clinic."

"So now what do we do? Give up?"

"Hell, no! I'm not going to give up. I think I'll talk to Lowell about it. He may be able to influence his father-in-law. What do you say?"

"I thought there was no love lost between those two?"

"I think they're on better terms now. You know, grandchildren are wonderful things. They bridge mile-wide gaps. I hear the old codger's a sucker for Lowell's and Phoebe's kids."

"Nothing like a small town, is there? Well, I'll let you be the judge. I'm going to lie low for a while. Keep in touch."

Emily came in with her knitting just as Arthur finished talking to Lowell, who had made a lunch date with him at the Anthracite Club for Thursday. She sat in a wing chair, facing away from him, where the lamplight was bright.

"I just talked to Lowell, Emily. He said that Phoebe and you had lunch together today. We ought to get together with them for dinner one of these days."

"Um-hmmm . . ." She was counting stitches. Arthur went back to his plan for the health clinic proposal, trying to cut costs, in view of the opposition they were likely to encounter. Emily was speaking, but he hadn't paid attention to her words.

". . . nice to know you weren't all work and no play in those days."

"Hmm? What did you say, dear?" he asked, looking up from his papers.

"I said that Phoebe introduced me to an old flame of yours today," she said in a gay, teasing tone.

"Really? An old flame of mine? Must've been pretty old," he answered, amused.

"Old, no! But pretty, verrry . . ." she said, exaggerating it.

He laughed. "Well, now, I wonder who that could have been?"

"Her name is Molly Tower—I think it used to be Shea?"

He was taken by surprise, both by Emily's words and by his reaction to them. It was as if someone had struck him. He felt a pounding in his head, a draining sensation in his legs. He was grateful that Emily was turned away from him. Otherwise she could not have failed to observe his stunned response. He wasn't sure how long it had taken him to say anything. "I didn't know she was in town." Even to his own ears his voice sounded unnatural.

"I think she told Phoebe her mother had died. . . . Anyway, she certainly is beautiful. Where does she live? She has a slight accent, almost British."

He let out a slow, unsteady breath. "I think she lives in Ireland. I really don't know much about her," he answered stiffly. "Emily, if you don't mind, I'd like to finish this tonight."

"All right, all right," she replied good-naturedly. "I can tell when I'm not wanted. I'm going up to take a hot bath and read myself to sleep. Are you planning to put in an all-nighter?" She rose, gathered up her yarn and the half-knitted sweater, and came around the desk to kiss him.

He looked up at her, trying to gain some reassurance from seeing her face, needing something to hold on to.

"Don't be too late, darling. You look tired," she said as she left the room. He listened to her retreating footsteps going up the stairs, muffled by the thick carpeting. He knew she would check on the children before going to their room. He sat there at the desk staring blankly ahead of him, dully aware of the sickening sensation in the pit of his stomach.

Wearily he rose from his chair and walked over to the window that looked south on an angle to the river just above the Great Bend. He was waiting for this feeling to pass. Surely it would. It was just the suddenness of it, the unexpected mention of her name, a name he had scarcely spoken or heard for almost eight years.

Why hadn't Father John called to tell him of Katherine's death? he wondered. . . . He leaned on the windowsill, pressing his forehead against the cold windowpane. A half-moon was shining on the dark waters of the Susquehanna. He started toward the side door, which opened to a terrace, then turned back and scribbled a note, leaving it on his desk just in case Emily came looking for him. It was not unusual for him to be gone at night, to the hospital or on a night call.

He walked down the footpath, a series of steps from the rise of Grandview Terrace to the boulevard below, and crossed over to the River Common. There was the fresh smell of springtime, the soft lawn of new grass underfoot, the trees in bloom, a promise in the air. He walked along the newly built dike all the way down to the end of Riverside Drive, passing no one along the way, hearing nothing but the night sounds of crickets and frogs, the whirls and eddies of the river, and the distant hum of traffic on the Market Street Bridge.

How long since he had thought of her? For so long he had trained himself to push thoughts of her out of his mind, it came as a shock to him that he was unable to do so now. Damn Phoebe Wintermuth! Why had she done it?

Introduced Emily to her . . . to Molly . . . there, he had thought her name, said it to himself. He whispered it aloud. *"Molly, Molly . . . oh God, Molly.* Are you really here, in this town, in this same place with me, and I didn't know it, didn't sense it?"

He turned back, walking north, the moon ahead of him, reflected in the water below, breaking into separate fragments and coming together, then rippling apart again. As he rounded the bend, the image of the bridge shone in the illuminated stream, its lights sparkling in the clarity of the night. The river had always brought him comfort. He remembered times in his younger days when he was troubled and would walk along its banks, looking down at the slow-moving current, taking heart from the eternity of it, the same river that had lapped at the shores of Hillside, winding its way between the mountains, rushing over the rapids, providing countless happy hours each summer of his childhood. . . . It brought him no peace now.

He walked up the slope of Grandview Terrace, past Hobson Carpenter's house, past Mason Forrest's, to his own driveway. He hadn't put his car in the garage when he'd come home from the hospital at dinnertime. The keys were in his pocket.

He backed out, not putting on the headlights until he was rolling down the curving road. Driving north, he went onto the bridge, heading across to Kingston, continuing west until he reached Wyoming Avenue. At Forty Fort he turned onto Monument Way to Sunset Lane. For eight years he had never once driven on this street, in the beginning taking pains not to do so, later finding it easy to avoid.

The large frame house was almost entirely dark. A dim light shone from an upstairs window. He stopped his car across the street, turning off his motor and lights. A "For Sale" sign was posted on the front lawn. The house already had a lonely, abandoned look—or was it that *he* felt lonely and abandoned?

Was it not preposterous for him to still feel the loss of her? After all this time? He and Emily . . . Emily was his wife . . . he loved her . . . didn't he? Their children, their home . . . it was a happy home, wasn't it? The entire fabric of his life seemed to be unraveling thread by thread, against his will.

As he watched, a shadow moved across the lighted window, and then back again. The light went out.

He started the motor and slowly drove homeward across the river, the waning moon now high in the sky, the spring breeze blowing chill.

When he slipped beneath the covers in their bed, Emily turned in her sleep and moved against him. Ordinarily, he might have put his arms around her, drawn her close to him, kissing her awake, loving her sensuality when she was drowsy. Tonight he moved away, turning his back, hoping she was truly asleep. He felt a cold fear.

V

Philadelphia   Winter 1939

Arthur would never have recognized Leisl Rosenmaier, now Leisl Brandt, as the same young woman he had met ten years before in Munich. Gone were the haughtiness, the aristocratic pride, the cool, erect demeanor. The Leisl who sat on the damask sofa in Herman Franke's drawing room was a shadow, an ephemeral spirit within the body of a woman. Her eyes were empty, her face expressionless, her mouth a thin straight line used only to answer necessary questions in a dull monotone.

Leisl's two little daughters played across the room, chattering to each other in German, their high, childish voices sounding at odds with the ponderousness of the language. Trudi, a five-year-old towhead with cornflower blue eyes, was showing her younger sister, Karin, how to string beads from the Indian belt-making game Arthur had brought for them. They did not look like American children, with their high-laced shoes, stockinged legs, and crocheted sweaters, all in muddy hues. Karin's brown hair was tightly braided and looped up close to her head, fastened with black ribbons.

Nathan sat across from them, quietly talking to Uncle Herman, explaining his plans for Leisl and her daughters to live in Rose's house in Wilkes-Barre with him and his mother. Herman Franke seemed at a loss. How to come to grips with this . . . this onslaught, the arrival of this broken woman and her young daughters . . . a concrete reminder to him of the vulnerability of the People among whom he was numbered? Leisl, the daughter of his second cousin, the Herr Professor Gunther Otto Rosenmaier, here in his parlor, a victim of the Brownshirts, a refugee from the Nazis. Cousin Gunther Rosenmaier, head of the most famous private clinic in Munich. . . . It was a burden almost too large for the tailored shoulders of the distinguished Philadelphian.

"I told him . . . I told him years ago to get out!" he had said, over and over, ever since his transatlantic telephone conversation with the Englishwoman, Millicent Tattlesworth. *"Now,* what is to become of them? Arrested? For what were they arrested?" He was bewildered. He failed to understand his own fear at the fate of the illustrious cousin who had become a victim.

Leisl had fled Germany with the two girls in the company of the Tattlesworth woman, whose husband was an officer at the British Consulate in Munich. They had all been issued permits to enter Britain—the entire family

—but as they made plans to leave Germany, there had been delays. The men had been detained at the clinic. Then, Eric, Leisl's and Armand's eight-year-old son, had been taken one day from his school in a truck with all the other Jewish boys. Frantically, they had tried to discover his whereabouts. Spencer Tattlesworth had made inquiries. He was assured that the boys had merely been sent to a youth education center for children of political suspects, where they would be housed and schooled for a brief period before being returned to their families. It was nearing the end of September 1938, and if they didn't leave soon, the British permits would expire.

Armand had insisted that Leisl go with Trudi and Karin, promising that the men would soon follow—just as soon as Armand could arrange for Eric's release. They had friends in high places. There were still good Germans . . . Baron Franz von Würtemberg, the former patron of Professor Rosenmaier . . . or Colonel Klaus Bahn-Funstnägler. . . . Why, the colonel had been a patient at the Rosenmaier Clinic—indeed, Gunther had performed life-saving surgery on Bahn-Funstnägler five years before. Surely, he would intercede for them! Eric was a little boy, a child. What would they want with him? It was all an error, a gross, horrible mistake.

Then had come the blow: Baron von Würtemberg's son, now a high-ranking officer in the SS, had denounced them, *and* his own father, who had been shielding them.

Leisl and her daughters were already in England with Millicent, while Spencer had promised to wait and accompany the Rosenmaiers and Armand as soon as Eric was again in their care. But it was not to be.

On November 7 in Paris, Ernst vom Rath, the third secretary of the German Embassy, was shot by a seventeen-year-old Polish émigré, a Jew. There followed a spasm of bestiality against Jews throughout Germany—a night of madness which shook the world. *Kristallnacht,* it came to be called . . . the night of broken glass. By November 10 reports reached London of mob violence in cities all over Greater Germany—attacks on Jewish citizens, old men, frail and defenseless, while other Germans stood in the street and watched. . . . The wrecking of Jewish businesses in fashionable shopping promenades of Berlin, Vienna, Frankfurt, Munich . . . the dynamiting and burning of Jewish synagogues, some of them hundreds of years old, works of art, national shrines . . . police looking the other way, arms folded, while organized youth gangs destroyed Jewish property, burned Jewish prayer books and Torah scrolls. If a non-Jew objected, he was turned on and beaten with the metal instruments these Nazi Party hoodlums carried. In less than forty-eight hours, virtually all Jewish businesses, institutions, and houses of worship in Germany had ceased to exist.

Leisl had been distraught. She must return to Munich immediately, to help Armand and her father, to go to Eric, to bring all of them out of Germany with her. Now that she was in London, back in a world that was sane and rational, it seemed outrageous that she could have left them at the mercy of the Nazis.

"No, Leisl, it is impossible for you to return," Millicent Tattlesworth had argued with her. "They won't let you in again. And if they do, they'll punish you. They'll never allow you to go to Armand. They'll arrest all of you. Wait! Please, just wait. Spencer will do everything he can. If anyone can help them, it's Spencer."

And so, she had waited.

The news dispatches continued. A group of Jews trying to enter the British Consulate in Berlin was arrested. Another line of Jews at the consulate of the United States in Vienna was rounded up, thrown into secret police vans, and driven away. Mobs invaded the homes of prominent Jewish citizens in Berlin, attacking them, seizing their valuables, destroying their furniture, hunting for weapons. Busloads of Jews were reportedly being sent to concentration camps from Berlin, Vienna, and Munich. Then came the announcement: All Jews were ordered to leave certain towns, including Munich, within forty-eight hours! What did this mean? Where were they to go? Leisl was hopeful this meant that her family would soon be out of Germany.

Spencer Tattlesworth arrived in London . . . alone. Gunther Otto Rosenmaier, his son, Kurt Wilhelm Rosenmaier, and Armand Herbert Brandt had been arrested in the early hours of the morning of Friday, November 11, during a roundup of Jewish leaders in Munich. They were being held at an unknown place. Armand had been successful in locating Eric, Spencer told them. The boy had been in his own bed in their home, with his father, on the very day they were to leave Germany, secure in the knowledge that they were in possession of an exit visa and a permit to enter England, when the police had taken them away.

For several weeks nothing was known about their fate. Then it was learned through diplomatic channels that they had been sent to the concentration camp ten miles outside of Munich . . . at a place called Dachau.

"Leisl's fortunate that your mother will take her in." Emily was sitting at the desk in their bedroom making out place cards for a dinner party they were giving on Saturday evening. Arthur had showered and climbed into bed, drained, after the disquieting experience of getting Leisl and the girls settled for their first night in Rose Hillman's house.

"Fortunate?" he mused. "I suppose so, if you consider the people who have nowhere to go." He shook his head in disbelief. "Leisl was the *loveliest* woman when I first met her. She was a beauty . . . elegant, sure of herself. To see her in this state is tragic! What's happening to the Jews of Germany is terrifying . . . and no one will do a thing to stop it!"

"What can anyone do? Who can stop it?"

"I think that if the leaders of other nations spoke out strongly enough . . .

if we refused to trade with Germany, recalled our ambassador . . . if Britain and France did the same . . . that would have some effect. A nation can't get away with treating people like animals unless they know other countries don't care enough to ostracize them for it."

Emily looked up from her guest list. "Would you be willing to go to war against Germany in order to stop what they're doing? I'm not sure I would."

Arthur realized that he and Emily had seldom had political discussions. He was surprised at her views.

"Go to war? If it came to that, I suppose I would. Not because it's the Jews they're mistreating. It's a symptom, Emily, a warning. If you let Hitler get away with this, there's no limit to what he may try." He put out his light and turned over. "I better get some sleep, honey. I hope you'll try to spend some time with Leisl, cheer her up a little. Poor woman is distraught, with her family in the hands of those monsters."

Emily spoke quickly. "Arthur, I hope you don't expect me to become a nursemaid to her. . . . I really can't see that we have much in common."

Arthur lifted his head. "Nursemaid? She doesn't need a nursemaid, Emily. She needs friends . . . some people who care and are a comfort to her. Thank your lucky stars you *don't* have anything in common . . . her experience is one you can do without!" He was angered, and his voice showed it.

"You needn't be sarcastic," she bridled.

"Emily, at times you disappoint me . . . you really do. You can sit there worrying about a dinner party when I have spent the past twelve hours with a woman who has lost her home, her security, her country—half her family is in a Nazi prison, possibly being tortured or already dead! And you are too self-absorbed to give a small amount of your precious time to show some commiseration. I wonder what goes on in that mind of yours."

"You have some nerve speaking to me like that! Of course, I have sympathy for her . . . for all of them. But I don't intend to have her completely disrupt my life, Arthur. What good would that do anyone?" Then, when he didn't answer, she added, "You know I'll be nice to her, Arthur. What would you expect me to do? I just meant . . . I . . . well, you can't think I should change my life all around because Leisl has arrived." She was trying to mollify him, to soften the impression of callousness she had given.

"All right, Em. I know you'll do what you can. I *don't* expect you to disrupt your life for her. Just try to be a little sympathetic."

Emily did make an effort to befriend Leisl, but it was apparent that the two would never take a great interest in each other. It was strange, Arthur thought. They had been alike in many ways, the stunning, proud Leisl of 1928 and the woman he had married. Both of them daughters of privilege and position, taking their acknowledged station as a matter of right.

In Emily's mind, though, Leisl was a "refugee," and perhaps it was all the more threatening that she had been a member of the elite. Were they not all, then, vulnerable?

Leisl, it appeared, preferred to stay at home in Rose's house, trying to be as useful as possible, greatly embarrassed to be causing these relatives—whom she had never known—so much inconvenience.

The girls quickly attached themselves to Nathan, who warmed to their affection. In the evenings his glance would return, time and again, to Leisl, looking for a sign of some emotion there. Grief, despair, anger, relief? Nothing. Total despondency and a vacant spirit. She went through the motions of living, rising in the morning, bathing and dressing the children with immaculate care, helping Rose in the kitchen, insisting on doing laundry and mending—any task that had to be done. If Leisl cried, she cried alone.

One evening Leisl had gone up to put the girls to bed. Nathan, who usually took the back stairs to his own apartment, walked up the front stairway instead. As he passed the bedroom that Trudi and Karin shared, the door was ajar. By the dim light from the lamp, he saw Leisl sitting in a rocker, the two children cradled in her arms. She sang to them in German. A lullaby, melancholy and sweet, in a low, soft contralto.

It was the saddest song Nathan had ever heard.

Wilkes-Barre   Spring 1939

Goldberger's Kosher Restaurant was about as unlikely a place for intrigue as even the wildest imagination could conjure up, Nathan thought. He selected a table in the rear of the long, narrow, tile-floored establishment. The table was covered with layers of starched white linen, so stiff you could have stood them on end. Each time a new customer was served, another clean cloth was laid over the others, until at the end of the day, there might be ten thicknesses.

Gertie, the big, friendly waitress from a Polish family in Swoyersville, brought a basket of cornbread and a plate of sour pickles. "How are you today, Mr. Hillman? Haven't seen you around for a while."

"Hi, Gertie! It's been busy. How's your sister doing? Everything all straightened out with her?"

"Yes, she's O.K. now. Boy, I'll never stop thanking you for helping her out. That louse of a husband of hers! Thought he'd get away without paying child support. . . ."

Nate smiled. "What do you recommend today?"

"Kreplach soup, stuffed cabbage, the brisket is good . . . stuffed derma, maybe?"

Nathan put his hand to his chest. "Spare me the indigestion! I think I'll just have the soup and some brisket." He handed her the menu. "Henry around?"

"I think he's in the back. You want to see him?"

"When he has a minute," Nate said in an offhand manner.

Nathan had finished his soup when Henry Goldberger, the youngest of the four Goldberger brothers and the only unmarried one, came over and seated himself at the table. Henry was a big man, well over six feet tall, with huge shoulders and a barrel chest. His reddish-brown hair grew in tight curls. He had thick eyebrows above cocker spaniel eyes, large and limpid. Women thought him attractive, finding the curved scar on his left cheek particularly intriguing. Henry had lived in Palestine on and off for years, reportedly fighting Arab fedayeen as a member of the Haganah, a self-defense group formed by Jewish pioneers. It was rumored around the valley that Henry had fathered no less than a dozen children in the various mining patches surrounding Wilkes-Barre. Nathan knew this to be no more than rumor. In fact, Henry had been long committed to a beautiful actress who lived in New York. But as long as his elderly mother was alive, he wouldn't marry her.

"How're things going, Nate?"

Nathan nodded, his mouth full of bread. He took a drink of seltzer. "Henry . . . your relatives, the ones who got out of Germany. Can you tell me how you arranged that?"

Henry looked him in the eyes without saying anything for a long moment. He leaned forward on his arms, lowering his voice. "It's not easy, Nate. It's dangerous . . . and the risks are on both sides. . . . I mean to you, as well as whoever it is you want to bring over."

"Can you tell me how to make contact?"

Henry made a gesture with his head. "Come upstairs when you're finished with your meal." He rose and walked back to the kitchen.

Nathan hadn't spoken French since he'd been in the hospital at Reims in 1918. His high school German was even rustier. Henry Goldberger had told him to trust his guides, to put himself entirely in their hands. He had his doubts, but what else could he do? Cursing his monolingual upbringing, typical of Americans one generation away from the immigration stigma, he vowed that if he got out of this alive, he'd go home and learn to function in as many languages as possible.

He'd come across France to Switzerland, stopping only one night in Paris to renew acquaintance with his distant relative, the son of his grand-uncle. Rafael Belkind was the doctor who had been so kind to him twenty-one years before, when he was gassed. Now fifty-eight, Rafael spoke no English, so their communications had been limited. His daughter acted as interpreter, informing Nathan that her only brother had immigrated to Palestine, where he lived on a kibbutz, an agricultural collective. Genevieve Belkind Solomon, her husband, Pierre, and their two children were the only remaining Belkind family in France beside her parents. They all looked at events in Germany with apprehension, worrying about the effects on the position of Jews in France.

Nathan had decided against mentioning the nature of his business in Europe. They knew he was en route to Zurich and assumed his purpose was financial.

They were correct in their assumption, Nathan reflected, as he fingered the flat packets strapped against his body. It was odd he felt no nervousness. Just a cold, steady determination. The wrappers contained 45,000 Swiss francs in new bills, which had been furnished him by a banker in Zurich, who *had* been nervous.

"Remember, you're just an American lawyer traveling on business to Munich," Bruno Toff, his contact in Switzerland, had instructed him. "We will not be together on the train. You will leave the train at Bad Tölz and walk to the restaurant in the Bahnhof. Sit at a table and order beer and wurst. Someone will join you. His name is Hans. He speaks little English. . . ."

"How am I to know he is the right man, then?" Nathan had interrupted.

"He will know you. He will mention my name." Toff had smiled an acerbic smile, with his mouth only. The eyes never lost their coldness.

"You don't approve of what I'm doing, do you?" he'd asked suddenly, knowing with utmost certainty that it was so.

"It's not my job to approve or disapprove," Toff had answered. "But since you ask . . . no, Mr. Hillman, American lawyer, I do not approve. What of all the thousands with no one to pay for their release?" He stubbed out his cigarette viciously. "I'm sorry," he'd said, and walked away without waiting for Nathan to follow.

Nathan caught up with him. "Look, I understand. If I could, I'd give everything I have to get all of them out. All American Jews would. The U.S. isn't the only country that hasn't opened its borders. What about England? What about South America?"

"You know what about them?" he'd replied. "They can all rot in hell." Well, he wasn't in the business of being a charmer, Nate agreed. As long as he did his job.

It was almost too easy. At the border the passport inspection, the customs. Getting in wasn't the problem, of course. At Landeck, a fat man in a black overcoat and homburg sat in the compartment across from him, not speaking, but staring at him through thick eyeglasses. Nathan felt as if those eyes could see through his clothing to the money belt he wore, a decidedly uncomfortable feeling. The sweat ran down the sides of his torso. Happily, the man got off at Innsbruck, and Nathan was alone in the compartment with one middle-aged woman who sat huddled in a corner of her seat reading.

The beauty of the Inn Valley and the staggering panorama of the Tyrolean Alps scarcely made an impression on him. As they crossed the border into Germany, Nathan felt a thrill of terror. Finally they approached Bad Tölz. He took his traveling case and stepped down from the railroad car.

In the Bahnhof restaurant, a dingy room with half a dozen tables, he ordered beer and wurst as he had been instructed. He had almost finished the unappetizing cold cuts, wondering why German sausages should be so famous, when a shadow fell across the table. He looked up to find a middle-aged man, a farmer, by his appearance, seating himself opposite him.

"*Grüss Gott,*" said the man. "*Bitte,* Bruno Toff . . ." Nathan nodded. "*Guten Tag. Ich bin Herr . . .*" The man held up his hand and gave an emphatically negative nod.

"*Kommen Sie . . .*" He led the way out of the deserted station to a small automobile.

Nathan waited in the isolated farmhouse for two days. He was alone most of the time, wondering whether he was the victim of a gigantic hoax. Late at night, Hans had departed, taking half the money with him. He had wanted all of it, but Nathan demurred, saying he would hand over the balance when the four prisoners were safely delivered to him. Hans had nodded gruffly and left him. There was bread, water, and cheese in the cupboard, which Nathan hoarded, not having any idea how long he would wait there.

On the third night he was awakened by the sound of a vehicle. Going to the window, he made out the silhouette of a dilapidated truck in the courtyard. Hans materialized in the darkness next to him.

"Hurry!" he hissed.

In the courtyard, standing at the back of the truck, was another man, looking furtively around.

"Vere iss de money?" asked this man.

"It's here," answered Nathan. "But first let me see the . . . merchandise."

He opened the rear of the truck. Inside were many wine kegs marked with the names of vineyards from the South Tyrol. By the light of a dim flashlight, Nathan could see the man lift one empty wine keg, pull back a tarp, and underneath the floor of the truck, on a matting lay one small, scrawny boy, fast asleep.

"What! . . . What is the meaning of this?" Nathan protested. "Where are the others?" Hans beckoned him into the house again. The other man followed after having a brief, heated exchange.

"*Nein* . . . not possible," Hans began. Somehow Nathan was able to understand that the Rosenmaier men had been transferred to a different section of the concentration camp. Dachau was a complex of detention centers. The arrangements made had been for a less secure unit, one where the guards had been approachable.

"They want more money," Nathan said.

No, that was not it, Hans told him. The money was the same if it could be done. But it was impossible. Men had risked their lives tonight and he had to be content with the results of their efforts, disappointing though they might be. *Disappointing?* He felt sick with the thwarted expectations he had held. Although he had told himself it wouldn't work, had steeled himself not to count on rescuing all of them, it was a blow. Thank the Lord, he hadn't told Leisl of his plans.

Nathan handed over the rest of the money. It had to be that way, even though the others had not been freed. To protect the interests of other people who could be rescued. Rotten goddamn Nazis . . . rotten goddamn Germans.

It all passed like a dream. The truck ride through the mountain passes on old, winding, seldom-traveled roads. The switch to another vehicle, carrying the still sleeping boy—drugged, Nathan realized—to the trunk and covering him with blankets. Crossing the border over into Switzerland at a point high in the Alps where the temperature was so low that he shivered in his light coat and worried that the child would take pneumonia. Hans bid him good-bye, *"Auf Wiederschaun! Good Luck!"* He suddenly looked heroic to Nathan in the gray predawn. At a chalet outside St. Gallen, Bruno Toff was waiting for them. For the first time, looking at the child he had bartered out of a concentration camp, a child he had never seen before . . . how was he to even know if it was the *correct* child? So undernourished, so neglected-looking, with bruises on his body, head shaven, deep dark hollows under the eyes. They undressed him and bathed him while he was still under the influence of the sleeping draught. Whatever it was, it was powerful. Nathan felt for the boy's pulse, looking down at the emaciated arm.

"Good God! What is that?"

"You don't know about the numbers, I see," said Bruno.

And Nathan knew that whatever child this was, whosoever son he had rescued, it was worth 45,000 Swiss francs, and he would spend all the gold in Fort Knox if he could arrange for the release of all the children, all the prisoners, in that evil, pesthole of a country whose soil he hoped never to step foot on again.

By the time they had the papers Bruno Toff had arranged, and after a few days in the care of Dr. Rafael Belkind in Paris, Eric Brandt had improved enough in appearance for them to board the S.S. *Champlain* at Le Havre on Saturday, June 4, 1939. The bewildered boy was apathetic throughout the crossing, but he ate greedily, wolfing down his food without enjoyment. Nathan had his meals served in the stateroom so other passengers wouldn't stare at Eric, whose appearance was bizarre, with his new-grown hair and skeletal face. Bruno Toff had explained to the boy that this was his cousin from America and that he was taking him to his mother and sisters. Eric had nodded dumbly, accepting it, showing no emotion. A week later, Arthur met them at the Forty-eighth Street pier in New York. No words were necessary when he saw the boy Nathan led by the hand.

"My God," Arthur whispered. "How will Leisl bear it?"

"She will," Nathan assured him. For Nathan was determined that he would shoulder whatever part of the anguish and heartbreak he could for Leisl and her three children, supporting them until the day that her husband, their father, was returned to them.

America held its breath while Hitler attacked Poland, then watched as Germany marched on Scandinavia and the Low Countries. Unbelievably, in June 1940, France fell.

"I doubt that Rafael Belkind got out of France in time," Nathan told Arthur. "I hope Genevieve and her family went to Palestine. Rafael's son was there and wanted them to come. The French are the most patriotic people—even more than the Americans. Rafael never did accept the idea that his son left France to go to Palestine."

They all knew, of course, that it was a matter of time until it became an American war.

Emily planned their annual pre-Christmas cocktail party for the first Saturday night in December in 1941. Their guests included doctors from the staff at St. Anne's, the Medical Society, the people who served on various committees with Emily, some faculty from Westmoreland College, and just plain friends. It was a party in the tradition of Claudia Grant. Arthur always thought of it as Emily's party, this holiday event that had become a custom with them.

Emily loved to mix people at her gatherings. "You'd think they lived in separate valleys with an impassable mountain in between," she often said to Arthur when speaking of the college faculty and their other friends.

"You've got Heinz 57 Varieties here, Arty," Nate teased Arthur that evening. Arthur had to admit that Lydia Matlin and Ida Finkelstein were an odd conversation pair, off in a corner together.

"What do you think they're talking about?" he asked Nate.

"Maybe Ida's giving Lydia her recipe for matzo balls!"

Arthur noticed that Nate never let Leisl out of his sight, taking her a plate of food, a cup of coffee, introducing her to everyone.

"Nate is so good to Leisl, isn't he?" he commented to Emily.

"Yes," she replied shortly. Then, because this had become a sore subject with them, she added, "But that's the way Nate is."

"It's a nice way to be," Arthur retorted.

The party went on until after two. They slept late the next morning, then had a large breakfast. Arthur liked to eat leftovers.

"Seafood crepes for breakfast?" Emily made a face.

"Sure, why not? I never got to eat any last night. I think you had too much food, honey." He brought his plate to the table and opened the Sunday paper.

"It's better to have too much than too little. It'll all be gone as soon as the children come home from Sunday school."

They lounged until midafternoon.

Arthur stood and stretched. "I have some house calls to make, and I must go to the hospital for a short time. I feel lazy today . . . I'd just like to do nothing." He went up to shower and dress.

As Arthur was knotting his tie, the telephone rang. He could hear Emily in the other room, speaking to someone. She sounded excited, urgently asking questions. I wonder who that is, he thought.

"Arthur! Arthur, the most awful thing. . . . That was Nathan. The Japanese have attacked our naval base in Hawaii. They say it means war!" She was white-faced, her eyes dark and round. "Oh, Arthur," she whispered. "I'm frightened. I've never been in a war."

VI

Wilmington, North Carolina   August 1942

Camp Edwards wasn't a bad post, considering. . . . Located on the North Carolina coast near Wilmington, its climate was endurable, even in the hottest part of the summer, which was when Arthur's field hospital did its training.

Fording icy streams up to his neck in March at Fort Monmouth, New Jersey, Arthur had been certain he was being trained for hospital duty in the European front lines, when an invasion should come. Then, abruptly, his unit had been dispersed, the men sent God knows where. He'd been put in command of another medical unit to be trained for base, field, evacuation, and portable duty, a jack of all medical trades, at Camp Edwards.

He'd been happy, working hard at making the hospital a smoothly functioning working unit, when Colonel Clarence Dreicher had taken over as his CO. It was mutual dislike at first meeting. Dreicher, a Regular Army man, who had graduated from the Citadel, had a whole bag of chips on his shoulder. He resented West Pointers, he resented enlisted men, he resented the new "civilian army" he was forced to deal with, and he despised people who were different from him—people like wops, niggers, spiks, chinks, and of course kikes. He called Catholics "mackerel snappers"—he had a whole vocabulary of epithets Arthur had never heard before. To Arthur's knowledge, there was only one species of human whom Clarence Dreicher did like . . . Southerners, of the Lutheran persuasion, who had graduated from the Citadel. Everyone else could fry in hell.

Back in February, when Arthur was separated from his 109th Field Artillery Unit, he'd been presented with a list from which he was to select the specialized duty and training for which he thought he was best qualified. He had requested the thoracic surgery cram course at the Mayo Clinic. He had paid little attention to that form, since it was well known that the Army mismatched job and profession almost to a point of scientific perfection. Just as he'd completed the line of assignments within his field hospital command —after eight weeks of drilling and scaling walls in the Carolina sun—he had received orders to report to the Mayo Clinic on September 1 for the surgeon general's course in thoracic surgery. He couldn't believe his good fortune, and despite feeling some sadness at being again separated from men he had trained and grown to like, he was eagerly anticipating the move to Rochester, Minnesota.

He must have looked too happy. It was with more than a little relish that Colonel Dreicher summoned him to his office three days before he was scheduled to go on a week's leave prior to reporting at the Mayo.

Trouble. The colonel was smiling. Arthur saluted and stood at attention, waiting for the big jolt. He had not miscalculated.

"*Major* Hillman," Dreicher said sarcastically, emphasizing the rank. (He had been furious when Arthur's promotion from captain had come through just days after he'd assumed camp command, on the recommendation of the previous commander, a no-nonsense brigadier from the Point who had been appointed to the General Staff.) "Your transfer orders have arrived."

Arthur was puzzled. "I received my transfer orders some weeks ago, sir."

Now, Dreicher smiled broadly, showing extreme delight. "Those orders have been changed, Major. You're to proceed to Fort Riley, Kansas, by the most direct routing, using commercial transportation if necessary." He handed Arthur a teletyped message marked "priority."

It had been a long time since he'd felt such a keen disappointment. He tried not to show it, but he knew his face sagged, and he looked down at the printed message to hide the hurt in his eyes.

"Well, Hillman," drawled Colonel Dreicher, "you're one sheeny who's not going to get a free ride on the Army."

Arthur closed his eyes, clenched his fists, and gritted his teeth. Control, control, he urged himself. "Will that be all, sir?" he asked tonelessly.

If Dreicher was hoping for something more, he didn't get it. Arthur went back to his quarters and packed quickly, cursing to himself. He spent the afternoon saying good-bye to his fellow officers, checking out the details of his command, signing over the controlled drugs to his next in command, determined to get the hell out of there as soon as he could. Back at the BOQ, he tried to reach Emily, but she was out. Expecting to meet him for a week in Philadelphia, she would be terribly disappointed. He'd been counting on that week together to try to set things right between them. Emily was lonely at home, he knew. Even though there had been a coolness between them before he went into the service, he thought she missed him. He certainly missed her. Sometimes, lying in bed at night, he longed to hold her in his arms . . . the longing a physical ache. They'd always been good together in bed. If only the rest of their marriage worked as well.

His phone rang, startling him. He heard an operator, her nasal eastern twang unmistakably Philadelphian. Then a male voice said, "Art? This is Roy McLean."

"Mac! What a surprise! How'd you ever find me?"

"It wasn't easy. I ran into Emily today, just as I was about to give up. She told me she was meeting you here on your way out to Minnesota."

It still hurt, the socko feeling in his gut.

"Ah, Roy . . . that's a long story. My orders were changed. Emily doesn't know yet." He told Roy what had happened—even about Dreicher.

Roy was appalled. "He said that . . . called you that to your face?"

"So help me, Roy."

"Jesus! Fort Riley . . . the pits. . . . Well, listen, I have a proposition for you."

"A proposition? Is it compromising?"

Roy laughed. "So compromising I'm not supposed to be talking about it over the phone. I'll just give you an idea. Will you put yourself in my hands if I tell you it'll be fast, furious, and you'll be in good company? Namely, mine and some other guys you know? And, ultimately, you might even get a chance to do some chest surgery."

"You bet!"

"O.K. Just sit tight for the next twelve hours. I assume you're packed and ready to go." Arthur told him he was. "Now, what's that bastard's name, your CO?"

"Colonel Clarence Dreicher. Why?"

"Dreicher? Well, Colonel Dreicher is about to get mud in his eye."

"Hey! Nothing that's going to backfire, Roy. That S.O.B. would love to have an excuse to bust me."

"Naw, don't worry. It's just that when he sees your new orders, he'll be gnashing his teeth," Mac assured him.

"Can't you give me a hint?" Arthur asked.

"Sure. Your first destination will be Carlisle . . . the School of Tropical Diseases and Jungle Sanitation."

Arthur whistled. "Gotcha, Roy! When will I see you?"

"One week, Art. At Carlisle Barracks."

On his way through Washington, Arthur had a brief meeting with John Riordan. Father John was in uniform, a chaplain, temporarily stationed at Fort Meade.

"I've got orders to serve with the Forty-second Infantry, the Rainbow Division," he told Arthur.

"That was my brother's division in the First World War, John. They saw plenty of action."

John looked good in a different uniform but Arthur preferred the clerical collar. They only had time for a quick drink, and then Arthur had to catch his train.

"I sure am glad I saw you, John," said Arthur.

"God bless you, Arthur. Take care of yourself," John said, throwing a comradely arm around him.

"You, too, John." And then he added, not understanding why, but the words came, "Pray for me, Father." John smiled.

When Arthur reached Carlisle, he found Mac, Frank Lucas, and another fifteen men he'd known at Jeff, all surgeons who still maintained an affiliation with Jefferson Hospital. They were being formed into a hospital unit to be attached to a medical battalion . . . destination to be revealed. Their course in tropical diseases and jungle sanitation was augmented by military lectures and drilling.

"It's essential you keep fit, gentlemen," they were told again and again. "Only the well prepared survive marches through the jungle."

This time it looked like he might do more than train another field hospital to go overseas without him.

Winter 1942

Emily had remained in Haverford with the children, waiting for him to get leave. He was closer to Wilkes-Barre at Carlisle, but he didn't raise any objections. There were enough differences between them.

Their orders came. They were shipping out. Arthur stopped in Wilkes-Barre to say good-bye to Rose, Nate, and his sisters. Rose bore with fortitude this second sending of a son to war. She would never burden him with her private fears.

"Be careful, Art," Nathan told him as they parted. "I hope you don't have to go out there, buddy. Don't be a fool and play hero." Poor Nate, the hero.

Arthur was pleased to see that Leisl and her children had become a happy addition to Rose's household. He noticed how crazy the children were about Nate. In a way, he mused, they were closer than he and his children were these days. Before, it had been his medical practice; now, being in the service. It left little time to sit with children in your lap, playing games.

The first thing Emily told him was that Claudia was having a large dinner party that night.

"Emily, I have only two days before I leave. Can't we spend them alone—just you and I and the children?"

She seemed distracted. "Darling, it's so difficult. Mother has dinner all planned. It would seem rude. Freddy and Martha are coming, and the Beckingers—Billy's parents. They'd think I was purposely avoiding them . . . they've never gotten over their disappointment that I didn't marry Billy. Did you know he's divorced from Peggy?"

"No, I didn't know," he answered dully. Maybe it's better this way, he thought. We'd probably end up saying all the wrong things. I'll be gone for a long time—better not to talk things out now. Who knows what would happen if we did.

The children looked wonderful! Jeff and Bobby, growing tall and strong . . . and Ellen, so like Emily, with her fair coloring. The missing front teeth only added to her appeal. They, at least, clung to him every moment, following him up the stairs to his room when he went to shower and change. They sat watching him lather his face and shave, the boys asking question after question about the Army.

Emily had put them in school in Haverford temporarily, when she'd delayed the return to Wilkes-Barre. Now she thought they would stay with her parents until the end of the Christmas holiday. He couldn't blame her. There were more diversions here for her.

"How do you like school?" he asked the boys.

They answered, almost as one, "We like it! We're playing soccer."

"That's a good sport. And what about you, Ellen?"

"I don't like it. I don't like the clothes," she lisped.

"The clothes?"

"She means the uniforms," Bobby explained. "They have to wear *bloomers*, and they stick out of the jumpers!" Both boys shouted out their laughter, and Ellen made a face at them. Ellen was at Finchley, the school that both Emily and Claudia had attended. It seemed they hadn't changed the uniforms since Claudia had gone there.

"It won't be for long, love," he comforted her.

It was one of the worst evenings he could ever remember spending with any group of people. Billy Beckinger came home unexpectedly from his desk job in Washington. He was in the Navy, a commander with the Naval Supply Corps, an important job for which his experience as an executive in the family chain of department stores qualified him. Naturally, the Grants had to ask him to dinner along with his parents. Emily's brother Freddy often came home on weekends. He was with the judge advocate general's department in Baltimore. The other guests included Freddy's in-laws, the Von Pforzens, and two of the senior partners in the Grant law firm.

"Where is Arthur being sent?" he overheard Billy inquire of Emily, across the table.

He knows better than that, Arthur thought. "We haven't received our orders yet," he answered, before Emily could say anything.

Over coffee and brandy, when the ladies had left the table, Arthur was shocked at the discussion of war profits, politics, and Billy's revelations of the kind of favors and influence peddling that went on in Washington.

Later, in the living room, the conversation turned nostalgic as the group who had grown up together reminisced about club dances, summer boating escapades, and people whom he knew only by name.

At 10:30, Arthur went over to Claudia and excused himself. "Claudia, would you mind if I went up to bed? I'm tired, and I have many things to take care of in the morning."

"Of course not, dear," she said, kissing him. She walked with him to the doorway, her expression softening as she looked at his face. "I'll explain to the others." Then, she added, "I'm surprised you and Emily joined us tonight. I told her you should spend your last evening alone."

"You're very nice to me," he said with unexpected feeling, realizing that Claudia cared about him. He suddenly felt tender toward her. "Good night, Claudia," he said gently.

Emily followed him into the hall, calling as he started up the curving stairway. "Arthur? Where are you going so early?"

"I'm going up to bed, Emily."

"That's awfully rude of you, to just leave like that. What about Mother's guests?" She stood on the stairs next to him, speaking in a loud whisper.

"Your mother said she would explain." Then he said, angrily, "I was bored stiff, Emily. How can you expect me to sit there listening to that conversation in which I can take no part and not be bored?"

Her cheeks flamed. "How many years have *I* sat through interminable evenings of conversation in Wilkes-Barre when you were with *your* friends, talking about things which I never shared? And how many medical conversations have I had to listen to—how many hundreds? Really, Arthur, you can be incredibly selfish at times." She turned and stalked into the living room.

Emily did not come up for another hour. By that time, Arthur had fallen asleep. He heard her come out of the dressing room, but he let himself drift back into slumber without speaking to her. She would have come to his bed, he knew, for she stood there looking down at him in the dark before getting into the other twin bed. That's how it had always been with them, their problems resolved in bed. That wouldn't work this time.

What had become of them? he thought, full of anguish. Where had those moments fled, those moments of glad grace? Once they had shared the joys of life together . . . love, laughter, children, sunshine. Now, all was dry as dust.

It would have been easy to cry when he said good-bye to his children. They knew only that he would be gone for a long time.

"Take care of Mommy and Ellen, boys. I'm counting on you to be young men." They kissed and hugged him, their nine-year-old bodies holding him tightly, feeling so young in his arms. Ellen's huge blue saucer eyes looked soulful. She had always wept when they parted, since early childhood.

Emily drove him to the station alone. In the car, parked there, she turned to him.

"I've made a mess of these two days, Arthur. It's all my fault. I'm sorry."

He started to protest, feeling guilty, knowing he had been equally at fault—it was no one's fault, he wanted to tell her. Just the way things were. She silenced him.

"Wait. Let me say what I want to say. You'll be gone for heaven knows how long. I'm not going back to Wilkes-Barre, Arthur. I'm going to stay in Haverford. The children are happy here, my parents love having us. I'm too lonely at home without you. It isn't even 'home' when you're not there."

"Is that why you've been remote—why you didn't want to be alone, to talk with me?"

"Yes. I knew you would try to change my mind. But I don't want you to. I simply hate the idea of staying there as long as you're overseas. I've already made arrangements for some things to be put in storage, and I'll go to close up the house." She could see his disappointment. "I'm sorry, Arthur. I realize I'm letting you down."

He sighed. "To say that I'm not unhappy wouldn't be true, Emily. It's so sudden. I guess I just pictured you being there in our house, waiting for me." Then he said something he had not intended to say. "Does this mean you're not ever going back?"

She looked frightened, but her eyes were steady. "We have things to settle between us, Arthur. This isn't the time. We're both under strain—you're leaving. I hope it doesn't mean that, but I can't say for sure."

He closed his eyes. Christ, what timing! In twenty minutes, he had to be on that train.

"Emily, this is *why* we should have spent the time together—this is a ridiculous moment to be having this conversation."

"I *know* it is . . . I . . . I'm sorry, Arthur. I didn't want to . . . I don't even know how it came out like this. I didn't intend to get into the future or what will happen with us—I just wanted you to know that I wouldn't be going home now, and I didn't want to either write it in a letter or to have any discussion about it."

He looked at his watch. "I've got to go now! Don't worry about it, Emily— you shouldn't have to stay in Wilkes-Barre if you don't want to. Will you keep in touch with my mother . . . and Nate?"

"Of course! Of course I will, darling!" She started to cry. "What's *happened* to us? Why does it have to be like this?"

There was a great heaviness in his chest. His throat tightened and his eyes prickled. "It's the war, honey. How can anything be right in this world now?" He put his arms around her. "Don't cry, Em. . . . We'll be all right. We'll get it straightened out when I come home." For a brief moment, her eyes shone with hope. "Kiss me good-bye?"

They embraced in sad desperation, both knowing the gulf between them was as wide as the ocean which would soon separate them.

BOOK SIX

———

At War
1943-45

I

Assam, India   1943

The monsoon arrived two months early in the northeasternmost region of India in 1943, while it failed altogether in Bengal, causing a great famine. For lack of rain, the rice crops shriveled and the streets of Calcutta embraced the dead and dying—for lack of rain, and for lack of the transportation needed to bring emergency supplies of food to stricken millions. Meanwhile, in one of nature's ironies, every ravine and gulley in the jungles of Assam became a raging stream with the premature arrival of the torrential rains. For an army preparing to fight a jungle war against a wily, hardened enemy, the monsoon made an already monumental task simply impossible.

In March, almost three months to the day of saying good-bye to Emily in Philadelphia, Arthur arrived at Lalitha, a remote tea garden in Assam state near the India-Burma border.

Seven weeks out of San Diego, aboard a converted Matson liner, the 24th Station Hospital had sailed past the Gate of India into Bombay Harbor. Arthur had stood at the ship's rail, taking in the riot of colors and sounds. The spectacle of the heaving, sweating, straining jumble of turbaned coolies in loin cloths, sari-wrapped women, bullock carts, two-wheeled *tongas,* and honking British Army trucks rushed in on him. Sharp splashes of crimson, ocher, and peacock blue met his eyes from the swirling skirts of peasant women who balanced heavy loads of bricks, for a construction project, on their heads. Half-naked children scurried among the uniformed Indian police, begging for *baksheesh* from every white *sahib* or prosperous-looking Indian they spied.

Arthur had been intrigued from the first moment he laid eyes on India's shore . . . stepped foot on her soil. Something gripped him, captivating his imagination. He felt a thrill of anticipation. India!

After a brief respite at a British Army station, they had endured a sweltering, dusty six-day journey by rail across the broad expanse of the Indian subcontinent, switching to a medium-gauge railroad in the Himalayan foothills, then to a slow-moving riverboat on which they steamed up the wide Brahmaputra until forced by rapids to take to land again. The final leg of this protracted itinerary was completed on yet a narrower-gauge trolly train, winding through dense tropical growth, until at last they were deposited in this forgotten corner of earth, India's northeastern frontier.

Two tin-roofed, one-story buildings—open to the elements, to the insects, and the free-roaming cows, whom they were forbidden to interfere with lest they cause a religious riot—were all Lalitha offered them in the way of permanent structures. These had comprised the infirmary for all the tea planters within a one-hundred-mile radius in the days before the war.

"I see it, but I don't believe it," Roy McLean said wearily as they surveyed the site where they were to carry out their assignment—setting up a station hospital for American flyers who flew "the Hump" from a nearby base, ferrying supplies into China. Later on they would be ordered to send portable surgical units to Burma, where Chinese screen troops were protecting the American engineers who were constructing the Ledo Road, a new land route connecting Assam to the war-torn Burma Road, which had been captured by the Japanese.

For the first two months, the Supply Corps seemed to have overlooked the 24th Station Hospital and its mission. "I don't *know* what happened to your equipment, Major," a frantic quartermaster lieutenant told Arthur, who was in charge of setting up a surgery. "The supply car seems to have been diverted to an unknown destination!"

"Well, find it, *dammit!* How do they expect us to set up a hospital without medicines and instruments?" Without plasma, linens, wire screening, generators, autoclaves, bandages, or electricity.

"Good old American know-how!" joked Frank Lucas, as they watched coolies from the surrounding hill towns clear brush, then construct rude huts of bamboo lashed together with cane and roofed with thatch.

How they managed to convert the abandoned British colonial health station into an American medical facility would forever remain a cause for wonder to Arthur and his fellow officers. They did it, though—securing a fresh water supply, bringing in electric lines, constructing wards and operating theaters, digging latrines, establishing lines of supply.

Their salvation had come in the form of an Indian Army Public Health officer, Major Ranjit Kar. Kar was the medical liaison between the General Staff for the Southeast Asia Command and the growing network of American hospitals assembling in India.

"Anything I can do to expedite things here for you, gentlemen, just say the word," Kar had told them when he paid his first visit toward the end of the second frustrating month in Lalitha.

"As a matter of fact"—Arthur had hesitated—"we're having some trouble getting our drainage and latrines straightened out." Because of the high ground water, it was necessary to keep adding more and more latrines, abandoning some of recent construction. With no automated equipment at their disposal, they had to use hand labor. But because most of the younger men from the villages were being drafted as porters into the Indian Army, workmen were hard to find.

Ranjit Kar had produced a work force within an hour, headed by a foreman who could carry out their instructions, since he understood English. On another occasion, Kar had managed to get them some air-conditioning equipment for the ward where the most seriously ill malaria patients were isolated. Arthur was fond of the urbane, smiling Indian major and looked forward to his infrequent visits. Thus far, this was the only Indian officer whose acquaintance he'd made.

They received their first combat casualties in the fall of 1943. Chinese, British, and Indian, they were in terrible shape by the time they reached Lalitha.

"We don't need a newspaper to know how *this* war's going," Frank Lucas remarked to Arthur after they had finished a particularly brutal series of surgery. Few of the wounds had been debrided at the front, where first aid and plasma were given. Infection was rampant, and after a long, tortured overland haul, the men were more dead than alive by the time they were admitted to the 24th Station Hospital.

In the early months, the cases had been almost all medical—routine fractures, malaria, dysentery. After a while they began to see many cases of scrub typhus. A virulent disease borne by mites, it was said to have been carried into Burma by the Japanese troops from Singapore. Whatever its origin, it had a dire outcome . . . almost 20 percent of the patients died. As American troops began to fight in Burma, they were found to be particularly susceptible to this lethal illness.

During those first days, the surgeons found themselves practicing general medicine for the first time since their internships. By the beginning of 1944 the reverse was true. Good surgeons were at a premium and all doctors were pressed into surgical duty in the base and field hospitals.

"Who is this guy, Michael Gentry, Colonel McLean?" asked Ralph Baum, a young surgeon who had recently arrived from the States.

"He's a missionary doctor, Captain. Served with Duncan Foster in Burma, made the march out with Stilwell's troops in '42." Roy McLean shuffled the cards and dealt. They were playing poker in the improvised Officers' Club to pass the tedious night hours at Lalitha. They'd been there for nine months. All of them were on twenty-four-hour call all the time, but this week had been strangely quiet.

"Duncan Foster? Isn't he the one who went on that lecture tour of American medical schools?"

"He's the one, all right," McLean answered. "Foster grew up in Burma, son of a Baptist missionary. Frankly, he's a second-rate doctor. Found he couldn't hack it in Stateside medicine, so he returned to the Burma hills, where he made a name for himself setting up a mission hospital. He meant to model it after Gordon Seagrave's hospital at Namkham, but it was never in the same class. . . . Your play, Lucas."

"The missionary doctors provided the only modern medical care available to the people of the Burma hills," Arthur explained to Baum.

"Did you ever meet Duncan Foster, Major?" Baum asked.

"Yes. I've met him a couple of times. He passed through, made his pronouncements, and went on his way," Arthur replied.

"You didn't like him, I gather."

"Not much. Typical missionary. Thinks he's better than most everyone else. Hell, you have to think you're better than people if your aim is to improve them by making them more like yourself!"

Before American medical personnel had been plentiful in the Burma-India theater, Foster's group had been used as a makeshift portable surgical hospital. The frequency of gangrene amputations from fractures set in tight plaster in the Foster unit had been double that of others, Arthur had been told. "I understand that Gentry, despite the missionary stuff, is a good doctor," he told Ralph Baum.

"If Gentry's giving us a chance for some action, I won't mind if he preaches at *me!*" said Frank Lucas, laying down his cards with a broad grin. "Full house!"

"Ahhhh!" McLean threw down his cards in disgust. "Gentry will be here first thing in the morning, so you'll get your chance to listen. That's it for tonight, fellas. I'm going to turn in. Will you take care of Gentry tomorrow, Art?"

"Sure, Mac. I don't mind. When do you think the first team will go?" Everyone turned to hear Roy's answer.

"Soon! It looks like they're really preparing an offensive. They're bound to need portable surgical units. It's Major Gentry's job to orient those of us who've never been out there in the jungle."

That was good news. Rumors had been circulating for weeks. An American combat unit was on its way to Assam in answer to General Stilwell's pleas.

An offensive. Finally, they would be on the offensive.

After checking on some of the most serious cases, Arthur walked across the muddy compound to the building that the staff officers shared as their quarters. Little more than a *basha*, it had a leaky mat roof overlaid with brushes. The walls were made of thick matting which let the breezes through, but also acted like a sieve during the heavy rains. Everything was damp all the time. Mildew and mold grew everywhere—in his locker, his musette bag, in the drawer of the table which served as desk and nightstand, the only surface on which to place anything he wanted to keep out of the puddles of water that formed on the concrete floor during each rainfall.

The walls separating his "room" from his neighbor's were other thickly woven mats, affording little privacy. He was uncomfortably aware that at least one of his fellow doctors wept at night, under cover of darkness. Arthur didn't know which one. He would like to have offered him some solace, but whoever it was preferred to keep his problems to himself. It was depressing, though, adding to the feeling of isolation and loneliness.

He began a letter to Emily.

Dearest Emily,

When all this is over, I'm going to find us a place in the desert to live! If I ever see rain again . . .

He ripped the page from the pad of stationery, balled it up, and threw it in the crate that served as a wastebasket. He began again, then threw that away too.

Turning out the kerosene lamp, he removed his boots and lay on his rope *charpoy* fully clothed, staring up through the darkness, listening to the sound of the sudden heavy rain on the roof, thinking of home and Emily, trying to remember what she felt like in his arms.

It was essentially not in his nature to pretend. He found it unnatural to profess love he did not feel, devotion that wasn't there. Yet, it was cruel to write letters to Emily, his wife . . . so far away, probably worried about him . . . and not express loving thoughts. Was it crueler still not to write?

He closed his eyes, envisioning the beautiful, self-contained young woman he had first met in Philadelphia . . . charming, a springtime maiden of fragrant pastels, smiling and graceful, with that unsuspected, hidden passion, reserved for him. How wonderful those days had been. . . .

That was the way he liked to dream of her. But when a letter from Emily would arrive, the image was shattered. Intruding on that illusion of serene beauty was a brittle, shallow woman who chattered about the trivialities of life in that close circle of Philadelphians which few outsiders could hope to penetrate.

If she still loved him, it was not apparent from their correspondence. Emily had always found it difficult to verbalize her deepest sentiments. He'd always known this and tried to understand her reticence. In the first years of their marriage, there had never been reason to doubt her love. They had been happy, contented, for the most part.

Where did it go wrong? Something had happened along the way—just when, he wasn't able to say. No one moment, no one incident. Rather a building of failures to meet each other's expectations.

In his hours of reflection here in this alien environment, first, to counter the boredom of Assam, then, the horror of the casualties, he knew that there hadn't been *one* pivotal episode, but a series of disillusionments, leading to a moment of recognition. . . .

He was no longer in love with his wife.

The wheels of the wider trucks hung over the edges of the precipice as they inched along the narrow, winding track. They were on a detour, bypassing a washed-out section of the Ledo Road. Rain had made the roadbed so soft that without warning the lead vehicle had plunged over the cliff, landing in a valley hundreds of feet below, exploding in a ball of fire.

Gingerly, the line of vehicles inched backward, one by one, until able to turn on a protected shoulder where they weren't in danger of following their unlucky companions to oblivion. Arthur watched, feeling deserted, as their transport departed, leaving them to march over the Naga Hills to the Hukawng Valley with two jeeps and an ambulance to carry the equipment for a portable surgery.

Arthur and Frank Lucas were the two senior medical officers. They were accompanied by a score of corpsmen, various technicians, a platoon of infantry, and fifteen porters who belonged to the wild hill people of the Garo tribes.

Arthur had said good-bye to Roy McLean at Lalitha.

"I've got a farewell present for you, Art," Mac had said, grinning. He held out a box and an envelope addressed to Arthur. In the box were the silver leaves of a lieutenant colonel. "Congratulations, Colonel Hillman! It's long overdue."

Arthur knew that this meant he wouldn't be serving again under Mac. They didn't waste two "light colonels" on a single hospital unit. As if in answer, Mac had handed him his orders:

PROCEED COMMAND 49TH FIELD HOSPITAL, NINGAM. LEDO TRANS-PORT POOL WILL PROVIDE VEHICLES; DETACH PORTABLE SURGI-CAL TEAM TO ACCOMPANY, SERVING AS NEEDED EN ROUTE.

It was signed by the medical field officer at HQ, Delhi.

As Arthur followed the track of their ambulance, he was grateful for those weeks of physical torment at Monmouth and Edwards. Whoever thought he'd actually be fording streams, carrying his pack over his head to keep it dry? But the leeches and insects were something they couldn't prepare you for. Nor the torrents of rain—so heavy at times he couldn't see. The steaming jungle, the night chills, the poisonous snakes, the mud . . . the uncertainty.

They had been halfway to Ningam when they'd had to halt. They were to proceed on foot to a deserted cluster of huts just north of Hkalak, a two-day march, until the washed-out road could be repaired and their transport catch up with them.

Only when they had finally stopped, set up their portable hospital, and started to receive sick and wounded was Arthur engrossed enough in his work to forget his own physical misery.

They had been stuck here for almost two weeks. The casualties were coming in large numbers, mostly Chinese. They were brought overland by native stretcher-bearers who scrambled up and down steep embankments, carrying the wounded in slings. As the days wore on, more and more Americans were among the wounded.

It was late afternoon. Arthur had finished the last surgical case. He and Frank Lucas had been working tandem on the two tables from before dawn, using kerosene lamps when it grew darker. Their gasoline was running low. Because the autoclave was gasoline-fueled, Arthur had insisted that they boil pots of water on a wood fire, keeping them on hand at all times to sterilize the instruments. They were in short supply of everything from surgical gloves to dressings. He wore no shirt under his gown, which was soaked with sweat, and he was dog-tired. For once, he knew what that expression meant.

"Colonel Hillman? Can you come out here, sir? We have a problem." It was Sergeant Morgan, who had been with the evac ambulance.

Arthur removed his gown and followed Morgan out of the surgery. Off to the right, near a clearing, stood the ambulance. Corporal Bailey, who had been part of the evac unit, was standing there, staring off into space, smoking rapidly, kicking stones viciously, mad as hell. An armed PFC stood sentry nearby, looking scared and uncertain. Morgan leaned his hand against the rear end of the ambulance, his arm extended across the door. Inside was a stretcher with a blanketed figure lying there.

"What's going on here, Corporal?" Arthur addressed Bailey.

"I say shoot the bastard or let him die! I'll be damned if I'll carry him to surgery!"

Motioning Morgan to step aside, Arthur looked in the interior of the ambulance at the wounded man lying on the stretcher. It was a Japanese officer —a major, still in uniform. He was conscious, but in shock. No plasma or other first aid had been administered. He was breathing in shallow, irregular gasps, his eyes dulled with pain.

A crackle of electrochemical impulses surged through Arthur. Shock, alarm, revulsion, compassion. The physician emerged victorious. He snapped an order to the two medical corpsmen.

"Get that litter over to surgery, on the double! Hear me, Bailey?"

Bailey threw down his cigarette, stamped it out, and, with a dark scowl, moved to obey, while Morgan already had the stretcher half out of the vehicle. The sentry looked at Arthur questioningly.

"Follow us, Private," Arthur said to the sentry, loud enough for Bailey to hear.

The last light was rapidly fading from the sky. Soon it would be pitch dark, the night of the jungle—darker than any night on earth.

They carried the wounded major into the surgery, where Arthur indicated they should place the litter to the side while he examined the man.

"Get an IV going, Morgan. Bailey, you're dismissed—and no nonsense, understand? We'll talk about this later." Bailey left. Morgan got the plasma and glucose going in an intravenous. Then he injected the patient with morphine and tetanus antitoxin, while Arthur cut away the clothes from the

Japanese's gaping chest wound. He whistled. "That's a nasty one, Sergeant. Let's remove the rest of these clothes and get him on the table."

"Yes, sir. Shall I call Major Lucas, Colonel?"

"No, Sergeant. He's asleep, and he badly needs that sleep. He's been operating for almost twenty-four hours without relief."

"So have you, sir," said Morgan.

"No. I managed to grab a few winks here and there. I'll be all right. Shall I get an assistant, or will you do it?" They both knew that Bailey wasn't the only one who might balk at giving aid to one of the enemy . . . the cruel, treacherous, unrelenting enemy who gave no quarter to their wounded.

The major had evidently put his hand up to shield himself when the explosion occurred. At any rate, the shrapnel that caught him in the chest had been deflected by the bone of the left forearm, which was fractured. They would attend to that after the more serious chest injury. Morgan administered inhalation anesthesia, while Arthur cleaned and debrided the wound. He was thankful for the ever-ready pots of boiling water which he'd insisted on. Morgan applied alcohol and iodine to the wiry, hairless chest and draped the prisoner with towels, and Arthur began his exploration. He located the shrapnel immediately. It had miraculously missed the vital organs by a hair, and lodged itself against a rib, which was chipped.

"Lucky bugger," Arthur muttered through his mask. He removed the segment—about three inches long and half again as wide—and suctioned out the blood from the chest cavity. He found a fragment of chipped bone in the process. No major blood vessels had been severed. The bleeding had almost stopped, probably because of the state of shock of the patient. Morgan took his pressure again and reported it had improved slightly since the administration of the life-saving plasma. Respiration was shallow but even, and the skin had lost its ghastly pallor.

Arthur sprinkled sulfonamide powder in the wound, then began the closing up. Throughout, he had been concentrating on the surgery, the vital signs, the mechanics of saving a human life—not even thinking about the fact that this was an enemy officer. Now he turned his attention to the fractured arm. Seeing the hand extended limply from the mutilated limb, something about the hand—its configuration—reminded him that he was operating on a member of the Imperial Army of Japan. It was a slim, well-shaped male hand—the hand of an aesthetic, educated man. No calluses on the palm, the nails surprisingly clean and cared for, considering the conditions of jungle warfare.

Arthur reduced and set the fracture. Fortunately, although broken in two places, it had not shattered. He cleaned and sutured the torn flesh. Morgan helped him with the plaster cast and drains.

"Light, and not too tight, Sergeant. We don't want any gas gangrene." Morgan regarded him with a long, enigmatic look.

Next they examined the patient thoroughly for other injuries. One foot was bruised and swollen, but didn't appear to be broken. "That may need strapping later. We'll wait until he's conscious," said Arthur.

"What are we going to do with him, Colonel?" asked Morgan.

"Do with him?" Arthur's voice had a puzzled tone.

"We're not set up for prisoners, sir. We can't afford a sentry."

"He's not going anywhere for a while."

"I wasn't thinking of that, Colonel Hillman. When some of the guys find out there's a Jap prisoner here, they're not going to like it much."

"Umm . . . I see what you mean. Well, I'll keep him near at hand until he's well enough to evacuate to the prisoner of war ward in Margherita or the camp at Ramgarh. What else would you suggest?"

Morgan shrugged. "I guess nothing else. Only I hope it's not too long. We don't need any trouble . . . it's a small unit."

Arthur nodded. "Sergeant," he said as Morgan began to clean up. The young man turned. "I've never lost a patient from neglect. Do you know what the Hippocratic oath is?"

"Yes, sir."

"Well, I take mine seriously, Morgan. And it doesn't leave room for exceptions, like Japanese or Germans. As far as I know, this man has never harmed an American." Morgan was looking down at the floor. "I think your thoughts are similar, Morgan. Or else you'd have let Bailey shoot him."

"I . . . I guess so, sir." He continued with his work. "Sir, you shouldn't be too hard on Bailey. He found that platoon they'd tied to trees and used for bayonet practice."

Arthur sighed. "I'm aware of that, Morgan. I'll talk to Bailey—don't worry about it."

Arthur had the Japanese major placed in a corner of the recovery area where they kept the most seriously wounded before evacuation. He himself slept in there on a cot that first night. The prisoner came out of the anesthesia, but was heavily sedated. He muttered in Japanese, half delirious. His temperature was 103, and Arthur was afraid that his wound would become seriously infected, despite the sulfa.

Sometime during the night, Arthur awakened and went over to the cot where the Japanese was moaning. He injected him with morphine and put a wet cloth on his head, gently bathing the perspiration from his face and neck. The dark eyes, clouded with pain, yet alert, followed his every move. Arthur looked back at his patient with a reluctant smile. He shook his head and said, "Don't ask me why I'm doing this, Major, but I want you to live. I'm afraid of the animal in me. If I let you die, the animal wins. . . ." Then he laughed. "You can't understand me . . . I'm talking to myself." Sometimes it was better to talk to himself. He'd sure be glad when they got to the portable hospital at Ningam. . . . Where the hell was their transport, anyway?

Bailey came in early in the morning while Arthur was preparing for the next onslaught of wounded. The corporal was sullen but docile. They sat in the alcove with the wounded Japanese in the corner. Arthur told Bailey he understood his hatred for the enemy. "This is a rotten, dirty war, Bailey. But there are rules to war, like everything else. And just because they don't obey the rules doesn't mean that we shouldn't. If we treat wounded prisoners that way—killing them, or leaving them to die—we're no better than they are. Can you understand how I view it?"

"Yes, sir, but I don't agree with you." He looked over at the cot in the corner. "I still wish I could've killed him."

"I wonder, Bailey, if you really do. Someday, when this is over, you may think about it and be glad you didn't have a gun." He put his hand on the boy's shoulder before dismissing him. To be so filled with hate at nineteen.

Arthur was alone in the surgery. They'd had word that they'd be moving on to Ningam in two or three days. That was a relief. Here they had set off to join the field hospital and been stranded for almost three weeks.

Arthur went into the "prisoner ward"—the place where he had set the Japanese major's cot. The man was asleep, breathing quietly. He was going to make it. The second night, Arthur hadn't been so sure. . . .

He had kept a vigil with the prisoner the entire night again, this time sleeping little, sitting in a camp chair next to the bed, frequently checking his pulse and temperature. He had been afraid that the man might have the dread scrub typhus. After peaking at 103, his temperature had begun to drop, and was hovering at 100 degrees. Arthur had looked through the prisoner's personal effects, which Morgan had collected from his clothes and placed in a hammock pocket tied on the side of his cot. There wasn't much—some worthless paper occupation money in a wallet containing identification and some photographs. Arthur had looked at the snapshots. A sweet-looking Japanese woman with small, almost artificial-looking features, and three doll-like children—two solemn little boys and a girl, who looked out with an angelic smile and large bright eyes. He had looked over at the sleeping prisoner, whose face was strong and appealing in repose—not at all like the Japanese soldiers in the American films they had seen . . . back in the days when he was near a movie theater. Glancing from the photographs to the father of this family, he had thought, *Are these my enemies?*

When he'd finished going through the wallet, gleaning nothing, since all the papers were in Japanese, he had looked up to see the major watching him gravely. Arthur had smiled, patted the man's arm, and put the wallet away, showing him where they stowed his possessions. The Japanese officer merely nodded. From time to time during the night, mostly to keep himself awake, Arthur had talked aloud, musing to himself about the irony of the two of them being there, the strangeness of the encounter. "I'm glad you're going to live," he'd said. "I don't know why it was so important to me. You're the first Japanese I've ever seen close at hand. . . ." The man had continued to regard him, but his features had relaxed and softened, as if reassured by the soothing tone of Arthur's voice. Maybe he can tell I bear him no ill will, Arthur had thought. . . .

Arthur sat in the chair, leaning his head back against a post, and rubbed his eyes. Lord, he was tired. He had almost drifted off when he heard the voice. Coming awake with a start, he looked around and saw no one. He must have been dreaming. He stood up and stretched.

"Colonel . . . do you think I might have a cigarette?"

Arthur turned sharply. There was no one else in the room. He looked out in the surgery. It was empty. Slowly, he looked around the room until his eyes met those of the Japanese major. The man was smiling.

"You speak English?" Arthur was incredulous.

The Japanese nodded. "Yes. I apologize for my rudeness in not telling you before this. I didn't know how it would affect my treatment."

"You not only speak English, you speak it like an American—perfectly, with almost no accent." He couldn't believe his ears. Then, he thought, he must be Intelligence! A spy? Even a spy couldn't do much with a chest wound like this man had sustained.

As if reading his thoughts, the man said, "You may ask me anything about myself and I'll answer you honestly, Colonel. I hope you won't ask me for information about my division, because I couldn't give you much—and even if I could, I wouldn't."

"That's not my job, Major. But I *am* curious to know where you learned to speak English like that."

"I spent seven years in Cambridge, Massachusetts. At Harvard. Studying biology and parasitology."

"That should come in handy here in Burma," Arthur said dryly. The Major laughed, then grimaced in pain and clutched his chest with his right hand. Arthur was sympathetic. He could imagine the pain from the incision and the trauma. When the Japanese was breathing easily again, Arthur asked, "Do you think you'd like to try a little liquid? I have boiled water in here."

"If it's hot," the man answered. "I can't abide cold water." After he'd taken a few sips, he seemed exhausted. He lay back, closing his eyes. In a brief time, he opened them again. "I would like a cigarette, if I may."

"Major, you shouldn't smoke with that chest wound. I'm afraid it would irritate your lungs. You've had anesthesia. You start coughing, and you'll wish you hadn't made it! It's as good a time as any to break the habit— besides, we probably don't have your brand," he joked.

"My brand is Lucky Strike, Colonel. I've been smoking them regularly lately."

"Where do you get Lucky Strikes in the middle of the jungle?"

"Your airdrops." The major smiled. "We were receiving food, cigarettes, and medical supplies at the generosity of the American Government."

"Good heavens! I wonder where they're dropping the bombs!" It wasn't surprising, though. The jungle was so dense, it was impossible to get a good reference point when dropping things by air—particularly if you were afraid of getting shot at.

Arthur set about finding out the essential details of his patient for his records. He took out his pen and report form. "Major, I have to ask you a few questions . . . name, please." Arthur tried to be totally businesslike. It was one thing to give medical care to the enemy—quite another to fraternize with him.

"Kenji Tokada, Major, Army of the Japanese Empire." Arthur did his best to exact more information, but his heart wasn't in it. Again, that wasn't his job. Morgan had told him they'd been taken to the officer by a Chin tribesman. When they found him, he was in a partly demolished jeep whose driver was dead, while another officer, a colonel, had blown his own brains out rather than be captured. Morgan had brought maps and papers found on the colonel's body, indicating that they were from the 18th Division, 114th Regiment. Evidently their jeep had taken a wrong turn in trying to keep up with the retreating Japanese forces. Major Tokada was acting as a medical officer, for he'd been wearing a cloth band, with an improvised insignia, around his arm. Things must be in total disarray for the 18th Division if they didn't have proper field hospitals traveling with them.

Two days later their transport arrived, and Arthur's surgical unit was again on its way to Ningam, on a spur off the Ledo Road where the 49th Field Hospital was established as a receiving station and evacuation point. The trouble was there was not a finished landing strip for C-47s to land. Work had been started on one, but the heavy monsoon rains and intense bombardment had stopped all progress. Now it was a muddy clearing on the edge of the jungle with ditches running at cross angles in a vain attempt to keep the ground around the hospital free from flash flooding. The only means of evacuation to a base hospital was overland to the airfield at Shingbwiyang—a muddy bumpy ride over the partly completed Ledo Road.

The planes could take only a few men at a time, and there was always a backup of over a hundred patients waiting to be evacuated. Everyone laughed when Arthur suggested that the Japanese prisoner should be evacuated. He'd have to wait his turn, and he was low priority.

Major Kenji Tokada remained at Ningam. The only prisoner of war in the "prison ward," he was either ignored or resented by most of the personnel. He was Colonel Hillman's patient . . . and he was Colonel Hillman's responsibility.

Arthur was examining Major Tokada's chest one afternoon during a lull.

Frank Lucas sat smoking a cigarette, still in his surgical gown, his square, ruddy face lined with fatigue.

"I'd like to know whether that gut case has amoeba or another parasite. Makes a difference in the handling. I don't want to spread that stuff around."

"Did you get a culture?" Arthur asked, as he swabbed the Japanese officer's chest. The drain had been removed, and the small opening sutured. Soon the dressing could come off.

"I can't get a damn thing in that scope. Christ, I had a better instrument in my high school chemistry class in Shenandoah," said Lucas.

Major Tokada spoke, apologetically. "Excuse me, Colonel Hillman, but it's a difficult diagnosis unless the patient's stool is examined immediately, while it's still at body temperature."

Major Lucas looked down at the tips of his boots, sucking in his cheeks. He had maintained total neutrality in the matter of "Arthur's Jap," as he thought of Tokada.

Arthur scrutinized the Japanese. "You're able to make that diagnosis, Major? You're a bacteriologist . . . a parasitologist, aren't you?" Major Tokada nodded. "Well," said Arthur, a gleam of humor in his eye, "how'd you like a job as a lab technician?"

Arthur congratulated himself that Tokada was a valuable addition to the staff. He identified organisms, typed blood, did cultures—even fashioned a still for distilling water. Once, when they ran out of intravenous fluid, Major Tokada asked for some green coconuts from the abundant supply growing around them. With interest, they watched while he cut away the outer shell. Using a sterile instrument, he pierced the inner husk and inserted an IV tube. There! A natural nutriment in liquid form, and it was completely sterile. Even Major Lucas was impressed with that one.

The Japanese stayed as much in the background as possible, permitted in the makeshift laboratory only when Arthur was in the adjoining surgery— and only on Arthur's direct orders. No one else wanted him there. No one else spoke to him. If Arthur hadn't been the CO, he wouldn't have been there at all.

When they were alone one day, Arthur asked, "How do you feel about aiding your enemies, Major Tokada?"

Tokada looked up from the microscope. "Probably about the same as you did, Colonel Hillman . . . confused." There was the hint of a smile.

"Touché," said Arthur. He looked out across the clearing at the tropical green hills in the distance. "To think what this place must have been like once . . . before all this." His hand swept in an expressive gesture.

"Mmm, yes. It's a brutal war," Kenji Tokada replied.

"You fellows started it!"

"Come now, Colonel! It could have been avoided. We were being strangled economically."

"You've been at war for years, Major. What about China, Indonesia? A nation that allows a bunch of militarists to take over gets what it deserves."

"They'll have us to thank for ending white colonialism. Never again will Asians accept the right of the West to rule them in their own countries! It's the end of the colonial era. That means India and Africa, too."

"So, now you're trying to tell me this war is a good thing?" Arthur laughed.

"Someday, I believe, they'll look back and decide it shouldn't have been fought." He was quiet for a moment, then said in a matter-of-fact voice, "Japan will lose, of course."

Arthur looked at him with interest. "*I* believe that, but I'm surprised to hear *you* say it."

Kenji smiled. "The United States has the manpower. And, as soon as she gets organized, will have the matériel to overcome our small nation. The European war is the important one for your country now. This, in Burma, is just a diversionary expedition, it would seem. . . . What I think our General Staff doesn't properly appreciate is that Americans—for all their love of the easy life and their reluctance to go to war—once committed, become a formidable adversary. If we don't win the Pacific soon, we've lost the war."

"Is it true that the Japanese soldier will fight to the death rather than be captured . . . as a matter of honor?" As soon as he'd asked the question, he realized his mistake. "Obviously, that isn't true, Major . . . or there would *be* no prisoners. I apologize if I've offended you."

"No need to apologize, Colonel. It is true. There is the code of *bushido* . . . total fidelity. Fight to the death; do not fall into enemy hands; if defeated, it is the duty of an honorable warrior to commit suicide. That is the ancient *samurai* code. Many military men still honor it." Kenji carefully put away the slides and materials he had been using. He was always so neat and precise in the way he placed each article, Arthur noted with fascination.

The Japanese faced him and said, in self-mockery, "I myself have been contaminated by my years in the West. I have acquired an unfortunate tendency to love my fellow man. I'm afraid I make a most unsuitable warrior. I loathe everything to do with this war."

There was a beautiful dignity about this man, Arthur thought. *Kenji.* It had a pleasing sound to it, that name. Kenji.

Another monsoon would begin in May. Truthfully, it was hard for the uninitiated Americans to differentiate between monsoon and the rains that plagued them throughout the year in Burma. The seasonal rains would only compound the misery of the troops, who regarded the climate and terrain with as much horror as they feared the fanatical enemy.

As March 1944 panted by, hour by hour, Arthur's field hospital was swamped with malaria and dysentery cases. The casualty count from tropical diseases rose higher and higher as the American combat unit dubbed "Merrill's Marauders" engaged the Japanese in the drive toward the strategic airfield at Myitkyina. Arthur saw illnesses he had read about, that had been described in a single lecture at medical school by a professor who had never seen a case in clinic. Yaws, sprue, scabies, dengue fever, schistosomiasis, cholera, and typhus. Venomous insect bites, ulcerated sores from huge leeches whose heads remained burrowed beneath the skin when frantic soldiers pulled them off in revulsion. As the humidity rose, some of the men developed a condition in which they lost their ability to perspire—life-threatening in temperatures of over 120 degrees. These cases had to be evacuated immediately.

Everyone was supposed to take quinacrine to prevent malaria. In the early days of the war, when the drug had first become available, the army doctors learned that there were serious side effects from its use, chiefly skin rashes and psychoses. Now some of the troops—particularly the Chinese—thought the quinacrine would make them impotent and refused to take it!

"Would you believe that they'd be worried about their sex lives out here?" a disbelieving Arthur asked Frank Lucas.

Lucas shook his head. "I dunno . . . unless they're making it with each other. I don't think there's a woman within a hundred miles."

Lucas was wrong. One day a platoon of battle-weary infantry was pausing for attention to their foot sores and other bodily miseries when two young women in Burmese dress wandered out of the jungle toward them. The two separated, one walking to a concentration of soldiers on a rise while the other continued toward the main group. The explosion from the grenades planted on the first woman's body caught most of them by surprise, warning the sentry, who shot her companion before she reached the men eating their K rations. What kind of fanatic would undertake such a suicide mission, allowing herself to become a walking bomb? Arthur wondered. They must be Japanese women, camp followers.

Each day became a new trauma. . . . Some of the men went mad with the heat and the tension. At the end of March, General Merrill, whose "Marauders" were taking the worst of the campaign, suffered a heart attack and had to be evacuated from the front. Morale in his unit, code-named Galahad, was at an all-time low.

In years to come, an occasional case—an automobile accident, a mine cave-in—would remind Arthur of the hospital in Burma. He would, for brief moments, relive the stench and the horror, the filth and disease, the severed limbs and hideous gaping wounds . . . the mutilated youth.

For they were all so young. Chinese, British, Indian, American—did it matter? They were young and glorious, formed for noble purposes. Set down here in this jungle hell, to fight a largely invisible enemy, they died nightmarish deaths.

Trying to repair their mangled bodies, Arthur was unashamed of his tears when he failed.

The order had come to prepare for evacuation. The Japanese were on the defensive and the field hospital was moving closer to Myitkyina.

Before retreating, the Japanese threw all their reserve of shells at the hospital, located on a road spur northwest of the Mogaung Valley. A seventy-millimeter shell made a direct hit on the building used as a surgery.

Kenji, asleep in his temporary prison ward, awakened at the loud explosion. He shouted for the guard. There was no response, so he left his cot and crossed to the entrance of the hut. Outside all was chaos. The dark jungle night was aglow with the reflection of fire while men were running from the tent ward in the direction of the main road where the transports had been loaded before moving on. He could see litter-bearers running with wounded men across the uncompleted airstrip toward the end where the evacuation ambulances usually parked. Some wounded soldiers, their heads or limbs wrapped in bandages, were helping each other across the road into the protection of the jungle.

Kenji looked around. His guard had disappeared. Cautiously, he left the building, raising his hands in case a sentry should be waiting to shoot. Coming around the corner of the converted schoolhouse, he saw fire, and by its light, the demolished surgery. Lucky no one was operating, he thought. Then he remembered . . . the surgeons had been preparing to split up the supplies for evac, for dispersal in three aircraft. He had heard them discussing their plans when he was making smears. The Americans often forgot that he understood English perfectly, and were sometimes unguarded when they spoke in his presence. They treated him the way some people treat children—as if he were incapable of comprehending anything more complicated than a simple direct order. Even then, they always spoke to him in a loud slow tone . . . everyone except Colonel Hillman . . . Arthur, as he thought of him to himself. A man he would like to have had for a friend in another time, in another world.

Now, seeing that part of the surgery was caved in, he scurried across the muddy compound, oblivious of the mortar fire. No one challenged him, no one noticed him. The smoking building, a part concrete, part wooden structure, had been an administration center for the agricultural district. The Americans had borrowed it for the surgery when they set up the field hospital at this station.

Kenji squeezed through the obstructed door. The main roof had collapsed at an angle, crushing the improvised wooden operating tables. Kenji could see a man's foot protruding from the debris on the left. He picked his way over there gingerly, careful not to dislodge anything that was acting as a support for the rest of the walls or the roof. His hands were shaking uncontrollably.

He reached the foot and felt the ankle for a pulse. Nothing. Pushing aside broken tiles and thatch from the roof, he uncovered the rest of the body. A head, almost severed at the neck by a jagged edge of sheet tin from the broken roof, fell to the side. It was Captain Lucas. Kenji felt the gorge rise up in his throat. Stepping over the body, he went down on his hands and knees, peering under the partly demolished tables across the room. He could see arms and legs twisted in a jumble on the far side of the surgery, near the shelves where the autoclave and the instruments had been stored.

To get through, he had to crawl on his stomach along the cement floor. His chest incisions pulled, causing him to wince, but he kept going, inching along, favoring his injured left arm, which was in a cast, so was protected.

Colonel Hillman and Corporal Bailey had been packing instruments into individual surgical personnel kits when the bomb hit. This end of the surgery had a low, supporting crossbeam which had cracked in the center from the force of the main beam's collapse but had broken the fall and deflected the beam from the two men who lay there. Bailey had been hit on the head from behind by the lower beam as it sagged. His skull was split open, a nasty, deep cut in the brain, but he was still alive. Colonel Hillman had thrown himself forward in an attempt to pull Bailey down with him, so had taken the thrust of the falling beam on his left shoulder and the left side of his head, while his right hip and leg had been caught by the edge of the counter and twisted under him as he fell. Kenji was sure the leg and shoulder had been broken and he probably had a skull fracture. But he was breathing, he was alive.

The Japanese major tried to lift the smaller beam from the bodies, but it was wedged tightly in its v-shaped position, and probably was preventing the entire roof and wall on that side from caving in. He gently disengaged Arthur's arms from Bailey, and by pushing him to the right was able to slowly slide him, with less than an inch to spare, under the pointed apex of the inverted triangle formed by the broken beam. The shoulders were too large to pass through, but by depressing the flesh with his fingers, Kenji was able to work the body under the beam. Pushing Colonel Hillman's head to the right, Kenji was able to just clear the space between the beam and the wall with the colonel's body.

He slumped down, exhausted. His chest was burning from the effort. He felt like every breath was tearing something inside. Cradling Hillman's head in his arms, he looked frantically around for medical supplies. No glucose or plasma intact. The crates of supplies had been smashed. He would never be able to locate morphine or tetanus antitoxin in the ruined surgery.

He became aware that the shells were still whizzing overhead and exploding around them. The whine of bullets could be heard in the intervals between explosions. Breathing easier now, Kenji put his hands under Arthur's arms from behind and, pushing himself backward with his feet, started toward the doorway, dragging the colonel's body after him. He could feel the bones shifting in Hillman's left collarbone, so he moved the body up into his lap more so that he could grasp him around the lower chest. He was a tall man, but his body weight was not beyond Kenji's strength.

It seemed like hours before they reached the doorway. People were shouting and running, jeeps and trucks rolling off loaded with wounded. Evidently no one thought there was anyone left in the surgery, for none of the orderlies or litter-bearers or anyone was paying any attention to the building. Then Kenji realized why! They were near the fuel dump and a crate of small arms ammo was burning, shooting off exploding bullets in all directions. If one of them should hit the cans of gasoline, that would be enough to blow them all to hell!

With a wrenching effort, he turned the colonel's body over and got it up over his right shoulder. Pulling himself up by the doorframe, he groped his way out into the night, tripping over the muddy, rocky ground, but not losing his balance. He bent almost double, like a coolie, and just able to see his direction by lifting his head a little, he staggered across the clearing to the edge of a revetment, where some vehicles had been parked. There was nothing there now except four demolished jeeps. Bullets zinged overhead. The Japanese units were pulling out, he knew, emptying their batteries at the field hospital in that insane policy they had of sparing no one or anything. He would try to make contact with the Japanese unit. It was his duty to try to escape. But first he must rescue Lieutenant Colonel Hillman, who had saved his life. And what about Bailey? His wound was almost certainly fatal. Wouldn't it be pointless to further risk his own life to rescue the corpsman, when he would die anyway? The man who had wanted to shoot him or leave him to die unattended?

Just then, in the darkness, illuminated by the flash of an explosion, he saw an evacuation ambulance. He thought he had seen some medics carrying a litter toward it, but he couldn't be sure. It was about fifty yards away, maybe more. Keeping to the scrub at the edge of the jungle, Kenji made his way along the periphery toward the place where he imagined he had seen the ambulance. He had to stop and crouch down several times when the firing came from both directions. He felt ready to pass out from exhaustion. Oddly enough, the pain in his chest had dulled, and his arm and leg were numb.

He came to the edge of the strip and called out, "Medic! Litter-bearer!" He was afraid for a moment they might be Chinese. If so, he was as good as dead. He called again, still making his way toward the spot where he thought the ambulance had been.

Then he heard them. "O.K., buddy. We're coming. Hang on." A wave of relief surged through him. And then they were putting the colonel onto a stretcher. "Careful," he gasped, "his collarbone is separated and he may have a broken hip or leg . . . head injuries too." In the darkness, noise, and confusion, they hadn't noticed him. He had a bush shirt over his trousers, and because there hadn't been time, he had no POW or other markings. His insignia were still in the pocket on his bed, but if they searched him his ID would be found in his shirt. He was suddenly cold with fear.

They had Colonel Hillman on the ambulance by now. He could just walk away before they asked him any questions. What about Bailey? He walked the few steps to the vehicle.

"There's another man who was alive in the surgery over there. An orderly. He's pinned under a beam. I couldn't lift him out."

The ambulance driver had a dim penlight with which he was writing up Colonel Hillman's tag. The corpsman had started an IV and was giving the colonel an injection. The driver turned the penlight on Kenji's face.

"Hey! What the hell . . . ?"

"Corporal, are you going to try to save Corporal Bailey? I'll show you the way."

The corpsmen were unarmed, but they could see that he was too. The two litter-bearers ran with him across the clearing to the surgery. When they saw the fire next to the fuel supply, they hesitated.

"You have time. It won't blow up yet," Kenji shouted. They followed him in and he pointed to Bailey. While the two supported the beam, Kenji dragged Bailey out, clear of the impending wreckage. They placed him on the stretcher, looked at Kenji uncertainly. He was obviously sick and in pain. They looked at each other, shrugged, and ran off toward the ambulance with the litter. Later, when they were inching their way along the muddy, rutted motor road toward the clearing station, they tried to reconstruct what happened.

"I could swear that guy was a Jap!" said the driver.

"He spoke English like an American, Zack."

"Whaddaya suppose happened to him?"

"I don't know. Stretch thinks he saw him go into the jungle. It was too dark and smoky back there to see. Shit! I'm glad to get outta there. I was sure we'd had it when I saw that shack on fire near the gas dump."

Major Ranjit Kar had boarded the C-47 at Lalaghat, his throat dry with apprehension. This was his second flight into the combat zone, and his first had not been reassuring. They'd clipped a wing on the treetops when landing at the roughly cleared jungle strip and been forced to wait for a liaison plane, smaller and lighter, to rescue them. However, Major Gentry had asked for a meeting, and as a veteran of the Portable Surgical Hospitals in the Burma campaign, he could hardly be denied. So, here he was, skimming over tree-tops, while the pilot looked for the landing strip, hoping to avoid drawing enemy fire.

They bumped down, bounced over the rough terrain, the plane vibrating and shuddering as if it would come apart with the next impact. *Hé, Ram!* We made it. Ranjit closed his eyes in prayerful thanks.

Three hours later, his head whirling with the dozens of assorted lists and priorities he'd been recording during his discussions with Gentry and his aide, he was aware of an evacuation ambulance bumping over the airstrip toward their C-47, which was loaded to capacity with wounded, ready for takeoff. He shook hands with Gentry and turned to climb up into the plane when the ambulance approached, its horn honking, siren wailing. He turned as the vehicle pulled up and two corpsmen jumped out.

"We've got a critical evac here," one of them shouted, while the other ran to the rear of the ambulance.

"Sorry, Corporal," the pilot shouted, holding up his hand. "We're over capacity, and I'll have a devil of a time clearing that ridge! You'll have to wait for the next plane."

"But, sir, this is an officer . . ." the corpsman protested. Even as he spoke, they were unloading the stretcher and carrying it to the cargo door.

"You heard me, soldier!" the pilot barked. He was in no mood for arguments. This run always made him nervous. He'd had enough near misses with this crate.

Something about the bandaged figure on the stretcher arrested Major Kar's attention. He walked over to the unconscious officer. "Where are you from, Corporal?" he asked the ambulance attendant.

"Forty-ninth Field Hospital, Ningam . . . sir." He eyed the insignia on the Indian officer's shoulder. A Southerner, he never had figured out how to deal with these dark-skinned Asians who spoke with an intimidating hauteur and outranked him.

Kar examined the ID tag attached to the wounded man. He turned abruptly. "Captain, make room for this stretcher in there! That's an order!"

II

Calcutta   June 1944

It was summertime, hot and breezeless, and he was at Hillside, because he was lying on his back rocking to and fro in one of the swings on the veranda, or was it his hammock in the birch grove? There was too much light, it hurt his head, the blinding, hot rays exploding in painful bursts into his eyes, expanding in his brain until he thought his skull could no longer contain its contents.

The searing pain spread outward and down. Like a cloak, it enveloped him in its folds, creating an aura about him, setting him apart, suspended from tubes which acted as lifelines. He longed to sink back into the dark nothingness again where he had been free of pain. He was growing larger and larger, until, high above himself, he looked down at Arthur lying in pain, rocking back and forth under the hot light.

Then the light went out and he was alone in the darkness, shrinking back into himself, feeling nothing.

Voices. A strident cacophony rushing around him, moving in against him in waves, then retreating, endlessly repetitious, pulling him back, pushing him out, urging him to go, imploring him to stay, a harsh metallic droning in the dark void . . . hemustnot hemustnot hemustnot lethimgo lethimgo . . . Go, begone . . . no stay, you belong to us . . . he can't go, he KNOWS, he knows it all now, knows everything . . . cannot go back . . . must go back . . . lethimgoooo . . .

Sticklike fingers clutched at his arms, pinching with a sharp, burning pain which shot up from his hand to his shoulder. He floated up from the darkness through liquid waves of light. Beyond were images he could not bring into focus. Then, back down into the void again, and his mother was there, calling his name, laying her firm hand on his brow, keeping the voices away from him in the other place. Arthur, be brave, be strong, she urged him, injecting some of her strength into his spirit. Come back. They won't let me. They have no power over you. But she began to fade . . . Mother, Mother, he called, Help me . . . but she was gone and again there was nothingness. His Grandfather Isaac was arguing with the voices in the other place. Arthur called to him, but he did not hear.

Then there were other voices, calling his name urgently now. "Arthur. Can you hear me? Speak to me."

Whose voice was that? He knew that voice. Who was she?

He saw the lighter place again, high above him. He floated up toward it effortlessly until he saw through a round place, through the ripples of the aqueous layer, a woman's face, blurred, with a crown on her head and a halo of light around her, smiling at him, entreating him to come with her.

The pain was severe now, his entire body gripped in pain, rigid, in a spasm of intolerable pain. He was sinking back down again, down, down into the other place and the voices were friendlier now. Stay! Stay with us. We're your friends, you belong with us.

But he didn't want to stay now until he saw the face of the beautiful woman with the shining halo of light once again.

With a mighty effort, against the restraining girdle of his pain, against the clutching wooden stick fingers which kept clawing at him, he struggled upward until he was able to see the round opening of light far above him at the end of a dark tunnel. Through the tunnel on the other side of the opening was a small image.

It was Molly's face surrounded by a blaze of sunlight and she was wearing a crown. She smiled at him and called his name from such a great distance. Molly, I'm coming to you, he answered, but his voice couldn't be heard. Don't leave me, Molly. Don't leave me here. Wait for me. But she just smiled. And then she was gone and he was in the void again, knowing that he would be there forever in this never-ending purgatory of pain and darkness and nothingness.

The voices came back now, deafening, roaring, in a frenzy, assaulting him from all sides, the sound waves crashing up against him, lifting him up, twisting him with a dizzying velocity, thundering away to a high place, then boring down, down, down on him in a swirl of rainbow spirals, boring into the nerve center of his brain like a buzz-saw Arthurarthurarthurarthurarthurarthurrrrrrr . . . arthur.

It was abruptly quiet, still . . . calm, peaceful.

A clinking of metal on glass, a soft footstep, the rustle of crisp fabric. In the background a muted hum.

He opened his eyes slowly, blinking in the dim twilight, confused. He lay in a bed in a white room, small, alien, unadorned. The familiar, acrid medicinal smells of a hospital, overlaid with the odors of India—smoke, cardamom, sandalwood. The distant sounds of India. A high trilling woman's song accompanied by a wooden flute, horns honking, the muffled drone of countless humanity.

Firm, yet tender fingers took his hand, pressing themselves against his pulse. Arthur turned his head slightly, feeling a great weight, a pulling sensation.

A quick movement caught his attention. Someone gasped and spoke his name.

"Arthur!" He moved his eyes, grimacing with the pain of it, in the direction of the voice. There was her face, the face that had beckoned to him.

"Molly?" He spoke hoarsely, with thickened tongue, a mere mouthing of the word.

"Yes. I'm here, Arthur." He wondered why she was crying.

"Don't leave me, Molly. Don't leave me again. Stay with me."

"I won't leave you, dear. I promise. I'll stay with you." She knelt beside the bed and laid her forehead down on the counterpane next to him, still holding his hand, and whispered through her tears, "Thank you, Lord. Thank you, thank you."

For the next week Arthur floated in and out of consciousness, but he never returned to the deep comatose state or delirium of the past. His fever steadily dropped until it was near normal. Still unable to take anything by mouth, he was fed intravenously. Now, when he was awake for longer intervals, he was lucid, although too weak for conversation. As a young child may go to sleep and, upon wakening, accept the presence of someone he knows who was not there before, so he now accepted Molly as a natural part of what was happening to him. He became accustomed to the sight of Molly in her stiff white nurse's uniform, taking his pulse and blood pressure, giving him an injection, changing the bottle for the IV, giving him a sponge bath, and adjusting his pillows whenever he was awake. There were others, of course. Doctors, other nurses. He was mildly irritated, resenting it, when she wasn't there at his side.

With each day there was improvement in his condition and less pain. By the end of that week, he awakened late in the afternoon with a new awareness of his surroundings. He realized that his left arm was immobilized across his middle, his right hand taped to a brace so that he wouldn't dislodge the intravenous apparatus. His right leg was in a hip cast. He was thinking coherently. That was good. His head felt tight. He couldn't touch it because his hands weren't free, so he tried moving it from side to side, gingerly, prepared for more pain. It was all right. His left leg was unhampered and felt fine—the only good part left, he was able to tell himself with wryness. He felt a mild discomfort in his genitalia and, lifting his head slightly with great effort, he saw the catheter going down the side of the bed to a bottle for the collection of measured urine. He shifted his position, moving his shoulders, and this caused more than a little pain in the chest and rib cage. "I am one helluva mess," he said aloud.

"Arthur? Was that you?" Molly moved from the doorway where she had been standing, believing him to be asleep.

"Where am I, Molly?"

"In the Royal Victoria Hospital in Calcutta. You were injured in the bombardment in Burma. You've been unconscious, and delirious with fever."

"How long have I been here?"

"More than three weeks."

"Does my . . . family know I'm all right?" he asked.

She nodded. "They sent a cable to your wife as soon as you regained consciousness."

"How did I . . . I was in the surgery . . . where did you come . . ." He had so many questions to ask and it was a struggle to think.

"Don't talk, Arthur. You'll tire yourself. I'll try to tell you everything."

Molly told him that he had been rescued by a Japanese prisoner, curiously enough. According to the report of the ambulance team from the evacuation unit, an English-speaking Japanese, an officer they had later been told, had carried him back to them from the destroyed surgery.

"Kenji! Where is he?"

"They said he . . . left. I think he must have escaped, or just walked away. It was pretty crazy there. They let him go. He found you when the roof collapsed. He went back for you and the others who were in the surgery with you . . . but they were dead."

"Lucas . . . Bailey . . . *dead*. God!"

"Who was the . . . Japanese man?"

"He was my friend."

"A Japanese prisoner, your friend?"

"Yes."

She caressed his arm. "You have a dislocated hip, a broken collarbone, broken ribs, and a severe concussion. In addition to scrub typhus. Your fever was a hundred and five for so long. We were *so* worried about you." She smiled at him, the most beautiful smile he'd ever known. "You're going to be fine now."

"Can't keep a good man down," he joked. He was feeling very weak.

"You *are* a good man, Arthur Hillman." Their eyes held.

He dozed for several minutes. Then he opened his eyes, afraid she had left, but she was still there at his bedside.

"And you? How can you be here, Molly? This is India."

"I know—isn't it amazing?" She shook her head in wonder. "I've been here at the hospital, nursing, for the past six months, with the Red Cross. I was making up the nursing schedule when I saw your name, Hillman, A.F., Lieutenant Colonel, U.S. Army Medical Corps." She didn't mention that his condition was listed as "grave." "I thought it couldn't possibly be you. That would be too much of a coincidence. But I put it down for my assignment, and it *was* you."

"Then you've been here all along?"

"Yes, for twenty-four days."

"Will they let you stay with me?"

"For a while."

His eyes closed again. He was weary, so weary, and his head hurt, but happiness lay over him like a blanket of comfort.

Getting out of bed for a few minutes was more exhausting than any effort Arthur had ever made. He forced himself to walk a few steps several times a day, as soon as the hip cast was removed. It couldn't be done alone. He needed help. Molly, or one of the other nurses, supported him.

After a week of slow walks down the hall, he began to feel on the road to recovery, able to sit up an hour at a time. In the afternoons, when she had finished her shift, Molly would stay in his room with him, talking or reading. She had been pulled off his case as soon as he was off the serious list. Special nurses were not available except in the most critical circumstances.

Arthur was content just to have her there. "Have you been happy these years, Molly?" he asked her.

"Happy?" she repeated in a faraway voice. "Happiness is relative, Arthur. There have been good times and bad. Sean is in detention—that's a euphemism for prison, I suppose. He was detained because he'd given a speech the night before some fires were set in Dawson Street in government offices. . . . They accused him of being an incendiary. He's being held now in preventive custody, the idea being that since Britain's at war with Germany, he may do something disloyal, I gather. I was told there is no possibility of his being released until the war ends . . . so I volunteered to come here. I'm still an American citizen, you see, so they couldn't prevent me from leaving."

"I'm sorry, Molly," he said sympathetically. "That sounds like things have been difficult for you." Then he said, "You and Sean have never had any children?"

She shook her head. "No." He knew he'd trespassed.

Once in a while, Ranjit Kar dropped by to see him. He and Molly had gotten to know each other during the time Arthur was so ill. One late afternoon in July when the weather was oppressive and they were thankful for the air conditioner Ranjit had provided, Molly said to him, "I never thanked you for what you did for Mother. She was grateful Arthur . . . and so was I."

"Unfortunately, there wasn't much anyone could do. I think the operation prolonged her life—I hope it didn't prolong her suffering."

Molly shook her head. "She suffered only at the end, but she was pretty sedated. By the time I arrived, she hardly knew me."

"I heard you were in town. With Father John in Washington, and your mother in Sunbury, I'd lost touch. I didn't even know she'd died until Emily —my wife—told me she'd met you." He smiled, remembering.

"Yes . . . we met. She's so elegant, Arthur! Just lovely. The kind of woman who makes you look to see if you have a run in your stocking."

"I'm not so sure that's a compliment, Molly!"

"I meant it as one," she assured him.

"That was a shock, when she told me she met you." He laughed to himself. "What? What's so funny?"

"Oh, it's kind of embarrassing . . . kid stuff, really."

"Tell me!" she teased him.

"All right. . . . I drove over to your mother's house that night. I was parked across the street, just looking at a light in the window until it went out."

"*You?* You were there! I wish I'd known. I wanted to call you, just to hear the sound of your voice. If the phone hadn't been disconnected, I think I would have. Luckily, my brother Kevin and his wife were in the house with me. That kept me from doing anything foolish. I left as soon as possible. Stayed only two days, attending to legal things."

Arthur leaned his head against the back of the chair, allowing himself to just look at her. "Do you suppose there's some design in your being here? Do you think that God of yours played a part in this?" He reached for her hand. "I know you won't believe me, but I wouldn't have made it if it weren't for you. I kept trying to surface to see if it was really you."

"I believe you. I *do* believe it's part of a grand design. There's no other way to account for it. Why else was I sent to India, if not to help you?"

The first week after Arthur came out of coma, he awakened from a nap one day to see a strange captain standing at the foot of his bed. The officer smiled and said, "I'm awfully happy to see you with your eyes open, Colonel Hillman."

"Have we met?" Arthur had no recollection of having seen this man before. He was of medium build, sandy-haired, in his thirties, with an open, friendly face.

"I've met *you*, sir, but you didn't have much to say when I last saw you." He moved around to the side of the bed and pressed Arthur's hand. "I'm Richard Blumenthal. I'm a rabbi."

Then Arthur noticed the insignia of the Jewish chaplain on the young man's lapel. He grinned—at least, he thought it was a grin. "I didn't know we had last rites."

Blumenthal laughed. "They say the return of a sense of humor is a sure sign of recovery."

The rabbi brought a chair to his bedside. "I've been looking in on you daily, but I was up in Assam last week, so I missed your big coming-out party." He sobered. "I thank God that you're on the mend, Colonel Hillman."

Arthur nodded. "I thank him, too, Captain Blumenthal."

"Is there anything I can do for you? Anyone I can write to—your wife—parents?"

Arthur thought about it. "My mother would appreciate that, I'm sure. My wife . . . ?" What would be Emily's reaction? he wondered. He hadn't heard anything from her in a very long time. How had the news of his being wounded affected her? "I don't know, Captain . . . she's not too religion-oriented. It might . . . worry her, make her think I'm worse than I am. . . ."

The chaplain understood, perhaps more than he revealed. He rose, preparing to leave. "I mustn't tire you. I promised the nurse I would stay only for a few minutes. If ever you want to talk about anything, Colonel—or if I can help you in any way, I hope you'll let me know." He added, as an afterthought, "I'm not only a rabbi. I've got a masters degree in psychology."

Arthur smiled weakly. "That's an interesting combination . . . should come in handy. I'd like to hear more about it sometime." The short visit had drained his energy. He closed his eyes and drifted off as Chaplain Blumenthal silently left the room. A minute later, when Molly looked in, Arthur was sound asleep. For a long time, she stood there, watching him.

Richard Blumenthal came to see him almost every day. He usually brought something to amuse or entertain Arthur . . . a tattered copy of *Life* magazine, an autobridge game, which he offered to play when Arthur felt up to it. One Friday afternoon he arrived with a thermos bottle containing homemade chicken noodle soup and some braided white bread which he said was *challah* but bore slight resemblance to the real thing.

"Wherever did you get it?" Arthur asked. The soup was almost as good as his mother's, as he remembered it.

"I know a Jewish nurse from the States. She came over to the bungalow I share with some other officers and fought her way into the kitchen. Our cook had fits, but she managed a pot of soup before he threw her out. I'm not so sure about the *challah.* She said they don't have the same kind of flour or yeast here. I thought you might enjoy having some, though."

"You bet! Thanks, Richard." Arthur liked the chaplain. He was the first nonvintage rabbi he'd ever known.

Richard Blumenthal told Arthur he'd graduated from Amherst, then studied at Harvard for a masters degree in clinical psychology, intending to go on for a doctorate.

"Somewhere in there, I felt this compulsion to study religion. I think it was a fulfillment of my own needs, more than a desire to minister to others."

"That's the psychologist in you speaking," Arthur replied. "You remind me of a priest I know. One of my good friends. He's always trying to rationalize why he's a priest, explain to himself why he's doing what he's doing."

"You're good friends with a priest? And yet you told me I'm the first rabbi you've ever been friends with!"

"Yeah . . . strange, isn't it? All the rabbis I've ever known had the dreariest personalities, truthfully. Sincere, admirable, but not your fun kind of guys." He appraised the chaplain. "You're different. You almost make me want to go to services."

"In that case, as soon as they spring you from this joint, I'm going to take you to a service such as you've never seen! It'll teach you something about Judaism."

The Indians assembled at Beth Shalom looked no different from the men and women Arthur had seen in the twisting bazaars or from the window of the train during his slow crossing of India. They were dark-skinned, handsome people, soft-featured, dressed in white to greet the Sabbath—the women in simple saris drawn over their heads, the men in the loose-fitting shirt of the Bengali merchant, except for those in the uniform of the Indian Army.

It was a small meetinghouse, occupying the first floor in a garden compound only a short distance from the hospital. Arthur and Richard Blumenthal removed their shoes at the door, walking in stockinged feet on the white cotton dhurries that covered the floor. They sat on a bench to one side of the *bimah,* which was placed in the center of the room, its ark of plain wood carved with the tablets of the Ten Commandments, singular in workmanship and design. An eternal light hung on a brass chain, its flame casting a flickering shadow on the ceiling high above.

All the women sat together, behind a wooden screen. Prayers were in progress, although few men were present. Arthur noticed men in the uniforms of the Allied Services—some Australians, a British lance corporal, and, off by himself in one corner, a Chinese officer, wrapped in a huge prayer shawl, *bentshing* and *davening* in earnest, his eyes closed, clasping his prayer book to his breast.

Richard was watching his reactions with bemused interest. Arthur smiled at him, leaning over to whisper, "I see what you mean. We're everywhere, aren't we?"

Richard nodded.

A distinguished-looking, light-skinned Indian, as simply dressed as the rest, came over to them. He shook hands with Richard and said, "Would you be kind enough to conduct our service this Sabbath eve, Rabbi Blumenthal?" His accent was pure Oxford.

"I'd be honored, Sir Samuel. May I present Colonel Hillman of the United States Army Medical Corps . . . Sir Samuel Benavram, the leader of this congregation."

"We are privileged to have you in our midst for *Shabbat,* Colonel Hillman. I hope you will accompany Rabbi Blumenthal to my home for our Sunday reception." Arthur thanked Sir Samuel, explaining that he was still convalescent.

"As soon as my doctor permits it, I'd be delighted."

The Sabbath service, as Richard Blumenthal had promised, was the most unusual he'd ever attended. It was a Tower of Babel, as Bengali, Urdu, Hebrew, Sanskrit, English, and Chinese prayers were offered by the various participants. Richard led the service in modern Hebrew, which was only faintly similar to the Sephardic dialect used by the Jews of Calcutta. Arthur joined in when he could follow, with prayers in the Ashkenazic Hebrew he had learned in his family's Conservative synagogue. For the most part, he listened and observed, the chants and customs of the Indians in the congregation often as strange to him as if he were in a Jain temple. Judaism, he was discovering, was not the familiar, orderly ritual that he'd known all his days but a many-faceted doctrine, as adaptable as it was universal.

As he looked around him at these Jews of India, they seemed to him as he imagined the Jews of biblical times had appeared—reminding him that the Jews were essentially an Eastern people. Their women, behind the open-work screen, saris covering their heads, were much the same as he had pictured Naomi and Ruth in the ancient land of Israel.

When Sir Samuel, as the leader of the congregation, carried the largest Torah scroll through the assemblage, followed by others bearing smaller Torahs, Arthur was moved as he watched the men, old and young, reach out with their prayer shawls to touch and kiss the sacred scrolls. He couldn't remember ever having felt more a part of his religion.

After the service Richard accompanied Arthur back to the Royal Victoria. This was the first time Arthur had been permitted to leave the hospital, and he was feeling shaky by the time he left the rickshaw, supporting himself with a cane.

"They're really Indians, Richard. How do they happen to be Jewish?"

"There are several groups of Jews in India, Arthur. Some, they say, go back to Solomon's time. Egyptian Jewish merchants traded with India—some of them presumably stayed and left descendants. And, no doubt, many are remnants from the beginning of the Diaspora. They've intermarried over the centuries, become assimilated. In Cochin, they are very dark-skinned, and shunned by some of the lighter-skinned Jews, who came at the time of the Spanish Inquisition." He shook his head sadly. "Whenever man has the opportunity to develop a class system, he will take advantage of it. India, of course, was the perfect society for that, with its castes. So . . . you've got a group of affluent, light-skinned Jews who remain an exclusive minority, another group of poor Jews who eke out a living as artisans or laborers, and then you have your urban, educated Jews, who practice law, are officers in the Army or successful merchants."

"Is Sir Samuel among those?"

"No. Sir Samuel is a different case altogether. His grandfather came here from Persia, made a fortune as the manager of estates for a wealthy nawab, and married an Indian woman of high caste who converted to Judaism. Sir Samuel's is a hereditary title, negotiated for his father by the nawab's son. It's a real tale of Arabian nights! Wait until you see his estate. He holds open house for Allied servicemen every Sunday evening. It's quite a sight! The whole community turns out."

The following week Arthur left the Royal Victoria Hospital for the faded splendor of Calcutta's Great Eastern Hotel, where officers were quartered. He had somehow convinced a skeptical Medical Corps major that he should remain in India instead of being rotated back to the States.

It was not long before Arthur had been assigned to administrative duties at the Institute of Tropical Diseases, taken over by the Armed Services. Soon he was able to work for two or three hours at a stretch.

Even to himself, he would not admit his reasons for staying on.

Major Ranjit SuRajat Kar liked to arrange picnic parties and excursions to one or another of his family estates in the Bengal countryside beyond Calcutta. Early on a Sunday morning he would drive by to call for Arthur at his hotel, then Molly at her guest house, and they would be off before dawn, driving through the streets of Calcutta—broad, tree-lined boulevards set along the perimeters of parks, twisting alleyways where the homeless slept on pavements, wrapped in threadbare blankets.

On one such morning, shortly after Arthur's discharge from the hospital,

they crossed over the newly constructed Howrah Bridge. Confronting them
was a scene lush with the endless expanse of rice paddies under cultivation.
Wherever they looked, India was at work. At the first glimmer of light in the
sky, men and women began their labor in the fields. Even small children had
their appointed tasks, herding water buffalo or donkeys, stopping to gape and
smile engagingly at the travelers as they sped by in Ranjit's jeep.

They passed many villages along their route where, despite the picturesque
quality of rural life, they were appalled at the filth and squalor. A village was
often no more than a cluster of mud-brick huts with thatched roofs, a tiny
bazaar, a miniature shrine, and a well—usually an open cistern in which
children splashed while women filled their water jugs.

"The community bathtub is also the community drinking fountain!" Ranjit
remarked.

"Can't they be made to understand that an open well becomes polluted and
causes disease?" Arthur asked.

Ranjit shrugged. "That's the way they've always done it, and they will
continue to do it that way until the government takes steps to improve sanitation."

Molly was enchanted with the slim, delicate-looking women in saris who
carried earthenware jars on their heads, striding barefoot, with arms swinging
freely at their sides, their hips swaying in a fluid, continuous rhythm. "India
is the most beautiful land I've ever seen, Ranjit. Although I must confess, the
condition of the poor, the malnutrition, the beggars, the cruelty of it all often
destroys the beauty for me."

"Yes," he answered. "For me, too, Molly. But one can't go about bleeding
all one's life. We become inured. . . . And that is the greatest cruelty of all."
He sighed and shook his head. "India . . . I doubt any one person can ever
know India—*all* of India. Certainly not a foreigner. We are *many* nations, not
one. Family, Community, Religion, Caste. More quarrels, more contentions,
more divisions than common bonds. . . . There are literally hundreds of
dialects, a score of languages . . . a Bengali is as much a stranger in Trivan-
drum as you would be. It is Gandhiji's mission to bring us to a sense of our
oneness. If we can forget our communal and caste differences long enough to
cooperate, we *will have* our independence."

More than once, Arthur had discussed British rule with Ranjit. Ranjit was
an ardent admirer of Mahatma Gandhi. In Gandhi's dream of an independent India, Ranjit saw the solution to all of his country's difficulties, social
and religious.

"This country has been kept in the Middle Ages because it would have
been impossible for the British to continue to exploit Indians, keep them
subjugated, if they were educated and modernized. People like my father, of
course, benefit from the Raj. But, for the whole of India, it is time to throw
off the yoke."

They crossed a stone ford over a stream on the fringe of a village on

Ranjit's family land. A group of unwhitewashed mud huts lay at some distance from the stream in a clearing.

"That's the untouchable quarter," Ranjit told them. "It's downstream from the caste part of the village, so that the stream won't become desecrated."

Women wrapped in bright cotton saris, pulled through their legs to hike up the skirts, were standing in the stream washing clothes, beating them on the rocks to clean them, then spreading them on grass to dry in the sun. Almost every woman was pregnant. There were dozens of small children, entirely naked or wearing only short shifts which exposed their bottoms, running barefoot along the edge of the stream. The women smiled broadly when they saw Ranjit, making the sign of greeting. Arthur noticed that only the youngest women had smooth skins and all of their front teeth. A wrinkled, painfully thin old crone stooped by the side of the brook, picking over a basket of *chik* patties, the cooking fuel made of dried cow dung and straw.

"How old would you say that woman is, Ranjit?" Arthur asked.

"She is perhaps forty, forty-two," Ranjit answered.

There was a shocked silence. "I don't believe it . . . are you sure?"

"Oh, yes, Arthur. Few women live beyond that age in the villages. She was married when she was a child, had her first baby when she was less than fourteen, and gave birth once a year until she no longer appealed to her husband. She eats no meat, has barely enough rice to fill her stomach each day, probably has had amoeba, trachoma, childbirth fever, malaria. She's one of the hearty ones . . . she survived." He spoke harshly. "That's my India. . . . That's the Raj. They're born, they reproduce, they die. Karma." He gave a short, bitter snort.

No one spoke for several minutes. They looked out over the fields to a grove of sal trees. Ranjit smiled affably. "We mustn't be downcast, chums! This is a holiday. Let's forget about India's problems, the war. We'll have a rollick."

Arthur felt a deep grip of pure affection for Ranjit. He's one of those people, my kind of people . . . like John Riordan and David Benjamin . . . like Kenji. I'm lucky. I need that sort of friend, wherever I am, even in a war. Kenji, what happened to you? You risked your life to save mine. Are you still alive, somewhere in the Burma jungle, that hell on earth? Most likely not. The war, the blood, the screams, the broken bodies, the hideous diseases, the steaming, rotting, putrid, infested foulness. Did that really exist on the same earth as this peaceful hinterland?

He turned and sought Molly's face. *I did love you so much. I think I still do. Or do again. Oh, God. What am I going to do? Nothing, I suppose.*

Just see this through to the end, he thought, and go home and be thankful that I saw her again, and knew Kenji, and know Ranjit . . . and am alive.

It was mid-September when Arthur and Molly went along with Chaplain Blumenthal to Sir Samuel Benavram's palatial residence in the north of Calcutta. A tropical palazzo, it sprawled in an immense park amid formal gardens, sprinkling fountains, and boasted a small zoo and an aviary with every species of bird known to India. Richard told Arthur and Molly that, in accordance with traditional Judaism, the Benavram kitchen distributed food to hundreds of poor every Friday before the Sabbath.

As the sun sank in a hazy sky, green lawns glittered with elegant Indian women in a rainbow of saris. Their husbands were polished and Western-educated, for the most part. Arthur met officers and enlisted men from all of the Combined Forces . . . all except British. Ah yes, he mused, I'm beginning to get the picture. They don't mingle with the natives.

"I understand you and Miss Tower knew each other before the war," Richard Blumenthal mentioned when Molly was in conversation with Sir Samuel's wife.

"*Mrs.* Tower . . . Yes, we both grew up in the same town in Pennsylvania." Arthur studied his drink. "The priest I mentioned, my friend . . . he's her uncle."

Richard nodded. "Oh, I see." Was it Arthur's imagination, or did the rabbi look relieved? "They should be sending you home soon, shouldn't they, Colonel?" he asked.

Arthur met his gaze levelly. "I refused a medical discharge, Captain. I'm feeling pretty good now, and I'm confident I can make myself useful in Calcutta until I'm well enough to return to active duty."

Blumenthal left them early. He was being sent up to Assam, to Margherita, to relieve the Jewish chaplain who'd been there for a year and a half. "He has malaria. They're shipping him home," the rabbi explained.

"I'm sorry to see you go, Richard. Let me hear from you," Arthur told him as they shook hands.

"Don't forget, if you ever need to talk . . . I'm a good listener. I'll be in touch from time to time."

If you only knew how much I would like to take you up on that. "Good-bye, Richard . . . take care of yourself," was all he said.

Arthur's hip and shoulder were throbbing from standing so long. Molly noticed him wince when someone jostled them.

"Arthur, I think we ought to go, too. This is too much for you."

"I *am* rather tired. I felt so great when we started out." They said good-bye to their host and walked through the formal gardens to the ornate wrought-iron gates where a jumble of cars were parked, their drivers squatting in a circle, smoking *bidis*. It was getting dark. They found a taxi and climbed in. Arthur leaned back gratefully as Molly gave the address of his hotel.

"I think we'd best get you home first, Arthur. I'll keep the taxi and go on alone."

"No, Molly, I'll see you home. You shouldn't take a taxi alone at night."

"Why ever not?"

"Women don't in India. It's an invitation to trouble." And as she protested, "Really, I'll drop you first."

When they reached her lodgings, she said, "I have some sherry, if you'd like to come in . . ."

He hesitated, then: "Yes, I'd like that."

Molly's rooms were on the second floor of Banarjee's Guest House. They sat on the hard couch in the sparsely furnished, darkened sitting room, sipping sherry and speaking in low voices.

Arthur's mind was hardly on their conversation. He watched the play of expression on Molly's face as she spoke, noting the shadow of her long lashes on her cheeks whenever she looked down thoughtfully, delighting in the small dimpling on the right of her chin when she smiled, recognizing the lines that had begun to form on either side of her mouth, but which seemed to add to her charm. The insouciant bloom of the exquisite girl he had loved had been replaced by a richly mature beauty which he found even more alluring.

"Arthur, you're not listening to me. I'll bet you haven't heard a word I said."

He shook his head. "I'm sorry, sweetheart . . . I was thinking. . . ." The old endearment slipped out, although he was unaware of it.

In the dim light, he didn't notice the color form in her cheeks. "What were you thinking about?"

He did not answer immediately. "I was remembering about us . . . how it was . . ." He paused. "How it could have been. . . ." It was the first time he had dared to give expression to the forbidden subject.

A terribly sweet sadness settled on her, a sigh escaped through her parted lips. "I have so often thought of you. . . ."

In the silence their eyes spoke to each other, of love remembered, of pledges made and promises broken.

"Why did you leave me?" His voice was bleak.

"I had no choice. They were so strong, so powerful. I was too young . . . I thought I couldn't fight them." She had a faraway look in her eyes. "It couldn't have been any other way. Even now, I know that."

He was too weary to contradict her. In any case, what would it matter now? "Is there nothing to be done?" he asked. Then, before she could answer: "No. You have a husband and I have a wife. We would both be fools to forget that." For the briefest moment a light of hope had shone from Molly's dark blue eyes.

She watched him . . . the contours of his strong face, the tenderness at the corners of his mouth, the fatigue lines which had been etched under his eyes and down his cheeks told of the deep sensitivity that lay beneath the surface fortitude. When he had been so ill, she had been free to touch him, to comfort him. Now he seemed remote, belonging to himself.

He turned and saw her studying him. She was still so beautiful—the most beautiful woman he had ever known. He leaned forward and softly caressed her cheek. "I had better be very careful," he said, "or I'll find myself hopelessly in love with you again."

He withdrew his hand. "I'd better go." They gazed at each other breathlessly. Molly's eyes were wide, unblinking, as if awaiting a judgment. Arthur's heart was thudding in his breast, his mouth felt dry, there was a weakness in his thighs. With a strangled moan he seized her and pulled her roughly against himself, crushing her mouth with his own, bruising her lips, forcing them apart. There was nothing of softness or tenderness or even devotion in his kiss. It was an anguished need—a need to erase the memory of war, of death, of horror. And the years of loneliness and longing.

Her arms held him tightly, her mouth welcoming his fierceness. Her hands moved over his head and face. She pressed her tear-streaked cheek against his. "Oh, my darling, my darling . . . you're the only one I've ever wanted."

But it was no good. It was too late now. His fingers hurt her shoulders as he put her away from him.

Breathing hard, his mouth a grim, straight line, he said, "You made your choice fourteen years ago, Molly. That can't be undone."

She sat there, the blood draining from her face.

He left her then, slamming the door behind him, leaden with fatigue. Molly heard the taxi drive away. She felt a rush of heat spread from her face to her shoulders. Mechanically, she undressed and got into bed. A hard numbness had settled over her. For a long time she stared out through the mosquito netting at the dark shapes in the room. Then tears seeped out of the corners of her eyes and slowly ran down the sides of her cheeks.

III

Calcutta   October 1944

Two weeks had passed since Arthur had seen Molly. He had purposely avoided going over to the Royal Victoria Hospital, knowing he'd probably meet her there. . . . What was the point? He tried not to think about her.

He was doing some surgery at the military hospital attached to the Institute of Tropical Diseases. Mostly repairs from hasty battle-station work, the results of poorly trained surgeons working under impossible conditions. The patients were brought into Calcutta before being flown home. Arthur found that he could work a full day now without feeling unduly fatigued. . . . The sooner he got back to his unit in Assam, the better.

Thanks again to Major Ranjit Kar, Arthur had moved into his own bungalow—an unheard-of luxury. It was near Garden Reach, complete with staff of cook, bearer, sweeper, *mali*, and *chowkidar!* A friend of Ranjit's had moved to Bombay and agreed to rent the bungalow to Arthur for six months. He'd grabbed it, tired as he was of hotel living.

In the late afternoon Arthur strolled out onto the veranda of the Officers' Club for the Combined Forces, intending to order a cold beer while he read several letters from home which had taken months to reach him, by the looks of the envelopes. *Chupprassis* were rolling up the *chiks* which shaded the porch, now that the sun was casting long shadows over the garden compound, not baking everything with its scorching, relentless rays. It was the end of monsoon; still, the air hung heavy with moisture. He was now accustomed to the heat of Calcutta, yet his shirt stuck to his back, even in this relatively cool time of the day. Heat and humidity were always on your mind in Cal.

He sat down at a small table off to one side and, after waiting for a few minutes, reluctantly clapped his hands for the bearer—a custom he loathed, but like so many things in India, he found it better to just go along rather than try to fight the established ways.

After ordering his beer, he spread out the letters, trying to organize them chronologically so that he could read them in proper order. It had been a long time since he had heard from Emily. Now, seeing her distinctive handwriting, he felt a flicker of dread.

> . . . I was relieved to hear from you, Arthur, and to know that you are recovering. I cannot tell you how frightening it was to receive word that you had been "wounded in action"—that sounded so ominous . . . they really shouldn't do that to wives, inform them in such a heartless manner.
>
> . . . The children seem happy, although they miss you terribly. Arthur, you should really try to write more often. They're getting old enough to receive their own mail, and although you're no doubt busy with your work, your children should be just as important.
>
> . . . Bill Beckinger is still in Washington, at that same desk job. He has all sorts of pull and can arrange for you to be sent back. But I'm afraid to suggest it without your approval. . . . Wouldn't it be just as well to come back to the States? We're having a war here, too. Sometimes I think the *real* war is on the home front. We have everything rationed—butter, sugar, coffee, meat. . . .

Arthur sat looking off in space at the green lawns with the *malis* working at the flower beds. The "whump" of tennis balls echoed from the grass courts to the left of the lawn, beyond the high hedges. What was there to say to Emily? The letter could have been from a stranger . . . a not very nice stranger. She sounded truculent, neglected, as if the war were a personal affront to Emily

Grant Hillman herself. And he *had* written to them, all of them, often. What was happening to his letters?

There was another letter from Emily. This one short and breezy, happier in tone. She was going to Washington to visit friends for a week. She would probably see Bill while she was there. What was that all about? Well, he supposed he shouldn't object to her being friendly with Bill Beckinger, considering that he had gone places with Molly. . . .

There were three more letters. A short one from his daughter in her careful, schoolgirl hand, sweet and loving, telling him about her classes in first aid.

> . . . I can help you with bandaging when you come home and are a doctor again, Daddy. . .

Tears sprang to his eyes, and he felt a lump in his throat. Ah, he did miss them so, his children! Even Emily . . . the old Emily. . . . He was so confused. This rotten war! That was the problem. He chided himself for his self-pity. Here you are, sitting in the lap of luxury in Cal, almost healed, with barely a limp to show for it. How many of those kids you were sewing up can say the same? Many of them are dead, many of them back in battle . . . most of them so young, they never even had the chance to marry and have a family.

He quickly read the letter from Nate telling him that his mother and sisters and their families were all well. They had received his letters and were reassured that he was fully recovered. Nate spoke about Leisl.

> She's a wonderful woman, Arthur. So brave. She knows her husband, brother, and father are probably all dead, but she won't give up hope. Her little boy, Eric, has made a fairly good adjustment. He's seeing Irv Goldberg for psychiatric help. Nice guy—he refuses to send a bill, even though I've offered to pay it. What should I do about that? What a question! You're over there in CBI, and I'm asking you about professional courtesy in Wilkes-Barre! Is that crazy? Take care of yourself, buddy. We all love you.

What the hell's wrong with me? he thought, his eyes blurred with tears. He decided to put the letter from David Benjamin away until later.

Ranjit Kar came across the lawn in his tennis whites, carrying a racket, a towel draped around his neck. "Arthur! I thought I saw you sitting there. I'm just going to have a shower and change. Will you wait?"

"Sure, Ranjit. I'll meet you in the bar. We'll have a drink."

"*Tikke.* Won't take a minute." He went off to the locker rooms. Arthur signed the chit for his beer and went inside to wait for Ranjit, glad to have a diversion.

He had become friendlier, if anything, with Ranjit Kar since Colonel Taylor had informed him that his associating with Indians was offensive to some of the British officers.

"That's *their* problem, Roger," Arthur had answered in anger. "I'll damn well choose my own friends."

Since then he had been treated coolly by a few of the British staff, whom Ranjit outclassed by a mile. Arthur thought, with some amusement, that they'd be falling all over themselves to be Ranjit's friends if they realized who he was. To the class-conscious British, a Rajkumar—a prince, the second son of a wealthy Rajah who had been knighted by His Majesty—was an acceptable Indian, one worth cultivating.

Ranjit came out of the locker room dressed in the dark grayish green of the Indian Army, looking like a Hollywood version of a handsome Indian prince dressed for war. His smile was blinding white in a face so arresting that it stopped short of beauty, his thin moustache clipped to perfection, his dark eyes, under straight shaggy brows, compelling.

"How are you, old boy? I haven't seen you for a spell."

"I'm fine, Ranjit. I've been working over in the Institute of Tropical Diseases. It's good to be busy again. I'll be glad when I'm back on active duty . . . another few weeks. What will you have, Ranjit?"

"Whiskey-soda for me. You?"

"I'm taken care of. They don't have bourbon, so I'll stick with beer."

The bearer served their drinks. Groups of British and American officers wandered in, occasionally glancing their way. It was unusual to see a white officer sitting in social conversation with an Indian, even in a club supposedly open to all commissioned men of the Allied Command. This was the former Gymkhana Club, denied to Indians—even princes—in palmier days.

As Arthur was leaving the club, about to enter his car, an attendant came running after him. "Colonel-sahib, there is a call for you!" He went back into the office, just off the main lobby.

"Colonel Hillman . . ." It was Meena Chaudhary, the executive secretary to the director of the Royal Victoria Hospital, a friend of Molly's. He and Molly had been some of the few Westerners to attend Meena's recent marriage, an elaborate ceremony performed by a Brahmin priest in an illuminated garden.

Meena sounded as if she were crying. "What is it, Meena? Is something wrong?"

"I've been trying to reach you *everywhere*. . . . There's been a fire, Colonel. At the hospital. A very serious fire." Her voice broke. "Molly is missing. She can't be found anywhere."

There was a roaring in his ears, a heavy darkness descending on him. He heard her voice, echoing from a great distance, *"Colonel Hillman? Can you hear me?"*

He was running out the door, moving as fast as his lame hip would permit. "Royal Victoria," he shouted to his driver. "Hurry! *Jaldi, jaldi!*"

Molly had been nursing in the ward of the most seriously injured: head wounds, amputees, chest and stomach cases, those least likely to make it. The ward was completely burned out. There had been a butane-gas fire which quickly got out of control. The ward, where oxygen was being used, was especially vulnerable. Half of the ward's beds contained corpses, burned beyond recognition.

The hospital wing was a shambles. Fire fighting, like every other procedure in India, was done by hand. Water pressure was notably poor in Calcutta. The hoses had been too short. There was every reason imaginable, every excuse, for the tragedy. Meena went with Arthur through the soggy ruins. It was impossible to determine where Molly had been. Numbly, he stepped over blackened debris, looking for signs of a nurse's white uniform, dreading the possibility of finding it. All the beds along one side of the ward had been empty, fortunately . . . yet, Arthur turned back to look again. There were charts on all of them. The charts were scorched, blackened, illegible, *but there had been patients in those beds*. Where were they now?

"Meena! Meena?" he called to her. She was out in the corridor now, speaking with some of the staff. Everyone was in a state of shock, hushed and serious. "Where are the other patients from this ward? The ones from the empty beds? All the beds along the right side are empty. There were patients in them—at least, it looks like there were."

"Yes, Colonel. Every bed was full."

"There are no bodies there. Were they evacuated?"

"I don't know." She looked questioningly at the others. They didn't know either.

For two hours Arthur was in torment, while they tried to locate the missing patients. The Royal Victoria was a huge H-shaped building with four wings extending from the main hospital, which had three floors. One wing had five floors, the others were under construction. The wing which had been so badly damaged was the oldest.

If they found those missing patients, Arthur thought, Molly might be with them. She may have helped to evacuate them before the fire got out of control. He clung to that hope.

Meena came running toward him, out of breath. "Colonel, it's terrible! They say almost no one got out alive from there. Most of the patients died of smoke inhalation. They've set up a temporary morgue over in the south wing in an unfinished ward. Shall . . . shall we go look there?"

"You stay here, Meena . . . I'll go," he said. "You've been through enough today."

He wanted to be alone when he found her body.

A British orderly was there, checking ID tags and records. He gave Arthur permission to go through to make a body identification. Arthur walked alone down the long, narrow hall and into the room where dozens of bodies lay on the floor in rows, each covered with a piece of canvas. The feet were exposed, with tags attached. With all of the death and horror he had witnessed these past two years, the sight hit him with an impact almost physical. God, please don't let her be one of them, he prayed.

Slowly, he walked along, stooping now and then to read a tag. Each one was marked with an "M" for male. At the end of the second row, a smaller body was completely covered. He lifted the canvas. Small feet . . . an "F" on the tag . . . his heart raced in panic. . . . Steadying himself, he knelt down on one knee and read the notation: *unidentified female nurse; need dental records.*

Steeling himself, he leaned over to draw the covering from the woman's head. The shock of it was too much for him. So terribly burned, so horribly disfigured . . . could this be Molly? Lovely Molly? Yes, he knew it could be . . . probably was. Gently, he replaced the canvas over the body, closing his eyes in grief.

He stood, bereft, wondering where to go. Then he leaned against the wall, laying his head against his forearm, allowing the tears to flood his eyes. Why had he permitted them to remain estranged? Why had he treated her so callously. He loved her. Despite everything, she would have been comforted to know that . . . and now, it was too late.

Arthur sat on a crate, his shoulders slumped, not wanting to leave this place. He heard workers' voices in the hospital compound, jabbering in Bengali or Bihari—whatever one of India's thousands of dialects they used—untouched by death and tragedy, which was a familiar part of their lives. The ever-present honking of automobile horns, a siren, the call of a *muezzin* in a nearby mosque.

There was a murmur of conversation from the outside corridor. The orderly was speaking with someone . . . soon he would be asked to leave. Arthur heard footsteps, someone was coming into the temporary morgue, walking down the aisle between the row of corpses, toward him. The footsteps stopped. Arthur looked up.

Molly stood there, disheveled, covered with soot, her uniform torn and soiled, one hand bandaged. She sucked in her lips, struggling for composure. Then her face crumpled, and she began to cry. Arthur went to her, folding her into his arms, holding her to him to comfort her.

He rubbed his cheek against her hair, aware of the smoke odor in his nostrils. "I thought you were dead," he whispered. "I thought . . . are you all right?" He looked at the bandaged hand.

She nodded. "I'm so tired."

"I'm taking you home now." He supported her with his arm as they left the darkened building and emerged into the crimson of a Calcutta sunset.

"Arthur, old boy, you and Molly ought to get away from Calcutta for a spell during the heat. In the old days, none of us ever stayed. You can use my house in Darjeeling. It's *pukka*, Darjeeling. Great spot for romance, too!"

"Ranjit, Molly and I didn't . . . that is, we aren't . . ." Arthur began.

Ranjit threw up his hands. "Come, Arthur. You owe me no explanations. I just meant that it would be nice for you to get out of the heat. The place is empty up there. I like friends to use it . . . keeps the servants on their toes. They tend to slack off when no one's there."

Arthur smiled at Ranjit's words. "In that case, Ranjit, I may do that. . . . I *am* grateful for your hospitality." Then he added with firmness, "But explanations or no, I think you should understand that Molly and I are good friends, that's all. While it's true that we once meant more to each other, that was long ago . . ."

"Yes, I know," Ranjit brushed it aside.

"How could you know?"

"Molly told me. When you were in the hospital, and she didn't expect you to live. I found her crying one day . . . she needed a friend to talk to, and I just happened along." Ranjit shuffled the cards. "Who has the crib?" Crisp, businesslike.

They were playing cribbage in the Officers' Club. The two of them were the only people in the lounge adjacent to the lobby this hot evening.

Ranjit's words excited Arthur. He wanted to ask more. More about what Molly had told him . . . about how she'd acted at the hospital when she'd thought he was dying. *I would have died, for sure, if she hadn't been there.* The only thing that kept him coming to the surface was wanting to see her face again, like a swimmer drowning, fighting to get to daylight, to air. . . . And, afterward, when he had come out of the coma, he remembered how she refused to let any of the Indian nurses change his IV or give an injection . . . standing over the orderlies when they had to lift or move him, to be certain they didn't dislodge a catheter. . . .

"Your play, Arthur." Ranjit was watching him with a small, private smile, drumming his fingers on the table, but not with impatience. Arthur realized he'd been daydreaming.

The big fan turned overhead, doing little to stir the oppressive humidity. A bearer came over to the table and removed the empty glasses. "Bee-roo, sahib?"

"No more beer for me. What about you, Ranjit?"

"I'll have *nimbu*-soda. You, too, Arthur?" The bearer moved away quickly and silently, the stiff coxcomb on his turban bending under the spinning fan.

"How would I get to Darjeeling?" Arthur asked, after they'd been served the cold lemon drink.

"Train," said Ranjit. "No need for you to worry, Arthur. I'll do the needful. I can get you a compartment any time you say. It could take forty-eight hours to get there, with the delays. The cars are off-loaded for portions of the way to make room for supply and troop transports. I'll see that you and Molly are met at Darjeeling."

Arthur looked at Ranjit from under lowered brows. "I think it's better if I go alone, Ranjit."

Ranjit shrugged. "Suit yourself, Arthur. It seems a bit selfish to leave Molly behind to suffer in the heat of Calcutta, when she could be enjoying the delightful mountain air of Darjeeling." He pronounced it musically, dahr-JEE-lingh, drawing out the syllables, while he absentmindedly toyed with the cribbage pegs, pushing them in and out of the holes. "It poses a little dilemma for me, I think."

"Why so?" asked Arthur.

"You see, the thing is this." He spread his hands. "I've already invited Molly to go! A problem, isn't it?" His eyes were twinkling, his smile beatific. Never was his English more clipped.

"Ranjit . . . you're not a prince at all. You're a crafty old banian, and not to be trusted for an instant!"

Arthur's heart was singing and his head taking wings, even as his inner self told him he was embarking on troubled waters.

They were in the foothills, the train moving slowly on an incline, rounding a sharp curve, so that they could see the front end from their car. Ranjit had been wise to insist they have a compartment. They had spent the night stopped at a siding while supply and troop trains moved by slowly and interminably in the dark, windows blacked out. They hadn't bothered to put on nightclothes. This wasn't exactly the Orient Express.

A fan spun on the wall opposite, pointed at a spot above their heads, turning the sooty air. Conversation stopped as they grew sleepy, falling off into short naps. Arthur woke to find Molly's head on his shoulder. He slipped his arm around her, contented to have her close to him. Her eyes opened as he looked down at her.

The train entered a long tunnel. They were in the most complete darkness. He bent his head to rub his cheek against hers. His lips sought her mouth, moving softly, slowly, in a kiss gentle and tender. As his arm tightened around her, drawing her closer, his other hand moved to her face, the fingers lightly touching her closed eyelids, moving over her hair, seeking the nape of her neck. Their lips drew apart for a moment, and in the darkness he felt her breath against his mouth.

"I love you," he whispered, so low she may not have heard him. Then they were kissing again, wanting never to stop. If only that long, dark tunnel could go on forever, enclosing them in its depths so that they need not ever do anything but stay in each other's arms, kissing like this. . . .

The tunnel came to an end and so did their embrace. They sat silently, his arm still around her, his other hand holding hers. Molly's head was turned away from him. She looked out the window at the terraced hills moving by, afraid to let him see the love in her eyes.

Arthur turned her slender hand over, stroking it with his own, looking at the lines in her palm, wishing that fortunes could be told and fairy tales come true.

At Siliguri they changed to a miniature train with a toy engine. Creeping, it wound through lush green tea gardens. It climbed along a tangle of fragrant, flowering jungle growth . . . tall dark green cryptomeria, stunted gnarled ilex, magnolias, and rhododendrons—magenta, pink, and white giants. The steeper the climb, the slower they chugged, until their engine lost a race with barefoot boys who ran beside the narrow roadbed, laughing and gesticulating at them.

Below Darjeeling, they alighted at Rajnager, where Ranjit's smiling major-domo, Parta Sing, was waiting. Borne aloft in *dandees* carried on the shoulders of men from the hills whose calf and shoulder muscles bulged from their years of scrambling up the mountainside—they arrived at the house, a white stucco, red-roofed summer palace clinging to the edge of a cliff, with a matchless view of the eternal snows of the Kanchenjunga from each of its many balconies.

Lunch was served on the lower veranda, facing away from the brightness of the afternoon sun toward an enclosed garden laden with hanging vines.

"It's like a fairyland!" Molly exclaimed. "I didn't know there was a place anywhere as beautiful as this."

"Hard to imagine one man owning all of this—not to mention his other houses. And he's only a *second* son!"

"Ranjit once mentioned his wife and children, but he never really talks about them. Have you met his wife, Arthur?"

Arthur shook his head. "No, I haven't. He told me she lives in Bombay now. Supposedly because of the war. But once, when we were sitting around having a drink, he said she doesn't get along with his family and that was the real reason why she left Calcutta."

"In-law problems!" Molly nodded. "That's a serious matter in India, so Meena tells me. An Indian wife has to live with her husband's family, and if she doesn't like her mother-in-law, her life can be really unbearable."

"Ranjit's such a nice guy, you'd think that would make up for the rest of his family," said Arthur.

A constant stream of bearers clad in Ranjit's family livery, some of them wearing the flat round toque of Nepal, served luncheon. Parta Sing approached when they had finished their coffee, after standing quietly in the shadow of the doorway until they noticed him.

"Rooms are ready, colonel-sahib, memsahib," he announced.

They followed the bearer up a broad stairway to the floor above, the entire surrounded by covered balconies, open to the winds. He led the way to the north end of the house through a pair of double doors to a luxurious suite, consisting of a high-ceilinged parlor, rich in oriental motif, and two sleeping chambers, each with its own dressing room and marble bath. Pale Lhasa wool carpets of Persian design covered the floors, shimmering where a shaft of sunlight beamed through the open shutters of the balcony. Molly sat in an intricately carved Tibetan chair with ivory inlay, appearing comfortable, satisfied, and entirely at ease . . . an ease that Arthur envied her.

Their bags had been unpacked and the contents placed in teak almirahs in the dressing rooms. Parta Sing moved a basket of fruit, adjusted a curtain, puffed up a pillow, and finally stood, stately in his Nepalese turban and hennaed moustache.

"Is every wishes met with satisfaction, memsahib?" he addressed Molly, having decided that she was in command of the situation.

"Yes, Parta Sing. Everything is *perfect,*" Molly assured him. "Thank you."

His lined face reorganized itself into joyful, smiling crags. "You'll be wanting tea?"

"Yes. You may serve it on the veranda at five o'clock. Meanwhile, we shall have a rest," Molly instructed.

"Very well, memsahib." He bowed and left, closing the double doors quietly.

Arthur had been looking out at the terraced hills of tea plants. He turned. "I think I'll take a bath before my nap. I feel a little grimy from the train. What about you, Molly?"

Molly was enjoying a private joke. "A bath? Yes, that sounds like a good idea." She walked quickly into her room and shut the door.

Arthur lay in the huge marble tub, each muscle in his body relaxing with the soothing effects of the warm jasmine-scented water. Total luxury, he thought, taking in the fluffy monogrammed towels with the princely crest, the hand-milled English bath soap, the silver-backed military brushes on the well-appointed toilet stand. It had been a good idea, after all, to come up here. The air was clear and clean, the breezes mild. He felt better already, just getting out of the oppressive humidity and heat of Calcutta.

And Molly? Had that been a good idea? Probably not. But the happiness of being here with her lent a special magic to Darjeeling.

After a doubtful glance at the lethal-looking straight razor, he shaved, using the silver shaving mug and brush provided. Arthur enjoyed the aromatic coolness of the sandalwood shaving soap. When he was finished, he splashed himself with astringent cologne from an ornate silver-encrusted bottle with a French label. Slipping on a robe which he found on the shelf, he walked across the large, sumptuous bedroom to the balcony, which overlooked a valley to the snow-covered peaks of the Kanchenjunga, shimmering in the brilliant sunlight. Wisps of clouds skimmed the edges of the massif against the clarity of the cerulean sky. Taking a deep breath of pure highland air, he had a sense of well-being which he hadn't experienced in years.

Arthur heard a step behind him. Molly came out on the balcony, which her room shared with his. She was in a dressing gown, looking fresh and rosy from her bath.

"I just had to follow my nose to find you," she laughed.

"I couldn't resist all those expensive-looking bottles! Is it awful?"

"No . . . it's sort of"—she gave a little shrug—"nice, appealing. . . ." She moved toward him, her smile a little uncertain, a look in her eyes, so vividly blue, that there was no mistaking . . . and he knew that nothing could prevent what was about to happen.

Arthur took her face between his hands, softly tracing its contours. He was overcome with an emotion so profound . . . love, yes . . . and more than that. Desire, certainly . . . but something apart from that, too. A wanting, a needing, a *compulsion* to be with this woman, anywhere on earth where the two of them could spend the rest of their lives together.

He spoke from his heart, as best he could. "There are no words to tell you how much I love you, my darling. I never did stop loving you. I never want to. I don't know what will become of me if I can't go on loving you." He let out a long, uneven breath as he took her in his arms.

With something approaching a prayer of gratitude, Molly's eyes closed. "I'm only yours," she murmured. "I've never belonged to anyone else. . . . Love me, darling! Please, let us take whatever we are permitted in this awful world."

He drew her to him slowly, savoring the moment. They kissed in a dream, unable to believe that this could be happening to them at last . . . to be there together, holding each other. How much of life is chance . . . that he had come to India . . . that he had been caught in the bombardment . . . that he had been brought to Molly. All this, he thought, as he pulled her down on the bed with him. And then, he thought of nothing . . . except Molly . . . Molly . . . Molly. . . .

"My love, my love," he called. And she responded with a shattering intensity, twining her arms and legs about him, kissing and touching and moving with him. Swept up on a tide of feeling beyond anything that had gone before, they heard no sounds, save for the other's voice, felt no awareness, except of each other. They existed in a time and place apart, until washed up on a shore of tranquility.

Gently, they became aware of the late afternoon sun filtering through the shutters into the room, a myna bird calling, the distant music of a gourd instrument in the hills.

"My God!" he whispered, looking at the beautiful face, its frame of shining dark hair spread across the pillow.

She smiled then, the smile of a thousand years of secret knowledge . . . womanly, triumphant.

A place inside him where there had been torment was at peace.

"There is the abode of the gods," said Parta Sing, his extended arm tracing an arc from east to west. "The mountains of snow are sacred. . . . From here is the beginning of all holiness."

Parta Sing had accompanied them to a place from which the splendor of the Himalaya was said to be seen at its best advantage. They had hoped to view the elusive Mount Everest, the world's highest peak. Like Kanchenjunga and Makalu, it lay remote and unconquered in Nepal, a land closed to foreigners. The Kanchenjunga dominated Darjeeling. It had appeared from behind its cloudy veil for them, but Everest hid herself from view like a shy bride.

"My village is there, beneath Sagarmatha, Everest." Parta Sing pointed.

"You are from Nepal?" Arthur asked, surprised.

Parta Sing's bright eyes danced in his leathery face. "Yes! I am Gurkha," he said with pride. "Many years, Parta Sing is being Gurkha Scout."

Arthur was thrilled. The Gurkhas were legendary. He had never before met one. "And, now . . . ?"

"Now my army service is finished. I am having pension. Many daughters for dowry . . . many sons. So I am serving the Rajkumar."

They walked from the carriage to a lookout where Parta Sing pointed out a high rope suspension bridge in the distance. "That way to Sikkim. Only by donkey or walking, to Gangtok," he explained. The bridge swayed in the wind, the only link between looming peaks, hundreds of feet above the yawning chasm separating India from Sikkim—another forbidden kingdom.

This place of mystery had cast its spell upon them. A richness of sights and sounds surrounded them, a voluptuousness of mood. They wandered through the streets of Darjeeling, along the Mall to the bazaar. They stopped to look at precious gems at a jewelry shop where they sat on cushions while they drank the local tea.

"Just see! Beautiful jewels for madam . . ." The jeweler had spread an array of sparkling gems on the silk-covered table before them. Rubies, sapphires, emeralds, peacock opals . . . great smoky topazes and amethysts. Arthur wanted to buy some for her . . . would have done so, if Molly hadn't protested. He returned alone the next day when Molly had accompanied Parta Sing to the fruit market, leaving Arthur to rest.

November the sixth was Molly's birthday—in a week. "Ah, good day, sir," the jeweler greeted Arthur when he parted the curtains to the shop. Removing his shoes, he entered and seated himself on a pillow. The tea ritual again. . . . Arthur was impatient, but in India one must observe the formalities.

We're in too much of a hurry, he thought. Here, life was timeless, suspended in motion.

The packets of stones were brought forth once again. "I am particularly interested in a topaz, as a gift for the lady," Arthur explained.

"Topaz is not good," answered the merchant.

"You mean, they're not good quality?" he asked.

"Oh, no, sir! Excellent quality. All stones are *pukka,* first-rate."

"Well, then, I don't understand. . . . Why do you say that the topaz is not good?" Arthur was puzzled.

"Topaz, it is bad luck." He put his head to one side, in pleading. "Maybe you like star ruby or lovely sapphire?"

"I never heard that topazes are bad luck! The lady's birthday is in November, so topaz is her birthstone."

"The lady is born under the sign of Scorpius! Then it is auspicious for her, the topaz!" He clapped his hands happily.

Out came the topazes. Hundreds of them. First, in shades of white, blue, and aquamarine, which the jeweler told him were not precious and, to Arthur, did not look at all like topaz. Then a selection of pinks and browns . . . still not what he had in mind.

The jeweler disappeared, leaving his "brother" to chat with Arthur and keep an eye on the gems. Several minutes passed, and Arthur was beginning to wonder whether he was wasting his afternoon when the jewel merchant returned with several little silken bags. He untied each, spilling out three golden jewels of precious topaz which caught the light overhead, reflecting it in glints of sparkling purity.

"The round one!" exclaimed Arthur. It was a beauty, the largest, most golden of the three. "How much is it?"

"For you, sir, a special price . . ." He placed the topaz on a balance and put little weights on the opposite pan of the scale. He gave Arthur a figure which, translated to dollars, seemed exceptionally reasonable. Arthur would have agreed immediately, but he remembered Ranjit's teasing when they stopped on Chowringhee once to buy a cane.

"You disappoint him by not bargaining, Arthur," Ranjit had said. "You rob him of the pleasure of the transaction. He would have only disdain for you if you didn't try to bring down the price!"

So Arthur gave a counter-offer for the jewel, and the jeweler mentioned another figure, higher than Arthur's. They agreed on the next round of bids, and had another cup of tea to seal the bargain.

"Now," said Arthur. "I'd like to have it set in something . . . a . . . an ornament, for her to wear."

Off they went, through the bazaar, to the gold merchant. Another cup of tea, another discussion about what to do with the beautiful stone. This merchant was a slender young man, with the dreamy look of one who appreciates things for their pleasure-giving qualities. He took Arthur to a rear room where four men sat cross-legged on the floor, working with gold, fashioning earrings, necklaces, and bracelets.

"Lover's knot!" The merchant took a piece from one of the artisans. It was a twisted rope of eighteen-karat gold, delicately scalloped around a ruby.

"Yes! That's exactly what I want," said Arthur. A lover's knot . . . how perfect. "But I need it in one week."

"It shall be done," said the goldsmith.

In the mornings after breakfast, arm in arm, they would walk down through the tea gardens to a rocky place at the side of a stream, foamy where it rushed over the crenellated stones in its bed, clear jade in its still pools. Arthur had bought a stout walking stick in the bazaar. His hip still pained him when he walked uphill, although he found the going easy on the way down.

Sitting on the ledge, they looked up to the silent sentinels of the snow-covered Kanchenjunga, diamond white in the bright morning sun, shadowy blue in its crevices as afternoon approached. They grew to love the majestic pinnacle in its various moods and colorations. Pink and crimson at sunset, mauve at dusk, it loomed above them. Even in the dark of night they felt its presence.

There, at their stream, in the shadow of the Kanchenjunga, Molly told him about Sean. Quietly, without self-pity, she repeated the story of her wedding.

"You mean . . . all these years, throughout your marriage . . . he's been impotent?" First, he was astonished. Then, aghast.

"Yes." It was a telling whisper, revealing her pain and loneliness.

"My poor darling!" He enveloped her in his embrace. "There's been no one else?" he asked, hating to say it, hoping for her sake there had been.

She shook her head. "No one else. There couldn't have been anyone else, except for you." She looked off in the distance. "The only part that is hard to bear is that I have no children. I had thought when I married Sean that at least I would be able to have children. . . ."

He seized her hands. "Molly . . . darling, *listen* to me! We were *meant* to be man and wife, you and I. You know it as well as I do. My marriage to Emily isn't working—hasn't worked. It's not her fault . . . it's no one's *fault.* I don't think it ever had a chance of being a truly happy marriage for either of us. We'll end up with a divorce regardless, I'm certain. . . . You can get an annulment!" She turned her head away sharply. "Please, my love! *Please!* Say you will, Molly. It's not too late for us. We can have all the children you want together. . . ." In all his life, he had never prayed for anything so much.

But Molly was frightened at the idea of an annulment. "It's such a serious step, Arthur!" she told him. "I know I have grounds for an annulment. No prior knowledge on my part of Sean's disability . . . a deception, although *he* certainly didn't intend it to be. The facts were withheld from me by a bishop of the Church. . . . That would be hard to prove, since the bishop in question is dead now." She looked down and sighed. "I suppose nonconsummation of the marriage would be the argument, even after all these years. I'm reluctant to put Sean through all that, Arthur. I'm not sure how he'd react at this stage in his life."

"If he cares anything for you, Molly, he wouldn't want to stand in your way. He would want you to be happy."

"I know. But we've been through a lot together, and he's been more than decent." She spoke with sudden feeling. "He's had such *rotten* luck. . . . It's *so* unfair! Sean's not an *incendiary!* He's a real patriot . . . an idealist! He's not against Britain so much as he's *for* Ireland." Her voice softened. "He's really an exceptional man, Arthur."

Arthur just swallowed and let it drop for the time being.

He told Molly about his children. "They're wonderful, Molly! The boys are twins, but so different, one from the other. Jeff is Emily's son—good-looking, self-assured, does everything well. Bobby is much quieter, sort of a dreamer. I never can figure out what's really going on in his mind. He's the sweetest kid, though . . . gentle and friendly. I wish he didn't defer to Jeff so much. It would be better if they went to separate schools, I think, but they always want to be together."

She watched his face as he spoke about his children, loving the play of emotions there, reading the depths of his devotion to them. "And your little girl?" she asked.

"Ellen is adorable. She and I have always had a special relationship, even when she was a tot." He gave a gentle laugh. "I suppose fathers always have a soft spot for daughters. . . . I remember you used to tell me that you and your father had that closeness."

It was a mistake to raise that. "Yes . . . we did. And it broke my heart to lose him."

Molly asked him about Emily, hesitantly. He praised Emily for her creativity, her sense of beauty. ". . . I don't know how she feels about me now, in all honesty. But I'm pretty sure she no longer loves me."

Molly couldn't imagine any wife of Arthur's not being in love with him. And his children . . . she couldn't get them out of her mind. "Imagine the effect on them if you were to be divorced."

"They'd still be my children, Molly. Plenty of other children have divorced parents—and worse. Think of all the children whose fathers aren't coming home from the war."

"That's different, Arthur. There's nothing anyone can do about that."

They talked in circles, accomplishing nothing. Finally, he said, "Promise me you'll at least make inquiries about an annulment, darling."

"All right. I will look into it, Arthur. That's all I can promise for now."

He had to be content with that. He had a sure feeling that he couldn't push too hard. That if he did, she would slip away from him again. And he knew he didn't want to go on without her.

Arthur took Parta Sing into his confidence. "Parta Sing, Monday is madam's birthday. Do you think we can plan something? A special dessert, perhaps?"

The kindly bearer was delighted. "Oh, yes! For memsahib, something very special. I tell cook. It shall be done."

"I'll need you to take memsahib away again, Parta Sing. So that I can go shopping without her," he added.

Parta Sing wagged his head in affirmation. "There is a special place for women only . . . a shrine for fertility."

"Uh . . . perhaps it would be better to take her to Observatory Hill, Parta Sing. I don't think she would care for the fertility shrine."

"Very well, colonel-sahib."

On the sixth of November, Arthur awoke with the sun. Molly was curled in a ball, her head buried in the pillow. He placed another blanket over her, thinking she looked cold. Arthur showered, shaved, and put on a terry robe. Then he opened the shutters to let in the cool morning light.

He sat on the bed as Molly stirred, kissing her awake.

"Ooooh"—she burrowed into the mattress—"I don't want to wake up. I was having the nicest sleep."

"Happy Birthday, darling," he said, nuzzling her neck.

Molly's eyes flew open. "I knew there was a reason why I wanted to sleep this day away. Thirty-eight! What a terrible old age to be."

"Come on, get up! I have a great day planned." He pulled her from the bed.

When Molly entered the sitting room, she found it transformed into a flower-filled fairyland. Sprays of meadow blossoms, fronds of trailing vines heavy with sweet-smelling white jasmine, great bunches of rhododendron, poppies, narcissus . . . in every space was a bouquet of colorful, fragrant blooms.

She clasped her hands together, her face rapt. "Arthur! It's . . . it's a dream!"

He took her by the hand, leading her into the room. "It's real, I assure you. . . . Come see what else is here."

On the banquette he had arranged the results of his second shopping expedition, spreading them out in careless array, like a trove of treasures.

There was a sari of purest silk, tissue thin, ice blue, richly embroidered in thread of pale gold. "It's from Banaras," he told her. "The best saris are supposed to come from there." He draped it around her, standing back to admire her. "You make it even more beautiful, my love."

There was a turquoise and silver ring with a tiny secret compartment for poison. "For a lady to use to protect her honor from invading hordes from the north," he teased. Reaching behind a pillow, with a theatrical flourish, he spread a large shawl of the softest, most featherweight Kashmir wool, in taupe and embroidered in silk. "It's from Ladakh, of the rarest wool from the chins of mountain goats . . . very special, madam!" Selecting a silver ring from a jumble of bazaar jewelry in a beggar's bowl shaped like an Aladdin's lamp, he took a corner of the shawl and inserted it in the small ring. Slowly, he drew the entire shawl through the ring. "It's called a ring shawl." Molly held her hands up to her cheeks, flushed with excitement.

Carried away with his role, Arthur produced a russet caftan of raw silk, a prayer wheel from Tibet, a necklace of amber, a small, carved sandalwood Lord Krishna playing his flute . . . "Here, smell it . . . isn't that lovely?" He held it to her nose as she inhaled the delicate scent of sandal. A little carved sheesham box lined in velvet was full of semiprecious polished cabochon stones of jade and amethyst.

"What do I do with them?" she asked wonderingly.

"Nothing . . . just look at them. I thought they were pretty." He reached for a gilt Tibetan Buddha, shaking it. "Hear that rattle?" She nodded. "There are prayer scrolls and supposedly precious gems inside . . . at least, the man who sold it said they were gems. I imagine they're pebbles, but the only way to find out is to open it and that would spoil it."

A pair of gold leather sandals with curled-up toes, an abacas, some worry beads. . . . In all, there were fifteen presents. "One for every year I've missed," said Arthur.

Throughout, Molly had been overcome, uttering small exclamations, her eyes wide like a child's on its first Christmas, unable to take it all in . . . allowing him to drape and adorn her, pile her lap full of exotic finery. By the time he produced a little silver flacon of pure lotus extract "from the Vale of Kashmir," anointing her temples and wrists with the scent, Molly had grown completely silent, bowing her head to look down at her folded hands.

Arthur knelt beside her, putting his hand under her chin, tilting her face up. The sapphire-blue eyes were liquid with tears.

"What is it, darling?" he asked.

"I've never been so happy in all my life," she cried, throwing her arms around his neck. "You're so wonderful! In all the world, there's no one as wonderful as you."

He kissed the tears from her eyes, murmuring soft words of love. Then he took her back to bed.

As if the gods wanted to give Molly a gift on her birthday, when they reached Tiger Hill, the filmy clouds hiding Everest's summit lifted like a curtain in the midday sun, revealing the magnificence of earth's tallest mountain, resplendent, majestic.

In the bazaar, as they passed an open stall, a turbaned man wearing a jewel in one ear called to them in an oily voice, "Come have your fortune told, madam. All things are revealed in the stars." Molly stopped.

"Come on, darling," Arthur urged in a whisper. "Let's go, before he starts working on us."

But it was already too late. The moment the man knew he'd caught their attention, he pursued them. "The lady-sahib must know her good fortune, sir," the man said in a wheedling tone, hurrying over to them, while children surrounded them and bystanders stopped.

"I am the most famous astrologer in all the Himalaya!" He handed them a card on which was printed in Sanskrit, Nepali, and English, "Swami V. L. Ramakrishna, Doctor of Astrology."

Arthur shook his head, but Molly was intrigued. "Oh, Arthur, it'd be fun. Let's see what he has to say."

Less than a moment later they were seated on dirty cushions in the curtained interior of the swami's shop. The air was thick with incense and other odors—cardamom, *ghee,* and unwashed bodies.

The swami removed his coat and donned a flowing garment which could have used the services of a *dhobi.* He seated himself opposite them.

"What is the date and exact moment of madam's birth?" he asked.

After a hesitant look at Arthur, she answered, "I was born on November 6, 1906, but I don't know the exact time. It was sometime early in the morning, before dawn."

"Sixth November," he exclaimed, his hands gripping each other in apparent ecstasy. "Then today is the anniversary of your birth! It is auspicious to consult the stars on one's anniversary."

From the recesses of a closed cabinet, he withdrew two thick, much-thumbed volumes with curling pages. Muttering, he peered closely at the pages as he turned them, stopping now and then to run his finger along a line of print here, a paragraph there. They watched him and glanced at each other, feeling foolish, wondering how best to extricate themselves from their situation. It was close and dusty within the room, and the odors were overpowering.

With a grunt, the swami closed his text and again seated himself on a pillow. He took Molly's hands, examining her palms, then, asking her to turn profile, he sketched some lines on a pad of paper. He dropped his head in meditation, placing his fingertips to his brow, closing his eyes.

Arthur's mouth was twitching with amusement. He dared not look at Molly. Just then the swami began to speak.

"You have known sorrow, madam, yet you wear a face of contentment. . . ." Molly's restless expression relaxed as the swami spoke in a hypnotic voice. ". . . sorrow breeds joy . . . and joy breeds sorrow. The heart that has not experienced sorrow cannot appreciate joy."

He frowned. "I regret to say that there are more sorrows ahead of you . . ."

All this talk of sorrow was getting to Arthur. Even though it was nonsense, he didn't like it at all . . . it was Molly's birthday and he had planned a day of unadulterated delights for her. Not this foolishness. About to interrupt and tell the man they were finished, he stopped, for he could see Molly's face and she was listening intently to the astrologer.

"Someone you love will have a great sickness, far away from you . . ." He paused. "Madam will live a long and full life . . . much love will be yours. . . . You will travel far . . . over the black water. . . . There you will find your ultimate joy and contentment."

The swami opened his eyes and looked at Molly as if he had just awakened from a trance. It was all part of a cheap act, Arthur thought.

"Come, Molly," he said quickly. He gave the swami some rupees, and they left the shop. "That place was filthy! I couldn't wait to get out of there. That's an experience we could have done without, sweetheart. Let's go have lunch." He guided her across the Mall to the Everest Hotel. "First thing I want you to do is go wash your hands," said Arthur. He was annoyed because he could tell that Molly's playful mood had been broken by the unfortunate visit to the swami.

After lunch, Arthur asked Molly to sit in the hotel lobby for a few minutes. "I have to go on a quick errand. Wait here for me. I'll be back in ten minutes." She didn't even ask where he was going.

They took a carriage back down to Rajnagar to their house, where silence reigned. Except for one of the assistant bearers who came out to attend them at the entrance, everyone was at rest. Tired after their long morning, they too went to their rooms for a nap.

Arthur knocked on Molly's bedroom door. "Are you ready, darling?" he called.

Molly opened the door. She was wearing the new russet caftan of raw silk with the gold sandals. Her high cheekbones lent an indefinable elegance to her face, emphasizing her wide-set eyes with their thick fringe of lashes. She had piled her hair into a loose chignon.

"Every time I see you, I fall in love all over again," he said, kissing her.

"Arthur, you just saw me half an hour ago!" she laughed.

"It seems much longer to me." He held a flat velvet box. "I have a birthday gift for you."

"But, darling, you've already given me so many gifts. Fifteen gifts in one day . . . I've never received so many beautiful things all at once."

"This is special. I had it made for you. Here . . . turn around." He placed the topaz, in its lover's knot of gold hanging on a heavy gold chain, around her neck.

"Ooh, Arthur . . ." Molly let out her breath. She lifted the heavy pendant in her hand, looking down at it. "I don't know what to say! I've never had anything like this before. . . ."

"Then it's about time you did," he said, kissing the tip of her nose.

"It's extraordinary! I didn't know topaz could be so magnificent."

"Not half so magnificent as the one who wears it." Arm in arm, they walked down the stairs to dinner.

A fire had been lit against the chill of the evening. Parta Sing served them a drink called *chhang,* a fermented potato liquor, much stronger than they suspected, they realized after a few sips. With the *chhang* they had *pakoras* and *papadams,* the delicious batter-dipped, fried vegetables and wafers flavored with ground chili pepper. Between the cheerful glow of the fire and the inner glow from the drink, Molly became animated.

Parta Sing announced dinner, leading the way to a room they hadn't seen before. A small, circular, turreted balcony, enclosed in glass, it hung out over the northwestern corner of the house, with an unobstructed view of the moon-silvered mountains of eternal snows. Ablaze with candelabra, the room was heated by a brass stove radiating warmth. Peach-colored linens covered the table. Someone had created a painstaking decoration of flowers on the table, laying the blossoms on the cloth in intricate designs. Starched napkins stood on end, twirled in spirals, and tucked into the overlapping layers were tiny rosebuds of crimson, pink, and yellow. At attention, Parta Sing anxiously awaited Molly's reaction.

Molly gasped. "Parta Sing! Did you do that for us?"

He smiled modestly. "Yes, memsahib. It is mogul banquet. When my Colonel Hilliard-memsahib had birthday, always we make mogul banquet."

"How kind of you to do that for me. I am honored. Thank you . . . thank you so much, Parta Sing." His ageless face was wreathed in smiles.

For dinner they were served barbecued pheasant, spit-roasted lamb, black *dhal,* sweet chutney, yogurt, a puffy bread of the mountains, and pickled vegetables. A chilled, light mango custard soothed the tongue after the hot spices.

"What a feast," Arthur groaned. "I can't eat another bite."

But Parta Sing was not finished. In he marched, followed by two bearers holding shining copper trays on their shoulders. They paraded around the table, ceremonially setting down a rich dessert made from boiled milk and sugar, covered with a tissue-thin layer of hand-beaten pure silver foil. On the second tray was a burnt-almond layer cake festooned with elaborate birds and flowers of spun, caramelized sugar. It was, without doubt, the most fantastic culinary triumph.

"Parta Sing, you must ask cook to come in here," said Molly. "This is incredible."

Cook was an old man with snow-white hair and great white moustaches. He had the round face and Mongol features of the Himalaya, and when he smiled, his eyes disappeared into his face. He, too, had spent his life serving the Raj in a garrison.

Arthur recalled what Ranjit and Kenji had said to him about Asian countries throwing off the yoke of Western colonialism. Not everyone in India would benefit when the British left, though. Those who depended on the English for their livelihood . . . what would become of them?

On their last day they visited all their favorite places. Two weeks had passed with a tranquility Arthur could not have imagined. Calcutta, with its teeming streets, the sweltering jungle of Burma, the war . . . for two weeks he had been able to forget.

The long morning walk had tired him, but Arthur was pleased that his hip had strengthened from the exercise of these two weeks.

After lunch they retired to their suite for a nap. Arthur lay back and folded his arms under his head. Molly thought he had fallen asleep.

"I'm going back, Molly."

She felt it, the cold dread in the sudden quickening of her heartbeat, the prickly feeling in her cheeks. "Back?" It had a constricted breathlessness.

"To Assam."

"You're not well enough yet!" she cried.

"I'm well enough."

"You tire so easily. You'll get sick again. Are they *making* you go?"

"No, they're not making me go. It's something I have to do. I'm needed there."

"You're needed in Calcutta, too. You're doing important work there."

"Nothing someone else can't do as well. The surgeons up there have been going twenty-four hours a day without a break for too long. They're short-handed. If I go up there, that'll relieve one or two men." He was quiet for a few minutes, thinking. "The tide is turning, Molly. There's going to be real action . . . I'm sure of it."

But Molly wasn't listening.

She was thinking of the swami's words: *Someone you love will have a great sickness, far away from you. . . .*

That night Arthur was restless. Finding it impossible to sleep, he went out on the balcony. The blue-black vault of the night sky stretched endlessly, enclosing him in an echoing stillness broken only by the distant barking of wolves in the hills. There was no moon to light the dark, yet billions of stars gleamed like jewels in the vastness overhead with a brilliance all their own. Here, at the top of the world, he felt a part of the endlessness.

Molly came out silently, leaning against him, laying her head on his shoulder. He placed his arm around her without a word, feeling her a part of himself. They stood there under the stars until she drew in her arms from the cold. Reluctantly, they returned to their bed.

His lips moved over her body in a celebration of love. She was all beauty, all truth, everything in life he wanted. There was a poetic perplexity in her spiritual nature and her intense sensuality. He loved nothing more than to bring her to undreamed-of heights of passion. Yet a part of her remained forever pure and virginal. Their love, for him, was proof that in a world filled with fear and hate, there was also hope.

Bearing silent witness to their ecstasy were the wild, snow-drifted peaks of Kanchenjunga, suspended on the edge of the universe, far from the intrusions of a cruel and violent war.

Back in Calcutta, a promotion awaited him . . . full Colonel. And, after the first of the year, Colonel Hillman would have his command . . . medical officer in charge of all military base hospitals, Bengal. He would be headquartered at the Royal Victoria.

He and Molly had snatches of time together. She was overwhelmed with the serious cases pouring in from the evacuation hospitals. He was preparing to leave for Lalitha.

While they had been in Darjeeling, the Allies had crushed the Japanese in the Battle at Leyte Gulf. The news, and its significance, came late to the troops in India and Burma. All they knew was that they had *their* enemy on the run and, at long last, they were receiving ample air cover and supplies. The constant battle with the jungle, the climate, the tropical diseases went on.

Molly was going to stay at his bungalow during his absence. "You might as well enjoy it, Molly. It's more comfortable than your rooms, and I've already paid the rent."

She held onto him when they said good-bye. She held him tightly, putting her face in his neck. "I'm so afraid. So terribly afraid. I don't want to lose you again." Her muffled voice had a desperation to it.

He rubbed her head with his big hand. "Ah, what kind of talk is that, sweetheart? You're not going to lose me, not ever. You and I are for keeps now." And when she didn't say anything: "Aren't we?"

"If I could only believe that!"

"You must believe it, darling. Have you written to Sean about an annulment yet?"

Her voice was shaky. "Not yet. I will, when I hear what the procedure is. It's so difficult for me, Arthur."

"I know it is, my love. I understand. But, please . . . don't wait too long."

He flew on an ATC plane from Dum Dum, making four stops along the way at American installations in Assam. It never ceased to amaze him how the American Army had mobilized itself into a war machine. The British had their military tradition in India, their colonial heritage. But these Americans who were sent out here, half a world away from their homes in Kansas or Maine, had proved to be up to the challenge of the war in CBI.

He marked the changes since his first arrival in Assam, and his optimism rose. Maybe there were inefficiencies, snafus, but a professional army, well supplied with men, machines, and ammunition, had been assembled there. As 1944 drew to a close, the new road to China was nearing completion, and it began to look like there might be an end to this war.

Not before thousands more lost their lives, though. How long? Two years? Three?

Calcutta   April 1945

"Feeling better, sweetheart?"

"Yes, Arthur. Much better, thanks," Molly said, her voice listless. She had been ill on and off with one of the frequent intestinal upsets that plagued most foreigners in India.

Arthur thought she looked poorly. There were shadows under her eyes, and she was wan. "I think you've been working too hard, Molly. Why don't you take a few days off?"

Molly didn't answer. She was standing in the living room of his bungalow, looking out at the garden with unseeing eyes. It was April, and the expectation of the monsoon hung in the air.

"What's the matter, honey?" He walked over to her, and when she turned, he knew. "Sean. You've heard from Sean."

She nodded. He felt that awful sense of loss before she spoke, knowing that the moment he dreaded most had arrived. He wanted to stop the words before she spoke them.

"He's sick, Arthur! *Very* sick. They think he has multiple sclerosis. He's being released from detention on medical grounds—a compassionate pardon. . . . He's asked me to come home," she finished lamely.

"And you're going?" His voice was cold, toneless.

"I *have* to go. It's my *duty* to go to him."

"And your duty to me? Or don't you have one?"

He knew he was making it twice as hard for her. He didn't care.

"He has no one else, Arthur."

"*Dammit!* It's not a fair fight. What can I say against a sick man? Am I always to sacrifice my happiness because of your duty—first to your Church, now to your husband, whom you can hardly call a husband!"

"Arthur, Arthur!" Molly cried. "Please, darling, don't be like this. You've never, *ever* said anything like that to me before."

"Well, it's about time I did! Do you think I'm made of stone, Molly? Must I go through that same heartache all over again?"

"It's *my* heartache, too. It's just as bad for me."

"Is it, Molly? Is it *really?* Or do you *enjoy* the role of tragic heroine? The martyr, giving up earthly pleasures for a higher reward?" He was completely unguarded now, lashing out, wanting her to hurt the way he was hurting.

She stared at him, her mouth an open oval in her bloodless face. He was frightened because he knew he had gone too far, saying things that, once said, could not be unsaid. Touching on a place better left alone.

Molly brushed past him. He tried to catch her arm, but she shook him off roughly, and ran out of the bungalow. Sick at heart, he let her go, knowing that in their present temper they would not make peace. Wait until she has time to think, he told himself. Wait until you get over the shock. *Fool!* What did you think was going to happen? You should have insisted she start annulment proceedings long ago. And *you* should have written to Emily about a divorce. Not only a fool, but a coward.

He slept poorly. Rising before dawn, he dressed in uniform and walked in the coolness of the early morning down toward the Hooghly, along Garden Reach and the Strand. The rising sun, already hot, shown pink and brilliant on Fort William. Vultures sat on monuments, their great wings spread out to dry in the misty dawn. Just yesterday the sight of this would have stirred him with its exotic flavor. Now he looked past it, unmoved, uncaring. Just get this damn war finished and let me get out of here, he thought.

When he reached the hospital, sweepers were doing their early morning mopping, moving along in a squat on their bare feet, swishing soiled wet rags back and forth across the marble floors, their hands leaving black prints on the walls, to be cleaned by the next caste of workers who would create their own dirty prints on still another's territory. Ordinarily, Arthur would have viewed this with amused tolerance for a centuries-old way of life. Today it irritated him. The dirt, the smells, the inefficiencies . . . the grinding, endless, hopeless poverty . . . How could the British have ruled here for three hundred years and kept things as they were?

His peons snapped to attention, while Gopi ran to open his office door. He wanted to scream at them that he was a mortal man like them, no better, no worse, and for godsakes stop the groveling.

"Colonel-sahib, *chai* coming." Gopi ran off, returning with a tray of dark hot tea. Arthur stirred two spoons of the coarse, granular sugar of workaday India into it. The hot liquid seared his throat, soothing his anger.

That evening after dinner, his bearer, Francis, announced, "Tower-mem-sahib coming."

Molly walked in and stood before him like a contrite schoolchild who has misbehaved. Francis closed the doors behind her.

Arthur rose, loving her beyond all reason, despite the sullen resentment that still lodged in his chest.

"I came to make up, Arthur. I can't bear for us to quarrel when we have so little time left together."

He had not moved. Something prevented him from taking that step toward her, making it easier. "When do you plan to leave?"

"In two weeks, as soon as I can get air transport." Arthur searched her face for a sign of weakness, of giving in. "You won't change your mind?"

Molly shook her head slowly. "No, darling. I can't change my mind."

"Is it Wilkes-Barre, Molly? I can leave. *Anywhere,* I'll go anywhere to be with you. We can go to California . . . come back to *India!* There's impor-tant work to be done here with independence coming. I'm not tied to Wilkes-Barre. All I want in life is to be with you somewhere on this earth, and to do my work, to help people who need help. Is that asking too much?"

"It's not Wilkes-Barre, Arthur. . . . Please, darling, don't make it harder. I wasn't honest with you yesterday. I had already decided. . . . It's not only because of Sean's illness, Arthur. I can't take my happiness from another woman's misery—an entire family's life destroyed. If Sean weren't ill, I would feel entitled to seek an annulment. However, you have a wife who *must* love you. How could she help but love you? And three children who need a father. The price is too high."

The lines of fatigue showed in her face, under the eyes and around the mouth.

"It seems to me it's a moot point now. Sean *is* ill. If I thought it would help, I would do or say anything to change your mind, Molly. . . ." He went over to her. "I don't want us to quarrel either. We've loved too much for that."

"Darling!" She put her arms around his neck. "Let's have a beautiful two weeks together."

"All right, my love," he whispered into her hair, although he was still hurting. "Somehow, it will be all right."

In later years he would think about these days from time to time, remem-bering them as the most bewildering period of his life. That Molly loved him with all the fierceness of his love for her, he never doubted. Why then must she persist in martyring herself and their love? Selflessness wasn't the answer. It *had* to be something else, something to do with her religion, something that eluded his understanding.

In the end he had to accept their parting, not wanting bitterness or recriminations to be their legacy to each other. They spent every possible moment savoring the joy of being together, drinking in the richness of the sights and sounds and odors of India. The vividness, the mystery, the allure of this strange and beautiful land would forever be joined in his memories of Molly. For him it was easier to imagine her in fantasy . . . in the setting of remote Eastern gardens, veiled in lustrous silks, scented with jasmine and sandal . . . a fairy-tale princess, a dream. To deal with the reality of a flesh and blood woman, a short ocean away in Ireland, became a torment, bearable only if he banished it from his consciousness.

On the day of Molly's departure, when it was still night, they drove to the airport. The British Air Transport plane would leave before the sun rose, for the Indian sun would heat the metal of the fuselage, creating an oven within.

It would be a long, grueling journey, with stops in Karachi and Cairo to pick up wounded men who were being flown home to England. Molly had volunteered to work as a nursing sister on the long flight. At least she would keep busy that way, easing the pain of parting. Arthur worried about her. She had not fully recovered from her intestinal upset—"gippy tummy," as the British called it.

At Dum Dum they stood to one side in the shadow of a shed, avoiding contact with others until the last moment. They had said their good-byes in the most meaningful way during the last two weeks. No longer caring about appearances, Molly had moved into his bungalow, sharing the nights as well as the days with him.

He took her hand, gazing at her, committing her beauty to memory. For them, even the luxury of a photograph would not be appropriate. "I'm supposed to say something important and memorable at a moment like this . . . and I can't think of a single thing."

"Neither can I!" They both laughed. He caught her against himself and thought, if we can still laugh together, we'll be all right.

"Oh, my darling," she cried. "I wouldn't give up these months for anything in the world! Our love will be a part of me always." She was struggling to keep her composure now.

"My love, if you ever need me . . . ." She looked so soft, so vulnerable to him.

"I'll *always* need you, every day. . . ."

Arthur brushed a tear from her cheek. "And I, you . . ." he whispered. There was a still calm within him now. He kissed her forehead and they turned toward the waiting plane.

One last look into the other's eyes . . . a last, lingering touch . . . the unspoken words . . . and she was gone.

There had been that last time . . . the last time forever. . . . It kept burning into his brain . . . tears welling behind his closed eyelids . . . the feel of her skin, the smoothness of her against him . . . the taste of her . . . the smell of her . . . the shattering ecstasy of a love so perfect. . . . How would he bear it? *How would he bear it?*

He watched the heavy transport plane roar down the runway and lumber into the lightening sky. He stood watching until it had become a distant speck on the horizon, its winking lights indistinguishable from the morning stars.

Farewell, my sweet, my only love. God keep you and protect you. He turned, finally, his shoulders bent in dejection. For now began the task of learning to live the rest of his life without her.

May 7, 1945   V-E Day

Arthur sat with Roy McLean in the Calcutta Officers' Club, having a drink in celebration. *Their* war was still very much with them. Roy's unit, the 24th Station Hospital, was on alert, everyone expecting to move up with Stilwell, whose forces had reached the China end of the Ledo Road.

"I've received orders to triple the number of beds in Calcutta," Arthur confided in Roy. "Certainly sounds like they're expecting some action out here."

Just four days before, British troops had recaptured Mandalay. The Japanese were really on the run. The Allied Forces were poised for an invasion of the Japanese homeland.

Mac shook his head. "I sure do wish you were with me, Arthur. Things just don't run the same when you're not there. You're looking good as new."

"I'd a lot rather be going along with you than staying here in Calcutta," Arthur told him. "I sure fouled things up by getting myself caught in that bombed-out surgery."

Mac rose. "What d' you say, Art . . . shall we go to the party?" There was a victory reception being given at the Bengal Club.

"I think I won't, Mac. See you back at the house later." Roy was staying with him as his house guest. The large, empty bungalow seemed a happier place with his genial friend there.

When he reached the walled compound of his bungalow, the *chowkidar* swung wide the wrought-iron gate, saluting him. A turbaned, blanket-wrapped figure rose from the veranda as Arthur stepped out of the automobile. It was Ranjit Kar's bearer.

"Gur Dev! What are you doing here?"

"Colonel-sahib, Rajkumarji is bad luck."

"What happened, Gur Dev?"

"Bad is burned. Is coming, ambulance plane. From Imphal, is coming."

"When?"

"Two days past." The proud bearer stood tall, tears streaming down his cheeks. Arthur's heart fell.

"Where is he now, Gur Dev?" he asked, his voice hushed.

Gur Dev struggled for control, lifting his head, standing at attention.

"In hospital. Military station, Barrackpore."

"Will you take me there? I can leave immediately."

"*Ji. Mehrbani,* sahib." Gur Dev's relief was evident.

Ranjit was a mummy, swathed in bandages from head to toe, tubes coming out of arms and nose, tubes carrying away body wastes. On the ride to the military station, Gur Dev told Arthur what had happened.

"Petrol tank explosion, sahib . . . four people killed."

Ranjit had been about to enter a staff car and, turning back, had taken the explosive rush of the fire full force. It was a miracle that he hadn't been among the dead.

Arthur spoke to the young Indian doctor in charge. "How bad is Major Kar?"

"Quite bad, sir. We're giving him whole plasma and fluids. Severe body burns. He'll need skin grafts if he survives. His eyes . . . I think he won't have sight. He should have eye surgery, if that were possible."

"Why wasn't he taken to the Twentieth General instead of all the way down here?" Arthur asked in irritation. The 20th General Hospital, staffed by medical faculty from the University of Pennsylvania, was a short airlift from Imphal, at Margherita. It was superbly staffed, with one of the best eye surgeons in the States. The lack of coordination in this army drove Arthur to distraction at times. . . . If it hadn't been for Ranjit, I might not have made it when I was injured, he remembered. Now he was determined to do the same for his friend.

"Can he be moved safely, Dr. Mukerjee?"

"That would depend, sir. He was moved here, but that was a necessity."

"I'm thinking. . . . I'd like to get Major Kar to Calcutta to my hospital. We have American surgeons and burn experts there."

"You'd have to get clearance, sir."

"If I can make the arrangements, will you help me on this end?"

"Yes, Colonel. You can depend on it."

He went back to Ranjit's bedside. "Ranjit? Can you hear me? It's Arthur." There was a muffled sound from the mummified figure.

"I'm going to get you moved to Calcutta, Ranjit. We've got the best people there. You just hang on, old friend. It may take a day or two, but we'll do it." He tried to muster as much cheer and optimism in his voice as he could. He would like to have touched Ranjit, to encourage him, but he wasn't able to find an unbandaged spot. Sick with pity and fear, he left the ward.

"Let's go back to Calcutta, Gur Dev. To the Royal Victoria Hospital."

This question of men and women was most complex. For the first time, Arthur had met Ranjit's wife, Sushila, when Ranjit had been brought to the Royal Victoria Hospital.

The Rajkumari, the princess, was a lustrous, spirited woman with skin like a lotus petal and flashing dark eyes. She wore her elegantly draped saris with authority, displaying a self-assurance beyond any woman of any country Arthur had ever met.

"Is he going to die, Colonel Hillman?" she asked Arthur directly on the first day.

Arthur measured his reply. "I have hope for him, Madam Kar. So far, he's resisted infection and his lungs are clear. We're using this new medication . . . remarkable drug, penicillin. However, I'd be less than honest if I told you he wasn't in grave condition."

She nodded. "Does he know I'm there? I can't see any reaction when I speak to him."

"He's heavily sedated. I think you can assume that he is comforted by your presence."

She smiled wryly. "You flatter me, Colonel Hillman. I have never been thought of as a comforting presence."

He patted her arm and looked pointedly into her eyes. "I know Ranjit is happy to have you here. We are good friends."

Miraculously, Ranjit Kar was going to recover. He was horribly disfigured. His face, his torso, and his arms were covered with scar tissue. The sight of one eye was gone, but the second eye had been saved, thanks to a fortuitous coincidence.

When Arthur had returned from the military hospital at Barrackpore, on the night of V-E Day, Roy McLean was waiting for him at his bungalow, concerned about the emergency that had taken Arthur away with no advance warning.

Arthur told him about Ranjit. "I feel terrible about this, Roy. I wish to hell there were a really top-notch eye surgeon on our staff."

"I ran into Lance Harper at the Bengal Club. He's down here for a short leave. Maybe he'd take a look at him, Arthur." Lance Harper was one of the best. Arthur had once watched him demonstrate a technique he had developed.

Harper had examined Ranjit, prescribing a strict regimen for the treatment of his eyes until he was well enough to consider surgery. At the end of June, Harper had flown down from Assam, bringing his own instruments and an assistant to perform the surgery.

"There'll be a big to-do if anyone hears that I had a special surgical team flown in for my benefit," Ranjit told Arthur, only half in jest.

"Rank has its privileges," Arthur answered. "If they can fly around the country for the generals, they can do the same for you."

"I can't do much on that right eye now, Arthur," Lance Harper had told him. "It's too soon to say whether there's irreversible damage to the retina. Maybe, in a few years, something can be done. But not in India. I suppose the cost would make it prohibitive for him to come to the States for surgery."

Arthur laughed. "You mean, you don't know who he is?"

Harper was puzzled. "Indian Army major is all I know."

"Well, first of all, he's an M.D., Public Health, from Edinburgh."

"Oh, why didn't you say so? He never mentioned it. Then he'd just have to manage to get himself to Philadelphia."

"I imagine he could do that, Lance," Arthur said dryly. "His father is one of India's wealthiest men, a Rajah. You just operated on a prince, Dr. Harper!"

Arthur often visited Ranjit and Sushila Kar at their large, sprawling bungalow with terraces and splashing fountains in its enormous garden. Ranjit's dry humor was intact, despite his ordeal.

"Every ill has its compensations, Arthur," he said one day in early August, as Sushila walked away from them into the house, her sari fluttering in the hot breeze like a giant butterfly. "It took this to bring Sushila back to Calcutta. She always had a sharp tongue, but now it drips with honey!"

Sushila was making the decisions now. Her strong character prevented Ranjit's family from interfering with their separate living arrangements. Arthur thought it a pity that it required a tragedy for them to rearrange their lives in this sensible manner.

The Kar children usually came to say hello to Arthur. Two sons, about the size of his twins, they were only a year apart. The youngest was a girl, named Leila—an exquisite child with a heart-shaped face and the longest, thickest eyelashes Arthur had ever seen. When she smiled, deep dimples formed in her cheeks. She leaned against Ranjit, shy before a stranger.

"What is it like in America, sir?" Ashok, the older boy, asked him.

"America is a big country, Ashok. About twice the size of India, so not every part of the country is the same. We all speak English, though, and most of the people seem the same to foreigners . . . the clothes we wear are similar in all parts of the country."

"What about the red Indians?" his brother, Nani, asked.

"There *are* American Indians who still wear their native dress and speak their own language within their community . . . but they, too, speak English when they go out to work. The American Indians make up a very small part of our population. Most American families have not been living there for so many generations. They all come from other countries."

"Then why do they speak English?"

Why indeed? "That's a good question, Ashok. I guess it's because we were an English colony, too, not so many years ago—let me see, one hundred and sixty-nine years ago, we fought for our independence."

"Will *we* fight for our independence?" asked Nani.

Ranjit exchanged glances with Arthur. "I hope we won't have to fight for it, Nani. I think we've earned it," he said. "Our main task will be to prove we can govern ourselves without tearing one another apart."

They heard a commotion across the terrace, in the entry to the house. Sushila came running toward them, her customary composure replaced by great agitation.

"Ranjit! Arthur!" she cried. "There's something extraordinary on the news . . . on the short-wave radio. A new weapon, a great bomb, has been dropped on Japan. They say it has destroyed an entire city!"

The war was over.

He should be jubilant. The Allies had won. Once again, the good guys had prevailed.

How many had died? How many *wished* they had died? The hospital was crowded with young men who, but for a day or an hour, might have been whole and strong.

He sat out in his garden under a star-filled Indian sky. The heavy smell of *raatki rani,* queen of the night, permeated the monsoon-washed air.

They had invented a great weapon . . . a bomb which had killed thousands of people . . . who knew how many? People whom it was easy to kill, because you didn't have to look them in the eye . . . and if you did, those eyes were different anyway.

A city . . . two cities. Entirely destroyed, so they said. People lived in those cities. Families. Women, like the woman in the photograph in Kenji Tokada's wallet . . . children, like the three Tokada children in the picture. . . .

He didn't even know what city Kenji had come from. A man who saved his life, and he didn't even know whether the bomb his country had dropped had obliterated that man's home and family . . . Kenji's widow and three children who would never know that their husband and father was a good man who valued life and peace more than the Japanese Empire's dreams of conquest.

Here in India he had found more than he had given. Love, friendship, heartbreak. They were the stuff of life.

He sighed. The war was over. Soon he would be going home.

BOOK SEVEN

———

At Peace
1945–59

I

Wilkes-Barre   Spring 1945

Leisl and her children made a charming domestic scene, eating their dinner at the kitchen table when Nathan sauntered in, his suit coat slung over his shoulder, hooked onto his finger.

"Hi, sport!" he ruffled Eric's hair, planted a kiss on each of the girls' heads, then threw down his briefcase and straddled a chair. His hand rested briefly on Leisl's shoulder.

"Mmm! That looks delicious." He eyed their plates.

Leisl's brows lifted. "Please! Would you like some, Nathan? I didn't think . . . expect you would be here tonight." Her voice had a compelling quality, rich and low, with minor undertones, the accent softly blurred around the edges.

"I'd love some, if there's enough." He laughed easily, a deep, warm masculine embracing of them.

Leisl served him chicken, potatoes, and vegetables. She watched intently while he cut his food and chewed. "You're a good cook, Leisl. D'you know that?"

The eyes warmed, glinty amber. "I don't have much opportunity to cook when Cousin Rose is home."

Rose had left that day to visit her sister, Celia, in Baltimore. The house had a different feeling without his mother—a Leisl feeling.

She smiled at him, the smile reaching out, touching him with golden light. Leisl was all tawny sunlit colors, mellow glimmers. She was beautiful in her own special Leisl way, although she took pains to hide herself behind reading glasses, wearing her autumn-leaf hair in that severe bun. . . . Nathan sometimes fantasized unraveling her hair, letting loose all that shimmeriness. . . . The tweedy skirts and sweaters suited her slim-hipped figure. She could have passed for a coed, if you didn't notice the care lines when her sweetly shaped mouth was in repose, or look too deeply into the eyes. What a metamorphosis, though, from the despondent woman who had first come to their home six years ago.

He watched her pour milk for the children, slice cake, hands neat and adept, the gold wedding band her single adornment. He remembered her saying that the English woman had worn it out of Germany. Leisl had given her a few valuables to carry . . . some jewelry that had belonged to her mother, some photographs. They would have taken everything away from Leisl, of course.

The children, excused from the table, ran into the sitting room to listen to Dick Tracy. Nathan helped Leisl with the dishes, taking pleasure in the sharing of a task with her.

"Not going out tonight?" she asked.

"No . . . I thought I'd stay home. Just relax, do some reading. . . ." She concentrated on the roasting pan. A stray lock of hair escaped and fell forward in her eyes. Nathan smoothed it back with his hand. That seemed too familiar a gesture, and he instantly regretted it, noting how her eyes avoided his. They finished the dishes in silence.

After the girls were in bed, Leisl read them a story, while Nathan sat talking with Eric in his room. This had become a ritual on the evenings when he was home. The boy was handsome, with a gravity in his blue eyes beyond his years. At his Bar Mitzvah, nearly two years ago, Eric had paid tribute to "four men for whom I feel love and gratitude—my father, my grandfather, and my Uncle Kurt, who are not with me today . . . and my Cousin Nathan, who is taking their place for me." The thronged synagogue had echoed with the sound of caught breaths and the clearing of throats, as the congregation had struggled for composure. *God, he had felt proud!*

It had been on Eric's Bar Mitzvah day that Nathan became aware of a change in his feelings for Leisl. . . .

In the beginning of 1939, when she had come to live in their house, he had gladly assumed the responsibility of their care. He insisted on taking the sole financial obligation upon himself, despite Arthur's desire to contribute, and the offers of his sisters' husbands to share the cost.

"Look . . . you just have to understand that this is something I want to do alone," he'd told them.

He didn't care what they said behind his back—that he was being noble, that he was sublimating, making up for the fact that he didn't have his own wife and children. Whatever label they put on it was all right with him. They were half right. Maybe he *was* making up for a lack in his life. He couldn't be bothered with analyzing his motives. If it gave him pleasure to do it, and the need was there, what did they care?

They all gave gifts to Leisl and the children, invited them to dinner, made grandiose offers of help, but as the novelty wore off, they went back to their own concerns. It was Nathan who became the surrogate for the father who was imprisoned in Germany, the man for Leisl to lean on in place of her husband, and her own father and brother.

Nathan had been absolute in his determination to obtain their release from the camp at Dachau. When he failed to barter the men from the concentration camp, he had devoted himself to restoring Eric to mental health.

Returning to Wilkes-Barre with the boy, Nathan had first prepared Leisl for the shock of seeing her son so altered in appearance . . . the son she still supposed to be a captive in Germany.

"Leisl . . . I have been in Europe, in Germany," he told her, sitting alone with her in the living room of Rose's house.

Her hands had flown to her face. *"You?* You have gone *there,* Nathan . . . to *Germany?* But, that was dangerous for you! Even for an American Jew, it is dangerous. . . ." She had not dared to ask even a single question.

"I tried to get your family out of the prison, Leisl."

She sat, straight and wooden, the tendons in her throat standing out, her hands tightly clasped in her lap.

"I have brought Eric home to you. . . . They would not free the others." He sat next to her, putting a restraining hand on her arm as she cried out. "Wait!" he cautioned. "You must be prepared, Leisl. He is changed. . . . He has been through an ordeal. Pretend to yourself that he has suffered a terrible illness . . . a plague. . . ." And Nathan had described how Eric would look, telling her about the number branded on his arm, not permitting her to see her son until she told him she was ready.

He had watched her face when Eric had walked into the room, watched as she clasped her son to her bosom, hugging and kissing him, holding him away from her to smile into the eyes that looked like marbles until she noted some human response there and the child had buried his head in her lap and sobbed. Not once did she falter, not once did she give in to her broken heart. Her courage, her fiber, had amazed him. Alone in his room, Nathan had wept.

From the moment Nathan had brought her son back to her, he had become a hero to Leisl. With Nathan's love and understanding to bolster him, Eric recuperated from his seven months of mistreatment. Leisl credited Nathan, far more than the psychiatrist, with the boy's recovery.

Eric had been abused in Dachau, the doctor told her. The child was unable to speak of his experiences himself. Leisl did not entirely understand what had happened to him there. But Nathan did. And it sickened him so much that he was filled with a murderous rage against the Nazis. They were perverted beasts, as well as inhumane bullies. Eric's malnutrition was not only the result of starvation, but a combination of inadequate food and a loss of the will to live.

Trudi and Karin had not suffered in the same way. They had been young enough so that they quickly forgot the indignities they had known as Jewish children in Germany. In Wilkes-Barre they went to school, joined the YWCA for swimming lessons, the YMHA for ballet lessons, went to Sunday school at the Reformed Temple, and became indistinguishable from all the other pretty little girls in their class after a year's time.

Each evening Leisl would sit knitting in the protection of Rose's house, seeing her children snuggled up to Nathan while he read to them or played a game of Monopoly or checkers or make-believe nonsense. His paternal exu-

berance was so much warmer and demonstrative than that which would have
been provided by their own father, had they but known it.

The mood of the house lifted the moment Nathan's step was heard at the
door. There would be a rush of small running feet, a clamor of glad cries,
"Nathan's home! . . . Nathan! Nathan!" A throwing of little arms around
his neck, while he hugged and kissed each one in turn.

"How 'bout a game of catch, Eric? . . . What happened to the doll,
Karin? Don't worry, I'll fix her." A recitation of Trudi's spelling lesson, the
multiplication tables . . . those were Nathan's province. He basked in the
happiness of their need for him.

Then came the Bar Mitzvah for Leisl's son, which Nathan arranged. A
quiet affair, compared to most such celebrations. Emily had come from Philadelphia with her children. Uncle Herman, too. . . .

There was a luncheon for family and close friends. A few toasts, a piano
and string trio providing some light background music. Nothing ostentatious
. . . just enough to mark it as a happy occasion.

Nathan danced with his mother and his sisters, then with Emily, more
stylishly elegant than ever. He twirled Trudi and Karin around the floor,
holding their hands as in a folk dance. His glance came to rest on Leisl, a
happy Leisl for this moment. Her eyes were alive, her smile like a gift of grace
bestowed on the assembled guests, her tawny shoulder-length hair loose, reflecting the glow of the overhead lights. On an impulse, he had asked her to
dance. Why shouldn't she dance? Is a woman to behave like a widow, in
anticipation of her bereavement?

"What a beautiful day this is for us, Nathan! And we have you to thank for
it!" she had said, her voice joyful, her head thrown back.

They had danced, and as she smiled up at him, as he felt her in the circle of
his arm, such a surge of emotion ran through him that the shock of it left him
speechless. Leisl saw a change come over him, felt him stiffen and withdraw
from her. She was puzzled, but the excitement of the event, the distraction of
so many people, diverted her attention.

After that, Nathan began to absent himself from meals. He had always
been active in civic affairs, in professional organizations, so he didn't have to
look far for excuses to be away from the house. With the war effort, there
were any number of jobs for him to do in the evenings . . . civil defense
warden, bond drives. He dated many women, as in the old days.

In her heart Leisl felt hurt when Nathan began to distance himself from
them, but she knew they had no claim on him. He had given enough of
himself to them. He was entitled to find diversion among his own friends
rather than be confined to the boredom of another man's family.

On the odd evening when they were all at home together, Leisl's emotions
were in tumult. She was so much an inward person that it was just one more

part of her life she must carefully monitor, revealing none of this inner turmoil as she worked in placid concentration.

"You're never at home with us these days, Nathan," Rose said, in an unusual show of reproval.

"Mother, I have to have *some* life of my own," he answered with annoyance. I should take another apartment, he thought. There was no longer any need for him to stay in his mother's house—indeed, there was a compelling reason for him to leave.

In his apartment Nate had set up the study as a retreat where he could read, listen to music, entertain friends if he wished—although he seldom had people over, and never women. It might be his own place, with its own back entrance, but it was still his mother's house. Tonight, however, it seemed rude not to spend the evening with Leisl when just the two of them were there. . . . He sensed she was lonely. Besides, Leisl wasn't "women."

"Why don't you come in and have a drink with me, Leisl?" he asked when she had kissed the girls good night.

"I have to correct papers, Nathan." Leisl had been teaching French at Westmoreland College for the past three years. She welcomed the chance to earn some money. Their dependence on Nathan, even after so many years, was still an unnatural feeling for her. Someday . . . someday, it would be repaid . . . somehow. She couldn't pursue that thought too long, because it led her to the war . . . to Germany . . . and to the reasons for her being here.

"Bring the papers in. I've got some work to do, too. Might as well keep each other company."

He put on some records, Chopin and Tchaikovsky, careful not to select Beethoven or Schubert, anything that might depress her, stir up memories. . . . He poured two brandies, setting hers on the low table in front of the couch.

They sat in companionable silence. Now and again he glanced over at her as she made swift marginal notes on a paper, her smooth forehead puzzling here and there over a student's words. Always in his life there seemed to be a forbidden woman, the sweet bitterness of a denied love. Abstracted, Nathan stared at his book with unseeing eyes, unaware of Leisl's attention focused on him, a soft hopelessness taking possession of her sensitive features.

At ten o'clock he switched on the radio to hear the latest war bulletins. General Patton's Third Army had crossed the Rhine near Mannheim, virtually unopposed, late the previous night, the announcer's staccato voice reported. . . .

"Mannheim is about two hundred and fifty kilometers from Munich . . . from Dachau. . . ." Leisl said, her voice curiously impersonal, a precise bell tone. She rose abruptly. "I must leave you now. Thank you, Nathan, for

keeping me company tonight. I know you did it so I wouldn't be alone. We
. . . I am grateful. Good night." And she was gone, leaving an emptiness
there in the room, a wanting in his heart.

He switched off the news, rinsed their brandy glasses, then stripped and
showered, letting the needle spray beat down on his head and against his
back. In his robe, he went down to lock up and turn out lights, as was his
habit. On most nights, he came in after the women had retired. He heard
Leisl's bath water running when he passed through the hall.

Lingering in the sitting room, he straightened pillows, picked up a stray
doll belonging to Karin. He knew this would be another one of those nights—
restless and solitary—when he couldn't sleep.

Nathan mounted the stairs, two at a time, in his bare feet, moving with
athletic ease. He paused at the top step, as Leisl, in her dressing gown, hair
brushed loosely around her shoulders, emerged from the girls' room, closing
the door quietly. The upper hall was in darkness. A beam of light from his
apartment illuminated the far end.

Leisl stood for a moment, turned away from him, looking toward the open
door of his study, unaware that he was standing there behind her. She held
her right hand up to her face, pressed against her mouth, as if to stifle an
outcry. Her other hand hung at her side, clenched in a fist.

At the sound of his step, Leisl turned sharply, a startled expression on her
face.

"Oh! Nathan, it's you. I thought . . . I didn't know you were there."

He placed a reassuring arm around her shoulders. He was stirred by her
soft loveliness through the thin wool of the robe. As she looked up at him, the
sorrow in her eyes had vanished, replaced by a glow of warm humor.

He drew her to him. "Leisl," he whispered.

She lifted her lips to meet his in a manner both natural and trusting. His
arms tightened around her as their kiss deepened.

When at length they drew apart, he said huskily, "You know that I'm in
love with you."

She sighed then. "I didn't know. I thought you just felt sorry for me."

He closed his eyes with a mirthless laugh. "No," he said shortly, "much to
my shame, I *love* you—the wife of another man."

She reached up to touch his cheek. "And I love you," she said simply. "I
don't know if I still have a husband, Nathan. It's been seven years since I've
seen Armand. I cannot even recall the sound of his voice. I have no tears
left."

"I don't wish him dead, Leisl. God knows I don't!"

"Nor do I. . . . I pray every day and night that he is alive . . . that he is
not suffering. . . ." Her voice trembled. "But I still love you."

Hours later, they lay in each other's arms, while Nathan gently stroked her hair, trying to still the qualms of conscience that troubled him.

The tear streaks had dried on her cheeks, her breathing was even now, following the catharsis of uncontrollable crying that had wracked her body.

"It's all right, darling," he had said. "It's all right," over and over. "I understand."

"No," she had sobbed. "You don't know. . . ."

And Nathan had told her that she needed to cry. It was the first time he had ever seen her cry in the six years since she had become a part of his world.

"You're feeling guilty because you're alive and safe and healthy, Leisl. Because you have food and a warm home and are cared for. . . . You're feeling guilty because you made love with me . . . and you enjoyed it."

"Yes. Oh, yes! You *do* understand, but not all of it. I never was able to love Armand this way, Nathan. He was so . . . so . . . *methodical.* I think German men are not so feeling as Americans, perhaps."

Nathan's laugh was gentle. "I'm certainly glad that German women don't suffer from that affliction!" He had succeeded in dispelling her apprehensions. But how was he to conquer his own misgivings?

Rose was in her sitting room, working on her ever-present knitting when Nathan knocked and entered the comfortable room. She patted the couch next to her, happy to have his company. Nathan looked so happy these days, the picture of good health. She almost forgot that he had ever been anything but robust.

"Mother, I have to talk to you," he began the conversation. He stood up and began to pace restlessly.

Rose nodded. "I've been wondering when you were going to do that, Nathan."

He stopped his pacing and looked at her. "You know, then?"

People in love were always so sure that only *they* knew what remained secret to everyone else!

"I'd have to be blind not to know what's going on before me in my own house."

Nathan colored. "Is it so obvious?"

"To a mother it's obvious!" Rose laughed. "No one else has suspected anything, as far as I know." She sighed. "Why is it my sons always seem to fall in love with a problem?"

"I didn't *want* to fall in love with her, Mother. It just happened," Nathan said.

"Are you sure, Nathan, you're not confusing love with pity?"

He'd thought that one through—for months. Pity . . . or he preferred to think of it as responding to Leisl's need for someone to lean on. That may have been the beginning of it. But that long ago had been replaced by love.

He shook his head emphatically. "No. I really am in love with Leisl. And she loves me."

"What will you do if her husband is alive?" Rose always came right to the heart of the matter with plain-spoken directness.

This was the very question that Nathan had been trying to come to grips with ever since V-E Day. He knew that Leisl, too, was tormented, each of them sensing the other's anguish from looks rather than any words that were spoken.

Nathan ran his hand through his hair. "God! I don't know! I swear, Mother, neither of us wants him to be dead."

"I'm sure you don't, Nathan. . . . I don't know what to tell you, dear. You must wait to see. Nothing can be decided until you know the truth."

"That's what we're planning to do. I just wanted you to know." He sat down, leaning forward, his elbows on his knees. "I've contacted the commission dealing with displaced persons, the Jewish refugee organizations, our government, everyone. Now that the fighting is over in Europe, I want to go to Germany as soon as it's possible for them to issue me a passport. . . . It's early, but I have friends with connections."

After Nathan left her, Rose sat, hands idle, looking into space. Had she made a mistake, bringing Leisl and her children into this house? Who could have foreseen such a thing?

Leisl was the granddaughter of her mother's first cousin, so the relationship wasn't close. Nevertheless, for Nathan to marry a woman who already had three children—they were *dear* children and Nathan was devoted to them—a woman whose husband, father, and brother had all perished in a concentration camp? For, from the stories they had read in the newspapers, it would be miraculous if they had survived seven years under those terrible conditions.

What a world they lived in! If Armand *had* survived . . . what then? Would Nathan have to bear the unhappiness of unrequited love all his life? Rose was not a praying woman, but if prayer helped, she now prayed that this would not have a tragic outcome. Either way, though, it would be a tragedy.

Leisl had become emotionally dependent on Nathan. They had not been lovers again after Rose had returned from her trip to Baltimore. It was better that way. The guilt was too difficult to bear, and the children were bound to sense something. All the strength and self-containment she had called on throughout the more than six years she had lived in Wilkes-Barre had deserted her. Now she leaned on Nathan, looked to him for support and reassurance.

This warm, tender man, so strong and yet so gentle, had become the most important person in the world to her, besides her children. He understood her. He knew she would never forget Armand and the others. Didn't expect her to forget.

Leisl was afraid. She always thought of Armand in the past tense now. What if he were alive? She wanted him alive. Of course she did! But it had been almost seven years since he had been arrested—seven long, awful years.

She couldn't remember him very well. She would look at his photograph, trying to think what he had been like. She had nothing else . . . no letters, no mementos to remind her of him. Only her wedding band. She knew he was dead. Either dead or suffering. Which was worse? And then she would think, What right had she to be alive when all of them were probably dead?

Nathan had so much love to give. It was endless. He loved his family, he loved his friends. He loved his country . . . his town . . . his work. He loved all of life. But most of all he loved Leisl . . . Leisl and her children. They were his world. He already thought of them as his own.

If Armand is alive, I'll spend the rest of my life on a psychiatrist's couch, he thought to himself. And if he's dead? I'll probably do the same.

In September he received an official letter:

A deposition from Maximilian Herzberg, released from Concentration Camp Dachau on June 15, 1945.
Re: *Prisoners Gunther Rosenmaier, Kurt Rosenmaier, Armand Brandt*

All three prisoners were known to me before the war in München. I was a laboratory worker employed at the München clinic of Professor Gunther Rosenmaier.

Gunther Rosenmaier died of malnutrition and heart failure in July 1942 in Block 41 at Dachau. Kurt Rosenmaier was shot with his brother-in-law Armand Brandt in February 1943 for refusing to carry out orders in the infirmary where medical experiments were being conducted on old men who were prisoners. They had engineered a plan for escape. Kurt had obtained clothing and papers to enable several people to escape. These articles were used by two prisoners who successfully left the camp. Both were returned and executed in front of the assembled prisoners.

This sworn deposition has been independently corroborated by the following eyewitnesses:

Heinz Rubinstein
Julian Zipper

Nathan told Leisl.

He read the report to her on a Sunday afternoon in September when they were alone. Rose had gone with the children to Frieda's house for the afternoon. He had asked her to keep them away as long as possible, explaining what he had learned.

Leisl sobbed in his arms, reading the deposition, then crying anew, as she digested first one fact, then another.

"They were brave, Nathan, weren't they? They died trying to save others. Together—the two of them!"

"Yes, dear, they were brave. We should be proud of them. The children will be. Their father and uncle were heroes." He let her cry. She needed a period of grief and mourning to release all the years of pent-up anguish, uncertainty, and guilt for being alive.

Nothing would ever diminish his anger.

They went to temple, to a memorial service, where the three names were entered in the Permanent List of the Dead, to be remembered each time the Yizkor service was held. Nathan ordered a memorial plaque in their honor.

It was Nathan who told the children, and it was to his arms the older two came with their tears. The youngest, not remembering her father, went to Leisl, crying tears of companionship for her brother and sister. They were a family, even before Leisl and Nathan were married.

Arthur arrived in New York one month later.

Arthur was worried about Nathan's plans to marry Leisl. Leisl seemed unstable, and he was concerned about Nathan having to shoulder the responsibilities of a delicate wife and three children, with his own history of ill health.

Leisl came to see Arthur in his office, asking for something to calm her. She told him she was having trouble sleeping. After talking to her for a while, he suggested that she see a psychiatrist, but she resisted the idea.

They talked about her dead family—her husband, her father, and her brother. She appeared on the edge of hysteria.

"Dead, all dead!" she cried. "You can't imagine what it means to have everyone you knew and loved dead. And killed by your own countrymen— not even by the bombs!" She buried her face in her hands. "Such beautiful, good men. . . . Kurt, he was a genius, an absolute genius, Arthur! They said there hadn't ever been a better student at the university as long as anyone could remember. And Armand—you remember him, Arthur! Trudi, she's just like him. Isn't she beautiful? Isn't she? . . . Oh, God, I look at Eric's arm and I see that awful number and I think my head will burst open. You must give me something to help me calm down, to sleep." She looked off into space. "Papa. The best people came to his clinic . . . he cared for them."

Arthur felt he had to say something about Nathan. "Leisl. I wonder about you and Nate. About your marriage. You have so many troubles, so many bitter memories. Wouldn't it be better to wait . . ." He stopped, feeling he had no right to say this.

"But, I *want* to marry Nathan! I *love* Nathan! He knows how I feel. He understands. He will not expect me to forget."

And so he wrote a prescription for a mild sedative, warning her that he would not refill it when she had used it all.

But he was determined to speak to Nathan.

"How about going for a ride, Nate?" Arthur called him on the first afternoon he didn't have office hours.

"Why sure, Art, I'd like that."

Arthur picked Nathan up in front of the Wyoming National Bank Building, where he had his offices. The weather was mild—a golden autumn day. They drove up East End Boulevard toward Bear Creek, chatting idly. Nathan leaned back, a serene smile on his face, allowing the breeze from the partly open window to blow his hair, squinting against the glare of the afternoon sun. He seemed relaxed and happy.

When they passed the sign for Thornhurst, Arthur turned into the old road, not expecting to find the mountain trail to the cabin, which he hadn't traveled for sixteen years. But in a few miles, there it was. He turned right and started up the sharp-curving track.

"You seem to know what you're doing, so I won't mention the fact that this looks like a donkey trail," Nathan joked.

"It's O.K. It doesn't go on for very long. There's a nice view at the top."

"You *do* know every inch of this territory, don't you?" Nathan grinned.

Arthur just shrugged. He felt detached.

When they reached the clearing, they saw the burned-out foundation of the cabin, the stone chimney rising scorched in the middle. Seeing it, for Arthur, was like the final closing of a book.

They walked up the forest path, Nathan breathing hard, but not faltering. Arthur slowed, but Nathan indicated that he was all right.

"I need more of this. It's good for my lungs."

"Since when are you such an authority on what's good for lungs?"

"Ask the man who owns one! If I'd been doing things like this all these years, I'd be in a lot better shape. Damn near made a total invalid out of me, with all the sighing and fussing!"

Arthur was reflecting on what Nathan had said when they reached the meadow.

"This is magnificent! Wouldn't I love to build a house up here," exclaimed Nathan. "Whose land is this?"

"This is state land, part of the forest conserve. An old friend of mind used to own the adjacent property—where the cabin burned down."

"An old friend?"

"That's right . . . an old friend."

They sat down on the boulder and were silent for a few minutes.

"O.K., Art . . . I gather you didn't bring me all the way up here on a Thursday afternoon to look at the view."

Arthur grinned. "I'm not sure I know how to begin, Nate."

"Why don't you begin with Leisl?" His tone was noncommittal, but there was a stubborn set to his jaw. "That is, of course, what you want to talk about."

"Yes, that's what I want to talk about. . . ." He paused. "Are you in love with her, Nate?"

" 'In love?' What's love, Art? Were you in love with Emily when you married her?"

Arthur just stared at his brother. Then he let out a long, slow breath. "That was different," he said.

"The only difference is that was you, and this is me. You were young, had your whole life ahead of you . . . and you were in love with someone else. . . ." As Arthur looked up, Nate continued, "Oh, yes, I knew you weren't over it." Seeing the pained look on Arthur's face, Nate was silent for a moment, wondering, was his brother yet over it, even after all these years?

Nate continued, "I spent the best years of my life waiting for death, and then when it didn't come, I felt better, but never perfect. How could I? . . . Mother watched over me . . . Father died grieving for me." He stifled Arthur's protest. "No! Let me say it all. . . . It was considered a small miracle when I finally went to law school. The cripple fighting on, despite the odds. Every client I handled in those days had the air of giving me a handout— their good work for the season. And surprised when I did a decent job! Sure, I don't have the energy that someone with two good lungs might have. But there are plenty who came back from that war, and this one, in a lot worse shape—or didn't come back at all. And I can't live out my life anymore feeling like half a man. Leisl wants me, and what's more, she needs me. And I need someone to take care *of* for a change, instead of the other way around." Nate looked at him with candor. "To answer your question, yes I *am* in love with her. We deeply love each other. We need each other."

"There's nothing to say, then, Nate. I'm happy for you. Really! I wish you joy, both of you."

Nate smiled at him fondly and threw an affectionate arm around his shoulders. "And don't worry, Arthur. . . . The marriage bed won't kill me. I've got testimonials to prove it!"

Arthur laughed—the big, hearty, wonderful laugh of old.

Sitting in the car before starting to drive home, he apologized to Nate. "I don't know why I think I have the right to interfere in your life, Nate. I guess you're right—I've always thought *I* had to take care of *you.*"

"Art, there were times when I used to look at you and I wanted to ask, 'Are you happy?' But I was afraid, because I knew what the answer would be. Now, I'm asking you."

Arthur looked away before answering, thinking about Nate's question.

"I'm not *un*happy, Nate. Does the absence of unhappiness constitute happiness? I'm not sure. . . . I have wonderful children, many fine friends, and I love my work." But he knew that wasn't what Nate was asking. He couldn't bring himself to give the real answer to his brother's question. "Emily and I . . . we care about and respect each other. I get much satisfaction out of my life."

"I'm glad to hear that, Art. I wasn't sure." Nathan's eyes still held a question as he smiled at Arthur.

"It hasn't all been good, Nate. But now, after the war, it seems Emily and I are destined to go on together. This war has changed all our lives. I don't think anything will ever be the same again."

Arthur started the car and they drove back in the lingering sunset. As they came down Wyoming Mountain, all of the valley lay below, bathed in a reddish light from the setting sun, the winding ribbon of the Susquehanna reflecting its glow.

If only Arthur would look at me that way, just once!

Emily stood in the rabbi's study at Temple B'nai Israel while Nathan and Leisl were joined in marriage. The devotion in Nathan's face as he looked down at Leisl, repeating the words of the marriage ceremony, was so moving that Emily's eyes grew misty.

How fortunate Leisl was to be marrying that loving, tenderhearted man, who so obviously worshiped her. Had Arthur ever felt that way about *her?* Even in the first days of their marriage? Emily didn't think so. Had he ever really loved her? He had *said* he did, but there had always been a part of him that was closed off from her.

During the war, when he was overseas, she had busied herself with every sort of volunteer work in order not to think about their problems—in order not to worry about him when he was injured—clinging to the hope that when he came home they would be reconciled. . . . Those few times in Washington, there had been Billy Beckinger. . . . It would have been so easy to have an affair with him, but she hadn't been able to because she loved Arthur so much that she couldn't imagine herself making love with another man. She had wanted to tell him that . . . had ached to write letters of love and longing to him, but she had been ashamed, too embarrassed to commit to paper the feelings in her heart. Unless he wrote love letters to her, how could she write those things to him?

Her eyes rested on Arthur's face, standing there next to Nathan as his best man, lean and handsome in the candlelight, the hair at his temples beginning to gray. After being his wife for fifteen years, she felt he was more remote and unattainable to her than ever.

It was eight months since he had returned from the war. Eight months that had been difficult, not so much because of their arguments and confrontations, but because there was so little of anything that meant something between them. Emily didn't know how to break through Arthur's reserve or her own sense of pride. And always she had to fight for *control*. She was constantly afraid that if she lost that control, she would slip away, beyond the place where her life was retrievable, into that yawning abyss that sometimes beckoned her.

Awaiting Arthur's return from overseas, Emily had been in an agony of nervous anticipation. She had gone to New York, arranging to meet him there, thinking it would be easier at an anonymous hotel than at her family's estate in Haverford. It had not occurred to her to go back to Wilkes-Barre, open the house, and wait for him there. Only after she had spent the second night alone in the suite she had reserved at the Plaza, awaiting Arthur's call, did it come to her that *of course* that would have been the thing to do—the idea that would have pleased him most—to move back to Wilkes-Barre, as he would want his wife to do.

Each morning, waiting to hear from him, she had dressed with care, hoping to look her best when he arrived, hair just right, makeup low-key, knowing that none of that mattered to Arthur. And after two days of this, he had finally let himself into the suite at 4 A.M., exhausted and haggard after an interminable flight from San Francisco, where the hospital ship had docked.

After all her careful plans, they had met for the first time in three years, Arthur fatigued and unshaven, Emily in her hairnet and nightgown, her breath smelling of sleep. But that hadn't seemed to matter, because after the first startled hello, she was weeping in his arms, and then they were in bed together, making love in a surge of passionate urgency, after which Arthur fell into a torpor of sleep from which he awakened twelve hours later.

Emily didn't know why she knew this—it was a certainty which she never doubted—that if it hadn't happened in the way it did, they might never have resumed their marriage at all. If it had happened in the storybook manner she had orchestrated, their distance would have become so apparent to them after an hour of forced conversation that they probably would never have shared the same bed again. At this stage of their lives that seemed to be the only satisfactory common ground in their relationship. . . .

They conducted the arrangements of their life together with the utmost decorum and consideration. Arthur engaged himself in his practice, which had grown almost too large for one man to handle alone. He involved himself in medical affairs of county and state. He was chief of staff at St. Anne's, president-elect of the Medical Society, and he was at last getting somewhere in the formation of a network of health clinics in the anthracite industry.

Once she was back in Wilkes-Barre, Emily had plunged herself into her own organizational activities. As she had in Haverford, she joined dozens of boards and committees in Wyoming Valley, as well as retaining some of her posts in Philadelphia, keeping busy and involved, finding this the best way to keep going . . . to keep that control she so desperately sought.

The strangeness of being back in Wyoming Valley had begun to wear off for Arthur. There were still times when he would awaken in the middle of the night, not remembering where he was for a few seconds, caught in that twilight between his dreams and wakefulness, feeling, smelling, almost *tasting* India. Then he would become aware of the darkened bedroom, the sheer curtains stirred by the breeze off the river, the quiet night sounds of Wilkes-Barre, and Emily's even breathing in the bed beside him.

At first he had had no sense of emotion about being home. He was neither happy nor sad, not even resigned. He merely was there.

He found many changes in the valley. New people in town, some who had come to run industries during the war and, liking it, finding it a place where they prospered, had stayed on.

There were new doctors who had opened practices in the community. During the war years his patients had gone to them or to other men, like Jack Lerner, who had not been in the service. Some of his old patients returned . . . many did not.

There were the men who had been killed in the war, the sons of families he knew, boys who should have been in college or graduate school or delivering the mail.

There were the people who had made a killing . . . profiteers from the war. Some of them—not content with the fortune that dropped in their laps—schemed to defraud the government in elaborate swindles. A congressman went to jail . . . several businessmen followed him. . . . The lawyer who had masterminded the plan, and *should* have served time, got off scot-free.

Ordinarily Arthur would have been outraged at such a miscarriage of justice. He remained indifferent.

He had his friends.

Jim Flannery was the same pal, the humorous, dependable fellow, back from serving in a field hospital in Europe. Hob Carpenter and Charles Means were still plugging along, getting older.

David Benjamin had been appointed a federal judge. He and Ruth had moved to Riverside Drive, next to the Wintermuths. Lowell had become the new president of Wyoming and Susquehanna after Phoebe's father died.

Some things remain constant. Arthur's mother had been the same, just a little grayer. Happy sharing her home with Leisl and the children, Rose had asked Nathan and Leisl to continue to live there after their marriage. It gave Arthur great comfort to recognize the steadfastness of his mother. She had looked at Arthur and seen something there. She sensed that more had happened to him than his physical injuries. Wise as she was, Rose couldn't begin to understand it.

Emily's rages began again.

It was over a trivial matter. But once she allowed herself to vent her anger, it was like opening a water gate. Such foolish things brought on her outbursts . . . neither of them knew how to deal with her anger.

The first time they had a terrible argument, the children were visibly upset, not looking him in the eye. *She's* the one who's shouting . . . why are they acting that way with me? He was troubled. Although he could only bring himself to keep a distant relationship with Emily, he didn't want a divorce. Having lost Molly, he *couldn't* lose his children.

Arthur forced himself to re-enter community life, to participate, to care. The way he had many years before, the first time Molly had left him.

And it worked. The patients who depended upon him, the hospital, the house calls, the surgery, the Medical Society . . . the new Lung Committee he had formed . . . his children, his friends. And Emily.

This was his life now. This would always be his life.

Autumn 1946

Arthur was preparing the first draft of the address he would deliver before the Medical Society when he was invested as its new president. He had thought about being discreet, giving a diplomatic speech that would ruffle no feathers, but had balled up the pages in self-irritation. What the hell! Since when had he taken the easy way out on issues?

He began to write, and as the words came flowing out, his pen raced across the pad. ". . . and I would hope that in my term of office, this society will support those who have come to recognize that social medicine is not a communist plot, that physicians have an obligation to see that preventive medicine is practiced in the community, that public health is a matter that concerns all of us . . . to deny health care to the poorest among us is to deny basic human rights. . . ." He was interrupted by the telephone ringing.

"Dr. Hillman speaking."

"Is that *the* Dr. Hillman—the Dr. Hillman who, it says here in the *Pennsylvania State Review* is an expert on occupational lung disease?" said a familiar voice on the other end of the wire.

It took Arthur only a breath to realize who it was. "Father John! How wonderful to hear your voice. Where are you?"

"Ask me where I'm going to be day after tomorrow," was the reply.

"All right." Arthur chuckled. "Where *are* you going to be day after to-morrow?"

"In Wilkes-Barre, P A, that's where. I'm coming in for a conference at King's College. Be there for three whole days. I'd really like to see you, Arthur."

John Riordan's voice had that same melodic timbre Arthur had always liked, but there was something . . . he couldn't grasp it . . . something different, a forced quality.

"Hey, John, why don't you stay here with us? Will they allow that?" Arthur asked.

John hesitated for a minute. *"Allow?* Listen, Arthur, I'm too old and getting too important for them to allow or not allow me anything! I'd love to stay. But let's not publish the news in the *Sentinel."* They finished the conversation on an up note, Arthur's spirits lifted in anticipation of the impending visit.

Emily was pleased to have John Riordan stay with them when he informed her. She told Mary, their housekeeper, to prepare one of the guest rooms, adding, "He's a priest, Mary, so anything special you think would be appropriate, please be sure to let me know."

Mary was aflutter with the cleaning and cooking for the next two days. "Maybe we ought to invite him more often, Arthur," Emily remarked. "I'll circulate him around, give him a different room each time. I've never seen Mary so happy in her work!"

Arthur laughed. "That's so funny . . . and so unnecessary, Emily. John Riordan's just a plain man, like everyone else."

"Not *quite* like everyone else," she answered. "I've never understood why a man as attractive and masculine as that would go into the priesthood. You'd think he would've married and had a pack of children, wouldn't you?"

That was the first trite reaction Arthur could remember from Emily. Tempted to say so, he replied instead, "I used to wonder about that when I first met him . . . but, no, I can understand why John chose his way. If all the priests, and all the rabbis and other clerics, were as good at their jobs and as sincere as Father John, I'd have a lot more use for religion."

The children were intrigued that a priest was coming to visit. "What should we *say* to him?" they wanted to know.

"You just say hello and act the same as you would with anyone else," Arthur told them.

John Riordan had aged. But, then, so had Arthur and all their friends. With John, it was not so much a question of gray in the hair or lines on the face. It was the eyes. Something had happened to John, and it was there, in his eyes. Or, rather, it wasn't there. A light had gone out.

They didn't have much time for conversation during the three days of the conference, because John had dinners and meetings each night. On Friday, when the conference was at an end, Arthur prevailed on him to stay over and spend the evening with them. John grasped at the invitation, seeming eager to be with him.

Mary served delicious filet of sole with mushrooms in a wine sauce for dinner and her extraordinary lemon meringue pie.

"What was this conference about?" Arthur asked his friend at the dinner table.

John smiled modestly and explained, "It was a meeting for deans. I've been made a dean at St. Mary's."

"No kidding? That's absolutely terrific, John! Congratulations! Let's drink to that."

John talked to Ellen and the boys with such naturalness that they soon relaxed in his presence, laughing at his amusing remarks, Ellen smiling when he complimented her on being as pretty as her mother.

"Where do you boys go to school?" he asked Jeff and Robert.

"We go to Wyoming Seminary, sir," Jeff answered for both of them. "We're going to Exeter next year."

Robert looked over at his father.

"Going away to boarding school, eh?" said John.

"My brother went there," Emily explained. "I think Bobby and Jeff will love it. Don't you, Arthur?"

Arthur smiled at Robert. "I certainly hope so."

"And you, Ellen? I guess you won't be going to Exeter!"

Ellen giggled. "No, Father John. I go to the Institute—but I want to go back to Finchley," she said, eying her mother. "I miss my friends there."

"Emily and the children spent the years when I was overseas in Haverford with her parents," Arthur explained to Riordan. "It's a difficult adjustment to make, coming back, making friends all over again." Emily pretended not to hear him.

After having coffee with the two men in Arthur's study, Emily excused herself. "I think I'll let you two reminisce about old times. I have some work to do for my arts committee." She said good night, missing only half a beat when John leaned over to plant an affectionate kiss on her cheek.

"Emily, I can't thank you enough for putting up with me. This has been such a pleasant and comfortable visit for me. I've had a real home for these few days." He held on to her hand, studying her face with satisfaction. "Arthur's a fortunate man," he said softly. He noticed the nervous parting of her lips, the small intake of breath at his words.

"Thank you for saying that, Father John. We've loved having you with us . . . Mary, especially, has loved it!"

"Ah, Mary! Now, there is a girl after my own heart—what a fantastic cook!" he said enthusiastically.

"You'll make her awfully happy if you tell that to her," Emily replied. "Good night." Even leaving a room, Emily had a special grace.

John looked over at Arthur, who was fiddling with liqueurs at the bar.

Arthur handed John a brandy, then sat in a chair opposite, crossing his long legs.

"I meant that, Arthur. You *are* a lucky man . . . she's lovely. And your children are terrific. You must be a very happy person."

Arthur was afraid to meet the priest's eyes, but when he looked up from his glass, he realized that for once Father John was not regarding him with that insightful discernment of old. John Riordan sat, shoulders slumped, eyes vacantly staring across the room.

"What's wrong, John?" Arthur asked quietly.

Carefully, John set his brandy glass on a table. He clasped his hands, looking down at them, rubbing them together in a wringing motion. Closing his eyes, he said, so low that Arthur had to lean forward to hear the words.

"My faith is being tested, Arthur." The anguish there was as real and as deep as ever Arthur had seen in his years of practicing medicine.

"Do you want to tell me about it? Maybe that would help."

The priest put his head against the back of the chair, rubbing his eyes with the heels of his hands, then running his hands through his hair in a rapid, nervous fashion. He didn't say anything for a few minutes, while Arthur waited, sensing the words were coming.

"I guess it was the war," he said, finally. "But that's too simple. What about all the other chaplains who went to war? All the other men, those who had to kill, and saw their friends die? I lost count of the number of times I administered last rites, gave extreme unction. I think I reached over a hundred in three hours one day.

"The kids, the scared, weeping boys . . . hardly over their childhood, so far from home and loved ones . . . afraid to die, but terrified of living and having to go out there again, or to go home without a limb, or blinded. I sat and held their hands, and had to tell them things I didn't really believe anymore . . . that they would go to heaven, that God loved them, that there was still good in man."

John formed a steeple with his hands, pressing his fingers against his lips to keep them from trembling. He swayed back and forth in the chair, like a talmudic scholar at prayer. He stopped and shook his head, sighing deeply.

He spoke in a grating monotone. "I was there when they liberated the camp at Dachau." Arthur's neck and scalp prickled, fearing, yet compelled to hear, the priest's words. "I saw those godforsaken souls"—his voice broke—"those souls forsaken by God, and I felt . . . *hate* . . . bitter, venomous hatred for the beasts who could bring themselves to do such unspeakable things to innocent people. I blame those who carried out the orders just as much as those who gave the orders. . . . There's a certain impersonality about giving orders if you don't have to see them carried out, or wield the instruments of torture yourself.

"There was a religious service for Christians . . . I wasn't there at the time. But the next day the commander of the brigade called for me. He was angry. . . . The place was . . . you can't imagine, Arthur, what it was like, what was going on there . . . our troops . . . some of our soldiers were so enraged when they saw the piles of bodies, the box cars full of corpses, the extermination camp . . . they went crazy, literally. They began machine-gunning German soldiers . . . the guards, the kitchen crews, anyone in uniform. One American officer ordered a sergeant to stop shooting, and the sergeant turned his gun on his own officer, actually shot at him . . . it was the worst thing . . . no, not the worst thing I've ever seen. . . . The worst was the Jewish section of the camp." He dropped his head in his hands, unable to go on.

Arthur swallowed. "I had some cousins who died at Dachau," he said. "My brother recently married the daughter. Her husband, father, and brother all perished there."

John continued, as if Arthur hadn't spoken. "The colonel said he wanted me to hold a service for the Jewish inmates of the camp. They couldn't locate a Jewish chaplain nearby. Wouldn't you think the Army would've had a rabbi on hand, knowing where they were heading? The Army!" He made a gesture of irritation. "Great planning. But the unbelievable thing was that when the Jewish prisoners asked to hold a service, the *Polish* prisoners raised objections! Can you *believe* that? They're all prisoners, they've all been starved and beaten and humiliated by the Germans . . . maybe not to the same degree as the Jews, but bad enough so that you'd think there might be some feeling of group solidarity, some commiseration for fellow sufferers . . . wouldn't you? But these damn Poles threaten to harm the Jews, to stage their own little pogrom in the middle of the parade ground at Dachau, if a Jewish service is held there! They said it would have to be held somewhere behind closed doors, in private. And these Poles were Catholics! *Christians,* they called themselves, followers of Christ, believers in Jesus and love.

"Well, the commander lines up all these MPs and, with an armed guard to protect them, we hold a service for those Jews." He smiled faintly and looked at Arthur. "I make a pretty fair rabbi, Arthur. You should've heard me." He had tears in his eyes. *"I cannot, and I will not, ever get the sight of those people out of my mind until the day I die.* If we are created in God's image, will you tell me who and what created the monsters who did those things?" John was silent.

Arthur began to speak. "I've often been grateful that I was in the Eastern campaign, John. It was horrible—the enemy was brutal, the bombs and bullets just as real, the wounds just as horrifying. When you're dead, you're dead, it's true. But on the way to being dead, if you had to deal with an enemy, I'd rather have dealt with the Japanese than the Germans. The Japanese have honor, and although I won't pretend they didn't do atrocious things to captives, they did it indiscriminately, as a matter of policy, for the purpose of instilling fear in the Allied troops. They didn't single out a group of people to wipe them off the face of the earth. They didn't invent a systematic killing machine, feeding millions of men, women, and children into it.

"I got to know a Japanese prisoner of war—an officer who was brought in seriously wounded, and I had to operate on him. I suppose I saved his life, but I was just doing my job as a doctor. He, on the other hand, risked his life to save mine when I was caught in a bombardment, unconscious and unable to save myself. I don't know what happened to him. I often think about him. He's probably dead now. But for the short time that I knew him, although we were enemies and that fact never escaped us, he did much to redeem my faith in people, when I was in danger of losing it."

John had regained his composure. He was calm. "I had a friend in Intelligence who told me that they captured some German documents—Gestapo, I think. Do you know they had information on almost every American city and town, with a list of community leaders, the Jews, the clergy—all the people they would need to round up and imprison when they got here! *Your* name was on that list, my friend! In Wilkes-Barre, Pennsylvania, given to them by Nazi sympathizers."

His words jolted Arthur. *Who?* he wondered, his mind flitting across the handful of German families he knew. Who in Wilkes-Barre would have done such a thing? He shook his head, and again concentrated on John's words.

". . . Germans, or former Germans who lived in this country, moved into a community, made friends, learned all about everyone, and then gave their names to the Gestapo for an extermination list. How's your faith in your fellow man after hearing that?"

"I like to believe that someone would've hidden me, tried to keep them from taking me, John . . . someone like you." Arthur sipped his brandy. "You once told me that work was the cure for all problems, John. I suggest that you try your own medicine. Your new job—the deanship—some of the same kind of community work with young people you did here so successfully. I imagine there is a great need for someone to do that sort of thing, even in our nation's capital. You'll regain your peace of mind. The war has reached *all* of us. It's left us in a state of shock, unable to believe such things can happen. You wouldn't be much of a priest if you weren't affected this way by the things you've seen."

John got up and walked over to the windows. "This is the first time I've talked about this to anyone, Arthur. Not even in Confession. I was afraid to . . . afraid to articulate it. . . . You can't imagine how good it feels to have gotten it out, to have spoken of it. I feel much different than I did yesterday. I won't be so simplistic as to say you've given me a miracle one-hour cure. But I do feel better. There are no friendships like old friendships, are there?" He smiled, that sweet, soft, slightly sad smile of his. "Priests aren't really supposed to have 'best friends,' Arthur . . . but I think I may have one."

If the telephone hadn't rung at that moment, Arthur would have told Father John about Molly and what had happened to them in India. The call was for Father Riordan, and Arthur left the study in order to give his visitor privacy. By the time John came looking for him, he had decided that he could not burden his friend with the knowledge of their meeting and their love.

Arthur took John to the train early the next morning. They bade farewell, promising to keep in touch. Arthur watched the train disappear down the track, a trail of smoke rising in the air, remaining there long after it had rounded the bend.

"Emily, I am not eager for the boys to go away to boarding school. I've missed four years of their lives as it is!"

"That's selfish of you, Arthur. And shortsighted. It's important for a man to go to a good school." Arthur recognized the steel in Emily's tone of voice.

"They *already* go to a good school. There's nothing wrong with Seminary. Plenty of students have gone to Yale from there, if that's where they want to go." This was too important for him to give in.

"Arthur, this is something they've been counting on for years." Emily was tooling up for an argument.

Well, then, he'd give it to her. "You mean, it's something *you've* been counting on for years, don't you?"

He saw her eyes flash. "It's only for them that I want it."

"Emily, I insist that they not go away now. We'll talk about it again next year. I want to get to know my sons."

She surprised him. "Living in the same house is not a guarantee of people being close . . . as you know. You've told me often enough that you weren't close to your father."

Was she trying to hurt him? "All the more reason," he said quietly. "I know what it's like to wish for a relationship and not have it." All sorts of relationships, he thought.

"They'll make valuable contacts there!"

"If you mean friendships, they'll make those at college. They'd better stay around here and make some friends in their home town," he retorted.

"Arthur, when will you realize that Wilkes-Barre is not the hub of the universe?"

"Emily, you get more and more like your mother with each passing day." He stormed out.

Arthur had no doubts that he was right about not sending the boys away. On a night when Emily was at one of her committee meetings, he had gone up to bed earlier than usual. He thought he heard something in the upper hall. Walking toward the children's rooms, there came the sound of weeping. Robert's door was open a few inches. It came from there.

"Bobby?" He opened the door.

No answer.

Arthur walked over to the bed. "Rob . . . ?" He touched the still form lightly. He felt a tremor under his hand.

"What?" said a small voice. At fourteen, Robert's voice hadn't found its proper register. Jeff was maturing earlier.

Arthur sat on the bed. "Something the matter, Bobby?" he asked.

"No . . . it's nothing."

"Sometimes it helps to talk about our problems. I'm willing to listen."

"Really, Dad, there's nothing to talk about," said the boy.

"You know, I can remember when I was your age, Robert. That must seem like a hundred years ago to you, but I can recall things that happened then as if it were yesterday. It's not an easy time of life. You're not grown up, and yet you're no longer a child. There can be lots of things that make you unhappy, confuse you." Bobby didn't say anything.

"Bobby, you know that I love you and your brother and sister very much, don't you? I missed you greatly when I was away overseas—I used to think about you all the time." He put out his hand to touch Bobby's face in the darkness. It was wet with tears.

Arthur took his son into his arms. "Oh, Bobby, don't be afraid to come to your father when you're unhappy! That's what parents are here for." The boy was crying hard now. His breath came in shudders. Arthur held him and patted his shoulders until the sobs subsided.

Arthur took his handkerchief from his pocket and handed it to Robert. "What is it that's troubling you, son?"

"That's the thing . . . I don't really know. I just sometimes feel sad . . . like . . . like awful things are going to happen."

That wasn't surprising. Awful things had happened in his son's short lifetime.

"What kinds of awful things, Rob?"

"Things like someone's going to die . . . or something like that."

"Are you afraid that Mommy or I might die?" he asked.

"Sometimes."

"Are you afraid that Jeff might die? Or Ellen?"

Robert sighed.

"That's a common worry, you know. Most people—even adults—fear things like that. Their own deaths or the death of someone they love very much."

"Do you?" asked Robert.

"I guess I'm kind of an optimist, so I don't generally worry about my family dying unless there's a good reason, like an illness. I'm a doctor, and I can be rational about death. I worry about other things, though."

"What kinds of things do you worry about, Dad?"

Arthur rubbed Robert's arm. "I worry about whether my children are happy, whether they'll grow up to be good people who are satisfied with their life's work . . . whether I've been a good father. . . ."

"You worry about that?" There was surprise in his voice.

"Yes."

"That's not something you have to worry about, Dad. You're a good father." Arthur's heart gladdened to hear those words.

"Here I'm supposed to be helping you get over your problems, and you're the one who's helping me!" he said.

Bobby gave a small laugh. "I feel better, Dad."

"Are you disappointed not to be going away to boarding school, Rob?" Arthur asked him.

"No. I didn't want to go. But Jeff did," he said.

"If Jeff wants to go, let him go without you. You don't have to do everything your brother does."

Robert shook his head. "I couldn't let him down . . . he expects me to go everywhere with him," he said. "Does this mean that we're never going to go?"

"No, it doesn't mean that at all. If you really wish to go to Exeter, you may. I wanted you home for at least another year. Once a boy goes away to school, Bobby, he never really lives at home again. I wanted us to be a family together for a while, before that happens." Then Arthur said, "Your mother and I had a disagreement about that."

"I know. I heard her." There was a note of sorrow in Robert's words. Arthur wasn't surprised.

"It upsets you when your mother and I have arguments, doesn't it?" Somehow, he'd known this . . . known Robert had heard Emily's anger.

"Yes. It scares me." Me, too, thought Arthur.

Robert was going to say something else, he could tell. "Dad . . . ? Are you and Mom going to get a divorce?"

"Just because a man and wife have an argument doesn't mean they're going to get a divorce, Robert. We can't always get along without disagreements." Arthur tried to put conviction into his words.

"Then you're not?"

"No, we're not."

Bobby seemed satisfied. "Thanks, Dad. For talking to me, I mean."

Arthur brushed back Robert's hair from his forehead. What a sweet boy he was! To think that he worried about such things. It was hard enough to grow up without fearing that your family was breaking apart. *Molly had been right!*

"There's nothing to thank me for, Rob. Anytime you feel like talking, you know who you can come to. And I don't want you to worry about people dying or things like that. Sometimes people do die before their time, but it's rare. It's not the end of the world, if someone should die, either. We go on. My grandfather used to tell me that the wonderful thing about the human spirit is that we find the strength to meet life's problems. Don't be afraid of life, Bobby. You'll be fine!"

He kissed his son good night, realizing that he had retrieved something of great value.

Arthur often thought about what those war years had meant for him in terms of his children's lives. Four crucial, formative years had been entirely lost to him, never to be retrieved. Robert and Jeffrey had been boisterous, affectionate, mischievous little boys when he left for India in 1942. He had returned to find two tall, handsome strangers wearing Haverford Friends School blazers, whose bodies stiffened in embarrassment when he hugged and kissed them.

In those few short years, other persons, other ways had imprinted their codes of behavior on his sons. At first they rose every time he entered the room until that became—even to them—ridiculously impractical. Their arms shot out in the firmest of handshakes even now, although Bobby, always the gentler and sweeter of the two, embraced him readily.

Jeffrey had light brown hair and Emily's lustrous gray eyes, while Robert was fairer, dark blond and blue-eyed. They didn't look alike. Most people were surprised to learn they were brothers, much less twins. Happily, they were close friends. Jeff was the more at ease, the more outgoing. Always the one to take charge, he counted on Robert to follow him in all of his undertakings.

Ellen, perhaps because she was a girl, or the youngest, was the child from whom he received unbounded affection. She was naturally demonstrative and effervescent, a free spirit with an irrepressible personality. Arthur thought she looked like Emily, but Emily said she was the image of him. Whoever Ellen resembled, she was an original in temperament!

Arthur had formed the habit of walking along the river on the top of the dikes in the evenings, when he wanted to think. After he left Robert's room, he was no longer sleepy. He let himself out the side door and walked across to the riverbank.

You were right, Molly. My children do need me. If Bobby feared that he and Emily would be divorced, was it not reasonable to assume that the others had the same hidden thoughts? He would have to reassure each of them in a special way. . . . Jeff wouldn't be as open or emotional as Bobby . . . he was Emily's child. Ellen would be easier. He found her more communicative than the boys.

Emily was away from the house so often, with all of her volunteer activities. Mrs. Kelly had left them before the war ended. They needed their father. Arthur must become the source of strength in their lives, the father they could come to with their problems, the one they would always be able to rely on for their emotional support.

Somehow, without being obvious about it, he must give them a sense of stability about their family, allay any fears they might have about their parents' marriage. After all that had happened to him in the past, after all the pain he had experienced, the dreams of love denied him—Arthur was not going to allow his family to fall apart. He would keep his marriage going, and he would make it work. He vowed his commitment to that.

Spring 1948

Ruth Benjamin seated herself in Arthur's consultation room, smiling wanly.

"If you have bad news for me, Arthur Hillman, I'll never forgive you!" She attempted to cover her nervousness with humor.

Ruth had come to see him several days ago. "I've never felt so rotten in all my life," she'd complained. "I know I must have some dread disease. I thought it was the flu—David had the flu two weeks ago—but this doesn't go away."

"I'll run some tests," he told her, after examining her carefully. "When was the last time you saw a gynecologist?"

She looked frightened. "Not for years. No need to. I never had any gynecological problems, except the one they couldn't do anything about. . . ."

David and Ruth had tried for many years to have a child. They had talked about adopting, but the years had passed and they kept putting it off. Now it was too late. David was forty-eight and Ruth was forty-three.

"Every woman should see a gynecologist, Ruthie—to prevent problems. Now don't you worry. You're fine. Come back to see me on Friday."

Now, it was Friday.

"Do you know what's wrong with me, Arthur?" she asked.

He nodded, smiling. "Uh-huh . . ."

"What's so funny?"

She was still in a state of shock when she left his office. How was she to tell David that they were going to have a baby . . . after twenty-three years of marriage?

There were many rewards in his life.

The Chest Fund. That was off to a fine start. Because of the broad interest in his local Lung Committee project and the miners' clinics, Arthur had been asked to join some public-spirited citizens in forming an organization to fund research in lung diseases. He had agreed to go on its board and succeeded in enlisting the support of his friend Senator Harry Steiger. Arthur had approached Emily's brother, and the fund had received a sizable contribution from Fred. (He had recently asked them to stop calling him Freddy. It seemed a reasonable request for a forty-six-year-old man.)

Arthur recommended John Riordan to the Chest Fund's board, since it was a Washington-based foundation. Father John was becoming well known as a charismatic speaker and a fine administrator at St. Mary's.

"It's good to know we'll be seeing each other at least three times a year, John," Arthur said to Riordan after their first board meeting together. "How are things at the college?"

"Terrific, Arthur. I've never been busier!" He looked fit, energetic, and satisfied. Arthur didn't ask, and John didn't mention their painful conversation after the war.

In October 1948, Arthur participated in the laying of the cornerstone for the first Diagnostic Health Center for the Northeastern Anthracite District. The governor gave a speech, the U.S. Secretary of Labor attended, as well as a number of officers of the United Mine Workers of America and representatives of the mine owners. The center was heralded as an example of cooperation between management and industry in the field of health care.

Eddy Valentine had come to the ceremony from his new job in Harrisburg in the Bureau of Mines.

"It's great to see you, Arthur!" Looking out over the crowd, he said, "You can take pride in this event. We wouldn't be here today if it weren't for you." Eddy still had that hoarseness in his voice, but his diction had improved.

"This should've happened fifteen years ago, Eddy. It's late in the game for the anthracite industry," Arthur replied. "You can thank all those disabled miners with their black lungs. They're the real reason this clinic is here." That and the willingness of one mine operator to join with the union, he thought, as he spotted Lowell Wintermuth coming toward them. Lowell had been that lone, courageous mine president who had taken the giant step, once the decision was his to make. Arthur felt a special warmth to see Eddy Valentine and Lowell shaking hands. More than a building had been started here today.

His practice was more demanding than ever. He was becoming known for his work in chest medicine and surgery. He had referrals for consultations from all over the state and even from out of state. Some patients did not like to go to a large teaching hospital, feeling it was too impersonal. Arthur could see that it would be easy for him to confine his practice to thoracic surgery, if he wished.

The hip dislocation had left him with some stiffness and pain, especially when he stood for long periods. That made the lengthier surgical procedures uncomfortable for him. Jim Flannery had looked at his X-rays and thought Arthur would develop some arthritis in that joint in the future.

"You've got to keep up some regular exercise, Art," Flannery told him. "Keep that joint moving!"

So Arthur walked every day, usually along the river, his old friend, the Susquehanna, and he played golf at Wolf's Head sometimes on the weekend, with some of the other doctors or his brother.

Nate and Leisl had a one-year-old son. The three older children doted on their baby brother. Nate had legally adopted Leisl's children. They went by the name of Brandt-Hillman.

"I don't think they should lose their identity with their father," Nathan explained to him. "But I want them to be my legal heirs, and to know that I think of them as mine."

Nate took Leisl to Israel on a UJA trip in early 1949. While there he made contact with Genevieve and Pierre Solomon, the cousins he had met in Paris. Genevieve told him that her brother, Jacques, who had settled in Palestine before the war, had been killed fighting for the British in the North Africa campaign. His three sons, all in their teens, were sabras living on a kibbutz in Galilee.

"Her father, Rafael Belkind—you know, the doctor who took care of me when I was gassed—died in a concentration camp, just days before it was liberated," Nathan told Arthur.

Life was gradually returning to normal, although the war years had altered forever the leisurely, carefree life they'd all enjoyed, even during the Great Depression. Never again could you look into another man's eyes, knowing for certain what you would find there.

His children, as always, were his chief joy.

Ellen, at fourteen, was becoming a beauty. She had Emily's long, supple body and delicacy of feature. Her coloring was more like Arthur's—her hair a golden honey-blond, her eyes a large, dreamy blue. The telephone rang constantly from the moment she entered the house after school. Arthur had always had a special closeness with his daughter. He noticed the subtle changes as she matured. . . . The years were passing too quickly! He wanted to hold on to his children's youth, jealous of their emerging independence, not wanting them to grow away from him.

He had finally acquiesced to the twins entering Exeter in their junior year.

"You really do want to go, Rob?" he'd asked. There had been no question about Jeff's eagerness to go to prep school.

"Yes, Dad. I'm ready now. I wasn't, back when we first talked about it, but I'm looking forward to it."

Both of the twins were such good-looking, popular boys. Jeff was the better student, but Robert was a superb athlete, with a warmer personality.

The house on Grandview Terrace seemed so empty now. Arthur couldn't wait for the boys' vacations. Why would anyone choose to send their children away any sooner than they had to, he wondered, wishing he hadn't agreed to it.

In February 1949, Ruth Benjamin gave birth to a healthy baby girl by Cesarean section. They named her Julie. She was a lovely child, with the most beautiful red hair and large hazel eyes.

Arthur had been greatly relieved when Ruth gave birth to a normal, healthy child. He had referred her to a new, young obstetrician who had trained in Boston. Much to Arthur's chagrin, he learned halfway through Ruth's pregnancy that she had been put on a new hormonal treatment, diethylstilbestrol, to prevent breakthrough bleeding. Ruth's obstetrician had told her that mothers who took DES, as it was called, gave birth to healthier babies. Arthur was conservative when it came to medication. He just didn't like prescribing elective medication, particularly for pregnant women. There were enough risks for babies whose mothers were over forty without adding the side effects from a new drug. He voiced his concern to the doctor, and the drug was discontinued. Thank heaven, all was well.

David, after recovering from the disbelief of being an expectant father, had immersed himself in a home-study course in obstetrics and neonatal care. "You have become an absolute *bore,*" Lowell Wintermuth, his next-door neighbor, joshed. "I swear, you'd think there was never a female born on the face of the earth before!"

"There never was one like this one!" David crowed in triumph, holding little Julie high in the air.

Ruth took to motherhood, as she did to every other phase of being David's wife, with tolerant equanimity. "I never thought I'd be changing diapers at my age, Arthur. But she's a love. Look at that silly fool, will you?" Her loving glance went to David, sprawled on the floor next to Julie's blanket.

Lowell traveled frequently. Wyoming and Susquehanna had recently diversified. It was now called W & S Industries, since Lowell had acquired other small companies in aeronautical metals and oil exploration. Phoebe was often lonely. She spent many hours of her day with Emily, doing volunteer work. Phoebe had been one of the few friends Emily had kept in close touch with during the years she had lived in Haverford when Arthur was overseas.

"Emily is the sister I never had," Phoebe told Arthur. "She's a wonderful friend."

Yes, Arthur reflected. He had many things to be thankful for . . . his family, his friends, good health, and satisfaction in his professional life—a sense of having contributed something of value to people in need.

If he wasn't *entirely* happy . . . if his life with Emily was not all that he could have wished . . . well, not everything could be ideal.

He and Emily would go on together.

Philadelphia   Autumn 1949

Ranjit Kar flew to Philadelphia in October of 1949 for surgery on his right eye. Dr. Lance Harper, now director of the new Eye Institute, performed the first of a series of delicate operations. It would be necessary for Ranjit to remain in the States for three months.

Arthur was thrilled to hear Ranjit's voice on the telephone. "Will you come to Wilkes-Barre to visit us, Ranjit? I'll drive down to get you."

"They tell me I have to remain very still, Arthur. That will be a test of will, won't it?" He sounded wonderful, chipper.

"Then I'll just have to come there to see you. Is Sushila with you?"

"Yes, indeed! She's never been to the States before. She insisted on joining me," Ranjit replied.

Emily's brother kept an apartment in a small residential hotel in Philadelphia. They arranged for it to be made available to the Kars.

"Ranjit was so hospitable to me, Emily," he told her. "It was a lucky thing he was there when I was brought in on the ambulance. He saw that I was flown to the hospital in Calcutta."

"You've never told me much about that, Arthur. When you were wounded, I mean," she said.

"Ah, Em . . . that's a part of my life I just want to forget about. I made it. That's all you really have to know." He looked away from her.

She liked it when he called her "Em." It reminded her of those early days, when she thought he loved her . . . a term of affection. *Did he still love her?*

They drove down to Philadelphia to see Ranjit and Sushila. The first moments were a shock. Arthur realized that in his mind he pictured Ranjit the way he had looked before the accident, without the scars from his burns.

"I'm in Delhi now, Arthur," Ranjit told him after they'd gone through the introductions with Emily. "In the Health Ministry. It's a new India! I hope you'll come back one day."

"There are some growing pains, from what I read in the papers," Arthur said.

"It was bloody awful," Ranjit replied. "It was what I always told you . . . . if we can't learn to get along with one another, we don't deserve anything better! Well, now we've got our India, and they have their Pakistan, and it'll be years, perhaps generations, before we can be friends."

When they were alone, Ranjit said, "Do you ever hear from Molly? Or shouldn't I ask?"

"You may ask, Ranjit. The answer is no . . . I don't expect we'll ever be in touch again. That's all in the past."

"Sorry I mentioned it, old man."

"No—I'm glad you did, Ranjit. You and I went through a lot together, and Molly was part of it."

Driving home, Emily said, "They're interesting, Arthur! I don't know when I've been so stimulated. Sushila is more knowledgeable about Western culture and art than most Americans."

"Yes, I know. They're probably the last generation of Indians who will be brought up that way."

Arthur visited Ranjit several times during his stay in Philadelphia. His operations were successful. Limited vision was restored to the right eye.

"I never expected to see out of it again, Arthur. I can't complain about the quality of the vision! Karma!" Ranjit was cheerful, uncomplaining, and a delight to be with. He and Sushila seemed devoted to each other. Arthur had a good feeling about them.

Lance Harper, now a celebrity in his own right, was still impressed with his Indian-prince-turned-government-minister. Roy McLean, whom Arthur saw frequently, reported that Harper had a standing invitation to visit Ranjit's family estates in India.

"Keep in touch, Arthur," Ranjit said wistfully, when they bid a final farewell. "God bless!"

Friends scattered so far and wide were a mixed blessing. Always having to say good-bye.

Exeter, New Hampshire   Spring 1950

"I've asked you to come up here, Dr. Hillman, because I'm worried about Robert. As I told you, he's had these blackouts twice, and the nurse tells me he has complained of headache on numerous occasions." The headmaster had called Arthur the previous morning. Arthur had flown to Boston immediately, trying not to alarm Emily.

"I'm sure it's nothing—probably sinusitis, dear. I'll take him to see Paul Rosenbloom at the MGH. Don't be upset." But he was terrified himself. Bobby, that wonderful boy, sweet and sensitive. God, please don't let anything be wrong with him!

Robert looked all right . . . a little thin and drawn. It was term paper and exam time, and he'd been working hard. "I'm sorry you had to come all the way up here, Dad," he apologized, shaking hands in the headmaster's office.

Arthur embraced him—he didn't care about their starchy Wasp customs.

"I'm glad to have an excuse to see you, Rob . . . we'll go down to Boston, get you checked out. I'm sure this isn't anything serious, son."

Robert turned to the headmaster. "My exams, sir . . . ?"

"Don't you worry about it, Robert. I'll speak to your teachers. You'll have extensions on everything."

Arthur visited with Jeffrey while Robert packed.

"How's it going, Jeff?"

"Fine, Dad. I'm doing real well. Say, what's with Rob? Is there something wrong with him?" Jeffrey looked anxious.

"I think he needs a thorough going-over . . . just to be sure. I doubt that there's anything serious wrong. He's probably been overdoing it. . . . Has he been studying too hard, d'you think?"

Jeffrey raised his eyebrows. "Well, Dad . . . we all work hard up here. I . . . uh . . . suppose he could be burning the midnight oil. But why would that make him pass out?"

"I don't know, Jeff. But we'll find out." Robert came in with his suitcase.

"Ready, Rob?" Arthur said.

Jeffrey looked unhappy. "Hurry back, Rob. The lacrosse team is counting on you!" The twins slapped each other on the back.

Half a dozen boys came out to wave good-bye to Robert as they drove off in the rented car.

Three days later, Arthur was sitting in Dr. Paul Rosenbloom's office at the Massachusetts General Hospital, where Robert had been admitted for observation and tests. Rosenbloom had interned at Jefferson when Arthur was chief resident.

"He's a fine young man, Arthur. Great physical specimen," the internist told him.

"Yes, Robert's quite an athlete, Paul. He's a good kid . . . we're close." Arthur looked down, took a deep breath, then raised his eyes. "Well? The EEG?"

Rosenbloom shook his head. "Nothing. Radiology . . ." He rose and went over to a light box, switching on the panel. "You can see, everything's perfectly normal here." Arthur joined him, while the physician described what they had looked for in Robert's work-up. He switched off the viewer. All the tests had been normal, he told Arthur.

"Blood pressure's fine." He leafed through the papers in Robert's folder. ". . . blood chemistry all within normal limits." Rosenbloom looked up. "I don't think we should do a spinal tap now. If the symptoms continue, then we can always bring him back in." He spread his hands and shrugged. "I see no pathology here, Arthur."

Arthur closed his eyes momentarily. "Thank God! But how do you account for it, Paul? Nerves? At his age?"

"Why not? Kids can be under pressure, just like adults. I see all sorts of illness brought on by tension . . . psychosomatic illness is a real phenomenon, Arthur."

"Yes, I know it is. But, somehow, when it's Robert . . . my own son. . . . I wonder what could be bothering him. He's away at school, so it's hard for me to know what's going on in his life all the time."

"Listen, my kids are at home in Brookline! Do you think I know what's going on in their lives?"

Arthur laughed. "I guess you're right." He sighed. "This is a tough year, the senior year, waiting to hear from colleges . . . he's supposed to be taking exams now. He's pretty preoccupied with the work he's missing . . . and lacrosse practice. Do you think that could be the problem?"

"Of course it could. I have no way of knowing. You could have him see someone . . . a psychiatrist. That's a fairly drawn-out process, and I'm not sure it's warranted at this time. Maybe he needs to relax for a week or two, unwind. Can he go home with you?"

"Sure. But I'm not confident that would be too relaxing. His mother would be worried about him. That might not be the best thing." Arthur thought for a moment. "We have a place up in Maine. . . . I wonder whether he and I should go up there for a few days. What do you think, Paul?"

Camp Repose, Maine

They tramped through the woods and fished together. They rode the old farm horses across fields, along winding rutted country roads. Their breath frosted in the cold northern spring air. They grilled steaks and fish, and made spaghetti and salad, sitting by the huge fireplace in the big beamed lodge to have dinner. For the first time, they drank beer together.

"I'm breaking training, Dad," Robert laughed when Arthur handed him a bottle of Moosehead the first night.

For two days they just enjoyed being there.

"What's wrong with me, Dad?" Robert had asked when Arthur came into his hospital room after his consultation with Paul Rosenbloom.

"There's nothing wrong with you, Rob, I'm happy to say." He'd been grinning, feeling marvelous, like a prisoner with a reprieve, ever since he'd left Rosenbloom's office. "I think you've been studying too hard, and I'm going to take you up to Maine. We'll spend a week up there, just the two of us. Nothing wrong with you, except that you need a vacation!"

Robert had looked doubtful. "Dad . . . my exams . . . and lacrosse . . ."

"Your exams will wait, Rob . . . so will the lacrosse team. I'll call the school and explain," he'd told him.

"What about Jeff? He'll think . . ."

"What will Jeff think, Bobby?" Arthur had asked.

"He'll think I'm goofing off, or letting the team down . . . something like that."

"You know something, Robert? I think you're too concerned about what Jeffrey thinks. . . . You don't have to live your life according to the way your brother wants you to live it."

Arthur had spoken to the headmaster at Exeter, and then to Jeffrey.

"Golly, Dad. He's missing the most important week in his senior year," Jeff had said.

"It's more important that he not get sick, Jeff. Rob needs a rest. He'll make up the exams later."

"Yeah, but if he wants to go to Yale . . ." Jeff had argued.

"Jeff, Yale is not the only college in this country. Maybe he won't go to Yale," Arthur had told him.

Now, sitting in front of a blazing fire at Camp Repose, Arthur said, "How are you feeling, Rob? Any headaches?"

"No, Dad. I feel terrific. That tight feeling in my neck and shoulders is gone, and I haven't been dizzy at all. It's good to not have all that stuff hanging over my head. Of course . . . it'll all be there waiting for me when I get back."

"Rob, you could take those exams tomorrow without studying for them and pass. You shouldn't be tense about them. As for lacrosse, Jeff says you're the best athlete there . . . so why does that worry you?"

"I have to do more than *pass* those exams, Dad." Robert looked into the fire. He had become a handsome young man . . . strong-featured. In the firelight, he looked like a rugged northwoodsman, wearing jeans and a heavy wool shirt. Soon he'll be a man, on his own, Arthur thought with a pang.

"Rob, what is it that's bothering you? The grades?" Robert's grades had never been as good as Jeffrey's, although they'd been decent enough to get him into Exeter, his average hovering just at the level that would allow him to participate in team sports.

Robert shrugged. "I guess so . . . I have to work so hard to get B's, Dad . . . sometimes, to get C's."

"Everyone can't be an A student, Robert."

"I have to have decent grades if I want to go to Yale." An edge had crept into Robert's voice.

"Does it matter so much to you if you don't go to Yale?" asked Arthur.

Robert looked up with surprise. "I thought . . . I mean, isn't that what you expect me to do? That's what I always was going to do . . . go to Yale . . . the two of us, Jeff and I."

"It's a nice idea, Rob . . . the kind of idle words parents say to their children. I never made a big thing of your going to Yale. Don't forget, I went to Penn State. I'll be happy with any college you decide to go to."

Robert looked him fully in the face. "I'm not going to make Yale, Dad. There's not a chance. I've known that for the past year."

"And that makes you unhappy?"

"It's Jeff . . . and Mom . . . I'm unhappy when I think how disappointed they'll be in me," said Robert.

"Rob, we're not going to leave here until I convince you that you have only yourself to account to . . . your own expectations are what matter. Neither your parents nor your brother have any right to set unrealistic goals for you."

Arthur began to talk to his son, the start of a week-long colloquy.

In later years, reflecting on the time he spent there in the woods of Maine with Robert, Arthur became almost thankful that there had been the necessity to take that brief time from his professional life, a time when he came to understand something of the beautiful nature of this young man, his son.

"You know, Dad, I feel like we're finally getting to know each other after all these years," Robert said one day as they stowed the canoe in the boathouse, after having been out on the lake.

"Rob, that's been a disappointment to me, the loss of time with you children—the war years, and now, with you boys away at school. It was selfish of me, I know, but I didn't want you to go away to prep school."

"Mom's . . . well, you know . . . when she makes up her mind that she wants you to do something—watch out! Jeff's a lot the same way. I remember when we lived at Briar Hill, when you were gone, it was that way about everything. Mom and Jeff would decide on something, and I'd just do whatever they asked." Robert looked unhappy when he said that.

"I've never asked, Rob. . . . How was it when I was gone? At your grandparents, I mean."

"It was lonely. I missed you. Mom was happier in Haverford than she is in Wilkes-Barre, I think." He looked off, searching for words. "You know how she is when we have company . . . sort of, well, gracious lady—that doesn't sound nice, does it? You know what I mean. Mom sort of has a special voice and special way about her when other people are around. Well, she was like that at Briar Hill. I always thought she was playing a role. Everyone in that house played a role—except Nellie! Grandma . . . she was the *grande dame*. We always used to kid, the three of us, that every time we brought a new friend home from school, Grandma would say, 'Yes, but who *are* they, dear?' She needed a pedigree on everyone. Aunt Martha, Uncle Fred . . . they all play-acted all the time, I thought. It just got to be that I knew what my part was and I memorized my lines. Mostly, I let Jeff write the part for me—Jeff's good at that."

Arthur was learning how wise Robert could be. "Rob, if you could do whatever you wanted, what would it be?"

"Up to now, it would be to live at home and go to school, come home every day to a house on a street—you know, like a regular street with small houses. I used to daydream about doing that . . . not having a nurse, just a mother and father like other kids had." Robert gave him an uncertain smile. "That sounds very ungrateful, Dad. I've had a pretty good life, and I should be glad I have. . . . As for the future, I don't know. I wish I could study medicine and be a doctor like you. That's what I *wish,* but I know I won't. . . . I don't like studying enough to go to medical school, even if I could get in."

"You have to really want medicine, Rob. The people who go to medical school because their parents want them to don't make good doctors," Arthur said.

"I don't know what I want to do, Dad. But I hope it's something good . . . something that's for other people, not just for myself."

Arthur decided that he didn't have to worry about Bobby. What a great world it would be if there were more men like Robert Hillman in it.

In June, two days after the twins had graduated from Phillips Exeter, Jeffrey was accepted as a member of the class of 1954 at Yale. Robert was rejected. Thanks to his uncle, Fred Grant, who was a trustee at the University of Pennsylvania and had taken a "special interest" in his application, he was admitted to Penn. Emily was reconciled to that. At least it was in the Ivy League.

Jeff was not happy. He had always taken it for granted that his twin brother would be there in New Haven with him. Robert was the friendly one, the one everyone liked, the good athlete, the great guy. Robert had let him down.

II

Wilkes-Barre   Autumn 1951

Arthur had been watching Emily with concern for months. She looked thin, taut, nervously stretched out. He thought she overextended herself, taking on too many commitments, expending too much on her numerous charitable and cultural activities.

Emily was on more boards and committees than there were days in the month. In addition to being a trustee of Westmoreland College, the Wyoming Valley Historical Society, and Temple B'nai Israel, she had just taken on the presidency of the Auxiliary to the Medical Society. Emily was serving out the last year of her term as president of the board of the Wilkes-Barre Institute, from which Ellen had graduated in June. In Philadelphia she spent several days each month attending board meetings of the Pennsylvania Museum of Contemporary Arts, the Philadelphia Conservatory, the Finchley School, and

Bryn Mawr Alumnae Association. There were a number of directorates in companies and banks in which her family had interests, as well as her responsibilities in the administration of foundations established by both the Grant and Allenberg families. And, just this week, the governor had appointed her to a new State Commission of the Arts. It was a deserved honor. Arthur was truly proud of Emily's accomplishments. However, she seemed to be desperately cramming activities into her life, always frantically rushing from one meeting to another.

"Emily, don't you think you ought to drop a few of your organizations?" he suggested from time to time. "It's hard to do a good job, or to enjoy it, if you're overcommitted."

"Yes. You're right," she would answer absentmindedly, but he saw no letup in her pace.

That tenacious stubbornness, the rages of anger, were more easily provoked now. Arthur had fallen into the habit of appeasement with Emily during the years when the children were still at home—almost anything to keep peace between them. Anything to protect Ellen, who bore the brunt of her mother's temper after the boys had gone away to Exeter.

More than once he'd found Ellen in tears. "I want to go away to school, Daddy. The boys are so lucky to be out of this house!" It had troubled him so much that he had almost decided to let Ellen board at Finchley in Haverford. But he kept postponing it, with the result that Ellen had continued at the Wilkes-Barre Institute, remaining at home through her high school years, with Arthur acting as a buffer between his wife and his daughter. There was nothing or no one to protect *him* from Emily's difficult personality, however, except his own defenses. He tried to keep a certain detachment, because to become involved in her swings of mood and restless energy invited confrontation.

Emily's father had died in his sleep one night in the fall of 1950. Emily moved her mother to Rittenhouse Square, where Claudia now lived with a maid and a cook. Since Claudia was limited in her ability to get around, she made unreasonable demands on Emily, expecting her to come to Philadelphia at her slightest whim. She had become argumentative and difficult, a feisty old dowager, still regal and attractive, hating the limitations imposed on her by the aging process.

Briar Hill had been sold to the president of a pharmaceutical company. . . . "*Nouveau riche,* of course," Claudia said. But who else could afford to keep up such an establishment these days? Claudia may have aged, but she was as class-conscious and imperious as ever. Arthur couldn't help but make the comparison to his own mother, who was so pleasant and easy to get along with that Leisl and Nathan never seriously considered moving into a home of their own.

Arthur rationalized about Emily's moods. There was nothing abnormal, he assured himself. Her temperament had always been volatile. At forty-six it was possible that she was menopausal, although he found that hard to believe, from her youthful appearance. It was understandable that she had become more difficult to live with . . . there *were* pressures on her. Some were of her own making, but enough of them were legitimate problems, frustrating to deal with.

He thought it would be beneficial for Emily to have a rest, put everything aside for a while. Maybe they should go up to the Maine house at Sunrise Lake for two weeks. They had spent some wonderful moments at Camp Repose. If they went up there together, just the two of them . . . even the best marriage needed occasional nurturing. *Their* marriage seemed in constant need.

It was something he would suggest, just as soon as he could find some free time in his own crowded schedule.

Autumn 1952

Emily rose from the perfumed bath and stepped into the shower stall. She had acquired the habit of rinsing herself in the shower after her bath. It had occurred to her . . . when was it? . . . oh, sometime not too many years ago . . . that it was an unsanitary practice to put on clean clothes immediately after coming from the water in which one had bathed. Why had she not thought of that before? Imagine all the people who sat in dirty bath water and dressed without rinsing themselves. . . . It made her shudder. Emily enjoyed her leisurely baths. They relaxed her, soothed away the tightness in her neck and jaws. A shower didn't have the same salubrious effect. . . . She luxuriated in her evening baths, followed by a rinse in the shower. She showered in the mornings or whenever she felt like freshening up. Emily would not have told anyone, but there were days when she had taken as many as six showers, in addition to her restful bath. . . .

Clean and rinsed, Emily toweled herself dry, then rubbed her body with *eau d'or* lotion, followed by Lily of the Valley dusting powder applied with a pouf. She frowned at her reflection in the full-length mirror. Reed-thin, Emily had not added an ounce in the twenty-one years of her marriage, but the freshness of youth no longer blushed on her body. Plain women were more fortunate in the end. Not having relied on their beauty, they could not mourn the loss of that which they had never possessed.

In her dressing room Emily slid the silver gray satin slip over her head. She sat at her makeup table, smoothing foundation under her eyes to cover the darkness of the circles—even in the flattering glow of the cosmetic lights, they were there. She never used to wear makeup to cover her skin . . . only a touch of lip color and eye shadow to enhance her coloring. Arthur was right. She *was* looking worn out. If only she were able to sleep at night. . . .

Now the gown. She removed it from its padded hanger. A gray crepe Mainbocher, it had simple lines, exquisitely tailored, with an intricate draped neckline as its only detail. She had bought it in Philadelphia at Nan Duskin, feeling a little guilty not to patronize a local shop for this important occasion. But several of the other gowns she would wear during the Arts Festival had come from stores in Wilkes-Barre.

Arthur hadn't seen the bills. . . . Oh, well, he had mellowed so much about her spending, showing the same detachment in regard to her extravagance as he did about everything else to do with her. Not that he couldn't be counted on to support her enterprises. He was the perfect spouse, always playing the role of ideal husband in public. In their private moments together —*what* private moments? she bitterly asked herself . . . he was so preoccupied with his work that she plunged herself into her committees and projects. . . . Alone with him, she longed to possess him. Completely. She never had. She knew she never would. When she tried to reach out, she found herself on the far side of an unbridgeable gap. . . . To pause to consider it, to attempt to discuss it with Arthur, that was a frightening idea. One that made her heart pound and her head buzz when she lay awake at night.

In the middle of the night, Emily often had episodes of "the daunts and the dreads," as her Scottish nurse, Cordie, used to call them. That's how she thought of them now . . . these periods of drifting, like a dismasted vessel, beyond the reef, to the unknown. At first, they had come only occasionally. She had stopped drinking coffee in the evening, thinking they were related to that. Now they were becoming worse. Rare was the night when she slept through till morning.

Emily fastened the clasp of the diamond bracelet, checked the diamond ear drops to see that they were secure. She seldom wore any of her important jewelry in Wilkes-Barre. They were family pieces, kept in the bank vault.

The Arts Festival, of which she was chairman, was being inaugurated with a gala. This was the premiere concert, with the Philadelphia Conservatory Orchestra under the direction of the Russian émigré conductor Dmitri Voitkevich. In all, there would be four weekends devoted to the festival, a fund-raising event for an Arts Center at Westmoreland College. It had been Emily's brainchild, the idea of a five-year drive for a center of the arts on the college campus, which would serve the entire valley. Emily saw no reason why Wyoming Valley could not build a tradition of cultural institutions in much the same manner as it was done in Philadelphia. She had learned the techniques of forming committees, soliciting large donations, and attracting the support of important names at her mother's knee, so to speak.

With a last look in the mirror, Emily went into the bedroom, where Arthur was waiting for her to adjust his bow tie.

Arthur whistled. "Lovely lady, you are *smashing!*"

She twirled. "Like it?"

"*Like* it? My dear, you've outdone yourself this time." He kissed her cheek. "I'm so proud of you, honey." There was that look of profound, vulnerable gratitude from Emily.

The children had come home from college for the premiere. Emily thought the twins looked marvelous in their tuxedos. It was hard to say who was the more handsome. Probably Robert. Jeff was smoother, though. They had each brought dates. Jeff's was a Wellesley girl, beautiful . . . Sharon Wolf, from Boston. Robert's girl was an art student . . . Camilla something . . . a little odd in her dress, wasn't she? She was pretty enough.

"Let me fix your sash, dear," Emily said to Ellen, who made a face, but turned around obediently to allow her mother to retie the bow on her gown. Ellen had brought her latest boyfriend, a Harvard student . . . a sweet, studious-looking young man who planned to go to medical school.

"His name is Tony Fontina," Ellen had said on the telephone, when she had called from college. Emily was relieved that Ellen's escort was such a presentable young man. Ellen seemed to want to defy her in everything these days. She had chosen Smith, rather than Emily's school. . . . "I won't go to Bryn Mawr, Mother. . . . I feel claustrophobic in Philly." Ellen knew it drove Emily wild when people called Philadelphia "Philly."

The concert was followed by a reception and glittering midnight supper. It was all perfection . . . everyone praised Emily.

When they retired that night, well past 2 A.M., Arthur complimented her, "Emily, that was you in your best style! Congratulations, dear. You must be tired. I hope you'll get a good rest now. Sleep late tomorrow morning." Arthur noted that she looked drawn in the overhead light, and was pleased that she fell asleep immediately. He heard her deep, regular breathing before he, too, slept.

The hands of the clock pointed to 3:30 when Emily awakened with a start.

Winter 1953

"Dr. Hillman!" It was Stella, his receptionist, on the intercom. She sounded frightened. "You'd better come out here . . . right away!"

Arthur was examining a patient, an emphysema case. He excused himself and went out to the waiting room, his stethoscope still around his neck. Two people, a man and a woman, were seated in the far corner of the room, reading magazines but taking an interest in what was going on in the reception cubicle where Stella's desk was situated. Emily was standing over the desk, looking down at a white-faced Stella.

"Is something wrong . . . Emily? . . . Stella?"

Emily did not turn to answer him, but continued to look down at Stella. "Yes, Arthur, something is very wrong!" she said in a loud, clear voice. Stella's eyes darted from Emily to Arthur. She rose unsteadily to her feet.

"Dr. Hillman . . . I . . . I haven't done a thing! I don't know what she's . . . what Mrs. Hillman is talking about." She was close to tears.

"Emily, what is it?" When she didn't answer him, but continued to glare at Stella, he said with growing impatience, "Emily, will you please tell me what this is all about? I have patients to take care of."

She whirled around then, and he was astonished to see that her face was suffused with held-in rage. She hissed at him, "You think I don't know what's going on in here? How you two are in a conspiracy against me? I know everything about it . . . the letters, the telephone calls . . . everything!"

Arthur took a deep breath. "Stella, please tell Mr. Conklin that I'll be tied up for a few minutes," he told the secretary. Taking Emily firmly by the elbow, he propelled her through the door that led to the main part of the house, across the back hallway to his study.

He closed the door behind him, then faced Emily. "Now, what in the *hell* do you mean by creating a scene like that?" He didn't ever remember being so angry. "What were you talking about in there?"

"I was talking about all the secrets you have behind my back—you and Stella, you and the children. I know you're all talking about me all the time, trying to keep me from entering into your life. *You don't want the children to love me!* You want to turn them against me. That's why you have Stella write letters to them, make phone calls to them. You think I don't know about all that?"

"Emily! I don't understand what you're saying . . . what you're thinking!" He was at a loss. In all her various moods and angers, he had never heard anything so irrational. "There is absolutely *nothing* . . . not a shred of truth to this. Why would I want to turn our children against you? Of course, I want them to love you . . . for God's sake, they *do* love you! If Stella writes to them, it's because I ask her to send a check or give them a message. . . . Really, Emily, you owe her an apology!" He glanced at his watch. "We'll discuss this later. I have to finish with my patients. Please, don't come into my waiting room again."

He returned to his office and got through the remaining patients, but he was in a state of agitation, and a dawning realization that Emily's strange moods had entered another phase.

"Please try to forget what happened, Stella," he said after he ushered out the last patient. "Mrs. Hillman was overwrought. She's been under a lot of pressure lately. I'm sorry she took it out on you."

"That's all right, Dr. Hillman. I just hope she doesn't think . . . well, that I would ever do anything to come between you."

"No! That's not at *all* what she was concerned about, Stella. It had something to do with the children . . . a misunderstanding. That's all."

And then he added, "I would appreciate it if you said nothing of this to anyone."

"I promise I won't! Why don't we just forget all about it?" She smiled reassuringly as she left for the day.

If only we could, Arthur said to himself.

Arthur could no longer deny that Emily was deeply disturbed. She was using tranquilizers in order to sleep at night. Afraid that she would take an overdose, he doled them out one at a time, watching her swallow each one. If she didn't have something, she wouldn't sleep. Although he didn't like the tranquilizers, her nighttime wandering was of even more concern to him.

Emily! Vibrant, energetic, healthy Emily . . . it was shocking to see her with dark circles under her eyes, strained and jumpy, her skin colorless. Argumentative and unreasonable at times, there would follow periods of depression when she seemed to care for nothing or no one.

Arthur consulted Irv Goldberg, the psychiatrist who had helped Leisl's son, Eric, when he had come to America.

"I can recommend several people for Emily to see, Arthur," the graying psychiatrist told him. Goldberg was now director of a private mental health facility near Hazleton. "I would see her myself, but I don't advise that. Emily would respond better to someone outside of the local community, from what you tell me. We should choose another institution."

"Institution?" Arthur felt the blood drain from his face.

"I didn't mean that she should be institutionalized, but I feel that you should consult someone who is prepared to give inpatient care if it appears necessary."

Dr. Goldberg arranged for Emily to visit a psychiatrist in the suburbs of Philadelphia. Their appointment was set up for the second Tuesday following Labor Day . . . shortly after their children left for college—Jeff at Yale, Robert at Penn, and Ellen in her sophomore year at Smith.

Arthur had tried to overcome the typical doctor's attitude about psychiatrists. *You'd think I'd be over that by now,* he chided himself. However, a little analysis was one thing . . . but an institution . . . for Emily, his wife? It preyed on his mind throughout August. He both anticipated the appointment, and dreaded it.

Arthur sat up suddenly, knowing something was terribly wrong, even before he was fully awake. He looked at the illuminated dial of the clock on his night table . . . 3:11. Cautiously, he put out a hand to Emily. She wasn't in their bed. She must have been unable to sleep again, gone out to read in the sitting room, or to have a cup of warm milk. She'd be annoyed if he went to find her, believing he was checking on her.

Yet, as he tried to fall back to sleep, it kept nagging at him. He swung his feet out of bed and padded across to the bedroom door, opening it quietly. The house was silent. There was a light in the lower hall, but the second floor was in darkness. Arthur went into the sitting room. Nothing there, the room dark and empty.

He felt a draft from somewhere. That was odd. Someone must have left a window open . . . it couldn't be the children, for they had left for school. He stopped, his movements arrested, as a chill coursed through him.

My God! He hurried to his closet. Jamming his feet into slippers and grabbing a robe, he donned it as he dashed down the stairs to the lower hall. The lamplight shown on the dark paneled walls, the rich Persian carpets. The ordered substantiality of the house reassured him momentarily. Everything was in its appointed place, just as it should be.

But the front door stood wide, allowing the uninvited intrusion of the night air.

He found Emily on the top of the dike, looking down at the dark, drifting surface of the river, the water reflecting the setting moon and the cold light of pinpoint September stars. She stood there in her thin nightgown and bare feet, oblivious of the chill night wind.

"Do you hear them?" she asked, as if she had been expecting him to join her.

He removed his robe and placed it around her, hugging her to him, kissing her forehead, smoothing her hair, wanting to drive out whatever awful thing was happening to her. His eyes glittered with unshed tears.

"Come home, darling . . . come back to bed," he said.

"But, don't you hear them, Arthur?" Her voice was thin and childlike, insistent.

"Hear what, my love?" he humored her.

"The voices . . . the river voices . . . they're always there. They were calling. It's so peaceful, the river . . . the only peaceful place for me. . . ."

He brought her back to their house, taking her into the big tile kitchen, where she sat while he heated milk for cocoa. She sipped from a mug, cradling it in her hands, looking down into the cup in the same searching way she had looked at the river. Arthur chafed her cold feet between his hands, warming them. Finally, he took her up to bed, tucking the covers around her, sitting there at her side and stroking her brow and her cheek. She closed her eyes, like a contented child, falling into a deep slumber. He sat there for the longest time, staring at her beautiful face, feeling the terrible weight of his sorrow.

Dr. Lawrence was younger than Arthur had expected the director of a private mental hospital to be. He looked more like a bank executive than a psychiatrist, dressed in a gray pinstriped suit, wearing a conservative tie, his hair smartly groomed.

"Your wife is suffering from anxiety syndrome, Dr. Hillman. A neurosis, with which she is having increasing difficulty in coping. Mrs. Hillman is a perfectionist. She is highly intelligent, as you know. This is common in patients of this sort.

"They are never able to measure up to their own standards, constantly expecting better of themselves, and of others. Therefore, they spend a lifetime adjusting to the imagined inadequacies of their own persons and those around them. You can see the strain this puts on the individual."

"What is the prognosis, Dr. Lawrence?"

"Quite excellent, I would say. There is nothing organic in her picture. All the tests on that score are negative. She has retained all her powers of deduction and reasoning, with only occasional impairment of the sense of reality. It is at those times that she lapses into this erratic behavior pattern. In order to deal with her anxiety, Mrs. Hillman has found it useful to retreat into a childish state, or one removed from the present. With a period of therapy and rest, she can come to understand her feelings of inadequacy and learn to come to terms with them."

Arthur's heart contracted. What was he talking about? Leaving her here—in this institution? He tried to concentrate on what the psychiatrist was saying.

". . . She is constantly aware of the need to control herself, the need to keep a grip on reality. I believe this has been going on for many years. Perhaps from her childhood on. It's an intricate case, but one in which I have no doubt that we can expect a fine result."

Arthur wet his lips. This was all so new to him. He had never known much about mental illness—had dealt with it as little as possible, which was not unusual in the years when he studied medicine. Now he wished he had devoted more study to it. "How . . . how long . . . will my wife have to remain in the sanitarium?"

"I would recommend that she remain here for several months. She is in an unstable period now . . . somewhat depressed. I think this acute stage will last a short time. She'll need support through this period, and we are equipped to give it. Then, as she emerges from this stage, we can see when she is ready to become an outpatient."

"There's no danger, is there? I mean . . . suicide . . . anything like that?"

"One never knows, to be frank. That's one reason why I want her to be hospitalized. She'll be watched constantly, and if there's any indication of that sort of thing, you can be sure we'll be on top of it." The psychiatrist was so self-confident! Arthur found himself looking for holes in the argument.

"You won't use anything like shock treatment or drugs, will you? I wouldn't want that, Dr. Lawrence."

"No, I don't think that will be necessary." He drummed a pencil on the desk. "Your wife tells me she has been taking tranquilizers regularly."

"Only for the past month or so . . . in place of a sleeping pill. She wasn't able to fall asleep at night, and she would get up to read. I found her asleep in a chair on several occasions. As far as I know, there has never been an incident like the other night before—when she walked out of the house.
. . ."

"We'll try not to use any drugs. I'll be certain to confer with you along the way. We would need your written consent before embarking on any mechanical or drug therapy." Dr. Lawrence rose, bringing the interview to an end.

"May I see her?" Arthur asked.

"Of course. But, then, I'd like you not to visit for a few weeks. Give her a chance to get into the routine. After that, we'll hope that regular visits will be helpful."

"Does she know she's staying here?" Arthur wondered how Emily would take the news, if she hadn't been told.

"Yes, she does. In fact, it was her suggestion. Mrs. Hillman said she has reached the end of her ability to achieve 'control'—that was the word she used—and she wanted to stay for a while." They walked out together. Dr. Lawrence escorted him to Emily's room.

"Your husband has come to say good-bye, Mrs. Hillman. I've told him that you've decided to stay with us." Emily looked up from the window seat where she was sitting, gazing out at the green lawns of Merrywood. Dr. Lawrence left them.

She came into his arms. "I've failed you," she murmured, her voice muffled against his chest.

"No! Don't say that, Emily. You haven't failed me . . . or anyone. You've been wonderful . . . just wonderful, in every way. If anyone has failed, it's I." He was filled with emotion. He longed so to sweep her up and take her home with him, afraid to leave her here with these professionals, who knew so much and cared so little.

"I want to stay here, darling," she said, seeming to read his thoughts. "I know I'll get well. I know I'm not really sick now, but I have to learn to cope with myself—to understand why I get these feelings of panic and depression. I just can't hang on and keep from going over the edge without some professional help. I realize that. I've known it for a long time."

"You really want to stay, Emily? I'm not forcing you to."

She looked up at him. "I'll miss you so much, Arthur. But, yes, I *have* to stay. For a while, at least."

He took her face between his hands. "Please get well, darling. . . . I love you, Emily."

Her eyes shone with hope.

Spring 1954

"It's important for Emily to have her work, Dr. Hillman. I would encourage her to do the things she enjoys most. But she mustn't go back to the overcrowded schedule she kept before she came to Merrywood. Emily understands that. She has made great strides in coming to terms with herself."

Arthur was annoyed at the paternalistic attitude the psychiatrist assumed toward his wife. She was "Emily." He remained "Dr. Lawrence." It was a tremendous relief to him when he took her away from Merrywood Sanitarium.

These had been the worse six months of his life. He had vowed that if she was returned to him in a whole, stable condition, he would do everything in his power to make her happy. He would devote himself to making their life and their marriage the secure bastion Emily desired and needed. He had come to realize, after the many discussions with her psychiatrist, how he had withheld himself from Emily, and how damaging that had been to their marriage, to her self-image.

"It is most important for the two of you to establish a dialogue with each other," the doctor had told him.

Home again, Arthur held Emily in his arms, as if she were a lost treasure that had been returned to him. "Emily, Emily . . ." He laid his cheek against her hair. "I never realized how much I needed you until this thing happened. How awful that it took this. I blame myself."

"If there's one thing I've learned from this, Arthur, it's that no one is to *blame* for what happened. It's not your fault, and it's not my fault!" She shook her head slowly. "Arthur, I was so in love with you . . . so wildly in love, you can't imagine. But you . . . you always *eluded* me. There was a . . . a thing there—a barrier. I was never able to put my finger on it, but it was there, between us. I didn't know how to get beyond it, to reach that part of you I wanted. Only once, in all the years of our marriage, do I remember a period when you loved me the way I longed for you to love me."

"When was that?" he asked.

"When I was expecting the twins . . . and when they were born. You were so wonderful then, so loving. It's funny. That gave me a value, a place in your affections that I didn't seem to hold on my own merits. I couldn't decide whether I was glad to be pregnant, or dismayed. I never felt at one with those babies, the way an expectant mother should. They had to be born before I could feel motherly toward them. I recognized this . . . this unnaturalness

. . . and disliked myself for it. I was so *consumed* with my love for you, and my inability to draw that same kind of emotion from you, that instead of being pleased that I could bring you such happiness, I was jealous—jealous of my own babies! With Ellen, it was better. Time had passed, my juices had settled, I guess. You were excited about another baby, and I was contented. But my wounded pride never recovered."

He stroked her head. "I wasn't very understanding, was I?"

"I was so alone here in this town, Wilkes-Barre. The outsider . . . not wanting to really belong here, yet not liking to be shut out, either. If it had been you and I together! But my own husband was part of that inside circle, keeping me from the inner warmth. It's no secret to you that in Philadelphia I was always favored. The Grant daughter, an Allenberg grandchild. Other girls envied me. Every mother in our set wanted me for her son." She smiled in irony. "And here I was, married to the man of my dreams." She put up her hand as Arthur nodded in protest. "Truly, Arthur, I *was!* My handsome husband, the healing physician, the darling of the community—and I didn't really have him at all. So, I did my best, played my role, and accepted that part of your love you were willing to give."

"Oh, Em." Arthur took her in his arms, holding her close. His eyes were moist and his voice was rough. "Forgive me, my dear. All these years, we've never talked like this." Would it have made a difference if they had? he wondered. How selfish, how unfeeling of him, not to have realized . . . Of course, he had always known she loved him more, but at this moment, he saw for the first time the depths of her unhappiness.

Yet, even now, he could not say the words she longed to hear—that she was the only woman he had ever loved. He did say what was in his heart though, and he knew it was true. "I *do* love you, Emily. I know I need you. We mean so much to each other—I hope we can go on together."

"Arthur, darling! How happy I am to hear you say that. I love you, and I need you, too."

And so, finally, Arthur and Emily were at peace. If someone were to ask him, Arthur would have said that he was happy.

Summer 1955

These were the best times. How many people were lucky enough to know that? Most of us look back with regret that we didn't make the most of the good years. Having escaped disaster, Arthur and Emily relished each day, drinking fully of the cup together. Even in moments of disappointment, the setbacks served to draw them closer.

Their children had some difficulties. Oddly enough, it was Emily who helped Arthur to accept Ellen's insistence that she marry Tony Fontina in the summer following her junior year at Smith. He might have expected Emily to object to the family background. . . . Tony hadn't been brought up in any religion, although his mother had been Jewish, which made him technically a Jew. His father, a professor at Princeton, had been an Italian historian, opposed to Mussolini back before World War II, when the couple married. Tony's parents lived apart now—a civilized arrangement, Arthur was told. Despite their upper-class attitudes, the Grants had always frowned on divorce. Yet Emily surprised Arthur by approving of their daughter's marriage.

"There's no point in trying to reason with Ellen, Arthur. I learned *that* when she was three years old!" Emily said, half in jest, when Arthur objected that they were too young. "We could do worse for a son-in-law."

"Tony's a fine young man, Emily. I just wish they would wait awhile. He has two more years of medical school and then his internship and residency. Those are tough years! It won't be easy for Ellen to be married to him when he's on duty for nights at a time . . . if you remember those days when you and I were going out."

"Oh, darling! If you're in love, none of that matters," Emily amazed him by saying.

"Ellen's a beautiful bride . . . almost as beautiful as her mother!" Arthur whispered to a dewy-eyed Emily when he seated himself next to her after leaving Ellen at the side of her groom. Emily squeezed his hand lovingly.

Jeff, in his first year at Harvard Business School, had been put in a romantic mood by the wedding. "Mom . . . Dad, I want to marry Sharon next June, after she graduates from Wellesley," he told them the day after the marriage. "I'm going to talk to Mr. Wolf about it when I go up there next week. . . . I thought I should ask you first, though."

Again, Arthur thought they were too young.

"She's such a lovely girl, Arthur. If they want to get married, I think we should encourage it," said Emily.

Arthur would have bet anything that Emily would be the one to object to early marriages, to question the choice of a partner. Not so. Well then, far be it from him to give them any problems! I ought to be the last person in the world to interfere with my children's marriage plans, he chided himself.

Robert worried him. Rob had been taking graduate courses in English at Columbia, intending to get his masters degree. He had abruptly left Columbia without completing the year, to take a job in a small boys' school in Ohio, teaching English and coaching lacrosse. Robert did not look happy to Arthur. He wanted to have a talk with him as soon as Ellen's wedding was over and the house had settled down. He had to do it soon. Robert had announced that he was going camping in New Hampshire for all of July and August. Robert was drifting . . . he had no idea of what he wanted to do with his life.

"Don't brood about him, Arthur," Emily said, when the talk proved to be inconclusive. "He's young. He needs to have some time to find himself. Robert will be all right."

"I always thought so . . . now I'm beginning to have my doubts."

"You know, he'll never have to worry about money, dear," she said as gently as she could, well aware of the problems her family's wealth had created for them in the past.

"I just hope that isn't the reason for his troubles, Emily. Sometimes it's good for a man to have to worry about money. If he had to make a living in order to support himself, he'd have no choice except to get himself set." Arthur prayed that the Grant fortune would not be the ruin of his son.

Brookline, Massachusetts Summer 1956

"Dr. Hillman . . . I mean, Dad . . ." Sharon stumbled over the name. It was hard to call someone "Dad" when you hardly knew him. ". . . our rabbi says he thinks he knows you. He's looking forward to seeing you."

A rabbi who knew him? "What is the rabbi's name, Sharon?"

"Rabbi Blumenthal. Richard Blumenthal."

A host of memories rushed in on Arthur . . . the hospital in Calcutta, the Indian Jewish service, the picture of a young man bringing him chicken soup that a Jewish nurse had made in his bungalow's kitchen. . . . To think that the same rabbi would be performing his son's marriage ceremony!

At the wedding rehearsal that evening, there was Richard Blumenthal, twelve years older, ten pounds heavier, but the same.

"How are you, Richard? I'm so happy to see you!"

"Colonel Hillman! I can't get over it. . . . When we signed the registry and Jeffrey said his father's name was Arthur and he was a doctor, I knew immediately it had to be you!"

"I haven't been called 'Colonel' for twelve years. You'd better make that Arthur!"

It was a beautiful wedding. Sharon's family were hospitable, attractive people who were obviously delighted to have Jeffrey as a son-in-law. The Wolfs were especially taken with Emily. Mr. Wolf knew the Grant law firm. He was a tax attorney. Was the whole world populated with lawyers? Arthur wondered.

At the last minute, Rose was not feeling well, so she was unable to attend. Leisl stayed at home with her, and Nate flew up for the ceremony, then returned that same evening.

The day after the wedding, in their hotel suite, Robert stunned them by announcing that he had resigned from his teaching post. He had no idea what he was going to do, he said. He thought he would travel around the country backpacking for a while. He had saved some money. He wanted to think.

Arthur loved Robert so, this big, brawny, gentle son of his. He was the closest to Robert among the three children. In the early years, he and Ellen had that special father-daughter relationship, but as Robert grew up, and especially after their time in Maine together, Arthur had come to admire this son's character more than that of anyone he knew. What was Robert's problem? He had so much to offer! He would have made a fine teacher, a wonderful physician, a sensitive social worker—even a good salesman, with his warm personality. Why couldn't he settle down? Why had he not found his interest?

"Rob . . . everyone has to have *something* they do in life. I think you better find out what your something is." He didn't want to smother Robert, or to undermine his confidence. That integrity of character was so rare, so special.

"You're not going to like this, Dad . . . but I think I want to be a poet."

"A poet?" Were people poets? Did they do nothing except write poetry? Maybe in Wordsworth's or Shelley's day. But in 1955 did someone just be a poet?

"Can you support yourself writing poetry, Rob?" Arthur asked.

"I'd like to try, Dad."

"Couldn't you be something like a newspaper correspondent, and write poetry on the side?"

Robert sighed. "I may have to settle for that."

Again, Emily was supportive to Arthur, and to Robert. "He needs to explore, Arthur. Some people don't have an easy time finding their space in life."

This, from Emily? Emily, who had been so disappointed when Robert hadn't made Yale? She helped Arthur to be more understanding. Robert went off to Maine, to live at Camp Repose for a while, to be at one with nature . . . to write poetry.

In the fall of 1956 they had a call from Ellen. "I'm pregnant!" she wailed. "I'm going to have a baby."

"That's wonderful news, Ellen! Aren't you thrilled?"

"Thrilled? *No*, I'm *not* thrilled. I don't want to have a baby now. I just started graduate school." Ellen was studying fine arts at Harvard. She wanted to be an art historian.

"Well, then why . . . ?" He stopped.

"I'll tell you why . . . the goddamned diaphragm didn't work!" She really did sound dismayed. "Boy! Women have it rough. . . . It's the woman who gets pregnant. You don't see Tony missing a beat over this. *He's* the one who's thrilled. I don't *want* to have a baby!"

"Ellen . . . you're not thinking of . . . ?" He couldn't finish.

Her voice softened. "No, Daddy. I couldn't do that . . . not to our baby. But I do wish it were a few years later." She had calmed down.

"Honey, you're not the first woman who's gone through graduate school and had children. It's harder, I know, but you can find a good nursemaid. Tony will do everything to help, I'm sure."

"You know, Daddy, there's something wrong with the way things are set up. I go to school all day and study at night. Tony works all day and a lot of the nights. So who is it who takes the shirts to the laundry, does the shopping and cooking? Me. I don't know why it's that way, but that's what happens. If he dries the dishes, I feel like I should say thank you."

Arthur thought it didn't sound good. Much of what Ellen said made good sense. But how could she expect Tony to do the housework when he was a resident? Arthur remembered his days of residency, when he was walking around like a zombie half the time.

"Let's face it," he said to Emily after they'd finished speaking to Ellen. "She's right. Men *don't* get pregnant!"

Seven months later, Michael James Fontina was born at Boston Lying-In Hospital.

What a feeling it was to hold his first grandchild!

"He's sweet, isn't he, Daddy?" Ellen was sweet herself, looking like a little girl with a blue ribbon in her hair, sitting up in bed, wearing the blue satin and lace bed jacket Emily had brought. Emily had gone on a wild shopping spree at the Kiddie Shoppe, buying the layette to end all layettes.

"He'll be a clotheshorse at twelve hours of age, Mother," Ellen had said groggily when they first arrived.

Ellen had the baby by natural childbirth, with Tony there, helping to deliver him.

"At least, with Tony, I didn't have to worry about the husband getting in the way," her obstetrician told Arthur. "It's really a lovely thing, this experience, when everything goes smoothly. I've had some ghastly times, though, when we ran into trouble . . . fetal distress or an abnormality."

For Ellen and Tony, it had been sublime. They said it was the most thrilling moment either of them had ever known.

"Imagine, Mom, having your husband there when your baby is born!" Ellen exclaimed.

Emily exchanged looks with Arthur. "I can imagine how wonderful that is, darling."

Emily hovered maternally over Ellen in a way she had never done when Ellen was a baby. How gentle and serene Emily was these days . . . that same serenity he had always loved in her when they'd first known each other.

Tony held Ellen's hand, looking at her lovingly. "Isn't she wonderful?" he asked them.

"I wonder whether Ellen realizes what a great husband she has," Emily said to him when they were driving home. "She takes an awful lot of Tony's love for granted."

"Why didn't you tell her I was there with you when our children were born?" Arthur asked her.

"And spoil her moment? Ellen likes to be an individual, Arthur. You know that. She thinks this is such a special experience for her—why should I steal her thunder?"

Arthur thought that was wise of Emily to have discerned that in Ellen.

In the midst of happiness came sorrow. Rose's health was failing. Arthur visited his mother often. She was bedridden most of the time with a weak heart.

"You're happy, Arthur?" she asked him suddenly one day.

"Yes, Mother. I'm very happy." He smiled at her.

She studied his face. He wasn't a young man any longer, she realized. Soon he would be fifty-seven, although he didn't appear that old to her. That pain was gone from his face, that look she had seen there for so many years. She believed him when he said he was happy.

"Your Grandfather Isaac used to say that living to an old age was the most overrated experience! He was right. You lose all your friends and many of your relatives . . . and you become a bother to those who are left."

"Mother! You're no bother to anyone. You must know that," he protested.

"It's a terrible feeling for someone like me to become dependent on others, Arthur. It takes all the joy out of life. Leisl and Nathan are wonderful to me, but I hate it when Leisl has to help me with everything."

"Mother, we wanted to get a nurse, but Leisl insists she will take care of you herself, so you couldn't be much trouble for her." He tried to cheer her up.

"You've been a wonderful son, Arthur." She lay back against the pillows, her face drawn, her hair loose around her shoulders. "Eighty years is a long time to live. . . ."

Two days later, when Leisl brought Rose's lunch to her on a tray, she refused it. "I think you'd better call the boys, Leisl. I don't feel so well, dear."

Both Rose Hillman and Claudia Grant died in the same autumn month of 1958. Rose was ready for death at the end, slipping peacefully away. Claudia fought to the last moment, terrified of the beyond.

Arthur and Emily went up to Maine after her mother's death. They drew comfort from each other, walking in the glorious fall, tramping on dry leaves.

"We're both orphans now, aren't we?" she remarked. "Somehow, as long as a parent is alive, you can still feel young, not fully grown up. . . ."

They were there at Camp Repose when Robert received a letter informing him that three of his poems had been accepted by *The Poet's Quarterly*. It thrilled Arthur to see how Robert basked in the warmth of Emily's pride.

In the beginning of November 1958, John Riordan called to say that he was being sent to Bolivia to teach at the sister university to St. Mary's. "I hope to develop a written language for the dialects spoken there by the Indians in the Andes. It's been a dream of mine for many years, Arthur."

John would be gone for four years. Arthur was happy for the priest, but he would miss seeing John at the board meetings of the Chest Fund. Since Father John would be leaving right after Christmas, he and Arthur met in Washington before Thanksgiving for a conference about the Chest Fund and to say good-bye. Arthur was feeling a letdown when he reached home, so it went especially hard with him when Ellen called that evening to tell them she and Tony were separating.

Emily was magnificent. "Ellen, dear, don't you want to come down here with the baby and talk to us about it? There's so much good in your marriage. Maybe you just need to get away from each other for a little while."

Arthur was extremely upset about Ellen's and Tony's separation. Tony was a wonderful person, a loving husband, and a fine doctor. What had gone wrong with them? He thought he knew. He'd seen it in his own marriage . . . the lack of communication . . . not recognizing each other's needs. . . . But he remembered that in those early days of his marriage, even when things were far from ideal, he had been determined to work it out. Where was that sense of serious commitment, of selflessness, in Ellen's marriage? He tried to talk to her. He thought she was at fault. Ellen couldn't seem to accept the fact that she was now a wife and a mother. He discussed it with Emily, who was much more understanding of Ellen's feelings.

Emily always seemed to be the stronger one about their children's setbacks. She bolstered *his* morale, helped him to accept the disappointments.

Ellen was there with them in Wilkes-Barre at the ground-breaking ceremony for the new Arts Center at Westmoreland College. The result of the five-year campaign Emily had begun was coming to realization. The center would be an ambitious project, encompassing a gallery, studios, an auditorium for the performing arts, and practice rooms for musicians. It would take almost two years to finish the construction.

"We have *you* to thank for this, Emily," the president of the college told her.

"For someone who always thought she didn't belong in Wyoming Valley, darling, you've certainly made your presence felt here," Arthur said to her that evening.

"Do you know, Arthur . . . there are times when I still feel like an outsider, trying to belong! Not often, but every now and then something happens, people talk about something that I can't share."

"Does it bother you as much?" he asked.

"No. We all come from the place where we were born. I've learned to accept that. When Briar Hill was sold, though, I think I realized that my ties to Philadelphia had been severed."

Wilkes-Barre   April 1959

"Where are you going dressed like that?" Arthur asked as Emily came running down the back stairs in a pair of old dungarees and hiking shoes, carrying a mackintosh.

"I'm going upriver to look for sites for the Historical Commission. We're planning great things for Susquehanna Day." Susquehanna Day was scheduled for the following year. A number of sites of historical interest that had been overlooked by the Parks Department were to be beautified and marked with plaques in an effort to increase public awareness and pride in the rich heritage of the Susquehanna River Valley. Emily was head of the committee that would select and plan the sites from Wyalusing as far south as Berwick.

"I'm really excited about this, darling. Wait till you see my report." She leaned over him as he sat at the breakfast table reading the morning papers. Reaching down, she gave him a hug. Arthur patted her arm and turned to kiss her.

"Who's going with you?"

"Phoebe was supposed to go, but she has the flu, so I'm going alone. It's such a beautiful day. After all the rain we've been having, I'm just dying to get outdoors."

Arthur eyed Emily's slim figure appreciatively as she helped herself to juice and coffee at the sideboard. "Where'd you get those jeans? They look like a second skin."

"Found them in Ellen's closet." She looked down at them over her shoulder. "I guess they *are* a little tight, but I wanted something old in case I have to trek through muck and mire."

"Somehow, Emily, I can't picture you in the muck and mire!"

"I choose to overlook that remark," she replied gaily, as she reached for some fruit to take with her. "I think I'll be on my way." She bent down to kiss him. " 'Bye, darling."

"Don't be too late, dear."

"I won't be that long," she said as she headed for the side door. "See you at dinner." She blew a kiss and was gone.

Through the breakfast-room window he saw her blue convertible go by in the driveway and noticed that she'd put the top down. It must really be a nice day, he thought.

Emily drove north along the river road on the west side of the Susquehanna. The fresh spring breeze caught her hair, blowing loose waves from the scarf she had knotted around her head. A bright sun shimmered on the sparkling surface of the river. If she didn't know how polluted the stream had become from a century and a half of coal and sewage wastes, she could have believed it to be the pure, limpid river inspiring verse and song in poets of a simpler age.

She turned the radio dial until she found some music. This was one of those perfect days, when she had that sense of herself, alive and full of purpose, an adventurous project ahead of her, and the prospect of coming home at the end of the day to spend a leisurely evening with Arthur . . . just the two of them for dinner. They would open a bottle of wine, light candles, eat in the small dining room, or perhaps the study. That would be nice. She'd tell Mary to take the evening off.

"A foggy day . . . in London town . . ." Emily sang along with Sinatra.

She knew why she was feeling so absolutely great these days. The trip in June—just five weeks away. They planned to spend four days in London, then on to Paris. She would show Arthur all her favorite places. Of course, Paris would be far different now, twenty-nine years later . . . the war . . . but the old marvelous buildings were still there . . . Notre Dame, the Louvre. . . . They must visit Les Halles before it was torn down . . . L'Isle St. Louis, with all the little bistros . . . the Left Bank. It had not been a happy time for her, in Paris . . . to be there with Arthur now would be heaven. They could rent a car, drive through the château country, to Nice or Monte Carlo. Then, on to Italy . . . Venice!

Venice with Arthur, what a fabulous thought! They would stay at the Danieli, have dinner on the roof by moonlight, glide along in a gondola together under the stars. From there to Florence. Then a drive through Tuscany . . . to Pisa, San Gimignano, Siena. South to Rome, Naples . . . Pompeii, Amalfi, Positano! There wasn't enough *time* for it all! Four weeks wasn't long enough. But Arthur had said he was keeping their return open.

"This is one summer that is just for you, darling . . . just for *us,*" he'd said when he gave her the tickets in that sweet, funny, dear way. He'd never done anything like that before. He'd always remembered her with beautiful gifts—lovely antique jewelry, art books. He was a romantic, her husband. And, to think, that after twenty-eight years of marriage, he would be more the romantic lover than he had been when they were newlyweds. To surprise her that way, with the tickets to Europe, taking the entire month of June . . . and maybe July.

Emily came to the bridge at Falls. Should she continue up the west side or cross over the river and go into Tunkhannock? The Historical Society might have a better map. The one she'd been given wasn't very good—hardly any road names appeared on it. Maybe it would be better to stop in town and ask about some of the sites.

The Wyoming County Historical Society was closed. Open Monday, Wednesday, and Friday from 10:00 A.M. to 3:00 P.M., said a lettered sign on the door. Today was Tuesday. Too bad. Well, she could organize things, get an idea of where the sites were, and then she and Phoebe could come back another day. It would take several weeks of tramping around to decide which sites to select. The other four members of the committee were screening the river from Wilkes-Barre down to Berwick. Then they'd all visit the sites together. Stanley Dubak, who had agreed to design the landscaping, had some wonderful ideas. . . .

Emily drove over the Tunkhannock bridge and turned north. The old Trading Post from the days of the fur trappers would be her first stop. She glanced at her watch. It was almost ten o'clock. She wouldn't have time to have lunch, if she hoped to visit all seventeen of the sites. . . . *Lucky I brought some fruit.* She hummed as the blue convertible skimmed over the winding country road.

The last patient had departed. Arthur threw his white coat in the laundry bin, shrugged on a tweed sport jacket, and went into the reception room, where his secretary was returning patient histories to the file.

"That about wraps it up for today, Stella. I better get down to the hospital. Be sure you have those latest statistics on black lung from the union headquarters for my talk at the Cartwright Foundation."

"I'll pick up your plane ticket for Washington, Dr. Hillman. You have a breakfast appointment with Senator Steiger on Thursday morning at seven-thirty." Arthur winced. "That was the only time we could find when you both were free! I'll type up your schedule, finish the final draft of your lecture, and call for the slides at the photo lab on my way in to work tomorrow."

"Terrific, Stella! What would I do without you?"

Stella handed him an index card. "Here are the house calls. Mrs. Agronsky's daughter sounded a little anxious, Doctor."

"Then I'd better go there first. . . . Good night, Stella. Have a pleasant evening. See you in the morning."

By the time Arthur reached the hospital, he was running an hour late. The switchboard operator signaled him through the glass window of the front office. "Sister Michael wanted to see you if you came in before six, Dr. Hillman. It's about the plans for the new wing."

Arthur glanced at his wristwatch. It was almost six o'clock. "Jeanie, would you please call my wife and tell her I'll be late for dinner. I should be home by seven."

An hour later, Arthur passed the front office on his way out. Jeanie called to him, "I left the message with your housekeeper, Dr. Hillman. She said not to worry about the time, because Mrs. Hillman wasn't home yet, either."

That was surprising. He thought Emily planned to return early. She probably got carried away with her creative ideas for the Historical Commission project.

It was almost 7:30 when he reached home. He was surprised not to see Emily's car in the garage.

"Mary, has Mrs. Hillman called?" he asked the housekeeper, who was sitting in the kitchen having her dinner.

"No, she hasn't, Dr. Hillman. That's not like her. She always calls when she's late."

"There's probably no telephone nearby. I imagine she'll be here any minute," he told her. "I'm going to take a shower. If Mrs. Hillman doesn't come soon, you can leave dinner and we'll warm it up."

The steamy shower felt good. He turned on the jets, feeling the tension ease in his muscles as the needles sprayed against his hip and lower back. His old hip injury often bothered him after sitting or standing in one position for a long time. That was one of the reasons he had given up surgery six years ago. The other reason, which he didn't like to think about, was Emily's illness. After all the discussions with her psychiatrists, he had concluded that a surgical specialty was too disruptive to married life. Up every morning to scrub at the crack of dawn, needing to get to bed early every night so he'd be able to operate in the morning. However, not practicing surgery hadn't done much for his free time. His days were usually nonstop. He rushed from hospital to house calls, to office, to clinic, and back to the hospital.

Arthur would take time for Emily this summer, though. The trip in June had been a surprise on her birthday, planned with care. He had wrapped the tickets in a large box, with masses of tissue inside, so that she was beginning to think it was a joke and that nothing was actually *in* the box. When she had discovered the envelope and withdrawn the airplane tickets, her eyes had moistened from emotion.

"You mean, you really will take a whole month off to travel with me?" she had said, not quite believing it. Something would interfere. An emergency . . . something.

Arthur knew then that the real gift to Emily was the gift of his time. The being alone together, traveling. It would be a care-free month. They might even extend it, stay longer. It would be wonderful to see Europe with Emily. She would be the perfect guide to places he had never seen . . . and they would discover the new together. So full of enthusiasm and humor, Emily was a delightful, mature woman—mentally strong.

Recently, she had said to him, "When I think of all the years I wasted worrying about such trivial things, darling—honestly, it's no wonder I went a little crazy!"

"I wasn't any help, Emily," he had answered.

Their marriage was good . . . a warm companionship, transcending the excitement of the first years in its depth and solidity. And there *was* excitement still, he reminded himself. Emily had always been a woman of tremendous allure. At fifty-four she looked years younger. He found her immensely attractive. The fires may have been banked, but there was a nice glowing bed of coals. . . .

Arthur turned off the shower, toweled himself dry, then quickly dressed in slacks and a sport shirt. Only lately had he broken the lifelong habit of wearing a coat and tie at the table.

Coming out of his dressing room, he frowned when he saw that Emily's dressing room and bath on the opposite side of their bedroom were dark. He picked up the intercom and buzzed Mary in the kitchen.

"Has Mrs. Hillman come in, Mary?"

"No, sir, Dr. Hillman. She hasn't called, either. She must have had car trouble." Mary sounded worried. In the recesses of his mind, an alarm rang.

"Don't worry, Mary. She'll be along soon. I'm sure there's a good reason for the delay." His tone was reassuring, from the habit of allaying the fears of others. But he felt a rising concern. Emily had been gone since 8:30 that morning. It was now almost twelve hours, and it was after dark. If she had trouble with a broken-down car or a flat tire, she would have gone for help and most certainly called by now. Unless she was on a deserted road in the dark, needing assistance.

He picked up the phone to call Phoebe Wintermuth. Phoebe was in bed with a flu-like virus. Lowell was in Chicago. Arthur told the maid that it was important, and shortly he heard Phoebe's congested voice on the line.

"Phoebe, I'm worried about Emily. She left at eight-thirty this morning to go upriver for the commission, and she hasn't returned. Can you tell me exactly where she was planning to go?"

There was a pause. "I have a list of suggested sites, Arthur. Emily said most of them were in the vicinity of Tunkhannock, on the west side of the river." He noted how uneasy Phoebe sounded. She was probably remembering that she would have accompanied Emily if she hadn't been ill, and was feeling guilty.

"Is there a map?" he asked.

"Emily took the only map we had. My list says things like 'Indian Campsite near Osterhout' and 'Burying Ground Outside Tunkhannock,' but it doesn't give any precise locations. Shall I bring it over, Arthur?"

"No. Thanks for offering, but I don't think that would be helpful. I'll make some calls. Maybe the State Police would know if there was an . . . if someone had car trouble."

"Oh, Arthur!" There was real alarm in her voice. "If anything went wrong
. . ."

"Now, Phoebe, nothing's gone wrong. It's probably foolish to call the police, but I'd rather do it now than wait until midnight. If Emily's stuck somewhere, she's probably mad as hell that I'm not there with a tow truck!" He thought his attempt at levity sounded flat.

"Call me the *minute* you hear anything, Arthur. I won't be able to stand it until I know where she is," Phoebe said. "You're sure you don't want me to come over?"

"And catch your virus? Are you kidding?" he joked. "Don't worry, Pheebs, I'll call back in a little while to tell you she's home safe." *Please, God.*

The State Police hadn't had any reports of an accident in the vicinity of Tunkhannock, at least not on the state highways. They gave him the number for the sheriff's office in Wyoming County.

The sergeant who answered sounded bored. Arthur explained the problem to him.

"Nope. Nothin' been reported here. She'll turn up." He yawned.

"Sergeant, I don't think you understand. My wife left at eight-thirty this morning, expecting to be gone for no more than four or five hours. She was all alone, and unfamiliar with the area. I'm afraid she's had an accident."

"There's not much we can do, sir, if you don't know where she was going."

"May I leave my number in case you hear anything, Sergeant?"

What the hell! This was ridiculous. Who did he know up there? He hadn't been to Wyoming County since before the war, since they'd sold . . . *Hillside! Joe Sanduski!*

Joe couldn't have been friendlier. "Arthur Hillman! That sure does bring back memories. How's the family, Arthur? Is your mother still livin'?"

"No, Joe. Mother died a little over a year ago. She was eighty." He inquired about Joe's family, then quickly told him about Emily.

"I'll call Clem Taylor, the sheriff. His pa's an old frienda mine, Arthur. Now, why don't you see if you can get holda that map you say she has. See if someone else has a copy—or, leastways, that list of places she was lookin' at."

"Good idea, Joe. Ah, I can't tell you how grateful I am to you. Let me give you my telephone number—I'll give you the office and the house. That way, if one's busy, you can still get through."

Arthur called Phoebe. She insisted he stay at home and she would bring over the list. Phoebe had the names and telephone numbers of all the committee members. One lived in Berwick, another in Plymouth . . . and a third in West Nanticoke.

Stanley Dubak, in Plymouth, had a copy of the map.

"I'll bring it right up there, Dr. Hillman," he offered. When Arthur apologized for inconveniencing him, he brushed it aside. "I'm a great admirer of Emily's, Dr. Hillman. If anything has happened to her, I don't know what I'd . . ." His voice trailed off. Arthur was moved. He hadn't ever heard of Stanley Dubak, wasn't even aware that Emily knew someone by that name . . . from Plymouth. . . .

He was suddenly in the grip of a cold fear. *Something terrible has happened! I know something has happened to Emily.*

He forced himself to remain calm. He had to *do* something. Call someone. . . . Nate!

He dialed his brother's number. Leisl answered. She called Nate to the phone. Just hearing Nate's voice was a steadying influence.

"Nate, Emily's missing . . . I mean, she hasn't come home from an excursion she made up around Tunkhannock. She should have been back by five at the latest. She was alone, near the river . . ." His voice broke.

"I'll be right over, Arthur. Don't worry, we'll find her."

He heard the door chimes. Down in the hall, Mary was speaking to a woman. Arthur raced down the stairs. It was Phoebe.

"Phoebe. I'm really sorry to get you out of bed like this."

"Don't be silly, Arthur. We'll all laugh about this in the morning." Phoebe handed him the list. He ushered her into the study.

"Drink?" he asked, automatically. Not waiting, he poured her a scotch. He would like to have had something himself, but he decided against it. He had a feeling it was going to be a long night. He glanced at his watch: *9:45!*

Emily, darling, where are you?

Mary appeared in the doorway, carrying a tray. "You have to eat some dinner, Doctor." She placed the tray on the desk in front of him. His stomach rebelled at the sight of food, but Mary stood over him until he began to cut into the roast chicken. The doorbell sounded again, so she left to answer it. Arthur put the tray aside.

It was Stanley Dubak. After hasty introductions, Arthur took the map and began checking it against Phoebe's list of historical sites.

The telephone rang. Arthur seized the receiver in prayerful expectation.

"Dr. Hillman? This is Clem Taylor speaking. I'm the sheriff of Wyoming County."

"Yes, Sheriff Taylor. Thank you for calling. Have you any news about my wife?"

"None, Dr. Hillman. I was hoping you could give me some more information. Joe Sanduski said you have a list of places Mrs. Hillman was visiting?"

There were seventeen different spots, and Sheriff Taylor had heard of only five of them. Arthur described the locations as they appeared on Stanley Dubak's photocopy of a hand-drawn map. A person would have to know the area well in order to find most of them.

"Sheriff Taylor, I'd like to come up there and look for her myself. I know some of that country along the river. I spent every summer of my younger days near Sanduski's farm. My family had a place there."

"Yes, I know. Joe told me. You come right ahead, Doctor. We'll give you all the assistance we can." The sheriff gave Arthur a number which he could leave at home in case any news came, or someone wanted to reach him.

As Arthur hung up, Nate arrived. Arthur had never been so glad to see his brother. Nate had always been a source of strength for him. When Nathan heard that Arthur had decided to go to Tunkhannock, he said he would go with him. Phoebe offered to remain at the house to monitor calls, while Stanley Dubak said that he was going to mobilize a search party to drive along both sides of the river, checking for Emily and her car. Arthur gave Dubak a description of the automobile and Emily's clothing that day. He remembered, with a pang, that she had looked like a lighthearted student in Ellen's old jeans that morning.

Ellen! And the *boys*. Should he call them? No, it was premature. In a few hours, he hoped this would all be a bad memory. There was no purpose served in alarming their children. . . . What could they do by long-distance?

Nate drove, while Arthur scanned both sides of the highway for a stopped car.

When they reached Tunkhannock, Clem Taylor was waiting for them. He was a big, barrel-chested man with a peculiarly hairless, immature face, baby-pink skin, and round, dark eyes behind wire-rimmed glasses. His head did not belong on that large, military body. Taylor had an earnest, eager-to-please manner. Arthur liked him. He was pinning his hopes on Clem Taylor—the way the family of a desperately ill patient had frequently pinned theirs on him.

"Still nothing to report, Dr. Hillman. I've sent four patrol cars out to cruise the roads in a radius of ten miles. If she's anywhere around here, we'll find her." The sheriff hesitated. "I have to ask you a few questions . . . you know . . . about your wife."

Arthur nodded.

"Was there anything that happened . . . something that might have caused her to . . . uh . . . not return home?" the sheriff asked.

Nate was horrified, Arthur could see. I better make it easy for all of us, he thought.

"No, Sheriff. Things were excellent when Mrs. Hillman left this morning. She was cheerful, happy, looking forward to her day . . . *and* to seeing me at dinner. I can assure you that she has not run away from home!"

The sheriff smiled. "I wasn't suggesting that, Doctor, but we have to consider everything." He made a note on his pad. "I must ask you another question. Difficult as this may be for you, I must ask whether Mrs. Hillman has ever been . . . suicidal."

If the sheriff had doused him with ice water, it couldn't have been more of a shock.

It had been five years since Emily had left Merrywood Sanitarium. Not once had he noticed signs of depression in her. . . . Not when Ellen had separated from Tony. . . . Not when Robert quit his job and took to the road. . . . Emily had taken it better than he had, reassuring him, bolstering his spirits, rationalizing that it was all for the best, would turn out to be a good thing in the end . . . using every cliché in her roster. *No,* Emily could not have taken her own life . . . impossible!

He shook his head emphatically. Too emphatically? "No, Sheriff, she was not suicidal."

Joe Sanduski came into the sheriff's office. Arthur recognized him immediately, and Nathan did, too.

"Arthur! Nate!" Joe held on to their hands, pumping them up and down. "I wish it wasn't your trouble that brought us together. I've often thought about you fellas when I read some news about you." He was an enormous man, like his father and uncles were. "I came to offer my help."

"That's good of you, Joe," said Arthur. "Let me show you this map. Maybe we can divide up the places Emily was visiting."

"These two are right near your old place, boys! Just next to Hillside," Joe exclaimed, pointing to markings near the river. "See this, where it says 'Twin Birches'?"

"Yes, I see, Joe. What's Twin Birches?" Nathan asked. "I don't remember that."

"That's what the new owners call Hillside. They bought it from the Hendersons and changed the name."

"Indian Rocks . . . I recall that," Arthur remarked absentmindedly. They decided to go there with Joe, while the sheriff and his men would fan out to the other sites. The sheriff sent a patrol car along with them.

It was strange to see Hillside again, after so many years. It looked smaller to Arthur. No one lived there now, Joe told them.

"The Hendersons lived here year-round, but these people just come in summer and during hunting season," he said. The house was desolate by dark of night.

Joe led them to Indian Rocks through a narrow footpath in the woods. It was deserted and overgrown. They stumbled in the brush, unable to see well by the light of the flashlights.

Arthur was discouraged. "It's so difficult to find anything at night, Nate. How would we know if Emily were around?"

"We'd see the car, Art," said Nathan.

"Not here, we wouldn't. She couldn't have driven in here."

"We would have seen a car out on the road if someone came here," said Joe. "There was no sign of one . . . unless . . . naw, I don't think she could have done that."

"Unless what?" asked Nate. "What could she have done, Joe?"

"There's a track the Hendersons put in a few years back. They wanted to build another house, but they gave up on it . . . ground was too rocky. They would've had to blast to put in a foundation. The road was never paved. It's sort of overgrown. I doubt we can follow it by dark. We'd be better off waiting till early morning."

"Couldn't we try?" asked Arthur. "Where is it? Is it on the map, Joe?"

Joe shined the flashlight on the map. "Here," he pointed. "See where the main road is? It's marked here."

"Let's try that, Joe. You never know." They walked back to Joe's farm, where the cars were parked.

The headlights picked out the dirt road easily enough. They bumped along the rough track.

"I don't think Emily would ever have driven in here, Art."

"I think you're right, Nate. She wouldn't. We might as well go back."

"We'll have to go to the end," said Joe. "There's a place to turn around there. . . . What time is it?"

It was 2:45. Arthur had a sense of impending doom. Nothing good can come out of this, he thought.

They reached the end of the wooded dirt road. Joe swung the car around a sharp corner, then backed up to turn around. As he pulled the car around to drive out, Nate caught the gleam of reflective metal through the trees.

"Stop!" he cried, peering out.

"What is it, Nate?"

"I thought I saw something in there. Back up and turn the headlights in that direction, Joe." He pointed east.

Joe did as he was told. He backed up and swung the car around, turning on the brights. There, in the beam of the headlights, was a blue Chrysler convertible, with its top down.

"Emily!" Arthur shouted, opening the car door with a wrench. He ran the thirty yards to the blue automobile. The car was empty, parked with the brake on, no key in the ignition.

"Emily," Arthur called. "Emily, where are you?" His voice echoed through the surrounding forest.

By three o'clock that afternoon, Emily had visited eleven of the seventeen historical sites. Unable to find three of them, she had wasted time, but those she had seen offered exciting possibilities. It was getting late. She decided to head for home.

Looking at the map, Emily realized that two of the remaining sites were located close together at a point a few miles south of Tunkhannock, off the river road. *I'll just find Indian Rocks before getting back on the main highway.*

The river road was narrow and curving, but it was so much more picturesque than the highway. She loved the scenery. This was marvelous country. Why hadn't she and Arthur ever done any driving around here together? *What an intriguing little shop . . . Hand-Mades.*

Three miles beyond the shop, she stopped her car to consult the map. Bear left at a fork in the road, near a red barn with a hex sign. After another half mile, she came to the red barn . . . the road forked, turning east. Emily passed a large, prosperous-looking farm. A mailbox at the gate bore the name "Sanduski."

The road grew narrower, but it had a good surface. She was looking for a sign that said "Twin Birches." Just beyond that there was an unmarked road that led to Indian Rocks. *This is a lot easier than I expected.*

Emily turned the automobile onto the narrow unpaved trail, two wheel tracks with grass growing between. Wondering whether this was a wise thing to do with the car, which was only a few months old, she drove slowly over the bumpy ground. There was a dense pine forest on either side of the road here. Emily inhaled the wonderful, piny aroma. The road turned to the right and came abruptly to an end at a huge boulder. She got out of the convertible.

I wonder how I'll ever manage to turn around here—it's pretty tight. She walked back to the turn. If she backed up, it looked as if she could maneuver the car just enough to turn it around and retrace her path. She'd better do it soon, though. It was getting dark in the woods. *I'll just take a quick look to see what's here, and then I'll leave.*

Indian Rocks was a group of five tall gray stone columns clustered together to form an almost solid wall of rock. In a crevice was a low, round opening to a cave. Emily saw an old, worn marker, bent sideways. She was able to make out the faded lettering: "Indian Cave. Here Indians camped on their journeys up and down the Susquehanna River. In the interior is a dungeon where the skeletons of three persons, presumed to have been captives, died. The skeletons were discovered in 1914. God Rest Their Souls. Wyoming County Historical Society."

Emily was thrilled. No one had said anything about skeletons or caves. She stooped to look into the cave, but it was black inside. She'd have to bring a flashlight with her when she came back with Phoebe. *I wonder how far this is from the river.*

She walked on through a grove of white birches, whose branches were in bud. The sun was warm here. Underfoot, the earth was soft and spongy with moss. In a few minutes Emily saw the river shining through the trees. She walked down through a glade of ferns, the new growth tightly furled. *This would be lovely in the summer . . . I have to come back.*

Standing on a boulder above the river's edge, she spied a small wooden dock downstream at a semicircular clearing on the shore. Leaning down, Emily balanced herself on one hand to jump the three feet to the rocky beach. She turned to look back up the embankment. The gray wall of Indian Rocks was hidden behind the grove of birches. Emily thought the rocks could be seen just over the treetops. If she went out on the end of that old dock, she would be able to see them. She placed her shoulder bag and the clipboard she was carrying with her Historical Commission papers on a boulder, setting a rock on top of the clipboard to keep the papers from blowing in the wind.

The dock was more rickety than she had supposed. It could not have been used for years. A wonder it still stood, considering that the waters of the Susquehanna reached flood level frequently, with the seasons.

Emily stepped onto the dock, bearing her weight on it to test its strength. It seemed sturdy enough. At one time there had been a railing because at intervals there were upright posts to waist level. Part of the wooden platform had washed away, and there were missing planks. In the riverbed, beyond the end of the wharf, stood pilings. Waterlogged and cracked, they had resisted the river's swift current for many seasons.

"I really shouldn't walk out there," she said aloud. "If anything should happen, there's no one around." Still, she was a strong swimmer. Up at Camp Repose, she swam a mile a day just for the exercise. The worst would be that she'd get wet!

Standing in the middle of the dock, she turned to view the shoreline. Up on the rise above the birches, Indian Rocks was clearly visible, five rounded ramparts like hooded monks—the three taller pillars close together behind the two in front. Putting her hand up to shade her eyes against the sun, Emily scanned the riverbank. Through the woods to the south, she could make out a substantial house with a great stone chimney. It looked dark and uninhabited.

Emily heard the rending sound of wood splitting as she took a step backward. She grabbed for one of the upright posts to catch herself as the planks gave way beneath her. Her foot went through the rotted wood, and she was thrown back off the end of the dock. As she fell into the water, her head hit one of the pilings a glancing blow, stunning her. She was dimly aware that her foot was caught between the planks of the pier, and she felt a searing pain as the bone above the ankle snapped.

The shock of the icy water revived her. She forced herself to the surface, despite the paralyzing pain in her left leg. Choking and sputtering, she broke from the water, gasping for air. She was sobbing from the pain. Trying to get a toehold, she realized that it was much deeper than she'd thought. The weight of her body was enough to pull part of the platform away from the structure. A section of it broke loose and turned over on top of her, forcing her under water again.

Frantically, she tried to free her foot with her hands, but it was wedged between two planks. If she could get her hiking boot unlaced, she'd be able to pull the foot out of it. The collapsed dock was heavy, weighting her down. Although the current was strong, the wreckage was not carried downstream because it had caught on the pilings.

If she didn't get her foot free soon, she wouldn't be able to hold her breath any longer. *There!* The laces were open. Her fingers worked at the laces, pulling them, loosening the high boot around the injured ankle. She would have to pull the foot out with her hands because she was unable to move it. . . . The pain was excruciating. . . . Her hands were so slow . . . so clumsy. . . .

She looked upward at the heavy wooden platform bearing down on her. Through the slats, she could see daylight. She turned her head . . . shafts of sunlight . . . through the ripples of the murky water. . . . Shafts of sunlight . . . warming the cold, green-brown watery grave in which she was trapped.

Arthur . . . Oh, Arthur . . . I wanted so to grow old with you. . . .

Up around this part of the Susquehanna, the river runs deep and pure in the spring. From Mehoopany down to Falls is one of the most beautiful expanses of the long, twisting stream which arises in New York's Otsego Lake and wends its 520 miles south to Chesapeake Bay.

Fishing was still a favorite pastime for locals in the summer months. But in the spring, when the fish are spawning, it was illegal to fish the river.

The two men who set out in a skiff from the boggy shore east of Eatonville did so stealthily in the darkest hours before dawn. They carried a bucket of decaying meat to use as bait for their drop lines and fat worms for their poles. They hoped to haul in as many bottom feeders and walleyes as they could in the short time they could remain on the river before daylight would reveal their presence.

They lay at anchor close to the eastern shore for almost an hour, without luck. The stream was swift there, for the channel was deep.

"No good, Max. We better get outta here," said one as he saw silver-gray traces of light appear on the upper rim of Sunrise Mountain.

"I tole ya we shoulda stayed on t'other shore, Ben! 'Smuch better over there where it's shallow 'n slower. . . . Why don't we give it a try?"

"Too late now," said Ben.

"Naw 'tisn't. We got a hour b'fore sunup." He pulled the starter on the outboard.

"Kill that motor!" hissed Ben. "Ya wanna bring the ward'n down on us?"

"Aww, none'll hear us now. The wind's too high." But he stopped the motor and moved to the oars. They pulled in the anchor and were quickly caught in the current, which swept them downstream. The man called Max strained at the oars, maneuvering the boat across the river toward the opposite shore. They proceeded on this diagonal, downstream course for a few minutes, until they broke free of the fast-moving channel. Then they rowed upstream against the current until they reached the gentle shallows on the west side. Max scraped the pebbly bottom with the oars. He turned the dinghy, its bow pointed south, so it would drift down along the western bank.

Max shipped the oars and began rebaiting the hooks. The boat floated along slowly, pointing first onshore, then offshore, according to the wind. Ben kept shifting nervously, peering through the darkness to the banks of the river, wondering whether anyone could spot them there. There was a steep fine for fishing out of season without a license.

The river began its big sweep to the east just below. They drifted down toward the bank there, where trees and roots hung off into the water, and flotsam was deposited by the freshets each spring. The river had been high this time last year, but it was normal this spring, despite the heavy rainfall the previous month.

"I'm headin' in, Max," Ben said in a voice that invited no discussion. "We ain't caught nothin', and we ain't goin' to." He started rowing into the bank.

The boat thudded against something resistant in the shallows, lodging there, the stern swinging around with the current. The lightening sky in the east made the dark shapes on the western shore all the more ominous.

"Catch us loose there, Max, will ya? I can't get us in."

Max was angry. He had counted on going home with some carp or drum-fish. He leaned over the bow to push the boat off from the obstruction. There was a bunch of soggy debris lodged there in the shallows near the rocky shore. He put his hands down to pull it away from the bow so they could beach their craft.

"What the hell is this?" he muttered. *"Jeesuz!"* And then he began to yell.

He'd seen death before. Hundreds of times . . . a thousand times? Painful death, merciful death, death by fire, death by sword. Death in all its forms, hideous and meek.

Emily! Emily, you are not meant for death. . . . Emily, my lovely Emily. That isn't you.

She lay there, silent, still, her story untold. Her flesh cold and pale, a deep pink blush across her face. Sodden strands of hair clung to her skull and brow. Her hands, no longer graceful, clenched air, forever frozen in the grasp for life.

In death, she should be beautiful, an angel sleeping. The white foamy froth of drowning lay across her features like a veil, masking the loveliness that had been Emily.

In his hopelessness, Arthur heard their voices in the room behind him. . . .

"A blow to the head . . . She was alive when she went into the river."

". . . missing shoe . . . broken ankle . . ."

"Not molested . . . clothing intact."

"Struck from behind? . . . Thrown into the water while unconscious? . . ." "Then, what of the shoe? . . ."

"What would be the motive?"

"Robbery. Her purse is missing. . . . She must have carried money. . . ."

"Arthur? Can't I get you a brandy or something? Well, then, some hot tea or coffee?" Nate put his arms around him. He leaned his head against his brother. Nathan was his strength.

"I can't leave until I know, Nate. . . . You understand, don't you?" Nathan understood.

Slowly, with the dawn, the story unfolded. The missing purse and papers revealed themselves in the early morning sunlight. The collapsed dock, with the hiking boot imprisoned between its planks . . . the rest was simple.

She had floated free out of the loosened boot, not soon enough. Downstream, her body had come to rest in the shallows near the shore, before the river widened and curved outward to the east.

They were all there. Their children, in anguished grief. His sisters, weeping and sorrowful. Leisl and Nathan, strong and comforting. Emily's brother, in mournful disbelief. And their friends, lamenting the beautiful Emily.

They moved around him in whispers, exchanging sympathetic, meaningful glances. They sorrowed and they proffered help, treading softly through the house.

At day's end, when he closed his door, he was alone in his bereavement.

She died at Hillside. She died in the Susquehanna, at the very place where he had spent his joyful youth. The treacherous, destructive river had taken her from him, had robbed her of her life.

Never again to breathe the same air. Never to share joy or sorrow. Never to reach out at night, knowing she was there, knowing that she loved him, that there was peace and meaning between them, that they would go on together, growing old.

BOOK EIGHT

A Pilgrim Soul

1960 – 62

I

Fukuoka City
Kyushu, Japan
22 May, 1960

Dear Colonel Hillman,

I am Kenji Tokada, the man whose life you saved in March of 1944. I hope you may remember me because I have never forgotten you.

For those few weeks in Burma, I saw that it was possible for decent men to rise above their enmities, for honor to prevail. If I had not believed that, I could not have survived.

I have often wondered what became of you. You can understand my pleasure when I saw your name in a recent issue of the World Health Organization newsletter announcing your appointment to a committee on industrial health. The article said that you are a consultant to the Cartwright Foundation, so I take the chance that this letter will reach you. I could tell from the photograph that you are the same man I knew in Burma.

There is a Japanese belief that if a man saves your life, you are forever tied to him in a spiritual bond which can never be broken. Therefore, Colonel Hillman, I feel that tie with you, and that is why I take the liberty of writing to you at this time.

If you care to reply to my letter, I shall be happy to hear from you. It is with that hope, I remain,

Your friend,
Kenji Tokada

---

3 Grandview Terrace
Wilkes-Barre, Pa., USA
June 30, 1960

Dear Major Tokada,

Your letter was forwarded to me from the Cartwright Foundation. You cannot imagine how excited and pleased I was to receive it. To know that you are alive and well is just wonderful. Frankly, I was doubtful that you had survived in that jungle, with your wounds not healed, and the terrible conditions there. How ever did you make it back to Japan?

If there is a Japanese belief about the bond with someone who has saved your life, then it is I who am bound to you in spirit. I was told it was you who carried me out of the surgery to the ambulance. I doubt that you owe your life to me, but there is no question that I owe mine to you.

In those days, during the war, there were times when all of us despaired of ever seeing friendship restored among nations. That was the cruelest war because we saw to what depths man is capable of sinking. Now, sitting here in my study writing to you, I find it difficult to believe that you and I were ever enemies, in a tent in the Burmese jungle, with men killing one another all around us. If only the world will learn to bring an end to war.

I would enjoy hearing from you. Tell me about your life, your work, and your family. Also, since we are no longer military men, I suggest that we dispense with the formalities. In my thoughts, you have always been "Kenji," and I am,

With warm regards,
Arthur

Wilkes-Barre   Spring 1961

"How are you, Dad?" It was Robert calling from Connecticut. "I thought I'd come home next weekend. There's something I want to discuss with you."

Arthur's heart lifted. "Wonderful, Rob!" He hadn't seen Robert for six weeks, since they'd met in New York for dinner with Jeff and Sharon. "How are things going at Prentice?" he asked. Robert was teaching English and math, and coaching lacrosse, at Prentice Academy, a small, well-regarded boys' school in western Connecticut.

"It's been going real well, Dad. They want me to come back next year—in fact, they've offered me a raise and a two-year contract."

Arthur was thrilled. He admitted to himself that he was still concerned about Robert. About what Robert was going to end up doing with his life. Here he was, twenty-eight, and Arthur did not yet have the feeling that Rob had "settled down." Maybe because he wasn't married, didn't have roots. That was silly, of course. Plenty of men didn't marry until well into their thirties. Robert seemed to always be on the edge of changing course, finding a new place for himself. . . .

"That is terrific news, Rob! They must really like you there," he said enthusiastically.

"I guess they do. I don't know, Dad . . . that's what I want to talk to you about. I'm not sure whether I want to sign myself up for two years."

That same thud in the pit of the stomach. "Oh . . . well, I'll be happy to talk about it with you. It sounds like a great opportunity to me. Two years isn't all that long," he said, trying to keep it casual. Two years . . . it can be an instant, or an eternity . . . two years since Emily had died. . . .

"I'll be there late Friday night. We can talk all weekend. Don't wait up for me, Dad. There's a girl I'm going to see in New York on the way down. We'll have dinner, so I won't get to Wilkes-Barre until after midnight."

"Fine, Rob. Enjoy yourself! Oh, do you have a key, or should I leave the side door open?"

"I still have a key, Dad—unless you've changed the locks."

"No, the locks are the same as they've always been. Rob . . . I just remembered. I'm having dinner at the Wintermuths that evening, in case you want to know where to reach me. I'll be there until eleven or so."

"O.K., Dad . . . say hello to Phoebe and Lowell for me. So long. . . ." He rang off.

Since when did he start calling them Phoebe and Lowell? *Robert, Robert . . . if only your mother were still alive.* She would tell me not to worry about you. She'd be the one to understand and point out how much worse it could be. It's true, you *are* working, but I keep feeling it's all temporary. Jeff's so solid, so ambitious, so successful. Never gives me a moment's concern. Except, he lacks heart. He doesn't have your sweetness, your goodness, your spirit. And Ellen, up there at graduate school in Cambridge studying fine arts, separated from Tony. . . .

"I'm still in love with Tony, Daddy. I know you can't understand why we live apart. I need to have some space from him. I need to develop my own interests, my own career. Then maybe we can get back together and live a sensible married life, where I do my work and he does his."

"Ellen, dear, you should've thought all that through before you insisted on marrying when you were only a college senior. When I pointed these things out to you, you wouldn't even consider them! You have a baby now. You can't neglect your child, relinquish your responsibilities as a parent."

"Daddy, I can't explain it. I realize everything you say is true. The problem is that you and Mother brought me up to be too moral! If I wanted to sleep with Tony, I had to marry him . . . so we got married."

Arthur found he could still be shocked. *"Ellen!* . . . Oh, never mind. Whatever you want, honey. Just remember that Tony isn't going to sit around waiting for you to come to your senses forever. There'll be another woman one of these days, and you'll be out of luck. He's a wonderful man, Ellen. I think you know that."

She had sounded subdued, as if she had been given a new thought, when she hung up. "Good-bye, Daddy . . . I'll come see you in a few weeks."

"All right, darling. I miss you. . . ." He'd felt twice as lonely when she hung up.

Am I a hypocrite? It's not all right for my daughter to tell me she wanted to sleep with a boy she loved? It was all right for me to do that . . . with Molly. Why was there nothing wrong with that, and there is when it's Ellen?

Even then, though, I didn't feel right about it, and neither did Molly. But things are different now. Standards have changed . . . new contraceptives. . . . It was hard to believe the changes within his lifetime. Let's face it, a lot of those are big improvements. Mainly, he just didn't want Ellen to be hurt, or Tony either. He was really fond of Tony. Arthur sighed. Did you ever stop worrying about your children?

Arthur tossed and turned, unable to get to sleep. *I thought my nights of lying awake until I heard a car in the driveway were over,* he said to himself as he looked at the dial of the clock—4:30. I suppose if Robert had a date, he wouldn't take her home until midnight, maybe stay and have a cup of coffee or something. It was a three-hour drive from New York, without traffic. He should have been here by now. There had been no message with the answering service when he'd called at 12:30, after the Wintermuths' dinner party.

They'd had him paired with a woman again; this time, an attractive divorcée from Harrisburg, ten years younger than he. Very nice, really, only he wasn't interested and it had showed. He hoped her feelings hadn't been hurt. There came a moment when he couldn't stand being in that room for another second, that room he'd sat in for so many afternoons and evenings with Emily. He'd left the living room and gone into the library to sit there alone. Phoebe had found him there.

"I'm sorry, Pheebs. I'm being a terrible guest. I just had to get out of there."

She had sat there with him, and she had been the one to end up in tears. "It's such rotten luck, Arthur! Emily was so wonderful. . . ."

So he had ended comforting Phoebe.

Arthur fell at last into a restless sleep. He awakened before seven, and walked down the hall to Robert's room. The door was closed. He opened it a crack. Rob was there, his long athlete's body sprawled out in the bed, bare-chested. His clothes were slung across a chair in a heap. *God knows what time he got here!*

Arthur knew he wouldn't go back to sleep, so he took a shower and shaved, dressing in slacks and a sport shirt. Now that he'd taken on a young associate in his practice, he didn't have to see any but the more serious patients on the weekend. He went down to breakfast, picking up the newspaper and taking his coffee and juice out to the screened terrace. It was a lovely morning, warm for April. The river sparkled in the sunlight and the newly budding willows swayed in the breeze.

"Good morning, Dr. Hillman," said Mary, coming out with a plate of scrambled eggs.

"Good morning, Mary. How are you today? Now, why did you make me eggs again? You know I have to cut down on my cholesterol!"

"Dr. Hillman, people have been eating eggs every day of their lives for thousand of years and it hasn't hurt them. If you didn't know about 'klor-ester-ole,' it wouldn't bother *you,* either!" Arthur ate the eggs.

He was reading the newspaper when the phone rang. It was Nate. "How about going out for dinner with us tonight, Arthur? We thought we'd go to Perugi's."

"Thanks, Nate, but Robert came home for the weekend, and we're just going to spend the time talking. He has some decisions to make."

"If you change your mind, we'd love to have Bobby, too."

"I know you would. I'll call if we do, but I think we'll stay home. Give my love to Leisl." He hung up.

They were concerned about him, he knew. Everyone was so thoughtful. He certainly didn't lack attention from his relatives or friends. The Flannerys, the Benjamins, the Wintermuths . . . Nate and Leisl, his sisters . . . many others. None of them let a week go by that they didn't invite him out to dinner or over for the evening. He was lucky. A lot of people didn't have that.

"Morning, Dad!" Robert, looking tousled, appeared in a robe, barefoot, carrying juice and coffee.

"Rob! I thought you'd sleep half the day. What time did you pull in?"

Rob grimaced. "Don't ask! I think it was close to five. The date in New York lasted a little longer than I expected!" He grinned.

"Nice girl?"

He nodded. "Nicer than I thought. She's a teacher at one of the girls' schools in the city. I met her at a workshop we had up at Prentice a couple of weeks ago. She's going to teach at a school for foreign service kids in Khatmandu next year. . . . Yeah, real nice girl." He gulped down his orange juice.

Mary came out. "Bacon and eggs, Robert? How are ya?"

Robert got up and hugged Mary. "How 'bout something like . . . uh . . ."

"Waffles, hot cakes," she offered.

"Yeah! Hot cakes with melted butter, maple syrup, and bacon."

Mary beamed. "I'm glad *you're* not worried about that 'klor-ester-ole.' " She winked at Arthur. "He's a growing boy."

"He'll grow in all sorts of ways if he continues to eat like that," said Arthur.

After Robert had eaten a stack of hot cakes and a rasher of bacon, Arthur asked him about his work.

"I like it there, Dad. It's a great place, with nice people. I have good friends on the faculty, and I know they like me. If I stay on, I have a feeling they'll make me dean of the lower school in a year or two . . ."

"What's wrong with that, Rob? It sounds wonderful. If you've chosen education as your field, that's the natural way for you to go, unless you just want to do nothing but teach, and not assume administrative responsibilities."

"No, it's not that." He played with a spoon. "It's just that . . . all the kids there . . . they're nice boys. I'm very fond of them. But there's not one kid in the place who hasn't had everything he could possibly want in life, or will ever know what it is to lack material things. I'm not sure I care to devote my life to teaching kids like that. I want to do something more useful, I guess. Something more important. If I weren't in these boys' lives, it wouldn't make much difference to them. I want to teach kids who wouldn't get to have an education unless it were for me, if you can understand what I mean." Robert looked at him seriously.

"Where will you find children like that, Robert? Even the poorest children in our country get an education. Only place I know would be the parts of the world where that isn't so, the underdeveloped countries."

"Exactly! That's precisely what I mean, Dad!" Now Robert was excited. "There's a new program that's being formed by the government. They just recently announced it . . . it's called the Peace Corps."

"Yes, I read about it." Arthur sounded doubtful.

"It's just the kind of thing I'd like to do. Live abroad in a poor country, with the people, working with them, helping them to develop their own schools, training teachers. I'm going down to Washington next week, during the spring vacation, to talk to them. I have an interview with one of Sargent Shriver's aides. Jane arranged it . . . Jane Abrams, the girl I had a date with last night. Her father knows everyone in the Kennedy administration. They've just started getting it all together. The applications aren't even printed up yet. They told me I'd be one of the first interviews!"

Arthur had seldom seen Robert so enthusiastic about anything. He had a light in his eyes when he talked about the kind of work he could do in this Peace Corps. Arthur didn't want to squelch his fervor, but he thought he ought to mention a few things that had escaped his son's attention.

"What would it mean, Rob, for you to interrupt yourself now, just as you're getting started, to take a position like this? From what I read, the program is really a volunteer project. It wouldn't lead to a career development opportunity. They don't really pay you, do they?"

"They pay your expenses, and a modest salary which they give you at the end of your tour of duty. You can sign up for varying periods of time. They want teachers." Robert looked down. "Dad, we both know I have enough money to live on whether or not I have a job. . . . I didn't ask for it. . . . It's just there, from Mother's estate, the family trusts. All three of us have more money than we can use. So why wouldn't it be a good thing for me to do something worthy with my life—something to help other people?"

Why, indeed, Arthur thought. Would it be better for Robert to spend his life working for IBM and living in Greenwich, like Jeff?

Nagasaki, Japan   June 1961

"This is Ground Zero, where the bomb exploded," said Kenji. "One and a half square miles was totally destroyed. At least forty thousand persons killed or missing." They were at the Peace Memorial.

On the remaining wall of a school building there was the outline of a person burned into the structure, as if that soul was forever emblazoned there, leaving its mute message for future generations.

Arthur didn't know what to say . . . he must say something. "I feel . . . a responsibility, Kenji. What an unspeakable horror my country has unleashed on the world."

"If it had been Germany that perfected the bomb first, don't you think they would have used it?" Kenji asked.

"I have no doubt they would. . . . That doesn't change matters. We are the ones who used it first, and we'll always have to live with that. It will come back to haunt us."

They stood on a hill, overlooking a new, modern Nagasaki. When a city is largely reduced to rubble in a millisecond, it can be entirely rebuilt. . . .

Standing next to his friend, Kenji Tokada, Arthur gazed out toward the distant harbor. How fitting that Madame Butterfly's house should be here in Nagasaki, city of dashed hopes.

The train trip along the Inland Sea had given him an idea of Japan's changing topography. From Tokyo, where he had participated in a panel on Lung Diseases in Industry at the meeting of the World Medical Association, Arthur had traveled alone to Kyoto. From there he had taken the train south to the island of Kyushu.

Kenji had met his train in Fukuoka City. Even in the milling crowd of Japanese figures, Arthur had known him immediately. There was that certain fineness of features, a shining quality in the eyes. With characteristic Japanese restraint, Kenji had greeted him . . . but there was a deep emotion beneath the surface.

"You're looking better than the last time I saw you," Arthur finally said, to ease the moment.

"I might say the same for you!" Kenji replied, laughing. "I've arranged a little tour. I hope you enjoy it."

He did not meet Kenji's family, but he'd been told to expect that. The Japanese rarely brought outsiders into the sanctity of their homes.

From Nagasaki they drove to Unzen National Park, where they stayed at a traditional Japanese inn. Together, he and Kenji took the hot bath, Kenji showing him how to first soap and rinse his body, then immerse himself up to his neck in the hot mineral water.

"Ahh! That is the most relaxing feeling," Arthur said, when he had adjusted to the intense heat of the bath. "If I could do this every day, my hip wouldn't trouble me."

"This isn't as hot as I usually take it, Arthur," Kenji told him. "It requires some getting accustomed to." Kenji's English was still smooth and as American as ever. "You have a hip problem? Is that from your injuries in the bombardment?"

"Yes. I had a dislocation—a bad separation. It took a long time to mend. I have arthritis in that joint now. Not enough to require any surgery, but it's stiff and painful at times."

After fifteen minutes, Kenji insisted they leave. "It's weakening at first," he explained. "Even I spend no more than half an hour in the bath."

They donned *yukatas,* cotton kimonos that were folded on the foot of a cot in the dressing room. Wearing slippers, they went to a private *tatami* room for dinner. Arthur noticed that all of the guests in the inn seemed to be men. The only women were the hostesses who conducted them to their table, and the waitresses—all traditionally lovely young women, wearing kimonos.

"Kyushu Island is known for its excellent *sashimi.* Have you had *sashimi?*" Kenji asked. Arthur had enjoyed the raw fish appetizers in Tokyo.

"Yes. I like it."

"I've ordered a very special *sashimi* for us this evening," said Kenji.

Their waitress entered the room, her feet shod in white cotton socks as she padded across the *tatami* floor where they sat on silk cushions. She knelt to place a lacquer platter in the center of the table. On the platter rested a large, live lobster. Its tail had been severed and turned over so that its ventral surface faced up. The tail meat had been neatly removed and sectioned into bite-size tidbits, then placed back in the shell in an artistic arrangement. The ultimate *sashimi!* Arthur found it deliciously delicate, although it *was* disconcerting when the lobster's feelers waved over his plate as he consumed its tail.

Kenji smiled. "What do you think of it?"

"Once you get used to the idea, it's wonderful!"

"You're a good sport, Arthur. You'll be sorry to know that the *real* delicacy, *shirauo,* is out of season . . . tiny white fish served live in a special broth! They are available for only one month each spring. We catch them with our chopsticks or a little net to eat them."

"Kenji, I can't promise that I would've eaten those!"

Back in his room alone, Arthur found his bed prepared for him on the floor —a thickly padded *futon* with crisp, smooth linens and an embroidered quilt. A mosquito tent had been arranged over the bed, because the *shoji* screens were open to a small balcony that overlooked a picturesque garden, softly illuminated by stone lanterns.

There was a low knock on the door. A young woman entered, dressed in a simple cotton kimono. She bowed, greeting him in Japanese, then in halting English said, "I . . . am . . . Noriko."

She carried a wicker tray on which jars and bottles were arranged. A towel was draped over her arm. She knelt, indicating that Arthur was to remove his *yukata* and lie on the *futon*.

He looked questioningly at the tray. She lifted the ceramic lids to show him. The containers held creams and lotions. Well . . . why not?

There are some sensations that cannot be described. Surely the person who had invented the technique of Japanese massage had been among the gods. One hour in the soft, pliable hands of Noriko convinced Arthur that he could easily spend the rest of his days in Japan. Her fingertips found tendons and nerve endings that *Gray's Anatomy* hadn't documented, he mused, as Noriko made a science of massaging his scalp. Slower and slower, softer and softer, she brought the kneading of his neck and shoulders to an end, as if reluctant to play the last note of a song.

Arthur sighed and opened his eyes. "That was very nice," he said, in a triumph of understatement.

She didn't understand his English. "You like . . . I stay?" she asked him.

Arthur smiled ruefully. "My dear, I'm afraid it would be a terrible disappointment—for both of us."

She looked puzzled. "You no like? Want other woman?"

"No, no!" he answered quickly. "I like. But too tired now. I sleep now. Thank you."

She bowed and left. *I hope I haven't disgraced myself. Good Lord! I hope I haven't offended her.* He was asleep before he could pursue the thought.

At the Fukuoka airport, he shook hands with Kenji. "Please come to the States soon, Kenji. I'd like the chance to show you some hospitality, although I'm afraid I couldn't match this wonderful trip. Thank you so much!"

"I've enjoyed having you here, Arthur . . . and I will be coming to the States one of these days. I may be giving a paper at a meeting at the Marine Biological Laboratory in Woods Hole in the summer of '63."

"That would be terrific! Let me know." He turned and waved to Kenji once again from the top of the ramp before entering the plane.

5 Tilak Marg
New Delhi 1, India
12 October, 1961

My Dear Arthur,

Imagine our happiness at receiving your son, Robert, in our home! What a gentle and considerate young man he is. Our family has fallen quite in love with him. Robert seems to have taken to our Indian way of life, enjoying the food and pastimes of our country.

My daughter Leila, who was just a small child when you knew her, has been showing Robert Delhi's main attractions. Leila is a medical student at the All-India Institute of Medical Sciences. She and Robert seem to get on well together.

Our sons are both fine. Ashok is doing graduate work in haematology at Edinburgh, my old school. He is married and has one son, little Pran. Sushila has become the doting grandmama! Nani was recently married to a cousin of the Prime Minister. Nani is in the Agricultural Ministry, interested in new strains of rice. And I continue with the Health Ministry, second to the top now. Soon, I expect they will retire me, like an old racehorse!

How are you getting on Arthur? Robert says it is lonely there for you, without Emily. Wouldn't you like to come visit for a time, old boy? It might do you good to get a change of scene.

Sushila joins me in sending love. The best news we could have is that you will soon arrive in Delhi.

All the best,
Ranjit

II

Washington, D.C.   February 1962

Rev. John P. Riordan, Vice-Chancellor. Arthur read the brass plate as he pressed the bell, absentmindedly counting the number of doors along the corridor of the Faculty Residence. A long way from Ashley, Pennsylvania, he thought, and was immediately ashamed of himself. He knew that the universe movers often came from the Ashleys of the world.

The door was opened by a handsome dark-haired youth in his late teens. Arthur thought he looked vaguely familiar.

"Arthur Hillman, to see Father Riordan."

"Come in, Dr. Hillman. Father John is expecting you. He'll be with you in a few minutes." The young man spoke with a slight accent, more like an inflection. British, Arthur guessed. "I'm Drew," he said, shaking hands. He took Arthur's hat and heavy winter overcoat to hang in the hall closet.

Arthur entered a living room with a dark red carpet. Its deep couch and armchairs were upholstered in midnight blue. An abstract painting—an oil, not very good, by an artist whose signature was unreadable—hung over the couch. The room looked little used.

John Riordan strode in, his stocky frame carrying more weight than in his younger days, his thick hair, with its widow's peak, entirely silver. He was wearing comfortable slacks and a sweater over an open-necked shirt. Arthur realized that it was the first time he'd seen John without his clerical collar, except for that once in his army uniform.

"Arthur!" John's greeting was full of warmth. "How grand to see you. A sight for these old eyes."

"John, you're looking wonderful! It's been a long time." He shook hands and embraced the priest. Arthur indicated the room. "I like your digs. How's life treating you? Are you glad to be back in the States?"

"No complaints, Arthur. I'm delighted to be here. Being around all these young students keeps me on my toes." His good-looking face creased in the same charming smile. "Come on in to the study. It's more comfortable." He led the way into a smaller room that was lined with book-filled shelves. Arthur recognized the priest's heavy desk from the rectory in Ashley.

Father John motioned Arthur to a couch as he sat opposite in an oversized leather armchair. "You have to bring me up to date on everything—the Chest Fund, the clinics, and your new work at the Cartwright Foundation. Are you there full-time?"

"I'm there part-time, as a consultant, John. That's a polite way of dealing with over-the-hill 'docs.' "

"Nonsense! They wouldn't waste their money on you if you didn't have an important contribution to make." He filled a pipe with tobacco, tamping it down, touching a flame to the bowl, and continued speaking as he puffed. "Have you left your practice in Wilkes-Barre?"

"No. I have a young associate, but I still keep the illusion of being a practicing physician. Can't cut the cord, I guess." He smiled at the priest, acknowledging their advancing years.

"And your house? Have you kept that?"

"Yes. My housekeeper lives there and takes care of things when I'm away. None of the children seems to want to live in Wilkes-Barre. It's such a big house. . . . I've lent most of Emily's art collection to Westmoreland College for the Arts Center—it's named after her, did you know that?"

Father John made a sympathetic expression with his mouth. "That's a fitting tribute, Arthur. Emily's death was a tragedy. I was so saddened to hear of it." John had written a warm letter from Bolivia after the accident. "You must be lonely."

Arthur sighed. "Yes. It doesn't seem like almost three years since she's been gone . . . but I'm getting used to it now. I keep busy. Work! That's your old medicine, isn't it?"

"Yep! That's still my medicine, Doc!"

They chatted about Father John's work in South America, the Chest Fund, the Kennedy administration, and people from Wilkes-Barre, like the old friends they were, the years making no difference.

"You're remarkable, Arthur! You never seem to age." John looked appraisingly at Arthur.

"Ah, John. We both know better," he laughed. "But I feel fine. Except for some trauma arthritis from the old hip wound, I'm in good shape."

The young man who had answered the door came in with a tray of glasses and ice. He put it down on a cellarette which stood in the corner. Father John rose. "You met Drew, didn't you, Arthur?"

Arthur smiled at the tall boy. "Yes, briefly."

Father John had busied himself with the drinks. "Still bourbon and soda?" he asked.

Arthur laughed. "What a memory! Yes, I'm the only Yankee in Washington who drinks bourbon. Confuses the hell out of everyone." He accepted the drink that Drew handed him.

Arthur turned his attention to the broad-shouldered youth, who lounged in a wing chair, casually draping one leg over an arm, comfortably at home in the priest's apartment.

"Are you a student here, Drew?" he asked.

"No. I'm a junior at Andover," the handsome young man replied. Arthur noted that his eyes were an intense dark blue under straight black brows—an unusual combination with the dark hair and warm complexion.

"You're English, I imagine."

Now Father John and Drew both laughed. "Some Irishmen would call out their seconds on that one, Dr. Hillman!"

Arthur grinned sheepishly. "I beg your pardon. I should have known. But your accent sounds English to me."

"You're right. I've spent a lot of time in English schools. My father was Irish, but I have an American mother," Drew said. He turned to Father John, who was holding out a ginger ale. "Thanks, Uncle John."

Arthur stared at Drew, unaware that John Riordan was observing him. His throat suddenly felt dry and constricted. He took a gulp of his bourbon, swallowing quickly. His voice was hoarse. "What . . . what did you say your full name was?"

Drew smiled, and Arthur knew of whom the lad reminded him. "I guess I didn't say, Dr. Hillman. It's Andrew Tower."

Arthur concentrated on keeping his breathing steady. With great effort he raised his eyes to meet his old friend's sympathetic gaze.

"I should have explained, Arthur. Drew is Molly's son. Molly's and Sean's."

There was a buzzing in his ears. He felt a thousand needles prickling in his scalp and shoulders. A voice inside him protested. *No! It's not possible!* She couldn't have . . . *Sean* couldn't have a son. How could this be their son?

Arthur realized they were looking at him, Father John with concern. Drew had evidently asked him a question.

"I'm sorry, Drew. What did you say?"

"I asked whether you knew my parents."

"Oh . . . yes, that is, I knew your mother. Many years ago. Before her marriage. I've never met your father." Arthur was surprised at the calm, natural tone of his voice.

"How did you know Mother?" It was an open, friendly question. The boy was interested.

"I'm from Wilkes-Barre. Your mother was a nurse at my hospital—and of course I was a friend of your Uncle John's." He continued speaking in a normal manner, although he felt bathed in sweat, as if he had passed through an attack of fever.

John looked sorrowful, like he was attending a wake, Arthur thought. Now that the shock of it was over, Arthur could not contain his curiosity about Molly's son. Aware that he sounded too eager, he asked question after question, purposely ignoring Father John's obvious distress.

Drew talked about himself easily. He told Arthur he had attended English schools in Geneva, and then a boarding school in Dublin for a year. "I hated it there." He looked at his Uncle John apologetically. "I came to the States for my junior and senior years. I hope to go to Dartmouth."

John shifted uncomfortably in his chair several times. Now he interrupted in a voice which brooked no argument. "Drew, I think you'd better get yourself ready for the plane, if you plan to go back to Boston tonight. It's getting dark and looks like we may have some weather."

Regretfully, Drew pulled his lanky body out of the chair. "Wish I didn't have to leave. This has been fun. But I've got to get back and hit the books. I'll pack up and come say good-bye." He left the room.

John shook his head impatiently. "Arthur, I am a stupid old fool. It never occurred to me about Drew. I should've told you to come another day."

"Don't be silly, John. It makes absolutely no difference. I'm glad to have met Drew. My heavens, that's all ancient history."

But the priest knew better. He sensed Arthur's heartiness was feigned. He had seen the naked look of pain, and a sort of recognition, on his old friend's strong face when he first realized that Drew was Molly's son.

Arthur rose. "I think I'll be running along now, John. Let's get together for dinner soon." Arthur felt impossibly restless. He had to get out of there, to think.

Drew was in the hallway when Father John saw Arthur out. They rode down in the elevator together, after saying good-bye to the silver-haired priest.

"Can I give you a lift?" Arthur asked.

"Isn't that out of your way? I'm taking the seven o'clock flight to Boston."

"No problem. National Airport is just fifteen minutes away. I'd be delighted." It was raining when they drove out of the garage, a freezing rain mixed with light snow. Arthur glanced up at the heavy sky, tinted pink from the glow of the city lights. "It looks pretty bad up there, Drew. I wouldn't be surprised if the flights are delayed or canceled."

"Yes. It's a bit of a fogger, all right. I suppose I could take the train."

"Tell you what! Why not stay over at my place? We can have an early dinner. You'll get a good night's sleep, and catch the eight-thirty flight tomorrow morning. I'd enjoy having you, and, frankly, this weather worries me. You won't save any time by taking the night train."

Drew hesitated only for a minute. "Thanks, Dr. Hillman. I think I'll take you up on that."

They had dinner in the pub in Arthur's apartment hotel—one of those dark-paneled steak houses modeled after someone's idea of an English men's club. Washington was full of them.

"Better than going out in this weather," Arthur explained to Drew.

"This is fine. You should see what I usually eat for dinner."

Arthur watched Drew as he devoured an immense slab of rare roast beef, baked potato lathered with butter and sour cream, vegetables, salad, dinner rolls, and ice cream. Between bites, he kept up a steady, unaffected conversation.

Molly's son. Arthur couldn't get over it. For all these years, not to know she had a son. He was very appealing. Just the right mix of self-assurance and deference.

"How's it going at Andover?" he asked Drew.

"Tough! I've never studied so hard in my life."

"You want to go to Dartmouth, hmm?"

"Yes," he answered. "They have a good premed program. I plan to go to medical school." That was natural enough, since his mother was a nurse.

"What kind of medicine do you practice, Dr. Hillman?"

"I'm an internist, with a special interest in pulmonary disease. Now I devote half of my time to the Cartwright Foundation, where I'm a consultant on industrial health."

Drew looked at him with interest. "How do you become a consultant in something like industrial health?"

"In my case it was a roundabout route. It grew out of my interest in lung disease related to the mining industry." Arthur leaned back against the wooden booth, warming to his subject. "I started my training in chest surgery at Jefferson Hospital in Philadelphia in the 1920s. . . . Then I went back to open a family practice in Wilkes-Barre—that was the only thing you could really do if you were a young physician starting out in those days. . . . I was pretty unhappy about it at the time, but everything has its compensations. I enjoyed those years of general practice. You get to know your patients. They come to depend on you. Great sense of satisfaction . . ."

Drew listened to Arthur's words, liking him. He thought the doctor was a nice man . . . he had a good face. . . . Drew wondered why he was sad.

". . . and so, one thing grows out of another," Arthur was saying. "I came to the foundation's attention when I was appointed to a committee for the WHO—the World Health Organization."

Drew looked alert. "Did you go to Geneva on that committee?"

"Yes. As a matter of fact, I still do—once every six months. I just returned from the last meeting in October."

"Sometime when you're there, Dr. Hillman, you should look up my mother."

Arthur looked down at his plate. "Your mother lives in Geneva?" His pulse quickened, contradicting the nonchalance in his voice.

"Yes. She works for Le Croix Rouge, the International Red Cross. She's director of nurses for their emergency medical teams. That's really home, Geneva."

"And your father, Drew? Is he in Geneva, too?"

"My father died when I was eight years old, Dr. Hillman. I never knew him very well. He was in hospitals a lot of the time that I can remember."

"I see. I'm sorry, Drew. I didn't know that," he apologized.

"That's O.K. No way you could've known."

"Has your mother remarried, Drew?" He thought his voice sounded natural, just conversational.

"No. Mum's a very independent woman, Dr. Hillman. She has a demanding job, lots of friends, and . . . well, I guess she thinks she doesn't really need a husband."

Arthur was aware that he was hanging on Drew's every word, staring hard at him. He signaled the waiter for the check. When it came, he signed it, concentrating on the numbers, fighting his rising excitement.

The morning sun streamed through his bedroom window, awakening Arthur. He sat up, glanced at the clock on his bed table, and realized he had overslept. In his robe and slippers, he hurried to the small library which also served as a guest room.

It was empty. The bed had been converted back into a sofa and the neatly folded sheets and blankets placed on a chair. Drew's suitcase was gone. Arthur felt a keen sense of disappointment. He had hoped to say good-bye to Drew before he left for Boston. There was a sheet of note paper on his desk.

Dear Dr. Hillman,

Many thanks for your hospitality. I thought I'd show my appreciation best by letting you sleep on a Sunday morning.

I hope I'll see you again when I get to Washington. I enjoyed last night very much.

Sincerely,
Drew

P.S. When you go to Geneva, say hello to my mother:

Mary Tower
5 Place de Ville
Geneve
Tel: 73202

He stood there for several minutes reading and rereading the message, written in a strong, angular hand.

Geneva   Spring 1962

Molly was nervous. Perhaps she shouldn't have agreed to see Arthur. After all this time, he was bound to have changed. It might be better to leave the old memories as they were, forever frozen in time. Golden, glorious, halcyon moments on distant mountains, with youth and time on their side.

To see each other now, their visages untempered by love, could only serve to erase the beauty of the past.

What would they say to each other? Too many years had passed. Too much had happened.

She hurried along the Rue de la Cité, oblivious of the evening strollers enjoying the mild spring weather, the punctilious Swiss husbands going home to their families after a day in their government cubicles at the Hôtel de Ville.

Molly had suggested Jeannine's because she thought it less likely that they would meet any of her friends from the international agencies community in this little family restaurant. No need to get involved in making introductions, giving explanations.

She'd taken a few minutes after work to bathe and change into a blue wool suit and fresh white blouse. She had studied her reflection carefully in the mirror, wondering—not for the first time—whether she should color her hair to remove the silvery strands that streaked its glossy blackness. In the end, she knew she wouldn't. At fifty-five, a few gray hairs were something she wasn't going to worry about. She had brushed on a trace of blue eyeshadow and a soft rose lip rouge, smiling ironically at her own image.

He will have to accept me as I am, she thought decisively . . . as I will accept him.

She arrived at Le Restaurant Jeannine, pulled open the door, and—restraining a vague impulse to cross herself—entered the candlelit interior.

It was not crowded at this hour. Molly spotted Arthur immediately, at a corner table in the rear. He rose when he saw her walk in. She made her way toward him, feeling strangely giddy.

He was a little heavier, perhaps. His hair was a distinguished silvery gray, and his face had the lines and creases that all caring doctors acquire with age. But, oh, he was still so handsome . . . that same warm magnetism emanating from him, that same wonderful smile! He was dressed, as always, in a conservative dark suit, well tailored to his tall, broad-shouldered frame.

Taking a few steps to meet her, Arthur extended his hands in welcome, bending to kiss her cheek.

"Molly! How wonderful to see you." He held on to her hands, continuing to smile down at her.

Her violet eyes crinkled at the corners. "I'm happy to see you too, Arthur." She paused. "I wasn't sure I would be!" He remembered her impish humor.

Arthur let her slide into the corner, then sat on the banquette adjacent to her.

"I've ordered wine. Is that all right?" She nodded, smiling delightedly, unable, nor even wanting, to disguise her pleasure at being with him again.

"You're really here in Geneva, Arthur! I can hardly believe it."

"I've been here a number of times in the past two years, Molly. It never occurred to me that you lived here. Not until I met Drew."

"He wrote me about meeting you." She ran her fingers along the stem of her wineglass, eyes veiled.

Arthur lifted his glass. "To . . . friendships . . . old . . . and new." As he smiled, he looked young and gallant.

She touched her glass to his and sipped the wine, her thoughts in confusion.

Molly was well known to the proprietors of the restaurant, so they did not mind when she and Arthur didn't order immediately. Nor did it concern them when they paid little attention to the food, once it was served. They smiled their patient understanding as monsieur and madame lingered over dessert, and then coffee, followed by Grand Marnier. . . .

Arthur listened to Molly, a bemused expression on his lips. ". . . I've been offered other jobs from time to time," she was saying, "but I think it's important for me to remain where I am. There are fewer and fewer Americans working in the international agencies now. The appointments are going to non-Americans, especially Africans and Asians, many of whom are *anti*-American . . . the same thing that's happening throughout the UN, Arthur. . . . Many Americans have been eased out, or have quit in disillusionment."

"Are most of your friends among the foreign residents in Geneva?" he asked.

"Almost one hundred percent! With a few exceptions, the Swiss are unfriendly to foreigners. They're aloof and unemotional people, sangfroid. They profit from the misfortunes of others, when you think about it. Swiss neutrality is a big business. They were actually pro-German in World War II. The only people who could flee to Switzerland were those who could afford to pay, and pay well!"

"One thing I can say for you, Molly—you haven't lost your spirit! I thought perhaps you would have mellowed." Arthur leaned an elbow on the table, resting his chin on his hand. He regarded her with a searching look. "At my age, I don't have an excess of time, Molly. I'll be here for the rest of this week. . . . I'd like us to spend as much of that together as possible."

She looked steadily back at him. "I won't even pretend that I don't want to do that, Arthur."

They walked up the Grande Rue toward the Hôtel de Ville. Molly lived on a cul-de-sac, in a house within a private courtyard, entered through a doorway in a high, thick wooden gate. It was late as they made their way along the empty streets, their footsteps echoing in the quiet.

"Geneva is not the liveliest city by night," she said.

"Yes. That surprised me the first time I came here," he replied.

At her door she asked, "Would you like to come in for a nightcap?"

He shook his head. "Not tonight, thanks. I have a busy day tomorrow. I'd better get some sleep. Shall we have dinner tomorrow evening?" She nodded. "I'll call you when I know what time we'll be finished with our meeting." He kissed her lightly.

It was such a pleasant spring evening that Arthur walked back across the bridge to the Hôtel de la Plage. In his mind he relived the last four hours, savoring each remembered word they had spoken, each mood he could recall from her expressive face.

He fell asleep that night with a lighthearted attitude, a sense of anticipation for the coming days.

On Thursday evening he said, "I'm supposed to leave for Paris on Saturday. There's a meeting there."

"I'll be sorry to see you go, Arthur," Molly answered. She looked beautiful tonight in a dark red dress, with a matching scarf loosely tied at the throat.

They had met at the WHO each evening, Molly driving out in her Fiat to wait for him in the lobby until his meeting was finished. Since Arthur was *rapporteur*, he'd had to stay at the end of today's final session to write up the proceedings. When he'd come down, ready to apologize for being so late, he had seen her talking to a distinguished-looking man dressed in diplomatic gray.

The man kissed Molly on both cheeks. "*À bientôt, ma chérie . . . je t'appellerai . . .*" he said with a wave as he left.

"I thought you might enjoy driving out to a restaurant I know on the Lausanne road," Molly said, when they were in the car.

Arthur had been wondering about the easy familiarity the man had shown toward Molly. He stifled the urge to ask her about him.

Soon they were on a mountain road, arriving at the picturesque restaurant, known for its fine wines and haute cuisine.

After they had given their order, the sommelier consulted with Arthur about the wine. Arthur enjoyed wine, but he didn't pretend to be knowledgeable about vintages. "We'll allow you to make the selection," he told the steward. The man seemed pleased.

"Congratulations," said Molly. "A man who admits he isn't an expert on wine!"

"I wouldn't expect him to choose his medication," he replied.

When they had finished an appetizer of crepes with a *sauce morilles,* and were enjoying the chateaubriand, Arthur said, "I don't really have to go to that meeting in Paris, Molly. . . ." He looked questioningly at her.

"You don't?" Her eyes were wide.

"I was thinking that maybe I would rent a car and drive somewhere for a few days. I've never seen the French Alps." She continued eating carefully. "Would you like to come along?" he asked.

She looked up. "Yes, I would," she answered, without hesitation. "We can use my car."

After the *fraises du bois,* they sat quietly, not speaking. Arthur studied her face. He sighed. "You're still so lovely . . ."

He saw the feeling in her eyes, the uncertain movement of her lips. He reached for her hand.

Sleep would not come to him that night. Had it been a mistake to see her again? he wondered. What had been gained? He'd always known Molly was an alluring woman. It shouldn't surprise him that it was still so. . . .

During those years that he had loved her . . . had been hopelessly in love with her . . . he had known joy such as few men ever experience. But he had also known much sorrow. Why should he open himself to being hurt again? Was he still vulnerable, after the things that had happened to him? After losing Emily?

For so long he had been numb, unable to feel anything. Now, he was afraid.

For the first time in the three years since Emily had been swept away in the waters of the Susquehanna, Arthur felt the stirrings of desire for a woman . . . for Molly.

Provence Savoie, France

They drove through winding mountain passes, stopping in tucked-away hamlets to dine on the fragrant, unpretentious dishes of the Alps. At Chamonix they rode the funicular to the summit, shivering in the cold air as they gazed at the snow-covered peaks of Mont Blanc and the spectacular panorama below. Young spring skiers were heading for the higher trails. The more adventurous were bound for Mer de Glace, the most challenging of the huge glaciers on the enormous mountain. The brightly clad, high-spirited young people added gaiety and color to the lodges along their route.

Away from the formality of Geneva, Molly and Arthur became more relaxed. There was so much to talk about, so much to tell. Their conversation raced from Wilkes-Barre to Washington, from Dublin to Delhi. . . .

Molly knew about Father John's new position. "Yes, he writes without fail at least twice a year. . . ."

"Did you hear about Ranjit Kar?" he asked.

"Ranjit? Don't tell me you're still in touch with him!" Arthur told her about the accident and how Ranjit's sight was saved.

"My son, Robert, is in India now with the Peace Corps. I think he's having a romance with Ranjit's daughter."

"Hands across the sea! Is it serious?"

"I'm not sure. I think I'd better find out. I don't think Ranjit would like that . . . we don't have princely blood." Molly's eyes told him that wasn't true.

Molly spoke of Sean and his illness. "It was so sad at the end . . . for that strong man, so large in his lifetime, to become totally dependent. It was a release when he died. There were a few years when he was fine—we had hope then, when we first came to Geneva. . . ."

Arthur told Molly about Emily's tragic death, and how lonely he had been ever since. She wanted to know about his children and his grandchildren . . . his work with the clinics . . . the foundation . . . the friends they had known together. Every topic, except one.

Soon it was time to drive on.

The small inn Molly had heard about from friends was romantic beyond their expectations. It perched on the edge of a precipice with a view of snow-crowned Alps and deep valleys. Monsieur and Madame Juniet welcomed them like old friends. They were the only visitors in the guest house.

Madame prepared for them a delicate meal—quenelles in a velvety white sauce, a veal ragout, and sorbet. The light, dry local wine was more to Arthur's taste than the fuller-bodied wines of the châteaux.

After dinner, in front of the fire, Juniet entertained them with harrowing tales of his adventures with the Résistance during the war while they sipped a colorless *poire* that seared their throats.

"Here in Bellevue," he said in his heavily accented English, "we had a station for people escaping to Suisse, mostly Jews. The Germans, *noirs salauds*, hardly knew we were here. Fortunate for us!" He gulped his *pastis* and stared into the fire.

Arthur watched Molly. In the rosy glow, she could have been the young woman he first had known. She turned her head slowly, her eyes answering the question in his.

Unhurriedly, they climbed the stairs to the charming suite which Madame had taken pleasure in reserving for them.

In the parlor Arthur gathered Molly into his arms, bringing her close against him and laying his cheek alongside hers. They stood that way for many heartbeats.

He looked down at the beloved face, the image which had haunted his dreams for half a lifetime. "You are my love," he whispered.

Their kiss contained all that they had felt for each other across the years . . . the longing, the heartache, and the devotion . . . since that first kiss on another mountain, so long before.

"I have never loved anyone but you, Arthur. In my whole life, only you, my darling. . . . I hope it's not too late for us."

In the high, carved wooden bed, with its fluffy *édredon piqué*, Arthur and Molly found, at long last, a safe harbor.

Geneva

Molly's apartment was set on the bastion wall of the old city, looking down on the Park of the Reformation and the university. Its small rooms were furnished for comfort and utility, with a pleasing blend of upholstered furniture and decorative pieces acquired for their beauty. The dining alcove opened to a roomy kitchen, filled with colorful pottery and a multitude of hanging copper pots.

Arthur looked around with curiosity at the shelves of books, the framed prints and watercolors, realizing that this was the first home of Molly's he'd ever seen—the first retreat of her own which reflected her tastes and pastimes. He ran his hand over a beautiful old quilt, which was draped across the back of a couch.

"So this is where you live. . . . It suits you, darling."

"I was lucky to find this. I moved here when Drew went away to school. It has a small second bedroom for him when he comes home."

Molly prepared a simple dinner . . . soup, salad, a crusty *baguette*, and Emmentaler cheese.

"No wine tonight, sweetheart," Arthur protested. "I feel like my liver must be well saturated with alcohol!"

Molly laughed and teased him. "You'd make a terrible Frenchman."

He had a feeling of peace, of well-being.

After dinner they sat holding hands in front of a fire, sipping coffee, feeling warm and contented.

Arthur decided it was the moment.

"Molly . . . there's something we must talk about."

"Yes, darling, what is that?"

"We haven't talked about Drew."

He felt her stiffen as she withdrew from his arm. "What about him?" She did not meet his eyes. Her slim shoulders looked slight and vulnerable, and for a brief time he hesitated.

"Molly . . . sweetheart, look at me."

There was everything in her eyes as she returned his look fully—courage, resolution, pride, and love. And Arthur knew the answer, even as he asked the question.

"He's my son, isn't he?"

Molly's chin trembled as she fought for control. She nodded gently, her shoulders sagging helplessly.

Arthur held out his arms to her. "I *want* him to be my son. . . . I want him to be *ours!*"

With a cry, Molly went into his arms, laying her head against his chest, holding on to him fiercely. Her breath came in harsh gasps. They clung to each other, so full of emotion they could not trust themselves to say anything.

Molly was the first to speak, her voice shaking. "Can you ever forgive me? He was all I had. If I couldn't have you, at least I could have your child."

He covered her tear-streaked face with kisses. "Forgive you? Oh, my darling! How can you ask? I just wish I had known. All these years, you and I have had a son, and I never knew."

"That's what I mean. I feel I must ask your forgiveness for that. But, you see, it was the only way . . . the only way I could have your baby."

Arthur smoothed back the softly waving hair from her forehead. "Do you want to tell me about it now?"

Molly closed her eyes in relief. "Yes. Oh, yes! I've wanted to tell you for all these years. I thought I'd never see you again . . . and even if I did, that it would not be possible to speak of it."

Molly told him how she had found herself pregnant in Calcutta, just as she had decided she could never allow Arthur to divorce Emily and leave his other children.

"I wanted your child, Arthur. *I wanted him so much.* I knew I could never have a child with Sean. You've been my only lover. Isn't that strange?"

Arthur nodded, terribly moved.

"An annulment for Sean and me . . . a divorce for you . . . those would have taken too long. The baby would have been born before either of those was final. I couldn't face that reality, all that it implied . . . what our families would have to endure." Her voice was low and her face sober as she looked into the dying fire. "Abortion was out of the question. So only one course was open to me: to return to Ireland and have the baby, and to hope that Sean would accept it."

"And he did?"

"Yes. If I'd never loved him before, I loved him for that. He was wonderful about it. He had known about us. I was honest with him. He said he was grateful to you for giving him the son he could never have had himself . . . he truly loved Drew."

"I should be grateful to *him,* for being a father to my son," said Arthur. "My son," he repeated, wonder in his voice. "He's a splendid boy, Molly."

She smiled at him. "He's been my whole life—everything! But that wasn't going to be good for him. That's why I sent him abroad to school. I wanted him to know America. He had to have some years away from me. Also, I had to become independent of him."

Arthur shook his head in admiration. "You are an amazing woman, Molly."

She sighed. "I'm glad you know. I'm glad it's all over—the deception."

"Drew? I think he doesn't suspect."

"No. I'm certain he doesn't. There would never have been any reason for him to question anything."

"We must keep it that way, Molly. . . . Who else knows?"

"No one."

"Confession?"

"No Confession. Not for years," she said, with a trace of a frown.

"I don't believe it!"

"It's true, Arthur. Not because of Drew, or us . . . well, maybe because of that, indirectly."

Arthur stood up, hands in his pockets, and walked to the windows. A spring rain was falling, creating watery halos around the lights of the opera house in the distance. Headlights of moving vehicles were reflected on wet pavement. He remained there, staring out at the darkened city for some minutes, weighing what he was about to do.

Turning abruptly, he went to her and grasped both of her hands in his.

"Molly, let's get married! I *swore* I wasn't going to ask you that ever again. You left me twice, and I wasn't going to be let down a third time! But we love each other, and I want us to spend the rest of our lives together."

"Arthur! Oh, darling . . . *yes!*"

Their kiss sealed the promise, and this time he knew it was a promise that would be kept.

"How did you know about Drew?" Molly asked.

"I didn't at first."

He remembered his shock when he had heard that Drew was Molly's son. "I knew that you and Sean hadn't been able to have children. I guess I thought he had suddenly regained his ability to father a child—that does happen. The idea even crossed my mind that the father could've been someone else. But when Drew wrote to me about a summer position with one of the clinics, he sent me his curriculum vitae. It had his date of birth on it." He still felt the stunned reaction he had known when he saw that date—December 16, 1945—on the printed page. He *has* to be my child, he'd thought. . . .

"I was pretty sure, then, although not certain. Not until you confirmed it did I dare hope it was so. I really wanted it to be so, darling. It means our love wasn't all for naught."

"Arthur . . . it never was 'all for naught,' regardless of Drew!"

"No, of course not. But when a man loves a woman as much as I love you, he wants nothing more than to have a child with her. I thought that had been denied us."

"I have photographs of him at every stage. I saved mementos. Always, in the back of my mind, was the possibility that maybe someday you would know about him." Molly brought out the leather albums and boxes of report cards.

They sat far into the night as Arthur Hillman pored over the life story of his love child, the child of his love.

Molly was in the grasp of single-minded purpose. As if, given this glimpse of a lost dream, she would capture and hold it, lest it slip away from her.

"I'll go home and wait for you," he said. "I have to prepare my children for this . . . make arrangements . . ." Arthur tried to sort it out in his mind.

"I'm going with you, Arthur! Let's just get married, and not waste any more of our lives apart from each other. Let's not worry about other people and what they think, ever again!"

She packed her bags, informed her office that she was taking an extended leave, and arranged for her apartment to be looked after. In two days they were aboard a Swissair flight for New York.

Wilkes-Barre   May 1962

There's magic on the Susquehanna in May. The air is temperate, the skies endless. Clouds chase themselves across the blue expanse in ever-changing images. Wind-tossed willows are reflected in the current where it flirts with its banks in flickers of light.

On a day fashioned for joy, amid the splash of azaleas, pink, cerise, and crimson, Arthur Franke Hillman and Molly Shea Tower were married on the bluff of Grandview Terrace as a small gathering of family and friends looked on.

Jeffrey and Sharon Hillman were there with their two small sons. Jeffrey had called his Uncle Fred Grant the previous week to seek reassurance. "Your father needs companionship, Jeff," Fred had told him. "He must be so lonely without Emily. In a way, his marrying again is a tribute to your mother. I think Arthur is entitled to whatever comfort he may find in a second marriage."

Ellen Hillman Fontina held her husband's hand, with little Michael standing between them, as they watched this wedding at the place where they, themselves, had been married.

Arthur had been unable to reach his daughter upon his return from Geneva. When she had answered his call, Ellen explained, "Tony and I went away for a few days, Daddy. We went up to Camp Repose. . . . We're going to try it again. Don't get excited! I'm not sure it will work, but I *do* love him." She had sounded tearful.

"Ellen, darling, I can't tell you what to do with your life. No one can. All I know is that we all need love in our lives, no matter what else we have." The words of his wise and loving grandfather, Isaac Hillman, so long ago imprinted on his spirit, were a lesson he had learned over and over again throughout his life, at dear cost. He remembered them still, as if it had been yesterday: "A man is nothing without the love of a woman, Arthur. To find love . . . that is happiness . . . that is success. Marriage, children . . . without those, all else is empty."

Robert was not with them today. Arthur missed him, the son he loved and admired so, far away in India. They would see Robert there in September when they took a delayed honeymoon trip. Autumn was the best season in India. . . .

Drew had been the one to react with unreserved delight when he heard they were to be married. Spontaneous and eager, he had told Molly, "I *knew* it! I knew he was the man for you the first time I met him!" He took full credit for bringing them together.

"What am I supposed to call you, Dr. Hillman? I mean, after you and Mum are married?" asked Drew.

Arthur had exchanged a smile with Molly. "You can call me Arthur, or whatever feels most comfortable, Drew. My children still call me Dad. . . ."

Drew had considered it. "I suppose Arthur is best. If I were younger, I might call you Dad, but I guess that would be kind of silly, wouldn't it?"

Arthur had not trusted himself to look at Molly.

Young Julie Benjamin smiled with her lips closed so the handsome boy whose mother was marrying Uncle Arthur wouldn't notice her braces. Standing next to her daughter, Ruth wiped a tear from the corner of her eye as she watched her husband perform this very special marriage ceremony. Justice David Benjamin spoke the words with unusual feeling, as he pronounced them man and wife.

Father John Riordan said a blessing over the couple. In his heart he gave a prayer of thanks to God and to His Son, Jesus Christ, for having united these two who were so dear to him, after their separate journeys in life.

Rabbi Eric Brandt-Hillman also blessed his uncle's marriage with Molly, asking "the God of Abraham, the God of Isaac, and the God of Jacob to cause His countenance to shine upon them in all the days of their lives."

Molly was a glowing bride. She stood at Arthur's side in all the elegant loveliness of her maturity, her deep blue eyes, wide and clear, reflecting the sure inner calm of dreams fulfilled.

Arthur's heart was engulfed with love. It was there in his face as he spoke the words which made Molly his wife, slipping the wedding band on her finger next to the sapphire and diamond ring—a ring which had rested in a vault for many long years, unworn by any other.

At day's end, their arms entwined, silhouetted in the mauve of twilight, Arthur and Molly Hillman bid good-bye to their wedding guests. A gust of wind sang from the mountain, down across the valley to the river, where it flowed on in its timeless journey.

They turned and, without a backward glance, closed the door behind them.

EPILOGUE

On Flows the River

June 1972

The day was cruelly beautiful. God's practical joke. From a bright blue sky, the sun smiled on denuded trees and mud-drenched lawns. The gentle summer breeze sought in vain for leafy fronds to stir.

Below, the sullen river moved, heavy and swift, laden with debris. Cold sparkles shone from its turbulent surface. Like an animal caged, it lowered, switching its tail, tossing its angry head with a vengeful, muffled growl. . . . With a swipe of its paw, it could annihilate.

Two men drove along the deserted streets in an army jeep. The older, bareheaded, dressed in khaki fatigues, stared straight ahead, anger turning his eyes to a flinty blue-gray. None of the wise men had anticipated the severity of the flood, thought Arthur with bitterness. Despite the warning signs of nature gone wild . . . despite the inadequate dikes.

Lulled by the drumming of rain on the roof and the false security of the defending dikes, Wyoming Valley had slept, until the raging waters of the Susquehanna, swollen with the torrents of Hurricane Agnes, lapped over the crest of the dikes, sending an alarm through the night. Frantically, the people had struggled in darkness to stem the flow of the river. Fighting their way up the muddy slopes, they piled bag after bag of earth and sand to shore up the failing levee. Blinded by rain, losing sight of loved ones in the dark, they heard the wail of sirens telling them they had lost the battle. Defeated, they had fled the valley, seeking refuge on higher ground. . . .

On the jeep rolled, through residential areas, like the advance guard of an invading army. Arthur half expected to see frightened survivors emerge from the rubble, their arms raised in surrender. In truth, he had never seen such devastation, even in the war.

Uprooted utility poles and broken trees lay like matchsticks. Some houses had been completely washed away, while others leaned crazily off their foundations. Household furnishings, carried along by the deluge, had alighted where they were deposited by the receding flood. Abandoned automobiles were coated with mud.

They rounded the bend of Riverside Drive, coming along the riverbank. There was Lowell Wintermuth's house, the entire facade . . .

"Gone!" Arthur exclaimed. "I can't believe it!"

The second floor hung there suspended, a bed caught against the upright window frame. The curving staircase was intact; it had stood against the force of the wave which cascaded down when the dikes burst. Every house they passed along the old, once lovely tree-lined avenue had been covered to its roof by the flood.

The young soldier driving the jeep was moved by the destruction. He asked, "Do you know the owners of any of these houses, Dr. Hillman?"

Arthur nodded. "Yes, I do, Corporal . . . in a town like Wilkes-Barre, you know most everyone."

They drove north, turning where the road curved. Ten days ago this had been a peaceful river common, a favorite picnic spot for the students of Westmoreland College. . . . Arthur shuddered. The street was alive with worms! Hundreds of thousands of huge worms, twisting in the mud. . . . On the college campus, the lawns and gardens were dun-colored wasteland.

He saw the outline of the Arts Center along the back campus. A massive effort had been mounted to save the works of art there, and the 250,000 volumes in the library. The river had crested at forty feet—eighteen feet above flood level. Arthur knew the loss would be in the millions of dollars.

He remembered the day when the new Arts Center had been dedicated. . . . He had stood looking at the bronze inscription on the face of the building: EMILY GRANT HILLMAN CENTER FOR THE ARTS. How proud she would have been, he had thought. . . . Emily's bequest, matched by the Grant Family Fund, had completed the endowment necessary for the center. That had been twelve years ago. So much had happened since. . . .

Arthur had been attending a meeting in Switzerland with Molly when they had received word of the flood. Trying to reach Wilkes-Barre by phone, he had been given the frightening information that it was impossible to get a line through because the valley was a disaster area. They had flown back to the States immediately.

Molly was waiting for him now in their Washington apartment. He wished she were here. Never once in ten years of marriage had they been separated, even for a night. As if to make up for a near lifetime apart, Molly had been determined to spend every moment together, traveling with him, helping him with his work, editing and typing his papers . . . ten years of a happiness reserved for the special few. He wondered how much longer it could last. His own mortality, the fragility of all life were manifest in this chance destruction caused by nature's hand.

They had reached his house on Grandview Terrace. The guardsman steered the jeep into the rutted driveway, avoiding a deep pothole filled with water. Arthur swung his feet out of the jeep and strode across the eroded lawn to the raised terrace. He stared at the leaded casement windows for a moment, then withdrew a key from his pocket and inserted it in the lock.

The gloom within was intensified by the dank odor of the scum which covered the floor and paneled walls. In the front hall the antique Persian carpet lay in a sodden heap on the warped parquet floor. The angry river had poured in, flinging furniture every which way, lapping to the ceiling. Everything—grand piano, couches, piles of leather-bound volumes from his library —had been immersed in the muddy, swirling water for three days, then tossed haphazardly aside, as the capricious stream receded, leaving a residue of filth.

A sense of futility enveloped him. . . .

Where to begin? How would they restore this house? They had been planning to sell it because they spent most of their time in Washington now. . . .

All through the valley, people must reclaim their homes from the river. The entire central city would need rebuilding. . . .

Arthur felt a rising excitement . . . a determination. They would return here, he and Molly, to see the city emerge again, to be a part of the new Wilkes-Barre!

The guardsman, standing respectfully aside, noticed the lift of the silver head with its strong-featured, still-handsome face. He saw the erect carriage of the doctor's undefeated figure as the shoulders straightened . . . the purposeful walk.

Arthur smiled at the soldier. "We'll be on our way now, Corporal. No point in lingering here."

Driving up Wyoming Mountain, they paused. Arthur Hillman turned to look back at the valley, still and uninhabited. The sun slanted lower, its golden light mirrored in the bends of the once bountiful Susquehanna as it traced its curving course through Wyoming Valley.

Arthur nodded to the corporal, ready to move on. If they hurried to the airport, he could be with Molly before sunset.

A Note on the Author

Harriet Segal has known many exotic rivers. Her life has taken her to the Ganges, the Nile, and the Yangtze, but the growing-up memories of Pennsylvania's uneasy Susquehanna River have never left her.

Born in Wilkes-Barre, the daughter of a distinguished Pennsylvania physician, she was educated at Wellesley College. Since her marriage to Dr. Sheldon Segal of the Rockefeller Foundation, she has been deeply involved in the international scientific community.

Ms. Segal has been an editor, a newspaper journalist, and an advertising copywriter. The author lives with her husband and three daughters in New York's Westchester County and spends her summers on Cape Cod. She is at work on her next novel.

THE SUSQUEHANNA RIVER

LAKE ERIE

MILES
0   60
0   KM   60

N
W   E
S

OHIO

PENNSY

State College

Pittsburgh

WEST VIRGINIA

M A R